BATTLECRY

BY CHRIS BUNCH AND ALLAN COLE

Sten
Sten 2: The Wolf Worlds
Sten 3: The Court of a Thousand Suns
Sten 4: Fleet of the Damned
Sten 5: Revenge of the Damned
Sten 6: The Return of the Emperor
Sten 7: Vortex
Sten 8: Empire's End

Battlecry: Sten Omnibus 1

BY CHRIS BUNCH

The Seer King
The Demon King
The Warrior King

The Empire Stone

Corsair

Dragonmaster 1: Storm of Wings

BATTLECRY

STEN OMNIBUS 1

Chris Bunch *and* **Allan Cole**

This omnibus edition includes

Sten

Sten 2: The Wolf Worlds

Sten 3: The Court of a Thousand Suns

www.orbitbooks.net

ORBIT

First published in Great Britain in 2010 by Orbit

Sten
First published in Great Britain in 2000 by Orbit

Sten 2: The Wolf Worlds
First published in Great Britain in 2000 by Orbit

Sten 3: The Court of a Thousand Suns
First published in Great Britain in 2000 by Orbit

A CIP catalogue record for this book is available from the British Library.

ISBN 978-1-84149-493-7

Typeset in Sabon by M Rules
Printed in the UK by CPI Mackays, Chatham ME5 8TD

Papers used by Orbit are natural, renewable and recyclable products sourced from well-managed forests and certified in accordance with the rules of the Forest Stewardship Council.

Orbit
An imprint of
Little, Brown Book Group
100 Victoria Embankment
London EC4Y 0DY

An Hachette UK Company
www.hachette.co.uk

www.orbitbooks.net

Contents

STEN

Dedicated to
Jason and Alissa
and
the late Robert Willey

BOOK ONE

VULCAN

Chapter One

[illegible]

[illegible]

[illegible]

[illegible]

[illegible]

[illegible]

[illegible]

[illegible]

[illegible]

Chapter One

Death came quietly to The Row.

The suit stank. The Tech inside it stared out through the scratched port at the pipe that looped around the outside of the recreation dome and muttered a string of curses that would've peeled a deep-space trader.

What he wanted more than anything was a tall cool narcobeer to kill the hangover drumrolls in his head. The one thing he didn't want, he knew, was to be hanging outside Vulcan, staring at a one-centimeter alloy pipe that wouldn't hook up.

He clamped his waldos on the flange, set the torque rating by feel, and tried another round of obscenities, this time including his supervisor and all the stinking Migs enjoying themselves one meter and a world away from him.

Done. He retracted the waldos and slammed the suit's tiny drive unit into life. Not only was his supervisor a clot who was an ex-joyboy, but he was also going to get stuck for the first six rounds. The Tech shut down his ground-zeroed brain and rocketed numbly for the lock.

Of course, he'd missed the proper torque setting. If the pipe hadn't been carrying fluorine, under high pressure, the error wouldn't have made any difference.

The overstressed fitting cracked, and raw fluorine gradually ate its way through, for several shifts spraying harmlessly into space. But, as the fracture widened, the spray boiled directly against the outer skin of The Row, through the insulation and, eventually, the inner skin.

At first the hole was pin-size. The initial pressure drop inside the dome wasn't even enough to kick over the monitors high overhead in The Row's roof control capsule.

The Row could've been a red-light district on any of a million pioneer planets – Company joygirls and boys picked their way through the Mig crowds, looking for the Migrant-Unskilled who still had some credits left on his card.

Long rows of gambling computers hooted enticements at the passing workers and emitted little machine chuckles when another mark was suckered into a game.

The Row was the Company-provided recreational center, set up with the Migs' 'best interests' at heart. 'A partying Mig is a happy Mig,' a Company psychologist had once said. He didn't add – or need to – that a partying Mig was also one who was spending credits, and generally into the red. Each loss meant hours added to the worker's contract.

Which was why, in spite of the music and the laughter, The Row felt grim and gray.

Two beefy Sociopatrolmen lounged outside The Row's entrance. The older patrolman nodded at three boisterous Migs as they weaved from one bibshop to another, then turned to his partner. 'If ya gonna twitch every time somebody looks at ya, bud, pretty soon one of these Migs is gonna wanna know what you'll do if they get *real* rowdy.'

The new probationary touched his stun rod. 'And I'd like to show them.'

The older man sighed, then stared off down the corridor. 'Oh-oh. Trouble.'

His partner nearly jumped out of his uniform. 'Where? Where?'

The older man pointed. Stepping off the slideway and heading for The Row was Amos Sten. The other man started to laugh at the short, middle-aged Mig, and then noticed the muscles hunching Amos' neck. And the size of his wrists and hammer fists.

Then the senior patrolman sighed in relief and leaned back against the I-beam.

'It's okay, kid. He's got his family with him.'

A tired-looking woman and two children hurried off the slideway to Amos.

'What the hell,' the young man said, 'that midget don't look so tough to me.'

'You don't know Amos. If you did, you would've soaked your jock – specially if Amos was on the prowl for a little fight to cheer him up some.'

The four Migs each touched small white rectangles against a pickup and Vulcan's central computer logged the movement of MIG STEN, AMOS; MIG STEN, FREED; MIG-DEPENDENT STEN, AHD; MIG-DEPENDENT STEN, JOHS into The Row.

As the Sten family passed the two patrolmen, the older man smiled and tipped Amos a nod. His partner just glared. Amos ignored them and hustled his family toward the livie entrance.

'Mig likes to fight, huh? That ain't whatcha call Company-approved social mannerisms.'

'Son, we busted the head of every Mig who beefed one on The Row, there'd be a labor shortage.'

'Maybe we ought to take him down some.'

'You think you're the man who could do it?'

The young patrolman nodded. 'Why not? Catch him back of a narco joint and thump him some.'

The older man smiled, and touched a long and livid scar on his right arm. 'It's been tried. By some better. But maybe I'm wrong. Maybe you're the one who can do something. But you best remember. Amos isn't any old Mig.'

'What's so different about him?'

The patrolman suddenly tired of his new partner and the whole conversation. 'Where he comes from, they eat little boys like you for breakfast.'

The young man bristled and started to glower. Then he remembered that even without the potgut his senior still had about twenty kilos and fifteen years on him. He spun and turned the glower on an old lady who was weaving happily out of The Row. She looked at him, gummed a grin and spat neatly between the probationary's legs, onto the deck.

'Clot Migs!'

Amos slid his card through the livie's pickup, and the computer automatically added an hour to Amos' work contract. The four of them walked into the lobby, and Amos looked around.

'Don't see the boy.'

'Karl said school had him on an extra shift,' his wife, Freed, reminded him.

Amos shrugged.

'He ain't missin' much. Guy down the line was here last offshift. Says the first show's some clot about how some Exec falls for a joy-girl an' takes her to live in The Eye with him.'

Music blared from inside the theater.

'C'mon, dad, let's go.'

Amos followed his family into the showroom.

Sten hurriedly tapped computer keys, then hit the JOB INPUT tab. The screen blared, then went gray-blank. Sten winced. He'd never finish in time to meet his family. The school's ancient computer system just wasn't up to the number of students carded in for his class shift.

Sten glanced around the room. No one was watching. He hit BASIC FUNCTION, then a quick sequence of keys. Sten had found a way to tap into one reasoning bank of the central computer. Against school procedure, for sure. But Sten, like any other seventeen-year-old, was willing to let tomorrow's hassles hassle tomorrow.

With the patch complete, he fed in his task card. And groaned, as his assignment swam up onto the screen. It was a cybrolathe exercise, making L-beams.

It would take forever to make the welds, and he figured that the mandated technique, obsolete even by the school's standards, created a stressline three microns off the joining.

Then Sten grinned. He was already In Violation . . .

He drew two alloy-steel bars on the screen with his lightpen, then altered the input function to JOB PROGRAM. Then he switched the pen's function to WELD. A few quick motions, and somewhere on Vulcan, two metal bars were nailed together.

Or maybe it was a computer-only exercise.

Sten waited in agony as the computer screen blanked. Finally the computer lit up and scrolled PROJECT COMPLETED SATISFACTORILY. He was finished. Sten's fingers flashed as he cut out of the illegal patch, plugged back into the school's computer, which was just beginning to flicker wearily back into WAITING PROGRAM, input the PROJECT COMPLETED SATISFACTORILY from his terminal's memory, shut down, and then he was up and running for the door.

'Frankly, gentlemen,' Baron Thoresen said, 'I care less about the R and D programs conflicting with some imagined ethical rule of the Empire than our own Company's health.'

It had started as a routine meeting of the Company's board of directors, those half dozen beings who controlled almost a billion lives. Then old Lester had so very casually asked his question.

Thoresen stood suddenly and began pacing up and down. The huge director's bulk held the board's attention as much as his rumbling voice and authority.

'If that sounds unpatriotic, I'm sorry. I'm a businessman, not a diplomat. Like my grandfather before me, all I believe in is our Company.'

Only one man was unmoved. Lester. Trust an old thief, the Baron thought. He's already made his, so now he can afford to be ethical.

'Very impressive,' Lester said. 'But we – the board of directors – didn't ask about your dedication. We asked about your expenditures on Bravo Project. You have refused to tell us the nature of your experimentation, and yet you keep returning for additional funding. I merely inquired, since if there were any military possibility we might secure an assistance grant from one or another of the Imperial foundations.'

The Baron looked at Lester thoughtfully but unworried. Thoresen was, after all, the man with the cards. But he knew better than to give the crafty old infighter the least opening. And Thoresen knew better than to try threats. Lester was too scarred to know the meaning of fear.

'I appreciate your input. And your concern about the necessary expenditures. However, this project is too important to our future to risk a leak.'

'Do I sense distrust?' Lester asked.

'Not of you, gentlemen. Don't be absurd. But if our competition learned of Bravo Project's goal, not even my close ties with the Emperor would keep them from stealing it – and ruining us.'

'Even if it did leak,' another board member tried, 'there would still be an option. We could possibly affect their supplies of AM_2.'

'Using your close, personal ties with the Emperor, of course,' Lester put in smoothly.

The Baron smiled thinly.

'Even I would not presume that much on friendship. AM_2 is the energy on which the Empire and the Emperor thrive. No one else.'

Silence. Even from Lester. The ghost of the Eternal Emperor closed the conversation. The Baron glanced around, then deliberately dropped his voice to a dry, boring level.

'With no further comments, I'll mark the increased funding as approved. Now, to a simpler matter. We're fortunate in that our maintenance expenditures on Vulcan's port facilities have dropped by a full fifteen per cent. This includes not only internal mooring facilities, but the pre-sealed container facility. But I'm still not satisfied. It would be far better if . . .'

Amos' eyes flickered open as the livie ended and the lights came up. As near as he could gather, the Exec and his joygirl, after they'd moved to The Eye, had gone off to some pioneer planet and been attacked by something or other.

He yawned. Amos didn't think much of livies, but a quiet nap came in handy every now and then.

Ahd nudged him. 'That's what I wanna be when I grow up. An Exec.'

Amos stirred and woke up all the way. 'Why is that, boy?'

''Cause they get adventures and money and medals and . . . and . . . and all my friends wanna be Execs, too.'

'You just get rid of that notion right now,' Freed snapped. 'Our kind don't mix with Execs.'

The boy hung his head. Amos patted him. 'It ain't that you're not good enough, son. Hell, any Sten is worth six of those cl—'

'Amos!'

'Sorry. People.' Then Amos caught himself. 'The hell. Callin' Execs clots ain't talkin' dirty. That's what they is. Anyway, Ahd, those Execs ain't heroes. They're the worst. They'd kill a person to meet a quota. And then cheat his family outa the death benefits. You becomin' an Exec wouldn't make me and your ma – or you – proud.'

Then it was his little girl's turn.

'I wanna be a joygirl,' she announced.

Amos buried his grin as he watched Freed jump about a meter and a half. He decided he'd let her handle that one.

Pressure finally split the pipe, and the escaping gas forced it directly against the hole it had punched through into The Row.

The first to die was an old Mig, who was leaning against the curving outer wall of the dome a few centimeters from the sudden hole in the skin. By the time he'd seen the fluorine burn away flesh and ribcage, leaving the pulsing redness of his lungs, he was already dead.

In The Row's control capsule, a group of bored Techs watched a carded-out Mig try to wheedle a joygirl into a reduced-rate party. One Tech offered odds. With no takers. Joygirls don't give bargains.

The pressure finally dropped below the danger threshold and alarms flared. No one flinched. Breakdowns and alarms were an every-shift occurrence on Vulcan.

The Chief Tech strolled casually over to the main computer. He tapped a few keys, silencing the *bong-bong-bong* and flashing lights of the alarms.

'Now, let's see what the glitch is.'

His answer scrolled up swiftly on a monitor screen.

'Hmm. This is a little dicey. Take a look.'

His assistant peered over the Tech's shoulder.

'Some kind of chemical leak into the dome. I'll narrow it some.' The Tech tapped more computer keys, cutting a bit deeper into the information banks.

AIRLOSS INDICATED; PRESENCE OF CONTAMINANT; POTENTIAL LIFE JEOPARDY; REDLINE ALARM.

The Chief Tech finally reacted with something other than boredom.

'Plinking Maintenance and their damned pipe leaks. They think we've got nothing better to do than clean up after them. I've got a mind to input a report that'll singe every hair off their hairless—'

'Uh . . . sir?'

'Don't interfere with my tantrums. Whaddaya want?'

'Don't you think this should be repaired? In a hurry?'

'Yeah. Figure out where – half these damned sensors are broke or else somebody's poured beer in them. If I had a credit for every time . . .'

His voice trailed off as he traced the leak. Finally he narrowed the computer search down, pipe by pipe.

'Clot. We'll have to suit up to get to it. Runs over to that lab dome – *oh!*'

The diagram he was scrolling froze, and red letters began flashing over it: ANY INCIDENT CONNECTED TO BRAVO PROJECT TO BE ROUTED INSTANTLY TO THORESEN.

His assistant puzzled. 'But why does it—' He stopped, realizing the Chief Tech was ignoring him.

'Clotting Execs. Make you check with them anytime you gotta take a . . .' He tapped for the registry, found Thoresen's code, hit the input button, and settled back to wait.

The Baron shook the hands of each of his fellow board members as they filed out. Asking about the health of their families. Mentioning dinner. Or commenting on the aptness of someone's suggestions. Until Lester.

'I appreciate your presence, Lester, more than you can imagine. Your wisdom is definitely a guiding influence on the course of—'

'Pretty good duck-and-away on my question, Thoresen. Couldn't do it better myself.'

'But I was not avoiding anything, my good man. I was only—'

'Of course you were only. Save the stroking for these fools. You and I understand our positions more clearly.'

'Stroking?'

'Forget it.' Lester started past, then turned. 'Of course you know this isn't personal, Thoresen. Like you, I have only the best interests of *our* Company at heart.'

The Baron nodded. 'I wouldn't expect anything else of you.'

Thoresen watched the old man as he hobbled out. And decided that old thieves get foolish. What could be more personal than power?

He turned toward the source of a discreet buzz and pointed. Six shelves of what appeared to be antique books dropped away, allowing access to a computer panel.

He took three unhurried steps and touched the RESPONSE button. The Chief Tech floated into view. 'We have a problem, sir, here in Rec Twenty-six.'

The Baron nodded. 'Report.'

The Chief Tech punched keys, the screen split and the details of the leak into The Row scrolled down one side. The Baron took it in instantly. The computer projected that the deadly gas would fill the rec dome in fifteen minutes.

'Why don't you fix it, Technician?'

'Because the clotting computer keeps spitting "Bravo Project, Bravo Project" at me,' the Chief Tech snarled. 'All I need is a go from you and I'll have this thing fixed in no time flat and no skin off anybody's – I'll have it fixed.'

The Baron thought a moment.

'There's no approach to that leak by now except through the Bravo Project lab? Can't you just put a vacuum maintenance Tech out?'

'Not a chance. The pipe's so badly warped we'll have to chop it off at the source. Yessir. We'll have to get into the lab.'

'Then I can't help you.'

The Chief Tech froze.

'But – that leak won't stop at Rec Twenty-six. Clotting fluorine'll combine, and then eat anything except a glass wall.'

'Then dump Twenty-six.'

'But we've got almost fourteen hundred people—'

'You have your orders.'

The Chief Tech stared at Thoresen. Suddenly nodded and keyed off.

The Baron sighed. He made a mental note to have Personnel up recruiting for the new unskilled-labor quotient. Then rolled the event around, to make sure he wasn't missing anything.

There was a security problem. The Chief Tech and, of course, his assistants. He could transfer the men, or, more simply— Thoresen wiped the problem out of his mind. His dinner menu was flashing on the screen.

The Chief Tech whistled tunelessly and slowly tapped a fingernail on the screen. His assistant hovered nearby.

'Uh, don't we have to . . .'

The Chief Tech looked at him, then decided not to say anything. He turned away from the terminal, and swiftly unlocked the bright red EMERGENCY PROCEDURES INPUT control panel.

Sten pyloned off an outraged Tech and hurtled down the corridor toward The Row's entrance, fumbling for his card. The young Sociopatrolman blocked his entrance.

'I saw that, boy.'

'Saw what?'

'What you did to that Tech. Don't you know about your betters?'

'Gee, sir, he was slipping. Somebody must have spilled something on the slideway. I guess it's a long way to see what exactly happened. Especially for an older man. Sir.' He looked innocent.

The younger patrolman brought an arm back, but his partner caught his wrist. 'Don't bother. That's Sten's boy.'

'We still oughta . . . oh, go ahead, Mig. Go on in.'

'Thank you, sir.'

Sten stepped up to the gate and held his card to the pickup.

'Keep going like you are, boy, and you know what'll happen?'

Sten waited.

'You'll run away. To the Delinqs. And then we'll go huntin' you. You know what happens when we rat those Delinqs out? We brainburn 'em.'

The patrolman grinned.

'They're real cute, then. Sometimes they let us have the girls for a few shifts . . . before they put them out on the slideways.'

Hydraulics screamed suddenly, and the dome seal-off doors crashed across the entrance. Sten fell back out of the way, going down.

He looked at the two patrolmen. Started to say something . . . then followed their eyes to the flashing red lights over the entrance:

ENTRANCE SEALED . . . EMERGENCY . . . EMERGENCY . . .

He slowly picked himself up. 'My parents,' Sten said numbly. 'They're inside!'

And then he was battering at the solid steel doors until the older patrolman pulled him away.

Explosive bolts fired around six of the dome panels. The tiny *snaps* were lost in the typhoon roar of air blasting out into space.

Almost in slow motion, the escaping hurricane caught the shanty cubicles of The Row, and the people in them, and spat them through the holes into blackness.

And then the sudden wind died.

What remained of buildings, furniture, and the stuff of life drifted in the cold gleam of the faraway sun. Along with the dry, shattered husks of 1,385 human beings.

Inside the empty dome that had been The Row, the Chief Tech stared out the port of the control capsule. His assistant got up from his board, walked over and put his hand on the Tech's arm.

'Come on. They were only Migs.'

The Chief Tech took a deep breath.

'Yeah. You're right. That's all they were.'

Chapter Two

Imagine Vulcan.

A junkyard, hanging in blackness and glare. Its center a collection of barrels, mushrooms, tubes, and blocks stacked haphazardly by an idiot child.

Imagine the artificial world of Vulcan, the megabillioncredit heart of the Company. The ultimate null-environment machine shop and factory world.

The Company's oreships streamed endlessly toward Vulcan with raw materials. Refining, manufacture, sub- and in many cases final assembly of products was completed, and the Company's freighters delivered to half the galaxy. To an empire founded on a mercantile enterprise, the monstrous vertical trust was completely acceptable.

Six hundred years before, Thoresen's grandfather had been encouraged by the Eternal Emperor to build Vulcan. His encouragement included a special C-class tankerload of Antimatter$_2$, the energy source that had opened the galaxy to man.

Work began with the construction of the eighty-by-sixteen-kilometer tapered cylinder that was to house the administrative and support systems for the new world.

Drive mechanisms moved that core through twenty light-years, to position it in a dead but mineral-rich system.

Complete factories, so many enormous barrels, had been prefabricated in still other systems and then plugged into the core world. With them went the myriad life-support systems, from living quarters to hydroponics to recreational facilities.

The computer projections made the then unnamed artificial world seem impressive: a looming ultra-efficient colossus for the most efficient exploitation of workers and materials. What the computer never allowed for was man.

Over the years, it frequently was simpler to shut down a factory unit after product-completion rather than to rebuild it. Other, newer factories, barracks, and support domes were jammed into place as needed. In a world where gravity was controlled by McLean generators, up and down were matters of convenience only. In two hundred years, Vulcan resembled a metal sculpture that might have been titled *Junk in Search of a Welder*.

Eventually, atop the catch-as-catch-can collection of metal The Eye was mounted – Company headquarters linked to the original cylinder core. The sixteen-kilometer-wide mushroom was, in Sten's time, only two hundred years old, added after the Company centralized.

Below The Eye was the cargo loading area, generally reserved for the Company's own ships. Independent traders docked offworld and were forced to accept the additional costs of cargo and passenger transfer by Company space-lighter.

Under the dock was the visitors' dome. A normal, wide-open port, except that every credit spent by a trader or one of his crew went directly into the Company's accounts.

The visitors' dome was as far South as offworlders were permitted. The Company very definitely didn't want anyone else dealing with – or even meeting – their workers.

Vague rumors floated around the galaxy about Vulcan. But there had never been an Imperial Rights Commission for Vulcan. Because the Company produced.

The enormous juggernaut delivered exactly what the Empire needed for centuries. And the Company's internal security had kept its sector very quiet.

The Eternal Emperor was grateful. So grateful that he had named Thoresen's grandfather to the nobility. And the Company ground on.

Any juggernaut will continue to roll strictly on inertia, whether it is the Persian Empire or General Motors of the ancients, or the sprawling Conglomerate of more recent history. For a while. If anyone noticed in Sten's time that the Company hadn't pioneered any manufacturing techniques in a hundred years, or that innovation or invention was discouraged by the Company's personnel department, it hadn't been brought to the Baron's attention.

Even if anyone had been brave enough or foolish enough to do so, it wasn't necessary. Baron Thoresen was haunted by the fact that what his grandfather created was slowly crumbling beneath him. He blamed it on his father, a cowering toady who had allowed bureaucrats to supplant the engineers. But even if the third Thoresen had been a man of imagination, it still would probably have been impossible to bring under control the many-headed monster the elder Thoresens had created.

The Baron had grown up with the raw courage and fascination for blood-combat – physical or social – of his grandfather, but none of the old man's innate honesty. When his father suddenly disappeared offworld – never to be seen again – there was no question that the young man would head the Company's board of directors.

Now, he was determined to revitalize what his grandfather had begun. But not by turning the Company upside down and shaking it out. Thoresen wanted much more than that. He was obsessed with the idea of a kendo masterstroke.

Bravo Project.

And now it was only a few years from fruition.

Under the Baron was his board, and the lesser Executives. Living and working entirely in The Eye, they were held to the Company not only by iron-clad contracts and high pay but that sweetest of all perks – almost unlimited power.

Under the Execs were the Technicians – highly skilled, well-treated specialists. Their contracts ran for five to ten years.

When his contract expired, a Tech could return home a rich man, to set up his own business – with the Company, of course, holding exclusive distribution rights to any new products he might have developed – or to retire.

For the Exec or Tech, Vulcan was very close to an industrial heaven.

For the Migs, it was hell.

It's significant that the winner of the Company's Name-Our-Planet contest, a bright Migrant-Unskilled worker, had used the prize money to buy out his contract and passage out as far from Vulcan as possible.

Fellahin, oakie, wetback – there will always be wandering laborers to perform scutwork. But just as the Egyptian fellah would marvel at the mechanical ingenuity of the Joads, so the twentieth-century assembly-line grunt would be awed by the like of Amos Sten.

For Amos, one world could never be enough. Doing whatever it took for a full belly, a liter of gutbuster, and a ticket offworld, he was the man to fix your omni, get your obsolete harvester to working, or hump your new bot up six flights of stairs.

And then move on.

His wife, Freed, was a backwater farm-world kid with the same lust to see what the next planetfall brought. Eventually, they guessed, they'd find a world to settle on. One where there weren't too many people, and a man and a woman wouldn't have to sweat for someone else's business. Until they found it, though, any place was better than what they'd already seen.

Until Vulcan.

The recruiter's pitch sounded ideal.

Twenty-five thousand credits a year for him. Plus endless bonuses for a man of his talents. Even a contract for ten thousand a year for Freed. And a chance to work on the galaxy's most advanced tools.

And the recruiter hadn't lied.

Amos' mill was far more sophisticated than any machine he'd ever seen. Three billets of three different metals were fed into the machine. They were simultaneously milled and electronically bonded. Allowable tolerances for that bearing – it took Amos ten years to find out what he was building – was to one millionth of a millimeter, plus or minus one thousand millionth.

And Amos' title was master machinist.

But he only had one job – to sweep up burrs the mill spun out of its waste orifices that the dump tubes missed. Everything else was automatic, regulated by a computer half a world away.

The salaries weren't a lie either. But the recruiter hadn't mentioned that a set of coveralls cost a hundred credits, soymeat ten a portion, or the rent on their three barracks rooms was one thousand credits a month.

The time-to-expiration date on their contracts got further away, while Amos and Freed tried to figure a way out. And there were the children. Unplanned, but welcome. Children were encouraged by the Company. The next generation's labor pool, without the expense of recruiting and transportation.

Amos and Freed fought the Company's conditioning processes. But it was hard to explain what open skies and walking an unknown road meant to someone who grew up with curving gray domes and slideways.

Freed, after a long running battle with Amos, had extended her contract six months for a wall-size muraliv of a snowy landscape on a frontier world.

Almost eight months passed before the snow stopped drifting down on that lonely cluster of domes, and the door, with the warm, cheery fire behind it, stopped swinging open to greet the returning worker.

The mural meant more to Amos and Freed than it did to Sten. Even though young Karl didn't have the slightest idea of what it was like to live without a wall in near-touching distance, he'd already learned that the only goal in his life, no matter what it took, was to get off Vulcan.

Chapter Three

'You gotta remember, boy, a bear's how you look at him.'

'Dad, what's a bear?'

'You know. Like the Imperial Guard uses to scout with. You saw one in that viddie.'

'Oh, yeah. It looks like the Counselor.'

'A little – only it's a mite hairier and not so dumb. Anyway, when you're in a scoutcar, looking down at that bear, he don't look so bad. But when that bear's standing over you . . .'

'I don't understand.'

'That bear's like Vulcan. If you was up The Eye, it'd probably look pretty good. But when you're a Mig, down here . . .'

Amos Sten nodded and poured himself another half liter of narcobeer.

'All you got to remember in a bear fight, Karl, is you don't *ever* want to be second. Most of all, you don't want to get caught by that bear in the first place.'

That was a lesson Sten had already learned. Through Elmore. Elmore was an old Mig who had the solo apartment at the end of the corridor. But most of the off-shift time Elmore was in the children's play area telling stories.

They were the never true, always wonderful part of the oral tradition that industrial peasants from a thousand worlds had brought to Vulcan, making their own underground tradition.

The Drop Settling of Ardmore. The Ghost Ship of Capella. The Farmer Who Became King.

And Vulcan's own legends. *The Delinqs Who Saved the Company.* The eerie, whispered stories of the warehouses and factory domes that were generations-unused by humans . . . but still had something living and moving in them.

Sten's favorite was the one Elmore told least often – about how, one day, things would change. How someone would come from another world, and lead the Migs up, into The Eye. A day of reckoning when the air cycling system would spew the blood of the Execs. The best was the last, when Elmore said slowly that the man who would lead the Migs would be a Mig himself.

The corridor's parents never minded Elmore. He kept the kids out of their hair, and, very grateful, they all chipped in to card Elmore some kind of present every Founder's Day. If any of them knew most of Elmore's stories were anti-Company, they never said anything. Nor would they have cared.

The end was inevitable. Some kid talked around the wrong person. Like the Counselor.

One off-shift, Elmore didn't return. Everyone wondered what had happened. But the topic became boring, and everyone forgot.

Not Sten. He saw Elmore again, on The Row. The man was a shambling hulk, stumbling behind a street-cleaning machine. He paused beside Sten and looked down at the boy.

Elmore's mouth opened, and he tried to speak. But his tongue lolled helplessly, and his speech was guttural moans. The machine whistled, and Elmore obediently turned and stumbled away after it. The word crawled out of Sten's mind: brainburn.

He told his father about what he'd seen. Amos grimaced. 'That's the secret you gotta learn, boy. You got to zig when they zag.'

'What'd I tell you about zigging, son?'

'I couldn't, pa. There were four of them, and they was all bigger than me.'

'Too bad, boy. But there's gonna be a lot of things bigger than you come along. How you gonna handle this one?'

Sten thought for a minute.

'They won't look nigh as big from the back, would they, dad?'

'That's a terrible thought, Karl. Terrible. Especially since it's true.'

Sten got up.

'Where you headed?'

'I'm . . . gonna go play.'

'Naw. First you're gonna let that black eye go away. And let people forget.'

Two weeks later, one of the four boys was shinnying up a rope in exercise period when it broke and dropped him twenty feet to the steel deck.

Three days after that, two more of the group were exploring an unfinished corridor. It was probably just their bad luck to be standing under a wallslab when the fasteners broke. After the boys were released from the hospital, the Counselor reprimanded their parents.

The leader of Sten's attackers was just as unfortunate. Out after curfew, he was jumped from behind and battered into unconsciousness. After an investigation, the Counselor said it had probably been a Delinq – a member of one of the wild gangs that roamed the abandoned sectors of Vulcan, one step ahead of brainburn.

Despite the explanations, Sten was left pretty much alone after that.

'Karl. Gotta have a word with you.'

'Uh . . . yeah, dad?'

'Me and the other folks been to a meeting with the Counselor.'

'Oh.'

'You wonderin' what he wanted?'

'Yeah. Oh, yeah. Sure I am.'

'Don't have any idea, do you?'

'Nossir.'

'Didn't think you did. Seems that some Mig's kid went and invented something. Some kinda spray. You don't know anything about that, do you, boy?'

'Nossir.'

'Uh-huh. This spray smells just like . . . well, like when the sewage recycler blew up down on Corridor Eighteen-forty-five. Remember that?'

'Yessir.'

'Kinda quiet tonight, aren't we? Anyway. So somebody went and sprayed this on the Counselor and four of those aides he's got. Sprayed on their pants where they sit down. Is that a laugh you're hidin'?'

'Nossir.'

'Didn't think so. The Counselor wanted all of us parents to find out who's got themselves an antisocial kid and turn him in.'

'What're you gonna do, dad?'

'Already done it. Dropped by the microfiles. Your ma talked to the librarian, while I sort of looked at who's been reading books on chemistry.'

'Oh.'

'Yeah. Oh. Unfortunately, I went and forgot to give them records back.'

Sten didn't say anything.

'My pa told me once – before you go setting a man's foot on fire, you best make sure there's at least six other people with torches in their tool kits. You follow what I mean?'

'Yessir.'

'Thought you might.'

One of the best times was what Sten always thought of as the Off-shift Xypaca.

Xypacas were incredibly nasty little carnivores that had been discovered on some hellworld by the Company's probeships. Nobody knew why the crew had brought back specimens of the psychopathic little reptiles. But they did.

Measuring barely twenty centimeters in height, the Xypaca had a willingness to use its claws and teeth on anything up to a hundred times its own height. One of Sten's teachers, originally from Prime World, said Xypacas looked like mini-tyrannosaurs, whatever they were.

If the Xypaca hated almost everything equally, it had a special hard place in what passed for its heart for its own species. Except during the brief breeding cycle, the Xypaca loved nothing more than tearing its fellow Xypaca apart. Which made them ideal pit-fighting animals.

Amos had just been rewarded by the Company for figuring out his mill would run an extra thousand hours between servicing if the clearing exhaust didn't exit just above the computer's cooling intake. With great ceremony, they knocked a full year off Amos' contract.

Amos, always one for the grand parlay, used that year's credit to buy a Xypaca.

Sten hated the reptile from the first moment, when a lightninglike snap of its jaws almost took off his little finger.

So Amos explained it to him. 'I ain't real fond of that critter either. I don't like the way it looks, the way it smells or the way it eats. But it's gonna be our ticket off of Vulcan.'

His spiel was convincing. Amos planned to fight his Xypaca in small-time preliminary fights only, betting light. 'We win small – a month off the contract here, a week there. But sooner or later it'll be our ticket out of here.' Even Sten's mother was convinced there was something to this latest of Amos' dreams.

And Sten, by fifteen, wanted off Vulcan more than anything else he could imagine. So he fed the Xypaca cheerfully, lived with its rank smell, and tried not to yell too loudly when he was a little slow in getting his hand out of its cage after feeding.

And it seemed, for a while, as if Amos' big plan was going to work. Until the night the Counselor showed up at the fights, held in an unused corridor a few rows away.

Sten was carrying the Xypaca's cage into the arena, following Amos.

From across the ring, The Counselor spotted them and hurried around. 'Well, Amos,' he said heartily, 'didn't know you were a Xy-man.'

Amos nodded warily.

The Counselor inspected the hissing brute under Sten's arm. 'Looks like a fine animal you've got there, Amos. What say we pitch it against mine in the first match?'

Sten looked across the ring and saw the obese, oversized Xypaca one of the Counselor's toadies was handling. 'Dad,' he said. 'We can't. It'll—'

The Counselor frowned at Sten.

'You letting your boy decide what you do now, Amos?'

Amos shook his head.

'Well then. We'll show them we're the best sportsmen of all. Show the other corridors that we're so bored with the lizards they've got that we'd rather fight our own, right?'

He waited. Amos took several deep breaths. 'I guess you haven't decided about the transfers over to the wire mill yet, have you, sir?' he finally asked.

The Counselor smiled. 'Exactly.'

Even Sten knew that handling the mile-long coils of white-hot metal was the deadliest job on Amos' shift.

'We – me and my boy – we'd be proud to fight your Xy, Mister Counselor.'

'Fine, fine,' the Counselor said. 'Let's give them a real good show.'

He hurried back around the makeshift ring.

'Dad,' Sten managed, 'his Xy – it's twice the size of ours. We don't stand a chance.'

Amos nodded. 'Sure looks that way, don't it? But you remember what I told you, time back, about not handling things the way people expect you to? Well – you take my card. Nip on out to that soystand, and buy all you can hide under your tunic.'

Sten grabbed his father's card and wriggled off through the crowd.

The Counselor was too busy bragging to his cronies about what his Xy would do to notice Sten shoving strands of raw soy into the large Xypaca's cage.

After a few moments of haggling, bragging, and bet-placing, the Xy cages were brought into the ring, tipped over, and quickly opened.

The Counselor's thoroughly glutted Xypaca stumbled from his cage, yawned once, and curled up to go to sleep. By the time he was jolted awake, Amos' Xypaca had him half digested.

There was a dead silence around the ring. Amos looked as humble as he knew how. 'Yessir. You were right, sir. We showed them we're sure the best sportsmen, didn't we. Sir?'

The Counselor said nothing. Just turned and pushed his way through the crowd.

After that, Amos couldn't get a fight for his Xypaca in any match at any odds. Nobody mourned that much when the Xypaca died – along with all the others – after a month or two. Lack of necessary trace elements, somebody said.

By that time, Amos was already busy figuring out another scheme to get himself and his family off Vulcan.

He was still scheming when Thoresen dumped the air on The Row.

Chapter Four

The Baron's words rolled and bounced around the high-roofed tube junction. Sten could pick out an occasional phrase:

'Brave souls . . . Vulcan pioneers . . . died for the good of the Company . . . names not to be forgotten . . . our thirty million citizens will always remember . . .'

Sten still felt numb.

A citizen, coming off shift, elbowed his way through the crowd of about fifty mourning Migs, scowling. Then he realized what was going on. He pulled what he hoped was a sorrowful look in his face and ducked down a tube opening.

Sten didn't notice.

He was staring up at the roof, at the many-times-magnified picture of the Baron projected on the ceiling. The man stood in his garden, wearing the flowing robes that Execs put on for ceremonial occasions.

The Baron had carefully picked his clothes for the funeral ceremony. He thought the Migs would be impressed and touched by his concern. To Sten he was nothing more than a beefier, more hypocritical version of the Counselor.

Sten had made it through the first week . . . survived the shock. Still, his mind kept fingering the loss, like an amputee who can ghost-feel a limb he no longer owns.

Sten had holed up in the apartment for most of the time. At intervals the delivery flap had clicked and every now and then he'd walked over and eaten something from the pneumatiqued trays of food.

Sten had even been duly grateful to the Company for leaving him alone. He didn't realize until years later that the Company was just following the procedure outlined in 'Industrial Accidents (Fatal), Treatment of Surviving Relatives of.'

From the quickly vidded expressions of sympathy from Amos' and Freed's supervisors and the children's teachers, to the Sympathy Wake Credits good at the nearest rec center, the process of channeling the grief of the bereaved was all very well calculated. Especially the isolation – the last thing the Company wanted was a mourning relative haunting the corridors, reminding people just how thin was the margin between life and death in their artificial, profit-run world.

The Baron's booming words suddenly were nothing but noise to Sten. He turned away. Someone fell in beside him. Sten turned his head, and then froze. It was the Counselor.

'Moving ceremony,' the man said. 'Touching. Quite touching.'

He motioned Sten toward a slideway bibshop and into a chair. The Counselor pushed his card into a slot and punched. The server spat two drinks. The Counselor took a sip of his drink and rolled it around his mouth. Sten just stared at the container before him.

'I realize your sorrow, young Sten,' the Counselor said. 'But all things grow from ashes.'

He took something from his pocket and put it in front of Sten. It was a placard, with KARL STEN, 03857-CON19-2-MIG-UNSK across the top. Sten wondered when they'd snapped the picture of him on the card's face.

'I knew that your great concern was, after the inevitable mourning period, what would happen to you next. After all, you have no job. No credits, no means of support. And so forth.'

He paused and sipped his drink.

'We have examined your record and decided that you deserve special treatment.' The Counselor smiled and tapped the card with a yellow fingernail.

'We have decided to allow you full worker's citizenship rights with all of the benefits that entails. A man-size monthly credit. Full access to all recreational facilities. Your own home – the one, in fact, in which you grew up.'

The Counselor leaned forward for the final touch. 'Beginning tomorrow, Karl Sten, you take your father's place on the proud assembly lines of Vulcan.'

Sten sat silent. Possibly the Counselor thought he was grateful. 'Of course, that means you will have to serve out the few years left on your father's contract – nineteen, I believe it was. But the Company has waived the time remaining on your mother's obligation.'

'That's very generous of the Company,' Sten managed.

'Certainly. Certainly. But as Baron Thoresen has so often pointed out to me in our frequent chats – in *his* garden, I might add – the welfare of our workers must come before all other things. "A happy worker is a productive worker," he often says.'

'I'm sure he does.'

The Counselor smiled again. He patted Sten's hand and rose. Then he hesitated, inserted his card in the slot again and punched buttons. Another drink appeared from the slot. 'Have another, Citizen Sten. On me. And let me be the first to offer my congratulations.'

He patted Sten again, then turned and walked down the street. Sten stared after him. He picked up the drinks, and slowly poured them on the deck.

Chapter Five

The on-shift warning shrilled and Sten sourly sat up. He'd already been awake for nearly two hours. Waiting.

Even after four cycles the three-room apartment was empty. But Sten had learned that the dead must mourn for themselves. That part had been walled off, though sometimes he'd slip, and some of the grief would show itself.

But mostly he was successful at turning himself into the quiet, obedient Mig the Company wanted. Or at least at faking it.

The wallslot clicked, and a tray slid out with the usual quick-shot energy drink, various hangover remedies, and antidepressants.

Sten took a handful at random and dumped them down the waste tube. He didn't want or need any, but he knew better than to ignore the tray.

After a few hours, it would retract and self-inventory. Then some computer would report up the line on Sten's lack of consumption. Which would rate a reprimand from the Counselor.

Sten sighed. There was a quota on everything.

Far up at the head of the line a worker touched his card to the med-clock. The machine blinked and the man shoved his arm into its maw. It bleeped his vital signs, noted he was free of alcohol or drugs that might be left over from last off-shift's routine brawl, and clocked him in.

The man disappeared into the factory and the line moved two steps forward.

Sten moved forward with the rest, gossip buzzing around him.

'Considerin' Fran was the loosest man with a quota on the bench, I think it was clottin' fine of the Company – so he lost an arm; only thing he ever did with it is pinch joygirls. They gave him a month's credit, didn't they? . . .'

'You know me, not a man on Vulcan can match me drink for drink – and next shift I'm rarin' for the line – I'm a quota fool! Bring 'em on, I says, and look out down the line . . .'

It was Sten's turn. He slotted his card, stared at the machine dully as it inspected and approved him, and then walked reluctantly into the factory.

The assembly building was enormous, honeycombed from floor to ceiling with belts, tracks, giant gears, and machines. The Migs had to inch along narrow catwalks to keep from falling or being jerked into the innards of some machine and pounded, pressed, and rolled into some nameless device that would eventually be rejected at the end of the line because it contained odd impurities.

After nearly two months in the factory, Sten had learned to hate his partner almost as much as the job. The robot was a squat gray ovoid with a huge array of sensors bunched into a large insect eye that moved on a combination of wheels and leg stalks that it let down for stairs. Only the eye cluster and the waggling tentacles seemed alive.

Most of all, he hated its high-pitched and nagging voice. Like an old microlibrarian that Sten remembered from his Basic Creche.

'Hurry,' it fussed, 'we're running behind quota. A good worker never runs behind quota. Last cycle, in the third sector, one Myal Thorkenson actually doubled his quota. Now, isn't that an ideal worth emulating?'

Sten looked at the machine and thought about kicking it. Last time he'd tried that, he'd limped for two days.

Sten's robot prodded him with its voice.

'Hurry now. Another chair.'

He picked up another seat from the pile in front of the long silver tube. Then he carried it back to where the robot squatted, waiting.

Sten and his robot were at the tail end of a long assembly line of movers, the capsules used in the pneumatic transit systems common to most industrial worlds.

The robot was the technician. Sten was the dot-and-carry man. His job was to pick up a seat from the pile, lug it inside the tube to the properly marked slot, and then position it while the robot heat-sealed the seat to the frame. It was a mind-numbing job that he never seemed to do quite right for his mechanical straw boss.

'Not there,' the robot said. 'You always do it wrong. The position is clearly marked. Slide it up now. Slide it up.'

The robot's heatgun flashed.

'Quickly, now. Another.'

Sten lumbered back down the aisle, where he was met by a worker whose name he couldn't remember. 'Hey. You hear? I just got promoted!'

'Congratulations.'

The man was beaming. 'Thanks. I'm throwing a big bash after shift. Everyone's invited. All on me.'

Sten looked up at the fellow. 'Uh, won't that set you back – I mean, put you even with the promotion?'

The man shrugged.

'So I card it. It'll only add another six months or so to my contract.'

Sten considered asking him why it was so important to rush right out and spend every credit – and then some – of his raise. How he could throw away another six months of his life on . . . He already knew the answer. So he didn't bother.

'That's right,' he sighed. 'You can card it.'

The Mig rushed on.

Leta was about the only bright spot in Sten's life those days.

In many ways, she was the typical joygirl. Hired on the same kind of backwater planet Sten's parents had come from, Leta just knew that when her contract ran out and she immigrated to one of the Empire's leisure worlds, she'd meet and sign a life-contract with a member of the royal family. Or at least a merchant prince.

Even though Sten knew better than to believe in the whore with the heart of gold, he felt that she got real pleasure from their talk and sex.

Sten lay silently on the far side of the bed.

The girl slid over to him and stroked his body slowly with her fingertips.

Sten rolled over and looked up at her.

Leta's face was gentle, her pupils wide with pleasure drugs.

'Ssswrong,' she muttered.

'Contracts. Contracts and quotas and Migs.'

She giggled.

'Nothin' wrong with you. An' you're a Mig.'

Sten sat up.

'I won't be forever. When my contract's up, I'll get off this clottin' world and learn what it is to be a free man.'

Leta laughed.

'I mean it. No carding it. No contract extensions. No more nights on the dome drinking. I'm just gonna put in my time. Period.'

Leta shook her head and got up.

She took several deep breaths, trying to clear her mind.

'You can't do it.'

'Why not?' Sten asked. 'Hell. Even nineteen years isn't forever.'

'You can't do it because its rigged. The whole thing. Controlled. Like your job. Like the games. Like . . . like even this. They set it up so you never get off . . . so you're always tied down to them. And they do it any way they can.'

Sten was puzzled.

'But if it's rigged, and nobody ever gets off Vulcan, what about you?'

'What about me?'

'You're always talking about what you'll do when you leave, and the planets you want to see and the men you want to meet who don't smell like machine oil and sweat and . . . and all that.'

Leta put a hand over Sten's mouth.

'That's me, Sten. Not you. I'm leaving. I've got a contract, and that gives me money and the drugs and whatever I eat or drink. I can't even gamble at the tables. They won't take my card. It doesn't matter what else I do. Just as long as I stay alive, I've got a guarantee that I'll get off of Vulcan. Just like all the other joygirls. Or the shills and the carders. They're all leaving. So are the Techs and the patrolmen. But not the Migs. Migs never leave.'

Sten shook his head, not believing a word she said.

'You're a sweet boy, Sten, but you're gonna die on Vulcan.'

He stayed away from Leta's place for a while, telling himself that he didn't need her. He didn't want somebody around that was going to tell him those kinds of . . . well, they had to be lies, didn't they?

But the longer he stayed away, the more he thought and the more he wondered. Finally he decided that he had to talk to her. To show her that maybe she was right about all the other Migs. But not about him.

At first, the people at the joyhouse pretended they'd never heard of her. Then they remembered. Oh, *Leta.* She was transferred or something. Yeah. Kind of sudden. But she seemed real happy about it when they came for her. Must've been a shift over at that new rec area in The Eye, for the Execs. Or something like that.

Sten wondered.

But he didn't wonder anymore when, late that off-shift, he stole into what had been Leta's cubicle and found the tiny mike planted in the ceiling.

He always wondered what they'd done to her for talking.

*

FIRST MONTH EXPENSES:

Quarters	1,000 credits
Rations	500 "
Foreman fee	225 "
Walkway toll	250 "
TOTAL:	1,975 credits

FIRST MONTH PAY:

2,000 credits less
1,975 credits expenses
25 credits savings

Sten checked the balance column on the screen for the tenth time. He'd budgeted to the bone. Cut out all recreation, and worked on the near-starvation basic diet. But it always came out the same. At twenty-five credits a month, he wouldn't be able to shorten his contract time at all, not by so much as six months. And if he kept on living the way he'd been, he'd go crazy in five years.

Sten decided to go over it one more time. Perhaps there was something he'd missed. Sten tapped the console keys and called up the Company's *Work Guidelines Manual*. He scrolled paragraph after paragraph, looking for an out.

'Clot!' He almost passed it. Sten rolled back up to the paragraph, and read and reread it:

> SAFETY LEVY: All migratory workers shall be levied not less than 35 credits nor more than 67 credits each pay cycle, except when performing what the Company deems to be extraordinary labor which increases the chances of accidental injury and/or death, in which case the levy shall be no less than 75 credits and no more than 125 credits each cycle, for which the Company agrees to provide appropriate medical care and/or death benefits not to exceed 750 credits for funeral arrangements and/or . . .

He slammed his fist on the keys and the vid screen did several fast flip-flops, then went blank.

They had you. No matter how you shaved it, every Mig would always be in the hole.

Sten paced back and forth.

The robot finished the mover and dropped out the exit, waiting for the next cigar tube to be on-lined. The completed car whooshed away, into the pneumatic freight tube and away toward the shipping terminal. But there'd been some error. Something or someone didn't have the next pile of seats ready.

Sten yawned as his robot whined at another machine about quotas. The second machine wasn't about to take the blame. They bickered back and forth electronically until, eventually, the ceiling crane slammed a seat consignment down between them. The robot slid into the mover. Sten hoisted a seat to his shoulder and lugged it aboard.

He set the chair in position and listened to the robot natter while he moved the seat back and forth.

The robot bent forward, heatgun ready. Sten felt a sudden bout of nausea wash over him. This would be it for the rest of his life, listening to the gray blob preach.

Sten lurched forward. The seat slid into the robot, and the machine yowled as it welded itself to seat and mover frame.

'Help! Help! I'm trapped,' it whined. 'Notify master control.'

Sten blinked. Then hid a grin.

'Sure. Right away.'

He ambled slowly off the mover to the line control panel, took a deep breath, and punched the TASK COMPLETE button. The doors of the tube slid closed, and the mover slid toward the freight tube.

'Notify . . . control . . . help . . . help . . .'

And for the first time since he'd been promoted to full worker, Sten felt the satisfaction of a job well done.

Chapter Six

Sten had been 'sick' for over a week before the Counselor showed up.

Actually, he really had been sick the first day. Scared sick that somebody might have discovered his little game with the robot. It'd be considered outright sabotage, he was sure. If he was lucky, they'd put him under a mindprobe and just burn away any areas that didn't seem to fit the Ideal Worker Profile.

But there probably was something worse. There usually was on Vulcan. Sten wasn't sure what something worse could be. He had heard stories about hellshops, where incorrigibles were sent. But nobody knew anybody who'd actually been sent to such a shop. Maybe the stories were just that – or maybe nobody ever came back from those places. Sten wondered sometimes if he wouldn't rather just be brainburned and turned into a vegetable.

The second day, Sten woke up smiling. He realized that nobody'd ever figure out what had happened to the robot. So he celebrated by staying home again, lounging in bed until two hours past shift-start. Then he dug out a few of the luxury food items his parents had saved and just stared at the non-snowing wall mural. He knew better than to stick his card in the vid and watch a reel, or to go out to a rec area. That'd make it even easier for the Company to figure out that he was malingering.

The flakes hanging in the air on the mural fascinated Sten. Frozen water, falling from the sky. It didn't seem very sanitary. Sten wondered if there was any way at all that he could get offworld. Even though those snowflakes didn't look very practical, they might be something to see. Anything might be something to see – as long as it was away from the Company and Vulcan.

By the third day, he'd decided he wasn't going to work anymore. Sten didn't know how long he was going to get away with malingering. Or what would happen to him when they caught him. He just sat. Thinking about the snowflakes and what it would be like to walk in them, with no card in his pocket that said where he was supposed to be and what he was supposed to do when he got there.

He'd just learned that if he squinched his eyes a bit, the snowflakes would almost move again, when the door buzzer went off.

He didn't move. The door buzzed again.

'Sten,' the Counselor shouted through the panel, 'I know you're there. Let me in. Everything is fine. We'll work it out. Together. Just open the door. Everything is fine.'

Sten knew it wasn't. But finally he pulled himself up and walked toward the door. The buzzer sounded again. Then something started fumbling in the Identilock. Sten waited at the door.

Then he hesitated, and moved to one side. The Identilock clicked, and the door slid open. The Counselor stepped inside. His mouth was already open, saying something. Sten leaped, both hands clubbed high above him. The blow caught the Counselor on the side of his head, slamming him into the wall. The Counselor slid down the panel and thumped to the floor. He didn't move. His mouth was still open.

Sten began to shake.

But suddenly, he felt calm; he'd eliminated all the possibilities now. He could do only one thing. He stooped over the unconscious Counselor and riffled quickly through his pockets. Sten found and pocketed the man's card. If he used that instead of his own, it might take Control a little longer to track him down. It'd also give him entry into areas forbidden by Sten's Mig card.

Sten turned and looked around the three bare rooms. Whatever happened next, it would be the last time he'd ever see them. Then he ran out the door, heading for the slideway, the spaceport, and some way off Vulcan.

He felt out of place the moment he stepped off the slideway. The people had begun to change. Only a few Migs were visible, conspicuous in their drab coveralls. The rest were richer and flashier: Techs, clerks, administrators, and here and there the sparkle of strange off-world costumes.

Sten hurried over to a clothes-dispensing machine, slid the Counselor's card into the slot and held his breath. Would the alarms go off now? Were Sociopatrolmen already hurrying to the platform?

The machine burped at him and began displaying its choices. Sten punched the first thing in his size that looked male, and a package plopped into a tray. He grabbed it and pushed his way through the crowd into a rest area.

Sten carded his way into the spaceport administration center, trying to look as if he belonged there. He had to do something about the Counselor's card soon. Everywhere he went, he was leaving a trail as wide as a computer printout sheet.

Nearby, an old, fat clerk was banging at a narcobeer dispenser. 'Clotting machine. Telling me I don't have the clotting credits to . . .'

Sten ambled up to him, bored but slightly curious. The man was drunk and probably so broke that the central computer was cutting him off.

'It's sunspots,' Sten said.

The clerk bleared up at him. 'Think so?'

'Sure. Same thing happened to me last off-shift. Here. Try my card. Maybe a different one will unjam it.'

The clerk nodded and Sten pushed a button and the man's card slid out. He took it and inserted the Counselor's card. A minute later the clerk was happily on his way, chugging a narcobeer.

Three hours later they grabbed him. The clerk was sitting in his favorite hangout, getting pleasantly potted when what seemed like six regiments of Sociopatrolmen burst in. Before he had time to lower his glass, he was beaten, trussed, and on his way to an interrogation center.

In front, the chief Sociopatrolman peered victoriously at the clerk's ID card. Except, of course, it wasn't his. It was the Counselor's.

Sten could feel it as soon as he entered the spaceport Visitor's Center. Even on the run, there was a sense of – well, what it was exactly, he couldn't tell. But he thought it might be freedom.

He moved through the exotic crowd – everything from aliens and diplomats to stocky merchantmen and deep-space sailors. Even the talk was strange: star systems and warp drive, antimatter engines and Imperial intrigue.

Sten edged past a joygirl into a seedy tavern. He elbowed his way through the sailors and found an empty space at the bar. A sailor next to him was griping to a buddy.

'The nerf lieutenant just ignores me. Can you believe that? Me! A projector with fifteen damned years at the clotting sig-board.'

His friend shook his head. 'They're all the same. Two years in the baby brass academy and they think they know it all.'

'So get this,' said the first man. 'I report blips and he says no reason there should be blips. I tell him there's blips anyway. Few minutes later we hit the meteor swarm. We had junk in our teeth and junk comin' out our drive tubes.

'Pilot pulled us out just in time. Slammed us into an evasion spiral almost took the captain's drawers off.'

Sten got his drink – paying with one of his few credit tokens – and moved down the bar. A group of sailors caught his eye. They were huddled around a table, talking quietly and sipping at their drinks instead of knocking them back like the others. They were in fresh clothes, clean-shaven, and had the look of men trying to shake off hangovers in a hurry.

They had the look of men going home.

'Time to hoist 'em,' one of them said.

In unison, they finished their drinks and rose. Sten pushed in behind them as they moved through the crowd and out the door.

Sten huddled in the nose section of the shuttle. A panel hid him from the sailors. They lifted off from Vulcan, and moments later Sten could see the freighter through the clear bubble nose as the shuttle floated up toward it.

The deep-space freighter – an enormous multi-segmented insect – stretched out for kilometers. A swarm of beetlelike tugs towed still more sections into line and nudged them into place. The drive section of the freighter was squat and ugly with horn projections bristling around the face. As the shuttle neared the face, it grinned open.

Just before it swallowed him, Sten thought it was the most beautiful thing he had ever seen.

He barely heard the judge as the man droned on, listing Sten's crimes against the Company. Sten was surrounded by Sociopatrolmen. In front of the judge, the Counselor loomed, his head nearly invisible in plastibandages, nodding painfully as the judge made each legal point.

They had found Sten in the shuttle, huddled under some blankets, stolen ship's stores stacked around him. Even as he messaged Vulcan for someone to pick Sten up, the captain kept apologizing. He had heard stories.

'We can't help you,' he said. 'Vulcan security sends snoopers on every freighter before it clears, looking for people like you.'

Sten was silent.

'Listen,' the captain went on, 'I can't take the chance. If I tried to help and got caught, the Company'd pull my trading papers. And I'd be done. It's not just me. I gotta think of my crew . . .'

Sten came awake as a Sociopatrolman pushed him forward. The judge had finished. It was time for sentencing. What was it going to be? Brainburn? If that was it, Sten hoped he had enough mind left to kill himself.

Then the judge was talking. 'You are aware, I hope, of the enormity of your crimes?'

Sten thought about doing the Mig humility. Be damned, he thought. He didn't have anything to lose. He stared back at the judge.

'I see. Counselor, do you have anything of an ameliorative nature to add to these proceedings?'

The Counselor started to say something, and then abruptly shook his head.

'Very well. Karl Sten, since you, at your young age, are capable of providing many years of service to the Company and we do not wish to appear unmerciful, recognizing the possibility of redemption, I will merely reassign you.'

For a moment, Sten felt hopeful.

'Your new work assignment will be in the Exotics Section. For an indeterminate period. If – ahem – circumstances warrant, after a suitable length of time I will review your sentence.'

The judge nodded, and touched the input button on his justice panel. The Sociopatrolmen led Sten away. He wasn't sure what the judge meant. Or what his sentence was. Except his mind was intact, and he was alive.

He turned at the door, and realized, from the grin on the Counselor's face, he might not be for very long.

BOOK TWO

HELLWORLD

Chapter Seven

'Simply a matter a' entropy. Proves it,' the older man said. And lifted his mug.

The younger man beside him, who wore the flash coveralls of a driveship officer, snickered and crashed his boots onto the table. His coveralls bore the nametag of RASCHID, H. E., ENGINEERING OFFICER.

'Wha's so funny?' his senior said belligerently. He looked at the other four deep-space men around the tavern's table. 'These is me officers, and they didn't hear me say nothin' funny. Did ya?'

Raschid looked around and grinned widely at the drunkenly chorused 'yessirs.' Picked up his own mug in both hands and drained it.

'Another round – I'll tell you. I been listening to frizzly old bastards like you talk about how things is runnin' down, and how they're gettin' worse and all that since I first was a steward's pup.'

The barmaid – the spaceport dive's biggest and only attraction – slid mugs down the long polished aluminum bar. Raschid blew foam off the top of his mug and swallowed.

'Talkin' to fools,' he said, 'is thirsty work. Even when they're high-credit driveship captains.'

The captain's mate flexed his shoulders – a move that had kept him out of fights in a thousand worlds – and glowered. Raschid laughed again.

'Man gets too old to stump his own pins, he generally finds some punko to do it for him. Tell you what, cap'n. You gimme one good example of how things is goin' to sheol in a handbasket, and maybe, jus' maybe, I'll believe you.'

The captain sloshed beer down and wiped the overflow from his already sodden uniform front.

'The way we's treated. Look'a us. We're officers. Contract traders.

Billions a' credits rest on our every decision. But look around. We're on Prime World. Heart'a the Empire an' all that clot. But do we get treated wi' the respect due us? Hell no!'

'We's the gears what makes the Empire turn!' one of his officers yelled.

'So, what d'ya expect?'

'Like I said. Respect. Two, three hunnerd years back, we woulda been fawned over when we made planetfall. Ever'body wantin' to know what it was like out there. Women fallin' over us. I tell you . . .'

The captain stood up and pointed one finger, an effect that was ruined by a belch that rattled the walls slightly.

'When an empire forgets how to treat its heroes, it's fallin' apart!' He nodded triumphantly, turned to his officers. 'That prove it or not?'

Raschid ignored the shouted agreement. 'You think it oughta be like the old days? Say, like when there were torchships?'

'You ain't gotta go back that far, but tha's good example. More beer! Back when they was ion ships and men to match 'em.'

'Torchships my ass,' Raschid sneered. He spat on the floor. 'Those torchships. You know how they worked? Computer-run. From lift-off to set down.'

The other spacemen at the table looked puzzled.

'Wha' 'bout the crews?'

'Yeah. The crews! Lemme tell you what those livies don't get around to showin'. Seems most'a those torch-ships were a little hot. From nozzle right up to Barrier Thirty-three, which is where the cargo and passengers were.

'After a few years, they started havin' trouble gettin' young heroes as crew after these young heroes found their bones turned green an' ran out their sleeves after two-three trips.

'So you know who these crews were? Dockside rummies that had just 'bout enough brains to dump the drive if it got hot beyond Thirty-three. They'd shove enough cheap synthalk in 'em to keep 'em from opening up the lock to see what was on the other side, punch the TAKEOFF button, and run like hell. Those were your clottin' hero torchships an' their hero ossifers.

'An' you think people didn't know about it? You think those drunks got torch parades if they lived through a trip? You think that, you even dumber than you look.'

The captain looked around at his crew. They waited for a cue.

'How come you know so much – Barrier Thirtythree – on'y way a man could know that he'd have to crew one.' The old man's mug slammed down. 'That's it! We come over here for a quiet mug or so – sit around, maybe tell some lies . . . but we ain't standing for nobody who's thinkin' we're dumb enough to believe . . .'

'I did,' Raschid said flatly.

The man broke off. His mate stood up.

'You sayin' you're a thousand years old, chief?'

Raschid shook his head and drained his beer.

'Nope. Older.'

The captain twitched his head at the mate . . . the mate balled up a fist that should've been subcontracted as a wrecking ball and swung.

Raschid's head wasn't there.

He was diving forward, across the table. The top of his head thudded into the captain's third officer, who, with another man, crashed to the floor in a welter of breaking chairs.

Raschid rolled to his feet as the mate turned. He stepped inside the mate's second swing and drove three knife-edged fingers into the inside of the mate's upper arm. The mate doubled up.

Raschid spun as the other two men came off the floor . . . ducking. Not far enough. The captain's mug caromed off the back of his head, and Raschid staggered forward, into the bar.

He snap-bounded up . . . his feet coiled and kicking straight back. The third officer's arm snapped and he went down, moaning. Raschid rolled twice down the bar as the mate launched another drive at him. Grabbed the arm and pulled.

The mate slid forward, collected the end of the beer tap in the forehead, and began a good imitation of petrification.

Raschid swung away from the bar, straight-armed a thrown chair away, and snap-kicked the captain in the side.

He lost interest for a few minutes.

Raschid, laughing happily, picked up the fourth man by the lapels . . . and the broken-armed third officer kicked his legs out from under him.

Raschid crashed down, the fourth man flailing punches at him. The old captain, wheezing like a grampus, danced – very deftly for a man his age – around the edge of the roiling mass, occasionally putting the boot into Raschid's ribs.

Two hands came from nowhere and slammed against the captain's ears. He slumped. Pole-axed.

Raschid scrambled to his feet, nodded at the new man in the fight, then picked up the third officer and slung him through the air at his sudden ally, a gray-haired behemoth with a nose that'd been broken too many times for anyone to be interested in setting it. He thoughtfully dangled the third officer with one hand, making up his mind. Then slammed the heel of his hand down just above the bridge of the man's nose, dropped him, and looked around for someone else.

The man who wore the Raschid nametag was sitting atop the fourth spaceman. He had a double handful of the man's hair, and was systematically dribbling his head on the bar floor.

The gray-haired man walked over, picked up the mate's unfinished beer and drained it. Then he grunted.

'I think you've made your point.'

Raschid peeled back the man's eyelids, and reluctantly let the man's head slam finally to the floor and stood.

The two looked each other up and down.

'Well, colonel?'

The gray-haired man snorted. 'H. E. Raschid. They get dumber every year. Or anyway somebody does.'

'That smacks of insubordination, colonel.'

'Sorry. Would the all-highest Eternal Emperor of a Billion Suns, Ruler of a Zillion Planets, and Kind Overseer of Too Many Goddamned People care to accompany his good and faithful servant back to the palace, where important business awaits, or – or you wanna stay the hell with it and go look for some more action?'

'Later, colonel. Later. Don't wanna corrupt the young.'

The Eternal Emperor threw an arm around his aide – Col. Ian Mahoney, O.C. Mercury Corps, the shadowy Imperial force responsible for intelligence, espionage, and covert operations – and the two men walked, laughing, into the thin sunlight of Prime World.

Chapter Eight

The Baron waited in the anteroom, pacing nervously, glancing now and then at the two huge Imperial Guardsmen playing statue at the entrance to the Eternal Emperor's chambers. If he thought about it – and Thoresen was trying hard not to right now – he was scared. Not a familiar emotion for the Baron.

He had been summoned by the Emperor across half the galaxy with none of the usual Imperial Palace formal politeness. The Baron had simply been told to come. Now. With no explanations. Thoresen hoped it had nothing to do with Bravo Project, although he was sure that even the Emperor's elaborate spy system wouldn't have uncovered it. Otherwise Thoresen was as good as dead.

Finally, the doors hissed open and a tiny robed clerk stepped out to bow him in. Thoresen was only slightly relieved when the guards remained at their stations. The clerk withdrew and the Baron was left in an immense chamber filled with exotic items collected by the Emperor over his thousand years of life. Odd mounted beasts from hunting expeditions on alien worlds, strange art objects, ancient books opened to wonderful illustrations far beyond any computer art conceivable.

The Baron gawked about him, feeling very much like some rube from a border world. Eventually he noticed a man waiting far across the chamber. His back was to Thoresen and he was apparently looking out over the Prime World capital through the large curved glass wall. He was dressed in simple white robes.

The Eternal Emperor turned as Thoresen approached and made his bows.

'We were told by our aides,' the Emperor said, 'that you had a reputation for promptness. Apparently they misinformed us.'

The Baron gobbled. 'I left as soon as—'

The Emperor waved him into silence. He turned and looked outside again. A long silence. The Baron fidgeted, wondering.

'If it's about the Company's latest prospectus, your highness, I can assure you there was no exaggeration. I'd stake my reputation on—'

'Look at that,' the Emperor said.

Confused, Thoresen peered outside. Below, members of the Royal Court flitted about in an elaborate lawn dance on the Palace grounds.

'Simpering fools. They think that because they are titled the Empire revolves around them. Billions of citizens work so they can play.'

He turned to Thoresen. A warm smile on his face. 'But the two of us know better, don't we, Baron? We know what it is to get our hands dirty. We know what it is to work.'

Now Thoresen was *really* confused. The man was blowing hot and cold. What did he want? Were the rumours about his senility true? No, he cautioned himself. How could they be? After all, the Baron had started them.

'Well?' the Emperor asked.

'Well, what, sir?'

'Why did you request this audience? Get to the point, man. We have delegations waiting from twenty or thirty planets.'

'Uh, your highness, perhaps there was some mistake – not yours, of course. But – uh . . . I thought you wanted to—'

'We're glad you came, anyway, Baron,' the Emperor interrupted. 'We've been wanting to talk to you about some rather disturbing reports.' He began to stroll through the room and Thoresen fell in beside him, trying hopelessly to get his mind on top of the situation. Whatever that was.

'About what, your highness?'

'We're sure it's nothing, but some of your agents have been making certain comments to select customers that a few of our – ahem – representatives construe as possibly being, shall we say, treasonous?'

'Like what, your highness?' Feigned shock from Thoresen.

'Oh, nothing concrete comes to our mind. Just little suggestions, apparently, that certain services performed by the Empire could possibly be done best by the Company.'

'Who? Who said that? I'll have them immediately—'

'We're sure you will, Baron. But don't be too harsh on them. We imagine it's just a case of overzealous loyalty.'

'Still. The Company cannot be a party to such talk. Our policy – in fact it's in our bylaws – is absolute.'

'Yes. Yes. We know. Your grandfather drew up those bylaws. Approved them myself as a rider to your charter. Quite a man, your grandfather. How is he, by the way?'

'Uh, dead, your highness. A few hundred years—'

'Oh, yes. My sympathies.'

They were back at the door and it was opening and the little clerk was stepping forward to lead an absolutely bewildered Thoresen out the door. The Emperor started to turn away and then paused.

'Ah, Baron?'

'Yes, your highness?'

'You forgot to tell us why you were here. Is there some problem, or special favor we can grant?'

Long pause from Thoresen. 'No, thank you. I just happened to be on Prime World and I stopped by to inquire – I mean, I just wanted to say . . . hello.'

'Very thoughtful of you, Baron. But everything is proceeding exactly as we planned. Now, if you'll excuse us.'

The door hissed closed. Behind the Emperor there was a rustling sound, and then the sound of someone choking – perhaps fatally – and a curtain parted. Mahoney stepped out from behind it. Doubled up with laughter.

The Emperor grinned, walked over to an ancient wooden rolltop desk and slid open a drawer. Out came a bottle and two glasses. He poured drinks. 'Ever try this?'

Mahoney was suspicious. His boss was known for a perverse sense of humor in certain sodden circles. 'What is it?'

'After twenty years of research it's as close as I can come to what I remember as a hell of a drink. Used to call it bourbon.'

'You made it, huh?'

'I had help. Lab delivered it this morning.'

Mahoney took a deep breath. Then gulped the liquid down. The Emperor watched with great interest. A long pause. Then Mahoney nodded.

'Not bad.'

He poured himself another while the Emperor took a sip. Rolled it around on his tongue and then swallowed. 'Not even close. In fact, it tastes like crap.'

The Emperor drank it down and refilled his glass. 'So? What do you think of him?'

'The Baron? He's so crooked he screws his socks on in the morning.

He ain't no toady, though, no matter how it looked when you were playing him like a fish.'

'You caught that, huh? Tell you what, if I weren't the biggest kid on the block I think he woulda cut my throat. Or tried, anyway.'

The Emperor topped off their drinks and then eased back in his chair, feet on his desk. 'Okay. We had our face to face – good suggestion, by the way. And I agree the man is just dumb enough and power hungry enough to be dangerous to the Empire. Now. Spit it out. What should I be worrying my royal head about?'

Mahoney scraped up another chair, settled into it and put his feet up beside the Emperor's.

'A whole lot of things. But nothing we can prove. Best bit I got is that a real good source tells me that Thoresen is spending credits by the bundle on a thing he calls Bravo Project.'

'What's that?'

'Hell if I know. Couple years ago I had my boy risk his old butt and come right out and ask. Thoresen ain't sayin'. Except that it's, quote, vital to the interests of the Company, endquote.'

'Who's your man?'

Mahoney grimaced. 'I can't say.'

'Colonel! I asked you a question!'

Mahoney sat up straight. He knew where the chain of command started. 'Yessir. It's a guy on the board of directors. Named Lester.'

'Lester . . . I know him. I was at his birth ceremony. Absolutely trustworthy in matters concerning the Empire. 'Course, in a hand of poker – well, nobody's perfect. So Lester is suspicious of this Bravo Project, huh?'

'Very. Thoresen is practically bleeding the Company dry to pay for it. He's maintaining barely enough profit to keep the stockholders happy. Even then, Lester thinks he's messing with the books.'

'That's not much to go on. Even I can't put the Guard on Vulcan on mere suspicion. I'd lose all credibility. Hell, I founded this Empire on the principles of free enterprise and zip government interference.'

'Do you have to believe your own propaganda?'

The Emperor thought about it a second. Then answered regretfully, 'Yes.'

'So what do we do about it?'

The Emperor frowned, then sighed and chugged his drink down. 'Hate to do this, but I got no other choice.'

'Meaning?'

'Meaning, I'm about to lose a great drinking buddy. For a while, anyway.'

Outraged, Mahoney came to his feet. 'You're not sending me to that godforsaken hole? Vulcan's so far out of the way even comets duck it!'

'Got any better ideas?'

Mahoney ran it over. Then shook his head. Slugged down his drink. 'When do I leave?'

'You mean you're still here?'

Chapter Nine

The airlock cycle clanked to an end. Thick yellow gas billowed into the chamber. Sten could barely see the other workers against the opposite wall.

The interior lock door slid open, and Sten walked toward his job station, across the kilometer-wide hemisphere of Work Area 35.

He figured that two years had passed, plus or minus a cycle or six, since he'd begun his sentence. How the time flies when you're having fun, he thought sourly.

The floor-level vats bubbled and boiled, gray slime crawling up onto the catwalks. Sten threaded his way around the scum, around huge, growing lumps of crystal.

He stopped at his first station, and checked the nutrient gauges feeding into one of the meters-high boulders. It took Sten half a very sweaty hour to torch off the spiralling whorls of a granular cancer from the second boulder in his area. He fed the crumbly residue to the atmosphere plants in the nearest vat, and went on through the roiling yellow atmosphere.

Area 35 was an artificial duplicate of a faraway world, where metals assumed a life of their own. Minerals 'grew,' 'blossomed,' and 'died.'

Samples of the various metals indicated one with rare properties – incredible lightness, yet with a tensile strength far in excess of any known alloy or element.

The Company's geologists found the mineral interesting and with enormous commercial potential. There were only two problems:

Its homeworld was a man-killer. That was the easiest part. The Company's engineers could duplicate almost any conditions. And with the condemned Migs of the Exotic Section to harvest the minerals, the casualty rate was 'unimportant.'

The second, and bigger, problem was working the material. After years of experimentation, metal-based 'virii' on the mineral's home-world were mutated, then used as biological tools to machine the crystal.

The shaped metal was used for superstressed applications: drive-ship emergency overrides and atomic plant core sensor supports as well as the ultimate in snob's jewelry. The cost, of course, was astronomical. Sten's foreman once estimated a fist-size chunk as worth an Exec's contract pay for a year.

The growth rate and size of each boulder were carefully controlled and computer monitored. But Sten had found a way to override the nutrient controls on one boulder. For six cycles, a small, unnoticed lump had been cultured, gram by gram, on one boulder.

Sten checked 'his' boulder. The lump was ready for harvesting – and machining into a useful little tool that Sten wasn't planning to tell the Company about.

He unclipped a small canister of a cutting virus from the bulkhead, and triggered its nozzle near the base of his lump. A near-invisible red spray jetted. Sten outlined the base of the growth with it.

He'd once seen what happened when a worker let a bit of the virus spray across his suit. The worker didn't even have time to neutralize the virus before it ate through and he exploded, a greasy fireball barely visible through the roiling yellow haze as the suit's air supply and Area 35's atmosphere combined.

Sten waited a few seconds, then neutralized the virus and tapped the lump free of its mother boulder.

He took the lump to his biomill and clamped it into position, closed and sealed the mill's work area, and hooked his laboriously breadboarded bluebox into circuit so the mill's time wouldn't be logged in Area 35's control section.

Sten set the biomill's controls on manual, and tapped keys. Virus sprayed across the metal lump. Sten waited until the virus was neutralized, then resprayed.

And he waited.

There were only two ways of telling time in Exotic Section. One was by counting deaths. But when the attrition rate was well over 100 per cent per year, that just reminded Sten he was riding on the far edge of the statistics.

The other way was with a handful of memories.

*

The hog-jowled foreman had waited until the guards unshackled Sten and hastily exited back into Vulcan's main section. Then he swung a beefy fist into Sten's face.

Sten went down, then climbed back to his feet, tasting blood.

'Ain't you gonna ask what that was for?'

Sten was silent.

'That was for nothing. You do something, and it's a whole lot worse.

'You're in Exotics now. We don't run loose here like they do up North. Here Migs do what they're told.

'Exotic's split up into different areas. Ever' one of them's a different environment. You'll work in sealed suits, mostly. All the areas are what they call High Hazard Envir'ments. Which means only volunteers work in them. That's you. You're a volunteer.

'You mess, sleep, and rec in Barracks. That's the next capsule down from Guard Section, which is where you are now.

'You don't come north of Barracks unless you figure your area ain't killin' you quick enough.

'One more thing. What goes on in Barracks ain't our business. All that matters is the machines are manned every shift and you don't try to get out. Those is the only rules.'

He jerked his head, and two of the Exotic Section's guards pulled Sten out.

The lump was almost down to the right dimensions. Sten rechecked his 'farm' and corrected the nutrients, then returned to the biomill and set up for the final shaping cut.

Sten's first area was what the foreman called a cinch shift.

It was a prototype high-speed wiremill. Nitrogen atmosphere. Unfortunately, it wasn't quite right yet. Extruder feeds jammed. Drawers put on too much pressure, or, most commonly, the drum-coiler gears stripped.

And every time the plant went down, someone died. Raw wire piling up behind the jammed extruder tore off a man's arm. Broken wire whiplashed through a man like a sword. A coil of wire lifted from its bin curled around a momentarily inattentive inspector's neck and guillotined him.

About a hundred 'volunteers' worked in that area. Sten figured there was one death per cycle.

He figured the foreman had been being funny. Until he graduated and found out how fast other areas killed Migs.

*

The virus had shaped that lump into a dull black rectangle, 10 × 15 × 30 cm. Sten tapped the STORE button, and the neutralizer control, then walked to another console. He quickly built up the three-dimensional model of the tool he would build, which included measurements of the inside of Sten's loosely closed fist.

This tool would fit only one man.

'Ya gon' gimme your synthalk for as long as I want?'

'That's right.'

'What'ya want?'

'You know how to fight. Foreman – his bullies – don't mess with you.'

'Clottin'-A they don't. Learned how to tight-corner all over the galaxy. Boy, I even had some guards training!' The little man beamed proudly. 'You want to be taught?'

'That's it.'

'Yeah. Yeah. Why not? Ain't nothin' else to do down here. 'Cept wait to die.'

Sten hit the TRANSFER switch and input his model, set up as a machining program, into the biomill. Waited until the PROGRAM ACTIVE light went on, then touched the START button.

Small, medium-power lasers glowed and moved toward the block of metal. Virus sprayed onto the block, and more metal crumbled away. Then the lasers 'masked' areas, and the virus shaped that block into the reality of Sten's model.

The shift hours dragged past, and the mill hummed on happily. Once Sten had to shut down when a guard came through. But he didn't stop at Sten's machine.

'Base position. Now. Clot! Stick always goes across your body. Just above the waist. Then you're ready for any kind of defense.'

'What about a knife?'

'You know stick – you'll be able to put that knife about eight inches up the lower intestine of the guy what pulled it on you. Now. One – swing your left up. Stick's straight up and down. Step in . . . naw. Naw. Naw! Stick's gonna go into the side of somebody's neck. You ain't askin' to dance with him. Do it again.'

An hour before shift-change, the TASK COMPLETE light went on. Sten began flushing the mill's interior with neutralizer. He knew better than to hurry.

*

'You in a bibshop. Man breaks off a bottle. Comes at you. What'ya do?'

'Kick him.'

'Naw. Naw. Naw. Hurt yourself that way. Throw somethin'. Anythin'. His arm's low, throw for his face. He's ice-pickin', slide a chair up his groin. Awright. You hit him. He goes back. What'ya do?'

'Kick. Kneecap. Arch if you can get close. Neck.'

'Awright! He goes down. What next?'

'Put his bottle in his face.'

'Sten. I'm startin' to get proud of you. Now. Get your tail in the head. Practice for the rest of the off-shift. Next off-shift, I'll show you what to do if *you* got a knife.'

Sten unlatched the work-area cover and lifted out his tool.

His. For the first time in his life, he had something that wasn't borrowed or leased from the Company. That the material cost was a merchant prince's ransom and the machining techniques used enough power for an entire dome made it even sweeter.

Sten held a slim double-edged dagger in his clumsy suit gloves. The skeleton handle was custom-fit for Sten's fingers to curl around in the deadly knife-fighter's grip the little man had taught him.

There was no guard, just serrated lateral grooves between the haft and blade that tapered from 1.25 cm width down 6.5 cm to a needle tip. The knife was 12.7 cm long and only 0.6 cm thick.

It was possibly the deadliest fighting blade that had ever been constructed. The crystal tapered to a hairedge barely 15 molecules wide, and the weight of the blade alone was enough pressure to cut a diamond in half.

Sten tucked the knife in an unused suit storage pocket. He already had the sheath built.

Hite had done that for him.

He and Sten had hidden out in a normal-environment disused area. He'd put Sten out with a central anesthetic. And then delicately gone to work.

The sheath was inside Sten's lower arm. With pirated microsurgery tools, Hite laid back a section of Sten's skin down to the dermis. He put an undercoat of living plaskin next to the subcutaneous tissue, then body-cemented into place the alloy U-curve that Sten had already built. That would keep the knife's blade from touching anything – including the U-curve.

A wrist muscle was rerouted across the mouth of the sheath to keep the knife in place. Then Hite replaced the layer of dermis and epidermis over the surgical modifications and body-cemented Sten back together.

It took several cycles to heal. But Hite was satisfied the plaskin was non-irritative, and the skin over the sheath would continue to regenerate.

The shift buzzer in Sten's suit blatted. Sten shut down the mill and headed for the lock.

Nobody knew exactly what Hite had done to get stuck in Exotic Section. It was known that he'd been a pioneer-world doctor. It was known that he'd taken a Tech contract on Vulcan for an unknown reason. And it was obvious that he'd done something incredibly wrong.

Hite never told anyone – including Sten – about what he'd done.

He was not only the only medic the Migs had access to but he'd been in Exotic Section for years.

He was also the only friend Sten ever had.

'Sten, lad. The problem with you is you don't laugh enough.'

'Laugh? I'm stuck in the anus of Vulcan . . . everybody's trying to kill me – they're gonna succeed – and you want me to laugh?'

'Of course, boy. Because what could be funnier than all that?'

'I don't get it.'

Hite leaned closer. 'It's because the gods hate you. Personally.'

Sten considered. Then smiled slowly. And started laughing.

'There's your other problem, boy. You laugh too much.'

'Huh?'

'What's there to laugh about? You're up the arse of Vulcan and everyone's trying to kill you. I'd get worried if I were you.'

Sten stared at him. Then shook his head and started howling.

In the shiftroom, Sten fed high-pressure disinfectant into his suit and resealed it. He waited. There was no leak. Sten dumped the disinfectant into the recycler and pegged the suit. In the Exotic Section, elderly vacuum worksuits, condemned by the Techs, were used. Leaks were very common. And in an area, there wasn't time to patch them. Sten yawned and pushed through the Barracks toward his bunk.

The knife was tucked inside Sten's arm. His open hand held it securely in position. Sten couldn't wait to show it to Hite.

Barracks smelled like The Row. Cubed and recubed. With no Sociopatrolmen. A couple of hulks were going through the meager effects of a young boy who lay sprawled in a pool of blood. One of them grinned up at Sten. 'Got fresh meat in today.'

Sten shrugged and kept walking. The ethanol stand was crowded as always. He stopped by his bunk. The female Mig who bunked over him had his blanket hung as a curtain, and paired grunts came from behind it.

Sten headed for Hite's square. The old man had been sick, and Sten hoped he was feeling semihuman. He wanted to ask him more about Pioneer Sector.

There was a knot of men around Hite's bunk. The foreman and some of his toadies. And beside them, a robot trundle.

Two of the thugs picked up a gray, frail, still form from the bunk and dumped it unceremoniously onto the trundle.

Sten broke into a run as the trundle automatically swiveled away. He smashed a fist into its control panel and the trundle stopped.

'Ain't no use,' one of the toadies said. 'Ol' basser's dead.'

'What happened?'

'Guess he just died. Natural causes.'

Sten started to turn . . . then pulled Hite's body over.

Blood still oozed from the slash in Hite's throat. Sten looked up at the foreman.

'He di'n't want to go on-shift. So, like Malek says, he just died. Naturally.'

The foreman made the mistake of laughing.

Sten came off the floor at the foreman. One thug body-checked him and Sten went to the floor, twisted, and came back to his feet.

And the little man echoed in his brain. *You're never angry. You never want anything. You are a response without a mind.*

A toady moved in, and Sten's foot lashed. The man's kneecap shattered audibly and he dropped.

'Take him.'

The toadies surged forward. One huge man had Sten from behind, crushing him with both hands. Sten wiggled an arm free and swung a fist back, thumb extended.

The tough dropped Sten and howled back, blood pouring from his eye socket.

Sten spun, his foot coming wide against the base of the bully's neck. It snapped and the man crashed to the deck.

'Get him, you clots!' the foreman thundered.

The two men left looked at the foreman and at Sten, trying to decide which was worse. One of the men ripped a bunk support free, and the second man's hand snaked into his pocket and flicked out with a gleaming knife, honed down from a hand chisel.

Sten dropped his right hand limply. Curled his fingers. The knife dropped into his hand. Cold. Comforting.

The man with the steel bar reached Sten first, swinging. Sten brought the knife up . . . and the blade razored through the steel. The man gaped for a second at the short steel stub he held, then Sten lashed in and cut his throat like soft butter.

The knifeman feinted once as Sten spun, then lunged for Sten's stomach. Sten overhanded a block . . .

The foreman stared, horrified, as his toady's arm, still holding a knife in writhing fingers, thudded to the deck.

Then the foreman turned and ran. The wrong way. Down, away from the guard capsule. Toward the areas.

Sten caught him just before the shiftroom. The foreman turned. Holding out both hands. Panicked eyes wide.

Sten slashed once.

The foreman screamed as his guts bulged out, and slopped wetly to the deck.

'That was for nothing.'

Sten ran for his suit as alarms began to shrill.

Inside Area 35, Sten could hear the banging on the lock. He wasn't too worried. He'd dumped the lock air and wedged the inner door open. That'd take them some time to get through.

The guards had to figure Sten was trapped. There was no interconnection to another area. All that was outside Area 35 was hard vacuum.

Sten gingerly lifted the viral spray tank out of his biolathe and muscled it to the dome's curving outer wall. He flipped the bleed valve open and scrambled back toward the overturned gravsled as the red viral spray hissed against the dome's skin.

The gravsled was the biggest thing he could get into position. He'd put all of its anchors down, and hoped it would hold when everything went.

The wall cracked and peeled and bubbled out until . . . the wall dissolved and became exploding blackness. A storm of escaping gasses howled into space. Mega-credits' worth of crystal boulders, vehicles, and tools pounded around the hole and then ripped their way out.

The gravsled cracked . . . anchors tore loose, and then, with a grinding crash, the sled came free and thundered toward the hole. It smashed across the hole but was just too large to fit between two main support beams.

And then the howling stopped. And what was left of Area 35 was silent.

Blood ran down into Sten's eyes where he'd slammed into his suit visor rim. He blinked it away and checked his suit carefully for leaks.

Then he slid around the sled and out the hole.

He swayed, momentarily vertiginous as blackness and harsh starlight rose around him.

One way or another, he was out of Exotic Section. And – he managed to grin wryly – achieving one of his dreams. He was out of Vulcan.

And then he was moving. Away from the hole, away from Exotic Section. Headed North, toward the only hole he could maybe hide in – the sprawling main mass of Vulcan.

He had no idea where he was going. First he took steps, then as he became bolder and realized there was enough magnetism left in the suit's boots to keep him from spinning off into space, in great meters-long bounds.

Several times he almost panicked and looked for a non-existent hiding place, when repair craft and patrol boats speared down toward him.

Then he realized . . . all they were worrying about was the sudden expensive explosion kilometers away in Exotics. If they even spotted him, one man in a work-suit wouldn't be connected with the destruction.

Not yet, anyway.

He held out as long as he could – until his suit's air supply began to rasp in his ears, and he could hear the regulator gurgle at him – then went to the first hatchway he saw. Sten guessed it was for routine maintenance.

He fumbled with its catches, and suddenly the hatch slid smoothly open. He crawled in the tiny lock chamber, closed the outer door, and hit the cycle button.

The inner door creaked open – at least there was air on the other side to carry noise – and Sten stepped out.

A long, deserted corridor stretched away before and behind him. Dust was thick on the walkway, and several of the overheads were burnt out. Sten slumped down against a bulkhead. He was free. He was home.

He considered those two thoughts. And smiled. His smile became laughter.

Free. Until they caught him. Home? On Vulcan?

But he laughed, as Hite had taught him.

It seemed like the right thing to do.

Chapter Ten

Thoresen hurried off the gravsled toward the shuttle. A few more minutes and he would be off Prime World and heading back to Vulcan. He was still nervous about the Emperor and half believed that at any second he would be arrested.

The Baron tensed as several guardsmen walked around a corner. But they were deep in conversation and were obviously not after him. He relaxed.

A certain wild part of him almost wished for a confrontation. Thoresen was not used to bowing to other men. He didn't like the feeling of terror. He walked past the soldiers, thinking that he could take them. Instantly. His mind fingered the possibilities. He would rip the throat out of the first one. The second would die as he broke his nose and drove the cartilage into the brain. The third – he shook off the feeling. He was breathing easier as he started up the loading ramp.

A little later, he was on the shuttle and heading for the liner orbiting around Prime World. Settling back – really relaxing for the first time since he left Vulcan – Thoresen thought over his meeting with the Emperor.

There were several possibilities: (a) The Emperor was senile. Unlikely; (b) The man was really trying to soothe a few aides. Nonsense. It wasn't his style; (c) The Emperor knew about Bravo Project. Wrong. Thoresen was alive, wasn't he? (d) The Emperor suspected something was up but couldn't prove it. Hence the meeting to feel Thoresen out and issue a subtle warning. Now, that was more probable.

All right. What would be the Emperor's next move? That was easy. He'd tighten the investigation. Send more spies to Vulcan.

The Baron smiled to himself, feeling much better about the situation. He closed his eyes to take a brief nap. Just before he fell asleep he made a note to himself. He'd order Security to clear with him the credentials of all offworlders. He looked forward to interviewing a few spies personally.

Chapter Eleven

Sten had been on the run for about a month when he met the girl. She was about fifteen and dressed in a shapeless, grimy black coverall. Her face and hands were smeared with grease. And she came within a hair of killing him. Her name was Bet. Sten thought she was the most beautiful woman he had ever seen.

Sten had made it that far by hiding in the ventilation ducts that warrened Vulcan. They varied in size from twenty-meter-wide central ductways to shoulder-wide tubes to individual rooms. The ducts were caked with the grease of years and periodically blocked by huge filter screens. Sten used a small powerdriver he had stolen from a warehouse to get through the screens.

The ventilation ducts went everywhere, giving him quick access to food warehouses and empty apartments when he needed to forage. The only real danger he ever encountered was when he chanced on work parties servicing the filter screens. But they were easy to avoid. He had also heard strange scrabbling and scratching noises which he figured were groups of Delinqs. So far, he had steered clear of them, pretty sure of his reception.

The only things he feared were the periodic extermination raids mounted by the Company against the Delinqs. From what he had heard back in his Mig days, the few survivors were guaranteed brainburn.

Still, he lived fairly well, and in fact had gained a kilo or two since his escape. He was just getting slightly bored and more than a little picky about his meals when he made a real find.

The hydroponics farm was a glistening green world that stretched out of sight into the mists. Towering purple ferns could be seen and row upon row of every conceivable plant, some in flower, some drooping with ripe vegetables and fruit. Sten had never seen anything like it before except at the vid library.

No humans were about. Only agricultural bots – the lowest form – tending and harvesting the plants. Sten dropped through the duct and landed on the ground. It was soft and green. Sten looked down at his feet. So that's what grass looks like.

He walked through the rows smelling – fresh air? Flowers? Soil? He picked a handful of what he thought might be grapes. Nibbled on them, his face lighting up at the fresh taste. Sten took off his shirt and started stuffing it until the seams nearly split.

A soft footfall. Sten whirled, his knife flashing out. Then he hesitated. It was a girl.

She carried a Sociopatrolman's stun rod, tied to a half-meter-long fiber rod. She hadn't spotted him yet and Sten started to slide back into a row of plants. Then he hesitated. She didn't behave like a Mig or a Tech. She had to be a Delinq.

Sten suddenly remembered one of his father's phrases: 'The enemy of my enemy is my friend.' He stepped from behind a huge fern into full view.

The girl saw him, froze, then flipped the stun rod on and drew back her arm, ready to hurl the improvised spear at Sten.

'Wait.'

The girl stopped. Still ready to throw. No fear at all. Her eyes widened as his knife hand flickered and the blade disappeared from view. He held out his hands, palms up.

'Who are you?'

'I'm Sten.'

'You on the run?'

Sten nodded.

'From where?'

'Exotic Section.'

The stun rod came up.

'Liar! Nobody's ever—'

'I blew out an area. Came across the outside in a suit. I've been living in the ducts.'

The girl frowned.

'We heard there was an accident. But that's impossible.'

Sten waited.

'You've got the muscles that come from lifting. And those scars on your legs . . . You're a runaway.'

'Then what am I doing here?'

The girl smiled humorlessly. 'Who knows? Trying to infiltrate us. Just weird. Maybe a real runner.'

Sten shrugged.

'Hold your hands out again,' the girl ordered. 'Palms up.'

Sten did as she asked. The girl inspected Sten's calloused and work-torn hands and looked closely at the grime-encrusted ragged nails.

'You could've faked that. Strip.'

'What?' Sten managed.

'Take off your clothes. If you're an infiltrator, you'll have a soft body like a socioslime.'

Sten hesitated.

'This stun rod,' the girl said evenly, 'is power-jumped. It puts out about two hundred per cent more force than it should for about two seconds. Then it burns out. But by then whoever it hits is ready for recycling.'

Sten fingered the fastener, then stepped out of the suit.

The girl walked completely around him, then stood, considering for a moment, in front of him.

The girl smiled slightly.

'It's a very good body.'

Then her smile vanished.

'Come on. Get dressed. I'm Bet.'

As he stepped into his clothes, she dumped his 'harvest' out of his shirt and handed it to him. She began picking through the vegetables and fruits, tossing some away as too green, stuffing others into a sack.

'You're lucky I came along,' she said. 'Most runners are caught after the first month.'

'You a Delinq?'

She gave him a disgusted look.

'I wouldn't be alive if I weren't. We know how to duck the sweeps. We know the places to hide, where they almost never look. A good Delinq can last . . . maybe five years.'

Sten was shocked.

'How long since you ran?' he asked.

'Three years now.'

She shouldered the sack and headed for a ventilation duct.

'Come on. I'll take you to Oron.'

She slid into the duct, motioned him past her, then replaced the filter screen. Then she pulled what appeared to be a tiny headband from her coveralls, flicked the light on, and wriggled by Sten to take the lead. The soft brush of her body against his turned Sten's mouth dry. He took a deep breath and crawled after her.

*

The Delinqs paid no attention to Sten and Bet as they dropped from the duct into the long-abandoned warehouse.

About thirty of them, dressed in the stolen finery of Vulcan's warehouses, were celebrating a raid on a particularly rich warehouse, and most of them were drunk or drugged. It was one of the strangest things Sten had ever seen: a party in almost absolute silence. Whispering – even in the safety of home base – was second nature to a Delinq.

Stranger still, they were all children. The youngest, he estimated, was no more than twelve – a girl rubbing oil on the body of a boy about thirteen. The oldest person Sten saw, as Bet led him through them, was in his late teens. Sten felt like an old man.

Oron was sprawled in the office section of the warehouse. At first glance, he appeared to be in his forties. A closer look showed that the white hair and withered arm belonged to a man only a year or so older than Sten.

His face was the worst. Half of it was mobile. The other frozen like a deathmask.

Beside him sat a pudgy girl, busily working her way through a pile of fruit. Behind him, on a fur-piled bed, were two naked girls. Both beautiful and sleeping – or drugged.

'This is Sten,' Bet said. 'He's a runner.'

Oron turned to the fat girl and pointed at Bet. 'Who is she?'

'Bet. You sent her out last shift to the hydroponic farm,' the girl said, not missing a bite.

Sten froze, arced his wrist, getting ready to spring out his knife. If this was Bet's gang, why didn't Oron know—? Oron caught Sten's expression. Half his face smiled.

'Fadal is my memory,' he said, gesturing at the pudgy girl. 'I am – am a . . .' His brow furrowed.

'Brainburn,' Fadal answered for him.

'Yes. I did something wrong when I was young, for which they . . . brainburned me. But something went wrong. It didn't . . . take. Or rather . . . it only partially worked.'

He motioned at his face and withered arm. 'My body. And part of my mind . . . So I am an . . . amnesiac.'

'Then how do you—?' Sten began.

'All that happens this shift is very clear to me. But the next shift, I do not know what went before. I remember how to talk. That I am a Delinq. That I am Oron. Although sometimes I forget that. And that I am the leader of these people. But . . . I must be reminded of . . . of . . . yes . . . of their names. And what I asked them to do.'

'He's the leader,' Bet said, 'because he can always figure out where to raid. And when to move just before there is another sweep.'

'Oron has been a Delinq for twelve years,' Fadal said.

She seemed to think it was a compliment. Sten guessed it just might be.

'So you are a runner,' Oron said. 'And you want to join us?'

Sten hesitated, looked at Bet, and then shrugged.

'Sure. Why not?'

'Do you vouch for him, Bet?'

Bet was surprised. Usually there was a test – and questions. Why was Oron willing to rely solely on her word? She glanced over at Sten, who was waiting for her answer. Then she could see it. The look on his face. He didn't care about the Delinqs or Oron. He was obviously confident in his abilities to survive without them. He was here for . . . her.

Sten felt his heart jump as she nodded.

'Do we team him?'

Bet met Oron's eyes. Suddenly she laughed.

'Yes.'

'Bet will be your team partner,' he said to Sten. 'Do what she . . . shows you . . . and you will live. Now, sit . . . have wine. And tell me . . . your story.'

Sten accepted a glass of wine and sprawled on the floor. He began his story, glancing over at Bet now and then as he spoke.

Chapter Twelve

'I wanna watch livie, mommie, I wanna watch livie.'

The Creche nurse hustled over to the boy, a warm smile on her face. She hugged him and palmed a button; the wall flickered, became a screen, and cartoon characters scampered in across it. The fourteen-year-old boy giggled in delight.

Bet's parents had sold her to the Company a few cycles before. The price: their contracts were torn up and the Mig couple was free to leave Vulcan. It was considered a remarkable bargain on both sides.

Normally the Company preferred Mig children to grow up into Mig men and women. But there were exceptions officials constantly sought. The Company psych who tested Bet whistled at her raw intelligence scores. Company reps approached Bet's parents, who told her she was going away to a much better place. They kissed her and put her to bed. Bet woke up in a Company Creche, surrounded by mostly younger children. The Company usually started with children of five, but Bet's score had been impressive. It decided to take a chance with the eight-year-old.

For the first time in her life, Bet was smothered by love and attention. The Creche Mothers hugged her, kissed her, and gave her toys. Very few things brought punishment or harsh words. Still, Bet never trusted the Mothers for a minute. No one ever discovered this, because Bet had learned very young to keep quiet, give answers only when asked, and always do what she was told.

It took Bet a long time to figure out what was terrifying her. It was the other children . . . her playmates.

Sten crowded past Bet and looked down into the warehouse. It was exactly like Oron's model. Towering stacks of crates and shipping tubes filled with everything from clothing to luxury food items for the Techs and Execs. It was a place that a human – on legal business – never had to visit as all functions and work were handled by bots, from tiny inventory clerks to giant, idiot-brained skip-loaders.

Bet and another Delinq began looking for the alarm system.

Oron had gone over the plan with him and then asked for suggestions.

'No, Sten,' he had said after listening. 'That way . . . there is no . . . escape. Look.'

His fingers traced the model of the warehouse's interior.

'Block the exits with crates. But even if you know they are blocked, you must still . . . think someone will come through. You must be prepared to . . . counter that. To have another . . .'

He fumbled for a word.

'Tactic . . . To be a Delinq, you must know tactics. Even when your plan is . . . perfect . . . you must assume it can go wrong. You must never get in a situation from which there is no . . . escape.'

Sten nodded. And Oron began showing him how to protect their backs.

'We will make a backdoor here . . . station lookouts here . . . and here.'

Bet had found the first alarm and disarmed it. Another Delinq was already unbelting the duct screen. A rope slithered downward and moments later they were on the floor of the warehouse.

Bet motioned for Sten to follow her to a computer terminal. The other three Delinqs began checking for other alarms.

'We can't leave any sign that we were here,' she whispered.

Her fingers flew over the terminal keys. First, she called up the SECURITY INSTRUCTIONS program and ordered the human body detector to ignore their presence. Then she called up the WAREHOUSE INVENTORY. She studied it carefully, made a few notes, and then altered the list.

'We can only take these items. No one will miss them.'

She signaled to the other Delinqs and they went to work, gathering their loot.

As a Delinq was lugging the last crate toward the piled loot near an opened vent, the Delinqs heard a slight squeaking noise. They leaped for cover as it grew louder.

The security bot rolled around a corner, feelers extended for signs of human life. The Delinqs held their breath as the feelers waved around in the air. Finally they retracted and the bot rolled toward the exit.

Suddenly, the bot squeaked to a halt. One of the Delinqs smothered a moan. He had left a crate standing in the middle of the warehouse floor when he dove out of sight. The security bot's power-hum rose. A stun rod snicked into view and the bot's sensors peered about, looking for the cause. No alarms. It wasn't sure yet. Although unlikely, a faulty worker bot might have left the crate unstacked.

Bet motioned to Sten. She pointed upward to a high stack of crates. They eased from their hiding place and slithered toward the stack. She clambered up Sten's shoulders, found a foothold and then picked her way up the stack of crates. She reached the top, then flattened as a crate creaked loudly underfoot.

The bot rolled toward the sound.

In a blur, Bet lifted a heavy crate and hurled it downward. The bot's stun rod came up and the crate smashed into it. The entire warehouse clouded with the most horrible odor Sten had ever smelled. Liquid gushed out of the crate, soaking the bot. It immediately began whirling around and around.

Sten caught Bet as she leaped down. Gagging from the smell, they covered their mouths and noses. Sten recognized the stink as Sensimusk. With a mechanical groan, the bot stopped its mad whirling and moved only its stun rod, waving the weapon feebly.

Sten looked over at Bet, who grinned and stepped boldly from behind the stack directly in view of the bot. It didn't even notice her. Sten followed as she walked casually to where the others were hidden. Everyone began shoving booty into the vent. Behind them, the bot waved its weapon indecisively.

Bet hated her doll. It was soft and cuddly and programmed to be the best friend a little girl could have. It made Bet's skin crawl when she held it close to her.

She was ten by then, and had moved to Ward B for the second stage. Love was still dispensed by the Creche Mothers, but it was used as a reward for nongroup participation – the children were encouraged to spend time with themselves. To watch livies instead of playing.

Bet never let on how she felt about the doll. She'd seen other children who maltreated or ignored their dolls punished. It seemed to be the only sin the children could commit. She didn't know why she felt as she did. Her doll was just like all the others – a little girl (boys had male dolls) with tiny, spindly legs and arms and a huge head. The face was a happy grin that Bet had decided was that of an idiot.

But one night she couldn't bear its snuggling up to her in bed and whispering in her ear, begging her to share her little-girl secrets. In a sudden rage, she hurled it to the floor. Instant horror. What had she done?

'Dolly, Dolly, be all right. Don't die—'

The doll opened its eyes again and began to croon.

'Bet, is everything happy?'

Bet nodded.

'Wouldn't you like to go lie down and hold me close and we can tell . . . can tell . . . can tell each other stories.'

'Yes, Dolly.'

She pulled it into the bunk with her and obediently lay down.

The doll seemed all right after that, even if it did repeat itself a little.

The dolls were actually highly sophisticated remote sensors for the Creche program's main computer. They were complete physical and emotional monitoring facilities. A small proximity director ensured that the computer and its human attendants would know if any child was out of range of her doll, for at night it was very important that each child cuddle his or her doll close. Only then could the device give its injections. Injections to dull physical perceptivity, to increase emotional dependence, and to reduce physical and, most important, emotional/sexual growth.

When Bet slammed her doll against the wall, she threw its sensors slightly out of kilter. They continued to report her as being at a ten-year-old's level of mental and physical development, so she was eventually classified a rapid-peaking retard and given the bare minimum of injections.

Within two years, Bet could see the change in the other children. The boys stayed round-cheeked and undeveloped. The girls still giggled and played trivial games.

Bet learned always to be alone and last in the refresher as her breasts and pelvic area began to develop. Fortunately she was slow enough maturing that menstruation did not occur.

But Bet knew something was dreadfully wrong. Wrong with the other children and wrong with the Creche Mothers. She felt that things were coming to some kind of awful development – but was powerless to do anything about it.

Sten thought Bet and Fadal had gone a little too far. Dressed as joygirls, they were teasing a brawny, off-duty Tech. Sten peered from his hiding place and shook his head. It wasn't what they were doing – that was part of the plan – it was their idea of what a joygirl looked like. He hadn't seen so much glitter since the crystal vat exploded back in the Exotic Section. He leaned closer, listening.

'You girls is a little young, aincha?' The Tech licked his lips as he looked them over.

'Don't worry, me and my sister have got lots of experience.'

'Your sister, huh? Now, ain't that somethin'. You sure your daddy won't – assumin' I was interested.'

'Why should he? It was his idea. He says two more years and his Mig contract will be clear, all the credits we're bringin' in.'

'His idea, huh? Well, I heard you Mig kids grew up fast, but I thought that was just stories.'

Bet and Fadal looped their arms through his and led him toward the apartment. 'Come on. Let's have a party.'

The Tech was half out of his clothes by the time Sten kicked in the door.

'The hell! What is this?'

The Tech nearly had a heart attack. He looked like a hairy maiden, trying to cover himself with one hand, struggling with his pants with the other. 'Uh – uh – Whaddya – Who are you?'

Sten brandished a large wrench. 'They're my sisters, that's who I am.'

He turned to Bet and Fadal, cowering on the bed in mock fear. 'Get home.'

They hurried out. Sten closed the door and took a step toward the Tech. 'Gonna teach you a little lesson. Mess with my sisters, will you?'

'Uh . . . listen . . . they said they was . . .'

'What? Calling them joygirls now? My god, you have a nerve.' He lifted the wrench high, getting ready to bring it down on the Tech's balding skull.

'Wait – Couldn't we talk this over?'

Sten lowered the wrench. 'Whatcha got in mind?'

The Tech fumbled in his pockets and pulled out his card. He waved it at Sten. 'I got lots of credits . . . lots of 'em. Just name your price.'

Sten grinned. Oron was right. This was easy money.

Voices. Bet stirred awake; the sedative the doll gave her was no longer enough for her twelve-year-old body. She leaned out of her bunk and peered across the Creche dorm. Lights. Faint mutterings. She climbed out of the bunk, looked at the doll, and hesitated. The doll 'knew' when it was being held. But could it tell by whom?

Bet lifted the blanket on the next bed. She never liked Susi much anyway. She tucked the doll into Susi's arm. Bet slipped into her coveralls and padded through the ward.

The semi-forbidden door to the corridor was open. She looked around. All the children were deep in drugged sleep. Bet took a deep breath and then walked through. The central corridor was brightly lit. At one end she saw the open window of what seemed to be a lab. Keeping close to the wall, she crept up to it.

The voices began again. One was high-pitched and sounded like it belonged to a very young child. 'I did all right today, didn't I, daddy? I moved that big liner all by myself all the way into the dock. Isn't that good?'

A second voice sounded. This one was deeper. 'Of course it is, Tommie. You're the best handler we've got. I told that doctor that, and he promised that he'd see that you got something extra for it.'

'Candy? I can have some candy? I like mint. You know I like mint, don't you, daddy? You'll get me some mint, won't you?'

'We'll see, son. We'll see.'

Bet looked around the edge of the door. She almost screamed. Sitting in a wheelchair was the emaciated body of a man. It looked just like her doll. A huge head, tottering on a pipe-stem neck. Powered implements lay ready at hand. The head had the hairless face, somehow enlarged, of a young boy. From its lips came the high voice. 'I saw some of those Migs you told me about today, daddy. I *am* glad that the Company didn't let *me* grow up like that. They have to walk, and they smell bad. They'll never know what it is to be like me. One day I get to be a crane, and then the next I'm behind the controls of a bot tug. They're so nice to me.'

'Of course the Company's nice to you, Tommie,' the second voice said. It came from a normal man, wearing the white coat of a lab tech. 'That's why we let you in the Creche, and why we help you now. We love you.'

'And I love you. You're the best daddy I've ever had.'

Bet let the door slip closed noiselessly, turned, and hurtled back down the corridor and out the entrance. She ran. She didn't know where she was running, but she kept going until she was exhausted. She was in a dusty, long-unused corridor. Bet huddled to the wall and tears finally came, then stopped as she noticed the corner had broken off the floor-level ventilating duct grill. She pulled at it and slowly worked the panel loose. Bet crawled into the cavity behind it and curled up. Eventually her sobs died away, and she fell asleep.

When she awoke, the half-dead, kindly face of Oron was staring at her.

The scrawny Delinq peered from the ductway, then motioned behind him. Six other members of the gang dropped quietly down into the empty commercial corridor.

There was a low whistle; the Delinq looked back up. Sten leaned out of the ductway and pointed out the targeted shop. The Delinq moused into the shadows and moved slowly toward it.

Sten settled back to keep watch.

He had been with Oron's gang for nearly nine months. Oron had taught him well and Sten had quickly progressed to trusted raider and now he was planning and leading his own raids. He was proud that none of his raids had taken casualties and very seldom did his Delinqs fail to return fully laden.

Still, he knew such luck couldn't last. Sooner or later, the Delinqs would be picked up by a sweep and destroyed. It was a fact of life. He'd seen the results of a sweep one time while scouting. The Sociopatrolmen hadn't even bothered to dispose of the bodies. Even though the remains were blackened and half skeletal, he could tell that some of the Delinqs hadn't died easily. Particularly the girls.

He thought about Bet. She was still – despite his friendship with Oron – the only reason he stuck with the gang. Sten loved her. Although he had never had the nerve to tell her. She was— She was . . . He shook himself out of his momentary reverie and went back to watching.

The Delinqs had reached the shop. Small cutting torches flared and the bars fell away. The scrawny Delinq – Rabet – reversed his torch and smashed the window. The Delinqs crowded in, scooping the display contents into their packs.

Sten looked back up the corridor. His eyes widened. Creeping down the corridor was a Sociopatrolman, stun rod ready.

Sten licked his lips, then reversed position. The Sociopatrolman slid into view directly under Sten. Sten levered himself out of the duct, crashing down on the big man, feet slamming into his neck. The Sociopatrolman thudded to the deck, stun rod spinning away.

Big as he was, the Sociopatrolman moved quickly, rolling to his feet, unclipping a riot grenade. Sten landed, spinning over one shoulder, feet coming back under him. Lunging forward, one foot reaching high up, then clear of the ground, the other foot joining, legs curled, snapping his legs out to full lock, as the Sociopatrolman's fingers fumbled with the grenade ring.

Sten's feet slammed into the Sociopatrolman's head. His neck broke with a dull snap. As the man dropped, Sten twisted in midair, bringing his legs back under him, landing, poised and turning, knife-edge hands ready.

There was nothing more to do.

The Delinqs looked at the dead Sociopatrolman, then hastily scooped the rest of the window display into their bags and dashed back toward the vent.

As Rabet clambered into the duct, he gave Sten a thumbs up and a flashing grin.

Sten shifted uncomfortably in his bunk. He couldn't sleep. He kept thinking about the Sociopatrolman he had killed and the scattered long-dead bodies of the Delinq gang. He had to get off Vulcan. He had to take Bet with him. But how? Plans swirled in his head. All carefully considered before. All doomed to failure. There *had* to be a way.

Something rustled. He turned and Bet slid through the curtains and into his room.

'What are you—?'

A soft hand went over his lips, silencing him.

'I've been waiting every night. For you. I couldn't wait any longer.' Very slowly, she removed her hand, then took Sten's and guided it to the fastener of her coverall. A moment later, she lifted the coverall off her shoulders and let it fall. Underneath, she was naked.

Bet moved up against Sten and began to unfasten his garment. He took her hand away.

'Wait.' He reached behind him, and pulled something from under his pillow. A small bundle. He shook it out. It was a long, flowing glasscloth robe. It danced and gleamed with a kaleidoscope of colors. 'For you. A gift.'

'How long have you had it?'

'A long time.'

'Oh . . . I'll try it on. Later.' Then she was in his arms and they sank back into the bunk. Locked together. But still in silence.

Bet followed Sten down the narrow ductway. It narrowed twice and they had to squeeze through. She had no idea where they were going. Sten had said it was a surprise. They turned a corner and the duct ended in a blank metal wall.

'This isn't a surprise,' she said. 'It's a dead end.'

'You'll see.' His pocket torch flickered into life and he began cutting. In a few moments he had cut a 'door,' with only a small piece of metal holding it in place. 'Close your eyes.'

Bet obeyed and heard the hissing sound of the torch cutting again and then a loud thump as the 'door' fell away.

'You can open them now.'

And Bet saw 'outside' for the first time in her life. A gentle lawn sloping toward a tiny lake. Tall green things that Bet thought were probably trees and at the edge of the lake a small – was it wooden? – house, built in the style of the ancients. Chimney, curl of smoke, and all. Sten tugged at her and she followed him out in a daze.

She looked up and saw a bright blue artificial sky. She shrank back, uneasy. It was so open. Sten put an arm around her and she relaxed.

'For a second I thought I was going to fall . . . off . . . or out.'

Sten laughed. 'You get used to it.'

'Where are we?'

'This is the private rec area of Assistant Personnel Director Gaitson. He left today for a two-cycle recruiting program offworld.'

'How do you know?'

'I played with the computer. I'm getting pretty good at it, if I say so myself.'

Bet was puzzled. It was nice, but – she looked around – 'What are we raiding?'

'We aren't. We're on a vacation.'

'A vacation? That's—'

'For the next two cycles we are going to do absolutely nothing except enjoy all the things that Gaitson has laid on. We'll eat the best, drink the best, and play. No raids. No patrolmen. No worrying. No nothing.'

Sten led Bet to the lake. He stepped out of his coveralls and slowly waded out. 'And right now, I'm taking a bath.' He waded out a few meters. Bet watched, waiting for something to happen. Sten turned around and grinned. 'Well?'

'How is it?'

'Wet.'

Bet smiled. And the smile became a chuckle. And then laughter. Shouting out, loud, full-bellied laughter. The way she used to when she was a child. Before the Creche. It was very un-Delinqlike.

She reached for the fastener of her coveralls.

*

'Sten?'

'Ummmm?'

'You awake?'

'Ummmmm . . . yeah.'

'I was just thinking.'

'Yeah?'

'I don't want to ever leave this place.'

Long silence.

'We have to. Soon.'

'I know that. But it just seems so . . . so . . .'

He hushed her and pulled her close. Brushed away a tear. 'I'm getting off,' he said.

'Off? What do you mean?'

'Off Vulcan.'

'But that's impossible.'

'So is living like a Delinq.'

'But how?'

'I don't know yet. But I'll find a way.'

Bet took his hand. Held it. 'Want me with you?'

Sten nodded. 'Always.' Then he took her in his arms and they held each other all night.

Chapter Thirteen

Mahoney arced off the slideway, over the barrier and into the machine shop's entrance. Balled in midair, hit on his feet, and was running.

He dashed down the assembly row, dodged a transporter, and rolled up onto the waste belt. The belt carried him from the shop, and a few feet over a second, southbound slideway. Mahoney slid to the side, went over the edge, hanging by his hands.

He let go, and rebounded onto the slideway. Took several deep breaths, and dusted off his coveralls. Shucking that tail, he thought, was getting harder and harder. Thoresen and his security section were entirely too interested in the movements of Quartermaster/Sergeant Ian Mahoney, Imperial Guards, Field Ration Quality Control subsection.

So far his tags were nothing more than Vulcan's routine paranoid surveillance on any offworlder. He hoped. But if they nailed him now, he'd be, at the very least, blown. So far Mahoney had managed to borrow a Mig's card long enough to produce an acceptable forgery, scrounge a set of Mig coveralls and head south.

He was miles below The Eye. Far off limits for any non-Company employee.

Down there, if he was uncovered by Security or any Sociopatrolman, the Company would probably find it simpler just to cycle him through the nearest food plant than go through the formalities of deportation.

Mahoney had put himself into the field quite deliberately. He'd been somewhat less than successful in recruiting local agents. Stuck in The Eye, all he had access to were obvious provocateurs and Migs so terrified they weren't worth the bother. At any rate, going operational was possibly less hazardous than red-lighting his mission and heading back for Prime World.

The Emperor, he felt, would be less than impressed with Mahoney's progress to date:

1. Thoresen was, indeed, in a conspiracy up to the top of his shaved head, and letting no one, including his own board of directors, in on the operation. Big deal. That the Emperor knew a year ago, back on Prime World.

2. Thoresen was working a gray and black propaganda campaign against the Empire, specifically directed at the Migs. But since he was using Counselors as the line-out, and had so many cutouts between himself and the campaign, he was still untouchable. Mahoney figured that operation had been going on, and all he'd been able to get was specifics and intensity.

Mahoney snorted to himself. Any buck private in Mantis Section's rear rank would have come up with that much or gone back to being a slime-pounder.

3. Offworld security systems were being beefed up and there were persistent rumors of some of the Company's production facilities being diverted to arms production. Unprovable, so far. And even if Mahoney could prove the allegations correct, the Company could always blandly claim to be planning expansion in Pioneer Sector.

'Zip-slant nothin' is what I got,' Mahoney muttered. And then froze. Far ahead, down the slideway, he could see a cordon of Sociopatrolmen checking cards with a portable computer. Mahoney's forgery wasn't that good. He quickly stepped off the slideway, onto a cross-passage. The slide-passage creaked along, into a large dome. On the other side, there was a second ID-check block.

Mahoney rabbited up a side-passage. Basics. Walk slow. Breathe slow. Look happy. A little zipped. You've just come off shift and are headed for your apartment. He went up a narrower corridor, then slanted off on still a third. Turned at the entrance then giant-stepped around the next curve.

Stopped. Waited. Listening.

Of course. Footsteps behind him.

Mahoney was being steered. But he didn't have a lot of options. Moving as slowly as he could, he let the ferrets push him deeper into the abandoned sectors of Vulcan.

The first man made the mistake of trying to blind-side Mahoney from a dead-end passageway. Mahoney went in under the blackjack, and put an elbow through the thug's epiglottis. Mahoney side-kicked the riot gun out of the second tough's hands, one-handed the gun out of the air and hauled in on the powerpack cord. The Sociopatrolman top-spun. Mahoney backpunched knuckles into the base of the man's skull.

Two. He turned, realizing that they were just the blocking element. Three more were coming around the corner. One had a gun up. Aiming.

A stun rod, spear-lashed to a rod, lashed out of the upper vent, burying itself in the gunman's eye. He screamed and went down.

Mahoney drove forward, knowing he wasn't close enough to the others, when a young man dropped out of the vent, right hand blurring back and forth.

Mahoney blinked as the second man's head bounced free, blood fountaining up to paint the overhead. The young man crouched, continuing his spin, and brought the knife completely through a circle, lunging up from the ground.

Mahoney noticed the young man kept his free hand on top of his wrist as a guide. Knows what—

And the third man whimpered at the knife deep in his chest. He toppled. The young man bent, pulled the knife out, and wiped it on the corpse's uniform. Young. Good. A bravo.

Mahoney stood very still and let the young man walk up on him. Another young man – no, a girl – dropped from the vent. She retrieved her spear.

About nineteen, fairly short, say sixty kilos. Second evaluation: nineteen going on forty. He looked like any street kid on any gutter world, except he didn't cringe. Mahoney figured he hadn't done a lot of crawling. A Delinq. Mahoney almost smiled.

Sten eyed Mahoney, then the two corpses behind him. Not bad for an old man. Looked to be in his mid-forties, and big. Sten couldn't place him, in spite of Mahoney's Mig coveralls. Not surprising, since Sten had only known three classes, and only face-to-faced two of them.

'There'll be more of 'em along directly, my friend,' Mahoney said. 'Let's keep the introductions short.'

'There's no hurry. For us. Never seen five patrolmen after one man. What'd you do?'

'It's a bit complicated—'

'Sten. Look.'

Sten didn't take his eyes off Mahoney. Bet stood up from the corpses and held three cards out to Sten. 'Those weren't patrolmen. They've got Exec cards!'

'Thoresen's security,' Mahoney said. 'They must've tracked me from The Eye.'

'You're not . . . you're offworld!'

'I am that.'

Sten made a decision.

'Strip.'

Mahoney bristled, then caught himself and swore. The kid had it. He tore off the coveralls, then pulled off his boots. Hefted one experimentally, then slammed it against the wall. The heel shattered, and bits of the tiny transmitter scattered across the deck.

Sten nodded. 'That's how they followed you. You can put the coveralls back on.'

He stirruped his hands, and launched Bet back into the vent. She reached down, gave him a hand, and he slithered up.

Turned, inside the vent, as Mahoney flat-leaped up, caught the edges of the vent with both hands and levered himself into the airduct.

'A bit tight for someone my age.'

'It isn't your age,' Bet said.

'We'll not be making light of our elders and their pot-guts.'

'Follow us,' Sten said shortly. 'And no talking.'

Mahoney blinked again as Sten put his knife away . . . seemingly into his arm. Then he ran after Bet and Sten, down the twisting duct.

Chapter Fourteen

'No, Fadal. for some reason I . . . remember what an empire is,' Oron said.

Mahoney started to ask. Sten shook his head.

'Intelligence?'

'Eyes.'

'Ah. And you will then want my people . . . and myself to be *your* eyes?'

'No,' Mahoney said. 'I'm too close to being blown.'

Oron looked inquiringly at Fadal. She was blank.

'Thoresen wouldn't have top Security men on me unless he was pretty sure who I was.'

'Thoresen . . . head of the Company. Your enemy,' Fadal whispered.

'You want?'

'I must have confirmation of Thoresen's plan. I've blue-boxed into the Exec and the central computers, and there was nothing on Bravo Project except inquiry-warning triggers.'

'This . . . Thoresen. He must have it personally.'

'Probability ninety per cent plus.'

Sten broke in. 'What happens if it's there? And you're right?'

'We'll send in the Guard. The Emperor will set up some kind of caretaker government. Things will change. For the Migs. For everyone.'

'Not good enough,' Bet said.

'We'll be dead by the time your clottin' Empire arrives. Or don't you know? Us Delinqs don't live to get old,' Sten said.

'Sten is right. A runner from another gang passed the word . . . when?'

'Two shifts ago,' Fadal said.

'He saw patrolmen in the warehouses. They were drilling with . . . riot guns,' Oron said, and smiled at his successful memory. 'They will be conducting an extermination drive soon. And we are now too many to evade them.'

'How many in your gang?'

'Fifteen now,' Fadal answered.

Mahoney calculated quickly. The tiny Imperial detachment had its own airlock. The inquiry wouldn't be too loud if he got what he wanted . . . 'Passage offworld. For *all* of you. To any Imperial world.'

Sten discovered he'd stopped breathing. He took a deep breath and looked disbelievingly at Mahoney.

'I can do it. You people raid Thoresen's quarters. Bring me anything that says Bravo Project. Which you can deliver on the ship. The Empire keeps its bargains.'

'I do not think there's any need to . . . debate this. Is there?'

Mahoney stood up.

There wasn't.

The patrolman stalked to the end of his beat and stopped. He yawned. Then turned and started back down the corridor.

Sten oozed from the vent in the wall . . . breathe . . . breathe . . . pace . . . pace . . . forward. Moving up on the guard. Keeping in time. Eyes on the patrolman's back. Closing. In step. Inside the three-meter awareness zone. Eyes off target. Mind blank.

Sten's left hand curled around the patrolman's neck. Cramped the big man's head hard back as he drove his knife deep into kidney. Breath whuffled. The man gargled. Sten sidestepped as the corpse voided, then dragged the patrolman back to the vent and stuffed him in. He ran down the corridor, to the beginning of the Exec section. Found the paneling and pried.

When the Delinqs had pored over the complete plans for The Eye that Mahoney had blind-dropped for them in the Visitors' Center airways, they'd found the key.

Evidently the Execs were more delicate than Techs or Migs. Most of the passageways, particularly those around the higher-echelon areas, were subdivided with an inner, noise-insulating wall.

The paneling came clear, and Sten beckoned.

The other fourteen Delinqs poured out of the vents and streamed toward him. One by one they slithered into the wallspace. Oron was in the middle, blank-faced. Fadal guided him into the inner wall. Sten cursed silently, and hoped Oron's memory would return quickly because if they failed, most of them would die in The Eye. Even if a few managed to get south again, into Mig country, there'd be an endless stream of extermination drives.

Again, Sten realized there was no choice. Bet grudgingly agreed. And then vacillated between eagerness to see new worlds and worry about whether they'd fit in. Sten figured that was a lucky sign.

The wallspace narrowed. Sten sucked his chest in. Must be a collision door. His chest stuck for a minute. Sten nearly panicked, then remembered to empty his lungs. He slid through easily.

They huddled outside the great double doors to Thoresen's quarters. Sten curiously touched the material. Rough. Grainy. Like fatigued steel. But rougher. Sten wondered why Thoresen didn't have the surface – it appeared organic – worked smooth.

Bet set the pickup to another frequency, and touched it to the door. Eyes closed . . . her fingers ran across the pressure switches. Inaudible pressure increased/decreased in Sten's ears. There was a click. The main lock was open.

Bet extracted a plastic rod from her pouch. Touched the heat button, and positioned it carefully in the middle of the door's panel. On the end of the rod, heated to human body temperature, was a duplicate of Thoresen's index fingerprint. Sten wondered how Mahoney had obtained it.

The door chunked – the Delinqs grabbed the weapons – and swung open.

Sten and the others cat-walked inside.

Time stopped. They were in space. They were in an exotic, friendly jungle.

They were in the very top of The Eye. Thoresen's quarters. The cover to the dome top was open, and space glittered down at them. Sten was the only one who'd seen off-Vulcan. He had enough presence to softly close the doors and look around.

There was no one else in the dome.

A garden. With furniture here and there, flowing gently into flowering wildness, as if someone had removed the walls, ceiling, and floor of a very large house, leaving in place all of the implements of living.

The Delinqs moved, recovering.

Sten spotted a motion detector swiveling toward them. He ran forward and leaped, knife plunging through the pickup. Sten spotted other cameras and pointed. The Delinqs nodded. Moved forward, fading into the unfamiliar shrubbery.

Sten, Oron, and Bet kept together, looking for what would be an office. At one side of the dome was an elaborate *salle d'armes*. Blades and guns of many worlds and cultures hung from the dome panels. And, on the other side, an imposing, free-floating slab that had to be a desk. Behind it, the most elaborate computer panel Sten had ever seen. Nearby stood a stylized sculpture of an enormously fat woman. Maybe.

Sten looked at Oron questioningly. His eyes gleamed bright. He waved them at the sculpture.

Sten and Bet slid up to it. It had to be. A narrow UV trip beam crossed in front of it. Sten took a UV projector from his belt, flipped it on, adjusted the intensity, and hung it in front of the pickup across the chamber.

It took several minutes to find the tiny crack in the sculpture. Sten fingered all projections on the sculpture. It wasn't that simple. Probably a sequence release that would take forever to figure out.

Oron turned, and Sten took the small maser projector from the ruck Oron wore. Opened it up, aimed the maser sights at the crack, and flipped it on. A little pressure on the trigger and the sculpture powdered. Underneath was a touch-combination door. Sten very carefully took a freeze carrier from his own pack and unclipped a tiny tripod.

He opened the freeze carrier and a white vapor spilled into the room from the near Kelvin-Zero cylinder inside. Sten pulled on an insulated glove and attached the cylinder to the tripod, aiming the release spout at the right side of the safe door. He armed the release and backed away.

Spray jetted from the cylinder and crystallized against the hull-strength steel door to the safe. Then Bet took a hammer from her pouch and tapped. The metal shattered like glass. The three grinned at each other.

They were in.

Papers, more papers, bundles of Imperial credits – Sten started to stuff bills in his pouch but Oron waved at him. No.

Then came a thick red folder. BRAVO PROJECT. They had it!

None of them noticed the young Delinq who'd wandered into the *salle*. Fascinated by an archaic long arm, he took it from the wall. The bracket clicked softly upward.

Sten handed the Bravo folder to Oron. The blank look suddenly returned to Oron's eyes. He looked, puzzled, at the folder and stood up. The folder spilled, papers scattering across the floor. Sten muttered and started gathering papers. No kind of order – scattered all over the floor. Sten worked as fast as he could.

The first blast caught three Delinqs in the chest, and side scatter from the riot gun blistered the foliage. The Sociopatrolman in the door pulled the trigger all the way back and swiveled.

The second blast caught a Delinq as he dived through some brush, burning away half his chest. Coughing screams broke the silence. Sociopatrolmen streamed through the door – guns out.

Bet pulled a grenade from her belt, thumbed the fuse, and pitched it, going flat, as death seared above her head.

Sten rolled toward the *salle*, ducking behind the first shelter he saw.

Three joined tanks, with a long hose and twin handles. Some kind of weapon.

The placard above the museum piece read: EARTH PRE-EMPIRE, RESTORED. FLAME WEAPON. It was Sten's luck that Thoresen, like many collectors, kept his weaponry ready for use. Sten grabbed the hose's two handles, and pulled them both. He saw the puff from the cone head at the nozzle, a small flare of fire, and then greasy, black flame spurted from the nozzle.

It spouted fifty meters across the chamber – a far greater range than its aeons-dead builders planned – and napalm drenched the Sociopatrolmen. They howled, for it was a very unpleasant series of deaths, whether a patrolman was lucky enough to have the oxygen sucked from his lungs by the searing flames, or, worse, as the sticky, petroleum-based napalm burnt through to the bone. But one man stopped screaming long enough to spray a burst from his gun just as a still-bewildered Oron walked forward. His head spattered through the chamber.

Robotlike, Sten stalked forward, hosing the nozzle back and forth. Finger locked on the trigger, eyes wide in panic. And then the flame sputtered and dribbled back to the nozzle.

Sten dropped it and just stood there.

Bet grabbed his arm.

'Come on!'

Sten came back to the world. The patrol team that had been blocking the entrance was gone. All dead.

Sten and Bet ran for the door, and only one other Delinq came out of his hiding place after them.

They went out the door and pelted down the corridor. There wasn't time enough to make it back to their rat paneling. All they could hope to do was put distance between them and Thoresen's quarters.

A running blur – the three of them down corridors, ducking as patrolmen came after them. Panicked Execs backing away and doors slamming and locking.

A floor grating. Sten and Bet heaving up. The grating coming clear.

Sten looked down. The passage went down, endlessly. No fans or acceleration ducting. He didn't know what it was for, but it didn't matter. A team of patrolmen was jogging down the corridor after them.

Narrow climbing cleats ran down the side, and Sten could make out some kind of tunnel about ten meters below the main passageway. He waved Bet into the hole. She clambered in awkwardly and Sten realized she'd been hit somehow.

Sten followed.

The other Delinq was still shaking his head when the riot gun blast caught him and blew him apart.

Bet slipped, one foot left the cleat and her leg fluttered into the passageway. Gunk. Grease. Something. She clawed at the cleat, lost her handhold. Screamed.

Too late, Sten reached for her as he stared down half a world. Bet, screaming endlessly, fell away from him.

Sten watched her body drop away. Until he couldn't see it. Then, somehow moving quickly, he slid sideways and began working his way down the passageway.

Mahoney paced his office. After he heard the alarms, he had monitored the patrol net and heard the riot squads being sent in.

The door opened suddenly and Sten walked into the room. Empty-handed. 'They caught us. They caught us. Bet's dead.'

Mahoney caught himself. 'Bet. That girl?'

'Yes. She's dead. Dead. And the file. What you wanted. Oron had it.'

'Where's Oron?'

'Oron's dead. Like Bet.'

Mahoney squelched his natural reaction to curse. 'All right. It's blown. But the bargain still stands. I've got the cruiser standing by.'

'No. I don't want to go.'

'Then what do you want?'

'A gun. Bet's dead, you see.'

'You're going back out there?'

'Bet's dead.'

'Yes. I keep two over there. In that desk.'

Sten turned around and walked to the desk. He never heard

Mahoney's step or saw the meat-ax hand snapping down. Sten crashed forward, across the desk.

Mahoney eased Sten around and gentled him into the chair. Then allowed himself a personal reaction. 'Clot!' He brought himself back, and took a copy of the *Articles* from a drawer. He laid Sten's right hand on it.

'I'm not knowing what religion you have. If any. But this'll do. Do you – whatever your name is – *Sten* it is. First name unknown. Swear to defend the Eternal Emperor and the Empire with your life – I know you do, boy. Do you solemnly swear to obey lawful orders given you, and to honor and follow the traditions of the Imperial Guard as the Empire requires? You do that, too. I welcome you, Sten, to the service of the Empire. You've not made a mistake, enlisting in the Guard. And it's a personal honor to me that you've chosen me own mother regiment, the Guard's First Assault.'

He put the book down, and stopped. Ruffled Sten's hair.

'You're a poor sorry bastard, and it's a shame things have worked the way they did. The least I can do is get you off this hellworld and let you be alive awhile longer.'

He tabbed the communicator switch.

'Lieutenant. In my office. A new recuit for the Guard. Seems to have fainted when he realized the awful majesty of it all.'

Mahoney took a bottle of synthalk from his desk and, without bothering with a glass, poured a long drink down his throat.

'With the wind at your back, lad.'

Chapter Fifteen

Thoresen was wading in excuses and assurances from the chief of security. The more he looked at the man's vid-screen image, the more he wanted to smash his earnest face. 'No *real* harm done,' the man said. How could he know?

Thoresen didn't really give a damn about the damage to his quarters or the charred bodies of the patrolmen. But what about Bravo Project? He had recovered the file. But he'd be a fool not to act on the assumption that someone had seen enough of the file to be dangerous.

Thoresen's head snapped up as he caught something in the drone from his chief of security.

'What did you say?'

'We have recovered the bodies of thirteen Delinqs and full identities have been made.'

'Not that. After.'

'Uh, one, possibly two of them escaped.'

So. He was right to worry.

'Who were they?'

'Well, sir,' the chief said, 'we recovered a hair particle in your quarters. A chromosome projection estimates the man would have been—'

'Let me see for myself,' the Baron snapped.

A computer image began to build on the screen as the chromo-analysis built the image of a man cell by cell. Finally, there was a complete three-dimensional figure. It was Sten. Thoresen studied the image carefully, then shook his head. He didn't recognize the suspect.

'Who is he?'

'A Mig named Karl Sten, sir. Reported missing in that Exotic Section explosion some cycles—'

'You mean the man responsible for *that* debacle is alive? How could he possibly – oh, never mind. That's all.'

'But, sir, there's more infor—'

'I'll go over the report myself. Now. That's all!'

The Baron scrolled the report that was Sten's life. It didn't take him long. There wasn't much to it, really, if you separated out all the legal and psych trash.

Suddenly, the connection was made. The Bravo Project. Sten was an orphan of Recreational Area 26. The Row had come back to haunt him.

He palmed the console board and the startled face of the chief leaped on the screen.

'I want this man found. Immediately. I want every person available on this.'

'Uh, I'm afraid that's impossible, sir.'

'Why is that?' Thoresen hissed.

'Well, we – uh . . . have located him. He's on an Imperial troop ship, bound for—'

Thoresen blanked the man out. It was impossible. How could—? Then he pulled himself together. He'd find this Sten. And then . . .

A few moments later the Baron was talking quietly to a little gray man on a little gray world. The hunt for Sten had begun.

BOOK THREE

THE GUARD

4 [illegible]

[illegible]

[illegible] cauldrons [illegible] and [illegible] in a dense [illegible] transparent gases.

The crowd [illegible] speaker [illegible] some [illegible] [illegible].

[illegible] leaped from the [illegible] and [illegible] launched a [illegible] down toward the [illegible] curling [illegible] the [illegible].

Close to the end of space, pure light flashed.

Chapter Sixteen

Nuclear fires bloomed up from the planet, silhouetting the warships hanging just out of the atmosphere.

'H minus fifty seconds and counting. Red One, Red Two detached to individual control. Begin entry maneuvers.' The command ship's transmission crackled in the assault ship's control chambers.

Controls went live, and the fleet transports swung in from their orbital stations. Braking rockets flared as the ships killed velocity and sank closer toward atmosphere's edge.

'Foxfire Six, I have an observed ground launch. Predicted intersection ... uh, thirty-five seconds. Interception probability eighty-three per cent. Beginning diversion ...' signaled an observation and interdiction satellite.

Foxfire Six's pilot cursed and slammed full power to the drive on his assault transport. He picked a random evasion pattern chip and fed it into the computer.

Deep in the ship's guts, Sten crashed forward against the safety straps. His platoon sergeant slammed against the capsule wall. The ceiling rotated around Sten, swung up crazily, and then went away as the artificial gravity went dead.

Sten and the other men in his platoon wedged themselves more tightly in the shock cocoons as gravity came and went in a dozen directions while the transport veered.

The control room speaker crackled: 'Four seconds until atmosphere. H minus thirty ... antimissile evasion tactics in progress.'

Pinpoint flames leaped from the O and I satellite as it launched a dozen intercepts down toward the six pencil lines of smoke curling up for the transport.

Close to the black of space, pure light flashed.

'Foxfire Six, I have a hit on one of your birds. Hit also tumbled gyros on second bird. Suggest you make diversionary launch.'

The transport's weapons officer dumped two batteries of gremlins to home on the upcoming missiles. The gremlins spewed chaff as they dropped.

A missile fell for the ruse, and diverted onto a gremlin. The others, probably ground-guided, homed on the huge troop transport.

'Foxfire Six, intercept now ninety-nine per cent. Suggest you launch troop caps.'

Inside Sten's capsule, the beeper went off, and a computer voice announced, 'Capsule launch on short countdown. Surface impact one minute twelve seconds.'

The transport pilot hit the launch key and the craft seemed to explode. The huge cone separated from the ship's main body, then spewed twenty long capsules into space. The capsules went to automatic regime, and targeted on the robot homer already in place on the target zone.

The grizzled corporal cocooned next to Sten said thoughtfully, 'Guess they got us targeted. Six to five they'll take us out before we ground. Naw. Make that eight to five. Want a piece?'

Sten shook his head, and the capsule rotated around him again.

Forty-six seconds had passed since the invasion elements, Red One and Red Two, had dropped away from the fleet.

The sky around the planet was blazing from nuke and conventional explosions.

Two missiles proximity-detonated on troop capsules. Sten's capsule juddered. 'In atmosphere,' the corporal said.

An idiot-level radar in the capsule nose *tsk*ed and told the capsule's computer to kill speed. Huge wings snapped out from the capsule's sides, and nose rockets bellowed. The capsule's vertical dive shallowed as the wings' leading edges went red then up into white. The air-howl was deafening inside the capsule.

Nearly simultaneously, the capsule's computer dumped three tear-away parachutes out the tail, and pulsed rockets to turn the capsule's course away from the ocean, back on track with the TZ homer. The computer deployed two sets of divebrakes to burn away before the capsule was subsonic.

Short-range ground/air missiles flashed up from the air defenses around the planet's capital below Sten's capsule. One- and two-man tacships skipped and skidded through the black blossoms, then tucked and went in.

Laser sights targeted launch sites, and glidebombs dropped, locked in.

The second wave of tacships swept across the city, scatterbombs cascading down. In the city's heart, a fire-storm raged, solid steel and concrete flowing in rivers as the city melted.

A terrain-following missile picked up Sten's incoming capsule, targeted and went to full boost, but lost the capsule in ground clutter. Unable to pull his bird out, the missile's officer manually detonated, hoping to do damage with a near miss.

The capsule pancaked in, up a wide avenue. Touch-down! – and the shockwave caught the capsule, one wing slamming against the street, and then the capsule pin-wheeled.

Sten's eyes came open. Blackness. Then the mini-charges blew and the capsule's bulkheads dropped away.

The men cascaded out, onto the street.

Sten stumbled, regained his feet, and automatically knocked down his helmet's flare visor. He hit the breakaway harness on the willygun; magazine in; armed; Sten went down on one knee. Ten meters away from his nearest squadmate.

Landing security perimeter complete.

A bellow from the platoon sergeant: 'First. Second squads. Maneuver. Third squad. Security. Weapons squad, set up over by that statue.'

'Come on. Diamond. Move it.'

Sten and his squaddies moved forward, hugging the side of the street. Sten's ears finally decided to return to life, and now he could hear the clatter of bootheels and the creak of his weapons harness.

The first missile from the weapons squad's launchers shushed into the air, and swung, patrolling for a target.

'Come on, you. You ain't got time for bird-watching. Keep your—'

The squad went flat as rubble crashed. Sten rolled through a doorway and came back up.

He ducked down, out of sight as the huge, gray-painted assault tank rumbled through a building and toward his squad.

Sten fumbled a grenade from his belt, armed it, and overhanded the small ovoid toward the track. The grenade burst, meters short, and Sten dove for the deck as one of the tank's two main turrets swiveled toward him.

His eardrums crawled and spine twisted as the tank's maser came up to firing pressure. The wall above him sharded as the soundwaves battered it into nothingness. Sten stayed down as the tank rumbled past.

One tread chattered a meter away from him. Sten heard the long gurgling scream as someone – his team partner – was pulped under the three-meter-wide tracks.

Sten rolled to his feet as the tank passed, caught the dangling end of the track's towing harness, and pulled himself clear of the ground, almost level with the rear deck. He unclipped another grenade and rolled it up between the turrets.

He dropped away and thudded to the pavement. The tank rolled on a few meters, far enough for Sten to be out of the sensor's dead zone.

An antipersonnel cupola spun toward him and the gun depressed, just as the grenade detonated. The blast ripped one main turret away. It cartwheeled through the air to squash two crouching guardsmen.

Sten lay motionless twenty meters behind the tank. Flame spouted from the crater in its top, then was smothered by the extinguishers. The second main turret ground back. Its AP gun sputtered fire, and bullets chattered toward Sten. He screamed as a white-hot wire burned through his shoulder, but came to his feet and dove forward, sliding across the pavement, under the track.

Pain. It hurts. Sten forced himself into the familiar aid mantra, and the nerve ending died, pain faded. His arm was useless. Sten awkwardly crawled from under the tank, then went flat as bullets spattered on the armor beside him.

A column of enemy infantry was infiltrating forward, through the ruins. They opened fire as Sten went around the tank's side.

The engine growled, and the tank rumbled forward. Sten edged along with it, keeping the tank between himself and the enemy troopers. He heard shouted commands, and bent down, peering through the track's idler wheels. He saw legs running toward the tank. Sten picked a bester grenade from its pouch and lobbed it over the tank. His flash visor blackened, covering the light explosion.

The soldiers went down. Stunned, their time sense destroyed, they'd be out of action for at least half an hour.

Gears crashed, and the tank ground down the avenue, toward Sten's platoon headquarters. Sten grabbed a cleat and awkwardly swung himself up onto the tank's skirts. The tank's remaining main turret was firing half-power charges down the avenue. The AP capsules were reconning by fire – spraying the buildings on either side of the track.

Sten crawled across the tank, toward the turret. An eye flickered in an observation slit, and an AP gun swung toward him. Sten jumped onto the top of the tank's main turret. He blinked—

Sten was sitting in a room, a gleaming steel helmet over his head, blocking his vision. Transmission tendrils curled from the helmet. But Sten was riding the top of a heavy tank, in life-or-death battle on a nameless world somewhere.

Sten's fingernails ripped as the turret swung back and forth, trying to throw him off. A hatchway clicked, and Sten shot forward while pulling a combat knife from its boot sheath. He lunged toward the tankman coming out, pistol ready.

The knife caught the man in the mouth. Blood gouted around Sten's hand. The man dropped back inside the tank. Sten levered the hatch completely open then jerked back as bullets rang up from the interior.

Sten yanked off his equipment belt, thumbed into life a time-delay grenade on it, then dropped the whole belt down the hatch.

He jumped. Landed, feeling tendons rip and tear, went to one knee, pushed away again, over a low ruined wall as behind him the tank blew; a world-destroying, all consuming ball of flame boiled up from the tank over the wall, catching Sten. He felt his body crackle black around him and sear down and down into death.

The recording switched off.

Sten tore the helmet off his head and threw it across the room.

A speaker keyed on.

'You just participated in the first assault wave when your regiment, the Guard's First Assault, landed on Demeter. The regiment suffered sixty-four per cent casualties during the three-week operation yet took all assigned objectives within the operations plan timetable.

'To honor their achievement, the Guard's First Assault was granted, by the Eternal Emperor himself, the right to wear an Imperial fourragère in red, white, and green. The battle honors of Demeter were added to the division's colors.

'In addition, many individual awards for heroism were made, including the Galactic Cross, posthumous, to Guardsman Jaime Shavala, whose experiences you were fortunate enough to participate in as part of this test.

'There will be thirty minutes of free time before the evening meal is served. Testing will recommence tomorrow. That is all. You may leave the test chamber.'

Sten clambered out of the chair. Odd. He could still feel where that bullet had hit him. The door opened, and Sten headed for the mess hall. So that's being a hero. And also that's becoming dead. Neither one of them held any attraction for Sten. Still, he thought to himself, thirty-six per cent is a better survival rate than Exotic Section had.

But he still wanted to know what valuable characteristics he could develop to qualify for Guard's First Assault Way Behind the Lines Slackers Detachment.

He sat on the edge of a memorial to some forgotten battle and waited for the long line of prospective recruits to shorten up.

Sten took a deep breath of non-manufactured air and was mildly surprised to find himself feeling happy. He considered. Bet? That wasn't something he was over. Any more than he had recovered from the death of his family. He guessed, though, that that kind of thing got easier to deal with with practice. Practice, he suddenly realized, he might get a lot of in the Guard.

Ah well. He stood and strolled toward the end of the line. At least he was off Vulcan. And he'd never have to go back. Although he did have dreams about what Vulcan would look like with a sticky planet buster detonated just above The Eye.

Very deliberately he shut the idea off, and concentrated on being hungry.

Chapter Seventeen

Rykor, too, was happy. Wild arctic seas boomed in her mind. Waves climbed toward the gray, overcast sky as glaciers calved huge bergs.

She rolled as she surfaced, exultantly spouting, then crashed her flukes against the water, and leapt free from wave to wave in powerful, graceful dives. There was a gentle tap on her shoulder.

Rykor rolled one eye open and sourly looked up at Frazer, one of her assistants. 'You want?' she rumbled.

'There's a vid for you. From Prime World.'

Rykor whuffled through her whiskers and braced both arms on the sides of the tank. She levered her enormous bulk up and over into the gravchair. Folds of blubber slopped over the sides until the frantic chair tucked them all safely in place. She tapped controls, and the chair slid her across the chamber to the main screen. Frazer fussed beside her.

'It's in reference to that new Guards recruit. The one you put the personal key on.'

'Figures,' Rykor muttered. 'Now I'll get more walrus jokes. Whatever a walrus is.'

The screen was blank, except for a single line of blinking letters. Rykor was mildly surprised, but touched the CIPHER button, and added the code line. She motioned Frazer away from the screen.

It cleared, and Mahoney beamed out at her.

'Thought I'd take a moment of your time, Rykor, and ask you to check on one of my lads.'

Rykor touched a button, and a second screen lit. 'Sten?'

'Now that'd be a good guess.'

'Guess? With your personal code added to the computer key?'

'That's always been my problem. Never known for bein' subtle.'

Rykor didn't bother with a retort. Too easy a target. 'You want his scores?'

'Now would I be bothering a chief psychologist if all I needed was a clerk to recite to me? You know what I'd like.'

Rykor took a deep breath. 'Overall, he should be what I've heard you call a "nest of snakes."' Mahoney looked puzzled, but decided to let it pass. 'Exceptionally high intelligence level, well integrated into temporal planning and personnel assessment.

'Which does not compute. He should be either catatonic or a raving psychopath. Instead, he's far too sane. We can test more intensively, but I believe he's primarily functional because his experiences are unassimilated.'

'Explain.'

'Analysis – bringing these problems, and his unexpressed emotions into the open – would be suggested.'

'Suggested for what,' Mahoney said. 'We're not building a poet. All I want is a soldier. Will he fall apart in training?'

'Impossible to predict with any certainty. Personal feeling – probably not. He's already been stressed far beyond our limits.'

'What kind of soldier will he be?'

'Execrable.'

Mahoney looked surprised.

'He has little emotional response to the conventional stimuli of peer approval, little if any interest in the conventional rewards of the Guard. A high probability of disobeying an order he feels to be nonsensical or needlessly dangerous.'

Mahoney shook his head mournfully. 'Makes one wonder why I recruited him. And into my own dearly beloved regiment.'

'Very possibly,' Rykor said dryly, 'it's because his profile is very similar to your own.'

'Mmm. Perhaps that's why I try to stay away from my own beloved regiment. Except at Colors Day.'

Rykor suddenly laughed. It rolled out like a sonic boom, and her body moved in undulating waves, almost driving the chair into a breakdown. She shut the laugh off.

'I get the feeling, Ian, that you are tapping the Old Beings Network.'

Mahoney shook his head.

'Wrong. I don't want the boy cuddled through training. If he doesn't make it . . .'

'You'd send him back to his homeworld?'

'If he doesn't make it,' Mahoney said quietly, 'he's of no interest to me.'

Rykor moved her shoulders.

'By the way. You should be aware that the boy has a knife up his arm.'

Mahoney picked his words carefully. 'Generally the phrase is knife up his sleeve, if you'll permit me.'

'I meant what I said. He has a small knife, made of some unknown crystalline material, sheathed in a surgical-modification to his lower right arm.'

Mahoney scratched his chin. He hadn't been seeing things back on Vulcan.

'Do you want us to remove it?'

'Negative.' Mahoney grinned. 'If the instructors can't handle it – and if he's dumb enough to pull it on any of them – that gives a very convenient escape hatch. Doesn't it?'

'You will want his progress monitored, of course?'

'Of course. And I'm aware it's not a chief psychologist's duties, but I'd appreciate it if his file was sealed. And if you, personally, were to handle him.'

Rykor stared at the image. 'Ah. I understand.'

Mahoney half smiled. 'Of course. I knew you would.'

Chapter Eighteen

'My name is Lanzotta,' the voice purred. 'Training Master Sergeant Lanzotta. For the next Imperial Year, you may consider me God.'

Sten, safely buried in the motley formation of recruits, glanced out of the corner of his eye at the slender middle-aged man standing in front of him. Lanzotta wore the mottled brown uniform of a Guards Combat Division and the pinned-up slouch hat of Training Command. The only decoration he wore, besides small black rank tabs, was the wreathed multiple stars of a Planetary Assault Combat Veteran.

He was flanked by two hulking corporals.

'Bowing and burnt offerings are not necessary,' Lanzotta went on. 'Simple worship and absolute obedience will make me more than happy.'

Lanzotta smiled gently around at the trainees. One man, who wore the gaily colored civilian silks of a tourist world, made the mistake of returning the smile.

'Ah. We have a man with a sense of humor.' Lanzotta paced forward until he was standing in front of the man. 'You find me amusing, son?'

The smile disappeared from the boy's face. He said nothing.

'I thought I asked the man a question,' Lanzotta said. 'Didn't I speak clearly enough, Corporal Carruthers?'

One hulk beside him stirred slightly. 'I heard you fine, sergeant,' she said.

Lanzotta nodded. His hand shot forward and grabbed the recruit by the throat. Seemingly without effort, he lifted the trainee clear of the ground and held him, feet dangling. 'I do like to have my questions answered,' he mused. 'I asked if you found me amusing.'

'N-no,' the boy gurgled.

'I much prefer to be addressed by my rank,' Lanzotta said. He suddenly hurled the recruit away. The trainee fell heavily to the ground. 'You'll find a sense of humor very useful,' Lanzotta added.

'There are one hundred of you today. You've been chosen to enter the ranks of the Guard's First Assault Regiment.

'I welcome you.

'You know, our regimental screening section is very proud. They tell me that less than one out of a hundred thousand qualify for the Guard.

'Under those conditions, you men and women might consider yourselves elite. Corporal Halstead, do these – whatever they are – look like they're elite to you?'

'No, Sergeant Lanzotta,' the second behemoth rumbled. 'They look like what's at the bottom of a suit recycler.'

'Umm.' Lanzotta considered. 'Perhaps not that low.'

He walked down the motionless ranks, looking at the trainees closely. He paused by Sten, looked him up and down, and smiled slightly. Then walked down a few more ranks. 'My apologies, corporal. You were right.'

Lanzotta went back to the head of the formation, shaking his head sorrowfully. 'The Imperial Guard is the finest fighting formation in the history of man. And the Guard's First Assault is the best of the Guard. We have never lost a battle and we never will.'

He paused.

'Some general or other said a soldier's job is not to fight, but die. If any of you fungus scrapings live to graduate, you'll be ready to help the soldier on the other side die for his country. We aren't interested in cannon fodder in the Guard. We build killers, not losers.

'You'll be in training for one full year here at the regimental depot. Then if I pass you, you'll be shipped to the field assault regiment.

'Now you beings have three choices for that year. You can quit at any time, and we'll quite happily wash you out into a scum general duty battalion.

'Or else you can learn to be soldiers.'

He waited.

'Are any of you curious as to the third alternative?'

There was no sound except the wind blowing across the huge parade ground.

'The third option is that you can die.' Lanzotta smiled again. 'Corporal Halstead, Corporal Carruthers, or myself will quite cheerfully kill you if we think for one moment that you would endanger your teammates in combat, and there's no other way to get rid of you.

'I believe, people. I believe in the Empire and I serve the Eternal Emperor. He took me off the garbage pit of a world that I was born on and made me what I am. I've fought for the Empire on a hundred different worlds and I'll fight on a hundred more before some skeek burns me down.' Lanzotta's eyes glittered.

'But I'll be the most expensive piece of meat he ever butchered.'

Lanzotta, as if unconsciously, touched the assault badge on his breast.

'Now, I will give you the first four rules for staying alive and happy. First, you should think of yourselves as two stages below latrine waste. I will let you know when I think you are qualified to consider yourselves sentient beings. Right now, I don't think that will ever happen.

'Second, when a cadreperson addresses you, you will come to attention, you will salute, you will address him by his rank, and you will do exactly what he tells you to do.'

He nodded sideways to Carruthers. The corporal ran forward to one recruit.

'YOU!' she shouted.

'Yes.'

The corporal's fist sank into the trainee's stomach, and he collapsed to his knees, retching.

Carruthers took one step to the side.

'YOU!' she screamed at the trembling woman.

'Yes . . . corporal,' the trainee faltered.

'JUMP!'

The girl gaped. Carruthers' fist blurred into her chin, and she went down.

'THEY AREN'T LISTENING, SERGEANT.' She sidestepped.

'YOU!'

'Yes, corporal,' the third trainee managed.

'JUMP!'

'Yes, corporal!'

The recruit started bounding up and down.

'THAT'S NOT HIGH ENOUGH!'

The trainee jumped higher.

Carruthers watched, then shook her head in satisfaction. She ran back to her position beside Lanzotta.

'Third,' Lanzotta went on as if nothing had happened. 'You will run everywhere except inside a building or when otherwise ordered.

'And fourth—' Lanzotta stopped. 'The fourth rule is that everything you can do is wrong. You walk wrong, you talk wrong, you think wrong, and you *are* wrong. We are here to help you start doing things right.'

Lanzotta turned to Halstead.

'Corporal. Take this trash out of my sight and see if there's anything you can do to improve them.'

'YES, SERGEANT.' The corporal snapped a salute, then ran to one side of the formation.

'Right . . . face!' he shouted.

Sten blinked as he found his body responding to hypno conditioning he'd been programmed with in the sleep lectures.

'Forward . . . *harch!* . . . double-time . . . *harch!*'

The formation of trainees stumbled forward.

'This is your home, children,' Halstead's voice boomed down the long squad barracks. Sten and the other recruits each stood next to a bunk.

'We give you a bed, which you'll be lucky to see four hours a night,' Halstead went on. 'You got one cabinet to put your equipment in. We will show you how to store it.

'I know most of you were brought up in a sewer works. You *will* keep this barracks clean. But it will *never* be clean enough.'

Halstead walked to the door. 'You have two minutes to gape around. Then fall outside to draw clothing and equipment.'

The barracks door slammed shut. There was silence for a moment, then the excited buzz of conversation. Sten looked around the room at his fellow trainees. They looked fit, healthy, and terrified. He wasn't quite the smallest of the group, but close.

'Farmers. All farmers,' the trainee beside the next bunk said. Sten looked at him. It was the young man from the tourist world. He held out a vertical palm to Sten. 'Gregor.'

Sten touched palms, and introduced himself. 'Is there something the matter with farmers?' he asked curiously.

'Not a thing. Just what the Empire needs to make into heroes.' Gregor might have curled a lip.

'But not you?'

Gregor smiled. 'You are on it. Not me.'

Sten lifted an eyebrow.

'Officer. That's the ticket. You hide and watch. When they start combing the losers out . . .' Gregor smiled again.

Halstead's whistle shrilled suddenly. Boots clattered as the trainees dashed for the door.

'YOU'RE TOO SLOW, CHILDREN, WAY . . . TOO . . . SLOW. THE LAST FIVE OUT ARE ON MESS DUTY!' Halstead bellowed.

'NEXT!' the corporal screamed. Sten, standing naked in the long line, wondered if Halstead could talk normally. Probably not, he decided. The trainee in front of Sten dashed to the large coffin, ran inside, put his toes on the mark, and Halstead banged the door shut.

He waited, then jerked it open. 'OUT OUT OUT,' he bellowed.

The man jumped out, and ran down the corridor to a dispenser trough that was already filling with packaged uniforms.

Sten pulled his head out of the ultrasonic barber. He ran his fingers dubiously over his suddenly bare skull.

Carruthers grinned at him and growled, 'Yeah, you look even dumber than you feel.'

'Thank you, corporal,' Sten shouted, and ran back to the waiting formation.

Sten, the clumsy transport bag dangling from one shoulder, ran back toward the barracks.

'FASTER, FASTER,' screamed Halstead. 'THAT ONLY WEIGHS FORTY KILOS, SCUM.'

Out of the corner of his eye Sten saw Carruthers kneeling on the chest of one recruit who'd gone down under the weight of the bag.

'You've got to understand,' Carruthers crooned, 'we're just trying to help you, skeek.' She suddenly bellowed, without getting off the panting man, 'NOW ON YOUR FEET!'

'Oooh,' Lanzotta moaned as he walked down the long line of trainees. 'You think you look like soldiers?'

He stopped in front of one traineee. Instantly Carruthers and Halstead were beside him. 'Son, your tunic lines up with your pants fastening.'

'DID YOU HEAR THE SERGEANT?' Halstead howled as he yanked the trainee's cap down over his eyes. 'HE SAID YOU LOOKED LIKE DRAKH,' Carruthers screamed in the boy's other ear. Lanzotta went on, as if the two bellowing corporals weren't there. 'We want you to look your best.' He shook his head sadly and walked on, as Halstead straight-armed the recruit back across his bunk, which collapsed sideways.

Lanzotta stopped in front of Sten.

Sten waited.

Lanzotta looked him up and down, then stared into Sten's eyes. A smile touched the corners of his mouth again, and he walked on.

There was a heavy whisper in his ear. 'I think the sergeant likes you,' said Carruthers. 'He thinks you'll make a fine soldier. I do too. I think you ought to show us all just how good you are.'

Pause.

'DROP! DO PUSHUPS! DO MANY, MANY PUSHUPS!'

Sten went down, caught himself on his hands, and started down. Carruthers sat on his shoulders, and Sten collapsed to the floor. 'I SAID DO PUSHUPS,' Carruthers shouted.

Sten fought to lift himself clear of the ground. Carruthers got up.

'ON YOUR FEET,' she howled. Sten snapped up, back at attention.

'I THINK WE WERE WRONG. I DON'T THINK YOU'LL EVER MAKE A SOLIDER,' Carruthers shouted. 'YOU WON'T EVEN MAKE A GOOD CORPSE.'

Sten stood motionless.

Carruthers glowered at him for a moment, then went on to the next victim.

'Your father didn't love you, did he, trooper?'

'NO, CORPORAL.'

'Your mother hated you, didn't she?'

'YES, CORPORAL.'

'Why didn't your mother love you?'

'I DON'T KNOW, CORPORAL.'

'She hated you because she was losing business until she had you aborted. Isn't that right, recruit?'

'YES, CORPORAL.'

'Who is the only person who loves you, trainee?'

'YOU ARE, CORPORAL.'

Sten winced as Carruthers hurled the recruit against the wall.

'WHERE ARE YOU FROM, SCUM?'

'Ryersbad Four, corporal.'

'WHAT? WHAT DID YOU SAY?'

'Ry – Ryersbad Four, corporal.'

'GET THAT TRASHCAN, RECRUIT.'

'Yes, corporal.'

'PICK IT UP, OVER YOUR HEAD.'

The garbage cascaded over the recruit's shoulders.

'GET IN IT.'

The trainee knelt, lowering the steel container over his body. Instantly Carruthers and Halstead thudded kicks into the can.

'SCUM' – *crash* – 'YOU DON'T HAVE ANY HOME' – *crash* – 'THE GUARD IS YOUR ONLY HOME' – *crash* – 'WHERE ARE YOU FROM?' – *crash*.

'Nowhere, corporal,' came the muffled voice from inside the can.

Halstead moaned, and tried to tear his cropped hair.

'It's hopeless,' he said quietly. 'Absolutely hopeless.'

Screaming again:

'RECRUIT, YOU WILL GET OUT OF THAT TRASHCAN.'

He helpfully kicked the container over. The trainee crawled out, his uniform stained and smeared.

'YOU LOOK LIKE YOU JUST FOUND A HOME, RECRUIT. NOW YOU TAKE THAT CAN OUT OF HERE TO THE MESS HALL. AND I WANT YOU TO STAND IN IT AND TELL EVERYONE WHO COMES BY THAT THAT'S YOUR HOME.'

'Yes, corporal.'

The recruit shouldered the container and stumbled toward the door.

'In your bunks,' Lanzotta snapped.

The naked recruits dove for their beds. Lanzotta walked toward the door.

'I want you to know something, children,' he said. 'I can truthfully say that I have never spent a worse first training day with a sorrier group of scum. I'm not even going to enjoy killing you. Don't you agree?'

'YES, SERGEANT,' came the shout from a hundred bunks.

'I really can't stand it. Good night, children.'

Lanzotta flipped off the light switch.

'Are you all exhausted?' came the question in the blackness.

'YES, SERGEANT.'

'What?'

'NO, SERGEANT.'

The light came back on.

'That's nice,' Lanzotta said. 'Five minutes. Fall outside dressed for physical training.'

He smiled and walked out of the barracks as the recruits stared at each other, stunned.

Sten ran the depil stick over his face again, just to make sure, reslotted it, and picked up his shower gear. He hurried out of the refresher to his bunk. Flipped open the cabinet and, checking the layout chart pinned to the inside wall, put everything away.

He checked the clock. He had a whole minute and a half until he had to dress. He sat down on the floor with a happy moan. His bunk was already S-rolled for the day, blanket folded in the prescribed manner on top of it.

'Sten. Gimme a hand.' Sten pulled himself back up, and grabbed the other end of Gregor's mattress.

The two men looked at each other, and both of them suddenly snickered. 'Definitely material for a recruiting livie,' Gregor grinned. 'By the way. You notice something interesting?'

'There's nothin' interesting on this clottin' world. Except that bed if I could crawl back in it.'

'Look around. Somethin' interestin'. There's women in this unit, right?'

'Good thinkin', Gregor. Guess they'll have to make you an officer.'

'Shaddup. But you know somethin' more interestin'? Everybody sleeps alone.'

'Probably some rule against anything else.'

'Rules ever stop anybody who's in the mood?'

Sten shook his head.

'They put something in the food. That's what it is. Chemicals. 'Cause they don't want anybody getting attached to somebody who probably's gonna wash out.'

Sten thought about it. Not likely. If everybody was like he was, they were just too tired to raise even a smile. He decided to change the subject. 'Gregor. You said something about you're gonna be an officer?'

'Sure.'

'How?'

'I have three things on my side. First, my dad. Don't say anything, 'cause I don't want to sound like I'm bragging, but he's a wheel. Our family owns most of Lasker XII. He's got touch. We've even been presented at court.'

Sten looked at Gregor thoughtfully. He guessed that was pretty significant.

'Second. I went to military schools. So I know what they're talking about. And I'll tell you, that's a lot better than the conditioning they pour in us while we're trying to sleep.'

'Military schools. Doesn't the Guard have some kind of academy? Just for officers?'

Gregor looked a little uncomfortable. 'Yeah, but my dad . . . I decided it'd be better to start at the bottom. You know, so you understand the troops that you're gonna command. Be one of them, and all that.'

'Uh-huh.'

'Third. Every now and then, they make an outstanding recruit award and commission the lucky choice. Right out of basic.'

'Which you think is gonna be you?'

'Pick somebody else. Look around. Go ahead. Pick somebody.'

Sten eyed the recruits, milling into their uniforms.

'Like Lanzotta said. They're just cannon fodder. I'm not saying I'm great, but I don't see competition. Unless . . . maybe you.'

Sten laughed. 'Not me, Gregor. Not me. I learned a long time ago, you keep your head down you don't get caught by the big pieces.'

The door crashed open. 'AWRIGHT, LISTEN UP. WE GOT A CHANGE IN THE TRAINING SCHEDULE SINCE IT'S GETTIN' COLD OUTSIDE. IT'S ALMOST TWENTY DEGREES CENTIGRADE, AND SO WE'RE GONNA PRACTICE. UNIFORM OF THE DAY WILL BE COLD-WEATHER GEAR.'

Gregor's mouth hung open. 'Cold-weather gear? It's the middle of summer!'

Sten jerked his cabinet door open and started pawing an arctic uniform out.

'Thought you'd already learned what Lanzotta said about us thinking.'

Gregor wearily nodded, and started changing.

'Report!'

'Sten. Recruit in training!'

Lanzotta leaned back in his chair.

'Relax, boy. This is just routine. As you know, the Empire takes a great deal of interest in seeing that its soldiers are well treated.'

'Yessir!'

'Therefore, I've got some questions to ask you. These will be filed with the rights commission. First question: Have you, since your arrival on Klisura, seen any instances of physical maltreatment?'

'I don't understand, sir.'

'Have you seen any of the cadre abuse any trainee? It's a severely punishable offense.'

'Nossir!'

'Have you witnessed any cadre member addressing any trainee in derogatory tones?'

'Nossir!'

'Do you consider yourself happy, trainee?'

'Yessir!'

'Dismissed.'

Sten saluted, whirled, and ran out. Lanzotta scratched his chin thoughtfully and looked at Halstead.

'Him?'

'Not sure yet. But probably.'

Chapter Nineteen

The assassin was methodical.

Mental notes: Sten; Thoresen; Time . . . time a question; Thoresen more so. Motive: personal. Possible – no, probable danger to me. Assignment questionable unless . . .

'There's a matter of payment,' the assassin said finally.

'We've already settled that. You'll be well paid.'

'I'm always well paid. It's a question of delivery. Uh . . . my back door?'

'You don't trust us?'

'No.'

The Baron eased back in his chair, closed his eyes. There were no worries. He was just relaxing and taking in a bit more UV.

'It seems, at this point, your problems aren't a back door – a way out – as much as they are your knowledge.'

'Knowledge?'

'Yes. If you choose to not accept the assignment . . . well, you're privy to a great deal, you must realize. Need I go further?'

The assassin casually reached over the desk and picked up an antique pen. 'If you even look at one of the alarms,' the killer whispered, 'I'll bury this pen in your brain.'

The Baron was still, then pushed a smile across his face.

'Do you have your own way out?'

'Always,' the assassin said. 'Now, when I complete the task, I have a bank in—'

Thoresen waved languidly. 'Done. Whatever the arrangements. Done.'

'It's not enough money.'

'Why not?'

'To begin. I must get inside the Imperial Guard. That may mean other deaths than your target.'

'You're thinking of joining the Guard?'

'Possibly. There is also the matter of the man who recruited Sten, this Imperial intelligence operative.'

'A minor agent.'

'Are you sure?'

The Baron hesitated. 'Yes.'

'I still need more money.'

'That is not a problem.'

'The time?'

'Yes. This must be done immediately.'

The assassin stood up to leave. 'Then I can't do it. No one can. If you'd still like to try, I'll give you a few names, but no one who would take the job is competent. Be warned of that.'

The Baron looked at him thoughtfully. 'How much time?'

'As much as I need.'

Thoresen was running ahead of the assassin. He had the best here. So . . . yes. It was the only way. 'Very well.'

The assassin started for the door.

'A moment, please,' Thoresen said.

The assassin stopped.

'The matter of the pen. How would you have killed me?'

'No.'

'I collect martial trivia – I'm quite willing to pay . . .'

The assassin named a price and Thoresen agreed. A few minutes later he was holding his elbow crooked in just the right position.

Chapter Twenty

Sten four-handed beermugs and pushed away from the vendor. He clattered the mugs down on the table, drained one, and grabbed another before the other two trainees could get to it.

'Whaddaya think, Big Time Trainee Corporal Sten?' Morghhan asked.

'Just like the clottin' world I came off. Anytime you get promoted, you end up payin'. Only difference is they take the credits now instead of later.'

'Y'got a bad attitude, troop,' Morghhan said as he sluiced down beer.

Sten poured more down his own throat and considered. Bad attitude? Not hardly. He was still pretty happy, in spite of the best efforts of Lanzotta and company. Maybe he was stuck in the Guard. But it was just for a few years. And nothing he did could extend that contract.

Also Sten had, if not friends, at least people he could sit and talk with. Even though most of their time was spent deciding what sewer pit Lanzotta crawled out of, he wasn't alone anymore. The new jargon everybody used wasn't much different from Mig-talk.

He put Bet back behind the wall quickly and turned to Morghhan, the skinny recruit he'd been sure wasn't going to make it through the last weeks of physical conditioning on that three-gee world.

'Damn right I got a bad attitude. I didn't ask for no stripes. They don't pay me better 'cause I gotta tell you clots when to wipe, do they?'

'If I was you,' Bjhalstred said softly, 'I'd be honored. Shows how much cadre thinks of you. Shows they think you'll make a real hero guardsman type.'

Sten snorted at Bjhalstred. He couldn't figure the agriworld boy out. Nobody could be so dumb. Or could they? Not that it mattered. Sten shrugged and dumped the spare beer in Bjhalstred's lap.

He yelped and grabbed at his crotch. 'Noncoms ain't permitted to discipline trainees. Ain't you listened to the regs? You wanna go outside?'

Sten stood up. 'You first.'

'Naw. You g'wan an' start without me. I'll work on your beer while you're gone.'

Morghhan interrupted.'Chop it. Here. Take Gregor's. Looks like he ain't gonna show.'

They drained their mugs, and Sten sourly held out another handful of credits. 'I'm buyin', somebody else is flyin'.' Bjhalstred headed for the machine.

'You got any idea why they gave you the stripes?' Morghhan asked.

Sten shook his head. 'I sure ain't been leechin' Lanzotta. Maybe they figure on trainee rank to wash out the weak ones, now they're finally gonna start teachin' us soldiering.'

'That don't compute.'

'Why not? We been nine weeks just doin' muscle-puffs, and we're down, what?'

'Seventy-three left. Out of a hundred.'

'Way too high, Carruthers was tellin' me. They only graduate ten per company. Should've dumped forty per cent by now, she said. Said they was gonna put everybody under the fine-line startin' right away.'

'So what? Either way they're gonna get you if they want.'

'Now there's a high-prob thought,' Bjhalstred agreed, coming back with the next round. 'Speakin' of high, here's ol' Lord Gregor himself.'

Gregor slid into a spare seat.

'Looks like you're nursin' a case of the hips,' Morghhan said. 'Who put it to you?'

'I was with Lanzotta.'

'For almost an hour? An' the bloodstains don't hardly show.'

Gregor smiled grimly. 'I'm not the one with bloodstains. But Lanzotta's gonna be.'

Sten waited.

'You went to him?'

'You have it locked. To tell him I'm sending off a letter to my father.'

'I'll bet he was very interested,' Bjhalstred said solemnly. 'Very important for a young trainee to keep his family posted.'

'It was about this clotting trainee stripe thing.'

Sten eyed Gregor over his beer. 'You still think you got raw 'cause they didn't give you any acting rank?'

'Straight. Hell, I deserve at least as much of a chance as anybody. They say these jack stripes are to pick out potential leaders. Why not me?'

'Maybe they figure you're nothin' but a potential wipe,' Morghhan said.

'Try me,' Gregor glowered.

'Shaddup, the both of you,' Sten put in before Morghhan had time to bristle. 'We are sittin' here, quietly drinkin' beer, and celebratin' that we can now get out of barracks for two hours a night an' get swilled.'

'Cadre gives us enough grief, we don't have to go out and synthesize our own,' Bjhalstred agreed.

Morghhan added a massive belch and went for more beer.

'I ain't just blowin',' Gregor said. 'You know my father's got influence. All I want is justice. Tell you what. I see all they gave you is a double stripe. Since you and I are the only ones in this company with any intelligence—'

'Appreciate the thought,' Bjhalstred said. 'Glad you two fleet admirals decided to split a beer with an ol' scrunchie like me.'

'That's not what I mean,' Gregor said irritably. 'Sten and I are the only two who're aware how much your whole military career depends on what happens right here in training.'

'Military career,' Morghhan said as he came back to the table. 'Whoo. Things getting serious around here.'

'Let 'im finish,' Sten said.

'So I told my father to go straight to the Imperial Court. Get an investigation. Why is the Guard wasting its finest potential because the instructors couldn't pour piss out of a spaceboot unless there was a printout on the heel?'

'Come on, Gregor. You mentioned my name. What's this got to do with me?'

'I'll use you as an example. You only got two stripes. You ought to have been trainee platoon leader. Or better. If I hadn't had training already, I got to admit you'd be almost as good a troop as me.'

'Yuh.'

'So I'm gonna mention you in my letter. Make a stronger case, and when my father takes care of things, it'll do you some good too.'

Sten started to say something, then decided to spend a few seconds unhooking Morghhan's fingers from the spare mug and inhaling it. Then he put the mug down.

'I don't think I want that,' he said, just as quietly as he could manage. 'I'll make my own way, thanks.'

'But—'

'Gregor. That's what it is, like you say. End program.'

Gregor stared at Sten, then nodded. 'Whatever you want. But you're making a mistake.'

'My mistake.'

Gregor got to his feet. 'Anyway. I got a letter to write.' And he was gone.

'Trainee Corporal Sten?'

Sten looked back from the doorway at Bjhalstred, who had snapped to rigid attention.

'You have my permission to speak, Trainee Bunghole Bjhalstred.'

'Request plus or minus reading on that last, over.'

'Stand by. Computing. Prog 1 – somebody's either gonna be trainee fleet general or Guard cesspool orderly with thirty years' time in grade. I dunno. Prog 2 – I'm gonna get imploded. Halstead said training was really gonna start tomorrow mornin', an' that's more than I can face without a hangover.'

Three mugs clanked solemnly.

'Awright,' Carruthers said in what were almost human tones. 'What you're about to get is the most carefully engineered way of killing someone known to man. Imperial engineers designed it so not even maggot-brains like you could screw it up. Which is almost unbelievable.

'I need one idiot volunteer. You.' She waved at Sten. 'Post.'

Sten slid out of the bleacher bench, double-timed to a position in front of the low stand, and waited at attention.

In the distance, behind Carruthers, ran the thousand-meter tree- and bush-studded emptiness of a firing range, lane-marked at its far end.

Carruthers opened the top of the lecture stand and took out a weapon. A smooth black triangle formed the stock/pistol grip, and a stubby inverted cone ended the seventy-centimeter-long barrel.

Carruthers handled the rifle reverently.

'You probably seen this, and handled it in the livies. This is assault rifle Mark XI. We call it the willygun. Tell you something strange about this. This was invented more'n a thousand years ago, on Terra, by a designer named Robert Willy.

'It was a fine design,' Carruthers said. 'On'y problem was that lasers weren't that good and nobody knew for sure how to handle hunks of antimatter, which is what makes this piece so deadly.'

She touched a stud, and a long tube slid out of the rifle's butt. 'This is the ammunition. Antimatter Two – AM_2 – the same stuff that powers spaceships. One tube contains fourteen hundred rounds. The bullet's a one-millimeter ball of AM_2, which is inside an Imperium shield, which is the only thing that keeps the whole magazine from exploding when it touches conventional matter.

'We once calculated, as a matter of interest, that one of these tubes has enough energy to power a scoutship all the way around this system at full drive level.

'Ain't that interesting, Bjhalstred?'

Bjhalstred jumped awake.

'You wasn't sleeping on me, was you, Bjhalstred?'

'NO, CORPORAL.'

'That's good. That's very good. But why don't you come on out here and get down in pushup position to make sure you don't *get* sleepy.

'Anyway. Fourteen hundred rounds. If the Empire ever sold these guns on the open market, which of course they never will, each little tiny AM_2 ball would cost a guardsman three weeks' salary. You see how good the Empire is to us?'

Carruthers waited.

'YES, CORPORAL,' came the shout.

'Aren't you all glad you went and joined up?'

'YES, CORPORAL.'

'You sounded a little weak on that one,' Carruthers growled. 'Assault rifle Mark XI. You got two controls. One is for your safety/single-shot/automatic fire mode selection, the other is the trigger. You got one dial, here on the butt, which shows you the state of battery charge. Each battery will give the laser enough energy for about ten thousand rounds, depending on atmospheric pressure, if any, and conditions.

'The laser is what is used to fire the particles. This means the only sight you got is this crosshair. You don't have to worry about trajectory or bullet drop or any of that other dust that's important with a conventional weapon.

'Which is what is special about the willygun. If you can point it at something, you hit that something.

'Demonstrator!'

Sten mounted the platform. Carruthers handed him the rifle. Sten handled it curiously. Light. Almost too light, like a toy. Carruthers grinned at him. 'That ain't nothing you'd give your kid brother on Empire Day,' she said, seeming to read Sten's thoughts.

Carruthers opened the stand again and took out an object wrapped in plastic and about fifty centimeters to a side. She jumped down from the stand and walked ten meters to a low table. Carruthers unwrapped the parcel.

'This here is meat,' she said. 'The stuff that soyacrap in the mess hall is supposed to taste like. It's got about the same consistency as a humanoid.'

Carruthers set the blood-oozing meat on the table and walked back to the stand. 'Shoot me that deadly charging chunk of beef, trainee,' she said.

Sten raised the weapon awkwardly to his shoulder, and aimed through the sight. He pulled the trigger. Nothing happened.

'Helps if you take the safety off first,' Carruthers snarled.

Sten flipped the switch just above the trigger, re-aimed, and fired. There was the low crackle as air ionized.

His eyes jumped open, and the recruits semidozing through the lecture snapped awake. The minute particle hit the meat. It looked as if the beef exploded, blood spattering for several meters to the side.

'Go take a close look, trainee,' Carruthers invited.

Sten climbed down from the stand and walked to the table. There were only a few chunks of the meat left. Sten stared at the spattered table and ground, then came back to the stand.

'Makes you think,' Carruthers said. 'just how healthy anybody on the receiving end of that round would be. The answer is,' she said, raising her voice, 'they wouldn't be. You hit anything humanoid or even anything close to it with one of those anywhere and they're dead. If the round don't make a hole big enough to stick your fist through, the shock will.'

Carruthers stood silently, letting the idea sink in.

'Something to think about, isn't it?' she said soberly.

'AWRIGHT, SLUGS, YOU SAT ON IT LONG ENOUGH. NOW UNASS THOSE BLEACHERS AND GIMME A COMPANY FORMATION. We're gonna let you kill some targets today.'

Carruthers waited until the recruits were on line, then added softly, 'So far we dumped less'n a third of you skeeks back to your home cesspits. Here's where we cut some more dead tissue out.

'Children, there ain't never been a soldier who couldn't shoot. If there was an army that'd let him, that army wasn't around long –

and the Guard has been around for a thousand years. This is where we start cuttin' clean.

'You either qualify on the willygun or you're out. Simple as that. If you more'n just qualify, there's bennies for that. More pay and better training.

'But first you best qualify. 'Cause I hear they're jumpin' those duty battalions into terraforming these days. I'd rather be making a first-wave drop myself. Figure the chances are better.

'Now. FIRST RANK, 'TEN-HUT. ONE MAN PER POST. AT A RUN. MOVE OUT!'

Ten recruits, in spite of extensive individual attention and minor batterings, failed to qualify. Their bunks were rolled and empty the next day.

Sten couldn't understand why anybody had problems. Carruthers had been right. Point the willygun, and you hit. Every time.

When the rifle course ended, Sten was qualified for the next stage: SNIPER-RATED.

It got him ten more credits a month, his first ribbon, and more training.

Carruthers thunked down beside him.

'You got the target?'

Sten peered through the sights of the rifle. 'Yes, corporal.'

Carruthers touched the control box beside him. The target shot sideways, out of sight behind the stone wall a thousand meters from Sten.

'Awright. Now. Focus on the wall. The crosshairs go out of focus, right? Use the first knob on your sight. Twist until you get the sight focused.'

Sten followed instructions.

'Got it? Now use the knob below your sight, and turn until the crosshairs are about where you think that target is, even though you can't see it. Got it? Fire one.'

Sten touched the trigger.

Sten's fortieth-century sniper rifle was, in essence, quite simple. The round was still the AM_2 shielded particle. But instead of using a laser as propellant, a modified linear accelerator hung around the barrel. The sight was used to give exact range to the target, then, when the scope was twisted to fix on the out-of-sight target, the accelerator 'spun' the round so that it could execute up to a ninety-degree angle if necessary.

A gun that could shoot around corners.

Sten heard the explosion and saw the wall crumble.

'Hit.'

Carruthers slammed Sten on the back.

'Y'know, troop, you keep up like this and Guard's First may get themselves a trooper.'

And for some reason, Sten felt very proud of himself.

Sten crashed the garbage bin down on the dump, then upended it. Clean enough. He shoved the nozzle of the ultrasonic cleaner to the bottom and touched the trigger. Then banged the can a few more times on the concrete and lugged it back into the mess hall. Most of the Guard's menial jobs were handled either by civilians or by the time-servers of the duty battalions. Except for the real scutwork. The Guard reserved those chores for punishment detail. It didn't bother Sten that much. It was still better than any on-shift back on Vulcan.

Besides, he didn't figure he could have gotten around the problem.

He'd been quite happy, sitting there on the sand watching Halstead posture at Lanzotta's commands.

'We are not building technicians,' Lanzotta had said. 'I've told you that. We're building killers. We want people who want to listen to the sound of their enemies' eyeballs pop, who want to see what happens when you rip somebody's throat out with your teeth.'

Sten looked around at the other trainees. Most of them looked mildly aghast. Sten blanked. He remembered quite well, thank you, sergeant.

'We need a demonstrator.'

Silence. The company had learned by now what volunteering generally got you. And then sombody said, 'Corp' Sten.'

Sten had a pretty good idea it was Gregor, but didn't worry about it. He was seriously into being invisible. Lanzotta heard the voice.

'Sten. Post.'

Sten grunted, snapped to his feet and ran forward.

'Yes, corporal.'

Halstead did another fast one-two move. Fair, Sten analyzed. He's open down low, though.

'Recruit Corporal Sten. That man is your most dangerous enemy. Your mission is to close with and destroy him!'

Sten ambled in. Held up his hands in what he hoped would look like an offensive move and went airborne. Sten rolled in midair, recovered, and held back as his feet touched. Allowed himself to crumple forward, face first in the sand.

That should do it. And he heard Lanzotta's whisper in his ear.

'You are faking it, recruit corporal. You know how to do it better. Now I want you to get back up, without letting your fellow skinks know what you're doing, and attack Corporal Halstead.'

Sten didn't move.

'The alternative is three days on garbage detail.'

Sten sighed and picked himself up.

Halstead moved in, hands grabbing. Poor. Sten flashed, and rolled toward the ground. Legs in the air, scissored about Halstead's hips.

Halstead crashed, Sten locked, using Halstead's momentum to bring him back up. Halstead rolling up, Sten incoming, shoulder under Halstead's waist.

Halstead went straight up in a curving flight. Sten had time enough to consider if he'd put a cadre into suborbital, then he was moving. Halstead slammed back down, still moving, and Sten slammed two toe kicks into his ribs.

Halstead stayed down.

Sten recovered and turned.

There was awed silence from the trainees. Sten looked at Lanzotta, who heaved a sigh and jerked a thumb.

'Hup, sergeant!'

Sten picked up his cap and double-timed toward the mess hall.

There it was. Spaced if you did, spaced if you didn't. Sten grabbed the other garbage can and lugged them back into the mess hall.

The mess sergeant grinned at Sten as he came through the tiny office.

'Guess you're glad to be goin' back to trainin' tomorrow, hey?'

Sten shook his head.

'Ya like it here?'

'Negatory, sergeant.'

'What's the problem, 'cruit?'

'Tomorrow we start knife training, sergeant.'

'So?'

Yeah. So. Sten suddenly started laughing as he dragged the cans back toward their racks. So? It was still better than Vulcan.

Even Sten felt a little sick as the medic worked swiftly on the gaping wounds. The body was riddled with shrapnel and gouting blood.

'The procedure hasn't changed in thousands of years,' the medic instructor said. 'First get the casualty breathing again. Second, stop the bleeding. Third, treat for shock.'

He finished, covered the humanoid simulacrum with an insulblanket, and stood up. Looked around the class.

'Then you yell as loud as you can for a medic. Assuming some bork hasn't decided we're the most important target he can hit and there's any of us left.'

'What then?' Pech, the fat recruit, asked.

'If there's no professional treatment, use your belt medpak. If the bleeding's stopped and the insides are more or less together, the antis in the kit should keep your buddy from getting the creeping crud.'

He laughed.

''Course if you're on some world where we don't know anything about the bugs, best you can do is try to leave a good-looking corpse.' The medic looked over Pech's steadily diminishing chubbiness. 'Which will be hard enough in your case, Pech.'

Sten and the others chuckled. The medic was the first instructor they'd had who'd treated them even vaguely like sentient beings.

The medic opened a large cabinet and motioned to Sten, who helped him lift out another simulacrum. This one was dressed in a battle suit.

'In a suit, things are different,' the medic said. 'The medpak should already be hooked up inside the suit and work automatically. Sometimes it does.'

Another snort of laughter from the medic.

'But if the suit's holed, all you can do is seal it and get the casualty to a medshelter. You get more on that in suit drill. Now, I need a sucker – I mean a volunteer.'

He glanced around the audience, and his eyes lit on Pech. 'Come on up, troop.'

Pech double-timed up to the stand and waited at attention. 'Relax, relax. You make me nervous. Okay. This dummy here is your best buddy. You went through training together. You chased . . .' He pretended to study Pech closely. '. . . uh – ameboids together. Now his arm has just been blown off. What are you going to do?'

The medic stepped back. Pech shifted nervously.

'Come on, soldier. Your best friend's bleeding to death. Move!'

Pech took a tentative step forward as the medic pressed the switch concealed in his palm and the simulacrum's arm exploded. 'Blood' sprayed across Pech and the stand.

Pech froze. 'Come on, man. Move.'

Pech fumbled for the medpak on his belt and moved closer. More pulsing 'blood' dyed his face. Pech unclipped the pak's base and took a pressure bandage off.

'Thirty-four, thirty-five, thirty-six, thirty-seven . . . forget it, soldier.'

Pech seemed not to hear him and fought to get the bandage in position. Finally, the gout of 'blood' stopped.

'Your friend just died,' the medic said harshly. 'Now, on your feet.'

Pech clambered up, numb. The medic stared around at the trainees to make sure they got his point. Then he turned back to Pech.

'The dye used in that blood won't wear off for two days. Maybe that'll help you think about how you'd feel if that dummy had really been your teammate.'

Pech never did recover from the incident. A few weeks later, after a series of foul-ups, he disappeared. Washed out.

Sten blinked as the world came back into focus. He and the five other recruits stared at each other blankly. Halstead flipped up the flash visor on his shock helmet.

'How long were you out?'

Sten shrugged. 'A second or two, corporal?'

Halstead held out his watch finger. Two hours had passed. He unclipped another of the tiny bester grenades from his pocket.

'Instant time loss. You don't know what's happened to you, and you don't think anything's gone wrong. These are some of the most effective infiltration weapons you'll use.

'The company's out on the dexterity course. Report to Corporal Carruthers.'

Sten saluted and the recruits ran off.

Sten couldn't get the man out of his mind. There had been nothing unusual about the incident, but for some reason the officer's image kept poking up from his brain at odd moments.

It had been his day as company runner and he had been dozing at the desk. He didn't hear the door open or close.

'You the only one here, guardsman?'

Sten snapped awake and was on his feet.

The man standing in front of him was tall and slender. Sten blinked and found himself staring at the uniform. Almost imperceptibly, it was changing shade to match the paneled wall background. The man wore a soft hat of the same kind of strange material that Sten later learned was a beret. It was tilted rakishly over one eye.

A winged dagger was pinned to the beret. The only other insignia on the uniform were captain's stars on one shoulder and on the other the black outline of some kind of insect.

For some reason, Sten found himself stammering.
'Uh, yessir – they're – they're all out in the field.'
The officer handed Sten a sealed envelope.
'This is for Sergeant Lanzotta. It's personal, so see it's delivered directly to him.'
'Yessir.'
Then he was gone.
A week later, Sten got a chance to ask Carruthers who the man was. The corporal whistled when Sten described the uniform.
'That's Mantis Section!'
Sten looked at her blankly.
'You mean you ain't heard?'
Sten shook his head, feeling like a pioneer-world idiot.
'They're the nastiest bunch of soldiers in the Imperial Army,' Carruthers said. '*Real* elite. They work alone – humanoids, ETs. The Empire takes the best the Guard has and then disappears them into the Mercury Corps – Intelligence.'
Sten remembered Mahoney and nodded.
'Anyway. Mantis wear those fancy trop-camouflage uniforms when you see them. Mostly, you don't see 'em at all and you'd better hope it stays that way.'
'Why is that?'
'If you see one of those boys in the field you know you're about to be in deep trouble. Any one of 'em's probably got about two thousand and three of the enemy on his butt.'
Carruthers smiled a rare smile. There was nothing she liked better than war stories. 'I remember one time on Altair V. We were down with a regiment on a peacekeeping mission and somehow we'd got ourselves surrounded.
'We were screaming for help on every wavelength we could reach and tryin' to hang on. We figured the next thing that'd happen is we'd have to die a lot.'
Carruthers laughed. Sten figured that she had just made some kind of a joke and laughed back.
'So, one night this woman shows up at the command post. A Mantis Section troopie. She'd come through the enemy lines, through our pickets, through the support lines and first thing we know she's sitting down with our CO eating dinner. When she finished, she borrowed some AM_2 tubes and bester grenades and disappeared again.
'I dunno what she did, or how she did it, but about twelve G hours later six Imperial destroyers showed up and bailed our tails out.'

Carruthers glared at Sten, which made him feel a whole lot better. A smiling Carruthers was something he didn't think he wanted to get used to.

'But that's not the way it usually works,' she told him. 'You ever see one of those guys again, troop, you crawl under something. 'Cause as sure as your tail is where your head ought to be, there's something big and nasty about to come screaming in – you just remember that, hear?'

Sten heard her real well.

'You will *all* learn about the fighting suit,' Lanzotta said. 'Chances are, some of you will even die in one. And you will discover, as I did, that the suit will kill you faster than the enemy, more often than not.'

At that point, Sten and the others turned their minds to 'doze.' They all thought they had Lanzotta figured now. All of his little lectures were structured the same. First, an introduction. Then – Lanzotta's favorite part – a history lesson. Followed by the information they really needed to know. At which point they snapped awake again.

'I am particularly fond of this subject,' Lanzotta continued. 'In fact, I have made a personal study of the suit. Because it was with this piece of equipment that the technicians reached the absolute height of absurdity.'

Click. Snap. Every recruit mind instantly slipped into a deeper state of unconsciousness. Lanzotta motioned to Halstead, who walked to a terminal and rapped on a few keys. There was a loud clanking and grinding and all the recruits came awake as a long rack of fighting suits ratcheted out into the lecture area.

Sten looked over the suits, and for once, he didn't have to fake interest. Many of them he recognized from the war feelies. They were huge, armored things shaped vaguely like humanoids. Some had what could pass for arms, but were track-based.

The first thing he noticed was they all seemed to be graded by size. At the beginning of the rack, they were small and flimsy-looking. From there they got larger and larger and more complex-appearing, until about two-thirds of the way down the line. Then they got smaller again, but with a more durable look about them.

Lanzotta paced along the line of suits, stopping at the largest one. 'Now here, as I can personally attest, is where the Techs really outdid themselves. It was all so logical, you see. To anyone but a guardsman. They made bullets, therefore they made bulletproof vests.'

Lanzotta looked his captive group over, as if anticipating a question. No one was that dumb.

'Now, I'm not going to explain what a bullet was,' Lanzotta said, 'except to say it was a projectile that was capable of creating a hole in you as big as the willygun. In some ways, it was worse.'

The way Lanzotta grinned at that, Sten *knew* he meant 'worse.'

'The larger the antipersonnel weapon,' Lanzotta continued, 'the more the Techs loaded on the armor. Until, finally, with this suit we could take anything. Lasers, nukes, bugs, null bombs, you name it, we were just about invulnerable.'

Sten was starting to get the drift of what was wrong with the suit.

'About fifty years ago, I had the great pleasure of testing this suit in action. Myself and about two thousand comrades in arms.'

Lanzotta laughed. And it was instant tension time for the recruits. Should they laugh? He obviously thought he had made a funny. But Carruthers and Halstead were stony-faced. They didn't think it was funny. Lanzotta ended their agony by not noticing anything and going on.

'Our orders were to put down a rebellion on a godforsaken planet called Moros. Besides the troops, we were supplied with everything known to modern military science – including the latest fighting suit.'

Sten studied it more closely. It was the largest, non-tracked piece of equipment on the rack. There were tubes and wires, minividscreens, and knobs and bulges everywhere. It looked like it weighed about five hundred kilos and would take a whole battery of Techs to operate.

'I love this suit,' Lanzotta said. 'It can do anything. It's AM_2-powered and pseudomuscled. Anyone inside it would be equal to thirty beings in strength. A small company dressed in these could advance through any kind of fire the enemy threw at them. It's impervious to almost anything and you can live in it for months without outside support.'

Lanzotta shook his head with the wonder of it all.

'Of course, no one thought to brief the natives on Moros. They weren't told what brave and fierce warriors we were. They didn't even know the word technology, so what could they think?

'We landed and they ran into the jungle. We advanced under fire – mostly spears and blowguns – and burned their villages. Then one day they grew tired of running.'

Lanzotta laughed again. But this time, Sten and the others were too caught up with his story to notice.

'What they discovered was this: Yes, we were big strong soldiers with the fire power of a small tank. But we couldn't maneuver. And we were cut off from our environment. So, they worked out this simple little trick.

'They dug pits, camouflaged them, and then fled before our advance. Of course, many of us fell in. The pits were lined with nets that tangled us up.'

Lanzotta wasn't laughing.

'And while we were struggling out of the nets, they'd run up to the pit and stick a big long spear through the suit's waste vent. The spear made large holes in the trooper inside.

'Naturally, the excrement was carried into the body. The wound festered so badly that the medpaks froze up – and many of us rotted to death.'

Lanzotta shook his head.

'We lost two-thirds of the guardsmen that made the assault. And more in another landing. Finally the only solution was to dust the planet, sit back, and watch Moros glow.'

Lanzotta patted the suit.

'Destroying planets isn't done in polite diplomatic circles. The Emperor was very unhappy.'

Lanzotta grinned as he came to his final point.

'The *new* Techs,' he said, 'started redesigning the suit.'

Sten wished he could find a place to hide. From the look on Lanzotta's face, he knew it would have to be very deep and made of something at least as strong as titanium.

'It is a sin and an abomination in the eyes of the Lord,' Smathers frothed. 'It was my duty to report their behavior to you.'

Lanzotta stared at him, then at the two men standing at attention nearby. Sten, he ignored – for the moment.

'Colrath, Rnarak, is he telling the truth?'

'YES, SERGEANT.'

Lanzotta sighed and turned to Smathers.

'Smathers, I have a distinct surprise for you. The Guard doesn't care about what beings do with each other when they're off duty, so long as everyone falls out for formation the next morning.'

'But—'

'But you come from a world settled by the Plymouth Brethren. Fine. Some excellent guardsmen have been produced by your beliefs. But all of them learned their ideas are not to be applied to anyone but themselves. And since when have you ever interrupted your sergeant?'

Smathers stared at the floor. 'Sorry. Sergeant.'

'Your apology is accepted. But have you ever been to bed with a man?'

Smathers looked horrified. 'Of course not.'

'If you don't know about it, did you ever consider that you're missing something?' Lanzotta said.

Smathers' eyes bulged.

'In any event,' Lanzotta said briskly. 'You are spending time worrying about something that is none of your business. And since you seem so preoccupied ferreting cesspools, I think we need one volunteer to clean the one in the barracks. You're accepted.'

'You're not going to—'

'I'm not going to,' Lanzotta agreed. 'Now move out.'

Smathers walked down the barracks toward the latrine. Lanzotta turned to Colrath and Rnarak.

'While the Guard isn't concerned with what you do or don't do with each other, we still must respect the beliefs of the other trooper. I am deeply distressed by the fact that you couldn't be bothered to find a private place for your recreation, and instead disturbed the sleep and happiness of other trainees. Go help him clean the cesspool.'

The two shame-faced men walked slowly away. Now Lanzotta turned his attention to Sten.

'Recruit Corporal Sten!'

'Yes, sergeant.'

'Why didn't you deal with this matter yourself?'

'I tried to, sergeant. Smathers insisted on seeing you.'

'As is his right. Especially when confronted with a recruit corporal incapable of handling a simple barracks dispute.'

'Yes, sergeant.'

'First, you will remove those stripes.'

'Ycs, sergeant.'

'Second, you will join those three on the cesspool detail.'

'Yes, sergeant.'

'Dismissed.'

Sten followed the others out. Next time, he thought, he'd save everyone a whole lot of trouble and just tear Smathers in half.

Chapter Twenty-One

Basically, Sten decided, he didn't give a Mig's ass. He touched the anodizer to the last bit of exposed metal on his weapons belt, then tucked it back in his cabinet.

Then looked up.

Tomika stood there, kitbag in hand.

He decided, for about the gigatime, she was the nicest-looking thing about training. And he'd tried. Indeed he'd tried.

'Who's paired with you, Sten?'

'My left hand,' he said.

She tossed her ditty on his bunk and started patting the pillow into shape. Sten's mouth dropped.

'Uh, Tomika? I asked before and –'

'I don't bag with NCOs. I got standards.'

Sten suddenly decided it not only wasn't important, but it was funny. Broke his laugh off as he looked at Gregor.

'You see what I meant,' Gregor said. 'And you were wrong.'

'I'm always wrong, Gregor. Howcum this time?'

'They are arbitrary. They wouldn't give me the rank I deserve. And they broke you. You see?'

'Nope. Far as I can see, I stepped on it.'

'It's right there. In front of you.' Sten decided that Gregor was getting a little shrill.

'DNC, troop. Does not compute.'

'My father taught me that any business that doesn't respond to new stimuli is doomed. That's the Guard. All they want is cannon fodder. Anybody who doesn't fit their idea of a moron hero, they'll put to scutwork. And if they make a mistake, like they did with you, they'll bust him down as soon as they see it.'

'You really believe that, Gregor,' Tomika said.

'Dash-A right I do,' Gregor said. 'I've written another letter to my father, Sten. He'll see things are rectified.'

Sten sat up. 'You, uh, mention me?'

'No, I did not. Just like you would have wanted. But you will regret it. You'll see.'

And Gregor laughed, turned, and walked back toward his bunk.

'Hey, Ex Recruit Trainee Small Time Corporal Sten? Is he two zeds short of a full count?'

Sten didn't answer her, just listened to Gregor's laughter as he clambered into his bunk.

'And what happens when I do this?'

Tomika giggled. Sten suddenly sat up in his bunk and put a hand over her mouth. Movement. A buried snicker. Tomika reached up and grabbed him, pulling Sten down to the pillow.

'No, Sten,' she breathed. 'Wait.'

Sten did – for a long count of heartbeats.

And then the shouting started.

Somebody hit the lights, and Sten bolted out of the bunk. The shouting came from Gregor's area.

Sten rolled out of his bunk, reflexively sliding up into an attack stance. And then he slumped down again, laughing helplessly.

Gregor screamed louder and started flailing.

Sten and the other recruits gathered around Gregor's area. The man did have problems.

'It's the Giant Spider of Odal,' somebody said in a mock hushed voice. 'You're in trouble, Gregor.'

Gregor was indeed in trouble. Somebody must've snuck a spray can of climbing thread out of the training area the day before. And while Gregor slept, he, she, or they had spun the thread from bunk to cabinet to boots to bunk to combat shoes to cabinet to end up connected to Gregor's nose.

The high-test, incredibly sticky goo made a very effective spider web, Sten decided. Whoever had spun the web had unclipped the hardener from the nozzle tip, so the more Gregor flailed, the more he became enmeshed in the strands.

Gregor by now had trussed himself neatly in the strands and was moaning.

Sten looked at Tomika. 'Who's got the real case at Gregor?'

She motioned blankly. 'Just about everybody.' The woman giggled. 'Guess he'll make a fine officer.'

'Bet three to one it won't straighten him out,' Sten said. 'Not just that, but prog—'

'Are we enjoying ourselves, children?' The recruits turned into instant statuary.

Sten could never figure how Carruthers managed a 116-dB(A) whisper. 'Is there any particular reason we aren't all at attention?'

'Ten-hup!' somebody managed. Carruthers waddled forward through the cluster. Looked at Gregor and clucked thoughtfully.

'The Giant Spider of Odal. Knew we had lice and a few rats, but thought we fumigated those spiders last cycle.'

Carruthers turned.

'Morghhan! Why don't you stroll down to supply and draw a tank of solvent. If you wouldn't mind.'

The squadbay door slammed on Morghhan before Carruthers finished her sentence.

'Giant spiders, hmm. Serious business.' Whisper into shout. 'Recruit Sten, what's the uniform of the day for spider hunts?'

'Uh . . . I dunno, corporal.'

'DROP, DROP, DROP. YOU ARE AN EXNONCOM AND YOU ARE SUPPOSED TO KNOW THAT! TRAINEE TOMIKA, YOU SHOULD HAVE TOLD HIM – DROP, DROP, DROP!'

Carruthers walked back to the door.

'You will fall out in five minutes in full spider-hunt dress, and prepare to spend the remainder of the night looking for what I estimate is five giant spiders.'

She slammed out. The recruits looked around. Bewildered. The door creaked open again.

'Anyone who is not in the proper uniform draws two days' kitchen detail. That is all, children. Time's a-wasting.'

When Bjhalstred ran over Corporal Halstead with a combat car, Sten knew he had been right all along. There was nothing stupid about the farmboy. Now, no one ever accused Bjhalstred of crunching Halstead on purpose. It was an accident. Sure, Sten thought to himself, sure.

'This,' Halstead proclaimed, 'is another Empire tool for wormbrains. One gauge shows you battery charge. Turn this switch, and the car starts. You adjust the lift level stick to the desired altitude. One to one-grand meters. Doppler radar keeps you automatically that far off the ground.

'Shove the control stick forward, you lift up. Farther forward, the faster. Max speed, two hundred kph. Move the stick to the side, the combat car turns. Do we have a volunteer?'

Halstead looked around the trainees until he saw someone trying to be invisible.

'Bjhalstred,' he crooned. 'Come on up here, my boy.'

Bjhalstred locked his wheels in front of the corporal.

'Never driven a car, hmm?'

'NO, CORPORAL!'

'Why not, trainee?'

'We don't believe in them on Outremer, corporal. We're Amish.'

'I see.' Halstead considered for a minute, then evidently decided not to say anything. 'In the car.'

Bjhalstred clambered in.

'You don't have any religious objections to driving, do you?' Halstead asked.

'NO, CORPORAL.'

'Fine. Start it, set it for two meters height, and drive out across the parade ground. Turn it around and come back.'

Bjhalstred fumbled with the controls, and the car silently lifted clear of the ground and hung there.

'Well?'

Bjhalstred looked puzzledly at the controls, then firmly took the control stick in his hand and yanked it to the right.

Halstead had just time to scream '*NOO*' as the combat car pivoted on its own axis, the bumper catching Halstead in the head and sending him spinning off the stand to the ground, and the car smoothly soared forward. Its radar had enough range to pick up the trainee-filled (but rapidly emptying) bleachers, and lifted the vehicle neatly up and over the bleachers, after which it turned neat fifteen-meter circles. Bjhalstred sat petrified at the controls.

Eventually Lanzotta and Carruthers got a second car and maneuvered alongside the aimlessly circling first vehicle. Lanzotta jumped lightly into the troop compartment, reached over Bjhalstred's shoulder, and turned the power off. The car settled down to the ground. Lanzotta levered Bjhalstred out.

'At the moment,' Lanzotta said, 'I do not love you, trainee. You have knocked one of my cadremen unconscious, and this is a Bad Thing.

'I am sure you will want to make Corporal Halstead happy when he finally comes to, won't you?'

Bjhalstred nodded.

'Otherwise he is liable to kill you, trainee. And then I'll have to write up a report on why he did that. So I'm sure you want to volunteer to do the poor corporal a personal favor, don't you?'

Bjhalstred nodded again.

'You see that mountain,' Lanzotta said, pointing at the kilometers-distant ridge. 'There is a creek on that mountain, trainee. Corporal Halstead is particularly fond of the water from that creek. So why don't you get a bucket and run up there and get him a bucket of water?'

'Huh?' Bjhalstred managed.

'That is, "Huh, Sergeant,"' Lanzotta said. 'And I think you heard me.'

Bjhalstred nodded, got slowly up from the seat, and started for the barracks.

Lanzotta watched him run into the building, dash out carrying a bucket, and disappear in the distance. Sten, watching from the company formation meters away, thought he saw Lanzotta's shoulders shake slightly. No, Bjhalstred wasn't that dumb.

Chapter Twenty-Two

Lanzotta looked happy.

Sten shuddered and wished he'd hit formation in the rear ranks. This would be a bad one.

Halstead started to call the company to attention. Lanzotta waved him into silence. 'Something very interesting just happened, children,' he said smoothly.

Pacing back and forth. This would be very bad.

'I just received the notification from, shall we say, a higher authority. It seems that I may not be performing my duty to best suit the needs of the Empire.'

Sten wanted to find a very deep, very heavily shielded shelter. He hoped he didn't know what was going on.

'I may not be giving some of my trainees the proper attention. Particularly in the area of acting rank. It seems this authority wonders if some very capable leadership might be squelched by this suppression.

'Yes. A very interesting letter.'

Lanzotta's smile vanished, replaced with a look of sincerity. 'I would hate to err on the Emperor's service, would I not? Gregor! Post!'

Sten thought right then would be a very good time to die. Gregor double-timed to the head of the formation, snapped-to and saluted.

'Recruit Gregor? You are now recruit company commander.'

Someone in the rear rank said 'Clot!' very loudly.

Lanzotta evidently decided to be deaf momentarily.

'Take charge of the company, Recruit Company Commander Gregor. You have one hour to prepare the unit for transshipment and combat training.'

*

It was possible, Sten decided, to think somebody had bad breath just by listening to them wheeze on a radio. He itched between his shoulder blades. It didn't do any good. Some genius had designed vacuum assault suits to itch a soldier everywhere it was impossible to scratch. Sten told himself he didn't itch, and went back to listening to Gregor wheeze on the command circuit.

Come on, he thought. Make up your mind.

'First Pla— I mean one-one.'

Sten keyed his mike.

'Go.'

'The ship is a Class-C patrolcraft. That means we go in through the drive tubes. I had my first sergeant take a reading. They're cool.'

Sten unclipped from the asteroid he and his platoon were 'hiding' behind and drifted out a little.

The old hulk hanging in blackness two kilometers away had been more or less tarted up to look like a C-Class, right enough. But . . .

Sten went on command. 'Six? This is one-one. Request seal.'

Gregor grunted and shut the rest of the company off the circuit.

'Going in the tubes is a manual attack, sir.'

'Of course, Sten. That's why . . .'

'You don't figure those bad guys maybe read the book? And have a prog?'

'DNC, troop. What do you want? Some weird frontal shot?'

'Clot, Gregor! We go up the pipe, somebody'll be waiting for us, I figure. If you could put out a screen, I'll take my platoon on the flank.'

'Continue . . . one.'

Sten shrugged. No harm in trying.

'We'll tin-can it. Peel the skin and bleed internal pressure off. That'll throw 'em off, and maybe we can double-prong them.'

More wheezing. Sten wondered why Gregor's father couldn't afford to get his son an operation.

'Cancel, one. I gave orders.'

Sten deliberately unsealed the circuit.

'Certainly, captain. Whatever the captain desires. Clear.'

Carruthers' voice crackled.

'One. Breaking circuit security. Kitchen detail.'

Sten heard Gregor bury a laugh in his open mike.

'This is six. By the numbers . . . leapfrog attack . . . maneuver element . . . go.'

Sten's platoon jetted into the open. Sten checked the readout and automatically corrected the line.

Diversion fire lasered overhead from the other two platoons. Sten tucked a random zig program into the platoon's computer. They continued for the hulk.

By the time they closed on the hulk's stern, half the platoon hung helplessly in space, shut down as casualties by the problem's computer.

Sten rotated the huge projector from his equipment rack and positioned it. He figured to go in just below the venturi and—

And there was a massive flash in his eyes, Sten's filter went up through the ranges to black, and Sten stared at the flashing CASUALTY light on his suit's control panel.

By now he'd gotten used to being 'killed.' As a matter of fact, this was the first time he'd enjoyed it. He did not think any of the casualties would collect the usual scut details when they got back to the troop area.

Lanzotta had a much bigger fish to barbecue. Or maybe much smaller, now.

Lanzotta was stone-faced and standing very still.

Sten relaxed, and flickered an eye toward Gregor.

'You went in by the book, recruit company commander?'

'Yes, sergeant.'

'Did you bother to check EM range?'

'No, sergeant.'

'If you had, you could have seen that your enemy modified those solar screens into projectors. Aimed straight back at their normally undefended stern. Why didn't you check, recruit company commander?'

'No excuse, sergeant.'

'Did you consider an alternate assault?'

'No, sergeant.'

'Why not?'

'Because – because that's how the fiche said to assault a C-ship, sergeant.'

'And if you didn't do it by the manual, you might have gotten yourself in trouble. Correct, Recruit Company Commander Gregor?'

'Uh . . .'

'ANSWER THE GODDAMNED QUESTION.'

Sten and the others jumped about a meter. It was the first time Lanzotta had ever shouted.

'I don't know, sergeant.'

'I do. Because you were thinking that as long as you stuck by the book, you were safe. You didn't dare risk your rank tabs. And so you killed half a company of guardsmen. Am I correct?'

Gregor didn't say anything.

'Roll your gear, mister,' Lanzotta said. And ripped the Guard Trainee patch off Gregor's coveralls. Then he was gone.

Carruthers double-timed to the head of the formation.

'Fall out for chow. Suit inspection at twenty-one hundred hours.'

Nobody looked at Gregor as they filed back into the barracks. He stood outside a very long time by himself.

But by the time Sten and the others got back from chow, Gregor and his gear had disappeared as if they'd never existed.

'First sergeant! Report!'

'Sir! Trainee Companies A, B, and C all present and accounted for. Fifty-three per cent and accounted six in hospital, two detached for testing.'

The trainee topkick saluted. Sten returned the salute, about-faced to Lanzotta, and saluted again.

'All present and accounted for, sergeant!'

'It is now eighteen hundred hours, recruit captain. You are to take charge of your company and move them via road to Training Area Sixteen. You will disperse your men in standard perimeter defense. You are to have them in position by dusk, which is at nineteen-seventeen hours. Any questions?'

'No, Sergeant Lanzotta!'

'Take charge of your company.'

Sten saluted and spun again.

'COMPANY . . .'

'Platoon . . . 'toon . . . 'toon . . .' chanted Sten's platoon leaders.

'Right *HACE!* Arms at the carry! Forward . . . *harch* . . . double-time . . . *harch*.'

The long column snaked off into the gathering twilight. Sten double-timed easily beside them. By now he could walk, march, or run – eyes open, seventy per cent alert – and be completely asleep. Lanzotta had been exaggerating when he said the trainees would only get about four hours' sleep a night.

Maybe that'd been so at the beginning. But as the training went downhill toward graduation, the pace got harder. There were fewer washouts now, but it was far easier to go under.

Lanzotta had explained to Sten after he'd given him the tabs of a recruit company commander. 'First few months, we tried to break you physically. We got rid of the losers, the accident prone, and the dummies. Now we're fine-lining. The mistakes you make in combat training are ones that would get you or other guardsmen cycled for fertilizer.

'Besides, there are still too many people in this cycle.' Too many people. Assuming – which Sten didn't necessarily – the one-in-a-hundred-thousand selection process, three companies of a hundred men each had been cut down to sixty-one.

Great odds.

Not everybody had been washed out. A combat car collision had accounted for four deaths, falls during the mountain training killed two more trainees, and a holed suit had put still another recruit in the awesomely large regimental cemetery.

Lanzotta thought it was impressive that a trainee was made a full member of the regiment before burial. Sten thought it was a very small clotting deal. Dead, he was pretty sure, was a very long time, and worm food isn't much interested in ceremony.

Ah, well.

By now they'd progressed from squad through platoon to full company-size maneuvers.

Sten wondered what joyful surprises Lanzotta had planned for the evening. Then he put the dampers back in his mind. He needed the rest. He let his mouth start a jody, put his feet on autopilot, and went to sleep.

Eyes closed, Sten sonared his ears around the hilltop. Four minutes, twenty-seven seconds. All night animal sounds back to normal. All troops in stand-to positions. Not bad.

Lanzotta crawled up beside Sten and flickered on a mapboard light. 'Fair. You got them out and down nicely enough. Second Platoon still bunches up too much. And I think you should've put your CP closer to the military crest. But . . . not bad.'

Sten braced. Lanzotta was being very polite. He knew for sure this exercise would be a cruncher.

Lanzotta: 'Briefing. Your company has been on an offensive sweep for two local days. You have taken, let's see, fifty-six – about seventy-five per cent casualties. *Tsk. Tsk.*

'You were ordered to assault a strongly held enemy position – there!'

Lanzotta took a simulator minicontrol from its belt pouch and tapped a button. On the hill across from them, a few lights flickered.

'Unfortunately, the position was too strongly garrisoned, and you were forced to withdraw to this hilltop. You are far in advance of artillery support, and, for operational reasons, normal air or satellite support is non-existent.

'You medvacked your casualties, so you have no wounded to worry about. The problem is quite simple. Very, very soon, the enemy will counterattack in strength. You probably will not be able to hold this position.

'Your regimental commander has given you local option command. Friendly positions are' – He pointed behind him and touched the panel. At the top of the ridge-crest, simulators set up a strong, not particularly well blacked-out position – 'there. Between your company and friendly lines are an estimated two-bridgade strength of bandits, operating with light armor and in small strike-patrol elements. All the options are yours. Are there any questions?'

Sten whistled silently.

'Recruit captain, take charge of your men. You have two minutes until the problem commences.'

Lanzotta slid away into darkness.

Sten motioned to Morghhan, his recruit first sergeant. They slithered away from the CP area. Sten dropped a UV filter over his eyes and flicked on a shielded maplight.

'*Sauve qui peut* and all that crud,' Morghhan whispered. 'You wanna surrender right now and avoid the morning rush?'

'Us killer guards never surrender.'

'You think he's setting you up?'

'Damfino. Prog – no. Retrograde movement's supposed to be a bitch, they told us.'

'You figure it, Sten. I'm gonna go practice up speaking fluent Enemy.' Morghhan low-crawled back to the CP and waiting runners.

'Four and three and two and one,' Lanzotta said, somewhere in the darkness. 'Begin.'

He must've started the simulator program. High whining . . . 'Incoming!' somebody shouted, and the ground rocked under him. Violet light lasered just overhead. Sten hoped the sweep-track automatic weapons which provided the 'enemy fire' weren't set too low or with random-center fire or with a movement homer.

Sten tapped the channel selector on his chest to ALL CHANNELS, and briefly outlined the plan to the listening troops.

'Six . . . this is two-one. We have movement on our front.' That was Tomika, acting-jack platoon leader of Second Platoon.

Sten overrode onto the command net.

'Estimation, two-one?'

'Probe attack. Possible feint. Approximate strength two platoons. One hundred meters out, on line.'

'Two-one . . . this is six. Hold fire. One-one? Any activity on your front?'

'Not— hang on. That's affirm. Got infiltrators working up the hill – will— aw clot!'

Lanzotta's voice broke in. 'Unfortunately the First Platoon leader exposed himself and was hit. Fatal.'

Sten ignored Lanzotta. 'One-two. Assume command. Estimation?'

'Affirm. Infiltrators. Company size. Prog – first prong attack. Shall we open fire?'

Sten thought quickly. 'Negative. When they cross fifty-meter line, they'll probably open fire. Prog – artillery support. First and third squads will withdraw twenty-five meters noisily. Second and fourth squads engage when they reach your positions and first and third counterattack. Prog – another feint. Top! Get weapons platoon to blanket their rear and break up the second wave. Take the CP, I'm shifting to Third Platoon.'

Clicked the mike off. 'Runner! Let's go!'

They went off into darkness, Sten navigating by treetop shadows. Fire intensified, and the ground under them quivered.

Sten jumped as what sounded like a thousand sirens went off. 'Psych,' he told the runner. 'Just noise. Let's move it!'

Sten dropped into the Third Platoon leader's dugout.

'What's out there?'

Sten held his breath and closed his eyes again. Listening. Sweeping his head from side to side. He swore. 'Clot hell! Armor!'

'I don't hear anything!'

'You will. Sounds like two units. Scrunchies pigback for support.'

Tagged the radio.

'Weapons . . . I want illumination. Stand by . . .'

The air hummed.

'Weapons, this is six. Do you receive?'

A runner materialized out of the night and slid into the hole.

'All units. Stand by. Scramble R-Seven.'

The communicator selected a simple code and keyed the company's transmitters to it. The code would be broken in a few seconds if the enemy had analyzers. But by then Sten would've finished the plan.

'Two-one. Sequence your troops past the CP, and reinforce one-two. Move! Two. On command, you will begin a frontal assault straight forward.'

Sten took a deep breath. This training was just real enough to make even simulated suicide work creepy.

'Three-one. Your men will hold the armor below your position. Your orders are to hold regardless. If we break out, you and your men are to exfiltrate solo.

'All units. The company will make a frontal assault against the feint in Second Platoon's sector. We will break out, and each man is on his own. You have the correct bearing on friendly lines. You will evade capture and join the regiment by dawn.

'That is all. Keep only water, basic weapon, and two tubes. Dump everything, including radios. Good luck. Move!'

Sten cut the radio. Lanzotta appeared beside him.

'Administrative note, Recruit Captain Sten. With dead radios, maneuver control can't inflict casualties.'

Sten found time for a grin, 'Sergeant, that never crossed my mind.' He was being honest.

Sten turned to his CP unit.

'You heard it. Drop 'em and let's chogie.'

'Lanzotta just wiped out weapons platoon. Sez it was counter-battery off your fire mission.'

Sten groaned.

'Lenden.'

'Go, Sten.'

'Honk down about five meters and gimme a handheld.'

'Then I'm gonna be dead?'

'Then you're gonna be dead.'

'Maybe they'll give us corpses a ride back.' The runner hunched out of the hole, pulling a launcher from his weapons belt. He touched the fire key, and the flare hissed upward. A scanner caught him, and pulled the plug. Simulator-transponder went red, and Lenden swore and started back for the assembly area.

The flare bloomed, and Sten saw two . . . five . . . seven assault tracks grinding up the base of the hill.

'Flash 'em.'

The platoon leader keyed his central weapons board, and high-pressure tanks, emplaced at the hill's base, sprayed into life. The gas mixed with the atmosphere, and the acting lieutenant fired the mixture.

A fireball roared across the hill's base, and three of the tracks caught and exploded.

'Leapfrog back. About sixty meters and set up an interior perimeter.'

Sten rolled out of the hole and skittered back toward the CP.

By the time he flattened beside Morghhan, he had a plan.

Shadows went across his front toward Second Platoon's area. Firing suddenly redoubled in volume from the Third's last-stand perimeter.

Sten gratefully shed his pack and command net, port-armed his weapon and went after them.

There was dead silence in the office.

Sten stared straight ahead.

'Four survivors, recruit company commander. You were wiped out.'

'Yes, Sergeant Lanzotta.'

'I would be interested in your prognosis of the effects of such an action in real combat. On the rest of the regiment.'

'I . . . guess very bad.'

'I guess very obvious. But you don't know why. Troops will take massive casualties and maintain full combat efficiency under two circumstances only: First, those casualties must be taken in a short period of time. Slow decimation destroys any unit, no matter how elite.

'Secondly, those casualties must be taken with an accomplishment. Do you understand, Sten?'

'Not exactly, sergeant.'

'I will be more explicit. Using last night's debacle. If you had held on that hilltop, and died to the last man, the regiment would have been proud. That would have been a battle honor and probably a drinking song. The men would have felt uplifted that there were such heroes among them. Even though they'd be clotting glad they weren't there to be with them.'

'I understand.'

'Instead, your unit was lost trying to save itself. It's very well and good to talk about living to fight another day. But that is not the spirit that ultimately wins wars. Failing to understand that is your failure as a company commander. Do you understand?'

Sten was silent.

'I did not say you had to agree. But do you understand?'

'Yes, sergeant.'

'Very well. But I did not relieve you and confine you to barracks for that reason. Your test scores indicate a high level of intelligence. I broke you because you showed me you are completely unsuited for the Guard or to be a guardsman. Effective immediately, you are removed from the training rolls.'

Sten's mouth hung open.

'I will explain this, too. You have a soldier. He takes a knife, blackens his face, leaves all his weapons behind. He slips through the enemy lines by himself, into the shelter of an enemy general. Kills him and returns. Is that man a hero? Of one kind. But he is not a guardsman.'

Lanzotta inhaled.

'The Guard exists as the ultimate arm of the Emperor. A way of putting massive force into a precise spot to accomplish a mission. The Guard will fight and die for the Emperor. As a fighting body, not as individuals.'

Sten puzzled.

'As a guardsman, you are expected to show bravery. In return, the Guard will provide you with backing. Moral and spiritual in training and garrison, physical in combat. For most of us, the bargain is more than fair. Are you tracking me?'

Most of Sten was wondering what would happen to him next – washed out to a duty battalion? Or would they dump him straight back to Vulcan? Sten tried to pay attention to Lanzotta.

'I will continue. A guardsman is always training to be more. He should be able to assume the duties of his platoon sergeant and accomplish the mission if his sergeant becomes a casualty. A sergeant must be able to assume the duties of his company commander.

'And that means no matter how tactically brilliant he is, if he does not instinctively understand the nature of the men he commands, he is worse than useless. He is a danger. And I have told you time and again . . . my job is to not just make guardsmen. But to help those men stay alive.'

'Is that all, sergeant?' Sten said tonelessly.

'Four survivors. Of fifty-six men. Yes, Sten. That's all.'

Sten lifted his hand toward the salute.

'No. I don't take salutes – or return them – from washouts. Dismissed.'

Sten ate, turned in his training gear and went to bed in a thick blanket of isolation. Emotionally, he wanted one of his friends to say something. Just good-bye. But it was better like this. Sten had seen too many people wash, and knew it was easier on everyone if the failure simply became invisible.

He wondered why they were waiting so long to get him. Usually a washout was gone in an hour or two after being dumped. He guessed it was the seriousness of what he'd done. The cadre wanted him around for a while as an object lesson.

It gave Sten time to make some plans of his own.

If they were sending him to a duty battalion . . . he shrugged. That was one thing. He didn't owe anything more to the Empire, so as soon as he could, he'd desert. Maybe. Or maybe it'd be easier to finish his hitch and take discharge into Pioneer Sector. Supposedly they never could get enough men on the frontiers, and anyone who'd been even partially through Guard training could be an asset.

But Vulcan . . . Sten's fingers automatically touched the knife haft in his arm. If he went back, the Company would kill him. He'd as soon go out quick before they got there. Besides, there was always a chance . . .

Not much of one, he decided, and stared blankly up at the dark ceiling.

Sten half felt a movement – his fingers curled for the sheath – and Carruthers' arm clamped on him.

'Follow me.'

Sten, still dressed, stepped out of the bunk. Automatically, he S-rolled the mattress and picked up his small ditty.

Carruthers motioned him toward the door. Sten followed. Dazed. He had just realized Carruthers had stopped him as if she knew about the knife. He wondered why they'd never confiscated it.

Carruthers stopped beside an automated weapons carrier. Indicated the single seat, and Sten climbed in.

Carruthers tapped a destination code, and the car hummed. Carruthers stepped back. And saluted.

Sten stared. Washouts didn't rate, but Carruthers was holding the salute. Sten was lost. He automatically returned it.

Carruthers turned and was double-timing away as the car lifted.

Sten looked ahead. The car angled out of the training area a few feet clear of the ground, then lifted to about twenty meters. Its screen flashed: DESTINATION RESTRICTED AREA. REQUEST CODE CLEARANCE. The car's computer chuckled, and printed numbers across the screen. The screen blanked, then: M-SECTION CLEARANCE GRANTED. NOTIFICATION. ON LANDING AWAIT ESCORT.

Sten was completely lost.

Chapter Twenty-Three

Mahoney ceremoniously poured the pure-quill medalcohol into the shooter, and dumped the pewter container into the two-liter beer-mug. He handed the mug to Carruthers, and turned to the other three in the room. 'Anyone else need refueling?'

Rykor lifted a fluke and propelled a minicascade from her tank at Mahoney. 'I have a mind that needs no further altering, thank you,' she rumbled.

Lanzotta shook his head.

Mahoney picked up his own mug. 'Here's to failure.'

They drank.

'How did he take it, corporal?'

'Dunno, colonel. Kid's a little shocky. Prob'ly thought we was gonna ship his butt back for recycling on that armpit he came from.'

'He's that dumb?'

'I crucified him, colonel,' Lanzotta said. 'I would assume he isn't guilty of any thinking at this moment.'

'Quite likely. You're pretty good at slow torture, Lan.' Mahoney paused. 'Rykor, sorry to bore you for a minute. But I got to tell these two. Obviously all this is sealed – saying that's a formality. But since it's closed, we can knock off the colonel drekh for a while.'

Carruthers shifted uncomfortably and buried her nose in her mug.

'I need a very fast final assessment. Rykor?'

'I have no reason to change my initial evaluation. His training performance, as predicted, was near record. His profile did not alter significantly. In no way could Sten have become a successful Guard soldier. His independence, instinctual animosity to authority, and attraction toward independent action are especially jagged on the curve. For your purposes, he seems ideal.

'The peculiar individual traumas we discussed when he entered training are maintained at close to the same level in some ways. But in others, since he has proven himself successful in training and in dealing with other people, he is far more stable an entity.'

'Carruthers?'

'I dunno how to put it, sir. But he ain't anybody I'd pick to team with. He ain't a coward. But he ain't for-sure either. At least not in, mebbe, a red-zone assault.'

'Only one sir! Thank you. Buy yourself another drink. And me one, too.'

Mahoney passed his mug across.

'I could probably elaborate on Carruthers' assessment,' Lanzotta said carefully, 'but there's no need. Gargle words don't explain things any better than she did.'

'Come on, Lanzotta. Like pulling teeth. You know what I want.'

'I'd rate Sten first rate for Mantis Section. He reminds me of some of the young thugs I tried to keep under control for you.'

Carruthers spun, spilling beer.

'You was in Mantis Section, sergeant?'

'He was my team sergeant,' Mahoney said.

'And I got out. Carruthers, you don't know any of this. But there's a clotting difference between going in hot, facing entrenched troops, and cutting the throat of some small-time dictator while he's in bed with a girl. Remember that, colonel?'

'Which one?'

Mahoney gestured, and Carruthers passed Lanzotta his shot/beer. Lanzotta stared into the amber distance, then upended the mug. 'I didn't like it. I wasn't any good at it.'

'Hell you weren't. You stayed alive. That's the only grade.'

Lanzotta didn't say anything.

Mahoney grinned and affectionately scrubbed Lanzotta's close crop. 'I'd still trade half a team if you'd come back, friend.' Then Mahoney turned business. 'Evaluations?'

'Transfer recommended, Psychiatric Section,' Rykor put in briefly.

'Recommend transfer,' Carruthers aped awkwardly.

'Take him, Mahoney,' Lanzotta said, sounding very tired. 'He'll be a great killer for you.'

Frazer slipped off the slideway and hurried toward the zoo. He was nervous about the meeting and the handivid burned in his pocket. He carded into the zoo and walked past the gate guard, waiting for the hand on his shoulder.

His clerk's mind told him there was nothing to be worried about – Frazer had covered all of his tracks. He was a master at the computer and the Imperial bureaucracy. No way could anyone know why he was there.

Frazer stopped at the saber-tooth tiger cages. He grew more edgy as the beasts paced back and forth. Like all the creatures in the zoo, the tiger was part of the gene history of humankind. If Frazer had gone farther, he would have encountered sloths and giant-winged insects and enormous warm-blooded reptiles. He could smell the reptiles from where he was, rotten meat and bubbling swamps . . .

The assassin moved in beside him. 'Got it?'

Frazer nodded and handed the assassin the vidpack. A long wait. And the assassin said: 'Excellent.'

'I chose someone whose record could be easily manipulated,' Frazer said. 'All you have to do is step in.'

The assassin smiled. 'I knew I could count on you. The best. You have the computer touch.'

Someone recognized Frazer's talents. Only he could dip into the informational pile and cut it out, one onion slice of information at a time.

'Ah – the money?'

The assassin handed him a slip of paper. Frazer studied it. 'It is untraceable?'

'Of course, pride in my work, and all that. You can see . . .'

Frazer was satisfied. His only regret was that Rykor could never know exactly how clever he was.

The assassin draped an arm over Frazer's shoulder as they walked away from the cages.

'You wonder about loyalty,' Frazer began.

'Yes. You do,' the assassin said.

The arm draped lower, curling around. Right hand circling around Frazer's chin, left hand snapped against the back of his head. There was a dull *snap!* Frazer went limp. Dead.

No one was around as the assassin dragged the body back to the edge of the cage. Lifted, braced, and Frazer's body lofted down.

The roars and the sound of feeding finished the matter.

Chapter Twenty-Four

The Emperor, Mahoney decided, had finally gone mad. He was hovering over a huge bubbling pot half filled with an evil-looking mixture, muttering to himself.

'A little of this. A little of that. A little garlic and a little fat. Now, the cumin. Just a touch. Maybe a bit more. No, lots more.' The Emperor finally noticed Mahoney and smiled. 'You're just in time,' he said. 'Gimme that box.'

Mahoney handed him an elaborately carved wooden box. The Emperor opened it and poured out a handful of long reddish objects. They looked like desiccated alien excrement to Mahoney.

'Look at these,' he boasted to Mahoney. 'Ten years in the biolabs to produce.'

'What are they?'

'Peppers, you clot. *Peppers*.'

'Oh, uh, great. Great.'

'Don't you know what that means?'

Mahoney had to admit he didn't.

'Chili, man. Chili. You ain't got peppers, you got no chili.'

'That's important, huh?'

The Emperor didn't say another word. Just dumped in the peppers, punched a few buttons on his cooking console, stirred, then dipped up a huge spoonful of the mess and offered it to Mahoney. He watched intently as Mahoney tasted. Not ba— then it hit him. His face went on fire, his ears steamed and he choked for breath. The Emperor pounded him on the back, big grin on his face, and then offered him a glass of beer. Mahoney slugged it down. Wheezed.

'Guess I got it just right,' the Emperor said.

'You mean you did that on purpose?'

'Sure. It's supposed to scorch the hair off your butt. Otherwise it wouldn't be chili.' The Emperor poured them both two beers, motioned to Mahoney to join him, and settled down in a huge, over-stuffed couch. 'Okay. You earned your check this month. Now, how about the next?'

'You mean Thoresen?'

'Yeah, Thoresen.'

'Zero, zero, zero.'

'Maybe we should escalate.'

'I was gonna recommend that in my report. But it's dangerous. We could blow the whole thing.'

'How so?'

'It's Lester. He says there's a lot more motion on Bravo Project. And he's got a way in. Trouble is, if he's caught, we're out an inside man.'

The Emperor thought a moment. Then sighed. 'Tell him to go ahead.' He drained his glass, filled it with more beer. 'Now, what about the other matter?'

'The gun smuggling? Well, I still can't prove it.'

'But it's happening? That's a fact, right?'

'Yeah,' Mahoney said. 'We know for sure that four planets – all supposedly our confederates – are shipping weapons to Vulcan.'

'Thoresen again. To hell with it. Let's quit playing games with the man. Send in the Guard. Stomp him out.'

'Uh, that's not such a hot idea, boss. I mean—'

'I know. I know. Lousy diplomatic move. But what about my "buddies" on those other four planets? No reason I can't take them out.'

'It's done.'

The Emperor grinned. Finally, a little action. 'Mantis Section?'

'I sent in four teams,' Mahoney said. 'I guarantee those guns will stop.'

'Without any diplomatic repercussions?'

'Not a whisper.'

The Emperor liked that even better. He got up from his couch and walked over to the bubbling pot. Sniffed it. Nice. He started dishing up two platefuls.

'Join me for dinner, Mahoney?'

Mahoney was out of the couch in a hurry and headed for the door. 'Thanks, boss, any night but tonight. I gotta—"

'Hot date?'

'Yeah,' Mahoney said. 'Whatever that is. Not as hot as that stuff.'

And he was gone. The Emperor went back to his chili. Wondering which members of the Royal Court *deserved* to share his company tonight.

Chapter Twenty-Five

The Baron watched the screen anxiously as a swarm of Techs moved quickly about the freighter's hold, making final connections and adjustments. This was it. A few more minutes and he would learn if all the credits and danger were worth it.

The Bravo Project test was taking place light years away from Vulcan, and far away from normal shipping lanes. The picture on Thoresen's screen changed as the Techs finished, then hustled out of the hold, crammed into a shuttle and started moving away from the ancient freighter.

Thoresen turned to the Tech beside him, who was studying swiftly changing figures on his own screen. Then:

'Ready, sir.'

Thoresen took a deep breath, then told the Tech to begin.

'Countdown initiated . . .'

The shuttle came to a stop many kilometers away from the freighter. The on-board Techs went to work, changing programs in their computers, getting ready for the final signal.

The inside of the freighter had been gutted, and at opposite ends the Techs had constructed two huge devices – they would have been called rail guns in ancient times – each aimed exactly at the electric 'bore' of the other.

Thoresen barely heard the countdown. He was concentrating on the two images on the screen. One was of a huge glowing emptiness inside the hold of the freighter. The other was of the outside of the freighter, the shuttle in the foreground. The Tech tapped him on a shoulder. They were ready to go. All of a sudden, the Baron felt very relaxed. Flashed a rare smile at the Tech, punched in the code that was the trigger.

The 'rail guns' fired, and two subatomic particles of identical mass were hurled at each other, reaching the speed of light instantly. Then beyond. Thoresen's screen flared and then it was over – literally almost before it began. Then his screen came to life again. Nothing. Just yawning space. No freighter, no—

'The shuttle,' the Tech screamed. 'It's gone. They're all—'

'Clot the shuttle,' Thoresen snapped. 'What happened?'

His fingers flew over computer keys as he ordered up a replay of the incident – this time at speeds he could see.

The particles floated toward each other, leaving comet trails. Pierced the magnetic bubble that was the glowing spot inside the hold, and then met . . . And met . . . And met . . . Then they vanished . . . reappeared . . . moved in and out of time/space . . . until they were replaced by a single, much different particle. Thoresen laughed – he had done it. Suddenly, the magnetic envelope began to collapse. There was a blinding flash of light and the freighter and shuttle disappeared in an enormous explosion.

The Baron turned to the Tech, who was still in shock. 'I want the timetable moved up.'

The Tech gaped at him.

'But those men on the shuttle? . . .'

Thoresen frowned, looked at his empty screen, and then understood.

'Oh, yes. The unfortunate accident. It shouldn't be too hard to replace them.'

He started out of the lab, paused a moment. 'Oh, and tell the next crew to back off a little more from the freighter. Techs are expensive.'

Lester smiled and patted the Tech on the shoulder. The man babbled something and tears began to roll down his cheeks. Lester leaned forward to listen. Just baby talk. And nothing more to learn.

It had been easy, Lester thought. Easier than he had expected. He had been working on the Tech for half a dozen cycles. Subtle hints of money, a new identity, a life-time residence paid up on some playworld. The man had been interested, but too afraid of Thoresen to do much more than listen and drink Lester's booze. Then one day he had cracked. He had been almost hysterical when he called Lester and asked to come to his quarters.

There had been some awful accident, he had told Lester, but when pressed he shook his head. No, the Baron . . . and Lester knew he had to take a chance.

He slipped up beside the man, pressed a hypo against his neck, and a moment later the Tech was a babbling idiot. But an idiot who would tell Lester everything he needed to know. Lester eased the man down on the bed. He'd sleep for a while, and then wake up with a huge narcobeer hangover. The Tech wouldn't remember a thing.

Now, all Lester had to do was contact Mahoney. What he would tell him about Bravo Project would guarantee an early end to Thoresen's career.

There was a loud smash and splintering of plastic. Lester whirled, then froze as the Baron stepped through his ruined door. He was flanked by two Sociopatrolmen. Thoresen looked at the sleeping Tech, grinned.

'A little party, Lester?'

Lester didn't say anything. What could he say? Thoresen motioned to his guards; they picked the Tech up and carried him out.

'So, now you know?'

'Yes,' Lester said.

'Too bad. I rather liked you.' He took a step forward, looming over the old man, and took him by the throat. Squeezed. Lester fought for air, felt his throat crush. Minutes passed before the Baron dropped Lester's corpse. He turned as one of the guards stepped back into the room. 'Make it look good,' Thoresen said. 'A sudden illness, *et cetera, et cetera*. And don't worry about his family. I'll take care of them.'

Chapter Twenty-Six

Sten whistled soundlessly and booted the door behind him shut. Flies were already starting to buzz around H'mid's severed head atop the counter.

Sten bent, touched his fingers to the blood pool around the body. Still a little sticky . . . no more than an hour. Sten reached over his shoulder and palmed out the tiny w-piece that hung between his shoulder blades.

Sten dodged around the counter and silently ran up the steps to the shopkeeper's living quarters. Deserted as well. No sign of search or looting. Very, very bad. He cautiously peered out one window, then ducked back in.

Two rooftops away, three Q'riya flattened, peering down on the street. And below . . . another one, down Sten's escape route. Very badly disguised, polished boot tips protruding from under the striped robes he was wearing.

Were they trying to drive him or was he trapped? Sten tried again. They were going to take him. The foodshop across the narrow dirty street was shuttered. Not at this time of day. Inside there'd be a squad of M'lan – the Q'riya tribe's private thugs.

Sten leaned back against the wall . . . inhale for count of four, exhale for count of four, hold for count of six. Ten times. Adrenaline slowed down. Sten started trying to figure a way out. He scooped up a handful of bracelets, the gems still unset, from H'mid's workbench, then the small carboy of acid from its shelf. Went back to the window and waited. He would probably have ten minutes or so before they decided they'd have to winkle the rat out.

A cart rumbled past below. Ideal. He carefully lobbed the carboy out, into the middle of its dry grain load. Aimed . . . hand bobbing, synched with the unsprung cart.

Fired. The carboy shattered. Smoke curled, and the cart seared into flames.

Shouts. Screams . . . smoke coiling back up the street.

The best he could do.

Sten tucked his robe ends up into his waistband, kicked off his sandals, and swung over the edge of the window. Hung by his hands, then dropped.

He thudded down, letting himself flatten. The shutter crashed open and a slug whanged out into the mud wall just above him. Sten came up . . . three hurtling paces across the street and a long dive through the open shutters.

Hit on the inside, rolling, and trigger held back to continuous fire as he sprayed the inside of the window.

Three M'lan gurgled down, the second howled air through a ripped open throat. Sten threw a second slug through the center of the man's forehead and was moving out toward the back door. He burst out then swore. Typical rabbit warren, creaky stairs leading down, past the tiny Fal'ici hovels. Sten went over the railing, and dodged into their midst. Shouts, screams, and shots from the street.

Sten wasn't worried. The Fal'ici wouldn't give any information to help the M'lan, even at gunpoint.

He came out of the slum maze onto another street. Excellent. First luck. Marketing. Thronged . . . including a heavy patrol of M'lan. They must have been tipped. When they saw the running figure, they went after him.

Sten yanked over a pushcart, leaped over a cart's tongue, then turned and tossed H'mid's bracelets high into the air. The gold caught the glittering sun and there was instant chaos. People came out of openings in the walls that Sten couldn't even see.

Somewhere in the boiling mob were the M'lan. Sten thought it very possible that one or another of the Fal'ici might just turn away from the gold for a chance to slip a couple of centimeters of polished glass into a trooper's throat.

He slowed to a walk, pulled his robe down, and casually strolled on. Tossed a flower vendor a coin, and pulled the biggest flower on her cart off. Shoved his nose onto it, and minced onward.

How . . . epi? Epi . . . clot it! He'd ask Doc when he got back to the cover house.

*

Sten took an hour to make sure he wasn't tailed. He didn't think much of the Q'riya's intelligence squads, but there were more than enough of them to run a successful multitail operation.

He was clean, so he walked quickly up to the gate of the unobtrusive house the Mantis Section team was working out of and went in.

To more chaos. Gear was going into packs neatly, but very, very quickly. Alex stood near the door, holding a breakdown willygun ready. Sten took it all in.

'We're blown?' Sten guessed.

'Aye, laddie,' Alex said. 'Th' clark Vinnettsa's been tryin' t' convince she's got buttons down her back wae taken.'

'And talked?'

'Wouldna you? Word is they could make a tombstone confess.'

'Somebody took H'mid's head off and left it for me to find.' Sten said. He crossed to a table and picked up a glass winer. Thumb over the cover, he eased the spout into his mouth and swallowed. After he'd set it down, he looked at the half-meter teddy bear sitting at ease in the room's only comfortable chair. The creature bore a near-benevolent scowl on his face.

'Doc?'

'Typical humans,' the teddy bear purred happily. 'You people could clot up a rock fight. Proof of the existence of divinity, I take it. You would still be in your jungles peeling fruit with your toes if there weren't a God of some sort or another. One with a rather nasty sense of humor, I might add.'

Vinnettsa hurried down the stairs coiling wire to the broadcast antenna on the roof.

'Come on, Doc. We don't have time for making love.'

Doc held his hands out in what he had learned was a human gesture, jumped off the chair, and began stuffing the hookup into a lift pack.

Ida came unhurriedly out from the closet that concealed the entrance to the comroom. Hefted her compack experimentally. 'Doc's right. You can't expect subtlety from anything other than us. Now, why they don't field an all-Rom team—'

Alex chuckled. 'For our Emp'rer whidny like havin' a worl' stole from under him, is why.'

Ida thought. 'If we did steal it – and that's a thought worthy of a Rom – then he wouldn't have to worry, would he?'

Sten looked around. Frick and Frack hung from the room's eaves, waiting.

'Do they have us spotted?'

'Negative,' Frick squeaked. 'We overflew ten minutes ago. We saw nothing.'

Maybe. The two batlike beings weren't high on anyone's intelligence list. Or maybe Sten hadn't worded the question correctly. But the information was probably correct.

The team was ready to roll. They huddled.

'We ken we're blown,' Alex said softly. 'D'ye think we redline an' evac?'

Jorgensen yawned. He was sprawled beside his pack, stocked pistol ready.

'Y'all sure we want to just pull pitch? Mahoney'll torch our tail for an incomp.'

Sten looked at Doc, who wiggled tendrils.

'Myitkina,' Sten said. It was Jorgensen's trance word. The rangy blonde sat immobile.

'Possibilities,' Vinnettsa snapped.

'A. Mission abort and withdrawal. B. Continue mission and assume nondiscovery. C. Begin alternate program.'

'Analyze it,' Sten said.

'Possibility A. Mission priority high. Currently incomplete. Consider as last resort. Survival probability ninety per cent if accomplished within five hours.'

'Continue,' Vinnettsa said.

'Possibility B. Insufficient data to give absolute prediction. Assumption that local agent broke under interrogation. Not recommended. Survival probability less than twenty per cent.'

The team members looked at each other. Voting silently. As usual, no one bothered to consult Frick and Frack.

'Two Myitkina.' Jorgensen came out of the trance.

'What's the plan?' he asked.

'Mobs 'n heroes,' Alex said.

'That ain't too bad,' Jorgensen said. 'All I gotta do is run a lot.'

Sten snorted. Alex clapped him on the back, a friendly gesture that almost drove Sten through the wall. Sometimes the tubby little man from the three-gee world forgot.

Sten wheezed air back into his lungs. 'Sten, you're a braw lad. A' they say, the bleatin' o' the kid frees the tiger. Or some'at like that.'

Sten glumly nodded and started shedding weaponry.

The assassin watched him from across the room. It would have to wait for a while. For better or worse, the assassin's future rode on the team's successes. For a while.

*

M-PRIORITY
OPERATION BANZI

Do not log in Guard General Orders; do not log in Imperial Archives; do not multex any than source and OC Mercury; do not release in any form. IMPERIAL PROSCRIPT.

OPERATIONS ORDER

1. *Situation:*

Saxon. Plus-or-minus well within Earth-condition parameters. Largely desert. Extensive nomadic culture (SEE FICHE A), predominant. Only port, major city and manufacturing complex Atlan (SEE FICHE B), situated in one of Saxon's few fertile valleys. Existence of large river and introduction of hydropower responsible for growth of Atlan. Atlan, and therefore Saxon's offworld policies, controlled by an extended tribe-family, the Q'riya (SEE FICHE C), believed to be an offshoot of main bedou culture Fal'ici. Manufacturing and all off-world trading controlled by Q'riya. In Atlan, their authority is enforced by the probably created semi-hereditary group known as the M'lan (SEE FICHE D). Q'riya authority does not extend beyond Atlan's limits, and semianarchy exists among the nomad tribes. Atlan's main export is weaponry, largely created by the introduction of major machinery by DELETED . . . DELETED . . . DELETED. Some primitive art, generally lowly regarded, also transshipped.

2. *Mission:*

To prevent offworld shipment of currently produced arms and, if possible, to significantly reduce or destroy that production capability.

3. *Execution:*

The team-in-place shall exercise the option of how the mission is to be carried out, hopefully by political means but, if necessary, militarily. Factors – this must not be attributed to an Imperial Mission. All extremes shall be taken to prevent evidence of Imperial involvement. Reiterate: All extremes (SEE ATTACHED, MISSION EQUIPMENT). Mission limitations: preference casualty rate among Fal'ici to be kept as low as possible. Continued existence of Q'riya in present position not significant. Alteration of existing social order not significant.

4. *Coordination:*

Little support can be given, due to the obvious conditions of OPERATION BANZI (see above), beyond standard evacuation deployment, which shall consist of . . .

5. *Command & Signal:*

OPERATION BANZI will be under the direct control of IXAL Code, Mantis Team operating under code schedule . . .

Chapter Twenty-Seven

The guards neatly lofted Sten into the cell's blackness. He thunked down on an uncomplaining body. Sten rolled off and started to apologize, then sniffed the air. About three days beyond listening, he estimated.

He got to his feet. The cavernous cell was very dark. Sten kept his eyes moving, hyperventilating. His irises widened. The view wasn't worth even one candle, he decided.

The prison was well within the anthro profile that fit Saxon. Build an unbreakable cell, and throw everybody into it you don't like. Feed them enough so they don't starve noisily, and then forget them. What happens in the cell is no one's concern.

He just hoped that Sa'fail was still alive.

Sten found a wall and put his back to it. Waiting. Lousy, he decided. It took about ten minutes for the bully-boy and his thugs to loom up in the blackness.

Sten didn't bother asking. The heel of his hand snapped the head villain's neck back, a sideslash dropped him while he gargled the ruins of his larynx. The second received a fist behind the ear as Sten bounced off the man's dead leader.

He threw the second corpse into the third man's incoming fists, then half turned, foot poised. The third man decided to stay down.

'Sa'fail. Of the Black Tents. Where is he?'

The toady grimaced. Thought was obviously not one of his major operational abilities. Sten was patient.

The toady looked at Sten's ready strike, grunted. 'In that corner. The dreadful ones keep their own.'

Sten grinned his thanks and snapped his foot out. Cartilage smashed, the man howled and went down. Sten bent over the man.

He decided he wouldn't have to kill him. The toady would be too busy bleeding for an hour or so to backjump Sten – and that, he hoped sincerely, was all it would take.

He worked his way through the bodies, softly calling the nomad's name. And found him. Sa'fail had an entourage. Sten looked them up and down. Surprisingly healthy for prisoners. He wondered if they'd gotten to recycling their fellow prisoners to stay healthy yet.

The nomad sat up and stroked his beard.

'You are not of the People,' the one who must have been Sa'fail's lieutenant said.

'I am not that, O Hero of the Desert and Man Who Makes the Slime Q'riya Tremble,' Sten said fluently in the desert dialect. 'But I have long admired you from afar.'

The nomad chuckled. 'I am honored that you found your admiration so overwhelming you must join me here in my palace.'

'Much as I would like to exchange compliments, O He Who Makes the Wadihs Tremble,' Sten said, 'I would suggest that you and your men get very close to that wall over there. You have' – Sten thought a moment – 'not very long.'

'What will happen?' the lieutenant asked.

'Very shortly most of this prison will cease to exist.'

The nomads buzzed then snapped silent as Sa'fail motioned.

'This is not a jest, I assume?'

'If it were, I would find it less funny than even you.'

'Even so, although your consideration might be for a brief time.'

Sa'fail considered. Then lithely came to his feet.

'We shall do what the outlander wishes. No matter what happens, boredom shall be relieved.'

The drom spat at Alex. He ducked and thumped four fingers against the beast's sides. It whuffed air and wobbled on its feet. The other members of the Mantis team hated droms, the stinking, recalcitrant transport beast of Saxon. They didn't bother Alex. He'd once been unlucky enough to serve with a Guard ceremonial attachment on Earth and had encountered camels.

But he didn't regret what was about to happen to his particular drom. The animal belched.

'Ye'll naught be forgettin' yer last meal,' he thought, and strolled away from the tethered beast. In trader's robes, carrying a forged day-pass plate, he'd been shaken down by the security guards surrounding the prison.

Search aboot as ye will, he thought. It's nae easy to find a bomb when it's digestin' in a beastie's guts. An' ye no saw the guns in that garbage in the wee cart.

He squatted by the wall and let the last few seconds tick away.

Frick banked closer to Frack. Half-verbal, half-instinct communication, nonwords: Nothing unusual. The other team members were in place. Frick's prehensile wing finger triggered the transceiver.

'Nothing. Nothing.' Flipped the com off and he and his mate banked for the city walls.

If there were any team members to link up with, they'd meet outside. In a few seconds.

Possibly when the charge goes, the assassin thought. Thought discarded. We will need every gun we have.

Jorgensen nervously fondled the S-charge looped around his neck. If life signs weren't continuously picked up by the internal monitors the ensuing blast would leave nothing to ID a Mantis trooper or his equipment.

One day closer to the farm, Jorgensen thought morosely. That's the only way to look at it. He unrolled the rug and lifted out the willygun.

'I realize you did this deliberately,' Doc purred. 'You know the antipathy we of Altair have toward death.'

'Nope,' Vinnettsa said. 'I didn't. But if I had, it's a clottin' good idea.'

Doc sat just in the entrance to a mausoleum, pistol clutched in his fat little paws. Vinnettsa made her final checks on the launcher and willygun, then let the elastic sling snap the willygun back under her arm.

'Revenge. A typical, unpleasant human trait,' Doc said.

'Your people never get even?'

'Of course not. Anthropomorphism. Occasionally we are forced personally to readjust the measure the – your word is fates – have made.'

Vinnettsa started to answer, and then the first blast whiplashed across the cemetery.

And the two of them were running from the tomb toward the guard quarters that ran inside a tunnel ahead of them.

A week before, bribed guardsmen had cemented the charge into the guardshack on the main gates.

The first explosion was minor. Alex had built it up of explosive, a clay shaping and, bedded into the clay, as many glass marbles as he could buy in the bazaar. Now the marbles cannoned out, quite thoroughly incapacitating the ten guards lounging around the gates.

Alex had set the charge below waist level. 'The more howlin' an' fa'in' an' carrin' on wi' wounded, the greater they'll be distracted.'

Vinnettsa set the range-and-charge fuse on the launcher's handle, brought it up. Aimed. As she counted ten, she heard the shouting of the officers who were mustering their riot squads to run them down the tunnel into the prison . . .

She touched the stud. The rocket chuffed out, cleared its throat experimentally, then the solid charge caught.

Vinnettsa flattened as the shaped charge blasted through the solid brick and exploded in the tunnel.

She picked herself up and watched the roof drop in. An added dividend, she thought. She headed for Alex's position.

'If Ah hadna been stupid, Ah wouldna been here. Second and third charges.' Alex hit the det panel under his robes. Two more diversionary charges blew on different sides of the prison.

'The Guard is mah home, Ah nae want for more. Fourth and fifth charges.' He blew those.

'An' noo 'tis time for us a' to be gone.' He fingered the main charge switch. And turned. Interested.

The drom ceased to exist. As did the wall.

The shock wave blew the main wall out, huge bricks hurtling across the brief space to shatter the inner wall of the prison. It crashed down. Prisoners howled in fear and agony.

Alex grabbed the willygun from the ground. Held it ready.

Dazed, blinking prisoners stumbled out.

'Go! Go!' he bellowed. They didn't need much encouragement. 'C'mon, Sten, m'lad. Time's a-draggin'. Ma mither's nae raised awkward bairns.'

Sten, an older, bearded man, and several men wearing the tatters of nomad gear ran into the street.

Alex saw a platoon of guards double around the corner toward him. 'Ye'll nae credit I thought a' that,' he grumbled, and hit the last switch. A snake charge positioned on the pavement moments before blew straight up, into the oncoming guards.

He flipped Sten a gun as he ran up. 'C'n we be goin'?' he said. ''M gettin' bored lurkin' aroun' wi' nothin' much to do.'

Sten laughed, dropped on one knee and sprayed bullets down the street. Then the nomads, still bewildered, followed the two soldiers at a dead run.

Doc waved his paw idly. Two willyguns crackled. The four guards at the gate dropped as the bullets exploded in their chests.

Jorgensen and Vinnettsa went down, guns ready, as Sten, Alex, and the nomads ran up. Alex continued on, up to the gates, unslinging a satchel charge. He bent over with it, and touched the timer. Turned and walked back. 'Ah suggest we be layin' doon, or we'll be starin' at all our own knackers.'

The nomads looked uncomprehending. Sten motioned furiously, and they chewed brick pavement along with the team.

Another blast, and the gates pinwheeled away. Bits of iron and timber crashed around the crouched soldiers.

'Miscalculated a wee on that one,' Alex muttered. 'Y'kn keek m f'rit.'

They were on their feet, running out into the desert.

'We wait here,' Sa'fail ordered. 'My men watch the city. They will be coming down to see who is stupid enough to come out of Atlan without soldiers to keep them safe.'

The team automatically set up a perimeter, then slumped behind rocks. Vinnettsa pulled a canteen from her belt and passed it around.

'The Fal'ici owe you a debt,' Sa'fail said to Sten after drinking.

Sten looked at Doc. This was his area. The bear walked into the middle and turned through 180 degrees. Tendrils waving gently.

Sten could feel the tension ebb. Automatically, everyone – soldiers and nomads – felt the small creature to be his best friend. That was Doc's survival mechanism. His species were actually spirited hunters who had nearly destroyed the wildlife of their homeworld. They hated everyone, including each other except during estrus and for a short space after a pup was born. But they exuded love. Trust. Pity the creature that stopped to bathe in the good feelings from the small creature.

'Why,' Sten had once asked, halfway through Mantis training, 'don't you hate us?'

'Because,' Doc said gloomily, 'they conditioned me. They condition all of us. I love you because I have to love you. But that doesn't mean I have to like you.'

Doc bowed to Sa'fail. 'We honor you, Sa'fail, as a man of honor, just as your race is honorable.'

'We Fal'ici of the desert are such. But those town scum . . .' Sa'fail's lieutenant spat dustily.

'I assume,' Sa'fail went on, 'that you liberated me for a reason.'

'Indeed,' Doc purred, 'there is a favor we wish.'

'Yours is anything the People of the Black Tents may offer. But first we have a debt to settle with the Q'riya.'

'You may find,' Doc said, 'that more than one debt may be paid at a time.'

The tent was smoky, hot, and it smelled. Why is it, Sten wondered, that a nomad is only romantic downwind? None of the princelings seemed to have any more water to spare for bathing than their tribesmen did.

He grinned as he saw Sa'fail, at the head of the table, ceremoniously bundle a handful of food into Doc's mouth. Lucky if he pulls back all his fingers, he thought.

But it is going well.

He unobtrusively patted Vinnettsa beside him. The tribesmen had only grudgingly allowed Ida and Vinnettsa full status with the other Mantis members. It had helped that Vinnettsa had been jumped one night by three romantic tribesmen and, in front of witnesses, used four blows to kill them.

Alex tapped him. 'Ah gie ye this as an honor, m'lad.'

Sten opened his mouth to ask what it was and Alex slipped the morsel inside. Sten bit once, and his throat told him this texture was not exactly right. He braced and swallowed. His stomach was not pleasant as it rumbled the bit of food down.

'What was it?'

'A wee eyeball. Frae a herdin' animal.'

Sten decided to swallow a couple more times, just to make sure.

The tents spread out for miles. The Mantis team and their charges had arrived at Sa'fail's home, and immediately riders had thundered off into the desert. And the tribes had filtered in. It had taken all of Sa'fail's considerable eloquence to convince the anarchic tribesmen to follow him, and only continuous, loud judgings held the tenuous alliances together.

One more day, Sten prayed. That is all we need.

He and Vinnettsa sat companionably on a boulder, high above the black tents and the twinkling campfires. Some meters away, a sentry paced.

'Tomorrow,' he said, thinking his way, 'if it works – prog not clottin' likely – what happens?'

'We get offworld,' Vinnettsa said, 'and we spend a week in a bathtub. Washing each other's . . . oh, backs might be a good place to start.'

He grinned, eyeballed the sentry, who was looking away, and kissed her.

'And Atlan is a desert and the Q'riya get fed into slow fires.'

'Will it be better, you mean?'

Sten nodded.

'Would it be worse is better. And, Sten, my love, do you really care, either way?'

Sten considered carefully. Then got up and pulled Vinnettsa to her feet.

'Nope. I really don't.'

And they started down the hill toward their tent.

The assassin watched Sten descend the hill and swore quietly. It would've been possible – and blamable on a tribesman. But that sentry. The chance was still too long. But tomorrow, there must be an opportunity. The assassin was tired of waiting.

The team split for the assault. Doc, Jorgensen, Frick and Frack went in with the nomad assault. It wasn't exactly Cannae.

The nomads slipped down from the hills in the predawn blackness, carrying scaling ladders. Positioned themselves in attack squads below the walls. The guards were not quite alert. The only advantage the attack had was that it had not been tried in the memory of man. Which meant, Doc told Sten, for at least ten years.

Nomad archers poised secret weapons – simple leatherstrip compound bows that the Mantis troopers had introduced to the tribesmen and helped them build over the month before the assault. Strings twanged and were muted. Guards dropped. And the ladders went into position.

The archers kept firing as long as they could – which meant until somebody successfully reached the walltop without being cut down, then whooped and swarmed up the ladders with the rest.

The four Mantis soldiers kept to Sa'fail. It would be helpful – to the nomads – if he survived the attack. And like most barbarian leaders, he felt his place was three meters ahead of the leading wave.

There were screams, and buildings crackled into flame to the butchershop anvil chorus of clashing swords. Civilians ran noisily for safety. And found none.

The M'lan fought to the last man. Too stupid to know better or, perhaps, smart enough to realize they weren't going to be allowed much bargaining.

Jorgensen shuddered, watching as waves of nomads swept into the Q'riya harem buildings.

Doc pulled at the bottom of the robe.

'Just children,' he purred. 'Having good, healthy fun.' His tendrils flickered, and Jorgensen forgot a transitory desire to put his foot on the pandalike being.

It went on, and on.

Vinnettsa stared down the valley at the burning city three kilometers away. 'Probably this is enough. Those nomads will take five years to put anything together.'

'Maybe,' Sten said. 'But these machines are mostly automatic. Cut the power, and we'll make sure.'

'Besides,' Alex put in, 'ye'll nae be denyin' me a great, soul-satisfyin' explosion, widya?'

Sten laughed, and they went to work in the powerhouse of the dam that bulked at the mouth of the valley, the source of power for all of the elaborate weapons factories scattered below.

At Alex's direction, they positioned charges carefully interconnected with time-fused det cord. They went by a very cautious book and set a complete backup system.

'Gie us two advan'ges,' Alex said. 'First, we mak siccar, an' second we'll nae hae t'be luggin' a' this home.' He effortlessly picked up a concrete block that must've weighed three hundred kilos, and 'tamped' his charge.

'Ye gae to yon end, an' final check. Ah'll dae this side.'

Sten and Vinnettsa doubled off down the long, echoing concrete corridor.

Sten bent over the first charges, checked the primer tie, tugged gently at the bedded primer, ran his fingers down the fusing for breaks.

Ten meters away, Vinnettsa lifted her pistol. Careful. Two-hand grip. And a job's a job.

Alex swore. Ah'm gettin' careless. Sten had his crimping pliers. He spun and ran lightly down the corridor. He came upon an unexpected tableau. He froze.

Vinnettsa was aiming, savoring the last second of accomplishment.

Alex, without thinking, spun. Ripped a wide disc insulator from the top of a machine, arced it.

The insulator spun . . . arcing . . . wobbling . . . almost too much force . . . as Vinnettsa increased pressure on the stud.

The edge of the insulator caught her just above the elbow. Bone smashed and blood rained as the insulator clipped her arm, gun and all, off.

Sten rose, his gun up, then he saw Vinnettsa. Her face was clenched in agony as she scrabbled one-handed for a second gun from her waistband, and swept up—

The first round exploded against the concrete, and Sten went sideways.

All on automatic, just like he was taught: right hand up, left hand around the trigger; trigger squeeze; squeeze; and held all the way back.

Vinnettsa's head exploded in a violet burst of blood and brains. Her body slumped to the pavement.

Sten's shoulder slammed into the pavement. He just lay there. Alex pounded up, bending over him.

'Are ye a'right, lad?'

Sten nodded. Not time yet to feel anything.

Alex's eyes were puzzled. 'Lass must've been crazy.'

Sten pushed himself up on his knees.

'Y'hit, Sten?'

Sten shook his head. Alex lifted him to his feet, then looked over at Vinnettsa's body.

'We nae got time to greet noo,' he said. 'But Ah feel Ah'll be doin' some tears later. She wae a good'un.' Paused. 'We hae work, boy. We still hae work.'

Alex's shot was a masterwork. The powerhouse shattered, walls crumbling. Huge chunks of the roof sailed into the lake, and a few thousand liters of water slopped over the edge.

But the dam held.

The team had time to see their handiwork, and to see the city of Atlan roaring in flames, before the Imperial cruiser touched down softly beside them.

Chapter Twenty-Eight

The Mantis Section museum was a small, squat building of polished black marble. There were no inscriptions or signs.

Sten walked slowly up the steps to the door. He inserted his finger in a slot and waited while somewhere a Mantis computer chuckled through its files then buzzed him through. He stepped inside and looked around. Behind him the door snicked closed. Twin beams of light flicked on, probed him swiftly and decided he belonged.

The museum was a single large room, lit only by spotlights on each exhibit. Sten saw Mahoney at the far end and started walking toward him, noting the exhibits as he went by. A twisted battlesuit. Charred documents, carefully framed. Blasted machines. The leg of what appeared to be an enormous reptile. There was nothing to point out what any of them were, or what incidents they commemorated. In fact, the only writing was on the wall where Mahoney stood. It bore names from floor to ceiling, Mantis Section casualties – heroes or failures, depending on your point of view.

Mahoney sighed, turned to Sten.

'I keep looking for my own name up there,' he said. 'So far, no luck.'

'Is that why you called me here, colonel? So I could carve in mine? Save Mantis the trouble and expense?'

Mahoney frowned at him.

'And why would we be doing that?'

Sten shrugged. 'I blew it. I killed Vinnettsa.'

'And you're thinking there was a choice?

'Battle fatigue? She cracked? And you should have been able to handle it?'

'Something like that.'

Mahoney laughed. A grim little laugh. 'Well I hate to spoil your romantic delusions, Sten. But Vinnettsa didn't crack. She really tried to kill you.'

'But why?'

Mahoney patted him on the shoulder. Then reached into a pocket, pulled out a flask. Handed it to Sten. 'Take a nip of that. It'll put you straight.'

Sten chugged down several large swallows. He started to hand the flask back to Mahoney, who waved it away.

'Keep it. You'll need it.'

'Begging the colonel's pardon, but—'

'She was an assassin, Sten. A very highly paid professional.'

'But she was cleared by Mantis security.'

Mahoney shook his head. 'No, *Vinnettsa* was cleared by security. The woman you killed was not Vinnettsa. It took us a while, but we worked it out. The real Vinnettsa died while on leave. It was a pioneer world, so we didn't get word right away. A clerk, named Frazer, noted the report, then disappeared it. Paving the way for the assassin to step into her place.'

'What happened to this Frazer?'

'Killed. Probably by your assassin to cover her tracks.'

Sten thought it over. It made sense. But it didn't make sense. 'But why would anyone go to all that trouble for me? It must have cost a pile of credits.'

'We don't know.'

Sten thought over his list of enemies, and yeah, he had a few. Maybe even the killing kind. But they would have settled it in a bar or back alley. He shook his head. 'I can't think who it would be.'

'I can. Vulcan.'

'Impossible. Sure, they were after me. But I was a Delinq. A nobody. No, even those clot brains on Vulcan wouldn't plant an assassin just to get somebody like me.'

'But they did just the same.'

'Who? And why?'

Mahoney gestured at the flask. Sten passed it to him, and he took a big slug.

'There's one way to find out,' Mahoney said.

'How?'

'Mindprobe.'

Sten's skin crawled as his mind called up images of brainburns and Oron. 'No.'

'I don't like it any better than you, son,' Mahoney said. 'But it's the only way.'

Sten shook his head.

'Listen. It's got to have something to do with that little mission I sent you and your friends on.'

'But we didn't get anything.'

'The way I look at it, somebody thinks you did.'

'Thoresen?'

'Himself.'

'I still don't—'

'I promise I won't look at anything more than I have to. I'll concentrate on the last few hours you were on Vulcan.'

Sten took the flask from Mahoney. Drank deep. Thinking. Finally: 'Okay. I'll do it.'

Mahoney put an arm on his shoulder, started leading him back toward the door.

'This way,' he said. 'There's a gravsled waiting.'

. . . Sten oozed from the vent in the wall, his eyes on the patrolman's back . . .

'No,' Mahoney said, 'it's not that.'

Sten was lying on an operating table. Electrodes attached to his head, arms, and legs leading to a small steel box. The box drove a computer screen.

Mahoney, Rykor, and a white-coated Tech watched the screen and saw Sten drag the patrolman back to the vent and stuff him in. Rykor checked Sten's vital signs on another display, then motioned to the Tech. He tapped keys and more images appeared on the screen.

. . . Sten and the other Delinqs were at Thoresen's door. Beside him was Bet. She took a plastic rod from a pocket. Positioned it in the middle of the door's panel . . . Bet . . . Bet . . . Bet . . . Be . . .

'Wait,' Rykor snapped.

And her Tech put the probe on hold. Bet's image froze on the screen. Rykor leaned over Sten and injected a tranquil. Sten's body relaxed. Rykor checked the medcomputer, then nodded at the Tech to continue.

. . . And Sten stepped into Thoresen's quarters . . . They were in another world . . . an exotic, friendly jungle . . . except . . . Sten spotted a motion detector . . . leaped . . . knife plunging into it.

'Almost there,' Mahoney said. 'Flip forward a few minutes.'

. . . Papers and more papers spilled from Thoresen's safe . . . And then Oron had it, a thick, red folder labeled BRAVO PROJECT.

'Hold it,' Mahoney said. 'Stop right now.'

'Is that what you're looking for?' Rykor asked.

'Yes.'

'And you want me – us – out.'

'Yes.'

Rykor signaled her Tech to wheel her out.

'Watch his vital signs,' she said. 'If they even flicker, shut the probe off.'

'I can run it,' Mahoney said.

Reluctantly, Rykor and her Tech left. Mahoney returned to the probe, started flipping through.

Oron's expression went blank and the folder spilled. Sten hastily tried to pick the pages up as they spilled over the floor. He wasn't even reading what was on them, but his mind registered images.

Mahoney cursed at himself as he froze the image of each sheet of paper. His fingers were clumsy at the computer keys as he hardcopied the display. Clot – it was there all the time in Sten's brain!

Chapter Twenty-Nine

Mahoney stood at full attention before the Emperor.

'AM_2,' the Emperor whispered to himself. 'Yes. Yes, it makes sense. He just might be able . . .'

He looked up at Mahoney, puzzled for a minute, then spoke. 'At ease, colonel.'

Mahoney slid to a smooth, formal at rest.

'You've told me the facts,' the Emperor said. 'Thoresen seems to be on the verge of artificially creating Antimatter Two. That's Bravo Project. Fine. Now, what are your feelings? Guesses. Half-thoughts, even.'

'The Empire runs on Antimatter Two,' Mahoney said. 'You control the source. No one, except you, knows where that source is. Therefore—'

'I am the Emperor,' the Emperor said. 'AM_2 makes me that. And since I am sane, and since I am . . . always, I provide absolute stability to the galaxy.'

'And Thoresen is thinking he can replace you,' Mahoney said.

The Emperor shook his head. 'No. You underestimate Thoresen. The Baron is a subtle man. If he could successfully manufacture AM_2 – which, by the way, no one, not even I, knows how to do – it would still be much more expensive than what I provide.'

'So what's his game?' Mahoney asked.

'Probably blackmail,' the Emperor said. 'It would be cheaper and far more rewarding to threaten. If everyone knows how to make AM_2, then I am not needed. Of course, he's not bright enough to realize that proliferation of this knowledge would mean the fall of the Empire. Which no one, including Thoresen, wants. But in the meantime, we must be prepared for Thoresen to suddenly quote us a very high price for something.'

'Which would be?'

'It doesn't matter,' the Emperor said. 'What matters is that we stop him. Now.'

Mahoney moved to attention again.

'I want this kept quiet,' the Emperor said. 'So. Use a Mantis Section team. First, foment revolt. Second, capture Thoresen – alive, you understand?'

'Yes, sir.'

'Then, with Vulcan in revolt, I shall officially be forced to land the Imperial Guard to restore order. Naturally, someone other than Thoresen will be chosen to head the Company.'

The Emperor picked up a drink, toyed with it, took a sip, frowned at the taste and put it down. Looked up at Mahoney again. Raised an eyebrow.

Mahoney snapped a salute. Wheeled. Marched to the door and exited. The Emperor studied his drink. Yes, he had seen to everything. Now it was up to Mahoney.

Chapter Thirty

Sten and the other members of his team were gathered around the briefing table. Mahoney was at the head.

'And so,' Mahoney said, 'with Sten's background on Vulcan, this team would be the logical choice for the mission.

'Now, for the mission itself, I visualize a four-step program . . .'

Sten didn't even hesitate when Mahoney had asked if they would volunteer for the mission. He had a special reason for wanting to go, and even if the others on his team had refused, he would have figured a way to squirm his way in.

Yes. A very special reason. When Mahoney had been flipping through his mind, he overlooked something. In the Bravo Project folder. Not that there was any reason why he should have noticed. It had been labeled: RECREATIONAL AREA 26: A SUMMARY OF ACTIONS. The Row. Thoresen had ordered it destroyed. And had killed his family.

Mahoney finished. He looked around at the members of the team, his eyes stopping on Sten.

'Any questions?'

'No, sir,' Sten said. 'No questions at all.'

BOOK FOUR

RETURN TO VULCAN

Chapter Thirty-One

Thoresen was pleased with himself. He strolled through his garden, pausing now and then to enjoy a flower. There had been a few glitches, but so far, everything was going according to plan. He was no longer concerned about threats from the Emperor. All possible leaks had been plugged. Even including that little matter of the Mig, Sten.

Sten was dead. Of that he was absolutely sure. Thoresen had just gotten the final information from his main contact on Prime World.

'I've breached Guard security,' Crocker had boasted. 'So this is straight from their computer.'

'What does that mean,' the Baron asked, 'except that you are going to charge me more?'

'It means your Sten is out of it for good. He was killed in a nasty training accident. A woman trooper was also killed.'

Thoresen smiled. How convenient. No final payment due to the assassin.

'Good work. Now, what did you find out about my relations with the Emperor?'

'You're fine, there,' Crocker said. 'The last time there was a complaint – and it was a minor one – about Vulcan, the Emperor sent a personal reprimand to the complaining party. He said he did not want a patriot such as yourself maligned.'

Thoresen plucked a flower. Sniffed at it. That, he didn't believe at all. He was sure the Emperor was playing some sort of game. But he wasn't worried. The only kind he could play was the waiting variety. And Bravo Project was almost complete.

Yes, the Baron had a great deal to be thankful for.

Chapter Thirty-Two

The drone tug shifted the huge boulder in its tractor grip and then nosed it against another. Ida cursed as she fought for control, slipped, and the boulders collided. Sten and the others slammed against the rock side, then tumbled toward the other as there was another loud thud.

'Would you get this clotting thing going?' Sten yelled at Ida. 'You're turning us into soyamush.'

'I'm trying. I'm trying,' Ida shouted back. She slid back into her seat and once again began to tap delicately at the computer keys.

Sten and the other members of the Mantis team were inside the boulder. It was actually a huge, hollowed hunk of ore fitted out as a minispaceship. Except, of course, there was no drive unit. Their tug provided that. Which was why everyone was cursing Ida, as she tried to maneuver the drone tug from inside the boulder.

'It's not my fault,' she complained. 'The damn drone doesn't have the brains of a microbe.'

'Dinna be malignin' the wee beastie,' Alex said. 'Ye're the one giein' the brains— Ouch! Clot you, lass.'

Ida grinned back at them. This time the big jolt had been on purpose.

'Maybe we better shut up,' Sten said, 'and let her drive.'

Ida caressed the keys. Finally, the tug began to respond more smoothly. The boulder next to them moved away to a safer distance. The drone's drive units flared, and they began to drift slowly after it, toward Vulcan.

Sten had figured the perfect insertion method. Vulcan sent only unmanned tugs to the mining world, where all work was done by bots. A hollow boulder nearby carried their gear.

On the final approach to Vulcan, Ida punched at her computer, setting up an ECM blanket to fool Vulcan's sniffers, then put a finger to her lips, warning them unnecessarily to be quiet. A security capsule sniffed them over, then gave the drone tug clearance.

A jolt, whispered curses, and the tug started to move them toward a huge, yawning port. Then, *slam*, they were down.

'Clot, Ida,' Jorgensen groaned. 'Gimme a little humanity.'

'That's her problem,'Doc said. 'She has too much of it.'

And then they were moving along a slideway toward the thundering sound of grinding, giant teeth.

'This is where we get off,' Sten said. 'And quick.'

They blew the port and scrambled out. About a hundred meters ahead of them waited the enormous jaws of a crusher. Sten and Ida popped the other boulder open and began hauling out gear. Jorgensen patted a knapsack he was carrying. Inside, Frick and Frack were whining to get out.

They carried the gear to the edge of the moving belt, then slid down after it.

'Next time,' Ida said as they stacked their things on a gravsled, 'you drive.'

'Can't,' Sten said. 'I think you broke my arm.'

He ducked under her swinging fist, then jumped up on the sled. As the others climbed on, Sten switched the sled controls to manual and headed for their hiding place.

He had spotted it when he was a Delinq. It was better than a hideout. It was a home, complete with access to food, drink and not-so-public transportation.

'The Emperor's got nothin' on us,' Jorgensen whistled.

Even Doc was gawking at Sten's find. They were standing in the main ballroom of what had once been a luxury passenger liner. It was from the earlier days of interstellar travel, when journeys took months, and competing liners boasted of the diversions they provided their well-heeled customers. There were staterooms, party rooms, and several other ballrooms like the one they were standing in, with glittering chandeliers and polished floors. In the perfect nonenvironment of Vulcan, everything was exactly as the Company had left it centuries earlier when the ship was used to provide quarters to Execs overseeing the construction of Vulcan. It had been bought from a belly-up corporation, bolted into place, and then abandoned as Vulcan grew.

Hundreds of meters up, near the ballroom ceiling, Frick and Frack wheeled about, squealing in delight at their regained freedom.

'Well,' Ida said, 'the bats like it, so I guess it's okay.'

She wasn't quite so happy when Sten showed her the ship's computer and put her to work. 'It's so clotting primitive,' she said, 'it belongs in a museum.'

Sten had had enough diplomacy drilled into him by now to know when to keep his mouth shut. And by the time he left, she was huddled over the board, stroking it back to life, and beginning the task of patching them into Vulcan's central computer.

'As I see it,' Doc said, 'our first objective is recruitment.'

He snuggled his tubby body back onto the chair, feet dangling. They were in the captain's quarters, wolfing down the Exec meal Ida had conjured out of the computer.

'Y'mean,' Alex said, 'Ah canna blow things oop yet?'

'Patience, Alex,' Sten said. 'We'll get to that soon.' He turned to Doc. 'You can't just walk up to a Mig and wiggle your finger at him. He'll think you're a Company spy and run like hell.'

Jorgensen burped, then tossed a couple of Peskagrapes over to Frick and Frack. 'Feed me some input, I'll see what I can plow up.'

Sten shook his head.

'No. We'll start with the Delinqs.'

'From what you told us about them,' Ida said, 'they'll try to cut our throats.'

'A suggestion?' Doc ventured.

Sten was surprised. Doc always stated facts. Never asked. Then he realized that despite their briefings, Doc was still feeling his way through the intricacies of Vulcan.

'Shoot.'

'No, no. You don't want to shoot them.'

'I mean – Clot! Never mind. Go ahead.'

'What we may need to do is establish a suprapeer figure. A hero for them to emulate.'

'I don't get it.'

'Of course you don't. Listen, and I'll explain . . .'

They didn't have to wait long to put Doc's plan into effect. Ida had patched into the Sociopatrol Headquarters' system, blue-boxed a monitor on it, then left orders for the ship computer to wake her at the appropriate time.

They had been nailed cold. All exits were sealed and the Sociopatrol was moving in reinforcements. It was a large Delinq gang armed with riot guns and obeying orders with almost military precision as the leader snapped out commands.

'You three, behind those crates. You and you, over there.'

There was a loud crump as the Sociopatrol peeled the outer lock door. The leader looked around. It was the best she could do. In a few minutes, they would all be dead. She took up position behind a stack of crates and waited.

Another, louder crump and the main door exploded inward in a shower of metal splinters. Screams from the wounded. The leader recovered, fired a burst at uniformed figures in the doorway. Ragged fire began behind her as the others started to fight back. Hopeless. The patrolmen advanced behind a huge metal shield.

A shout above them.

'Down!'

The leader looked as a slim figure dropped from a duct onto a mountain of crates. He was behind the advancing spearhead of Sociopatrolmen. She lifted her weapon. Almost fired. Again, there was a shout.

'Flatten.'

She dropped as Sten sprayed the patrolmen with his willygun. Mass confusion and hysteria began among the attackers. A few tried to fight back. Sten worked his willygun like a hose, spraying from left to right and then left again. And in a moment it was over and there were twenty dead Sociopatrolmen.

Sten jumped down and walked toward the Delinqs. They came out of hiding, dazed. Staring at Sten as he advanced. One boy took a cautious step forward.

'Who's your leader?' Sten asked.

'I am.' A voice behind him.

He turned as the woman came from behind the stack of crates. And froze.

Bet.

She fell. And fell. And fell. Screaming for Sten. Every muscle tensed for the hurt. A child again in nightmare fall.

And then there was a softness. Like crashing into a soft pillow, but still falling. And the pillow stiffened, and she hit . . . bottom? And was flung upward, tumbling over and over. Then falling again. Slower.

Until Bet found herself suspended in midair over a huge machine. A McLean gravlift that workmen used to hoist heavy equipment through the ducts.

Cautiously, she slid off the pillow and dropped to the floor. She peered up into the darkness. Nothing. She shouted for Sten. There were sounds above her, then a beam of light speared down. She threw herself to one side as patrolmen fired at her. Came to her feet and sprinted away.

Bet stretched luxuriously on the bed. Nuzzled up to Sten.

'I never thought—'

He silenced her with a kiss. Drew her closer.

'What's to think? We're alive.'

Ida paced back and forth, glaring now and then at the door to Sten's quarters. She was *very* angry. 'That's just great,' she snarled at Alex. 'She bats her eyes and no more Mantis trooper. Just another loverboy.'

'Ye nae hae a sliver a' romance in yer bones, lass?'

Ida snorted but didn't even bother to answer.

'We all ken aboot Bet,' Alex said.

'Sure,' she snapped. 'We all know each other's psych profile. Just like I know you mourn for your mother's home-cooked haggis. But that don't mean I have to let your dear old momma join our team.'

'Now, dinna be malignin' me mither. Had an arm a' her could stop a tank wi' one blow.'

'You know what I mean.'

'Ah do. An' y'be wrong. Wrong a' wee lil body cou' be.'

'How so?'

'I'ye nae see it, whidny bother a' explain. Ah'll be havin' Sten do it f'me.'

Ida snorted again, then grinned. 'To hell with it. Let's have a beer.'

*

'We don't have a chance,' Bet pleaded. 'Let's just get out. Off Vulcan. Like we always dreamed.'

Sten shook his head.

'I can't. And even if the others let me, I wouldn't. Thoresen—'

'Clot Thoresen!'

'Exactly what I plan to do.'

Bet started to tell him that killing Thoresen – even if he could – wouldn't bring his family back. But that was obvious. She sighed. 'How can I help?'

'You've been running that gang since I . . . left?'

Bet nodded.

'From what I saw, they're pretty good.'

'Not as good as Oron's,' she said. 'But the best, now. We're armed and not running like Oron did.'

'And you have the respect of the other Delinq gangs?'

'Yes.'

'Good. I want you to set up a meeting.'

'A meeting? What for?'

'Listen, and I'll tell you.'

The Delinq chieftains eyed each other warily. Even with Bet's assurances, they were suspicious. The meeting could be a setup for the Sociopatrol – or a takeover.

About fifteen of them were spread around the huge table, muttering to each other and trying not to be impressed by the huge banquet or the luxurious dining room.

The meeting place was a new restaurant scheduled for opening in a day or two. The latest servant bots purred around the room offering the Delinqs delicacies reserved for Execs. Ida had found it after Sten had told her he wanted an impressive meeting place for the gang leaders, someplace that would show them just how powerful the Mantis team was. Ida had first patched into the personnel computer, and ordered all of the prospective restaurant employees to remain on their current jobs. The tap of a few more keys showed restaurant construction seriously delayed because of needed materials. And just to make sure, Sten had a few worker bots put a sign on the main entrance: DANGER. DO NOT ENTER. VACUUM CONDITIONS BEYOND.

Bet was at the head of the table. Beside her sat Sten. She put a hand up for attention and got it. 'Look at us all,' she said. 'Look at the faces around this table.'

Puzzled, they did.

'This is the first time the leaders of every gang have been in one room. Better yet, nobody's cut any throats.'

True, some of them thought. But maybe not for long.

'Think about what that means. All of us together. Representing a combined strength of maybe three hundred or four hundred Delinqs.'

A stir.

'What's that get us?' a gang chief named Patris snarled.

'Normally,' Bet said, 'nothing. All of us against the Sociopatrol would mean just a little bit more splatter than usual. Normally.'

'So who's talkin' about goin' against the patrol?' asked a gang boss named Flynn.

Bet pointed at Sten. 'He is.'

The muttering became a loud grumbling.

'This is Sten. You've heard about him. He was with Oron.'

Even louder grumblings.

'Sten's been offworld. Off Vulcan. And now he's come back to help us.'

Stunned silence. But mostly because of the enormity of the lie.

'You all heard about what happened to my gang?' Bet said.

Nods all around.

'And you heard about what happened to the patrol clots that almost got us?'

Slow nods. Glimmers of what she was getting at.

'Sten killed them,' Bet said. 'All of them. If he wasn't who he says he is, then how could that even be? How could I be here talking to you?'

'She's right,' Patris noted. 'My best runner saw them cleanin' up the clottin' bodies.'

Flynn sneered. 'So he's a hero. Big deal. Now, what's he want with us?'

Sten rose. Instant hush.

'It's very simple,' he said. 'We're gonna take over Vulcan.'

The effort to overthrow Vulcan began with a series of what Doc called 'gray actions.'

'We want to increase the discontent among the Migs,' he said. 'Then impress on them the vulnerability of the Company.'

Doc thought the proposed gray-action incidents his best work yet. Jorgensen thought they were just plain dirty tricks, and what Alex called them was not repeatable, even in his brogue. Only Ida was charmed. She saw infinite possibilities in enriching herself.

'That'll have to wait,' Sten warned her.

'For what? I got this computer singin' any song I want.'

'Then you found Bravo Project?'

Ida sighed. 'Well, almost any song.'

Doc glared at her.

'I'll start on the radio broadcasts,' she grumped.

Even Doc was impressed with the device she worked out. It took up an entire stateroom aboard the old liner. Basically, it was just a simple radio broadcaster beefed up with enough power circuits to boost Vulcan out of orbit. She rigged it to a Mantis minicomputer and set it to monitoring the Company band that broadcast Mig news and entertainment.

'Flip this switch,' she said, 'and we're on their band. Anything we say sounds like it's coming from their station.'

'You mean like "Thoresen does it with Xypacas"?' Sten asked.

'A little more subtle than that,' Doc broke in. 'The idea is to make it *sound* like it's a Company-approved script.'

Incomprehension registered on Sten's face. He waved them away in disgust. 'Never mind,' Doc said. 'I'll work out what we're going to say. You just worry about your end.'

Sten and Bet ambled past the factory. They strolled unhurriedly along like two Migs just off-shift and heading for a narcobeer. Several workers came out of the factory and stepped on the slideway beside them.

Sten nudged Bet with an elbow.

'Will you looka that,' he said loudly. 'That's Bearings Works Twenty-three, ain't it?'

'Yeah,' Bet answered. 'Sure is. I heard about that place.'

Sten shook his head.

'Poor clots. I sure wouldn't wanta work there. Oh, well. Guess the Company's workin' on a cure.'

A beefy Mig glared at them. 'Cure? Cure for what?'

Sten and Bet casually turned toward him. 'Oh, you work there?'

The Mig nodded.

'Sorry,' Bet said. 'Never mind.'

The beefy Mig and his buddies pushed over to them. 'Never mind what?'

Sten and Bet appeared a little nervous. 'Say,' Sten said. 'Not so close, if you don't mind. No offense.'

'What'sa matter with you? Waddya mean not so close? We got the crawlin' crud or somethin'?'

Bet tugged at Sten. 'Let's get out of here. We don't want any trouble.'

Sten started away, then stopped. 'Somebody's gotta tell them,' he said to Bet. He turned back to the puzzled Migs. 'We work at the Mig Health Center.'

'So?'

'So we been gettin' some real strange cases from that place.' He pointed at the factory the men just left.

'What kinda cases?'

'Not sure,' Bet said. 'Has somethin' to do with the lubricants you use.'

The Migs stiffened. 'What's wrong with 'em?' the beefy man asked.

'Can't tell. Seems to be some kind of virus. Hits only males.'

'What's it do to them?'

Sten shrugged. 'Let's just say, they ain't been havin' much of a sex life lately.'

'And probably never will,' Bet chimed in.

The Migs looked at each other.

Sten grabbed Bet by the arm and pulled her away. 'Good luck, boys,' he yelled back over his shoulder.

The Migs didn't even notice them leap over the barrier and hurry off down another slideway. They were too busy looking impotent.

Ida positively purred into the microphone. Doc sat beside her, checking his notes, making sure she made the right points in the right untrustworthy tone of voice.

'Before we begin our next request, fellow workers, we have an announcement. This is from the Health Center, and the people over there are very concerned about a rumor that's been going around.

'A silly rumor, really. It has to do with viral contamination of lubricants at Bearing Works Twenty-three.

'Ah, excuse me – I mean with the *non*contamination of lubricants at . . . Never mind. It is totally without foundation, the Health Center informs us. And there is no cause for alarm.

'It is absolutely not true that it causes impotency among males – Correction. There is no contamination – but if there were, it would not affect the potency of males.

'Uh . . . I guess that's it. Now, for our next selection—'

Ida flipped the switch and the regular broadcast boomed in. Just as a song was started. She turned to Doc, beaming.

'How'd I do?'

'I am happily considering all those poor, suffering Mig libidos.'

The following shift, only eight Migs showed up for work at the bearing factory. Within fifteen minutes those eight had also heard about the broadcast denial and were on their way out.

Patris, disguised as a Sociopatrolman, leaned casually against a wall. Watching the Migs at play in the rec area. Another Delinq – a woman dressed like a joygirl – chatted with him. Pretending to be on the make.

A tall, skinny Mig caught their attention. He was working a gambling 'puter. Inserting his card, waiting as lights and wheels flashed. Cursing as he kept coming up empty-handed. In the card went again for another try.

'He's been at it an hour,' Patris whispered to the girl.

She glanced over at the Mig.

'Probably just added six months to his contract,' she said.

She turned, slipped over to a duct, stumbled against it.

'There's our mark,' she whispered to the Delinq inside. A scuttling sound and he was away.

Hours later, the Mig was still at it. Inside the wall, behind the gambling machine, the Delinq manipulated the controls with a blue-box of Ida's evil devise. He kept the Mig just interested enough by feeding him a few wins. But steadily, the man was losing.

'Clot,' he finally shouted.

Turned and stalked away from the machine. Patris flicked an invisible speck from his uniform and strolled over to the gambling 'puter. He waited just until the Mig looked his way. Inserted a card. Instant sirens . . . bells . . . lights going wild.

The loser Mig froze.

'Clot,' he said to a Mig beside him. 'See what that slime just did?'

'Yeah. Got himself a fortune.'

'But I been playin' that thing half the day. Don't gimme a clottin' credit. Then he walks up and . . .'

Other Migs gathered at the sound of the winning machine, overheard the loser Mig, then cast nasty looks at Patris. Patris finally pretended to notice. He stalked over to the crowd, swinging his stun rod.

'On your way,' he ordered. 'Quit gawkin' and git.'

The angry crowd hesitated. 'Stinkin' cheat, that's what it is,' somebody yelled from the back. The somebody being the 'joygirl' Delinq.

'You should'a seen him,' the loser Mig shouted. 'He stole what I should'a won.'

More angry grumbling. Patris hit the panic button and in a flash a squad of patrolmen were rushing to his rescue. He waited until they closed on the crowd, then faded out of sight.

'Fellow workers,' Ida said. 'We all must be grateful for the marvelous recreational centers provided by the Company. At no small expense, I might add.

'For instance, the gambling 'puters, which give us all good, clean, honest fun. Company statistics prove that the machines pay off more credits than they take.

'But there are always losers, who now are spreading a terrible rumor. So terrible it almost embarrasses me to repeat it— However, there is no truth to the story that the machines are set to pay off only to high Company officials. No truth at all. Why, some liars have even indicated that the machines only pay off to Sociopatrolmen. Can you imagine that! The *very* men hired at no small expense by the Company to . . .'

Jorgensen came up with the masterstroke.

'That's lightweight stuff,' he said. 'You gotta hit a guy where it really hurts.'

'Such as,' Doc sniffed, a little hurt.

'Like beer.'

The following shift break swarms of Migs streamed into the rec domes. Offered their cards and settled back for a cool one. Nothing. Not one drop. The machine merely swallowed the card, deducted credits, and then chuckled at the Mig to go away.

'Clot I will,' shouted one big Mig. He shoved his card in again. Still nothing. He slammed a meaty fist into the machine. 'Gimme!'

'I am Company property,' the machine informed him. 'Violation of my being carries severe penalties.'

The Mig kicked the machine in answer. Alarms went off at five Sociopatrol centers. They steamed to the rescue. Only to find empty domes. Empty except for the twisted hulks of beer machines. All looted of their contents and groaning on the floor.

Doc shook his head.

'No. Too obvious. Not gray enough. Skip talking about the beer, Ida, and go to the food situation instead.'

Ida turned on her microphone.

'Fellow workers, the Company is pleased to announce a new health program. They have discovered that we are all getting much too overweight.

'Therefore, beginning next shift, all good rations will be reduced thirty per cent.

'That thirty— Sorry, we're in error. That program will not take effect until . . . until— What? Wrong announcement? Oh, kill it! The program is no go!

'Fellow workers, there is no truth to the report that food supplies will be cut thirty per cent next . . .'

Sten side-stepped a drunken Mig, sloshing a little beer, then pushed through the crowd to Bet. Set down their beers and settled into a seat beside her.

'I'll tell ya,' a Mig said to his companions, 'they've gone too far now. Too clottin' far.'

Sten winked at Bet, who smiled back.

'They cheat us. Mess with our sex lives, try to screw with our beer. Now they're gonna increase all work contracts one year.'

'Where'd ja hear that?'

'Just now. From that woman on the radio.'

'But she said it was just a rumor.'

'Yeah. Sure it is. If it's a rumor, how come they're tryin' to deny it so hard?'

'He's got a point,' Sten broke in.

The Mig turned to Sten. Peered at him, then grinned. Slapped him on the shoulder.

'Sure I do. That's the way the Company always works – feed you a rumor, get the reaction, then spring it on you for real.'

'Remember last year,' Bet said. 'There was that rumor we were all gonna lose three paid holidays? What happened?'

'We lost 'em,' the Mig said sullenly.

His friends all sipped beer. Thoughtful. Angry.

'What the clot,' someone sighed. 'Nothin' we do about it 'cept complain?'

Nods of agreement.

'I tell ya,' the first Mig said, 'I'd sure do something about it if I could. Hell, I got no family, I'd take the risk.'

The other Migs glanced about. The conversation was getting dangerous. One by one they excused themselves. Leaving only Sten, Bet, and their Mig friend.

'You mean what you said?' Sten asked.

''Bout what?'

'About gettin' even with the Company.'

The Mig stared at him suspiciously. 'You a spy?'

He started to stand up.

'Well, so what if you are. I'm fed up. Nothin' make me feel better'n to break you—'

Bet took him by the arm. Gently pulled him down and bought him a beer.

'If you're serious,' Sten said, 'I got some people I want you to meet.'

'To do what? Gripe like all the others?' He waved an arm at all the Migs in the bar.

'We gonna do more than gripe,' Sten said.

The Mig eyed them. Then smiled a big grin. His hand reached across the table. 'I'm your man.'

Sten shook his hand.

'What are you called?'

'Lots of things from the clottin' supervisor. But my name's Webb.'

They rose and left the bar.

'I think I finally got the idea how this whole thing works,' Bet told Ida and Doc.

'The gray actions?' Ida asked.

Bet nodded.

'Poor humans,' Doc said, 'torturing what little brain they have over the obvious.'

Bet gave him a look to shave his tendrils at neck level. Turned, and started out the door.

'Wait,' Ida said.

Bet stopped.

'Doc,' Ida said. 'You're the all-seeing being, but sometimes you miss what's in front of your pudgy little face.'

'Such as?'

'Like maybe we ought to find out what Bet has on her mind.'

Doc thought about it, tendrils wiggling. Then exuded his warmest feelings at Bet. 'My error,' he said. 'Blame it on genetic tendencies to rip and tear.'

Mollified, Bet returned and settled into a chair. 'What I was thinking about,' she said, 'was the ultimate gray action. For Migs.'

'Like?' Ida asked.

'Like the old legend that's been going around Vulcan since the first Mig.'

'Legends?' Doc said. 'I like legends. There's so much to build on.'

Bet took a deep breath.

'Story says someday there's gonna be a Mig revolt. A successful revolt led by an offworlder who was once a Mig himself.'

Doc was still feeling a little slow – his apology had put him off.

But Ida got it right away. 'You mean Sten?'

'Yes. Sten.'

'Ah,' Doc said, finally getting it. 'The mythical redeemer. Sten leads the way to salvation.'

'Something like that,' Bet said.

'The perfect rumor,' Ida said. 'We spread the word that the redeemer is here.' She looked at Doc. 'Have we reached that point yet?'

'Yes,' Doc said. 'It's the perfect intermediate stage.'

Bet hesitated. 'One problem.'

'Such as?' Doc was anxious to be about his work.

'What will Sten think about it?'

Ida shrugged. 'Who cares? Just wish it were me. There's a lot of money in redemption.'

The rumor spread like a virus colony on a petri dish. All over Vulcan, Migs were tense, angry, waiting for something to happen. But knowing, still, that nothing ever would. Without prodding, the dissension would dissipate to everyday acceptance.

'You see?' the old Mig told his grandchildren. 'It's like I been tellin' your dad all along. There is a way off Vulcan. And clot the Company.'

His son and daughter-in-law ignored the obscenity. Nodded to their kids. Gramps was right.

'And like I been sayin' all the time, it's a Mig that'll shove our contracts right up the Company's—'

'*Dad*,' his daughter-in-law warned.

'Tell us about him, gramps,' a child said. 'Tell us about the Mig.'

'Well, to begin with, he's just like us. A workin' clot. And then he got offworld. But he never forgot us, and . . .'

'Ah didna ken Ah was servin' wi' th' Redeemer,' Alex said. He bowed ceremoniously and held the mug out to Sten.

'Sharrup,' Sten growled. Bet giggled.

'Ay, Bet. 'Tis wonderful ye brought th' weenin' hole in m'theology to light. Here Ah was, servin' in darkness, havin' naught save th'Trinity t' keep me safe.'

'Trinity?' Bet asked.

'Aye.' Alex bent, and picked a struggling Sten up by the hips. Held him high overhead . . . then to either side, then dumped him back in the chair. '*In nomine* Bobby Burns, John Knox, an' me gran'sire.'

For once, Sten couldn't find an Imperial obscenity dirty enough to fit the occasion.

Chapter Thirty-Three

'Begging your pardon, sir,' the Counselor said, 'but you don't know what it's like out there. Lies. Rumors. Every Mig ready to cut your throat.'

'Nonsense,' the Baron said. 'It's a normal Mig stage.'

The Counselor sat in Thoresen's garden, waiting for the axe to fall. But it wasn't what he expected. Here he was with a drink in his hand, chatting with the Baron. That's not what usually happened when Thoresen summoned an employee. Especially with all those stories going around about the Counselor.

'I asked you here,' Thoresen said, 'because of your well-known frankness.'

The Counselor beamed.

'And that matter,' Thoresen continued, 'of certain, ah, shall we say, alleged indiscretions on your part.'

The Counselor's face fell. It was all a setup after all.

'There have been accusations,' Thoresen said, 'that you have been dipping a bit too deep into Mig credits.'

'I never—' the Counselor began.

Thoresen held up a hand, silencing him.

'It's expected,' Thoresen said. 'It's the way it's always been done. The Counselors make a little extra for their loyal efforts, without cost to the Company, and casual labor contracts are extended without expensive book work.'

The Counselor relaxed a bit. The Baron's description was accurate. An informal system that had worked for centuries.

'My difficulty,' the Counselor said, 'is the rumors. I promise you – on my life – I've never taken the amount I'm being accused of.'

Again, Thoresen motioned him to silence. 'Of course you haven't.

You are one of my most trustworthy – well, at least, discreet – employees.'

'Then why—?'

'Why did I summon you?'

'Yes, sir.'

Thoresen rose and began pacing. 'Actually, I'm calling in all of my key officers. The Migs are moaning and groaning again. It happened in my grandfather's time. And my father's. I'm not worried about them. What I'm concerned about is the overreaction of my own people.'

The Counselor thought about the ugly looks he had seen lately. It was more than Mig grumbling. He started to say something. Then decided not to.

'As I said,' Thoresen continued, 'it's just a cycle. A normal cycle. But it must be handled delicately.'

'Yes, sir,' the Counselor said.

'The first thing to remember,' Thoresen said, 'is not to aggravate them. Let them blow a little hot. Ignore what they say. And identify the leaders. We'll deal with *them* after things calm down.' He looked at the Counselor. 'Am I understood?'

'Yes, sir.'

'Good. Now I plan to take a personal hand in all this.'

'Yes, sir.'

'I want all incidents – no matter how minor – brought to my attention.'

'Yes, sir.'

'No action – no matter how minor – is to be taken without my go-ahead.'

'Yes, sir.'

'Then it's settled. Now, is there anything else I should know about?'

The Counselor hesitated, then said. 'Uh, yes. The broadcasts on the Mig radio. They've been a little heavy-handed?'

'An excellent example of what I've been talking about. Overreaction. The people responsible have denied releasing that information, but facts are facts.'

'If I may ask – what did you do?'

Thoresen smiled. 'Dismissed them. And ordered all broadcasts cleared by me.'

There was an uncomfortable pause, until the Counselor realized he had been dismissed. He rose, almost bowing.

'Thank you for your time, sir.'

'That's what I'm here for,' the Baron soothed. 'To listen to my people.'

He watched the Counselor exit. Measured him. A clumsy man, he thought, but valuable. If things got worse, he could always throw him to the Migs. No. Not necessary. Not now. Events were just being blown out of proportion.

Chapter Thirty-Four

For a person who had just pulled off a minor coup, Ida looked glum. She had found Bravo Project. Even with Sten's help, it had been a nasty problem. It was, obviously, near The Row. Or, what had been The Row. But the whole area was a warren of corridors, factories, homes. And specially constructed computer dodges, worked out by a genius whom Ida had grown to admire.

'What I did,' she told the group gathered around her terminal, 'was make the assumption that Bravo Project was sealed from the rest of Vulcan.'

'Naturally,' Sten said.

Ida glared at him. 'That means all the people who worked there have to be kept under ultratight security. But these are special people. Not prisoners. So I figured they gotta be kept happy. The best food. Drink. Sex. The whole shot.'

Doc smiled a nasty little teddy-bear smile. Ida had more brains than he gave her credit for.

'I set up a monitor on gourmet food shipments. Livies for high-brows, things like that.'

'What's the problem, then?' Sten asked.

Ida tapped some keys. A three-dimensional model of the Bravo Project lab blossomed out. Silence as they all studied it.

'Projection,' Jorgensen said. 'Direct assault unacceptable casualties. Mission in doubt with conventional tactics.'

Doc looked it over. His tendrils waved in agreement. The others waited for his conclusions.

'Under the present circumstances,' he said, 'Jorgensen is correct. But what if we move it up a stage?'

Jorgensen ran it through his brain. '*Black* operations . . . Input flux increased . . . Bravo target . . . Yes . . . alternatives . . . but too numerous to compute.'

They discussed it.

'I vote we push to the next level,' Sten said.

'What the clot 'm I supposed to say?' Sten whispered.

Doc was trying to learn a sneer. He didn't have the expression quite right yet. 'The usual inspiring drivel. You humans are easy to impress.'

'If it's so easy, why don't you get up on those crates?'

'Very simple,' Doc said blandly. 'As you keep telling me, who believes a teddy bear?'

Sten looked around at the other team members.

'Tell 'em aught but the truth, lad,' Alex said. 'They're nae Scots so they'd no ken that.'

Bet just smiled at him. Sten took a deep breath and clambered to the top of the piled boxes.

The forty-odd assembled Migs in the warehouse stared up at him. Behind them, their Delinq guides eyeballed Sten curiously.

'I don't know what the Company will think of you,' Sten said, 'but you scare clottin' hell outa me!'

There was a ripple of mild amusement.

'My da told me, most important tool you had was a four-kilo hammer. Used it to tap his foreman 'tween the eyes every once again, just to get their attention.

'I'm lookin' at forty-seven four-kilo hammers just now. You and your cells are gonna get some attention. Starting next shift.'

A buzz rose from the cell leaders below him.

'You all got jobs, and you and your folk've run through them enough. I'm not gonna stand up here and tell master craftsmen how to set your jigs.

'Just remember one thing. There's only a few of us. We're like the apprentice, with half a tool kit. We go breaking our tools early on, we'll end up not getting the job done.'

The men nodded. Sten was talking their language. Doc's tendrils wiggled. Correct procedure, he analyzed, even though he didn't understand the analogies.

Sten waited until the talk died. Raised his arm, half salute.

'Free Vulcan.'

He waved the Delinqs forward to guide the Mig cell leaders back through the ducts to their own areas, and jumped down from the crates.

'Well, Alex?'

'Ah nae think it's Burns . . . but it'll do. Aye, it'll do.'

The Mig eyed the weapon skeptically. It wasn't confidence-inspiring. A collection of 20-mm copper plumbing pipe, brazed together. He unscrewed the butt-cap, and took two of the sodium thiosulfate tablets that fell onto his palm, shoved the weapon back into his coveralls and went down the corridor.

Breathe . . . breathe . . . breathe . . . normally . . . you're on your way to report a minor glitch to your foreman. There is no hurry . . .

He touched the buzzer outside the man's door. Footsteps, and the bespectacled foreman peered out at him.

He looked puzzled. Asked something that the Mig couldn't hear through the roaring in his ears as he brought the weapon out and touched the firing stud. Electric current ran into tungsten wires; wires flared and touched off the ammonium-nitrate compound.

The compound blew the sealed prussic-acid container apart, whuffing gas into the man's throat. He gargled and stumbled back.

The drill took over. The Mig dropped the gas gun on the dead Tech's chest and walked away. Took the amyl-nitrate capsule from his coverall pocket and crushed it – completing the prussic-acid antidote – stripped off his gloves and disappeared into a slideway.

Ida swam a hand idly, and the robot's lid opened. She stared in at the ranked desserts in the server.

'Y'all gettin' fat,' Jorgensen said.

'Correction. I am not getting fat. I *am* fat. And intend on getting fatter.'

She began stuffing some megacaloric concoction into her face with one hand and tapping computer keys with the other.

'Did you wipe them?' Sten asked.

'Hours and hours ago.'

'Then what in the clot are you doing now?'

'I randomed, and got the key to the Company's liquid assets pool. Now, if I can get a linkup, I'll be able to transfer whatever I want into some offworld account.'

'Like a Free Trader roll?'

'That could— *oops!*' Her hand flashed across the keyboard and cut her board out of circuit. 'Suspicious bassids got a security key hidden in there.'

Sten started to say something, then turned away. Bet had been watching, confused.

'What's she doing?'

'Setting up her personal retirement fund,' Sten said.

'I figured *that*,' Bet said disgustedly. 'I meant the wiping.'

'We figured Company security and the patrol kept records on troublemakers. Migs who didn't rate getting brainburned or pulverized yet. Ida located the records and wiped them.'

'I did better than that,' Ida said, wiping her hands on the bot's extended towel. 'I also put a FORGET IT code in, so any more input will be automatically blanked.'

Bet looked impressed. Ida turned back to the keyboard.

'Now. Let's have another squinch at those assets.'

'This is Free Vulcan,' the voice whispered through a million speakers.

Frantic security Techs tried to lock tracers onto the signal source. Since the signal was initially transmitted via cable to a hundred different broadcast points, randomly changing several times a second, their task was hopeless.

'It has begun. We, the people of Vulcan, are starting to strike back. Seven Company officials were removed this shift for crimes against the workers they've ground down for so many years.

'This is the beginning.

'There will be more.'

Sten slumped into the chair and dialed a narcobeer. Drained it, and punched up another.

'Any casualties?'

'Only one. Cell Eighteen. The contact man got stopped on the way in by a patrol spotcheck. His backup panicked and opened up. Killed all three of them.'

'We'll need the name of the man,' Doc said. 'Martyrs are the lubricant of human revolutions.'

Sten put his nose in his beer. He wasn't in the mood just yet.

'There goes the little guttersnipe now,' Doc said approvingly.

Lying beside the panda in an air vent high above Visitors' Center, Sten focused the glasses. He finally found a Delinq wearing Mig coveralls darting through the crowds of offworlders.

'You had him take a bath, I trust,' Doc said. 'He is supposed to be the angelic little child every human desires for his very own.'

Sten swung the glasses to the four Migs wearing Sociopatrolman uniforms, as they hue-and-cried after the Delinq.

'Slow down, boy,' Sten muttered. 'You're losing them.'

As if listening, the boy zig-zagged aimlessly for a few seconds and the 'patrolmen' closed in on him. Shock batons rose and fell.

'Ah,' Doc sighed contentedly. 'I can hear the little brute scream from here. What's going on?'

'Mmm . . . here they come.'

Spacemen boiled out of the bar the Delinq had allowed himself to be caught at.

'Are they righteously indignant?'

Sten panned the glasses across the spacemen's faces. 'Yep.'

The offworlders knotted about the struggling group. One of them shouted something about bullies.

'Come on,' Sten muttered. 'Get 'em moving.'

The Delinq was a better actor than the four adults. He went down, but swung his head then dug his teeth into one man's leg. The phony Sociopatrolman yelped and brought the shock baton down.

That did it. The spacemen became an instant mob, grabbing bottles, smashing windows. The four 'patrolmen' grabbed the boy and ran for the exit.

Sten hit the key of the minicomputer beside him, and the riot alarm began shrilling.

'Tell me what's happening,' Doc said impatiently.

'Our people have cleared the dome. All right, here comes the riot squad in shock formation.'

'What are the spaceclots doing?'

'Charging.'

'Excellent. Now, we should see the first couple or three real patrolmen going down. Somebody should be panicking and putting his baton on full power and . . .' Doc smiled beatifically.

'Sure did. Took out a first officer. Drakh!'

'What you are telling me is that the morally outraged foreigners, having witnessed the brutal beating of a charming young child, and having been attacked by thugs, are reacting in the most strenuous manner possible. Tell me, Sten. Are they eating the Sociopatrolmen?'

'They aren't cannibals!'

'Pity. That's a human characteristic I haven't been able to observe at firsthand. You may proceed.'

Sten grabbed a hose, shoved it through the grill and triggered the tanks of vomit gas into the Visitors' Center, grabbed Doc, and they quickly slithered away.

'Excellent, Sten, Excellent. Free Traders are insatiable rumor-spreaders. At the least, the Company appears in a bad light. With luck, a few of those space sailors are moralists – which I doubt – and will refuse cargo. Especially after they wonder why the Company not only involved them in a riot, but gassed them in the bargain.'

Sten decided the only thing that could make Doc happier would be a massacre of orphans.

*

COMPANY DIRECTIVE – TO BE IMPLEMENTED IMMEDIATELY

Due to poor productivity, the following recreational domes provided for Migrant-Unskilled workers are to be closed immediately: Nos. 7, 93, 70.

There's some'at aboot explosions in vacuum, Alex decided for the hundredth time as he watched the lighter become a ball of flame. Almo' a puirfec' circle it makes.

He picked up his explosives kit and edged out of the loading dock.

Four other crates, besides the one that had just vanished the off-world loading ship, were booby-trapped. With a difference. Only somebody with Alex's experience would realize they would never go off. One explosion was to draw the attention of the Free Traders – destroying only a robot lighter – and the other bombs to discourage Free Traders' shipping Company cargoes.

COMPANY DIRECTIVE – SECURITY PERSONNEL ONLY

Effective immediately all ID cards issued to personnel whose duties are in the following areas: Visitors' Center, Cargo Transshipping, or Warehouse Divisions are rescinded. New passes will be issued on an individual basis. Thereafter, any member of patrol or security staffs failing to detain persons using old-style (XP-sequence) IDs will be subject to firm disciplinary proceedings.

The secretary checked Gaitsen's desk carefully. Light pen positioned correctly, Exec-only inputs on STANDBY, the chair set carefully so many centimeters from the desk.

Efficiency is all, Stanskill, Gaitsen had said repeatedly. Clottin' surprise, the secretary thought, he never said that in bed. Too busy worryin' about his heart, maybe.

She went to the door, palmed it, and looked around for the last time. Everything familiar and in its place, just the way the Exec wanted. She passed through the doorway, and, as instructed, left her carryall on her desk in the ante-chamber. She checked the clock. Gaitsen should just about be out of the tube.

She knelt by the duct, and the Delinq waiting impatiently held the screen open. The woman crawled inside and disappeared.

As she awkwardly bent around a ninety-degree turn in the ducting, the secretary was sorry she wouldn't be able to watch as Gaitsen plumped down in his favorite seat.

'Alvor?'

'Yuh?' The bearded cell leader peered over Sten's shoulder.

'Did you have your team take this Braun out?'

'Never heard a' the clot.'

Sten nodded, and scrolled on up the security report. Whoever killed Braun – low-level Exec in Product Planning Division – must've been settling a private grudge. He considered a minute. No. Free Vulcan would not claim that killing with the others. Might get the Company even more upset.

COMPANY DIRECTIVE – SECURITY PERSONNEL ONLY

Prior to beginning routine patrols, consult route with shift team director and chart R79L. Areas marked in blue are to be patrolled *only* by four-man teams equipped with riot gear. DISCUSSION OF THIS POLICY MODIFICATION IS FORBIDDEN TO NON-CLEARED STAFF.

'This is the voice of Free Vulcan,' the speakers resonated. 'We would like to know how you Executives and security people feel.

'As if there is a noose tightening around your necks?

'Things have been happening, haven't they? What happened to that Sociopatrol that was sent out to Warehouse Y008? It never reported back, did it?

'And Exec Gaitsen. That must have been very unpleasant. Not a very fast way to die, either. Perhaps you executives who use your secretaries as joygirls might reflect on Gaitsen for a few moments.

'Yes. There is a noose. And it is getting steadily tighter, is it not?'

'Do you have a tracer?' Thoresen glowered.

'Nossir. And, Baron, I don't think we'll be able to get one.' Thorensen blanked the screen, and keyed up another department.

'Semantics. Yes, Baron?'

'Do you have an analysis of that voice?'

'We do. Very tentative, sir. Non-Mig, non-Tech. Even though the voice of Free Vulcan—'

'You have been directed not to use that term, Tech!'

'Sorry, sir. Our theory is that the voice is synthesized. Sorry.'

Thoresen flicked off, noted the time, and headed for the *salle d'armes*. He pulled a saber from its hanging and spun on the instructor.

'Come in,' he growled. 'As if you mean it!'

Sten eyed the hydroponics farm dubiously. It looked just as it had before Alex bustled off. The agribots still lovingly tended the produce intended for Exec consumption. 'You sure it's gonna go?' he asked skeptically.

Alex patted him patronizingly. 'Ah ken ye dinnae know what ye're glassin', lad. But dinnae tell your gran'sire how to suck eggs.'

Sten followed him to the shipping port and ducked inside. Alex let the door almost close, then blocked it with a small metal bar. 'Now ye see it—'

He touched off a small emergency flare, lobbed it into the middle of the farm, and yanked the bar out. As the door snapped closed, Sten saw the compartment fill – deck to ceiling – with a mass of flames.

'Ye ken,' Alex said, as the shock slammed against the lock, 'i's what's known as a dust explosion. Ye mere put the intake in the fertilizer supply, burn awa' the liquidifier, an' dust sprays aboot the room. Touch i' off' – the little man chuckled happily.

EXECUTIVE PERSONNEL EYES ONLY

> We have noticed an inordinate number of applications for transfer, early retirement, or resignation. We are most disappointed. During this admittedly unsettling time, the Company needs its most skilled personnel to be most attentive to their duties. For this reason, all such applications shall be disapproved until further notice.
>
> Thoresen.

Webb slit the dying Sociopatrolman's throat from ear to ear, stood, and brushed his hands off. He walked over to the only survivor of the ten-man patrol, held against the wall by two grim Migs. 'Let 'im go, boys.'

The surprised Migs released the patrolman.

'We're makin' ya a bargain,' Webb said. 'You ain't gonna get splattered like the rest of your scum. We're gonna let you go.'

Webb's two men looked surprised.

'You just wander back to your barracks sewer, and let your friends know what happened.'

The patrolman, near rigid with terror, nodded.

'An' next time they put you out on patrol, you don't have to crud around like you're a clottin' hero. Make a little noise. Don't be too anxious lookin' down a passage where somethin' might be goin' on you don't want to know about. Let 'im run, boys.'

The patrolman glanced at the Mig bush section then he backed away. He sidled to the bend in the corridor, whirled and was gone.

'Y'think he's gonna do like you want, Webb?' one of his men asked.

'Don't matter. Either way, he won't be worth drakh anymore. An' don't you think security's gonna wonder why he got away without gettin' banged around?'

'I still don't understand.'

'That's why you ain't a cell leader. Yet. C'mon. Let's clear.'

The five-man patrol ducked as Frick and Frack hissed down from the overhead girders of the warehouse. One man had time to raise his riot gun and blast a hole through some crates before the white phosphorus mini-caps ignited.

The two creatures swooped back over, curiously eyeing the hell below them as the phosphorus seared through flesh and bone, then banked into the waiting duct above.

'You! What's that? The brown drakh?'

'Soybeef stew,' Sten replied. 'May I offer you some?'

'Nawp. Don't need any extra diseases. I'll help myself.' The med-Tech ladled stew from the tureen onto his tray, then slid on down the line.

Sten, face carefully blank, looked down the line of servers to Bet. They both wore white coveralls and were indistinguishable from the other workers in the Creche staff mess. Part of Sten's mind began the countdown, while another caught bits of conversation from the technicians at the tables.

'Clotting little monster! Daddy this, an' daddy that an' daddy I got to be a spacetug today and—'

'If we didn't need 'em, Company oughta space the little clots—'

'Tell 'em stories, pat 'em on the head, wipe their bungs when they mess. The Company don't pay us near enough.'

'How you doin' with Billy?'

'Me an' that clot are reaching an understanding. I put him in a sewer supervisor, and just left him there for two shifts. Clottin' booger's gonna learn.'

'Actually, doctor, there's no reason the Company has to maintain these creatures in the style it does. I'm theorizing that the program could be implemented with the use of atrophy amputation.'

'Hmm. Interesting concept. We might develop it . . .'

Time.

Sten snapped the stock of the willygun to lock and brought it up, finger closing on the trigger. The two Sociopatrolmen lounging at the entrance dropped, fist-size holes in their chests.

'Down! Get down!' Bet shouted . . . the servers stared, then flattened as Sten lobbed two grenades from his pouch into the middle of the hall.

Bet showered a handful of firepills across the room, then the two fell alongside the servers.

Seconds passed and there was stunned silence from the other side of the serving line, then screams. And an all-enveloping blast.

Sten lifted his head and eyed Bet. She was laughing. He scrambled to his feet and pulled her up. Shook her. She came back to reality as he pushed her toward the garbage vent that was their escape hole.

He did, in fact, understand her a little better.

'This is the voice of Free Vulcan. We know what it is to be a Mig. To live under the bootheels of the Company. To know there is no law and no justice, except for those who have the stranglehold of power.

'Now, justice will come to Vulcan. Justice for those who have lived for generations in terror.

'Migs. You know what a terrible joke your Counselors are, and how your grievance committees are echoes of the Company's brutality.

'There is an end to this. From this shift forward, Free Vulcan will enforce the rights that free men know everywhere in the galaxy.

'If your foreman forces you to work a double shift, if a co-worker is toadying to the Company, if your sons and daughters are being corrupted or stolen by the Company – these evils will end. Now. If they do not, Free Vulcan will end those who commit them.

'If you have a grievance, talk about it. You may not know who is Free Vulcan. Perhaps your shiftmate, another worker down the line, the joygirl or joyboy in the Dome – even a Tech. But your words will be heard and our courts will act on them.

'We bring you justice, people of Vulcan.'

*

COMPANY POLICY – ALL COUNSELORS AND
SECURITY EXECS – EYES ONLY

The sudden lack of participation by Mig-Unskilled workers in our grievance program has been brought to my attention. It is our opinion that concern about the tiny band of malcontents that styles itself 'Free Vulcan' is excessive, since, in fact, we are now able to grasp terror by its throat.

Security Executives are evaluating the main areas reflecting such lack of involvement since the absence pinpoints areas where malcontents are located. Appropriate measures, of the severest kind, are imminent. It is strongly suggested that all Counselors make the workers for whose welfare they are responsible aware that, once these malcontents are dealt with, those who have encouraged them by participating in their kangaroo 'justice' system will also be disciplined.

Thoresen.

'The thought has occurred to me,' Ida drawled as she passed around glasses of alk, 'that none of us are the people our parents wanted us to associate with.'

'Some of us,' Bet said evenly, 'are the kind of people who wouldn't want to associate with our parents in the first place.'

'Are we no bein' grim, lass?'

'Parents?' Frick shrilled. 'Why would, colony, our colony care?' Frack squealed agreement.

'If you humans aren't creating traumas for other people,' Doc said, 'you can't wait to set them up for yourselves, can you?'

Sten was interested. 'How do pandas get along with *their* progenitors, Doc?'

'It is not a factor. First, in the breeding process the male sheds his member after copulation and quickly – bleeds would be an analog – to death.' Doc waved several tendrils. 'Once the young hatches, inside the female, it exists . . . ah, as a parasite until born. Birth, naturally, occurs at the moment of female death.'

Bet blinked. 'That doesn't leave you with much of a sex life, does it?'

'I have wondered why the human mind isn't physiologically below the umbilicus,' Doc said, 'since most of its thought is concerned with that region. But, to answer your question, those of us with a proper concern for the future arrange to have ourselves neutered. The operation also extends our life span for nearly a hundred E-years.'

Sten couldn't decide whether to laugh or be embarrassed.

'I can see it now,' Jorgensen drawled. 'Amblin' up the road. Farm spread out in front of you. You duck down behind a bush, spray the windows for snipers, then zig-zag up to the door, boot it open, heave in a grenade, roll in firin', and come to your feet, "Ma! I'm home!"'

'Ah no ken why ye gie wha' we are so much concern,' Alex finished. 'Th' none a' us'll get oot'a Mantis alive.' He upended his drink and went for another, not looking particularly concerned.

Sweat dripped from the Counselor's face onto his torn, filthy robes. 'There was simply no truth to that story. My dealings with you Migs—'

'Mebbe we use that word,' a brawny Mig said, 'but that don't make it sound right comin' from you.'

'Excuse me. You're quite right, of course. But . . . truthfully, I never attempted to deprive any . . . migrant worker of his rightfully earned time for personal benefit. It's a lie. A story created by my enemies.'

The five cell leaders managed to look disbelieving in unison.

Sten watched closely from behind the one-way panel to one side of the 'court,' set up in an abandoned warehouse. He found it interesting that he didn't hate the Counselor that actively anymore. On the other hand, he felt less than no desire to intervene.

'You can examine my record,' the Counselor went on. 'I've always been known for my fairness.'

Bitter laughter drowned whatever else he was going to say. 'We'll cut you a skate on that one,' Alvor said. 'Still leaves you assignin' Migs to shifts to get 'em killed 'cause they wouldn't give you whatever you wanted. I know two, maybe three people you set up for brainburns.'

The Mig at the end of the table, who'd been silently staring at the Counselor, suddenly got up. 'I got a question, boys. I wanna put it to his scumness personal. What'd you want from my Janice, made her cut an' run to the Delinqs?'

The Counselor licked his lips. The Mig grabbed him by the hair and lifted the Counselor out of his chair. 'You ain't answered my question.'

'It – there was – just a misunderstanding of my attempt to communicate.'

'Communicate. 'Sat it? She was ten.'

Sten got up. But the Mig holding the Counselor was keeping himself back. He looked over at the other cell leaders. 'I don't need any clottin' more. Vote guilty.'

And the chorus answered in agreement.

'Unanimous,' Alvor put in. 'What's the sentence?'

Sten kicked the screen over. 'Give him to his friends. Outside.'

The Counselor's eyes flared open. Who? And then he was screaming and clawing as the cell leaders had him. They jerked the double doors open and pushed. The Counselor half fell, half staggered into the arms of the workers waiting outside.

Alvor pulled the door to. But the sound of the mob outside was very clear.

That was the first.

'Just like pushin' dominoes,' Sten said. He and Alex were headed back for the ship. 'Three more cycles and we can stop hidin' behind bushes, start the revolution, and get the Guard in motion.'

'Dinna be countin' your eggs afore they're chickened.'

'What the clot does that mean?'

'Ah no ken. But ma gran used it t'mean things gang aft aglay.'

'Would you speak Imperial, for clot's sake?'

'Ah'm spikit proper, it's just your ears need recalibratin', lad.'

'Bet me. But look. We're all set. A, we get a resistance set up. B, we start rightin' wrongs and killin' every Exec we can get and every Tech that can count above ten with his boots on.'

'Aye. There's naught wrong so far.'

'C, we build weapons and train the Migs how to use 'em. D, we set up our own alternate government, just like the conditioner taught us. Then, E, we're gonna snap our fingers in three cycles and the revolution has started.'

Alex unslung his rifle – their sector was secure enough for most of the Migs to go openly armed now – and stopped.

'You no ken one thing, Sten,' he said. 'Man or woman, once they get their hands on th' guns, there's no callin' what'll happen next. Ah gie ye example. Mah brother, he was Mantis. Went in to some nice barbarian-class world our fearless Emp'rer decided needed a new gov'ment.

'Ye trackin' me yit? Aye, so they raises the populace, an' teaches 'em how to stand an' fight. Makes 'em proud to be what they is, 'stead of crawlin' worms.'

'I am not trackin',' Sten said.

'So they runs up the blawdy red flag a' revolution, an' it starts. People slaughter a' th' nobility in th'r beds. My braw trots up wi' the gov'ment they've set up to replace the old baddies. An' the people're so in love wi' blood an' slaughter, they turns the *new* gov'ment inta cattle fodder like they done the first. My braw gets offworld wi'out an arm, an' the pro' don't take. So he's back tendin' sheep on Edinburgh, an' I goes out to keep the clan name fresh. Now, I'm takin' the long road aroun' – but best ye rec'lect. When ye're giein' bairns the fire, ye no can tell what'll be burnt.'

He reslung his willygun, and he and Sten walked in silence to the airlock into the ship.

To be welcomed by Ida screaming, in a dull roar, 'Clot! Clot! Clot!' A computer terminal sailed across the room to slam into a painting.

'What's wrong?'

'Nothing at all. But look at what your clotting Migs did!' She waved at the screens around the room. Sten noticed the other members of the team and Bet were silently staring.

'These are all the security channels. Look at those fools!'

'Dammit, Ida, tell me what happened!'

'As far as we can estimate,' Doc said, 'the Sociopatrol was transferring several unregenerate Migs South, to Exotic Section. One of the Migs in the shipment must've had some friends.'

Sten glanced at the screens then walked to the alk container and poured himself a shot.

'So they decided to rescue him,' Ida continued. 'Naturally, the patrol reinforced, and so did the guy's friends. Which sucked in most of our cells in South Vulcan. Look.'

Sten stared at the sweeping screens. Every now and then he recognized a face from the resistance.

''Pears,' Jorgensen said, 'like they dug all the weapons out and went huntin' for bear.'

Ida sneered at Sten, then started cutting in sound from the various screens. Fascinated, Sten sat down to watch.

He saw screaming Migs charge a formation of patrolmen sheltered behind upended gravsleds. Riot guns sprayed and the Migs went down.

On another monitor a Mig woman, waving the severed head of a patrolman, lead a vee-formation of resistance fighters into a wedge of patrolmen. The camera flared and went out, but it looked like there were more patrolmen down than Migs.

A third screen showed a static scene at the entrance to Exotic Section. The lock was barricaded, and patrolmen had blockades set around it. Migs sniped at them from corridor and vent openings.

Sten turned away and poured the drink down. 'Clot. Clot. Clot.'

'I already said that,' Ida noted.

Sten turned to Jorgensen. 'Miyitkina.'

Jorgensen's eyes glazed. He went into his trance.

'Observe occurrence. Prog.'

'Impossible to compute exact percentages. But, overall, unfavorable.'

'Details.'

'If a revolution, particularly an orchestrated one such as this, is allowed to begin before the proper moment, the following problems will occur: the most highly motivated and skilled resistance men will very likely become casualties, since they will be attacking spontaneously rather than from a given plan; underground collaborators will be blown since it becomes a matter of survival for them to come into the open; since the combat effort cannot be mounted with full effectiveness, the likelihood of the existing regime being able to defeat the revolution, militarily, is almost certain. Examples of the above are—'

'Suspend program,' Sten said. 'If it's blown, how long does it take to put things back together again?'

'Phraseology uncertain,' Jorgensen intoned. 'But understood. Repression will be intensified after such a revolution is defeated; reestablishment of revolutionary activity will take an extended period of time. A conservative estimate would be ten to twenty years.'

Sten didn't even bother to swear. Just poured himself a drink.

'Sten!' Bet suddenly shouted. 'Look. At that screen.'

Sten turned. And gaped. The screen she was pointing at was the one fixed on the entrance to the Exotic Section.

'But,' he heard Doc say, 'those are none of our personnel.'

They weren't. 'They' were a solid wall of Migs. Unarmed or carrying clubs or improvised stakes. They were charging directly into the concentrated fire of the patrolmen grouped around the entrance. And they died, wave after wave of them.

But they kept coming, crawling over the bodies of their own dead, and, finally, rolling over the defenders. There was no sound, but Sten could well imagine. He saw a boy – no more than ten – come to his feet. He was waving . . . Sten swallowed. Hard. There were still threads of a Sociopatrol uniform clinging to it.

More Migs ran forward, teams with steel benches ripped from work areas. They slammed at the doors to the Exotic Section, and the doors went down.

Jorgensen, still in his battle-computer trance, droned on. '. . . there are, however, examples of spontaneous success. As, for example, the racially deprived citizenry of the city of Johannesburg.'

'Two Miyitkina,' Sten snapped.

'Ah hae a wee suggestion,' Alex said. 'Ah suggest we be joinin' our troopies, or yon revolution may be giein' on wi'out us.'

*

Sten stepped through the smashed windows of the rec dome's control capsule and looked down at the faces staring up at him in their thousands. Sweaty, bloody, dirty, and growling.

It made no sense. Militarily. One rocket could take out not only the assembled Mantis team, but all the resistance workers they'd so laboriously trained and recruited over the months.

Clot sense, Sten thought, and flipped the hailer on.

'MEN AND WOMEN OF VULCAN,' his voice boomed and echoed around the dome. He assumed that there were still functional security pickups, and he was being seen. He wondered if Thoresen would be able to ID him.

'Free men and women of Vulcan,' he corrected himself. He waited for the roar to die. 'We came to Vulcan to help you fight for your freedom. But you didn't need our help. You charged the Company's guns with your bare hands. And you won.

'But the Company still lives. Lives in The Eye. And until we can celebrate that victory – in The Eye – we have won nothing.

'Now is the time . . . Now is the time for us to help you. Help you make Vulcan free!' Sten chopped the hailer switch and walked back into the capsule.

Alex nodded approvingly. 'Ah, ye can no dance to it, but Ah gie yer speech a' fair. Now, if we through muckin' aboot, ye ken we'll shoot away our signal, an' gie on wi' our real business?'

MYOR YJHH MMUI OERT MMCV CCVX AWLO . . .

Mahoney moved aside and let the Emperor read the decoded message:

STEP ONE COMPLETE. VULCAN NOW IN COMPLETE INTERNAL TURMOIL. BEGINNING STEP TWO.

The Emperor breathed deeply.

'Deploy Guard's First and Second Assault according to Operation Bravo, colonel.'

Chapter Thirty-Five

The Baron stared at the figure on his screen. Frowned. It was familiar. He tapped keys, and the camera moved in on Sten. Thoresen froze a frame. Studied Sten's face. No. He didn't know him. Thoresen punched the keys ordering the computer to search its memory for a possible ID. With a little luck, it would just be some Mig with a loud mouth and tiny brain. Somehow, Thoresen didn't think it would work out that way.

Ida's model of the Bravo Project lab looked like a gray skinny balloon, half full of water at one end. There wasn't much to study; Ida had still been unable to penetrate security.

The team members and Bet eyed the model morosely. Sten, Alex, and Jorgensen wore, for the first time since they'd been on Vulcan, the Mantis Section phototropic camouflage uniforms. Ida and Bet were fitted into the coveralls of a Tech/1st and /3rd Class.

There wasn't much to say. Nobody was interested in inspirational speeches. They shouldered their packs, silently got into the gravsled, and Sten lifted it off, into the corridors of a Vulcan gone insane.

Vulcan was quickly collapsing as the Migs took to the streets. Images of pitched battles, looting, and Sociopatrol defeats floated up on the Baron's vidscreen.

The Baron turned the vid off. It was hopeless. There was nothing more he could do to put down the revolt. He would just have to let it burn itself out, then try to put his empire back together again.

A light blinked for attention. Thoresen almost ignored it. Just one more report from a hysterical guard. No, he had to answer. He flicked his computer on.

His heart turned to ice. The computer had identified the Mig leader. Sten. But he was— How? – And then the Baron knew that his world was about to end.

There was only one possibility: Sten; the Guard; Bravo Project. The Emperor knew and the Emperor was responsible for the Mig revolt. Sten was part of a Mantis Section team.

Desperately, Thoresen searched for a way out. What would happen next? How was he supposed to react? That was it: the Emperor was looking for an excuse to land troops. Thoresen was expected to call for help. He would be arrested, Bravo Project uncovered and then . . .

And then Thoresen had it. He would go to the lab. Get the most important files. Destroy the rest and flee. The Baron would still have the Emperor where he wanted him as long as he had the secret to AM_2.

He rose and started for the door. Paused. Something else. Something else. The Emperor would have ordered the lab destroyed. Sten and his team could be on the way now. He hurried to his comvid.

The frightened face of his chief security man came into view. 'Sir!'

'I want as many men as you can spare. Here. Now,' Thoresen snapped.

The security chief started to gobble.

'Get yourself together, man.'

The chief stiffened. 'Yes, sir.'

He disappeared. Thoresen thought quickly. Was there anything else? Any other precautions? . . . He smiled grimly to himself, opened a desk drawer, and pulled out a small red box. He shoved it into his pocket and raced out the door.

Chapter Thirty-Six

Frick and Frack arced back and forth, high above the deck of the Bravo Project lab. Hugging the ceiling, they'd gone straight down the entrance corridor, above the security teams.

They hadn't been seen by human eyes. There were, after all, no birds or even rodents on Vulcan. What the human eye doesn't understand, it doesn't see.

The security watch officer eyeballed his fingernails. He'd chewed them to the quick last shift. And he'd systematically racked every patrolman within twenty meters. There wasn't anything to do but sweat and count his problems.

And he had a lot of them. Guarding a lab whose purpose he had no idea of, for openers. Plus the clottin' Migs were going crazy – his best off-shift buddy had been found with a half-meter glass knife through his chest. And now he'd been tagged that Baron Thoresen was on his way down.

The last thing he needed was the computers being as berserk as they were, he thought. He glanced at the screen. Experimentally slammed it with one ham fist. Didn't change things. It still indicated flying objects were inside the lab proper.

The watch officer wondered why he'd taken the Company's job. He could have been very comfortable staying on as head of secret police on his homeworld. He looked up at the two Techs trundling down the corridor. 'Bout clottin' time, he decided.

The beefy first-class Tech swaggered into his office and lifted a lip. Clottin' joy, the watch officer thought. I gotta get a deesl-dyke. All I need now is hemorrhoids.

He smiled sympathetically at the poor third-class Tech behind Ida.

Poor kid, he thought. Shows you. Bet that first-class clot tried somethin', an' her assistant didn't go for it, so the dyke makes her lug the toolboxes.

''Bout what I'd expect,' Ida snarled. 'Computer cracks up, an' all you can do is sit there puttin' your thumbs up your nose.' She turned to Bet. 'Men!'

The watch officer decided it was going to be a very long shift. He tried to keep it formal. 'We're getting readouts,' he began.

'I know what you're gettin',' Ida said. 'We got terminals too.' She eyed the watch officer. 'I tol' you, kid, it'd turn out to be somethin' simple.'

'What do you mean?' the security officer asked.

'That bracelet. You hang that much alloy near a terminal, it's gonna get crazy. Figures.'

'But that's the automatic screen. We've always worn them. And nothin's happened before.'

'Yah. An' those clottin' Migs haven't tied up the computers before either. You tellin' me every one a' you patrol geeks wears them?'

'Yes.'

'Dumb, dumber, dumbest. Get 'em out here.'

'Huh?'

'Everybody on the shift, stupid. Maybe this one'll be easy, an' the only problem is somebody's got a bracelet that's signaling wrong.'

'We can't call in every patrolman,' the watch officer started. Ida shrugged.

'So great. Me an' cutie here'll go on back and file that we couldn't properly evaluate the situation. Sooner or later somebody else'll come around and try to fix that computer.'

The officer eyed the screen. The flying objects were still there. Looked at the third-class Tech, who slipped him a sympathetic and very warm smile. Made a decision. Turned to the com and keyed it open.

'Third shift – no emergency – all officers report immediately to central security. I repeat, all officers report immediately to central security.'

Bet slipped two bester grenades from her pouch and stood up. Bravo Project's security officers were crowded inside the small office. Ida stood near the door.

'This everybody?'

The watch officer nodded.

Bet hit the timer on the grenades and dived for the door. She landed on top of Ida.

The two grenades detonated in a purple flash.

The Bravo Project patrolmen crumpled. Bet rolled off Ida and helped her up. Ida wheezed gently, muttered something in Romany, and shrilly whistled between her fingers.

Sten and the other members of the team hurried into sight, running toward them.

'We'll hold the back door. You stand by.' Ida stepped inside and lifted the toolbox tray, extracted two folding-stocked willyguns, readied them, and tossed one to Bet as Sten and the others ran into the Bravo Project lab.

Meanwhile, Ida had turned the watch commander over. 'What're you doing?' Bet asked curiously.

'Private revenge,' Ida replied, planting one hoof firmly in the unconscious man's groin. 'I suspect he thought nasty things about me.'

She lifted her other foot off the ground. Bet winced and turned back to look down the long empty corridor.

'Wouldnae it be simpler,' Alex suggested, 'to just blow th' whole shebeen?'

'Clot, yes,' Sten said. 'But if we did' – he gestured up to the ceiling – 'we'd be soyasteaking all those Techs up there.' He grinned. 'Damfino why I'm stickin' up for 'em.'

'Because,' Doc said, 'mission instructions were to obliterate this lab with minimum loss of life.' He waggled tendrils at Alex. 'Ignore him. Simple minds find simple solutions.'

Alex ignored Doc. 'Ah gie ye pocket-size destruction, i' ye'll tell me where Ah begin.'

The lab ceiling lofted high above them. High enough, Sten decided, for the hangarlike building to have its own weather. Frick and Frack curvetted among the ceiling lights. In the middle of the lab was a small space freighter, its cargo doors agape. Mysterious apparatus sat around it on the main floor. Doors opened off the sides into rabbit warrens of minor labs.

'Set charges on any information storage file,' Sten decided. 'Any computer. And any piece of equipment that doesn't look familiar.'

'Finest kind,' Jorgensen moaned as he shouldered back into his pack. 'That means he's gonna shoot anything that don't look like a sheep.'

Alex wagged a finger. 'Frae yon teddy bear Ah take abuse a' that nature. But no frae a man wi' his feet still i' the furrows.'

And they went to work.

*

Thoresen, in spite of his fascination with weaponry and martial arts, had never been in combat. Nevertheless, as he entered the corridors that led to Bravo Project, he had sense enough to drop back and put two squads of the fifty-strong patrol company in front of him. Thoresen was still analytical enough to realize he was in a response situation. He might, he considered as he unobtrusively dropped back in the formation, still be running late.

Bet wiped sweaty hands on the plastic willygun stock. 'Deep breaths,' Ida said calmly. 'Worry about them ten at a time.' She suddenly realized what she'd said, and chuckled. 'On the other hand, do you think a surrender flag would be a better idea? Now!'

Bet pulled the willygun's trigger all the way back. The gun spat AM_2 slugs out into the packed mass of oncoming patrolmen.

Screams. Chaos. Ida thumbed a grenade and over-armed it down the corridor, then crawled under the deck plating as riot guns roared.

Bet dropped the empty tube from her gun and slammed a new one home. She was mildly surprised that she wasn't as scared as she'd been watching the patrolmen come in. 'Ida!'

'Go,' the heavy woman said, without taking her eyes off the corridor. She squeezed the trigger.

'If I was with Delinqs,' Bet managed, 'I'd say the time has come to haul butt.'

'But you ain't. You're with a big-time Mantis Section team. So what we're gonna do is haul butt.'

Ida rolled out the door, finger locked on the trigger, then through the entrance to the labs. Bet slid after her. The two women turned, and sprayed down the corridor, then dashed toward the main lab.

Alex sang softly to himself as he unspooled the backup firing-circuit wire back toward the center of the lab.

'Ye'll set on his white hause-bane,
An I'll pike out his bonny blue een;
Wi' ae lock o' his gowden hair.
We'll theek our nest when it goes bare . . .'

Clipped the wire and fed it into the det box. Ran his firing circuitry through his mind, and glanced at Sten. Sten high-signed him, and Alex closed the det key.

'Ye ken we best be on our way. An hour an' yon labs'll be a mite loud for comfort.'

Then Ida and Bet doubled into the room. Ida crouched next to the door and sprayed down the corridor.

'The patrol,' Bet shouted. Slugs spattered through the lab doors, and the team members went flat, scuttling for cover. Ida emptied her magazine and scrambled toward the ship.

The team formed a semicircle perimeter just before the freighter. Sten ducked behind a large machine resembling a drill press as the first of Thoresen's troops burst into the lab.

'Can you stop the charges?' Sten shouted.

Alex cut down the patrolmen inside the lab, then said calmly, without turning his head, 'Ah may've outsmarted mesel' on this one, lad. Each an' every one a' those charges I fitted a antidefuse device to.'

'Sixty minutes?'

'We hae' – Alex checked his watch – 'nae more'n fifty-one, now.'

Tacships, darting in front of the Guard's assault transport, hammered through the drifting security satellites off Vulcan, not knowing that Bet's massacre of the Creche workers meant most of them were unmanned.

Monitors moved straight for Vulcan. Over the past months, Thoresen had acquired some moderately forbidden antimissile devices and installed them in blisters on Vulcan's outer skin. The combination of the Guard's sudden attack and the half-trained status of their crews, however, meant only a few went into action before the monitors' own missiles wiped the positions out.

Obviously the normal canister-dispersing assault transports couldn't be used. Conventional freighters had been laboriously modified for clamshell-nose loading and unloading. Proximity detectors clacked, braking rockets shuddered the transports down to a few kilometers per hour, then still slower as the pilots dived out of the control positions, sealing locks behind them as the transports crashed through Vulcan's outer skin, half burying themselves into the world.

The noses dumped away, and suited guardsmen spilled out. There was little resistance. None of the patrolmen inside had realized what could happen in time to suit up.

The Guard smoothly broke down into small, self-contained attack squads and moved out. Behind them moved their semiportable maser support units and, around the ships, combat engineers went into action, closing off the vents in the outer skin.

Resistance, compared to the Guard's usual opposition, was light. The Sociopatrolmen may have thought themselves elite thugs, but, as they discovered, there was a monstrous difference between larruping unarmed workers or crudely armed resistance fighters and facing skilled, combat-experienced guardsmen.

Mercenaries make rotten heroes, Thoresen decided as he watched the Sociopatrol officer wave his squad forward. About half of them huddled even closer behind the improvised barricades Thoresen had ordered set up just inside the lab's entrance. The other half reluctantly came to their feet and moved forward.

The Mantis troopers across the room opened fire. The fastest-moving patrolman made it three meters before legs exploded and he sprawled on the bodies of previous waves.

The accountant part of Thoresen's brain shuddered at the tab. They have five men – Thoresen hadn't seen Frick and Frack, sheltered high above him on a beam – we came in with almost seventy. They've taken no casualties, and we've lost *thirty* patrolmen?

The com at his belt buzzed. Thoresen lifted it. He listened, then hastily muted the speaker. Slowly going white as anger washed over him. Mostly at himself. He had assumed the Emperor wouldn't move in without some pretext, but the panicked communications center Tech had notified him that the guardsmen were already in. Including the rebels' sectors, almost a third of Vulcan was taken.

Thoresen slithered backward to the patrol officer. 'We'll need more men,' he said. 'I'll coordinate them from the security office.' The wall above his head exploded as he snaked his way out of the lab into the corridor.

He got up and ran down the corridor toward the end. Stopped and took the tiny red control unit from his pocket, touched the fingerprint-keyed lock, and opened the unit. He tapped .15 onto the screen and closed the circuit, then forced himself to calmness as he walked away from the Bravo Project labs. A gravsled waited for him. 'The Eye,' he ordered, and the sled lifted.

Behind him, under the floor of the lab's main controls, the timer started on Thoresen's own Doomsday Device – a limited-yield single megaton atomic device that would obliterate the entire project lab and give Thoresen his only chance at remaining alive.

Ida raked fire across the patrolmen's barricades and grunted.

'Alex. You realize that if we stay pinned down and your charges go off, I'll never take you drinking again.'

Alex wasn't paying attention. His eyes were locked on one of the instruments from his demopack. 'Sten. We hae worse problems tha' the charges Ah set. Ah hae signs a' some nuclear device's running.'

Sten blinked. 'But where? Who set it?'

'Ah dinnae. But best we find it. Mah name's Kilgour, nae Ground Zero.' He set the detector to directional, and swept its pickup around the room. 'Ah, tha's so fine. Yon bomb's right across there.' He waved across fifty meters of open space toward the central controls.

'Gie us some interestin' thoughts,' he said. 'Firs', we manage t'gae 'crost that open space wi'out gettin' dead. An' then Ah hae the sheer fun a' tryin' a' defuse it, wi'out knowin' when it's gonna go.'

'Mad minute!' Sten used the aeons-old shout, and the team opened fire, spraying rounds at the barricades.

Alex grabbed his pack and rolled to his feet. Running, zig-zag. Riot shells crashed around him.

'Over there!'

Jorgensen elbowed out of cover and sprayed the patrolman shooting at Alex. Exposed for only a moment, and the patrol officer fired. The riot round armed and exploded halfway across the lab, and barbed flechettes whined out.

Jorgensen's shoulder and arm were momentary pincushions, then the flechettes exploded. The Mantis troopers stopped shooting momentarily, but discipline took over, and they continued mad-minute fire. Sten watched Alex as he ripped the meter-wide floorplates up and slid down belowdeck.

'Our broodmate, almost. Yes he—' and Frick and Frack launched themselves from the dome. Frack armed one of her tiny wingbombs and folded her wings.

Plummeting in a vertical dive, she and Frick made no attempt to release. They died instantly as their tiny bodies slammed into the patrol officer. Then the bombs went off. The officer became a fireball, and shrapnel sliced through the squad crouched beside him.

Sten saw Doc crawl from his hiding place near Jorgensen's body and move toward the dead man's willygun. The small panda awkwardly turned the willygun toward the barricades, then staggered up with the crushing – to him – weight. One hand pulled the trigger back and held it until the magazine went empty. More shock. *Doc* really isn't . . .

Sten swept his sights over the barricade, and blew off the arm of a momentarily exposed patrolman. As the man reared up, screaming, Bet finished him.

Alex knelt beside the nuclear device under the floor-panels. Ah ken on'y hope, he thought, the amat'oors who built this lashup hae some respect f'r betters an gie some shieldin'. Ah c'd build a better A bomb then this be wi' a crushin' hangover an' mah teeth, he thought.

The bomb was an idiot-simple device. A metal ball covered with what resembled modeling clay. Small, directional blasting charges studded the surface, hooked to a radio pickup and what Alex assumed was a timer.

He started to yank the wires off, then squinted. There were extra wires he didn't see any purpose for. Booby traps, he decided.

Thin, he thought, we'll gae the hard way. And began gently lifting each blasting charge out of its slot. Ah wonder how many ae these Ah'll yank out afore this wee bomb blows? He wiped sweat away.

The driver pushed the sled wide open, and he and Thoresen ducked behind its shield. The sled flashed down the corridor, and the Mig resistance fighters ducked. They spun, and the few with riot weapons opened up.

Far too late as the sled banked around the corridor and out of sight.

Thoresen looked up. Ahead of him was the entrance to The Eye. He sighed in relief – it was still held by a detachment of Sociopatrolmen.

'Ah hae it! Ah hae it!'

Sten saw, out of the corner of his eye, Alex's rotund form bounce out of the below-floor space and bound across the open area. He dived and skidded across the last five meters into shelter. 'Yon wee beastie's safe'n mah gran,' he said.

'Leaving us only one problem.'

'Aye,' Alex said. 'Figurin' how we haul butt afore we're hoist wi' our own petard.'

At least fifteen patrolmen were stubbornly holding behind the barricades. 'I don't think,' Ida said, 'they'd be much interested in a mutual truce.'

'Correct,' Doc added gloomily. 'Prediction: since they've been cut up so badly, they'll assume we're bluffing.' He ran another few rounds through the willygun that Sten had wedged into position for him. 'Kilgour. You realize this is all your fault. Now I'll never be able to have my own practice.'

'Nae tha's an advantage Ah no considered,' Alex managed. 'Tae many bloodybones aroun' as 'tis.'

Bet shook her head in disbelief.

'Ida,' Sten said suddenly. 'Come on. Alex. We're going to try a superbluff. Flank 'em if they go for it.'

Ida rippled to her feet, and the two dodged out, toward the freighter's lock. Puzzled, Alex, Bet, and Doc opened up with covering fire.

Sten wedged the flare to the freighter's control room window, and shoved the portable com into his coveralls. 'You think they'll believe it?'

Ida lifted her hands helplessly. 'Rom don't believe in death songs. So we might as well go out trying.'

Sten checked his watch. Alex's charges had only ten minutes to go. He and Ida hurried to the lock and began firing at the patrolmen. Alex, momentarily unobserved, sidled out of the Mantis Section's improvised fort toward the patrolmen's flank.

The patrolman waited. Sooner or later, one of them would show himself. Sooner or later . . . he jerked as what looked to be an explosion flared across the lab in the freighter's control room. Wild shot, he guessed. Then the freighter's external speakers blossomed out of their compartments and crackled to life. A siren warbled up and down its range and a metallic voice announced: 'Two-minute blast warning, two-minute blast warning. All units clear blast area. Repeat, all units clear blast area . . .'

For the first time the patrolman realized the exhaust nozzles of the freighter were aimed almost directly at him. He didn't know what to do.

'Must've hit the computer,' the man beside him muttered.

'What happens if it fires?' the patrolman managed.

'We fry,' his companion said.

Sten coughed, then touched the transmit button on the portable com. Ida had linked it directly into the freighter's broadcast net. He tried to sound as much like a computer as possible.

'This is a thirty-second warning, thirty-second warning. Override. Thirty seconds from out-of-sequence computer lobe. All units, thirty-second correct transmission. Time to blast now fifteen seconds . . .'

The near-panicked patrolmen didn't see Alex break cover. Even if they had, assuming normal human reactions, they would not have had time to stop the high-gee trooper's charge.

Alex dived as he came over the barricade. The first patrolman he hit died with a crushed skull. Alex let the body cushion him while he rolled, feet lashing out, smashing through the stomach walls of two men.

He was on his feet, one-handed swinging the body of the second man like a meaty club.

Sten and Ida came up, offhanded aiming, firing. Sten gaped as Alex tore the head off another patrolman, then disappeared.

The two troopers ran for the barricades. Screams. Then silence, the two patrolmen broke, running for the exit. Alex jumped to the top of the barricade, picked up a three-meter-long steel work bench and hurled it like a spear.

It crunched into the two men, smashing their spines. Doc and Bet darted across the room. 'I would suggest,' the panda managed as he passed them, 'we avoid the usual imbecile human congratulations. We have four minutes.'

The four Mantis troopers and Bet sprinted down the corridor. Sten slammed the emergency panels as they went down the corridor. Hoping that would be enough.

The charges went just as Alex said they would. Sten, Bet, and Alex stared at the intestine-shaped lab through a port in the main passage. Ida held Doc. Light winked, winked, and again. They felt a low rumble through the plates under their feet. Then Bravo Project blew. The shaped charges blew out and down, ripping the floor and supply sections out of the lab like it was a fish being gutted.

'That's what The Row must've looked like,' Sten thought suddenly.

The rumble crescendoed, and emergency alarms clanged. Debris cascaded out the bottom of the lab into space. But the top section, the Tech's housing, was still intact.

Ida and Doc looked at Alex. 'Ah'm a wee bit disappointed,' he said, not meaning a word of it. 'I nae counted a' that sympathetic second blast. It whidny be hon'rable to say Ah done that.'

And then Bet noticed Sten was gone.

Chapter Thirty-Seven

It was done. All traces of Bravo Project eliminated in the explosion. For the first time in hours, Thoresen felt safe.

He poured himself a celebratory drink. Odd, he thought. His dream lay in shambles, but he still felt elated. He'd beaten the Emperor after all. All he had to do was wait for Guard officers to come through his door, thank them for rescuing him from the Migs, and put himself in their hands.

What could the Emperor do? Put him on trial? For what? There was no evidence. Besides,Thoresen thought, the Emperor would be reluctant to admit publicly that an alternative to his AM2 monopoly might exist.

Thoresen would probably have to accept a lesser position in the Company's leadership. He shrugged. It would take a few years, but he would be back up on top again. And then they'd see. They'd all see.

Suddenly, Thoresen realized he was quite mad. He laughed. What a strange thing to realize about yourself. It was like being another person on the outside, watching yourself, taking note of thoughts and actions. And examining them like a Tech observing a microbe. Something crawled at the back of his brain. Was Sten really dead? That explosion? It wasn't quite what he expected. Different, somehow. Thoresen found himself wishing Sten were alive. His fingers curled, imagining them crushing into the soft Mig throat. Sten, he thought. Sten. Come to me.

There was a sound behind him. Thoresen smiled to himself and turned.

Sten was a few meters away and padding softly toward him. A knife glittering in his hand.

'Thank you,' Thoresen said, 'for being so prompt.'

Sten hesitated. Puzzled.

'You know me?'

'Yes. Intimately. I killed your family.'

Sten was on him in a rush, knife hand blurring at his throat. Thoresen dodged, gasping slightly as the knife point touched a shoulder, leaving a trail of blood. He kicked sideways and felt a crawl of pleasure as he heard the dry snap of Sten's wrist breaking. The knife went flying and disappeared in the grass.

Sten ignored the pain, twisted to avoid a blow, and struck out with his good hand. Fingers clawing Thoresen's face. And Thoresen was backing away from him. Sten went into a crouch, anticipating a charge. Then he realized that the Baron wasn't coming at him. Behind him, a few meters away, was the arms collection. Thoresen was going for a gun.

Sten sprinted for the wall, hands closing on an ancient blunderbuss as Thoresen reached his choice – Sten realized it was a pirated willygun – and opened fire. Sten dove to the ground, whipped the shotgun up. Fired. The charge ripped into the overhead dome lighting. Darkness. And he was rolling over and over again as the AM_2 bullets stabbed through the darkness, searching for him.

He crawled behind a tree. Chunks of earth and wood exploded around him. Then silence. Sten listened. He heard a slight rustling as Thoresen moved in the darkness. Sten thought he was coming toward him. Gathered himself for a leap.

A click. A long rasp. And Thoresen opened the cages.

The tigers came out of the cage running. Two huge mutated gray Bengals. Growling softly. Lashing their tails. Thoresen punched a control button. A tingling in their collars, and they turned, then moved swiftly away from him.

Sten moved through the brush. Where was Thoresen? Why didn't he come? A rustling behind him. Soft padding. Sten whirled as the tiger charged. Bounding. Then a huge leap, straight at him.

He dropped backward, bringing his feet together and – straight up with all his strength. They connected, and the tiger went flying over him. Landing, convulsing. Tried to get up, then went down. Dead, its throat crushed by Sten's kick.

Sten came to his feet, fighting back the pain in his useless wrist. Sickness crawled in his stomach. Then. Over there! A sound. Thoresen, he was sure.

The dome lights came on. Sten was frozen for a moment, blinded by the glare. Then he dived for cover as the willygun opened up. He was behind another tree. How many shots? He hadn't heard

Thoresen reload. He had to be getting low on ammunition. Sten looked around wildly, searching for a weapon.

The tiger stood there, lashing its tail. Gathering itself for a leap. Then it screamed to freeze him in place.

Sten forced himself to laugh, a wild almost hysterical giggle.

'I got the other one, Thoresen,' he shouted.

The Baron opened up with the willygun. Catching the tiger just as it jumped for Sten. It turned end over end, and crashed to the ground, dead. Thoresen kept firing. And then there was a dry clacking sound as the gun was empty. Sten charged from the brush.

Thoresen saw him, searched desperately for another magazine. Nothing. He moved back quickly – grabbing for the first weapon he could find. The saber blade rasped as he pulled it off the wall and slashed.

Sten grunted in pain as the tip of the blade grated across ribs. He dodged the backhand stroke, grabbed for a weapon. Any weapon.

The rapier flashed up as Thoresen struck. A loud clang as the blades met. Sten twisted his wrist slightly, almost in reflex, and the saber slid off. He lunged forward, felt the tip hit the softness that was Thoresen, and then the blade was almost ripped away as Thoresen parried. Sten dropped back.

He flexed the thin foil. Trying to come up with the right hold. Then thought of a knife, loosened his grip. Thoresen took a step forward, smiling and whipping the saber blade back and forth.

Not a chance, Sten thought. The saber Thoresen held was too powerful and fully edged. Sten was fighting with just a slim piece of pointed steel. Flexible steel. Sten suddenly realized there might be an advantage. The flexibility. No matter how hard Thoresen struck, he could turn the blade away.

And Thoresen struck. The blades met. The rapier was like a snake as it twisted around the saber, using the force of the stroke to turn it away. And Sten lunged forward, felt his point find flesh, heard Thoresen moan as it slipped through.

Sten stepped back just as the saber ripped at him. Pause. Thoresen stood before him, panting and leaking blood from several wounds. But seemingly unfazed.

He charged forward, slashing hard. Sten tried to parry, but the blade foil slipped, and he felt the saber cut deep into his arm, then the limb twisted away, out of range.

Thoresen knew he had Sten now. The way the rapier point dropped, he was sure his last cut had made Sten's fighting arm useless. Like the other.

He stepped toward him, slashing down. Missing as Sten parried the blade, but still leaving an opening. And Thoresen began the back-handed swing that would decapitate Sten.

Screamed in agony as the rapier point speared into his elbow. The saber fell and Thoresen grabbed desperately, his fingers closing on steel. He ripped the foil away while feeling the flesh of his fingers turn to raw meat.

The Baron struck out with his good hand, the palm a knife edge, aiming for Sten's collarbone. He felt bone give and struck again. But Sten blocked the blow and fell back, one arm dangling. He was trying to keep his footing.

Thoresen threw another punch and Sten knew horrible agony as he caught the blow on his useless arm. He speared out hard, fingers like a blunt blade. Feeling Thoresen's ribs snap like dry wood. He stepped back quickly, to avoid a counterblow, but tripped to one knee. And Thoresen was on him, hand cracking down for Sten's neck.

Sten struck up with all his strength. Below the ribs. Bone giving again. Giving. Giving. Soft wetness.

Thoresen screamed in pain.

Sten ripped the heart from his chest.

For an awful frozen moment Thoresen stared at Sten. And then he was falling.

Sten looked numbly at the dripping heart in his fist. Then down at the Baron's body. He turned, and threw the fibrillating organ far into the brush, where the tigers lay.

Unexpectedly, he heard a shout and peered up. A shadowy figure was rushing toward him. He tried to strike out at it.

Bet caught him in her arms. Lowered him unconscious to the ground.

Chapter Thirty-Eight

The emperor's face was stone. Cold. Mahoney stood before him, frozen to attention.

'All traces of the AM_2 have been destroyed?'

'Yessir!'

'And Vulcan under a new government?'

'Yessir!'

'And Thoresen?'

'Uh . . . dead, sir.'

'I see. I thought I ordered him taken alive?'

'You did, sir!'

'Then why weren't my orders obeyed?'

'No excuse, sir.'

'No excuse? That's all you can say, no excuses?'

'None at all, sir.'

Mahoney loomed over Sten, who was trying his best to stand at attention. Very difficult when you are head-to-toe in a hospital L5 system.

'I just came from the Emperor.'

Sten waited.

'He had some rather loud comments to make. Specifically, trooper, the small matter of direct disobedience to orders. Imperial orders.'

Sten imagined that he did, took a mental deep breath and prepared for the worst. Execution, probably.

'Do you have anything to say for yourself, lieutenant?'

Sten did. But thought better of it. Why waste his breath? He was already a condemned man . . .

'I'm waiting, lieutenant.'

'Uh, begging your pardon, sir,' Sten croaked. 'But you just called me lieutenant.'

Mahoney laughed, then sat on the edge of the hospital bed. 'A direct commission from the Emperor himself, lad.' He reached into his tunic and pulled out a pair of small silver bars. And Sten's knife. He laid them on the bed.

Sten was sure he was either dreaming or Mahoney was mad, or both. 'But, I thought I, uh . . .'

'The boss man was happier than a piece of beef snuggled up to a hot cabbage,' Mahoney said. 'He'd had second thoughts about those orders. But there wasn't time to get to you.'

'He wanted Thoresen killed?'

'In the worst way. Saved a lot of explanations.'

'Yeah, but a commission,' Sten said. 'I'm not the officer type.'

'I couldn't agree more. But the Emperor thought otherwise. And a good trooper always obeys his commander. Ain't that so, lieutenant?'

Sten grinned. 'Almost always, anyway,' he said.

Mahoney got up to go.

'What about Bet?'

'Unless you got any objections,' Mahoney answered, 'she's joining your Mantis team.'

Sten had no objections at all.

The Eternal Emperor reverently dusted off the bottle, popped it open, then poured two healthy drinks. Mahoney picked up one. Looked at it suspiciously.

'Scotch again, boss?' he wanted to know.

'Yep. Except this time it's the real stuff.'

'Where from?'

'I ain't saying.'

Mahoney took a sip. Gagged.

'What the—?'

The Eternal Emperor beamed. Took a big slug. Rolled it around his mouth, savoring it.

'Just right,' he said.

Filled up his glass again.

'You took care of everything? On the Sten matter?'

'Just like you said, boss.'

The Emperor thought a minute.

'Let me know how he works out. I think that Sten is a boy to watch.'

'He sure is, boss. He sure is.'

Mahoney forced himself to finish his drink. And then held out his glass for more. In his job, you made sure you always kept the boss happy.

And the Eternal Emperor hated to drink alone.

STEN 2: THE WOLF WORLDS

Dedicated to
Kathryn and Karen
. . . for the usual godzilla reasons
and
The real *Alex Kilgour*
. . . 'Who Cares Who Wins . . .'

BOOK ONE

ABSENCE OF BLADE

Chapter One

The GQ sirens ululated through the Jannisar cruiser. The thunder of crashing boots died away. The ship's XO nodded in satisfaction as the STATIONS READY panel winked to green. He made a mental note to assign extra penance to one laggard ECM station, then spun in his chair to the captain. 'All stations manned, Sigfehr,' he reported.

The captain touched the relic that hung under his black tunic, then opened his intercom mike. 'Bow, ye of the Jann, as we make our prayer to Talamein.

'O Lord, ye who know all things, bless us as we are about to engage the unbeliever. We ask, as our right due, for your assistance in victory.

'S'be't.'

The chorus of 'S'be't' echoed through the ship. The captain switched to a double channel.

'Communications, you will monitor. Weapons, prepare launch sequence, LRM tubes two, four, six. Target onscreen. Commercial ship. Communications, establish contact with target ship. Weapons, we will launch on my command, after surrender of enemy ship. This is bridge, clear.'

The cruiser's prey appeared to be just another obsolescent *Register*-class mining survey ship wildcatting through the galaxy's outer limits.

Its oval hull was patched, resprayed, corroded, and even rusty from its very occasional atmospheric landings. Its long, spindly landing legs were curled under the ship's body, and the mining grab claws were curled just below the forward controls.

It resembled nothing so much as an elderly crab fleeing a hungry shark.

Actually, the ship was the IA *Cienfuegos*, an Imperial spy ship, its mission complete and now speeding for home.

Extract, Morning Report, 11 Saber Squadron, Mantis Section:

> The following detached this date, assigned temporary duty Imperial Auxiliary Ship *Cienfuegos* (x-file OP CAM-FAR):
> STEN, (NI), Lt. OC Mantis Section 13, weapons;
> KILGOUR, ALEX, Sgt., NCOIC, Demolitions;
> KALDERASH, IDA, Corporal, Pilot & Electronics;
> MORREL, BET, Superior Private, Beast Handler;
> *BLYRCHYNAUS*, Unranked, Anthropologist, Medic.
> Team detached with Indiv Gear, Units 45 & 46.
> NOTE: OP CAMFAR under dir O/C Mercury Corps, subsq. entries t/b cleared thru Col. Ian Mahoney, Commander Mercury Corps.

Sten stared approvingly at the nude woman strobe-illuminated by the hydroponic lights. He walked to the edge of the plot and gently picked his way past the two huge, black-and-white Siberian tigers.

One of them opened a sleepy eye, emitted a low growl of recognition. Sten ignored it, and it returned to licking its mate's throat.

Bet turned then frowned, seeing Sten. Sten's heart still thumped when he saw her. She was small, blonde, and muscles rippled under her smooth, tawny skin.

She hesitated, then waded through the waving plants to the edge of the plot and sat beside him. Sten was only slightly taller than Bet, with black hair and brooding black eyes. He was slender, but with the build of a trained acrobat.

'Thought you were asleep,' she said.

'Couldn't.'

Bet and Sten sat in silence for a moment – except for the purrs of Munin and Hugin, Bet's two big cats. Neither Bet nor Sten was particularly good at talking. Especially about . . .

'Thought maybe,' Sten tried haltingly, 'we should, well, try to figure out what's going on.'

'Going wrong, you mean,' Bet said softly.

'I guess that pretty well is it,' Sten said.

Bet considered. 'I'm not sure. We've been together quite awhile. Maybe it's that. Maybe it's this stupid operation. All we've done for a long time now is sit on this clottin' ship and play tech.'

'And snarl at each other,' Sten added.

'That, too.'

'Look,' Sten said, 'why don't we go back to my compartment? And . . .' His voice trailed off. Very romantic approach, his mind snapped at him.

Bet hesitated. Considering. Finally she shook her head. 'No,' she said. 'I think I want things left alone until we get back. Maybe – maybe when we're on R and R . . . maybe then we'll go back to being like we were.'

Sten sighed. Then nodded. Perhaps Bet was right. Maybe it was best—

And the intercom sang: 'If we aren't disturbing the young lovers, we seem to have a small problem in the control room.'

'Like what, Ida?' Sten asked.

The tigers were already up, ears erect, tails swimming gently.

'Like a clottin' great cruiser haulin' up on us from the rear.'

Bet and Sten were on their feet, running for the control room.

A relatively short man, about as wide as he was tall, scanned the display from the ship's *Janes* fiche and grunted. Alex was a heavy-worlder with steel-beam size bones and super-dense muscles. And his accent – Scots because of the original settlers of his homeworld – was as thick as his body.

'Naebody w'knae th' trawble Ah seen,' he half sung to himself as he glanced over the description of the ship that was pursuing them.

Sten leaned over his shoulder and read aloud: '619.532. ASSAULT/PATROL CRUISER. Former Imperial Cruiser *Turnmaa*, *Karjala* class. Dim: 190 meters by 34 . . . clottin' chubby ship . . . Crew under Imperial manning: 26 officers, 125 men . . .'

'Four of us, plus two tigers, against 151 troops,' Ida broke in. The Rom woman mused over the odds. She was as chubby as she was greedy. Ida had her fingers in every stock and futures market in the Empire. 'If anyone's taking bets, I'll give odds . . . against us.'

Sten ignored her and read on: 'Armament: six Goblin antiship launchers, storage thirty-six in reserve . . . Three Vydall intercept missile launchers, storage forty-five in reserve . . . four Lynx-output laser systems . . . usual in-atmosphere AA capability . . . single chain gun, single Bell-class assault laser, mounted unretractable turrets above A deck. Well-armed little bassid . . . Okay, now, speed . . .'

'Ah'm kepit my fingers linkit,' Alex murmured.

'Clot,' Sten said, 'they can outrun us, too.'

It was Ida's turn to grunt. 'Clottin' computer, all it tells us is that we're swingin' gently, gently in the wind. Any data on who those stinkin' bad guys are?'

Sten didn't bother to answer her. 'What's intercept time?' he snapped.

Ida blanked the *Janes* display and the screen relit: AT PRESENT SPEED, TURNMAA WILL BE WITHIN WEAPONS RANGE IN 2 SHIP SECONDS FOR GOBLIN LAUNCH CONTACT WILL BE MADE IN—

Bet cut the readout. 'Who cares? I don't think those clowns want to shake our hands.' She turned to Sten. 'Any ideas, Lieutenant?'

Ida's board buzzed. 'Oh-ho. They want to talk to us.' Her hand went to the com switch.

Sten stopped her. 'Stall them,' he said.

There was a reason for Sten's caution. The problem wasn't with the control room – the *Cienfuegos* was indeed an Imperial spy ship – but except for its hidden super-computer, a rather sophisticated electronic suite, and overpowered engines, it still was pretty much the rustbucket inside as it was on the outer skin.

The problem was its crew: Mantis section, the Empire's super-secret covert mission specialists. Mantis troopers were first given the standard one-year basic as Imperial Guardsmen then, assuming they had the proper nonmilitary, nonregimented, and ruthless outlook on life, seconded first to Mercury Corps (Imperial Military Intelligence) and then given the two-year-long Mantis training.

Clot the training, Sten thought while trying to come up with a battle plan that offered even a one-in-ten chance of survival. The problem was really the team's physical appearance: Munin and Hugin, two four-meter-long mutated black-and-white Siberian tigers. One chubby Scotsman. One fat woman wearing a gypsy dress. One pretty woman. And me, Sten thought. Sten, Lieutenant, commanding Mantis Team 13, suicide division.

Whoopie, he thought. Oh, well. Sten motioned to Doc while Ida fumbled with the com keys, making confused responses to the cruiser.

Doc waddled forward. The tendriled koala's real name was *BLYRCHYNAUS*, but since no one could pronounce his Altarian name, they called him Doc. The little anthro expert (and medic) held all human beings in absolute contempt. Though he was mostly considered a pain in the lower extreme, he had two indispensible talents: He could analyze culture from small scraps of evidence; and (as one of the Empire's most formidible carnivores) he had the ability to broadcast feelings of compassion and love for his adorable self and any companions.

'Any idea who they are?' Sten asked.

Doc sniffed. 'I have to *see* them,' he said.

Sten signaled Ida, who had taped a crude frame to the com pickup so that she would be the only creature visible on the ship.

'Once more onto the breach of contract,' she said and keyed ANSWER.

Three stern faces stared at her from the screen.

'G'head,' Ida yawned. 'This is *Hodell*, Survey Ship P21. Ca' Cervi on.'

'You will cut your drive instantly. This I order in the name of Talamein and the Jannisars.'

Out of sight of the Jann captain, Doc studied the man. Noting his uniform. Analyzing his speech patterns.

Ida gave the captain a puzzled look. 'Talamein? Talamein? Do I know him?'

The eyes of the two men beside the captain widened in horror at her blasphemy. The senior officer glared at Ida through the screen.

'You will bring your vessel to an immediate halt and prepare for boarding and arrest.

'By the authority of the Prophet, and Ingild, his emissary in present-time. You have entered proscribed space. Your ship will be seized, you and your crew conveyed to Cosaurus for trial and execution of sentence.'

'Y'sure got yourself a great justice system, Cap'n.' Ida rose from her chair, turned, and planted her bare, ample buttocks against the pickup. Then, modestly lowering her skirt, she turned back to the screen. She noted with pleasure she'd gotten a reaction from all three black uniforms this time.

'And if nonverbal communication ain't sufficient,' she said, 'I'd suggest you put your prophet in one hand and your drakh in the other and see which one fills up first.'

Without waiting for an answer, she broke contact.

'A wee bit d'rect, m'lass?' Alex inquired.

Ida just shrugged. Sten waited patiently for Doc's analysis.

The bear's antenna vibrated slightly. 'Not pirates or privateers – at least these beings do not so consider themselves. In any case authoritarian, which should be obvious even to these odiferous beasts of Bet's.'

Hugin understood enough of the language to know when he was being insulted. He growled, warningly. Doc's antenna moved again, and the growl turned into a purr. He tried to lick Doc's face. The bear pushed him away.

'I find interesting the assumption of absolute authority, which would suggest either a fuehrer state of longstanding or, more probably, one of a metaphysical nature.'

'You mean religious,' Sten said.

'A belief in anything beyond what one can consume or exploit. Metaphysics, religion, whatever.

'My personal theory would be what you call religious. Note the use of the phrase "In the name of Talamein" as a possible indicator.

'My estimation would be a military order, based on and supporting a dictatorial, puritanical religion. For the sake of argument, call this order the Jannisars.

'Note also that the officer has carefully positioned two aides to his either side. Neither seemed more than a bodyguard.

'Therefore, I would theorize that our Jannisars are not a majority in this . . . this Talamein empire, but an elite minority requiring protection.

'Also note the uniforms. Black. I have observed that in the human mind this indicates a desire for the observer to associate the person wearing that uniform with negativism – fear, terror, even death.

'Also, did any of you notice the lack of decoration on all three uniforms? Very uncharacteristic of the human norm, but an indicator that status is coupled with the immaterial – in other words, again, an indicator that we're dealing with metaphysical fanatics.'

Doc looked around, waiting for appaluse. He should have known better.

'Ah a'ready kenned they wa' n'better'n a lot'a Campbells,' Alex said. 'The wee skean dubhs th'had slung a' they belts. No fightin' knives a man wae carry. D'ble-edged. wi' flat handles. A blade like tha's used for naught but puttin' in a man from the rear.'

'Anything else, Doc?' Sten asked.

'The barrel that walks like a being said what I had left out,' Doc said.

Sten rubbed his chin, wishing, not for the hundredth time, that Mantis had been able to assign them a battle computer before the mission. Finally he looked up at everyone. 'The way I see it, we have to let them play the first card.'

Chapter Two

'On my command,' the Jannisar captain said harshly. 'Goblin tubes two, four, six, prepare to launch. Launch.'

Metal clanged as the three long-range missile tubes lifted above the cruiser's outer skin. Oxygen and solid fuel boiled from the tubes as the Goblins fired.

'We have a launch on missile six and missile two . . . launch on missile four . . . missile four, misfire.'

'Attempt reignition,' the captain said.

'Reignition attempted,' the weapons officer droned. 'Attempt unsuccessful. Missile failed to ignite. Primary ignition circuits defunct . . . secondary ignition circuits defunct, missile falled to self-arm.'

A Jannisar will never show emotion, the captain thought. He cut off the weapons room circuit, then looked at his executive officer. His expression was also blank. Malfunctions weren't, after all, that unexpected. By the time an Imperial warship was sold, it had generally seen a lot of combat. But still, the captain thought furiously, with the proper tools, what we Jannisar could do in the name of Talamein!

Then he refocused his attention on the missile tracking screen, as the two 5kt missiles homed on the fleeing *Cienfuegos*.

'Guess he told me,' Ida said 'They've launched missiles.'

'How long?' Sten asked.

'Impact in . . . eighty-three secouds. We've got a whole lifetime.'

'Not funny,' Sten managed as he dropped into a weapons seat and tugged on the helmet.

Into a gray half-world. Part of him 'saw' the ghost-images of the other soldiers in the control room. But suddenly he was the missile.

The weapons control system was, of course, no different from the feelies. The helmet's contact rested on the base of the skull and induced direct perception to the brain. The operator, using a standard joystick and remote throttle, kamikazied the missile directly to the target.

Sten 'saw' the port open before him . . . a froth of air expired . . . then the streaked blackness as his CM missile launched. He flipped another switch on the panel and launched 'himself' again. He kept the second antimissile-missile on a slave circuit, holding a path to his flank.

Sten dimly heard Bet, from another panel, snap, 'Gremlin flight nine launched . . . all ECM A-A-A operational . . . waiting for contact . . . waiting for contact.'

The Gremlins were small antimissiles that provided a false target signature identical to the *Cienfuegos*. Dead silence, waiting either for the Gremlins to divert and explode the Goblins or for Sten to close his own missiles into range.

Alex noticed that sweat had beaded on Ida's lip hair. Then blinked as salt droplets rolled down his forehead, into his eyes. He deliberately looked over at Doc, Hugin, and Munin.

The tigers were pacing back and forth, their tails lashing. Doc sat perfectly still on the tabletop.

'I have a diversion on missile one,' Bet called suddenly. 'The bassid's turnin' . . . come on, you. Come on . . . right on and . . .' She blanked her pickup as one Goblin, idiot sure its mission was accomplished, blew a meter-long diversionary missile into nothingness.

'Dummy,' Bet said triumphantly, pulling off her helmet.

Sten suddenly muttered obscenities, yanked stick and controls back: 'Stupid missile's got a misfiring engine . . . no way to get a track on it.'

The second Goblin arrowed straight into Sten's vision – and Sten desperately stabbed at the manual det switch.

The small nuclear head on his missile fireballed . . . but Sten had already switched 'himself' to the second countermissile, spun it on its own axis, and pushed full drive.

'You have a negative hit on that,' Ida said, keeping her voice calm.

Sten didn't answer. He was slowly overhauling the Jann missile. He closed in . . . and his helmet automatically switched him from radar to realtime visual.

Gotcha . . . gotcha . . . gotcha . . . he thought as the blackened drive tubes of the Goblin grew visible.

'Seven seconds till contact,' Ida said, wondering how her voice stayed level.

And Sten fired his missile.

Another atomic fireball.

'I still have a – nope, I don't. Radar echo. We got 'em all, Lieutenant, old buddy.'

Sten took off the helmet; he blinked around the control room. He'd stayed with his missile right until det point – and his mind insisted that the explosion had temporarily flare-blinded his eyes. Slowly the room went from negative to overexposed to normal.

Nobody applauded. They were, after all, professionals. The only comment was Alex's: 'An' noo y'ken whae a Scotsman wearit kilts. It's so he noo hae to change trews when aught like this happens.'

'Fine,' Sten said. 'First problem out of the way. With only two long-range launches, that's probably all they've got. Which means they'll close with us in . . .'

'Four hours,' Ida said.

'Four hours. Perfectly lovely. Find us a place to hide. Preferably some nice world about 6AU wide with one hundred per cent cloud cover.'

Ida swung the scope console down on its retracting arm and started scanning the space-globe around them.

'Here's the plan. Ida'll find some world where we can go to ground,' Sten said, in his best command voice. 'Maybe we'll be able to reach it before the bad guys catch up with us. We'll go in-atmosphere, set it down—'

'Set *this* clunk down in-atmosphere?' Ida asked.

'—then we'll sit on what hopefully is a tropic isle until they get tired of lurking and we can go home.'

'You call that a plan?'

'Doc, you got an alternative to sitting around up here and dying a lot'?' Sten asked.

The team got to work.

'The enemy ship has diverted course, Sigfehr,' the Jann XO said. 'Probability is they are plotting landfall on Bannang IV.'

Involuntarily the captain started, then composed himself. 'That ship cannot be from any world in Lupus Cluster.'

'Obviously not, sir.'

'That increases my interest. An out-cluster ship, with enough antimissile capability to deter even us. Obviously a ship with what must be considered a valuable cargo. What is our closing rate?'

'We will be within intercept missile range in three hours, sir.'

'And Bannang IV?'

'They could in-atmosphere at approximately the same time.'

The captain allowed himself a smile. 'Were I not interested in their cargo, it would be tempting to allow them to land on Bannang. It is true – Talamein will revenge his own.'

'Your orders, sir?'

'Unchanged. Continue the pursuit. And destroy them.'

'It ain't much of a world,' Ida said, 'but it's the best I can do.'

Sten eyed the screen, half-consciously read it aloud: 'Single solar system. Sun pretty much G-one yellow dwarf . . . five worlds . . . That's too close to the sun. Desert world . . . two methane giants.'

'Unknown IV looks like home,' Ida put in.

'Unknown IV it is. Let's see . . . about twelve thousand km on the polar axis. Spectograph – where the hell – okay: acceptable minims on atmosphere. Grav's a little lighter'n normal. Mostly land . . . acceptable bodies of water . . . single source of electronic emission.'

'So it's inhabited,' Bet said from the galley area.

'Which is where we won't put it down. Maybe they're related to these clowns on our tail. You're right, Ida. That's our new home.'

'*Maybe* it's our new home,' Doc said. 'Both screens, you will note, show about the same figure. We'll reach your Unknown Four just about the same time as the *Turnmaa*. The suspense should be most interesting.' He pulled a chunk of raw soyasteak from Munin's plate and swallowed it.

Sten itemized: ground packs, weapons, surface suits, survival gear, first-contact pouches . . . as ready as possible.

The computer clacked and spat out seven small cards. Each duplicated the data held in the *Cienfuegos'* computer – the data the spy ship had been dispatched to gather, an analysis of a mineral found on a world in the now-distant Eryx Cluster.

Sten wondered if he'd ever find out why the Emperor was so interested in the gray rock that sat on the mess table in front of him. His but to do, keep from dying, and not ask classified questions.

He distributed the cards to the team members and tucked one each into Hugin and Munin's neck pouches.

'Ah hae to admire a mon wi' organization,' Alex said. 'Noo a' wha Ah hae to worry aboot is splittin' yon sample. Ah gie it a whirl an hour ago.'

'And?' Sten asked curiously.

'Two iridium drills, two shipsteel crystals, an' one scratch in m' mum's heirloom diamond. It's hard, it is.'

Sten's hand dropped, fingers curled. From the sheath in his arm a crystal knife dropped into his hand. Sten had grown it on Vulcan while doing time in the deadly industrial Hellworld for labor sabotage.

Double-edged, with a skeleton grip, the knife had a single purpose. To kill. There was no guard, only grooves on the end of the haft. The knife was about 22cm long and only 2.5cm thick.

Its blade, however, was barely 15 molecules wide. Far sharper than any razor could be. Laid against a diamond, with no pressure, it would cut smoothly through.

Sten carefully held the ore sample in one hand and started cutting. He was somewhat surprised – the blade met some resistance.

'Aye,' Alex said. 'Ah nae ken whae we're doin' aie this. A substance ae tha' . . . it's price is beyond reckon.'

'Worst abortion anybody's ever seen,' Ida said proudly.

'Worse than that,' Doc added. 'Ugly. Misshapen. Improbable. It should work just fine.'

While the others in the team were readying themselves for landing, Doc and Ida had been building the decoy, three Gremlin antimissile missiles. The first was rebuilt to broadcast a radar echo like the *Cienfuegos*. The second was modified to provide an extremely eccentric evasion pattern, and the third was to provide diversionary launches, much as the *Cienfuegos* would under direct attack.

Finally the entire team stood around the three welded missiles, deep in the cargo hold of the ship.

'Pretty,' Sten said. 'But will it work?'

'Who the hell will ever find out?' Bet said. 'If it does, we're fine. If it doesn't . . .'

She turned and headed for the bridge. Hugin and Munin paced solemnly behind her.

'Closing contact,' the Jannisar XO reported.

The captain ignored him for a moment. He was running tactical moves through his brain – the enemy ship will (a) engage in combat . . . and be destroyed; (b) surrender . . . impossible; (c) launch a diversion and enter atmosphere.

Only possibility . . .

'ECM room,' he called up. 'Report readiness.'

The delay was long. 'Most units in readiness, Sigfehr. Interdiction system standing by, target/differ system plus/minus forty per cent, blocking at full standby.'

His screen broke: 32 MINUTES UNTIL INTERCEPT . . . 33 MINUTES UNTIL TARGET BREAKS ATMOSPHERE.

The crab *Cienfuegos* continued its so-far-successful scuttle.

Inside the control room, Mantis troopers were tightly strapped down – including the tigers who, isolated in their capsules, were somewhat less than happy about the state of the world. The battle was, from then on, in the hands of whatever gods still existed in the fortieth century.

Except for the tigers, all were clad in the phototrope camouflage gear of operational Mantis soldiers. They wore no badges, no indication of rank, just the black on their left collar tabs and the flat-black Mantis emblem on their right.

Three screens glowed dully – the proximity detector locked on the Jann cruiser, the main monitor on the upcoming world, whose atmosphere had already begun to show as a hazy glare, and Ida's central nav-screen.

Doc provided the needless and somewhat sadistic commentary: 'Sixteen minutes until atmosphere . . . 15 minutes until the *Turnmaa* is in firing range . . . 15 minutes/fourteen minutes . . . 14.90 minutes . . . 14.30 minutes; congratulations, Ida, you've picked up a lead.'

Alex broke in. The tubby three-gee-world Scotsman was lying on his accel couch. He'd insisted that if he were going to die, he was going to die in uniform. And the others agreed.

'It wae back ae Airt . . . ane, b'fore the Emp'ror, even. In those days, m'ancestors wae called Highlanders, aye.'

'Twelve minutes, even, and closing,' Ida announced flatly.

'Now, in th' elder days, tha' Brits wae enemies. E'en tha, we Scots ran th' Empire tha had, wi'out tha' known it.'

In spite of the tension, Sten got interested.

'Howinhell, Alex, can anybody run an empire without the boss knowing about it?'

'Ten minutes to atmosphere,' Doc said.

'Ah 'splain thae some other time, lad. So, one braw day, there's this reg'mint ae Brit guards, aw braw an' proud in their red uniforms an' muskits. An' th' walkin' along thro' this wee glen, wi' they band playin' an' drumits crashin' an singin' and carryin' on, an' all ae sudden, they hears this shout frae th'crags abouve 'em. "Ah'm Red Rory a' th' Glen!"

'An' th' Brit general 'e looks up th' crag, an' here's this braw enormous Highlander, wi' his kilt blowin' an' his bearskin o'er one shoulder an' aye this braw great claymore in his hand. 'E has this great flowit beard on him.

'An' yon giant, 'e shouts just again, "Ah'm Red Rory a' th' Glen! Send oop y'best pickit man."

'An' so the Brit gen'rl tums to his adj'tant an' says, "Adj'tant! Send up our best man. Ah wan' tha' mon's head!"'

'Hold on the story,' Ida cut in coldly. 'We're on launch.'

Dead silence in the control room . . . except for the increased panting of the lashed-down tigers.

Consider three objects, the target/goal, the pursurer, and the pursued. Seconds . . . now milliseconds in the light-year chase . . . as the *Cienfuegos* tries to hide in-atmosphere. Three factors in the equation. And then an unexpected fourth as the decoy-missile launches.

'Captain! I have a double target!'

'Hold course. Repeat, hold course. ECM room, do you have a selection?'

'Negative, captain. We have a negative . . . Talamein help us . . . all systems lost in ground-clutter.'

The captain closed the com circuit. Forced down the sailor oaths that rose unasked in his regimented memory. Substituted a prayer. 'May the spirit of Talamein – as seen in his only true prophet Ingild – be with us. All stations! Stand by for combat!'

The Jann cruiser suddenly looked more like a dolphin school as the Vydal close-range ship-to-ship missile stations fired. Fired, cut power, and looked around for a target.

VYDAL-OPERATOR INPUT. TARGET. NO TARGET. CLUTTER ECHO HAVE TARGET. TARGET TARGET DOUBLE TARGET DOUBLE LAUNCH. FIRST TARGET NONACTIVE FIRST TARGET POSSIBLE POWER. TARGET I HAVE A TARGET HOMING ALL SYSTEMS HOMING. ALL OTHER UNITS SLAVE TO HOMING. HOMING.

New, the Vydal-series missiles were not the brightest missiles the Empire ever built. After twenty years' hard service, several in the less-than-adequate maintenance the warriors of the Jann used, they were no longer even what they had once been.

Most of the Vydals obediently followed the tarted-up decoy launch as it blasted into deep space. But one, more determined, more bright or more iconoclastic than its brothers, speared flame from its drive tubes and homed on the *Cienfuegos*.

In the Jann cruiser, its operator cursed as he tried, without success, to divert the Vydal to its 'proper' target. But the lone missile detonated barely 1000 meters from the *Cienfuegos* as the ship began the first white-hot skip into the atmosphere of the unknown world.

Ida had been trying to bring the *Cienfuegos* – a vehicle with the glide characteristics of an oval brick – successfully in-atmosphere for a landing, but the one kt detonation of the Vydal put paid to the plan. The *Cienfuegos* flipped, turned, spun. No problem in deep space – down was only where the McLean generators defined it – but entering a world?

The explosion crushed the *Cienfuegos*' cargo holds and flipped the crablike ship a full 180 degrees. Top-to-bottom, of course, since disaster never comes as a solitary guest, just as the *Cienfuegos* finally hit solid atmosphere.

Doc was the only being who might have found the situation humorous as the craft spun wildly out of control, beyond the skewpath Ida had plotted, beyond even a conventional dive, beyond any kind of sanity.

But Doc was not chuckling. He was, after all, seconds from death.

As were Sten and the other members of Mantis.

The ship crackled out of the skies and plunged into the upper atmosphere. Sensors sniffed wildly for surface . . . any kind of molecular surface at all.

Figures danced and swirled across the ship's computer screen and Sten shouted strings of changing numbers at Ida. Her fingers flowed across the controls, tucking in the impedimenta of the mining ship, sliding out two stubby wings. She tensed, as she felt the beginnings of atmosphere. Brought the nose down gently . . . gently . . . The ship hit the first layer of air and spun wildly.

Ida slammed on the right thruster, a short violent flare, then off again. Hit the left. And slowly brought the ship back under control. Nose in again. Just right. Slicing deeper into the air a degree at a time. Then the ship settled out, behaving like a ship again.

Sten glanced around. Bet was pale in her seat but steady. Alex was flexing excess gees out of his muscles. And Doc had the fixed stare in his teddy-bear face that he got when he was plotting revenge on someone. Ida shot a grin over her shoulder.

'Now let's find a place to hide,' Sten said.

She just nodded and turned back to the controls.

Suddenly the jet stream hit them at twice the speed of sound. On the *Cienfuegos* girders bent and groaned. Cables snapped and whipped, sparking and hissing like electric snakes.

The massive air current tossed the *Cienfuegos* again, further out of control and driving it helplessly down toward the surface of the unknown planet.

Ida cursed and fought the control board, trying not to gray out. One viewscreen flashed a possible crashlanding site, then blanked out.

Ida jammed out everything the ship had that resembled brakes from the stubby emergency landing foil to the landing struts to the atmosphere sampling scoops.

The ship juddered and jolted as the little winglets bit into the atmosphere, and Ida punched the nose thrusters, momentarily pancaking the *Cienfuegos* into something resembling control.

A moment later the *Cienfuegos* topped the high walls of the huge volcanic crater Ida had targeted on and then was booming low over a vast lake, sonic blast hurling up waves.

Everything not fastened down hurtled forward as Ida reversed the Yukawa-drive main thrusters and went to emergency power.

A prox-detector screen advised Ida that the current landing projection would impact the *Cienfuegos* against a low clifflet rimming the lake's edge – something that Ida was quite aware of from the single remaining viewscreen.

Ida did the only thing she could and forced the *Cienfuegos* into a 10-degree nose-down attitude.

The ship plowed into the lake, slashing out a huge, watery canyon.

And Sten was back on Vulcan, running through the endless warrens after Bet, Oron, and the other Delinqs. The Sociopatrolmen were closing in on him and he shouted after his gang to turn and fight. Help him.

Something stung at him beyond dream-pain and Sten was clawing his way back up into bedlam. Every alarm on the ship was howling and blinking.

Doc was standing on Sten's chest, methodically larruping him across the face with his paws. Sten blinked, then wove up to a sitting position.

The other Mantis soldiers were scrambling around the room, in the careful frenzy that is normal Mantis-emergency.

Alex was lugging gear to the open port – wrong, Sten realized, it was a gaping tear in the ship's side – and hurling it out into bright sunlight. Bet had the tigers out of their capsules and was coaxing the moderately terrified beasts out of the ship. Ida was piling up anything electronic that was vaguely portable and self-powered.

Alex lumbered over to Sten and slung him over one shoulder. With another hand he grabbed Sten's combat harness and rolled through the tear in the *Cienfuegos*' side.

Alex dumped Sten on the pile of packs and went back for another load. Sten staggered to his feet and looked at the *Cienfuegos*. The ship was broken almost in half longitudinally, and various essentials like the winglets and landing struts had disappeared into the lake mud. The *Cienfuegos* would never fly again.

Sten battled to clear the fog from his brain, trying to conjure up a list of the supplies they'd need. He stumbled toward the rent in the ship.

'Wait. We should—'

But Alex ran out with more gear then spun Sten around turning him away. 'W' should be hurrin', lad. Tha wee bugger's aboot t'blow.'

Within seconds, the team was assembled, packs shouldered and stumbling up the low clifflet.

They had barely passed over its crest when, with a rumble that echoed around the vast crater walls, the *Cienfuegos* ceased to exist save as a handful of alloy shards.

Chapter Three

The egg-shaped crater they had crashlanded in was huge, almost seventy-five kilometers long. The lake itself filled about half of the area, even though it was obviously drying rapidly, from the 'big end' of the egg toward the 'point,' where Ida had glimpsed a break in the crater's walls.

The ship had cashed it in about ten kilometers from the gap, leaving the team with a nice hike to clear their still muddled brains.

By now they'd taken stock of their situation, which bore a close resemblance to dismal. They'd lost almost all their gear in the wreck, including emergency protective suits and breathing apparatus. They did have their standard ration/personal gear/water filtration packs that, rumor had it, no Mantis soldier would walk across the street without.

The arms situation was equally bleak. The only weapons they'd brought out were their small willyguns, a sufficiency of the AM_2 explosive tube magazines for those guns, and their combat knives.

No demo charges. No hand-launched missiles.

A slackit way f'r a mon, Alex mourned to himself. Ah dinnae ken Ah'd ever be Alex Selkirk.

'Does anyone have any plans?' Bet asked mildly as she pushed her way through a clump of reeds. 'How the clot are we gonna get off this world?'

'Plans could be a bit easier if Ida would tell us where she committed that landing.'

'Beats me,' the heavyset woman growled. 'If you recall. I didn't have much time for little things like navigation.'

'Regardless,' Bet put in. 'It's all your fault.'

'Why?'

'It always has to be somebody's fault,' Bet explained. 'Imperial Regulations.'

'An' who better'n the wee pilot?'

Alex should have kept his mouth shut. It had been a very long day for Ida, and she decided the joshing was no longer funny. She turned on Alex.

'I'd push your eyes out,' she said, 'except it'd only take one finger, you bibing tub of—'

And Sten stepped in before tempers could in fact heat up. 'Words. Just words. They don't cross klicks.'

'Leave them be,' Doc suggested. 'At the moment, a little spilled blood would cheer me enormously.'

Alex whistled suddenly. 'Willna y'have a lookit this!'

They'd broken out of the reeds and were crossing an open section of terrain. Here the ground had once been covered by fine, volcanic ash, which had hardened over eons into solid rock.

Alex was pointing at a cluster of enormous footprints, bedded deeply into the rock surface. Sten followed the prints with his eyes: they came out of what must've been the lake's edge, moved about twenty meters along it, then the being who had made them stopped for a moment – the prints were deeper there. Then they turned, hesitated as if the being had looked at something, then went on, disappearing gradually.

Sten stood in one of the humanlike prints and raised an eyebrow. It was at least twice as large as his own foot.

'I hope we don't meet his cousin,' he said fervently.

Ida turned her little computer on, measured the rock. She laughed and snapped it off again.

'You're safe,' she said. 'Those footprints are at least a million years old.'

Sighs of relief all around.

'I wonder who they were?' Bet asked.

'The People of the Lake, obviously,' Doc answered.

Alex gave him a suspicious look. 'An' how w'ye be knowit thae, y' horrible beastie?'

Doc shrugged his furry shoulders. 'What else would a being call itself if it lived on the shores of a lake this size?'

'Doc,' Ida said, 'if I were a gambling woman – which I am – I'd say you just outfoxed yourself. You couldn't possibly know something like that.'

Everybody chortled in agreement.

Doc trudged on without comment.

*

The spectacle from the top of the low rise was interesting enough, Sten admitted as he frantically scrabbled the willygun off his shoulder.

First was the slow descending of the crater walls as the crater opened out to flatlands and brush.

Second were the tiny thatched knots of huts scattered around the crater's opening – possibly two or three hundred of them, clustered in knots and hidden on tree cover.

But far more significant was the solid wall of warriors. Lined up, almost shoulder to shoulder, were hundreds of beings, each nearly three meters tall. Evidently Ida was wrong and the beings that'd left the mooseprints in the rock were still alive and quite healthy.

Also hostile.

They were huge, slender creatures, with straw-colored skin like the savannah around them. They wore bright-colored robes, caught at one shoulder with elaborately carved pins.

And each was armed with a spear that towered even higher than himself.

'What was that you said about being safe, Ida?'

'I haven't been calling them very well lately, have I?'

'What do we do?' Bet asked.

'I think somebody's coming to tell us.' Sten nodded in the direction of one warrior who was advancing up the hill.

Guns came up, level.

'Put 'em down,' Sten hissed. 'We don't want to look threatening.'

'Threatenit? Ah dinna ken who threatenit who, Ah must mention.'

The being stopped about ten meters away. Closer up, he was even more formidable. His height was accented by an impossibly long, narrow face, with flowing, feathery eyebrows and hair greased high into a tan helmet shape. He was carrying a bundle of what appeared to be weapons.

The group jumped involuntarily as he hurled the bundle toward them. It dropped in front of Sten.

'/Ari!cia! /Ari!cia!' the being shouted, pointing at a low grove of trees lining one side of the hill.

'What's he want, Doc?' Sten asked.

Doc shook his head.

'Except for the fact that he is speaking a heavy glottal-stop language, I haven't the faintest idea.'

'/Ari!cia!' the being shouted again.

Then he turned and strode back down the hill and disappeared into the trees.

'Projection,' Doc theorized. 'Given a primitive culture . . . warrior-herdsmen. No longer nomadic, their wars have most likely become raids and meetings of champions.'

'Oh.' Sten got it and walked forward. He knelt and took the weapons from their hide wrap. There was quite an assortment: one short spear; one atlatl, throwing-stick; one medium-size club; one long war spear; and one hand-shaped and polished curved chunk of hardwood. A throwing-club, Sten theorized, wondering about the open vee at one side.

'We have been challenged,' Doc continued. 'One of us is supposed to face him in that grove. If our champion loses, our lives shall all be forfeit.

'If we win, they will call us brothers and try to fill us with whatever mind-altering potion these primitives have been able to create.' Doc preened at his own instant synthesis.

'The question is,' he continued, 'which one of us heroes will enter that grove? I might suggest . . .'

Guard – and Mantis officers – are trained to lead from the front. By the time Doc had begun his suggestion, Sten had already shed his combat harness, picked up the weapons, and begun sprinting down the hill toward the grove.

His sprint became a dead hurtle as Sten hit the treeline at a run as behind him he heard the eerie ululating cheers of the warriors on the savannah outside.

Brush smashed up at Sten, and he flat-dove over a bush, twisted in midair, and hit the ground in a left-shoulder roll. Ground scraping, and then knees under him and *don't do that* as Sten did a fast bellyskid to his right.

The air hissed and a short spear did a stomach-high deathdance in a tree where he would have been.

Sten stayed down. Diaphragm breathing. His hands running over the weapons. Trying for some kind of familiarity. He remembered something from Mantis Section's thoroughly hateful primitive weapons instructor – if you have to even think about it, troop, you're dead.

Don't think. Automatic. Listen. See. A soft breeze, carrying the scent of unknown flowers, and a soft rustle. Dead ahead, Sten thought, sweeping his head from side to side, tracking the sound of the warrior moving away from him, deeper into the grove.

Sten was on his feet, the short spear notched into the atlatl.

Move forward. Deep shadows became masses of vines and ancient tree roots. Silence became the rustling of small animals and insect buzzings.

Half crouched, Sten moved after his challenger. Ah. A snapped twig. The warrior had waited at that spot.

Nothing else – and then the frantic buzz of an insect and a blur as Sten snapped back the throwing-stick, hurled, and dove away in one motion.

Sten almost felt his enemy's spear bury itself in the ground next to him. He heard a muffled yelp of pain – satisfaction, hit – and was on his feet again and plunging forward, the war club coming up to strike.

He smashed down at a tangle of brush. Nothing.

Wrong, and Sten spun behind a tree for cover.

Waiting.

If you will not come to me, he thought, and went flat, belly-crawling forward under that bush he'd clubbed. Not that far wrong – there was bruised vegetation, immense footprints in the soft soil, and a rusty smear of what he assumed was blood.

But from the amount, Sten was sure he'd done little damage. He scanned the area, looking for a sign. Grudgingly Sten had to admire his opponent. How could a creature that size disappear without a trace?

Up, and slowly moving deeper into the grove.

'/Ari!cia!'

It was a muffled shout.

'/Ari!cia,' it came again.

Sten had been listening to the shout for nearly fifteen minutes. And for at least five of those, he had been trying to figure out what to do.

He gently parted a few stems and peered out. The warrior was standing at one end of a large glade smack in the middle of the grove. A large, *well-tended* grove, where, Sten was sure, many beings had met and fought and died before. The warrior had dropped all of his weapons except for the huge, woodenlike war boomerang. He was brandishing it and yelling '/Ari!cia!' for Sten to come out to fight.

Sten had quietly circled the grove twice, trying to logic out the warrior's game. Obviously this trial by combat, or whatever it was, consisted of formalized rules: creepy-crawly through the grove and then if everyone survived that, another test in the glade. One on one, one weapon at a time. At the moment it looked like it meant they were supposed to stand out in the open and hurl boomerangs at each other.

Sten had several problems with this proposition. First off, although this was obviously a fight to the finish, he was sure that the being's many friends, relatives, and stray drinking acquaintances wouldn't be too pleased if Sten cut the warrior's head off. Sure, it was probably a great way to get invited to a drinking feast, but leaving alive afterward might be a problem. Second, there was the problem with the boomerang. Sten hefted it for the eighteenth time. He had thrown such things during primitive-weapons training, but they were all built for beings pretty much Sten's size, give or take a quarter meter or so. This weapon, on the other hand, was built for three-meter-high beings. Sten could barely pick it up, much less throw it in his enemy's general direction.

Sten ran his troubles through his mind a few more times. And kept on coming up with the same answer. He grunted and walked out onto the glade.

The warrior spotted him instantly and the shouting stopped. What could only be an enormous grin split his face. To Sten it looked like it might be a relieved grin, as if the warrior had been worried that Sten wouldn't be much of a contest.

The warrior went into a crouch, holding the boomerang edge-on in front of him. Sten, feeling like a damned fool, tried to copy the stance.

The attack came without warning. It was an explosion of motion, like a huge coiled steel cable whipping out. The throwing-club snicked out, knee-high across the grass, and Sten leaped upward, almost clawing the air to get higher. And then to his horror, he saw the boomerang slowmotion upward in a molten-edged glide. Sten was tumbling over in midjump . . . a numbing shock as something crashed into his arm and he thudded into the ground.

Sten rolled up to his feet spitting earth and grass. He checked to see where he had been hit, what was left him. and then he heard the hooting laughter of his opponent. At Sten's feet lay his own boomerang neatly splintered in two.

A slight bloom of anger as Sten realized that his enemy was laughing because Sten had nothing to throw back, as if that would have done any clotting good, and the weird duel was dead-even again.

The warrior snatched up his huge spear and came running at Sten like an enormous cat. Sten ignored his own war spear, curled his fingers, and felt the tingling response and then a coldness in his hand as the knife leaped into his waiting fingers.

He stalked across the grass, bracing for the leap and the slash as the warrior hurtled toward him. Just before the collision, the warrior spun his spear end over end and then suddenly . . . he wasn't there.

Instinctively Sten dropped flat and rolled. And in that instant of the roll, he saw the most incredible thing: the warrior had pole-vaulted over him. Sailing, sailing, like a giant heron, over Sten's body . . . hitting the ground . . . spinning and laughing back all in one motion.

Sten back-somersaulted. And again and again like some mad tumbler, leaping more than two meters with every turn.

Stop.

Forward somersault, dodging under the spear, slicing over and downward with his knife.

And the warrior was standing there, in an instant of helplessness, gaping at his half spear. Sten tackled him, trying to put all his weight into the fall, and he heard the warrior's breath woosh out, and then Sten was astride the warrior. Knees locked on each shoulder. His knife at his enemy's throat. A long hesitation.

'/Ari!cia!' Sten finally said, pressing knife against skin.

The warrior looked up at him. Panting. And then a long, slow, grin. '/Ari!cia,' he gasped. 'Clotting hell! You won!'

If the warrior had taken advantage of Sten's amazement, he could have killed him on the spot.

Chapter Four

'My friend, the gourd is with you.'

'Wanna 'nother drink?'

'Clot me! Am I not circumcised? Must I wail like a woman when the elder passes?'

'Gotcha. Ya wan' 'nother drink?'

Ida took a long draw off the gourd, burped, and passed the gourd to Acau/lay. It was a neat trick, since they were sitting across a fire from each other, about a meter and a half apart. But Acau/lay, Sten's former enemy, simply hiccuped, grabbed, and chugged.

Sten had to admire the being. When you are three meters high, you have a helluva drinker's reach, among other advantages. Speaking of reach, Sten plucked the jug from his new old buddy Acau/lay and took a deep swallow, passed it on, and bleared at the scene.

Prior to his present drunkeness, Sten had learned several things. To begin with, his hard-found friends were one of many tribes on this planet. They called themselves the Stra!bo. Which translated into The People of the Lake. Recalling Doc's mocking laughter over that discovery, Sten winced.

The postcombat celebration was being held in the Stra!bo tribal hall, which was a single chamber the size of a warehouse. The circular 'building' was made of an enormous bush. As near as Ida could tell, the bush was a single plant, thousands of years old. As generations passed, the outer edge of the bush had expanded to its present enormous size, while the inner area died back, leaving bare ground – one huge bald spot. The Stra!bo had only to put a thatched roof in place to provide themselves a feasting hall.

The place was crowded with partying Stra!bo. Males and females all getting drunk on their thin (but highly alcoholic) grain beer and telling lies about what great warriors they were.

Acau/lay thumped Sten in the ribs and passed him a big, foul-smelling pot. Sten took it, raised it to his lips, and smothered a gag. The pot was filled with a grayish-pink matter with large globules of stringy red floating and bubbling about.

'The drink of life,' Acau/lay said by way of encouragement.

Sten contemplated his own life and liver, then sipped. The smell and flavor hit him like a missile.

'Thanks,' Sten croaked to Acau/lay, and passed the pot to Doc, who looked at him with pleading in his eyes.

For a moment Sten almost sympathized. Then he remembered the mocking laughter and gave Doc a grin. 'Delicious,' he said.

Doc suppressed a shudder and drank. And a remarkable thing happened: For the first time since they'd met, Sten saw Doc beam. Beam without benefit of tragedy or gore. Doc took another gulp. Nem!i, the Stra!bo chieftain, almost had to rip the pot away to enjoy his own 'drink of life.'

'What is that stuff?' Sten whispered.

'Blood and milk,' Doc said with unseemly satisfaction. Then he smacked his lips.

'You're . . . smapsolute . . . I mean . . . absoluteshly . . . Clot it. You're right. It's delushhious.'

Doc burped and grabbed the pot back from his host, Nem!i. Guzzled the vile mixture down.

Sten was in awe. Doc was drunk. From the blood. Then he understood. As one of evolution's most perfect carnivores, Doc was in butcher's heaven. The blood was hitting him like 200-proof alcohol.

'Sm-watch schmiling at you . . . foul hu . . . hu . . . human?'

Doc glared at Sten and turned to Nem!i. Patted him on the knee with a tiny paw.

'Ya' know,' Doc said, 'you're not too . . . uh . . . bad . . . for a life-form. Now gimme that pot back.'

'Aye, and it must be a lone life y' be livint, lass. Herdin' thae bloody great coos, wi' nae boot the wind in y'r ear ae company.'

Alex placed a sympathetic hand on the tawny knee of Di!n, one of the Stra!bo women. She patted his hand back, her palm engulfing even one of Alex's huge meat hooks. She was thanking him for his understanding.

'What is a woman to do?' she asked. 'Hour after hour staring at the buttocks of beasts. Once in a doublemoon I get to practice my javelin throwing on a hungry Tsar-cat . . .'

She drank deeply. Wiped away a tear. She lowered her voice to a soft whisper.

'But I have dreams,' she said.

Alex smiled, moved closer.

'You promise you will not laugh if I tell you?'

Alex nodded a solemn promise. Fingers tracing the knee a little higher.

'I dream that somewhere, someplace, there is a strong and handsome enemy. An enemy just for me. Who will love me and I can love in the killing.'

She gave Alex a deep soulful look. Alex slowly pulled his hand away.

'Do you think,' she began, then: 'No. I could never ask. I am still an unblooded warrior. How could a man like you . . .'

Alex tried to be kind.

'Nae, lass, it cannae be. Ahm beit sorry, but we must be friends noo. Nae more.'

Di!n sighed a maidenly sigh of disappointment, belched, and passed the gourd back to Alex to drink.

'Fascinating,' Bet said. 'Fascinating.'

She politely covered a yawn. It wasn't just the beer, although beer had always made Bet sleepy. It was the beer plus her companion, Acau/lay.

The warrior Sten had defeated was the tribe's champion. And as champion, it was also his duty to be the Stra!bo historian. Just then he was giving Bet a thrust-by-parry account of the tribe's beginnings.

The history of Stra!bo was its wars. Normally there was nothing Bet liked better than war stories. But some time ago, the Stra!bo and the other tribes had realized that the millennia of slaughter had to stop. Still, there remained the problem of how young warriors could be blooded, to become adult men and women. Thus the creation of the highly formalized champion-against-champion combat.

The ritual, Bet guessed, had begun about two hundred thousand years ago. And Acau/lay knew the details of each combat. It was a strange kind of a Jacob begat whomever history.

'. . . And then in the year of the burning grass,' Acau/lay droned on, 'Mein!ers slew Cal/icut and there was a great feasting . . . In the following year, Ch!intu slew the Stra!bo champion, Shhun!te, and there was a great mourning . . .'

Bet glanced over at Sten for possible help, then cursed to herself. He was pointedly staying out of it, drunkenly babbling to the chief.

'. . . And in the year of the rains, the Trader's champion . . .'

Bet came wide awake.

'Traders?' she asked. 'What traders? And when?'

Acau/lay was delighted at her sudden display of interest. He had at one point begun to suspect his guest was bored, but on reflection dismissed the thought for the silliness it was.

'Just traders,' he said. 'Beings like you. It was – perhaps five hundred combats ago. Our champion defeated theirs. We exchanged many presents, and they left.

'Let me see now, I think their champion's name was—'

'Never mind that,' Bet broke in. 'Do the traders still come?'

'Of course,' Acau/lay said with some surprise. 'They come very regularly. Are we not friends? Do friends not wish to visit often and exchange gifts?"

'How often do they visit?'

'About every thirty days. In fact, they were here not long ago.'

Acau/lay took a slurp from the gourd. 'We thought you were their rivals.'

Bet jabbed Sten.

'These . . . traders,' Sten asked carefully. 'Different, you say.' He hiccuped. 'Are you sure they aren't just from another part of this world?'

'Could I, Nem!i, chief of all the Stra!bo' – he belched – 'become that confused?'

'Drinkin' this yak-pee,' Bet said, 'easily.' Acau/lay had already passed out beside her.

'Do herdsmen have gray rafts that float in the air instead of the water? Do herdsmen have their huts shaped like fish, that can also fly through the air?'

'Offworlders,' Sten said with satisfaction.

'And will you take us to these traders?' Bet asked. She sounded almost sober.

'For my new friends, who have been blooded by the rites of the Stra!bo . . . tomorrow or the next feast day I will send you, accompanied by my best warriors.'

'We thank you, chief,' Sten said, realizing he was starting to sound about as formally drunk as Nem!i.

'It is, I must say,' the old chief wheezed, 'a long and hard journey of some thirty risings and settings of the sun.'

'Nem!i, what're the hazards that . . .'

Bet stopped. Nem!i had sagged gently against Sten and started snoring. Sten and Bet looked at each other. Bet shrugged and picked up another gourd.

'Well,' Bet said, 'I guess we'll be able to get off this . . . charming world and not have to spend the rest of our days drinking blood and pushing calcium critters around. So shall we follow the example of the noble Nem!i?'

'Why not,' Sten said, and took the gourd. It seemed as good an idea as any other.

Chapter Five

Sten came awake to the glare of an evil, yellow sun that was hurling spears through the cracks of the hut. He moaned gently and shut his eyes.

His head felt like a thousand – no, two thousand – ungulates had hooved through his brain, then paused to graze and defecate on his tongue.

Someone stirred next to him.

'I think I'm gonna die,' he said, holding his eyes tightly shut.

'You are,' Ida answered.

'Shut up, Ida. I'm not kidding.'

'Neither am I. We're all gonna die.'

Sten came fully awake. Sat up and stared through bloody eyes at the rest of the group already up and glooming around the sleeping hut.

'For once,' Bet said, 'Ida isn't exaggerating. We've got some kind of bug. And it's gonna kill us in about . . .'

'Twenty days,' Ida said.

'Clot on that,' Alex said. 'At the moment Ah need a wee bit of the dog that gnawed the dirty Campbell if Ah'm gonna see the end of this day.'

Sten ignored this. 'Would you mind explaining what's going on?'

Ida flicked her hand scanner on Medic-probe and gave it to Sten. He peered at the tiny screen. And found another creature staring back at him with DNA hate in its single-glowing protein eye.

The Bug, as Bet had called it, was a rippling blue ribbon with the thinnest of green edges to mark the boundaries of its form. Spotted about its perimeter were tiny, bright red dots, like so many gun nests.

'What the clot is it?'

'Some kind of a mycoplasm,' Ida said. 'Note, it is a cell, but it has no cell walls. It's probably the oldest life-form in the Galaxy. It's mean, lean, and hungry. And we've been breathing in millions of them since we landed. Interesting that mycoplasms do occur in areas of volcanic activity.'

'I'm not interested in its lifestyle, Ida. What about our own?'

'Like I said, Sten, twenty days.'

'No prophylaxis?'

'None – except getting offworld.'

'Twenty days,' Bet mused. 'Which puts us ten days short of the traders' post.'

Sten rubbed his head, which was moving from the gong solo to the tympani section of the program, then looked back up at his equally gloomy friends.

'Fine news. Now what else can go wrong?'

And above them the air split open with a blinding shriek. The hut shook, and a cloud of insects from the thatched roof floated down about them.

Sten and the others ran outside, to see the Jann ship scuttling across the sky.

Alex turned to Sten, smiling oddly. 'Y'beit tha luckiest lad Ah'm knowit,' he said, then pointed up at the *Turnmaa* as it climbed, then banked back toward the Stra!bo village, braked, and settled for a landing.

'If die we mus', tha wee beastie'll hae to stan' in line.'

Chapter Six

'IN THE NAME OF TALAMEIN WE DEMAND THAT YOU DELIVER UP THE OFFWORLDERS.'

The Jannisar captain's voice boomed across the savannah, drowning out even the chants of a thousand warriors drawn up before his ship.

A forest of spears shook back in defiance.

'It's bloody foolishness,' Alex said.

Sten, Alex, and the others were hiding in a small grove of trees watching the confrontation.

Sten had to admire the Janns' efficiency. They were very well trained soldiers. The ship had landed. Before the dust of the ship's landing had a chance to settle, the Janns had swarmed out, dug in, sandbagged, and set up their squad automatic projectile weapons.

On the ship itself, the top-turret chain-gun moved back and forth, tracing the line of warriors.

It reminded Sten of the volcanic mycoplasm hunting in their veins. The mycoplasm with its hateful DNA swinging back and forth, waiting for the pounce.

'IN THE NAME OF TALAMEIN . . .'

'We can't let this happen,' Bet said, rising to her feet. The others – even Doc – rose with her. Sten started out of the trees first.

And then they heard Acau/lay's cry for combat.

'/ARI!CIA!'

'/ARI!CIA!'

Acau/lay stepped away from the crowd and stalked toward the ship. He was carrying the bundle of weapons – a gift for the enemy he would slay with love in the grove.

'/ARI!CIA!' He cried again. Coming to a stop in front of the waving turret of the chain-gun.

'S'BE'T,' the Jann captain's voice boomed back.

Acau/lay hurled the bundle of weapons down on the ground. Drew back, pointing at the grove of trees and urging the ritual combat.

'/ARI!CIA!'

'/ARI! . . .'

And the chain-gun boomed out. Cutting off Acau/lay's final cry to fight. The projectiles stitched across him, literally cutting him in half.

As one body, the warriors hurled themselves forward, and all the Jann guns opened up instantly, cutting and spewing fire. Before the Mantis team could move, a hundred Stra!bo were dying on the ground and the others were fleeing.

In a crazy moment, Bet remembered Acau/lay telling her of the Stra!bo pride. In their two-million-year history they had never broke and run.

The tear-runnels had dried, but still marked Nem!i's cheekbones. He and Alex lay below the crest of the low hill overlooking the Jann cruiser.

'If these men are beyond custom, then they are beyond the law,' the alien whispered.

'Y'ken right,' Alex said. 'Ae Ah said b'fore, they're naught better'n ae scum a' Campbells.'

Sten lay on the hilltop, binoc-lenses carefully shielded from reflection, staring down at the cruiser.

'If they do not have the law, then we cannot surrender our friends to them.' Nem!i continued his careful analysis. He was still deeply shocked by Acau/lay's murder. 'So this will mean . . .'

Sten clicked the binocs off and back-slithered down the hill beside them. He'd overheard the last of Nem!i's whisper.

'This will mean,' he interrupted flatly, 'that at night's fall we kill them. We kill them all.'

As the sun was occulted by the crater wall, an exterior speaker crackled:

'Evening stand-to. All bow. Talamein, we thank thee for thy recognition of our might. We thank thee for our strength as Jannisars and for proclaiming our duty on this world of unbelievers.'

There was no movement around the cruiser as the black-uniformed troops listened to the prayer, except the endless, automatic sweep of the chain-gun's turret atop the ship.

'We thank you in advance,' the captain's voice rasped on, 'for the boon which you will grant us on the morrow as our due for pursuing these unknown raiders. S'be't.'

The soldiers moved quietly into their nightwatch positions.

'Why did your Sten not pick one of us, one of the Stra!bo to begin the attack?' Di!n asked furiously.

Bet deliberately kept stroking Hugin, even though both tigers had been given their instructions and should have been on their way. Ida didn't volunteer, either.

'Because Sten respects your customs,' she finally improvised. She picked herself up and eyed the ranked formation of Stra!bo warriors, hidden deep in the battle grove.

'Knowing little of your laws, he felt that perhaps his methods – the methods of our team – might violate your customs.'

Di!n grunted in satisfaction. She returned to the endless stropping of her spearblade on the leather strap curled around her fingers.

Bet looked down at the tiger. 'Munin. Hugin. The cattle. Now.'

The tigers spun and bounced off into the gathering dusk, bounding deeper into the grassland that led out of the crater.

Ah, nae ye're bonnie wee boys, Alex thought, watching the five-man Jann patrol approach the clump of brush he was flattened in.

Ye hae not jus' the wee perimeter laddies, but rovin' patrols goin' to an' fro throughou' the night.

Aye, an' here they come. Point mon, all alert an' strikit . . . patrol leader . . . aye, two weapons mons, an' th' wee tailgate.

C'mon, laddies. Alex's waitin'.

The patrol crept through the now almost total blackness past his clump of brush. Kilgour shouldered out of his weapons harness. Waiting.

Eyes awa' fr'm 'em, he needlessly reminded himself. Dinna be lookin' . . . ah, they be passin'. Pass on, pass on horseman, his mind misquoted.

The patrol, moving at a well-trained slowstep, silently passed the clump.

And Alex came up and fell into step behind them.

Step an' step an' y'ken we're in rhythm . . . an' now comin' up behind yon laddie . . .

Alex's enormous fist, three-gee-world muscles bunched behind it, smashed into the back of the rearguard's neck. The Jann dropped without a sound. Alex caught him, eased him to the ground.

There was no sound. The patrol eased forward. and Alex continued his creep.

Nae, these twa'll be linked by th' weapons belt. A nit tricket if y'can solve it. His fist went flat at belt level, flashed forward, into the base of the fourth man's spine.

He contorted, back broken, and fell. Alex pivoted around the falling corpse and sideslammed one meaty paw into the base of the third man's neck. Then swore to himself as the loosely held squad weapon crashed to the ground from the dying man's shoulder.

The Jann noncom had time to whirl and start his weapon up, finger coming back on the trigger. Alex one-handed the weapon away, the barrel cracking, and his open palm went straight into the man's throat.

Gettin' a wee sloppy, m'boy. Cartilage crackle and a gurgle, his mind reprimanded as Alex flat-dove forward. Hit the ground in what looked like a curled bellyflop as the point man heard his noncom's deathrattle, came around, and Alex was rolling, his legs thrashing, and the man came crashing down, his weapon flying a meter away.

The pointman scrabbled for a knife, and Alex, now moving almost slowly, brought his knee up and then crashing down into the man's ribcage. He heard the dull sound of ribs crunching, and the Jann contorted and was dead.

Alex held, flat. Waiting. Nothing. Up on his hands and knees, and looked back down the path.

Y'mum'd be proud, lad. Five for five. Ah, well. Roll on demob.

And Alex went back down the path to wait for the attack to begin.

Nem!i had never seen so small a being run so fast. He and Doc had taken position about one kilometer outside the crater's mouth, deep in the grasslands. Between them and the craters, the Stra!bo cattle moved leisurely toward the corrals.

Doc was crashing through what was to him a jungle of grasslands, holding a heavy – again for him – bag of powder carefully to one side.

The ripped corner of the bag was trickling powder onto the ground. Doc looked up, saw that he was parallel with the crater's far wall, turned, and – still at a dead heat – dashed back toward the Stra!bo chief.

Came to a halt. The small bear and the tall chief looked soberly at each other.

'A being such as yourself deserves the highest respect,' Nem!i said soberly. 'To these eyes, you were an elder advisor to your youths. But now to find that you are yourself still a warrior, in spite of your advancing years. And that your body can still function, even though you are as fond as I of feasting – it is an amazing sight.'

Doc ground his sharp little teeth and wished that the Empire hadn't done such a good job of conditioning him out of killing people who thought well of him.

'I thank you, Nem!i,' he managed. 'Your pleasure can only be exceeded by mine, when I see you personally lead the charge against the black ship.'

Nem!i shook his head sadly. 'I am afraid not, my friend. Men of my age are fit only for the mopping up and to congratulate the young warriors after their success. I will not be able to seek battle this night.'

Doc swore six words Alex had taught him and touched the toggle switch.

And the powder caught, flashing high into the night. The tinder-dry grasslands roared into life, and, almost instantly, the two-kilometer arc of savannah outside the crater was a crescent-inferno, burning straight into the crater.

The cattle caught the scent of the flames and lowed nervously. Their amble became a trot. Behind them was wildfire – a prairie firestorm.

Burning brands flew high into the night, and the fire began over-leaping itself, almost burning itself out.

A blazing clump of bushes landed on one emasculate bellwether's back. He howled in dismay and broke into a gallop.

The panic spread, and the ground thundered as the herds of the Stra!bo stampeded directly toward the crater's mouth.

Hugin yowled nervously across the crater gap. Educated and mutated he may have been, but part of his tiger genes remembered what happened when large cats stood in the way of buffalo herds.

Munin coughed back, comfortingly. Then squatted and urinated. Hugin, too, followed orders.

The herd was just beginning to turn, unable to channel into the narrow crater pass, when the lead animals caught the scent of urine. What little ideas they had vanished in the acrid smoke and the scent of a hunting animal.

Hugin and Munin had not only channeled the stampede into the crater but almost doubled the stampede's drive forward.

Into the crater.

Directly toward the Jann cruiser.

The Jann com center was a confusion of gabble:

'Negative observation on firestart' . . . 'Alpha patrol, this is base. Alpha patrol, do you receive this station?' . . . 'In the name of Talamein, stop them!' . . . 'All stations . . . all stations to General Quarters' . . . and then a long, blood-chilling shriek from one speaker.

The shriek came from the lone Jann soldier on observation point as the charging cattle broke through the savannah and reached his position. He held the trigger back to full automatic on his projectile weapon, and three animals rolled and were swallowed up as the rest of the herd boiled over the Jann.

The cattle thundered on. Even though they had heard the rush of the charge, the men in the weapons pits outside the floodlit glare had little time. To a man, they died under the axe-sharp hooves of the herd.

The Jann cruiser was barely twenty meters ahead of them.

There was no way or time for them to turn.

Sten, crouched high in one tree in the grove closest to the cruiser, didn't even have time to finish his flashed-curio equation:

To calculate the changes in velocity of a body (the *Turnmaa*) when a certain force is applied (stampeding cattle), the formula is – clottin' hell!

That solid black wave of cattle hit the equally solid Jann cruiser . . . and the stampede kept on coming.

And like a wave, it crested higher as animal dove over dead animal into the cruiser.

Fifty meters away, Sten could hear the alarms roar inside the cruiser.

The huge ship tottered on its landing jacks . . . rocked . . . and one small phalanx of animals slammed into it.

The Jann cruiser rolled, jack supports bending and snapping, and crashed to the ground.

Sten could feel the smash, even over the rolling thunder of the stampede.

Which was . . . just below him.

And, of course, the animals broke neatly, dividing around the trees, and continued their panic run off into the blackness.

Sten dropped out of the tree and hurtled toward the cruiser, clambered over the dead and dying animals, just as the *Turnmaa* settled on one side. The weapons in the top turrets were parallel to the ground.

Sten's willygun came off his shoulder, and he scrabbled up the cruiser's side, feeling a fingernail tear and break away. The turret hummed into life, just as Sten shoved his willygun's muzzle into the shrouding around the chain-gun's barrels.

He yanked the trigger all the way back and held it.

The willygun contained 1400 rounds. Each 'bullet,' while barely 1mm in diameter, was made of Antimatter Two, the same substance used to drive starships. Each 'bullet' was in its individual Imperium shield, and laser-fired.

One round, on impact, would have about the same explosive force as a twentieth-century handgrenade.

It took twenty rounds to sledgehammer through the shrouding, into the turret's inside. And then:

Picture liquid dynamite exploding. Picture the heart of a fusion reactor, *sans* lethal radiation.

The picture of hell.

Sten let 500 rounds whisper and crash into the turret, then dove straight down, as the explosion boiled up, spraying the steel of the turret out the gun mounting.

Sten tuck-rolled in midair, then thunked down on a fairly convenient steer. He whirled as footsteps thudded up and:

'Ah tol' you there be naught ae useful like ae coo,' Alex said, helping him onto his feet.

And then the world turned into chaos as:

Di!n, Bet, and the Stra!bo warriors roared out of the darkness; Hugin and Munin, seemingly enjoying themselves immensely, loped out to join the Lake People's charge; Doc panted up, muttering unintelligibly, and . . .

Ida was standing beside them, her willygun spitting out measured bursts as Jann warriors tried to retake the turret, and:

'Ah'm Red Rory a' th' Coos,' Alex bellowed, and leaped straight up the cruiser's side. Caught hold of some ripped hull plate and dove into the hole where that turret had been.

Sten, somehow, was right beside him, and then they were inside.

Flashing moments of red gore:

Di!n, a fixed smile on her face, as she slowly spitted a Jann officer against a bulkhead;

The whistle of spears wailing down a long corridor into a knot of panicked Jann troops;

Alex ripping a compartment door off its dogs and spinning it into a squad weapon as its gunner tugged uselessly at a jammed tripod;

Ida calmly snapping shots as a platoon of Jann, assembled in one hold, maneuvered forward;

Bet, on the back of a not particularly pleased Hugin, Munin soaring ahead of her, smashing down three Jann.

And then silence.

The red fog faded, and Sten looked around.

They were in the ship's control room. Bodies were scattered across the room, and blood seemed to trickle everywhere.

On one side, a handful of Stra!bo warriors, spears ready. The cats. The Mantis troopers. Sten.

And, his back to the semicircular main control panel, the Jann captain.

In full uniform.

'Talamein spoke against us,' the captain said. 'We have not found favor in his eyes.'

Sten didn't answer, just walked toward him.

'You are the leader of this rabble?' the captain asked.

He took Sten's silence for assent.

'Then it is only right and fitting,' the captain said, slowly drawing the saber at his side. 'I shall fight a warrior worthy of my stature.'

Sten considered. Suddenly Di!n was beside him, pressing a spear into his hand. She nodded – yes. You.

Sten hefted the spear, then dropped it, and, in one motion, lifted his willygun and fired twice.

The rounds caught the captain in the head, splattering his skull back across the twin view panels.

Sten turned away, holstering the gun. Nem!i was looking shocked, and then his expression cleared. He smiled.

'Ah,' he said gently. 'For Acau/lay. You do understand our culture.'

'Is it gonna lift, Ida?' Bet asked, slightly worried.

'Of course it is,' the Rom woman snorted. 'So we've got half the ship sealed against leaks, we're taking off with no landing gear, there's a bad fuel leak, and I haven't had a bath in a week.'

'No problem for a lass like you,' Alex agreed.

Her thunder somewhat stolen, Ida snorted and hit keys. Maneuver drive belched, hiccuped, snorted, and the *Turnmaa*'s nose lifted.

'Now, as long as I can keep this computer from realizing what I'm doing . . .'

And she slammed both drive pots full forward.

Somehow both Yukawa drive units caught at once, and the *Turnmaa* clawed its way upward, searing the ground as the ship lifted for space.

Below it, only a handful of the Stra!bo were watching. They'd buried their dead, held their feast, and life went on.

Di!n, at the head of her phalanx, watched the *Turnmaa* flame upward and out of sight, silently thinking her own thoughts for many minutes after the last wisps of exhaust floated away and became indistinguishable from the clouds.

BOOK TWO

GARDE

Chapter Seven

The man in the river appeared to be in his mid-thirties. His long fishing rod was bent in an almost complete half-circle and the near-invisible line sang out from the reel almost to the growling rapids a few dozen meters upriver.

The man was muttering a steady stream of curses, half under his breath – curses and almost-prayers.

'Run on me again like that, y'clottin' guppy, and I'll turn you loose. Come on, salmon. Come on back down. Come on.'

Suddenly the salmon broke water, a silver arc flashing in the gray spring sunlight, and came downriver.

The curses doubled as the man touched the wind button on his reel, one thumb held on the reel itself to prevent overwinding.

The meter-long fish torpedoed directly at the fisherman, and he stepped hastily back, swayed as his rib-booted foot slipped on a rock and he almost went under.

Then the salmon was past him and running again.

He flipped the reel switch and now let line run out, braking with an already seared thumb on the line.

Mahoney cut the power on the combat car and it dropped gently to the moss-covered ground. He stepped out of the wind-screened sledge and eyed the grove of soaring redwoods with extreme skepticism. Perfectly safe, the logical side of his mind said. The other side, the side that had kept him alive on half a thousand primitive worlds, insisted there be ghosties and ghoulies and four-pawed critters with appetites inside.

As usual, he listened to that part of his mind and fished a combat harness from the back of the seat, slid the shoulderstraps on, and buckled the belt. On it hung a mini-willygun, a grenade pouch, and his combat knife.

'So if I'm wrong I'll feel like a clottin' fool,' he subvocalized, and grabbed the small daypack from the floor of the car.

Looking cautiously about him, he paced very deliberately forward into the trees.

And, quite suddenly, standing in front of him was a small, bow-legged, muscular man wearing the mottled brown uniform of a guardsman and a rakishly-tilted bellman's cap with a chinstrap. The soldier's willygun was slung across his back.

Held in his right hand, at a forty-five-degree port-arms, was a fourteen-inch-long knife that looked like a machete, but its blade flared to double its size at the tip. The soldier's left hand held, almost caressingly, the back of the knife.

'Lieutenant-Colonel Ian Mahoney. Mercury Corps. On His Imperial Majesty's service,' Mahoney said, being very careful not to move, trying to remember when and why he'd had himself hypno-conditioned to speak Gurkhali.

The soldier was perfectly motionless. Very cautiously Mahoney extended his right hand, palm down.

The guard took his left hand from the knife and unclipped his remote sender. Half-stepped forward and ran the computer's pickup over the back of Mahoney's wrist.

The computer read the implant and fed it back to the guard company's watch-computer. A beat, and then one light glowed green.

The Gurkha stepped back and brought his kukri to the salute. Mahoney returned it and walked deeper into the woods.

He was very, very glad there hadn't been a glitch – he'd once been permitted to attend the praetorian unit's birthday and seen one soldier, no taller than the meter-and-a-half trooper who'd challenged Mahoney, lop a bullock's head off with one stroke, using the long ceremonial knife.

He half grinned, remembering the drunk that had followed the religious ceremonies and the blessing of the unit's weapons. Tradition. How long, he wondered, had the short mountain men from Earth's Nepal served as soldiers? Perhaps, he thought, longer than even the Eternal Emperor.

And then the roar of the river was loud in his ears, and he stepped through the scrub bush and stood looking down the sloping bank at the fisherman.

It was quite a sight. The man had the rod held high and horsed back. The salmon writhed in the rolling water around the man's knees.

'Ah, if I had one more hand . . . get in here, you clottin' fish.'

The problem, Mahoney decided, was that the fish wouldn't fit the landing net the fisherman held in his other hand. The fisherman turned the chill air a little bluer, dropped the net to dangle from its waist-strap, pulled from his back pocket something Mahoney thought was remarkably like a sap, and smacked the fish.

The salmon convulsed and went limp.

'That's all you needed,' the fisherman said with satisfaction. 'A priest to administer the last rights.'

He swung the creel from his back, opened the top, and started to stuff the overlength fish into it.

'Nice to see a man happy at his work,' Mahoney said dryly.

The fisherman froze, then turned and eyed Mahoney with a very cold eye.

'Is that any way to speak to me?'

Mahoney ceremoniously doffed his beret and knelt. 'You are of course correct. Accept my most humble apologies, and allow me simultaneously to apologize for disturbing your vacation and to greet His Imperial Majesty, the Eternal Emperor, Lord of Half the Universe and All Its Worshipful People, including that half-dead aquatic in your purse.'

The Eternal Emperor snorted and began wading toward the bank.

'I have always appreciated,' Mahoney went on, 'serving a man who, in spite of his position, appreciates the simple pleasures of life.'

The Emperor stopped dead in the calf-deep water.

'Simple, you clottin' idiot? Do you know what this clottin' salmon cost me? Three hundred years, you oaf. First I must convince Earth's government that granting me a small vacation spot would in no way interfere with their local half-wit ancestral policies.'

He clambered out of the river and began walking toward the campsite.

'Next I purchase from the province of Oregon the whole clottin' Umpqua River. Then I purchase the towns up and down the river and relocate each and every yahoo to the world of his choice with a proper pension.

'Then I spend several million credits cleaning up the pollution and programming these clottin' fish to swim up it to lay their clottin' eggs.

'Nah. Do not give me a simple.'

Mahoney followed the Emperor, smiling to himself. It was obvious the Emperor was having an excellent vacation. He hoped he'd be as happy once he finished Sten's report.

It was quite a campsite. A low, staked-down vee-tent almost into the bushes. A half-decayed log had been muscled up to a flat boulder. Stones had been piled nearby to form a three-sided fireplace.

Other than that, there were no signs that the Emperor had been camping in this spot for more than fifty years.

In the fireplace was tinder under a teepee-shaped collection of wood that went from twigs to some fairly sizable logs. The Eternal Emperor walked out of the brush, whistling softly. He was deftly bending a green sapling into a snowshoe-shaped grill. As he passed the fireplace he took out a disposable firestick, fired it, and pitched it at the wood. It roared into a four-foot pillar of flame.

'See that, Colonel? Good firebuilding. Woodsy lore and about half a gallon of petroleum. Now we wait for the fire to burn down, and I clean this here monster.'

Mahoney watched curiously as the Emperor took out a small knife and deftly cut the fish from below its gills to venthole. He carried the fish guts into the brush, then walked over to the riverbank to wash the now degutted salmon.

'Why don't you have one of the Gurkhas do that, sir?' Mahoney wondered.

'You'll never make a fisherman, Colonel, if you ask that question.' Almost without a beat: 'Well?'

'The rumors were right,' Mahoney said, suddenly sober.

'Drakh!' the Emperor swore as his hands, seemingly moving with their own will, slit the salmon down its back and split it neatly into two halves.

'The samples the Mantis team procured from the Eryx Cluster match, according to preliminary analysis, all the capabilities of Imperium-X.'

'You can ruin a man's first vacation in ten years, you know, Colonel.'

'It's worse. Not only is this X-mineral able to replace Imperium-X for shielding purposes, but it evidently occurs in close to a free state. Of the four worlds surveyed by my team, this X-mineral is present on at least three of them.'

'I hear the sounds of a gold rush,' the Emperor muttered. 'And I'm starting to feel like John Sutter.'

'Pardon, sir?'

'Never mind. More of the history you refuse to learn.'

'Yessir. You want the capper?'

'Go ahead. By the way . . . did you bring a bottle?'

Mahoney nodded glumly. He fished a bottle of what the Emperor had synthesized and dubbed scotch from the pack and set it on the boulder between them.

'Too good,' the Emperor said. 'We'll start on mine.'

He walked to his tent and came back with a glassine jar full of a mildly brownish liquid. Mahoney looked at it suspiciously. One of the problems of being the Emperor's head of Secret Intelligence – Mercury Corps – and his confidant/aide/assassin was being subjected to the Imperial tastes for the primitive. Remembering a concoction called 'chili,' he shuddered.

'They called this 'shine,' the Emperor explained. 'Triple-distilled, which was easy. Run through the radiator of something those hillpeople called a fifty-three Chevy, which I never bothered finding out about. Then aged in a carbonized barrel for at least a day or so. Try it. It's an experience.'

Mahoney lifted the jar. He figured the less the taste, the better off he'd be, and poured a straight gurgle down his throat.

He realized he'd never noticed that the river was a nova and that he seemed to be standing in the middle of the fireplace. But somehow he didn't drop the jar. Eyes watering, seeing double, he still managed to pass it to the Emperor.

'I see you're wearing a gun,' the Emperor said sympathetically 'Would you mind holding it on me while I have a drink?' Mahoney was still gasping as the Emperor chugged a moderate portion.

'Continue, Colonel, with your report. You are planning to stay for dinner, aren't you?'

Mahoney nodded. The Emperor smiled – he *did* hate to eat alone, and his Gurkha bodyguards prefened their far simpler diet of rice, dhal, and soyasteak.

'I ran a computer project, sir,' he went on. 'We can supress the existence of this X-mineral for perhaps two, possibly three E-years maximum. And at that time every footloose wanderer and entrepreneur in the Galaxy will start for the Eryx Region to make his fortune.'

'As I said, a gold rush,' the Emperor murmured. He was busy dressing the fish. He'd picked a handful of berries from a bush on the outskirts of the clearing and a small clump of leaves from each of the two bushes nearby.

'Juniper berries – they grow wild here; two local spices, basil and thyme, that I planted twenty years ago,' he explained. He rubbed berry juices on both sides of the split salmon, then crushed the leaves and did the same.

Mahoney continued with his report. 'Per your orders, sir, I

instructed my Mantis team to take the most direct way back from the Eryx regions toward Prime World.'

'Of course – that'll be the route all my eager miners'll follow if word gets out.'

'The plot led through the Lupus Cluster,' Mahoney said.

'What the hell is that?'

'A few hundred suns, planets . . . mostly inhabited . . . back of beyond.'

'Inhabited by whom, might I ask?' the Emperor said.

'My team's ship got jumped by one of your majesty's ex-cruisers. The *Turnmaa*.'

'Are they all right?' the Emperor asked tersely. All pretense of casualness was gone.

'They're fine. The cruiser starting shooting, my team put down on some primitive world. The *Turnmaa* came after them. So they took the ship. Two hundred dead black-uniformed crewmen later, they came home in the *Turnmaa*.'

'Hostile group of boys and girls you breed over there in Mantis,' the Emperor said, relaxing. 'Any idea why these baddies jumped my ship? It was supposed to look like a tramp miner, wasn't it?'

'They started out by screaming "In the Name of Talamein,"' Mahoney said, as usual preferring the indirect explanation.

The Emperor slumped down on the log. 'The Talamein! I thought I put a stake through their heart ten generations ago!'

No psychohistorian has ever been able to explain why, throughout human history, waves of false messiahs come and go. Never one at a time. Witness, for example, the dozens of saviors, from 20 B.C. until A.D. 60, who gave the Romans a rough road to go.

A similar wave had swept the Galaxy some four hundred years previously. Since the Emperor knew that a culture must be allowed religious freedom, he could do little until a particular messiah would decide he was the Entity's final fruition and declare a jihad. Until then, all the Emperor could do was try to keep the peace and endure.

There was much to endure.

Such as the Messiah of Endymion VI, who decided that all women on the planet were his sole property and all the men were unnecessary. The first item of interest is that the entire male population, believers all plus or minus a few quickly sworded atheists, suicided. Even more interesting is that the Messiah was impotent.

There was an entire solar system that believed, like the early Christian Manichees, that all matter, including themselves, was evil and to be destroyed. The Emperor never learned how they managed to blackmarket a planetbuster nor how they managed to launch it into their sun, producing both a solar flare and a sudden end to the movement.

A dozen or so messiahs preached genocide against their immediate neighbors, but were easily handled by the Guard once they off-planeted.

The messiah of one movement took a fairly conventional monotheism system, added engineering jargon, and converted several planetary systems. The Emperor had worried about that one a bit – until the messiah absconded to one of the Imperial play-worlds with the movement's treasury.

One messiah decided Nirvana was a long ways off, so his world purchased several of the old monster liners, linked them together, and headed for Nirvana. Since their plot showed Nirvana to be somewhere around the edge of the universe, the Emperor quit worrying about them, too.

And then there was the faith of Talamein. Founded in reaction to a theology in decay, a young warrior named Talamein preached purity, dedication of life to the Entity's purpose, and putting to the sword anyone who chose not to believe as he did.

The old religion and the new were at gunspoint when the Emperor stepped in. He offered the Talameins and their Prophet enough transport to find themselves a system of their own. Overjoyed, the warrior faith had accepted, boarded ships, and disappeared from mortal man's consciousness.

The Emperor was fairly proud of his 'humanitarian' decision. He had interceded not because he particularly cared who would win the civil war but because he knew that (a) the old, worn-out theocracy would be destroyed, (b) the people of Talamein would have themselves close to a full cluster as a powerbase, and (c) that faith would inevitably explode out into the Galaxy.

The last thing the Eternal Emperor needed, he knew, was a young, virile religion that would ultimately find the Emperor and his mercantile Empire unnecessary. The result would be intragalactic war and the inevitable destruction of both sides.

Not only did the Emperor defuse the situation, but he also guaranteed that if the faith of Talamein survived, he would always be thought of as Being on Their Side.

All this the Emperor remembered. But, being a polite man, he listened to Mahoney's historical briefing.

*

'More fish, Colonel?'

Mahoney burn-cured a slight case of the hiccups with a shot from their second jar then shook his head.

After the birchwood fire'd burned down to coals, the Emperor had put the salmon on the sapling grill. He'd left it for a few minutes, then quickly splashed corn liquor on the skinside and skillfully flipped the slabs of fish over. The fire flared and charred the skin, and then the Ernperor had extracted the fish. Mahoney couldn't remember when he'd eaten anything better.

'So the people of Talamein ended up in this – this Lupus Cluster,' the Emperor said.

He smiled to himself, remembering that when he had picked out the system for the young fanatics, a court wag had translated it 'The Wolf Worlds.' How appropriate, he thought, thinking of the attack on his Mantis team.

'Then, following them, it seems as if every renegade, degenerate, and bandit warlord in their sector headed for the Lupus Cluster and sanctuary because they, of course, were True Believers in the Faith of Talamein all along.'

'Tell me more,' the Emperor said. 'I'm morbidly fascinated on how much worse things can be.'

Things were, indeed, much worse.

About 150 years before, the Faith of Talamein itself had split, conveniently ending with the Talamein A people on one side of the roughly double-crescent-shaped cluster, the Talamein B fanatics on the other.

Talamein A had the 'True Prophet,' the man who claimed the most direct descent from Talamein himself. But this 'original' faith deteriorated into opulence, schismatic politics and a succession of less-than-prescient Prophets. This not only split the faithful, but the real power came to rest with a merchant council.

The council was made up of most of the baronial trading families, who were more than willing to provide leadership in the confusion. Each family, of course, secretly felt that the council was only temporary, until it managed to seize full power for itself.

So this 'True Prophet' of Talamein A was indeed a figurehead, but was also the only thing keeping one crescent of the Lupus Cluster from absolute anarchy.

On the other side were the 'renegades' of Talamein B, who had vowed a return to the purity of their original warrior faith. Purists need proctors, so the 'False' Prophet of Talamein B had created a ruling class of warrior-priests. Black-uniformed, they publicly eschewed worldly goods though their bleak fortresses were known to 'store' many 'for the common good.' Such were the Jannisars. The Jann had needed barely one generation to become the rulers of the people of Talamein B.

'So on one side,' the Emperor said, 'we have these merchant princes. The top man is . . .'

'A rogue named Parral. He currently heads the council.'

'His Prophet is?'

'Theodomir. When he was young he massacred a few lots of disbelievers then settled down to his real interests, which seem to be bribes, antiquarian art, and the martyrs of the faith. Sanctus – the homeworld and the capital – is sometimes called the City of Tombs.'

'Who's the Jannisars' Prophet?'

'A killer named Ingild. Among other things, my agents report, he's addicted to narcotics.'

The Emperor put both hands to his temples and rubbed slowly, thinking.

'Our analysis—'

'Enough, Colonel Mahoney,' and suddenly the Eternal Emperor was cold sober and his voice shifted into the metallic command tone.

'Here is your analysis,' he said. 'First, there is no way to mine this X-mineral without the word getting out. Second, when word *does* seep out, all those rich-miners-to-be will move straight through the Lupus Cluster. Third, either the merchants will turn privateer or the Jann will become bandits. Fourth, there will be a monstrous slaughter of those rushing to the gold fields. Open the scotch, Colonel.'

Mahoney passed the Emperor thc bottle.

'Fifth, the bloodbath will force me to send in the Guard – to keep the spaceways open and all that drivel. Sixth, it will be interpreted as the Eternal Emperor's violating his most sacred word and supressing a religion. Here, have a drink.

'Sixth – no, I did that. Seventh, before word of this discovery gets out, the entire Lupus Cluster must be under the control of one entity. By the way, does Theodomir the Vacillating have much longer to go?'

'He's probably got another one hundred years under him, boss,' Mahoney said. 'His main heir's named Mathias. About thirty years old. Thinks religion and politics don't mix. Unmarried. Lives a pure life. Thinks the faith of Talamein is sacred.'

'Uh-oh,' the Emperor murmured.

'Nope. He thinks the faith of Talamein is for the vastnesses – he did say that, 'cause I can't pronounce that word – and so he's got a small troop of young men. They spend their time in manly sports, hunting animals, fasting, retreats, and so forth.'

'Mmm.' The Emperor was deep in thought again.

'What's the problem, boss?'

'I can't remember whether I was on seven or eight.'

'Eight. I think. Can I have the bottle?'

'Royalty has its privileges,' the Eternal Emperor said, swallowing twice before he handed the jug to Mahoney.

'Eighth, we want the cluster controlled by one entity, but one that's . . . amenable to reason. Which means he'll listen to me without my having to send in the Guard. Nine, these Jannisars are impossible. No way am I going to be able to keep a bunch of thug priests under control.'

'Uh, you're saying you want ol' Theo to come out on top?'

'Not at all. I want somebody on his side to come out winners.'

'Anybody in particular?'

The Emperor shrugged. 'Hell if I care. You pick a winner, Colonel.'

Mahoney felt himself sobering up. 'Obviously this is to be a deniable operation?'

'Brilliant, Colonel. Of course I don't want the hand of the Emperor to be seen meddling in a cluster's private politics.'

Mahoney chose to ignore the sarcasm. 'That means Mantis.'

'By the way,' the Emperor said, neatly plucking the bottle from between Mahoney's feet. 'That team that took the samples?'

'Yessir. Team Thirteen. Lieutenant Sten commanding.'

'Sten?'

'He's handled some difficult assignments for us in the past, sir.'

'Give him a couple of medals, or something,' the Emperor said.

'Or something,' Mahoney said.

'Any decision, Colonel?' the Emperor asked. 'Before we get thoroughly drunk – which Mantis unit do you intend to use?'

Mahoney took the bottle back and drained it. Oddly, when he was drinking or angry, he spoke with the faint whisper of what used to be called a brogue. 'Could I be troublin' you for some of your 'shine, Emperor? And in answerin' your question, indeed, I think I have just the lad in mind.'

Chapter Eight

It took a while for Sten to hunt down the rest of his team members to let them know he was being detached. They'd scattered across the Guard's Intoxication and Intercourse world as completely as they could.

Bet, true to their agreement, had gone her own way – picking up a hunting guide and disappearing into the outback with Hugin and Munin. Sten had given her the message briefly, over a com in Mantis voice-code, then gotten clear. He wasn't sure he was that sophisticated yet.

Ida had been easy; she'd been comfortably ensconced in a casino, trying to see if her beat-the-game system would bankrupt the casino before the officials threw her out.

Doc had disappeared into the wilds of the recworld's only university and was finally located growling contentedly at anthropology fiches in the media center. Before him was a flask of Stra!bo blood-milk drink that he'd conned a slightly revolted Guard tech to put together for him.

Detached service wasn't unusual for Mantis soldiers. But this was the first time it had happened to Team 13 and to Sten. But the Emperor orders, and man can but obey.

Sten was feeling a little homesick-in-advance and he was puzzled about how one man could accomplish what Mahoney had ordered. Meanwhile he was scouring bibshops. He knew he would find Kilgour in one of them.

He heard Alex before he saw him, as the voice boomed out the screen opening of the shop. 'So the adj'tant sae "Sah," an' dispatchit thae best Brit sol'jer, who fixit his bay'nit . . .'

'What's a clottin' bayonet?' another voice asked.

'Y'dinnae need to know. Jus' keepit silent an' list'n. So this braw Brit sol'jer goes chargint opp yon hill. An' in a wee second, his head come bumpit, bumpit, bumpit back down.

'An' then yon giant skreekit e'em louder, "Ah'm Red Rory ae th' Glen! Send opp your best squad!"

'Ah the Brit gen'ral, who's turnit purple, sae, "Adj'tant! Ah wan' that mon's head! Send opp y'best squad." An' th' adj'tant sae "Sah!" an' opp go thae regiment's best fightin' squad.'

And Sten, wondering if he'd ever hear the end of the Red Rory saga, walked into the bar.

Alex saw him, read the expression, and grunted to the two totally swacked guardsmen who were pinned against the wall by the table. 'Ah gie y' a wee bit more ed'cation some other time. Be on wi' ye, lads.'

He pulled back the table, and, relieved, the two guardsmen stumbled away. Sten slid into an empty chair.

'Gie me th' worst, lad. An kin handl't.'

And Sten repeated Mahoney's briefing, the anti-tap pak on his belt turned up to high.

'Ah wae wrong! Ah noo can handl't,' Alex moaned. He was even too depressed to order more quill.

'Whae m'mither sae i' she findit out Ah been cashier't frae th' Guard?'

'It's just a cover, dammit. Your mother'll never hear.'

'Y'dinnae ken m'mither.' Alex groaned. 'Ah whae y'be't, lad, if Ah'm a busted-out Guards RSM?'

'Obvious. I would like you to meet ex-Captain Sten, Third Guards, decorated, wounded, mentioned in dispatches, and cashiered for committing nameless atrocities.'

Alex groaned again, brought a paw out in what Sten thought would be mock-salute, and turned into a grab for Sten's mug.

'Ah knewit, Ah should'a stayed Laird Kilgour.' He sighed.

Chapter Nine

According to church dogma, Talamein had ordered his fleet of émigrés to set down on Sanctus because a vision told him that the water-world was particularly blessed by the spirit of the cosmos.

Actually, Talamein had diverted for the first E-normal world that swam onto the scopes since he was faced with near-mutiny and his people were developing a moderate case of the cobblies.

Sanctus had one major city – the City of Tombs – a few minor fishing villages, one minor port, and hundreds of villages. Its population was composed of those in the theocracy, those who exploited the pilgrims to the World of Talamein, and peasants – fisherfolk or farmers.

And Sten.

He shifted uncomfortably on the stone bench and massaged the stiff place in his neck. A cold breath of air needled his spine. The Prophet's guardsman eyed Sten just as coldly as the breeze caressing his spine. Sten grinned at him and the guard turned away.

He had been sitting on that bench for three hours, but patience was a virtue learned quickly on Sanctus. Especially in the City of Tombs, with its drab bureaucratic priests, massive monuments to the long-dead, and ghostly cold spots.

Not exactly soft duty, Mahoney, Sten thought, looking around the ancient anteroom in pure boredom. Like everything else in the City of Tombs, it was constructed of yellowing stone that had once been white. The chamber was enormous, decorated here and there with chiseled faces, gilded statuary, and elaborate tapestries.

And the room was thick with the scent of incense.

But like everything else on Sanctus, everything in the room was worn and threadbare. The tapestry had been torn and then mended, the gilded figures chipped.

Even the guard, with his ceremonial halberd and unceremonial projectile weapon, was threadbare, his uniform far from clean and patched many times.

Sten, on the other hand, wore the brown undress of the Guards division, his chest hung with the decorations he and Mahoney had decided were appropriate. Conspicuously absent was a Guards Division patch on the sleeve – but there was a dark patch where it might have been ripped off following a court-martial. He stood out in the poverty that was Sanctus.

Money was the number-one problem on the World of Talamein, far more important than the state of a being's soul. Bribery, Sten had learned, was a surer path to salvation than prayer.

Fortunately, Mahoney had supplied Sten with more than enough credits. He had already been a week on Sanctus, humbly seeking an audience with Theodomir the Prophet, but it had taken awhile to grease his way up the chain of command.

A helluva way to run a religion, Sten thought.

He had paid a last big bribe the day before to purchase a bishop. So far the bishop had kept his promises.

Sten had been ushered through the streets of the 'awesome' City of Tombs, with its vast monuments and towering chimney-like torches. A few of the torches spouted huge columns of flame. They were turned on, like fiery praywheels, when the families of the very rich made their offerings for the recently departed.

To Sten, the city looked like a huge valley of factories in mourning.

Sten eased himself down the bench another half meter to escape the cold. Besides the tawdriness of the place, the cold spots were one of the first things Sten noticed. They seemed to be scattered all through the long hallways and chambers, rising strangely from seemingly solid stone. Careful, Sten warned himself, or pretty soon you'll start seeing Talamein ghosts.

He heard a *click click click* in the distance and looked up just as the guard snapped to attention. The clicking footsteps stopped for a moment, and then a huge door boomed open. And Sten rose to greet the man his bribe had bought.

'Welcome. Welcome to Sanctus.'

And Mathias, son of the Prophet, strode over to greet Sten.

Even though Sten had studied his fiche, Mathias' appearance was a surprise. In a world of fishbelly-pale ascetics, the tall young man had the ruddy look of an outdoorsman. He wore an unadorned red uniform that smacked more of the military than the priesthood.

And, more interestingly, he greeted Sten with the palm-out gesture of equal meeting equal.

Sten hesitated, then muttered the proper greetings, trying to get a measure of the young man, as he found himself taken by the arm and escorted down a long, dark hallway.

'My father is most anxious to meet you,' Mathias said. 'We have heard much of you.'

Of me and my money, Sten thought a little cynically.

'Why did you not approach us straightaway? The Faith of Talamein is most ready to accommodate a man of your . . . abilities.'

Sten mumbled an excuse about wanting to look around Mathias' delightful city.

'Still. You should have come direct to the palace. To me. I have been hoping to meet a man such as yourself.'

It occurred to Sten that Mathias meant what he was saying and, possibly, knew nothing about how one bribed one's way into the Presence.

'I hope my father and yourself reach an – an understanding,' Mathias said.

'As do I.'

'Perhaps . . . if such is the case . . . you will find time to meet some of my Companions. My friends.'

'That would be interesting,' Sten said. Prayer meetings! The things a man must do to kick over a dictatorship.

Mathias suddenly smiled, warmly, humanly. 'I suspect you are thinking my friends sit around by the hour and drone from the Book of Talamein?'

Sten looked away.

'We are familiar with the words of the Prophet. But we find our faith is . . . best realized . . . away from the cities. Trying to teach ourselves the skills that Talamein used to find freedom. Nothing professional, of course. But perhaps you might offer us some pointers.'

He stopped as they stopped at the end of the corridor, and the double doors thundered open.

And Sten found himself standing in what could only be described as a throne room. Threadbare, for sure, but a throne room just the same. Here the tapestries were much thicker and (originally) richer. And it was crammed with statuary. And at the far end, nestled in thick pillows on a huge stone chair, was Theodomir, the Prophet. Behind him was a huge vidmap of the water-world that was Sanctus. With the single island continent that was the Talamein Holy of

Holies. A large ruby glow lit the location of the City of Tombs. The picture was framed by two immense torches – the cleansing symbol of the religion.

Suddenly Sten realized Mathias was no longer standing beside him. He glanced downward. The young man was on his knees, his head bowed in supplication.

'Theodomir,' he intoned. 'Your son greets you in the name of Talamein.'

Sten hesitated, wondering if he should kneel, then settled for a courteous half bow.

'Who is that with you, Mathias?'

The Prophet's voice was thin and rasped like sawgrass.

Mathias was instantly on his feet and urging Sten forward 'Colonel Sten, father. The man we have been speaking of.'

Sten blinked at the sudden promotion, then stepped toward the throne, all parade-ground military. He clicked his heels and semi-relaxed into a parade-rest stance.

'A poor soldier greets you, Theodomir,' Sten intoned smoothly. 'And he brings a humble soldier's gift.'

There were gasps around the room, and Theodomir went pale as Sten's hand went in his tunic and came out with a knife. Out of the corner of an eye he saw a guard start forward, and Sten laughed to himself, as he very carefully and very ceremoniously laid the knife at the Prophet's feet.

The knife was very valuable and very useless. It was made of precious metals and inlaid with gleaming stones. Sten glanced at Theodomir's frayed robe and wondered how quickly the Prophet would put the gift up for sale. If the fiche was correct and Theodomir's tastes were as earthly as it indicated, Sten figured it would take about an hour.

Theodomir recovered and motioned for a cupbearer to hand him a chalice of wine. He took a long, unholy gulp and then burst into laughter.

'Oh, that's very good. Very good. Slipped it past security, did you? Through the scanners and skin search.'

The laughter stopped abruptly. The Prophet turned a yellow eye at an aide cowering nearby. 'Have a word with security,' he said softly.

The aide bowed and scurried off.

The Prophet took another gulp of wine, then began chortling again. He turned his head to a curtain beside him and toasted the shadowy recess.

'Well, Parral. What do you think? Can we make use of our clever Colonel Sten?'

The curtain parted and a small, thin, dark-faced man stepped out. He gave Theodomir a slight bow and then turned to Sten, smiling.

'Yes,' Parral said. 'I think we should have a little chat.'

They sat in a small, dusty library. The chairs were cracked and ancient, but quite comfortable, and the walls were lined with vidbooks. Sten couldn't help but notice that the dust lay thick on the religious works and reference texts. A few well-worn erotic titles caught his eye.

Mathias refilled their cups with wine – all except his own. The Prophet's son preferred water.

'Yes, we are indeed quite fortunate to find a man of your talents, Colonel Sten,' Parral said smoothly. He took a small sip of his wine.

'But I can't help but think we might be too fortunate. By that I mean you appear, shall we say, overqualified for our remote cluster. Why is a man with talents in the Lupus Cluster?'

'Simple,' Sten said, 'like all things military. After I, ah, resigned from the Guard . . .'

'Ah. Perhaps cashiered would be a better word?'

'Don't be rude, Parral,' Mathias snapped. 'From what we've heard of the colonel's background, the Empire appears to hold in low esteem a soldier who fights to win. The details of his leaving Imperial Service are immaterial to us.'

'I apologize, Colonel,' Parral said. 'Continue, please.'

'No apologies necessary. We are, after all, both businessmen.' Sten raised the glass to his lips, catching the startled looks around the room. 'You are in the business of trading. I am in the business – and I mean business – of fighting.'

'But what about loyalties? Don't soldiers fight for causes?' Theodomir asked.

'My loyalties are to the men who hire me. And once the contract is signed, as a businessman, I must keep my word.'

He gave Parral a conspiratorial merchant-to-merchant look. 'If I didn't, who would ever buy what I sell again?'

Parral laughed. A cold bark. He leaned across the table. 'And what exactly do you have to sell, Colonel?'

'To you, a vastly expanded business empire. The first trading monopoly in the Lupus Cluster.'

Sten turned to Theodomir. 'To you, a church that is whole again.'

After a moment, Theodomir smiled. 'That would accomplish my grandest wish,' he said dreamily.

Parral remained unconvinced. 'And where is your army, Colonel?'

'Within reach.'

'To topple Ingild – and to destroy the Jann – would require an enormous force.'

'You have beautiful forests on Sanctus,' Sten replied obliquely. 'I imagine with very tall trees. Trees that die, but still stand. How much force does the woodsman need to exert to topple that tree?

'Where my force excels,' Sten said, 'is knowing, just as the woodsman knows, where and how to exert the proper force.'

'To destroy Ingild,' Theodomir whispered. 'All those worlds would be mine again. That's quite a lot.' He turned to Parral. 'Don't you think so, Parral? Don't you think that's quite a lot indeed?'

To Theodomir's delight, Parral nodded his agreement.

'Since you come so well, ah, provisioned,' Parral said dryly, 'I assume you have a budget describing the costs of your operation?'

Sten took the fiche from his inside tunic and passed it to the merchant.

'Thank you, Colonel. Now, if you'll excuse us, the Prophet and I shall discuss your terms.'

Sten stood up.

'Although,' Parral said quickly, 'I'm sure we'll have no difficulty meeting them.'

'I will show you to your rooms,' Mathias offered. 'I assume you will be willing to move into the palace?'

Sten smiled his thanks, bowed to Theodomir, and followed Mathias. The door had hardly closed before Theodomir poured down the rest of his wine and started worriedly pacing the room. 'What do you think, Parral? What do you really think? Can we trust him?'

Parral shrugged and refilled the Prophet's glass. 'It really doesn't matter,' he said. 'As long as we watch our backs.'

'Oh, I'd love to see it,' Theodomir said. 'I'd love to see that idol-worshipper Ingild chased down and crushed – Do you really think we can do it? Is it worth the risk?'

'The only thing we can lose,' Parral said, settling back in his seat, 'are a few of my credits and the lives of his men.'

'But if Sten wins – if he wins, what do we do with him?'

Parral laughed his cold laugh. 'What you always do with a mercenary.'

Theodomir smiled. And then he joined in the laughter. 'I'll find a nice little tomb for him,' he promised. 'Right beside the place I'm going to put Ingild.'

Chapter Ten

The Jannisar stood quaking by the missile launch tube. Sten could see his eyes rolling in fear above the big wad of stickiplast slapped across his mouth. His hands were bound behind him. His knees buckled and the two hulking figures on either side of him jerked him up.

The Bhor captain lumbered forward, his harness creaking in the silence. The bloodshot eyes of fifty crewmen swiveled, following him, as he paced up to the Jann and stopped. Otho peered up at his victim through the two hairy bushes the Bhor called eyebrows.

'S'be't,' he mocked.

He turned to his crew and raised a huge hairy fist, holding an enormous stregghorn.

'For the beards of our mothers,' he roared.

'*For the beards of our mothers*,' the crewmen shouted back.

In unison, they drank from the horns. Otho wiped his meaty lips, turned to the Bhor tech waiting by the missile bay door. He raised a paw for the command and Sten could hear the Jann squeak through the stickiplast. He almost felt sorry for the poor clot, guessing what was coming next.

'By Sarla and Laraz,' Otho intoned. 'By Jamchyyd and . . . and . . . uh . . .'

He looked at an aide for help.

'Kholeric,' she stage-whispered.

Otho nodded his thanks. 'Bad luck to leave a clotting god out,' he said.

He cleared his throat, belched. and continued. 'By Jamchyyd and Kholeric, we bless this voyage.'

He brought his hand down, and the Bhor tech slammed the BAY

OPEN switch. The doors hissed apart, and the two Bhor guards lifted the wriggling Jann prisoner into the tube. Otho roared with laughter at his struggles.

'Don't fear, little Jann,' he shouted 'I, Otho, will personally drink your heathen soul to hell.'

The crew hooted in glee as the doors slid shut. Before Sten could even blink, the tech slammed the MISSILE FIRE switch and the ship jolted as air blasted the Jann into vacuum. He barely had time to moan before his body exploded.

The ship's metal floor thundered with the footsteps of cheering Bhor crewmen as they rushed and battled for room at the porthole to watch the gory show.

Sten fought back a gag as a smiling Otho heaved himself over to him. His breath whooshed out as the Bhor slapped him on the back, a comradely jackhammer blow.

'By my mother's beard,' he said, 'I love a blessing. Especially' – he thumbed toward the missile bay doors and the departed Jann – 'when it's one of those scrote.'

He bleared closer at a pale Sten. 'Clot.' he cursed at himself, 'you must think me a skinny, stingy being. You need a drink.'

Sten couldn't argue with that.

'It is good,' Otho said, 'that the old ways are dying.'

He poured Sten a horn of stregg – the pepper-hot brew of the Bhor – and heaved his bulk closer.

'You won't believe this,' he said, 'but the Bhor were once a very primitive people.'

He'd caught Sten in mid drink, and he nearly spewed the stregg across the table. 'No,' Sten gasped, 'I wouldn't.'

'The only thing left now,' Otho said, 'is a bit of fun at a blessing.'

He shook his huge head. Sighed. 'It is the only thing we have to thank the Jann for. Before they came along and started killing us, it had been . . . in my grandfather's time that we last blessed a voyage.'

'You mean, you only use Jannisars?' Sten asked.

Otho frowned, his massive forehead beetling.

'By my father's frozen buttocks,' Otho protested, 'who else would we use? I told you, we are a very civilized people.

'We had almost forgotten the blessing until the Jann arrived with their clotting S'be'ts. But when they slew an entire trading colony, we remembered. We clotting remembered.'

He drained his horn, refilled it. 'That scrote we just killed? He was one of fifteen we captured. What a treasure trove. We shared them out among the ships. And one by one we used them in the blessing. Now, I must admit a small regret. He was the last.'

Sten understood completely. 'I think I can solve that for you,' he said quietly.

The captain belched his agreement. Pushed the jug of stregg away. 'And now, my friend, we must discuss our business. We are three days out from Hawkthorn. My fleet is at your disposal. What are your orders after planetfall?'

'Wait,' Sten said.

'How long?'

'I assume that the credits I have already paid will hold you for quite a while.'

The Bhor raised a hand in protest. 'Do not misunderstand, Colonel. I am not asking for more . . .' He rubbed thumb and hairy forefinger together in the universal gesture of money. 'I am merely anxious, my friend, to get on about this business.'

Sten shrugged. 'A cycle at the most.'

'And then you go to kill Jannisars,' Otho asked.

'And then we kill Jannisars,' Sten said.

Otho grabbed for the stregg again. 'By my mother's beard, I like you.' And he filled the horns to overflowing.

The Bhor were a wise choice in allies. If ever there was a group noted for fierce loyalties, fiercer hatreds, and the ability to keep a single bloody goal in constant sight, it was they. They were the cluster's only native people, the aborigines of a glacier world, an ice planet pock-marked with a thousand volcanic islands of thick mist and green.

In times of legend, the Bhor lived and died in these oases. Growing what little they could. Bathing in their steaming pools. And, when they became brave enough, hunting on the ice.

At first, it was really a question of who was hunting whom. No one knows what the streggan looked like in those days. But Bhor stories and epic poems describe an enormous, shambling beast that walked on two legs, was nearly as intelligent as a Bhor, and had a gaping maw lined with row after row of infinitely replacable teeth.

Starvation drove the Bhor out on the ice. A dry professor in a room full of sleepy students would say it was merely a need for a more efficient source of protein.

Tell that to the first Bhor who peered over an ice ledge, considered the streggan crunching the bones of a hunting mate, and thought fondly of the empty – but safe – vegetable pot back home.

It must have been an awesome sight when the first Bhor made the historical decision. Compared to the streggan he would have been a tiny figure. Compared to a humanoid, however, the Bhor was solid mass. Short, with a curved spine, bowed but enormous legs, splayed feet, and a face only a 'mother's beard' could love. His body was covered by thick fur. A heavy forehead, many cms thick. Bushy brows and brown eyes shot with red.

Although about only 150cms tall, the average Bhor is one meter wide – all the way down – and weighs about 130 kilograms. As far as mass equivalent, this equals the density of most heavy-worlders like Alex.

And so what the streggan was faced with was enormous strength in a small package. Plus the Bhor ability to build cold-heat-tempered tools. All the Bhor had to figure out was how to club the streggan down.

There were many mistakes. Witness the gore of early Bhor legends. But, finally, somebody got it right and the streggan became a major source of that missing protein.

There was an early error, quickly corrected. The first thing a Bhor did at a kill was to rip out the liver and devour it raw. With a streggan, the Bhor might as well have been consuming cyanide. The lethal amount of vitamin A found in a streggan liver would be double that of an Earth polar bear (also lethal) or that of a century-old haddock. Eating the liver of your enemy was the first of the Old Ways to go.

Before they could expand offworld, the Bhor first had to master the ice of their native world. With the streggan at bay, the Bhor then learned to trade. With that came the ability to kill their own kind. After all, what else was left to brag about in the drinking hall?

Unlike those of most beings, Bhor wars over the centuries were small and quickly settled into an odd sort of unity through combat.

Basic principle of Bhor religious emancipation: I got my gods, you got yours. If I get in trouble, could I borrow a couple?

When the Bhor first began expanding their 'oases' by melting the glacier ice, the great cry came to 'Save the Streggan.' The Bhor had killed so well that their previous Grendel of enemies was nearly extinct. Today the only examples left are in Bhor zoos. They are much smaller (we think) than before, but still fierce. Enough for a Bhor mother to still use them for traditional boogey-men.

The streggan are now as much a legend as the saying 'By my mother's beard.' All Bhor have a great deal of facial hair to hide their receding chins. The females have slightly more than the males. In ancient times, it was a long, flowing beard for their children to cling to when mother was gathering veggies – or was faced with a shot at pure-protein streggan.

By the time the streggan were nursery legends, the Bhor had already established themselves as traders throughout the Lupus Cluster. Even though the People of Talamein – both sides – were moderately xenophobic, they knew enough to leave the Bhor alone.

As long as the Bhor kept to themselves and stayed within the trading enclaves, there was no trouble as the humans expanded through the cluster. The Bhor did not think much one way or another of most people anyway, so coexistence was possible.

Until the Jannisars decided they needed an Enemy. Which put the rogue, one-god fanatics against casually pantheistic armed trader-smugglers.

When Sten met them, the outnumbered Bhor were as headed for extinction as their old enemies, the streggan. But with no one to drink their souls to hell.

Chapter Eleven

'Hawkthorne control, this is the trader *Bhalder*. Request orbital landing clearance. Clear.'

Otho closed the mike and looked over the control panel at Sten. 'By my mother's beard, this be an odd world. Last time we put down here there were three different landing controls.' Otho rumbled slight merriment. 'And they swore great oaths that if we followed anyone else's landing plot they'd blow us out of the atmosphere.

'Enough to drive a Bhor to stregg, I tell you.' He grinned huge yellow teeth at Sten. 'Of course, that doesn't take much doing.'

Sten had noticed.

The speaker garbled, then cleared. 'Vessel *Bhalder*. Give outbound plot.'

This is the *Bhalder*. Twenty ship-days out of Lupus Cluster.'

'Received. Your purpose in landing?'

'My chartermate is hiring soldiers,' Otho said.

'Vessel *Bhalder*, this is Hawkthorne Control. Received. Welcome to Hawkthorne. Stand by for transmit of landing plot. Your approach pattern will be Imperial Pilot Plan 34Zulu. Caution – landing approach must be maintained. You are tracked. Transmission sent.'

'And if we zig when this pilot plan says to zag,' Oth grumbled, 'we'll be introducing ourselves to interdiction missiles.'

Even mercenaries have to have a home – or at least a hiring hall. Hawkthorne was such a 'hiring hall' for this sector of the Galaxy. Here mercenaries were recruited and outfitted. Hawkthorne was also where they crept back to lick their defeats or swaggered back to celebrate their victories.

It was a fairly Earth-normal world around a G-type star. Its environment was generally subtropical.

And Hawkthorne was anarchic. A planetary government would be created by whatever mercenary horde was strongest at any given time. Then they'd be hired away and leave a vacuum for the smaller wolves to scrabble into. Other times the situation would be a complete standoff, and total anarchy would prevail.

The mercenaries hired themselves out in every grouping, from the solo insertion specialists to tac-air wings to armored battalions to infantry companies to exotically paid logistics and command specialists. The only coherence to Hawkthorne was that there wasn't any.

The *Bhalder* swung off final approach leg, Yukawa drive hissing, and the flat-bottomed, fan-bodied, tube-tailed ship settled toward the landing ground.

Weapons stations were manned – the Bhor took no chances with anyone. The landing struts slid out of the fan body, and the *Bhalder* oleo-squeaked down. A ramp lowered from the midsection, and Sten walked down, his dittybag in one hand.

A dot grew larger across the kilometer-square field and became a gravsled jitney, Alex sitting, beaming, behind the tiller.

Alex hopped out of the jitney and popped a salute. Sten realized the tubby man from Edinburgh wasn't quite sober.

'Colonel, y'll nae knowit hae glad Ah be't t'sae y', lad.'

'You drank up the advance,' Sten guessed.

'Thae, too. C'mon lad. Ah'll show y' tae our wee hotel. It's a magical place. Ah hae been here n'more't aye cycle, an' thae's been twa murders, aye bombin' an' any number't good clean knifint's.'

Sten grinned and climbed into the gravsled.

Alex veered the sled around two infantry fighting vehicles that had debated the right of way and now blocked the dirt intersection with an armored fenderbender.

The main street of Hawkthorne's major 'city' was a marvel, filled with heavy traffic, which consisted of everything from McLean-drive prime movers with hovercraft on the back to darting wheel-drive recon vehicles to a scoutship doing a weave about forty feet overhead.

The shops, of course, sold specialty items: weapons, custom-made, new or used, every conceivable death tool that wasn't under Imperial proscript (which of course meant the Guard-only willyguns, as well as some other exotica). Uniform shops. Jewelers who specialized in providing paid-off mercs with a rapidly convertible and portable way of carrying their loot and accepting on pawn whatever jewels a loser needed to hock.

And through the chaos marched, swaggered, stumbled, crawled, or just lay in a drunken babble the soldiers. All kinds, from the suited pilots to the camouflage-dressed jungle fighters to the full-dress platoons that specialized in guarding the palace.

Then Sten noticed a very clear area on one side of the street. It was a small shop, with the dirt walk neatly swept, the storefront freshly painted. The sign outside read:

JOIN THE GUARD!
THE EMPIRE NEEDS YOU!

Sten glanced in the door at the recruiting post's only occupant, a very dejected, lonely, and bored Guards sergeant, wearing his hashmarks, medals, and unhappiness for all to see.

'Ah nae understand't our Guard,' Alex said, seeing Sten's gaze. 'Dinnae thay ken half ae thae troopies ae deserters in the first place an' in the secon't place men whae na sane army'd hae in th' first place?'

Sten nodded glumly. Alex was quite correct – Hawkthorne was quite a place. Mahoney, Sten thought, was a jewel. Here, son. Go hire a few hundred psychopaths and crooks and topple two empires.

And see if you can't get it done before lunch . . .

But that was the way Mantis Section worked. Sten probably wouldn't have wanted it any other way.

Chapter Twelve

COMMANDOS!

200 OF THE FINEST NEEDED!

DEFEND THE FAITH OF THE CENTURIES!

PAY GUARANTEED

Colonel Sten, late of His Imperial Majesty's Third Guards Assault Division, is hiring 200 elite soldiers to assist in the protection of one of the Empire's most respected social and theocratic orders.

NONHUMANOID FREELANCES UNFORTUNATELY CANNOT BE CONSIDERED DUE TO ABOVE RELIGIOUS CONDITIONS

Only the Best Need Apply!

The Lupus Cluster and the Faith of Talamein is under attack by a godless and mercenary horde, attempting to invade and destroy some of this sector's most beautiful and desirable worlds, inhabited by peace-loving people. Needed individual equipment: individual weapons, cold-weather suits, space combat suits. Combatants should expect little ground leave.

A SHARP SHOCK NEEDED!

Colonel Sten, highly regarded in the Guard both for his extensive combat experience (18 major planetary assaults, numberless raids and company-size actions), is noted for having the lowest casualty rate in the Third Guards.

THOSE ACCEPTED WILL BE PROVIDED WITH USUAL SURVIVOR'S INSURANCE

PROVEN COMBAT EXPERIENCE NECESSARY

To include covert operations, lifts, jugular raids, smash-and-grab, ambush, harassment, and diversionary. Background in following units preferred: Imperial Guards, Trader Landing Force,

Tanh, some specific planetary forces allowed (please check with recruiter).

CONDITIONS OF DISCHARGE
WILL NOT BE INQUIRED INTO

Standard Contract

Individual acquisitions by proficient individuals or units will not be logged, provided point of origin is *not* from friendly forces. Commando-qualified soldiers, individuals or units, should apply Colonel Sten. Breaker House, WH1 . . .

Sten read the onscreen ad and winced slightly.

'You wrote this?'

'Aye,' Alex said, upending his half liter of quill.

'It's gone planet-wide?'

'Aye.'

'You think you're pretty clottin' funny, don't you?'

'Aye,' Alex agreed smugly and keyed for another drink.

Chapter Thirteen

Sten looked at the man across the bar table from him and decided he was potentially lethal. About two cms taller than Sten, a kilo or two heavier. Part of his hawkface moved stiffly – a plas reconstruction, Sten guessed.

The man probably had a hideout gun trained on Sten, under the table. And I really hope he doesn't think about using it, Sten thought, eyeing Alex, who slumped, seemingly half asleep, on a stool nearby.

'It's all what they used to call a crock, you know,' the hawkfaced man said cheerfully.

Sten shrugged. 'What isn't?'

'I've got seventy-eight men—'

'Seventy-two,' Alex broke in, without opening his eyes. 'Twa b'hospital, one kickit y'stday, three in a wee dungeon an' y' wi'out th' credits to gie 'em oot.'

'Good men,' the man went on, seemingly unperturbed. 'All with battle experience. About half of them ex-Guards, some more used to be Tanh, and the others I trained myself. You can't ask better than that, Colonel.' He carefully put quotation marks around Sten's rank.

'I'm impressed, Major Vosberh,' Sten said.

'Not from the contract offer you're not,' the lean mercenary officer said. 'I read the fiche. Religious war. Two clottin' Prophets. Council of merchants, for hell's sakes. And these – these Jannisars.'

'You did understand the fiche,' Sten agreed.

'And you expect me to commit my people into that maelstrom for a clotting *standard* contract?'

'I do.'

'Not a chance.'

Sten leaned forward. 'I want your unit, Major.'

'But you won't get it at those prices.'

'I will. Item – you signed on for Aldebaran II; your side lost. Item – Kimqui Rising; the rebels won and you offplaneted without most of your hardware. Item – Tarvish System. They signed a truce before you got there. You're broke, Major. As my sergeant-major said, you can't even afford to bail your troopies out of jail!'

Vosberh rose slowly, one hand moving, very casually, toward his tunic button.

'Don't do that, Major,' Sten went on. 'Please sit down. I need your soldiers – and I need you alive to lead them.'

Vosberh was startled. Sten hadn't moved.

'All right. I apologize for my temper.'

Sten nodded wordlessly, and Alex got up and headed for the bar. He returned with three liter glasses. Sten sipped from one.

'Say I'm still in the market,' Vosberh said, after drinking. 'The job's to take out these Jannisars and their boss, right?'

Sten grunted.

'Ah,' Vosberh said, interested in something he must've caught in Sten's expression. 'But we'll get back to that in a minute. How do we do it? Specifically.'

'I haven't chosen specific targets yet. We'll base on a planet named Nebta, which should make your troops happy.'

Alex handed Vosberh a fiche, which the man pocketed.

'No major campaigns. No advisory. Assassination. Nitpick raids. No land-and-hold. Get in, get out, few casualties.'

'They always say few casualties.' Vosberh was starting to relax.

'Since I'll be with the landing forces, I have certain personal interest in keeping the body count low,' Sten said.

'Okay. Say I take standard contract. How's it paid?'

'Half in front, to the men's accounts.'

'I handle that.'

Sten was indifferent.

'How's the payment handled?' Vosberh continued.

'A neutral account on Prime World.'

'Prime World? What about the Empire?'

'I checked. They don't even know where Lupus Cluster is. Private war. No Imperial interests in the cluster. Believe me I looked.'

Vosberh was getting steadily friendlier. 'When's the payoff? When this Ingild gets crucified?'

'When the job's finished.'

'We're back to that, aren't we? Maybe . . . maybe, Colonel-by-the-grace-of-this-Theo-character Sten has some plans of his own? Maybe when the Jann are history there'll be another target?'

Sten took a drink and stayed silent.

'A forgotten cluster,' Vosberh mused. 'Antique military and a religion nobody takes seriously. This could be very interesting, Colonel.'

He drained his glass, stood, and extended a hand. Sten stood with him.

'We accept contract, Colonel.' Sten shook his hand, and Vosberh was suddenly, rigidly, at attention. He saluted. Sten returned the salute.

'Sergeant Kilgour will provide you with expense money. You and your unit will provide yourselves with all necessary personal weapons and equipment and stand by to offplanet not later than ten standard days from this date.'

Chapter Fourteen

Sten lowered the binocs and turned to Alex, more than a little puzzled.

'If this Major Ffillips is the clottin' great sneaky-peeky leader you say she is, how in the clot did she get herself this pinned down?'

'Weel,' Alex said, thoughtfully scratching his chin, 'yon wee major makit ae slight error. The lass assumit whan sh' nae pay h' taxes, th' baddies'd show up, roll a few roun's, an' then thae'd g'wan aboot thae bus'ness. Sh' reckit wrong.'

Sten gaped. 'You mean those tanks down there . . . are tax collectors?'

'Aye,' Alex said.

Below the hillock they lay on was a wide, dusty valley. At one end the valley narrowed into a tight canyon mouth, barely twenty meters wide.

In the valley were ten or fifteen dozen infantry attack vehicles – laser- and rocket-armed, five-meter-long tracks, each carefully dug in. In front of them were infantry emplacements and, Sten's binocs had told him, a very elaborate electronic security perimeter.

'Taxes ae Hawkthorne.' Alex continued, 'be't a wee complex. Seems ae mon whae sayit he be th' gov'mint – if he hae enow firepower to backit hae claim, well, tha' be what he be.'

'So when this instant ruler asked for credits, Ffillips told him to put the tax bill where a laser don't shine, and then they put her under siege?'

'Aye, yon Ffillips 'raps is a wee shortsighted ee her thrift,' Alex agreed.

'And all we have to do is break through the perimeter, get inside that canyon, convince Ffillips that we can pull her tail out, and then break the siege?'

Alex yawned. 'Piece ae cake, tha.'

Sten took out a cammie face-spray and wished desperately that he'd been able to bring two sets of the Mantis phototropic camouflage uniforms with him.

'What Ffillips dinnae ken we knowit,' Alex mentioned, 'is tha twa weeks ago, sappers infiltrated her wee p'rimeter an' blew her waterwells to hoot.'

Sten eyed the tubby man from Edinburgh and wished, for possibly the ten thousandth time, that he wouldn't hold *all* the intelligence until the last minute.

A piece of darkness moved slightly and suddenly became Sten, face darkened, wearing a black, tight-fitting coverall. Behind him slipped Alex.

In front of them were the manned and the electronic perimeters. They'd passed the emplaced tracks easily – armor soldiers traditionally believe in the comforts of home. Which means when night comes they put on minimal security, electronic if possible, button up all the hatches, turn on the inside lights, and crack the synthalk.

Sten and Alex had moved forward of the armor units walking openly, as if they belonged to the tax-collecting unit.

The manned post to their left front was no problem. The two men behind the crew-served weapon were staring straight ahead. Of course there was no need to watch their rear.

The problem was the electronics.

Sten dropped flat as his probing eyes caught an electronic relay point. He moved his hand forward, closed his eyes, and finger-read the unit. Clot me, he thought in astonishment. This thing's so old it's still got transistors, I think!

Alex passed him the Stealthbox. Sten touched it to the relay and the box clicked twice. Then a touchplate on the stealthbox warmed, signaling to Sten's hand that the relay would now send OK OK OK NEGATIVE INTRUSION even if a track ran over it. The two men crawled on.

Sten and Alex were barely fifteen meters in front of the manned position when, without warning, a flare blossomed in the night sky.

Freeze . . . freeze . . . move your face slowly away . . . down in the dirt . . . wait . . . and hope those two troopies back in the hole aren't crosshairing on your back.

Blackness as the flare died and crawl on.

The second line of electronics was slightly more sophisticated. If Sten and Alex didn't need to crawl back out, it would have been simple to put a couple of 'ghosts' into that circuitry, so that the perimeter warning board would suddenly show everything attacking, including Attila's Hordes.

Instead Sten took a tiny powerdriver from his waistbelt and gently – one turn at a time – backed off a perimeter sensor's access plate. The stealthbox had already told him there were no antishutdown sensors inside.

Sten set the access plate down on the sand and held one hand back. Alex gingerly fished a very dead desert rodent from his pouch and passed it to Sten. Sten shoved the tiny corpse nose-first into the sensor. That sensor flashed once and went defunct.

Sten then carefully bent the access plate to appear as if the rodent had somehow wormed its way inside. He reinstalled the plate on the box and all looked normal again.

As they crawled past the now-dead electronic line, Alex suddenly tugged at Sten's ankle.

Sten froze, waiting.

Alex slithered past him and sabotaged a second, independent-circuit alarm. Then he swept the area in front of it with his stealthbox. Finally he took a small plastic cup from his pouch and positioned it, open end down, over the pickups for a landmine trigger.

Sten glanced at him. Alex yawned ostentatiously and waved Sten onward.

'I agree, Major,' Sten said politely. 'You and your force would be a valuable addition. I've never had the chance to operate with three-man commando teams and I'd like to see them in action.'

Ffillips was a short, muscular woman with ramrod military posture. She was middle-aged, with silvery hair as immaculate as her uniform. She had cold, assessing eyes that warmed now as she boasted about her troops.

'Trained 'em myself.' Ffillips said proudly. 'Took the best I could find from the planetary armies. Gave them pride in themselves. Taught 'em to look like soldiers. And, I tell you frankly, without bragging, they're very damned good. Think of 'em like my own children, I do. I'm like a mother to them.'

Ffillips' people did look pretty good, Sten had to admit, even though he and Alex had been able to penetrate the canyon and infiltrate Ffillips' camp without being challenged. Sten's mild egotism was that there wasn't another soldier in the Galaxy who could see a Mantis soldier until the knife went between the third and fourth ribs. Sten was probably right.

The canyon opened up into a broad, green, high-walled valley. Caves dotted the cliff walls, and there had been possibly half a dozen natural artesian wells in the valley.

Ffillips' troopers, broken down into their three-man (or -woman) squads, were strategically positioned. Antitrack positions lined the canyon and the high walls probably had dug-in antiaircraft positions.

And the valley was now completely dark, from the fighting positions to Ffillips' own headquarters-mess cave. Good light discipline.

Since no track or soldier could attack down that narrow canyon, Ffillips' mercs could have held the position for a century, assuming they weren't hit with nukes or human wave assaults.

Except that their wells had been destroyed.

Ffillips finished reading the contract by hand-cupped penlight and shook her head.

'I think not, Colonel. Frankly, I could not, in all conscience, offer my young men and women an offer as penurious as this one.'

Sten shrugged and looked around the cave. He saw a fist-sized boulder, picked it up, and walked over to a nearby well.

He let go, and they all heard the echoing thuds of the rock as it clattered down into dryness. Sten walked back and sat down across from Ffillips. Alex was looking very interestedly at one canyon wall, trying to keep from laughing.

Finally the silver-haired woman said, with obvious reluctance, 'Lift the siege for us. Then give us three days to resupply.'

Sten smiled.

Sten's first analysis was that mercenaries work for pay, or for beloved/feared/respected leaders, or possibly even for idealism. Ho. Ho. Ho. None of the latter two applied to these tax collectors.

Second analysis, as he and Alex crouched in the brush behind the 'tax collector's' headquarters, was that no matter how high they promoted him, he better never get so lazy, luxury-loving, and sloppy.

The setup was pretty plush. Five tracks, which should've been on line, were semicircled in front of the headquarters. The headquarters unit was three com tracks, two soft-skinned computer vehicles, one security-monitor half-track, and one extended-base track that was the unit leader's quarters.

Most of the tracks had their rear ramps dropped, and light gleamed through the small camp. What perimeter human guards there were had been positioned well within the light circle, so Sten knew they'd be night-blind.

Sten kicked Alex's outstretched foot. 'Time to take the palace, Sergeant.' Alex rolled to his feet, and the two cat-footed forward toward the headquarters.

Sten was within two meters of the first guard when he was spotted. The man's projectile weapon came off his shoulder – on his clottin' shoulder! – to somewhere between present and port arms.

'Halt.' Bored challenge.

Sten didn't answer.

Simultaneous: guard realizing two men were coming in on him/his weapon coming down/hand toward trigger/Sten inside his guard.

Very smoothly . . . step in . . . right hand back, left forward. Hip snap and Sten's cupped right hand shot forward. It crashed into the sentry's chin, and his head snapped back. The man was probably dead, but Sten continued the attack, one sidestep and the edge of the hand straight across the man's larynx. Catch the body and ease it to the ground.

And then they were both running.

Alex rolled a fire-grenade into the security-monitor half-track, flat-dove as another sentry fired a burst into his own camp, rounds whining off armor, and was back on his feet just as an alarmed tech peered out of one of the computer vehicles, saw Alex, and yanked the door closed.

Alex's fingers grabbed the door, centimeters from slamming, and three-gee muscles yanked. The door *skrawked* completely off its hinges and went spinning away.

One of the techs inside was grabbing for a pistol. Alex one-handed a console through the air at him. It crunched the man's chest, and he sprawled, blood spurting and shortcircuiting the main computer. Lights flashed and then the inside of the vehicle was plunged into darkness.

'Cask? Cask?' The other tech's terrified whisper.

Ah, wee lad, Alex thought. M'moon's in benev'lence, an' Ah lie y' t'livit.

And he was out the door, moving toward the second vehicle. He picked up its ramp and slammed it sideways into the track's now-clamped-shut door. Door and ramp gave way at the same time. Bullets seared out, and Alex flattened to one side.

Ah c'd use m'willygun ae thae very moment, he thought, and then saw what looked like a hydraulic jack nearby. Alex rolled to it, took the meter-long handle in both hands, and twisted. The handle, only half-inch mild steel, snapped off cleanly.

Alex rose to his feet, hefted the handle, then hurled it through the vehicle's door. Followed it with a thermite grenade. A howl gurgled down and then sparks began flashing and Alex could see flames crackle.

He picked himself up, dusted his knees, and looked around for something else to demolish. The headquarters was in chaos – it seemed as if everyone was shooting. But not at Alex.

Since panic spreads, the line units opened up. Alex wondered idly what they thought they were shooting at, then wandered over to see if Sten needed any help.

He didn't.

Alex started to enter the command track, then checked himself. 'Ah'm wee Alex a' th' Pacifists,' he said softly.

Sten chuckled and emerged from his lurking place just inside the track's entrance. He wiped his knife-blade clean and slid the knife back into his arm.

The two men stood, slightly awed by the high explosive and pyrotechnics on the plain around them.

'C'mon, laddie. Thae clowns'll be ae it a' night, an' Ah'm thinkit Ah buy y' a wee brew.'

And, as silently as they came, Sten and Alex disappeared back into the night.

'Ah dinnae like to tell the wee laddie no,' Alex explained.

'PREEEEE-SENT . . . HARMS!'

And the ragged formation of beings brought their weapons up. At least those that had them did.

'Aw,' Alex said, entranced, 'ae likit ae wave an' all.'

'You,' Sten said, 'have even a lousier sense of humor than Mahoney.'

'HIN . . . SPECTION . . . HARMS!' A bucket-of-bolts clatter as the assembled hopeful mercenaries snapped their boltcarriers open. The young man wearing captain's bars, khaki pants, and a blue tunic managed a salute.

'Unit ready for inspection, Colonel,' he said.

Sten sighed and started down the line. He stopped at the first person, who was trembling slightly. Sten snapped out a hand for the man's rifle. The prospective merc didn't let go.

'You're supposed to give it to me when I want it,' Sten explained. The man released the rifle. Sten ran his little finger around the inside of the firing chamber, then wiped off traces of carbon. He glanced down the corroded barrel and gave the weapon back. Then he moved on to the next person.

The inspection took only a minute.

Sten walked back to the captain. 'Thank you, Captain. You may dismiss your men.'

The captain gaped at him.

'But, uh . . . Colonel . . .'

All right. He wants an explanation, Sten thought.

'Captain. Your men are not trained, are not experienced, are not combat ready. Their weapons – those they have – are ready for recycling, not for killing people. If I hired your unit, I'd be . . .'

'Like takit wee lambkins t'slaughter,' Alex put in. Both Sten and the captain wondered what the hell he was talking about.

'I'm sorry, Captain,' and Sten started away.

The young officer caught up with Sten, started to say something, reconsidered, then began again.

'Colonel Sten,' he finally managed. 'Sir, we . . . my unit . . . need this assignment. We're all from the same world, all of us. We grew up in the same area. We've used all our savings just to get here. And we've been on Hawkthorne for five cycles, and so far, well . . .' He suddenly realized that he sounded like he was begging and shut up.

'Thank you for your time, Colonel,' he finished.

'Hang on a second, Captain.' Sten had a thought. 'You and your men are stranded, yes? Zed-credits? And nobody, justifiably, will hire you?'

The captain nodded reluctantly.

'Captain, I can't use you. But in the center of the city there is a man who can.'

The man's expression grew hopeful.

'He's an old sergeant, and you'll find him at Imperial Guard Recruiting. Now, here's what he'll want to see from you . . .'

Sten ignored the boy sitting across the mess table from him and glowered at Alex.

'Another joke, Sergeant?'

'Nossir. Ah dinnae ken whae tha' lad comit frae.'

The boy was about nineteen years old. About Sten's height and possibly fifty kilos in weight with an anchor tied around his ankles. Even in the daylight Sten could see the glitter of the boy's surgicorrect lenses.

'*You* want to enlist?'

'Certainly,' the boy said confidently. 'By the way, my name's Egan. And I'm speaking for twelve colleagues.'

'Colleagues,' Sten said amazedly.

'Indeed. We would like to sign on. We've read your contract and accept the terms for the duration of service.'

Sten moaned to himself. It was turning out to be a very long day.

'If you read my, uh, proposal, you'd have seen that—'

'I saw that you want a hardy crop of killers. Daggers in their teeth or wherever you people carry them.'

'Then why—'

Again an interruption. 'Because you can't fight a war without brains.'

'I assumed,' Sten said, 'that I could possibly provide those.'

'You? Just a soldier?' It was Egan's turn to sound amazed.

'I manage.'

'Manage? But you need battle analysis. You need projections. You need somebody to run logistics programming. You need somebody who can improvise any ECM system you might require. You need – Colonel, I'm sorry if I sound cocky. But you really need us.'

'Not a chance. You and your friends – I assume they're like you?' Sten tried another, somewhat more polite tack. 'First of all, how can I tell if you're really the brain trust you say?'

'Possibly because I know your payee account on Prime World is 000–14–765–666 CALL ACCOUNT PYTHON, account depositor one Parral, world unnamed, and your current balance, as of this morning, was $72,654,080 credits.'

Very silent silence. Sten decided he was getting tired of gaping. It was time to start laughing. 'Howinhell,' he managed, 'did you find that out? We are operating through cutout accounts.'

'You see why you need us, Colonel?'

Sten didn't answer immediately. Oh, Mahoney, his mind went. Why did you put me out here by myself? I don't know what the clot kind of people you need to run a private war. So far all I've done is fake it. I wish I were back with Bet and the tigers and doing something simple like icing some dictator.

Stalling, he asked, 'Egan. One question. Who are you and your friends?'

'We . . . up until recently, we were advanced students at a lycée.'

'Which one?'

Egan hesitated, then blurted, 'Prime World.'

Both Sten and Alex looked impressed. Even soldiers knew that the Empire picked its brightest to attend the Imperial Home World Lycée.

'So what are you doing here?'

Egan looked around the mess. No one was within earshot. 'We were experimenting one night. I built a pickbox – that's something you use to get inside a computer—'

'W'ken whae i' be,' Alex said.

'And I guess it seemed like a good idea at the time, but somehow we ended up inside the Imperial Intelligence computer.'

Sten, carefully keeping a straight face, held up a hand for silence. Egan shut up. Sten motioned to Alex. They rose and walked to the far end of the mess, both automatically checking for mikes.

'D'ye ken whae yon wee but wickit lad done? He an' his boyos got aeside Mahoney's files. Ah nae wonder wha' thae b'doint ae Hawkthorne. Espionage's good frae ae penal unit f'r life.' Alex chuckled.

'What, good Alex, do you think of our Colonel Mahoney right now?'

'Ah'm thinkit h' beit puttin' us in ae world ae drakh. Ae this momit, Ah nae b'thinkit kindly ae th' boss.'

'So we hire these kids?'

'Frae m'point, Sten lad, there be nae ither choice.'

Computer printouts littered the room. Sten dragged a paw through his now-longish hair and wondered why the clot anybody ever wanted to be a general in the first place. He never realized how much paperwork there was before you got to say 'Charge!'

Alex was sprawled on the couch, placidly going through a long, fan-folded report, and Egan hunched over the computer keyboard. He tapped a final series of keys and straightened.

'Ready, Colonel. All units are on standby.'

'Aye,' Alex agreed, tossing the logistics printout to one side and reaching for a nearby bottle.

'Sten's Stupidities,' Sten said, coming to mock-attention and throwing a salute to the winds. 'Ready for duty, saaah! I have two hundred who're—'

'Two hundred and one,' the voice rumbled from the corner of the room.

Alex was on his feet, pistol ready, as Sten hit attack stance.

The voice shambled forward. Sten decided the man must be both the ugliest and most scarred humanoid he'd ever seen.

He held both hands up, palms forward, waist level, in the universal I-bear-no-arms symbol. Sten and Alex relaxed slightly.

'Who the drakh are you?'

The man looked down. Picture a giant, two-and-a-half meters tall, looking hunch-shouldered and shamefaced.

'Name's Kurshayne,' he said. 'I want to go with you.'

Sten relaxed and grabbed the bottle. 'We closed recruiting yesterday. Why didn't you apply then?'

'Couldn't.'

'Why not?'

'I was in the clink.'

'Nae problem wi thae,' Alex said, trying to be friendly. 'All ae us bin thae. E'en m'mither.'

'But I ain't with any mob,' Kurshayne said. 'There weren't nobody to stand my bail.'

'If you're solo, what are you doing on Hawkthorne?' Egan asked.

'Lookin' for work.'

'Any experience?' Sten asked.

'I guess so,' the giant answered. 'I got this.'

He pawed through his waistpouch, dug out a very tattered and greasy fiche, and reluctantly handed it to Sten.

Sten took it and dropped the card into the pickup. It started as a standard Guard Discharge Certificate:

THIS IS TO CERTIFY THT THE BEARER IS
KURSHAYNE, WILLIAM

PRIVATE
TERM OF ENLISTMENT: 20 YEARS
ASSIGNMENT: FIRST GUARDS ASSAULT MILITARY
SCHOOLS: NONE
DECORATIONS AWARDED: NONE
HISTORY: 27 Planetary Assaults, First wave. 12 Relief Expeditions, 300 support assaults (TAB X1 FOR DETAILS), Brought up for following awards: Galactic Cross, four times; Imperial Medal, eight times; Titanium Cluster, sixteen times, Mentioned in Dispatches, once. Reduced in rank, 14 times (TAB X2 FOR DETAILS).

The fiche continued scrolling. Sten looked up at the giant with considerable awe. Four times this Kurshayne was up for the Empire's highest medal? And . . .

'Why'd you get busted fourteen times?'

'I don't get along with people.'

'Why not?' Egan asked.

'Dunno, really. I guess I like 'em okay. But then – then they do things. Things that don't look right. And I gotta do something about it.'

I have more than enough troubles, Sten thought, and took the man's fiche out of the pickup. He handed it back to the man.

'Kurshayne, if we weren't fully manned . . .'

'Beggin't y'r pardon, Colonel.' Alex.

Sten held. Alex paced slowly around the giant.

'Ah knae ye,' he said, very, very softly. 'Y'r a mon whae knowit th' right, but y' dinnae ken whae thae be't betters'n y'. Aye, Kurshayne, Ah knae y'ilk.'

Kurshayne glowered down at the rotund sergeant.

'Nae, Ah proposit ae wee game,' Alex said silkily. 'Y' ken aye punch?'

'I know one punch, little man,' the giant said. 'Do you want to play it with me?'

'Aye. Ah do thae,' Alex said.

'You go first.'

'Nae, m'lad,' Alex said, a grin flickering across his broad face. 'Y'be't thae applicant. Ah be't thae mon. Gie i' y'best shot.'

Without warning Kurshayne swung, an air-whistling roundhouse punch that caught Alex in his ribs. The punch tumbled him, rolling and spinning back against the couch, the couch crashing over, and then Alex slammed flat against the wall. He lay motionless for a moment.

Then he picked himself up and came back. 'Aye, tha be ae braw slug, m'lad,' he said. 'B'nae i' be't mae turn.

'An' Ah be't fair. Sportin', likit. Ah gie y'warnin'. Nae likit yae, wha hie me ae sucker punch ae i' y'be't ae Campbell. Nae, Ah w'hit ye, mon.

'But since Ah want ye in m'troop, Ah nae will damage y' severe't. So Ah tell y' whae Ah'll be hittint y'. Ah be strikit y' ae th' center chest. Light-like, f'r Ah nae want y' hurt.'

Sten had never heard Alex's dialect so thick. Correctly, he figured Kilgour was angry. Sten decided he was sorry for what was about to happen. Illogically, he was starting to like the dumb giant.

Kurshayne braced for the punch.

Instead, Alex delicately reached forward and picked Kurshayne up with . . . clottin' hell, one hand, Sten realized . . . and lifted him clear of the ground. And then, seemingly casually, threw Kurshayne.

Two hundred kilos of Kurshayne, as if the laws of gravity had been put on hold, flew through the air. Hit the wall – two meters off the ground – and the wall went, crumbling into plas destruction in the corridor outside.

Kurshayne pinwheeled after the wall, out into the corridor. And, moving very, very fast, Alex went after him. He bent over the semi-conscious relic and near whispered.

'Nae, nae, y'wee mon. Y'hae ae job, Ah reck. But y'll no playit thae game twice, Ah reck.'

Kurshayne fogged his way to his feet. 'Nossir.'

'Ah'm nae sir. Ah'm nae but aye sergeant. Yon Sten, h'be't sir.'

Kurshayne struggled into rigid attention. 'Sorry, Sergeant.'

'Ah ken y'be't sorry, lad,' Alex crooned. 'Nae, y'be't off aboot i', an' Ah wan' y'back here in ten hours. clean't up an' ready t'fight.'

'Sir!'

And Kurshayne saluted and was gone. Sten and Egan were still gaping as Alex turned.

'W' noo hae 201 soldiers, Colonel Sten,' he said. Then staggered to the console and snagged Sten's bottle.

'Clottin' hell!' Alex groaned. 'Yon lad nie near kilt me! Th' things Ah do't frae th' Emp—th' cause!'

Chapter Fifteen

And I had a great future as a cybrolathe operator, Sten thought mournfully, looking at his assembled troops. They were standing in what could only be called Parade Motley on the landing ground, just in front of the *Bhalder.*

Oh, Mahoney, I will get you, Sten groaned. There were Vosberh's troops. Unshaven, unbathed, but well armed and, Sten conceded, fairly lethal.

Beside them, giving many hostile looks, were Ffillips' commandos. Spit and polish.

There were other one- or two-at-a-time pickups and Egan's crew of studious-looking Lycée kiddies.

Why me all the time? Sten wondered.

Beside Sten were flanked Vosberh, wearing a simple brown uniform, Ffillips in her personally designed dress uniform (suspiciously close to Guards full-dress), Alex, and Kurshayne.

Kurshayne had evidently decided he was cut out to be Sten's personal bodyguard and had equipped himself` with what he thought was an ideal weapon.

As far as Sten could tell, since Kurshayne refused to let anybody examine it, it was a full-auto projectile weapon, with about a one-gauge barrel.

Sten knew that no human could fire it without being destroyed by the recoil. Whether Kurshayne could do it was still a moot point.

Oh. Mahoney, Sten thought again.

Then, business. One pace forward.

'UNIT . . .'

'COMP'NEE . . . COMP'NEE . . .'

The shouts rang across the wind of the landing field.

'Unit commanders. Take charge of your troops. Move them into the ships.

'We're going to war!'

And then nothing but the howl of the wind and the drumbeat of bootheels.

And then nothing but Sten looking at Alex and both of them knowing why they'd chosen the profession they did.

And so, without banners, without bugles, they went off to war . . .

BOOK THREE

TAKING THE BLADE

Chapter Sixteen

The Jann Citadel hugged the plateau crest of the high, snow- and ice-covered mountain. Three sides of the mountain dropped vertically. Only the fourth featured a machine-carved road that S-snaked up toward the crest. A road with manned and electronic guardposts every few dozen meters.

The Citadel was more than just the theological center of the warrior faith/caste – it was also the training ground for all Jann cadets. And it was Sten's first target.

The Citadel had been located on a not especially welcoming world, near the tip of a northern continent. It promised, by its very appearance, monastic dedication, asceticism, and lethality – quite an apt summary of the Jann beliefs, in fact.

Sten and his 201 mercenaries had been able to insert easily, using the talents and the ground-lighters of the Bhor.

Now they lay crouched at the foot of one vertical precipice, the sheerest that Sten could pick from the vidpics aerial recon had taken. The sheerest and the least likely to be guarded, especially now.

Far above him, atop the crest, the Citadel itself sprawled on the plateau. It closely resembled a black cephalopod, with its humped center section and, finger-sprawling out from the central bulk, the four tube barracks that held the Jann cadet cells.

Lights were on in the barracks, red against the snow. And, in Sten's mind, he could see the top of the 'hump' – the massive building containing the temple itself, gymnasium, arena, and administrative offices, see its weather membranes 'breathing' in and out as they adjusted and readjusted the environment within. Even from the base of the cliff, Sten could see one of the membranes, glowing yellow-red from the lights inside and gently moving in and out like a living thing.

He pushed out of his mind the fear response that the entire Citadel was a living, brooding entity – an entity one of the mercenaries had immediately dubbed 'the Octopus.'

Snow crunched behind Sten as Alex moved beside him. A second crunch as the ever-present Kurshayne snow-crawled up on his heels.

Sten tapped Alex on his shoulder and passed him the night glasses, then turned to check the rest of the mercenaries on the rock-strewn hillside behind him.

The 200 men and women wore white thermal coveralls and were snuggled deep into snowbanks. Sten's practiced eye could pick out a movement here and there, but only because he knew where to look. Not only were the troops white-cammied, but so were their weapons and faces.

Which is why Sten started slightly when Alex lowered the night glasses and looked at him, peering through large, white eyes. White-camo contact lenses were very hard to get used to.

Sten smiled about the obvious joke about holding your fire until you can see . . . Alex raised a questioning eyebrow over a pure white eyeball. Sten covered, smile gone. He didn't think even Alex would appreciate the joke under the circumstances.

Which were: the Citadel. A deadly octopus in profile. On top of a sheer mountain. With black spots of soft shale where even snow couldn't stick. And where it did, the rock was old and rotten. Blanketed with ice and snow. Sten wasn't worried about the crumbling rock. That he could handle. But the ice sheets were waiting, ten-meter-long razorblades.

Sten shuddered.

Alex took one more look at the kilometer-high cliff. Leaned close to his side.

'Ah dinna lovit tha heights.' the heavy-worlder confessed in a whisper. 'Aye lads bounce whenit tha fall. Th' Kilgours squash.'

Sten chuckled and Alex whispered into his throat mike for Vosberh and Ffillips to come forward.

Expertly the two swam-crawled through the snow until they were on either side of him. Sten gave his last instructions. He was pleased when the two professionals didn't even raise an eyebrow as they saw the climb that faced them. Ffillips, however, put in a word for bonus money, and Sten shushed her.

'I want to hit them where it hurts,' he reminded. 'The chapel. A legitimate target. Torch it. Melt it.

'Ffillips? Your group has responsibility for the chapel. Vosberh – the barracks. They should be empty now. Blow them to hell for a diversion.

'If you see an officer – a teacher – in your way, kill him.'

He paused for emphasis.

'But if you can help it, don't kill any cadets.'

Vosberh hissed something about baby roaches growing up to be . . .

'They're kids,' Sten reminded. 'And when the war's over. I'd rather face some ticked-off diplomats than angry parents or brothers and sisters with short-range murder in their thoughts.'

Vosberh and Ffillips – very much the professionals – remembered wars they had won and coups they had then lost, and agreed with Sten's reasoning.

The cadets – unless some got in their way – were not valid military targets.

There was a thump at Sten's boot. He looked back and saw Kurshayne. The man had Sten's pack of climbing gear. Sten sighed. Accepted.

'All right, you can come with me,' he said.

Still, as he crawled forward to begin his climb, he felt a little bit better.

Chapter Seventeen

It was a temple of guttering torches. Deep shadows and oiled gold. A thousand young Jann voices were lifted in a slow military chant generations old. And the thousand-cadet procession moved in measured, slow-motion paces through the temple. The cadets were dressed in ebony-black uniforms, with white piping.

At the head of the procession was the color guard, carrying two heavy golden statues. One was of Talamein. The other was Ingild, the man the Janns called the True Prophet. Mathias and his father, Theodomir, would have called him many other things. True, or Prophet, even, would not be among them.

The procession was in celebration of the Jann Sammera: the Time of Killing. In Lupus Cluster history, it was a revenge raid by a small band of Jann. They hit one of the small moons off Sanctus that keep the potentially great tides in check, and slaughtered everyone. And then, trapped, they waited for the inevitable reprisal from Sanctus. When it came, there were no Jann survivors. A bloody historical note of which the Jann were immensely proud.

The procession moved through the temple, past enormous statues of Jann warriors and the flags of the many planets the Jann had converted or destroyed. The temple was the Jann holy of holies.

The cadets moved out of the temple, and huge metal doors slid closed as the last row of men passed. Then the cadets slow-marched down a hallway so enormous that in the summer months humidity brought condensed 'rain,' into an equally huge dining room.

In the dining room, the color guard marched straight forward down the main aisle, toward the huge stage and podium where the black-uniformed guest of honor and the school's military faculty waited.

The others shredded off and wove black and white ribbons through the long aisles created by the dining tables set for a thousand young men who were soon to join the Jann.

As the color guard approached the stage, General Khorhea – the guest of honor – and the hundred or so faculty members rose. From the wall behind them came a *hiss* as a twenty-meter-wide flag dropped from the ceiling. It was black with a golden torch.

Gen. Khorhea raised a hand. 'S'be't.'

And the color guard bowed, wheeled, and then began the slow march back to the chapel. Where they would return the statues to their positions and then quietly filter back for the celebration.

General Suitan Khorea despised personal ostentation. Except for silver-threaded shoulderboards and a thin silver cord on his left arrn, he wore no clues that he was the head of the Jannisars. In his prayers he reminded himself often of the line from one of the chants of Talamein – 'O man, find not pride of place or being/But gather that pride onto the Glory that is Talamein/For only there is that pride other than idle mockery.'

Mostly Khorea was proof that, even in a rigid theocratic dictatorship, a peasant can rise to the top. All it takes is certain talents. In Khorea's case, those talents were an absolute conviction of the Truth of Talamein; physical coordination; a lack of concern for his own safety; total ruthlessness.

Khorea had first distinguished himself as sub-altern when a Jann patrol ship had stopped a small ship. Possibly it was a lost trader, more likely a smuggler.

Khorea's commander would have been content merely to kill all the men on the ship as an object lesson. But before he could issue orders, Khorea's boarding detachment had slaughtered the crew and then, to guard against accusations of profiteering, had blown up the ship.

Fanaticism such as that earned its reward – a rapid transfer by Khorea's unsettled CO to an outpost located very close to the 'borders' of Ingild's side of the cluster, a transfer probably made in the hope that Khorea would make himself into a legend in somebody else's territory. Hopefully a posthumous legend.

But luck seems to select the crazy, and, in spite of the best efforts of the Janns' enemies, Khorea survived, even though he inhabited a body that looked as if a careless seamstress had practiced hemstitching on it for a few months.

In his rise, Khorea had gathered behind him a group of young Jann officers, either as fanatical or as ambitious as he was.

Eventually Khorea ended as ADC to the late General of the Jann, who one evening had confessed to Khorea that he was struggling against a certain . . . desire . . . for one of his own orderlies. Before he finished speaking, the man was dead, Khorea's dress saber buried in his chest.

Khorea faced the court-martial with equanimity. The officers on the court were trapped. Either they executed Khorea, which would make him a convenient martyr for his following, or they blessed him and . . .

. . . And there were no likely replacements to head the Jannisars.

The answer was inevitable.

Khorea returned to the court-martial room not only to find his dress saber's hilt pointing at him (point would have meant conviction), but lying beside it the shoulderbars of a Jann general.

Now the Jann priest's voice droned on. He was nearing the end of the traditional reading of the Book of the Dead, the list of the casualties of Sammera. The cadets were drawn up at attention. Except for the priest's voice, the hall was silent. Finally the priest finished and closed the ancient, black-leather-bound book.

General Khorea stepped forward, a golden chalice in his hand. He raised it high in a toast. As one, the thousand cadets wheeled to their tables and raised identical chalices high.

'To the lesson of Sammera,' he roared.

'To the Killing,' the cadets roared back.

The liquid in the chalices burst into flames, like so many small torches. And, in unison, Khorea and the cadets poured the flaming alcohol down their throats.

Sten craned his neck back, looking up the sheer cliff of ice that towered above him. It was a near-impossible climb and therefore, Sten reasoned, the route where the Jann were most vulnerable.

He looked at Alex and shrugged, as if to say: 'It ain't gonna get any easier.'

Alex held out one hand. Sten stepped into it, and the heavy-worlder lifted him straight up. Sten scrabbled for his first handhold, found a crack in the ice, jammed a fist into it and the spiked crampon points into the ice, and began his climb.

The most important thing, he reminded himself, was rhythm. Slow or fast, the climb had to be constant steady motion upward. After all these centuries, science had done little to improve the art of climbing. It was still mostly hands and feet and balance. Especially on ice. His eyes scanned for the next hold, so he would always know where he was going before he committed himself. If Sten trapped himself on the cliff, with no way down, in the morning, when the Jann troops found him, he would be a very embarrassed corpse.

Then he reached the first nasty part of the climb, a yawning expanse of glass-smooth ice. He looked quickly about, searching for handholds, already making his decision and digging out the piton gun.

Sten aimed the gun at the ice and pulled the trigger. Compressed air hissed as the gun fired the piton deep into the cliff face. Quickly he snapped the carabiner onto the piton, laced the incredibly lightweight climbing rope through it, and spooled the rope from his climbing harness down to Alex.

Climbing thread would have been far easier to manipulate, but it was not suitable for a main rope 203 men would have to use. Alex clipped his jumars onto the rope and slid up after Sten.

Sten set the next piton, and then another, weaving his way up the cliff. By the time he reached the end of the sheet ice, he was tiring. But he kept climbing, thankful for the massive amount of calories he'd choked down before landing.

Sten found a long, slender crack in the ice and jammed his way into and up it. He took advantage of the brief respite to suck in huge gulps of air to steady his trembling muscles. Still, he was constantly watchful, making sure that he kept his weight balanced over his feet. Behind him, he sensed Alex and Kurshayne.

And then it happened. Just as he was reaching up for the next handhold . . . straining . . . straining . . . one spiked boot broke through rotten ice and Sten was scrabbling for a hold and then he was falling . . . falling . . . falling. He tried to relax, waiting for the shock when the rope brought him up short of the first piton.

There was a jolt. And then a *ping* as the piton pulled out, and then he was falling again and . . . and . . . *crack*. The next piton held, and Sten was slammed up against the face of the cliff.

He hung there, dangling, swaying, for a long time, momentarily numb. Then he recovered, ignoring the pain of bruised muscles and doing a quick inventory of his body parts. Nothing broken. He peered downward and saw Alex's anxious face looking up at him. Which immediately broke into a smile, when Sten flashed him a weak grin and gave him a thumbs-up sign.

Sten spun around on the rope and looked up at the cliff's mass looming over him. He took two shuddering breaths and started climbing again.

*

Sten chinned himself on the cliff's summit. He kept tension in his fingers and shoulder muscles so that he could finally relax most of his body and turn the problem over to his eyes and brain.

The main body of the Octopus humped up at him black and glowing in the snow. The Citadel was merely a building constructed for a purpose. But it was a live thing. It was an animal that had to do animal things. It had to eat fuel, it had to breathe, and its enormous body had to retain heat and expel cold.

The last function was the constantly moving weather membranes. Sten's way in.

Sten checked the plateau in front of him, hummocky ground rolling slightly uphill toward the Citadel. Even though it was impossible for any intruder to attack the Jann from this side of the mountain, they obviously put little faith in the impossible. The hundred meters or so of rolling ground between the cliff edge and the first building was thoroughly covered by sensor-activated guns.

The multibarreled lasers constantly swept the area, looking for movement. Sten slithered over the clifftop and snow-crawled forward, thankful, for a change, that he had hired Egan and his Lycée kids.

Sten halted just outside the first sensor's pickup point. He fingered open his pack and slid out a powerdriver and a little metal box with dangling wires and heat clips. Sten dug into the snow and found the plate that guarded the sensor control system from the elements. He hesitated at the screws that held the plate in place and reminded himself of potential boobytraps. He placed the driver's bit into the first screw and flicked the button for reverse. The first screw whirred out smoothly and Sten was alive.

He quickly removed the plate, fused in the heat clips, and then glanced at the nearest sensor guns that were 'sniffing' at the night.

It was an illusion, of course. The guns didn't do anything but shoot. However, buried across the landscape were very efficient sensors that ignored the stray rodent but ordered the guns to cremate anything approximating man-size.

Sten turned the dial on the box until it told the sensor he'd just become a small furry creature, not worthy of a killing burst from the guns.

He stood up. And the guns kept searching. Ignoring him for larger game. The Lycée kids were right.

'Come on up, Alex,' he said in a perfectly normal voice. He braced himself for the hiss of the guns. Nothing. And he knew again that he was safe.

Alex effortlessly lifted himself over the cliff. 'Y' be takit tea oop here f'rit sae long?' Then he glanced at the scanning guns. They didn't react even to Alex's body mass. 'Aye' was his only comment.

Alex turned to throat-mike the orders down to the rest of the mercenaries.

Kurshayne was the first up with all of Sten's equipment, then Egan and his Lycée crew, who moved out and began permanently defusing the sensor guns. Next came Vosberh and his boyos. As Sten walked toward the curving hump of the Citadel, he consciously shut off any worry about his troops. He had to assume they were professionals. And that everything Sten had in mind would work.

Chapter Eighteen

Khorea bowed to the Citadel Commandant and stepped to the forefront of the podium. He had prepared a speech for this graduating event. But then he felt the movement deep in his mind – a feeling that he *knew* was the spirit of Talamein.

It could have been described more prosaically as a result of alcohol drunk by a near-teetotaler, adrenaline-response, and egotism. It was, however, doubtful that any Jann psychologist would have had the temerity to do so.

Khorea forgot his prepared speech and began: 'We are being tested today. Tested as we, the Jann, have never been tested before.'

He looked out at the thousand before him and thought that the officers would be the most important graduates the Citadel ever produced. He also sensed that most of them would be dead in not too many months.

'It is fitting,' he continued, 'that while we celebrate the Killing and your acceptance as Jann I tell you of the trials that we shall face.

'Trials which we shall only overcome by strength. Our strength, the strength of our arms, our minds, and our Faith in Talamein.'

The cadets stirred. The speech was quite different from what they had expected and from what they were accustomed to hearing from their cadre.

'These trials I shall now warn you of. They have been building for some time. We know the babblings of the madman Theodomir. And we know how dearly he would love to destroy the flame of truth, so it could be perverted into his own ashes.'

More like it. The cadets relaxed, and a few of them even smiled grimly. They were quite used to Theodomir diatribes.

'But the madman has gone beyond ravings. He has determined to try us by force of arms.'

Large smiles from some of the cadets – in their final training cycle most of them had participated in raids against the poorly trained, ineffectual levies of Theodomir. Khorea understood their smiles.

'This night you will become Jann. And then you will go out to face the armies of Theodomir. But be warned – these are not the rabble you have known.

'Theodomir has chosen mercenaries. Men who have trained to the peak of killing madness in the gold-souled ranks of the Emperor of the Inner Worlds.'

Khorea ceremoniously spat.

'Mercenaries. But a mercenary can fight, regardless that he defends an evil cause. This then is the trial you will face, Jann-to-be.

'At this moment Theodomir, the False Prophet, is raising an army against our peaceful worlds. An army that does not believe. An army that, if it conquers, will ensure that the Truth of Talamein and we, his servants, will cease to exist. If they win, it shall be as if we had never existed.

'Tell me, Jann-to-be – to keep that from occurring . . . is that not worth the Death? My death, your death – the death of every man in this room?'

Silence. And then one cadet came to his feet. Khorea automatically noted him proudly as the cadet screeched:

'Death! Long live death!'

And the cadets howled, the long, enraged howl of hunting beasts.

Sten whirled the fusion grapnel twice, then cast it straight up. The line coiled at his feet disappeared upward, into the obscuring snow, and then the head of the grapnel hit the outer skin of the Citadel about twenty meters up and instantly melted itself into bond.

Sten gave a tug. Solid contact. He began catwalking his way upward, keeping his body almost ninety degrees out from the curving surface of the Octopus.

When he reached the grapnel's head, he braced himself against it and hurled a second grapnel upward. Even with the crampons, he almost slipped and fell, before the grapnel hit, skidded, and then caught.

Sten leaned back onto the rope then began the next stage of the climb to the roof of the Jann sanctuary.

Below him Alex, Kurshayne, and Ffillips' commandos began

swarming up the awesome curve of the Octopus like so many ice flies. Grapnel, gloves, and boots found every protuberance in the smooth surface to keep from coming off.

Sten was the first to reach the weather membrane. He peered down through its red glow into the chapel below. It was empty. Alex pulled up behind him and tapped Sten's boot.

Sten reached back for the blister-charge, and Alex, panting after the climb, slid it into his gloves. Sten gave one fast look at the charge, thanked the whiz-kids again, licked the charge, almost freezing his tongue in the process, and slapped the charge to that 'breathing' membrane. Then, still in one motion, he slid back down the rope.

The charge fused to the membrane, glowed, and then the whole membrane surface began a slow melt. It peeled back and up, leaving a gaping hole directly into the heart of the Jann Citadel.

Sten took yet another grapnel from Alex, anchored it on the edge of the hole, and then unreeled the line down into the chapel below.

Then he descended, hand over hand, into the Citadel. Alex, Kurshayne, and Ffillips' men and women followed. They landed, then spread out through the chapel, checking for intruders and setting up security.

Sten stood in the middle of the room. It was awesome. Sten could almost feel evil flowing from the walls. In the flickering torchlight, the huge military statues loomed at him like gargoyles, about to leap through the forest of wall-hung regimental banners. It was indeed a temple – a temple for the worship of violent death.

Behind him Sten heard Alex's breath hiss. His friend shivered. 'Ah nae hae seen aught s'cold.' he whispered. Sten nodded, then looked over at Kurshayne.

'Blow it,' he ordered.

The Jann cadets were eating in silence. On the huge stage, the officers were also at their meal. General Khorea nibbled politely at each dish, then pushed it away. He refused when a servant offered to refill his wine glass.

Khorea looked around at the cadets and felt a great stirring of pride. Soon, he thought, all these young men would be joining him in the great Jann cause. Many would die, he knew. He also wondered if one of these young men at the tables would someday be a general like him.

And at that moment there was an enormous, soul-shattering explosion. For one of the few times in his life, Khorea felt an instant of fear. The enemy had struck where no Jann had ever believed possible. The Citadel was under attack.

Vosberh and his men raced toward the barracks. Minutes later, Jann guards, reacting to Vosberh's diversionary blast, poured out of the barracks and died as Vosherh's men sprayed them with a withering fire.

Vosberh snapped a command and his fire team hustled forward. Quickly they set up the tanks of the flamethrower, twisted the controls, and a sheet of flame gouted out.

The first barracks complex exploded into fire.

Kurshayne hustled up to a statue and draped a heat-pack on one huge metallic arm. Around the chapel Sten, Alex, and Ffillips' men were doing the same.

Sten slapped his last heat-pack into place, whirled, and ran for the huge door. He and Kurshayne were the last men out. Sten barked an order, and Kurshayne hit the det button while still on the run. Behind them in the chapel the heat-packs detonated, one by one.

The fire began as a slight red glow, gradually growing larger and larger, and then a blinding flash of white.

Each pack was like a miniature nova. The heat radiated out, farther and farther, with white glow blending into white glow, until the whole chapel was blinding white.

The drapes and regimental banners were the next to go, crisped in the instant fire-storm. And the golden statues began to bubble and then melt. A molten river of gold streamed across the floor as the statues melted like so many giant snowmen.

Air howled through the hole in the roof and the open door like two tornadoes as atmosphere rushed to fill the semi-vacuum created by the fire.

And then, with a roar, the entire temple exploded.

That second blast shook the Citadel to its foundation. It hit the dining room like an earthquake, flinging Jann to the floor.

The enormous room was in chaos. Men shouted meaningless orders that no one was heeding anyway. On the stage Khorea dragged himself out from under the table, pawing for his weapon. He was appalled at the hysteria raging about him. A wild-eyed Jann officer ran toward him, waving his gun. Khorea grabbed the man, but the officer struggled free and ran on.

Khorea grabbed for a mike. In a moment his voice boomed

through the huge dining-hall speakers, demanding order. It was a voice trained on a hundred battlefields and brought almost instant response. Men froze in place, recovered, and then turned to stare up at him.

But before he could issue any orders, the main doors blew open and Sten's killing squad waded in. They punched through the unarmed cadets, ignoring them, and fanned out across the room in three-man teams, firing into the Jann officers on the stage.

A young cadet lunged at Sten with his ceremonial dagger. Kurshayne grabbed the boy with one hand and hurled him across the room. Behind Sten, Alex lifted an enormous table and threw it into a group of charging cadets. It sent them reeling back, effectively out of the fight.

Sten flipped a pin grenade into a group of officers, and they disappeared in a hurricane of arms and legs and gouting blood. The wall beside him exploded, and he whirled to see a Jann officer getting ready to fire again.

Kurshayne swung that monster shotgun off his shoulder and triggered it. The officer shredded in the hiccuping boom of the cannon.

Ffillips plunged forward onto the stage itself just as Sten and his team got moving again, up the other side.

Sten spotted Khorea instantly, recognizing him from Mahoney's briefing. He slashed his way forward, going for the ultimate target. But there were dozens of men between him and the general. They died bravely, but they died just the same, trying to protect their general.

And Khorea saw Sten and instinctively recognized him as the leader of the attack. Khorea clawed his way forward. He wanted desperately to kill Sten.

A group of Khorea's aides rallied, grabbed the general, and, ignoring his shouts of protest, did a flying-wedge toward the rear of the stage. Sten had one last, fleeting look at the man's white, spitting face as the aides carried him through the rear door and disappeared.

Then Sten went down under a pile of bodies.

They punched and kicked at him, fighting each other in their blind fury for revenge. Sten slashed and slashed with his knife. And still they kept coming. Sten could feel numbness spread through his body.

Alex and Kurshayne fought desperately to get to him. For fear of killing Sten, they had to use their hands. Hurling men away, smashing skulls, and literally ripping limbs from bodies.

And suddenly they were there. There was no one in front of them but a battered and torn Sten, bleeding from a dozen superficial cuts.

Alex pulled him to his feet. They looked around for more Jann to kill. There was nothing but pile after pile of black-uniformed bodies and Ffillips' commando teams, grimly making the same search.

Sten spotted Ffillips across the stage. She gave him a large smile and a thumbs-up sign. It was over. Before the Jann cadets could rally at the loss of their cadremen, the mercenaries were moving across the stage and out a side door.

Outside the Citadel, the mountaintop ran with rivers of fire. Vosberh had done his job well. All the barracks were crackling and exploding.

Sten, Ffillips, and their people linked up with Vosberh and Egan's troops at the start of the exit roadway. They were in loose formation, ready to move out.

'Casualties,' Sten snapped.

'Three killed. Two stretcher cases. Ten walking wounded. It was a walkover,' Vosberh reported.

'None,' Egan said proudly.

Ffillips looked mournful. 'Seven dead. Twelve more wounded. All transportable.'

Sten saluted his subcommanders and turned to Alex, pointing at the downward S-curving roadway.

'We'll walk this time.'

'Ah'm w'y', lad,' Alex said. 'M'bones ae t' oldit to play billy-goatgruff wi' again.'

The mercenaries moved out briskly.

Behind them, the Citadel and its dreams of death and glory flamed into ruin.

Chapter Nineteen

The doctors hovered over the wriggling, leechlike creatures, waiting for them to shoot their potent narcotics into Ingild the Prophet's veins. They were the perfect parasites for an addict, creatures who traded euphoria for a few calories. Ingild waved at the doctors impatiently, and they carefully coaxed the tiny bulbous monsters free of his skin.

Ingild sat up and motioned the men away. The doctors scattered, not bothering with their usual professional bowing and posturing. The 'False' Prophet (as Theodomir would have called him) was in a snit. He glanced around the throne room at his guards, trying to compose himself before the comforting ego-drug took effect.

A little over half the guards in the throne room were black-uniformed Jann. Ingild fought back instinctive paranoia, even though he knew that in this instance it was a correct psychosis. The Jann guards, he realized, were more interested in watching Ingild than in protecting him from possible assassins. The rest of the guards were members of Ingild's own family, which made him relax a little. He pushed aside the thought that there was an excellent possibility they had been subverted by the Jann.

The symbiotic narcotics began to filter through, and he felt a faint wave of relief.

He *was* Ingild, and before him all men owed allegiance.

Ingild, like his counterpart and opponent Theodomir, was a middle-aged man, not too far into his second century. But unlike Theodomir, he looked as if he was near the end of his time. Ingild was wizened, his skin blotched and peeling. His head featured a bald dome with unhealthy strings of hair dangling from the sides.

A traveling medico had given him the reasons for his scrofulous appearance many years ago. The doctor had said that Ingild's deep-seated fears counteracted the benefits of modern longevity drugs. Ingild had the man executed for his advice, but had kept the compu-diagnoses and scrolled through them several times a day for insight.

A Jann guard walked over to him, very correct and military, but Ingild could sense the contempt.

'Yes,' Ingild said.

'General Khorea,' the guard announced.

Ingild covered the wave of fear and nodded at the guard. Khorea entered, made a slight bow, and strode over to the throne couch.

The ego-drug cut in for an instant, and Ingild did a mental sneer at Khorea's appearance. The man had not even bothered to change, he thought, after the debacle at the Citadel. His uniform was torn and there were streaks of dried-blood on the exposed skin.

Khorea drew up before him and snapped a very respectful salute. Ingild just nodded his acceptance. Then Khorea shot a look at the guards, made a signal, and, to Ingild's horror, all of them withdrew.

When the last man had gone, Khorea sat on the edge of Ingild's couch. Ingild fought back an angry scream. Instead he smiled at Khorea and gave him a fatherly pat on his arm.

'At last, my general,' he said, 'you have returned to me. I have prayed for your safcty.'

Khorea made an impatient motion. 'Listen very carefully. I have had an address prepared. It minimizes the damage to the Citadel.

'Basically it says we fought back a cowardly surprise attack. We drove the enemy away and killed many of them.'

'But,' Ingild protested, 'your report—'

'Forget my report,' Khorea snapped. 'That was for my officers.' Then, almost as an afterthought: 'And for you.'

Ingild swallowed his indignation.

'You will emphasize the casualties to the cadets. They were mere children, after all.'

Ingild looked at him in surprise. 'But there were few cadet casualties.'

Khorea gave him a withering look, and Ingild bit back any other protest.

'Everything is ready for your system-wide address,' Khorea continued. A small pause for effect. 'My speechwriters have appended an appropriate prayer.'

'What do we do next?' Ingild blurted, hating himself for it.

Khorea smiled.

'We fight,' he said. 'Total war. These are only mercenaries, after all. They will collapse after a few engagements.

'Especially when this amateur Sten, who leads them, is proven only to be lucky and not in fact a qualified leader at all.'

'Who is he?'

Khorea grimaced. 'Ex-Imperial Guards. Court-martialed and thrown out. Hardly a worthy opponent.'

Khorea stood up. 'But Sten and the mercenaries are the worry of the Jann. You must see that the faith of our people is behind us.

'I wouldn't advise any more stimulants before your address,' he warned.

Ingild shivered, but involuntarily nodded obedience.

Khorea smiled his cold smile again, drew himself up, and delivered a perfect salute. Followed by a low, mocking bow. 'The Jann will await your further orders, O Keeper of the Flame.'

He wheeled and marched out. Ingild looked after him, hating the clicking heels and the ramrod back.

A moment later, his guards drifted back in.

Chapter Twenty

Even pioneer clusters, settled by dissidents, fanatics, and malcontents, and crippled by two warring religions, can have a minor Eden.

Such was Nebta, the temporal version of Sanctus. Parral's power base.

The Nebtans controlled mainstream trade, which meant whatever merchanting the Bhor weren't able to wangle, connive, blackmail, or smuggle.

Nebta was a very rich and very beautiful world, a world where even the poor were rich – at least compared to the other habitable Lupus Cluster planets.

Nebta's oceans were slightly salty and its minor moon provided gentle tides. It swam in a perpetually mild climate, and most of its small continents were located inside the planet's temperate region.

The ugly necessaries of warehouses, landing fields, and brokerage houses had been sensibly located on the large, equatorial, desertlike main continent.

Nebta's merchant princes preferred their mansions, luxury, and indolence to the realities of trade. Sten had wondered how long it would take Ida to own the entire planet if she were there.

The government of Nebta was based on strength. Each of the merchant princes had his private army and generally confined himself to his own fortified city and fortress mansion.

Nebta was 'ruled' by a council of these merchant princes, a council that had been suborned, subverted, and threatened into acquiescence by Parral many years before.

Inside the fortified cities lived the clerks, shipping specialists, bankers, and such. The farmers lived outside the cities and were, by mutual agreement, kept out of the constant political connivings of the merchants.

Parral's own fortress-estate was actually a series of mansions, covering more than 150 square miles of hand-manicured parkland. Grudgingly Parral had housed Sten and his mercenaries in one of those mansions, a sprawling marble monstrosity the mercs were happily turning into a cross between a barracks and a bordello.

After the astonishing rapier stroke against the Jann Citadel that had opened the war, Parral had decided a masque was in order.

According to Parral's social secretary, those invited were the best, the most beautiful, and the brightest men and women from Nebtan high society.

Plus, slightly reluctantly, the guests of honor. This did not mean all 201 mercenaries: this portion of the guest list was restricted to Colonel Sten, his executives Ffillips and Vosberh, and, at Sten's insistence, Alex. And at Kurshayne's insistence, Kurshayne.

Sten and Alex had decided the monster's protectiveness was going too far. They didn't know if telling Kurshayne no party would produce tears or a battle royal. Besides, it was just a party.

But, Sten admitted as the five soldiers walked up the sweeping steps to Parral's main mansion, past too many rigid guards, it might be quite a party.

The invitation had specified uniform, so Sten had tucked himself into the Third Guards' blue full-dress and shako that his cover identity required. Ffillips was also in Guards uniform, wearing medals that Sten knew damned well she wasn't entitled to.

Vosberh moved behind them, wearing a neat, undecorated brown uniform that Sten theorized was of his own design.

Kurshayne's uniform, on the other hand, *was* his Guards parade uniform. The sleeves still had the thread-patterns where rankstripes had been laboriously sewn on and then ripped off a dozen times. He wore none of his campaign ribbons, having explained, worriedly, that he'd hocked them all for quill and was that a problem?

Sergeant Alex Kilgour was the glamour, though.

Somewhere – Sten didn't think it'd been in his kit, although he never knew exactly what Alex chose to lug around in that elderly, battered leather trunk – Alex had put together the following: flat, low-heeled, very shiny black shoes; knee-high, turned-down stockings of a horrible, clashing-colored pattern of squares; a black, silver-mounted, jeweled dagger tucked in the right silk-flashed stocking. Above that Alex wore a hairy skirt in the same pattern as the stockings. In front of his groin a pouch made from the face of an unknown animal hung from silver chains. The chains were attached to a broad, silver-buckled leather belt, with a diagonal support strap running over one shoulder.

Suspended from the belt was not only the pouch, but a half-meter-long, single-edged, hiltless dagger on the right as well as a long, basket-hilted broadsword.

Sten didn't know if Alex thought he was going to a party or an invitational massacre.

To continue: under the belt was a black doublet and vest, both with silver buttons. At Alex's throat was a ruffled silk jabot and, at his wrists, more lace.

Over that was another couple of meters of the hairy, colored cloth, belted to Alex's belt in the rear and then attached to his left shoulder with a silver brooch.

Finishing off the outfit was what Alex called his bonnet – looking a bit like an issue garrison cap, but with more silver and some kind of bird-feather pluming rising from it.

Also, Sten knew, tucked out of sight in that pouch was a nasty little projectile pistol.

Sten couldn't decide exactly what was going on and wasn't sure he wanted to ask.

Naturally, all of the sentries outside the mansion saluted Alex and ignored the others. Only Ffillips seemed upset by the error. They went into the hall.

Just inside the door Sten gratefully parked the shako and walked into the central ballroom.

The first thing he saw was a woman wearing nothing else but a quiver of arrows with a bow tucked beside it taking three glasses of some beverage from a servibot.

Startled, he looked around the ballroom. From the nude Amazon on, his impressions became a little chaotic.

The princes of Nebta seemed to have a vague idea about uniforms but a very definite idea about making these uniforms unique.

Sten saw a pastiche of every army that had ever fought in the thousand years of the Empire and the prehistory before it.

Sten thought he recognized about one tenth of the uniforms. But just barely. There was, for instance, a podgy, red-faced man wearing the fighting cloak of the Thanh, but under it was an aiguelette-crowded purple tunic. There was someone wearing a skirt like Alex's, but of common cloth, with a broad, short-bladed sword, hammered metal helmet, greaves, and shoulder-plate, and even somebody wearing a full metal suit.

He turned to Ffillips in puzzlement.

'That's called armor, Colonel,' Ffillips said as she passed Sten a glass.

'But . . . those holes in the facemask? Wouldn't it leak in space?' Ffillips laughed for some reason and Sten decided to quit showing his ignorance.

Then Parral was standing in front of him, in a costume as fantastic as any of his guests: a long, embroidered robe, a square hat, a huge sword – swords were evidently very popular – and slippers.

'Welcome, gentlemen,' Parral silked. 'Since this fete is in your honor, we are delighted.'

'The pleasure is ours,' Ffillips replied smoothly. 'We can only hope that our campaign is successful enough to provide many other occasions as wonderful.'

Parral looked at Ffillips, then ostentatiously turned his attention to Sten.

'Colonel, there are a few minutes before the meal. Perhaps you and your . . . underlings would care to circulate?'

Sten nodded stiffly.

Sten's ideal party was a certain amount of quill, beer, four or five congenial companions, and a bright woman he hadn't bedded yet. Certainly not this kind of panoply – there must've been a thousand people milling around the ballroom.

But Sten smiled his thanks to Parral and then moved slowly off through the crowd, flanked by Alex and the silent, non-drinking Kurshayne.

'It ain't the heavy haulin' that 'urts the 'orses 'ooves,' Alex murmured, 'hit's the 'ammer, 'ammer, 'ammer on the 'ard 'ighway.'

'What are we doing here?'

'Bein' heroes,' Alex said. 'An' gie'in these wee parasites a chance to dress up.'

'Oh,' Sten said, and set his untouched glass back on a passing tray.

'W'll lurkit around here until they feed us, makit our 'pologies, an' gie back to our wee homes an' gie drunk like civilized sol'yers,' Alex said. 'Dinnae tha' be a plan?'

Sten agreed and started looking at his watch.

The merchant princes of Nebta religiously held to a pattern for the banquet. Dinners were multicourse – a twenty-course meal was regarded as vaguely bourgeois. Each course consisted of a main dish, the cooked barley that had originally sustained the first settlers on Nebta, coupled with a highly exotic side dish.

Of course the princes ignored the barley side dishes and concentrated on the goodies.

Sten had decided the only way to survive terminal obesity was to nibble a lot. He sampled something strange from a dish, then nodded to his waiter, who promptly removed the dish.

He wasn't much impressed by the supposedly exotic dishes. In Mantis he'd relentlessly eaten anything that didn't (a) poison his skin when rubbed on it; (b) move too much; or (c) try to eat him.

The waiter bowed up with the next sample, and Sten tried to behave the way he thought an experienced ex-Guard officer, experienced in affairs of state and the gut, would behave.

Kurshayne hulked behind him. He'd not only refused drink but food as well. Sten thought he was taking this bodyguard thing entirely too seriously.

Alex, on the other hand, was enjoying himself. And eating most of everything in sight. His table area looked a little like ground zero on a very sloppy nuclear test. Sten could not understand where the man was putting all the food – perhaps in that pouch.

The waiter removed the dish. Sten waited. And then heaved a sigh of relief, when he saw other servitors removing the plates. At last it was over.

A few more minutes, listen to some speeches, and then Sten would head for the mercenaries' mansion and bed. He did, after all, have an appointment to keep a few hours before dawn . . .

Parral hissed politely for silence, and the conversational hum in the room died away. Parral stood and lifted his glass.

'I thank you, honored guests, for joining me as we, the defenders and supporters of the True Faith of Talamein, celebrate the victors of the battle of . . .'

And Sten shut his ears off. He was sure this speech would not tell him anything he already didn't want to know.

And the speeches went on, and the toasts went on. Sten barely touched his glass to his lips at each toast.

And then, mercifully, Parral finished, there was applause, and, from some unseen niche, music began.

'Colonel Sten,' Parral said. The man had an odd ability to materialize unseen. Not that Sten noticed, because beside the prince stood a young woman. About Sten's own height; close-cropped dark hair that Sten could already feel on a pillow beside him. She would have been nineteen, perhaps twenty years old.

Her costume was not a uniform; instead it was a high-necked, dark-colored tunic skirt, very conservative until you noticed the hip-high slit up one side of the skirt and until the lights caught the dress.

It turned translucent under certain lighting and at certain angles, suddenly promising flashes of the tanned, smooth skin underneath.

Sten would have thought that his suit radio was suddenly malfunctioning with a static-rush – but he was not wearing a suit.

Dimly he heard Parral: 'This is my youngest sister, Sofia. She expressly wanted to meet and congratulate you.'

Sofia extended a soft hand. 'I am honored, Colonel.' Her voice was low and throaty and full of promises.

Sten stumbled his return greetings, realizing he sounded like an utter clot. He couldn't help staring at her, and then he realized with a start that she was staring at him too. Sten was sure it wasn't true, but it seemed as if she was just as taken as—

'Perhaps,' Parral broke in, 'you would do Sofia the honor of dancing with her.'

Sofia blushed.

'I've never – I don't—' and Sten shut up, because he suddenly knew he was going to learn how to dance in record time.

He took Sofia by the hand and led her around the table.

Trying not to look at her, trying to eye the moving feet of the dancers already on the floor. Hell, it can't be that hard, he reasoned/rationalized. First they move a foot to the side, then the other comes up beside it and – what was the Bhor prayer? . . . By the beard of my mother, don't let me blow it.

Then, somehow, it was all natural as Sofia was all softness melting into his arms. He could smell the perfume in her hair, and Sten, who had never cared much about music, felt something in the dance and was floating across the floor with her. He felt a building tightness in his throat as he found himself drowning in intense deer-eyes staring solemnly up at him.

'Are you enjoying the party?' she whispered to him.

'Not until now,' he said. It was a statement, not a flirt.

'Oh,' she said, blushing again.

Then, if it was possible, she was snuggling closer in his arms. Sten thought he had died and gone to whatever heaven was sanctioned in this part of the Empire.

Suddenly, nearby, he heard a table crash over. Sten spun, Sofia forgotten, his right hand started to curl to bring the knife out.

The center table was overturned and, standing in the rubble was Alex and a young, heavily muscled man that Sten vaguely remembered as being Seigneur Froelich.

'I do not challenge underlings,' Froelich was saying. 'I merely wished to convey my compliments to your superior, express my admiration for his abilities, and then to allow my considerable dismay that he had decided to company the lady Sofia.'

Sten was across the dance floor, costumed Nebtans scattering before him.

'Sergeant!'

'Beggin' your pardon, Colonel.' Alex's voice was down into that deep brogue and almost whisper. 'Ah hae a wee bit a business ae th' moment.'

Sten, properly, shut up. And then there was a tap at his shoulder. He turned, and fingers flicked across his face.

Momentarily blinded, Sten dropped into attack stance, clawhand coming out to block-feint . . . and then he caught himself.

Another man was there, someone who looked enough like Froelich to be his twin. It was Seigneur Trumbo.

'As Seigneur Froelich's cousin, I must also confess to being offended. I also wish to extend my compliments.'

Sten caught a glance of Sofia as the crowd gathered around. Very interesting, he flashed. In a dueling society like Nebta, she doesn't seem delighted. She looks scared. For me? Come on, Sten, he reprimanded himself. Shut your clottin' glands off.

And now Parral. 'This is bccoming an interesting evening,' he said. 'Colonel, perhaps I should explain some of our customs.'

Sten shook his head. 'Don't bother. These two bravos want to fight. S'be't,' Sten mocked.

'Then, tomorrow,' Froelich's cousin began . . .

'Tomorrow I am very busy,' Sten said flatly. 'We fight now. Here.'

A murmur floated through the crowd, and then eyes brightencd. This would indeed be a fete worth talking about.

'As first challenger, then,' Froelich said, 'I believe I have precedence, if you'll excuse me, Seigneur Trumbo?' He bowed to his cousin.

'Ye hae a problem, lad,' Alex said. 'Ye'll nae b'fightin' m'colonel. It's be me.'

'I have already told you that—'

And the great sword hung in Alex's hand and then crashed down, splitting the thick overturned table down the middle.

'Ah said ye'll be fightin' me. Ah challenge you, as Laird Kilgour ae Kilgour, frae ae race thae was noble when your tribe was pullin' p'raties in ae wasteland. Now ye'll fight me or ye'll die here ae y'stand.'

Froelich paled, then recovered, smiling gently.

'Interesting. Very interesting. Then we shall have two bouts.'

The dance floor was cleared and sanded in a few minutes, and the Nebtans ringed the fighting area. Alex and Sten stood fairly close together at one side of the floor, Trumbo and Froelich across from them. The two soldiers were flanked by Vosberh, Ffillips, and the still-unworried Kurshayne.

Since Sten and Alex were the challenged parties, they had choice of weapons as well as location and time.

Alex, of course, had chosen his claymore, and Parral had been delighted to provide Froelich with a basket-hilt saber that nearly matched the Edinburghian's weapon.

Sten had thought wistfully of his own ultimate knife, then discarded the notion. He was, after all, supposed to be a bit of a diplomat as well as a soldier, and he figured that Parral would not be overly thrilled by having one of his court bravos butchered two seconds into the fight.

So he'd picked poignards – long, needle-tapered, double-edged daggers, almost 40cm long. Parral had lovingly selected a matched pair from his own extensive collection.

Sten hefted the weapon experimentally – it was custom-built, of course, and made of carefully layered steel, in the eons-old Damascus style. To compensate for the blade-weight and consequent imbalance, the maker had added a weighted ball pommel. It would do.

Alex padded softly up beside Sten. 'How long, wee Sten, d'Ah play't wi' th' castrati t'makit appear bonnie?'

'Give him a minute or two, anyway.'

Alex nodded agreement and walked to the center of the floor. Froelich stood across from him, testing his saber's temper by tension-bending the blade. And trying to look deadly, dashing, and debonair.

Alex just stood there, blade held casually in eighth position. And then Froelich blurred forward, blade slashing in on a high attack. Alex's hand crossed over, point still down, and blades clanged.

'Ah,' he murmured. 'Y'fight th' wae ae mon should, wi'out skreekit an' carryint on.'

But Sten could tell by the expressions of the Nebtans that Froelich had already broken etiquette. Probably, he guessed, there was supposed to be some kind of formal challenge, offer to withdraw, and all the rest of the boring business. So? All Froelich was doing was shortening the time span before he became wormfood.

Froelich went back on guard. Alex still waited patiently. The next attack was a blinding flurry of strokes into first and third. Or at least it was supposed to have been. Alex locked hilts with Froelich's second stroke in a *prise de fer*, forced the man's saberhand up level, and then shoved.

Froelich clattered back, falling, rolling, coming up, quite respectably fast, Sten thought, and then going on guard. Breathing hard, he closed in, cautiously clog-stepping forward.

And now Alex attacked, brushing past Froelich's parry with a strong beat and flicking the claymore's blade. The tiny cut took off most of Froelich's ear. Froelich riposted and backhanded across Alex's gut – which was no longer there.

Alex had leaped backward, almost ten feet. Again he stood waiting. As Froelich, leaking blood and reddening, howled and came in, Alex flicked a glance at Sten. Now?

Why not? Sten nodded back, and Alex's blade snaked out, clashed Froelich's saber out of the way and then Alex, seemingly in slow motion, brought the claymore's hilt back almost to his neck and hewed.

Froelich's head, gouting blood, described a neat arc and splashed into the punchbowl. The corpse tottered, then collapsed. Alex sheathed his claymore and strode off the floor to dead silence.

'You might really be Laird Kilgour,' Sten whispered.

'Aye. Ah might be,' Alex agreed.

Parral, looking a little shaken, walked up to the two soldiers. 'That was, uh, quite a display, Sergeant.'

Alex gravely nodded his thanks.

'Colonel? Seigneur Trumbo? I should caution you, the man is one of Nebta's best. He has fought more than a score of duels and operates his own *salle*.'

Sten kept silent.

'I am in a bit of a quandary. You should be aware,' Parral went on, 'that this man goes for the kill. On one hand, I do not wish to lose the able captain of my mercenaries.'

'But on the other?'

'The Trumbo family and mine have somewhat of an alliance. His death would be equally inappropriate.'

'The question then, Seigneur Parral,' Ffillips said quietly, 'is which death our colonel would find least appropriate then, is it not?'

Parral had the good grace to smile before walking to the center of the dance floor as a servitor finished sweeping the last of the gore aside and sprinkling fresh sand. The body was being lugged out by two of Froelich's long-faced retainers, who must've bet on their ex-leader.

'It would appear,' Parral said, relieved at finally being able to go through the rigamarole, 'that both challenged party and challenger are unable to settle their differences except by blood. Am I correct?'

Sten nodded, as did Trumbo as the two men walked toward each other, each gauging his opponent.

'Then blood is the argument,' Parral intoned, 'and by blood it shall be settled.' He bowed twice and backed off the floor.

Trumbo went on guard. At least he wasn't holding his poignard like an icepick. Instead he had his left hand flattened out in front of him, fisted into a guard and held chest-high. His poignard was held low, pommel lightly resting on his left hip. He crab-walked toward Sten.

Sten stood nearly full-on, with right hand, fingers curled, held forward, waist high. His poignard was held slightly to the rear and slightly lower than his right hand.

Sten, too, began crab-walking, trying to move to Trumbo's offside. Come on in, friend, he thought, eyes carefully wide open. Come on. A bit closer. And who trained you, clot? as Trumbo's eyes narrowed and predictably he lunged, going for Sten's chest.

But Sten wasn't there to meet the blade. He sidestepped and snapped his right palm into Trumbo's temple. The man staggered back, then recovered.

And came in again. And Sten's knife flicked out, flashing under Trumbo's guardhand, into the flesh of his knife wrist. Blood started dripping slowly as Sten went back on guard.

Trumbo was becoming canny. First thing in a knifefight is try for the cheap kill. But if you're facing an experienced man, the only way of winning is to bleed your opponent to death.

And so he next tried an underhand slash, coming straight up for Sten's knifehand. Sten easily parried the stroke, arm-blocked the blade, and stepped close inside Trumbo's guard. The razor tip of his poignard sliced Trumbo's forehead open.

And Sten doubled back, ready position, moving, moving, shuttling from side to side. Trumbo closed in again and . . . oh, clottin' amateur . . . tried the old knife-flip, tossing the knife from his right to his left hand. The maneuver should've thrown Sten off-guard, and Trumbo would have continued his lunge, driving the poignard deep into Sten's gut.

But somewhere between Trumbo's right and left hand was Sten's snap-kicked foot, and the poignard pirouetted high into the air, gleaming blade flashing reflection, and Sten reversed his grip on the poignard and smashed the pommel into Trumbo's chin.

Trumbo thudded back, stunned. Sten waited for movement, then flipped his own poignard into the air. It thunked, point-first, into the dance floor. The fight was over.

Sten bowed to Parral, who was again looking surprised, and started back toward . . .

'No!' was the scream from what Sten thought/hoped was Sofia, and he was crouched, head-down, duck-spinning as Trumbo came off the floor, grabbing Sten's poignard and driving it forward, and Sten's fingers scooped, his own knife came out of his arm and he overhanded a slash from his knee.

His knife blade hit the poignard's keen steel and cut through it like cheese.

Trumbo's eyes gaped at the impossible and then Sten backrolled and was on his feet, Trumbo still stumbling forward as Sten side-stepped, whirled, and slashed again.

The knife neatly parted Trumbo's skin, ribcage, heart, and lungs before Sten could pull it free. The body squished messily to the floor.

Sten sucked in air that tasted particularly sweet and decided he'd try another bow to Parral.

Chapter Twenty-One

'You disappoint me, Colonel,' Parral said gently.

'Ah?' Sten questioned.

'I thought all soldiers were hard drinkers. Poets. Men. I believe someone wrote, who have an appointment with death.'

Sten sloshed the still-untouched pool of cognac in the snifter and smiled slightly.

'Most soldiers I've known,' he observed dryly, 'would rather help someone else make that appointment.'

Parral's glass was also full.

The two men sat in Parral's art-encrusted library. It was hours later, and the fete had broken up with excited buzzings and laughter. Parral had let Alex and Sten freshen and change in his chambers and then had wanted to talk to Sten alone.

Reluctantly Alex, Kurshayne, Ffillips, and Vosberh had left the mansion. After all, Sten had pointed out reasonably, I'm in no particular danger. No one except an absolute drakh-brain would kill his mercenary captain before the war's won.

'I find you fascinating, Colonel.' Parral observed. touching his glass to his lips. 'First, we in the Lupus Cluster are . . . somewhat isolated from the mainstream of Imperial culture. Second, none of us have had the advantage of dealing with a professional soldier. By the way, aren't you rather . . . young to have held your present office?'

'Bloody wars bring fast promotions,' Sten said.

'Of course.'

'The reason I asked you to stay behind is, of course, primarily personally to compliment your prowess as a warrior . . . and to gain a better knowledge of what you and your people intend.'

'We intend winning a war for you and for the Prophet Theodomir,' Sten said, being deliberately obtuse.

'No war lasts forever.'

'Of course not.'

'You assume victory, then?'

'Yes.'

'And after that victory?'

'After we win,' Sten said, 'we collect our pay and look for another war.'

'A rootless existence . . . Perhaps . . . Perhaps,' Parral continued, staring intently into his snifter, 'you and your men might find additional employment here.'

'In what capacity?'

'Do you not find it odd that we have two cultures, both very similar, at each other's throats? Do you not find it odd that both of these cultures espouse a religious faith that you – a sophisticated man of the Galaxy – must find somewhat archaic?'

'I have learned never to question the beliefs of my clients.'

'Perhaps you should, Sten. I know little of mercenaries, I admit. But what little my studies produce is that those who survived to die without their swords in hand became . . . shall we say, politically active?'

Parral waited for Sten's comment. None came.

'A man of your obvious capabilities . . . particularly a man who could develop, let us say, personal interests in his clients, might find it more profitable to linger on after his contract was fulfilled, might he not?'

Sten stood and walked to one wall, and idly touched a gouache of a merchant's tools – microcomputer, money converter, beam scales, and a projectile weapon – that hung on the wall, then turned back to Parral.

'I gather,' he said, 'that the key to success as a merchant is an ability to fence with words. Unfortunately, I have none of that. I would assume, Seigneur Parral, that what you are asking is that, after we destroy the Jannisars, you would wish us to remain on, with a contract to remove Theodomir.'

Parral managed to look shocked. 'I would never suggest such a thing.'

'No. You wouldn't,' Sten agreed.

'This evening has run extremely late, Colonel. Perhaps we should continue the discussion at a later date. Perhaps after more data has become available to you.'

Sten bowed, set his full glass down on a bookcase, and walked to the door.

Chapter Twenty-Two

Sten walked down the steps and yawned broadly at Nebta's setting moon. A very long night, Sten, he thought to himself. And you still have four hours to go until you make contact.

'You look tired, Colonel,' came the silken voice from the shadows.

Kill a man, love a woman, Sten hoped. It could turn out to be an interesting evening. He nodded to Sofia as she rose from her seat on the balustrade.

Not to mention interesting things like my dawn meeting yet to come, not to mention Parral's wanting me to sell out the Prophet, not to mention this incredible woman who I do not believe wants to make love to me because of the cut of my hair.

And I will momentarily ignore the fact that my gonads are suggesting it's perfectly proper to sell out Emperor, mercenaries, Theodomir, and Uncle Tom Dooley for this woman. He smiled back at Sofia.

'You provided quite an entertainment,' Sofia said.

'Not my idea of an enjoyable evening.'

'After they removed your opponents, I looked for you.'

'Thought it best to leave, Sofia. I do not think it's proper to dance with a woman with blood up to your elbows.'

Sofia was surprised. The script was not going as it should.

'The only thing I could be sorry about,' Sten improvised, 'is thst my late friends intervened before I could tell you how lovely you are.'

Sofia brightened. Things might proceed. And Sten suppressed an urge to laugh. MANTIS SECTION/COVERT OPERATIONS Instruction Order Something, Clause I Forget, Paragraph Who Remembers: 'When approached on a sexual level, covert operators should remember that they have not necessarily been found attractive beyond the moon and the stars but rather that the person making the approach is allied with the opposition and attempting to subvert, to maneuver into a life-threatening situation, or to provide the opposition with blackmail material. In any event, until a life-threatening situation occurs, it is recommended that operatives pretend to be seducible. Interesting intelligence has been produced in such situations.'

And so Sten stepped very close to Sofia, lowered his voice, and gently touched a finger to her cheek.

'Perhaps we might walk. Perhaps I might have a chance to tell you what I wasn't able to.'

Sofia's smile vanished. Then it returned to her face. Very interesting. The woman is an amateur, Sten concluded. Parral, you should never have sent your little sister to do a whore's work.

Then, arm in arm, the two walked down the steps into Parral's sprawling garden.

Chapter Twenty-Three

It was quite a garden.

At one end – almost a kilometer from the castle – the garden narrowed, then spread into a soft meadow where a gentle river flowed.

And of course there was a small dock in midmeadow.

And of course there was a boat.

You aren't that far removed from Imperial technology, Sten thought as he stood on the dock, romantically put an arm around Sofia, and looked at the boat.

It was clear plas, with an illuminated strip to mark its gunwale. No sign of power, no oars, just several soft cushions.

What a setup, Sten thought.

And so he kissed Sofia.

And again the world went soft around the edges as her lips caught him and brought him in. At that moment, Sten was having trouble remembering who was seducing whom.

He gently broke the kiss and touched her lips at the corners with his, twice. Then bent, took off her shoes, and stepped her down into the boat.

Noiselessly, the boat moved along the river. Above them hung the waning moon, and below them, Sten could see the luminous flash of fish as they slept below him.

And so we will round this bend in the river, Sten thought, and then the boat will dock itself in a lovely grotto. And what will I find there besides taps? Assassins? Kidnappers? Parral working a badger game? And good luck to 'em all. Sten bent over and kissed Sofia again.

It was a helluva grotto, Sten realized as the clear boat silently touched the grassy bank. Rocks had been sculpted to form a secluded hideaway. And down over them splashed a waterfall, illuminated with what Sten guessed were a couple of low-powered meth/HC1 lasers, lasing from UV down toward yellow in the spectrum.

A helluva trap, too, as he lifted Sofia in his arms out of the boat, ready to peg her into the arms of any waiting killers.

But there was nothing.

'Your brother has quite a taste in gardens,' he said.

'Parral?' Sofia was puzzled. 'He doesn't know about this. I designed it.'

The situation had gone awry slightly. Sten lowered Sofia to the grass, then stood again. She put both hands behind her head and eyed him quizzically. Sten lifted one boot behind him and touched a bootheel. The tiny indicator light stayed dark. How odd. No monitors.

For Sten, the situation was very rapidly getting out of hand.

He knelt beside Sofia, one leg curled under him, his hand ready to bring out the knife. She was still staring at him.

'Did you know Parral ordered me to dance with you?'

Sten hesitated, then nodded.

'You did?' she said, slightly surprised. 'And did you know he wanted me to wait for you, outside the library? And I was supposed to take you – take you to my chambers?' Her voice was suddenly fast, confessional.

Sten was starting to realize that, at least in this case, the *Covert Operations Manual* was a tad lacking. He had the sense to keep his mouth shut.

'Do you know what Parral wanted me to do?'

'I can imagine.'

And Sofia stopped.

Embarrassed, Sten suddenly realized that he had carried his basilisk act a little too far.

He swung a leg over Sofia and, balancing himself on his knees, slowly brought both hands down the sides of her face, down across her chest, moving to the side of her breasts, across her stomach.

Sofia sighed gratefully and her eyes closed.

Sten's hands moved gently back up, then down, caressing her bare arms and hands.

Sofia's hand moved blindly to the catches on her gown and snapped them free. Sten, moving very slowly, slid the gown down to Sofia's waist, and her erect nipples on small breasts gleamed in the reflected laser-light from the waterfall.

He kissed her then, on the lips, on the throat and then down across her breasts to her stomach.

Then stood and dropped away his uniform.

And there was no sound except the whisper of her gown coming away from her body and the arabesque of two bodies meeting.

Chapter Twenty-Four

It was minutes before dawn as Sten, now clad in black coveralls, moved from dying shadow to alleyway through Nebta's main street.

It ain't the killing, he thought sleepily to himself, that makes sojering hard. It's the fact the bassids never let you go to bed.

He preferred not to reflect – not then, anyway – on making love to Sofia. He wasn't sure what it all meant – other than Sofia was the first woman since Bet who had added star drive to her sexuality.

Besides, there was still this clottin' meeting.

After dark no one in his right mind went down Nebta's streets, which then became the province of the killer gangs and the only slightly less lethal night patrols who reasoned (with some justification) that anyone out after dark was either a villain or desperately in need of escort service. Payment up front, please.

Sten slid down an alley that stank of death, garbage, and betrayal. Waiting at the end of the alley was the only other person he'd seen on the streets besides one half-drunk patrol team. A beggar. A scrofulous beggar, whose sores gleamed luminous in the near dawn.

'Giveen me, gentleman, y'blessing,' the beggar wheezed.

'Mahoney,' Sten said frankly, 'you're clottin' hard to bless. Lesions that glow in the dark. Give me a break.'

The beggar straightened and shrugged. 'It's a new lab gimmick.' Mahoney shrugged as he straightened to his full height. 'I told them it was too much, but what the hell.'

Sten shook his head and leaned against one slimy wall, one eye on the alley mouth.

'Report,' Mahoney said briskly.

Sten ran it down – how he'd successfully recruited his mercs, none of whom had yet tried to knife him in the back. How he'd done his first by-the-book raid on the Jann, aimed at getting them into a reactive position and operating emotionally rather than logically. How Parral had opened negotiations to sell Theodomir down the creek.

'No surprises so far,' Sten finished.

'What about Sofia?'

Sten's mouth dropped as Mahoney grinned. 'You see, m'lad? The day I don't know far more about what's going on than you do is the day you'll take over Mantis. But—'

'Brief me,' Sten said.

'Nineteen. Convent – no, you don't know the term – religious/sexual exclusionary training. Parral is trying to marry her off for an alliance. Non-virgin. Bright, near genius. Prog – looking for her own alliance, which I assume . . .' Mahoney decided to be delicate. Sten decided to keep his mouth shut.

'Sounds as if you're doing quite well, lad,' Mahoney went on. 'You have only one problem.'

'Which is?'

'Unfortunately, our estimates were that it would take three E-years for word of the Eryx discovery to seep out.'

'But?'

'But somebody talked. I am truly sorry, m'lad, but current estimates are that within two E-years every wastrel, geologist, and miner in this sector will be heading for the Eryx Region – and coming straight through the Wolf Worlds!'

Sten grunted. 'You don't make it easy, Colonel.'

'Life does not make it easy, Sten. So your timetable is moved up. The Lupus Cluster must be pacified within one E-year.'

'You can ruin a man's entire day, boss.'

'After the grotto,' Mahoney said gently. 'I think it would take a great deal more than me to do that.'

And then he was crouched, cloak across his face. He sidled down the alley and was gone, leaving Sten in the shadows, watching the first glisten of the rising sun and wondering how the hell Mahoney knew about *that*.

Chapter Twenty-Five

It was a small gray building in a small green glen, located almost one hundred kilometers north of Sanctus' capital. A young man in the blood-red uniform of Mathias' Companions escorted Sten to the entrance, waved him inside, and left him.

Sten entered, somewhat tentatively.

To a tourist the glen would have looked deserted. But Sten had heard rustling in the undergrowth as he and his escort had passed through. And the smell of many campfires. And the forest was silent – a sure clue to human presence.

The walls on the inside of the little building dripped with the sweat of the high-humidity water world that was Sanctus. No one waited for him inside.

He moved through what seemed empty administrative offices filled with desks, coms, and vid-file cabinets, then was brought up short by a glass wall.

Through the glass he could see Mathias.

Except for a modest breechcloth, the young man was naked. Sten watched quietly as Mathias inserted his hands into two metal rings, attached to three-meter-long chains. The chains themselves seemed to hang from nothing, but were grav-bonded into position.

Mathias' body was all one gleaming, rippling muscle. And even Sten was impressed as the Prophet's son lifted himself effortlessly on the rings, supporting himself on upper-body strength alone. The young man's stomach muscles knotted as he lifted his legs straight up above his head and did a handstand on the rings. Mathias did an unbelievable number of arm presses, then swung his body in a long, slow, 360-degree loop. Again and again, and then he let go, doubling himself into a somersault. He landed perfectly on his feet as if he were on a low-grav planet.

Sten whistled to himself softly, and then opened and walked through the glass door.

Mathias spotted him instantly and shouted a greeting. 'Colonel. Your presence is our blessing.'

Mathias grabbed a towel from the floor and began to wipe away the sweat as Sten moved forward to meet him.

Sten shook his hand, eyed the rings then the young man as he pulled on a plain, rough-clothed robe. 'Pretty impressive,' he said.

'Oh' – Mathias smiled – 'my friends and I believe in the fitness of our bodies.'

'Your friends?' Sten remembered the smell of campfires.

'The Companions,' Mathias said, taking Sten by the arm and leading him toward the back door. 'You know about them?'

Of course Sten did. They were the six hundred young men – all very wealthy and all very religious – who were Mathias' couterie. They delighted in all forms of sport, physical deprivation, challenge, and prayer. They were totally devoted to Mathias and the ancient ways of the religion of Talamein.

'Yes, I know about them.'

He was on Sanctus at the mysterious request of Mathias, a polite plea for a visit. An important one, Mathias had assured him. Sten didn't have the time, but he thought it was politic to go.

'I have been following your exploits,' Mathias said as they exited the door and started down the path into the fern forest.

Sten didn't reply. He was waiting.

'I must say, Colonel, I'm impressed.' And with just enough hesitation to qualify for an afterthought: 'As is my father.'

Sten just nodded his thanks.

'I have been thinking,' Mathias continued. 'You and your men are bearing the brunt of this fight yourselves. For which we are grateful. But it isn't proper.'

If Sten had *really* been a mercenary, he would have agreed. Instead he made a polite protest. Mathias raised a hand to stop him. 'If we are to be truly victorious,' Mathias said, 'Sanctus must dare to spill its own blood. Not just that of – if you will forgive me – beings who might be viewed as mere hirelings.'

A self-deprecating smile to Sten.

'Not that we are not convinced that all of you are committed to the cause of Talamein. And that of the True Prophet – my father.'

Sten accepted his apology. Very wary now.

'And so, I have a proposal for you, Colonel. No, an offer.'

They turned the corner of the path, which spilled into a broad glade.

Mathias pointed dramatically. Drawn up in line after blood-red line were the Companions. Six hundred young men in their spotless ceremonial uniforms. Without an apparent signal, they all raised a hand in salute.

'MATHIAS,' they shouted in unison.

And Sten gave a slight jolt as Mathias shouted back: 'FRIENDS.'

The young men cheered deafeningly. Mathias, all smiles, turned to Sten.

'Colonel Sten, I offer you my life and the lives of my companions.'

Sten wasn't quite sure what to say.

'What the clot could I do?' Sten asked Alex.

The big man was pacing back and forth in the control room on the Bhor ship.

'But the'r't nae professional, lad.'

Sten slumped into a chair. 'Look, Mahoney has moved the whole operation up one entire year.'

'We'll recruit some more men,' Alex responded.

'No time,' Sten said. 'Right now we need bodies. Anyplace we can get them.'

'Cannon fodder,' Alex said.

Sten shook his head. 'They're not professionals, but the Companions have trained – after a fashion. And they will take orders. All we have to do is form them into our mold.'

'An Ah dinnae ken wh'll be trainit' them,' Alex continued suspiciously. 'Ffillips? Trainit th' lads ae commandos? Th' nae be't time f'r thae.'

'Possibly Vosberh,' Sten said, keeping his face straight.

'Nae, nae. Tha' be't e'en more silly.'

Sten grinned at him. 'Then we have the answer.'

Alex was aghast. 'Me,' he said, thumping a meaty thumb into his chest. 'Y'nae be't suggestin' ae Kilgour wae y'?'

'I thought it was your idea.'

Sten handed Alex a fiche. 'Now, I was thinking, Red Rory of the Advertisements, you should begin their training with . . .'

Chapter Twenty-Six

Alex keyed his throat-mike. 'Ye'll be awake noo an' be lookit across yon field.'

Fifty of Mathias' Companions were dug in across the military crest of a wooded hill. Most of them looked puzzled, having no idea what the purpose of the exercise was.

It wae, Alex thought to himself, a wee bit ae argument against heroism. He tucked behind a bush as, far across the brush-covered field, another fifty of the Companions came into sight, weapons ready. They were spread out in standard Guard-type probe formation.

He yawned and scratched, waiting for the soldiers to come closer. They did. A Companion next to Alex lifted his rifle, and Alex backhanded him on his shrapnel helmet. The Companion thudded down, unconscious, and Alex reminded himself yet again that the wee light-grav folk had to be treated with ae gentleness.

Wait . . . wait . . . wait . . . and then Alex hit the airhorn's button. The blast rang down the hill, and the entrenched Companions opened fire.

With blanks.

Down on the flats, some of the Companions dove for cover, others began howling and charged.

The firing doubled in volume. Alex let it continue for six seconds, then bounded up and down into the open. With his mike open.

'Cease fire, y'bloodthirsty reeks! Cease FIRE!'

The popping died away. On the flats, the probing Companions, following instructions, froze in place – in the exact positions they were stopped in when Alex gave the ceasefire signal.

Alex waved the other fifty out of their hidey-holes and down onto the fields. They trailed out and assembled in two-platoon formation.

Each man carried a plas target. The plan was to replace the real men with the targets. After that, Alex chuckled to himself, the real fun would begin.

Alex walked around the attacking formation. A Companion who'd sensibly found cover was replaced with one type of target – if the cover he'd found would withstand projectile fire, the target was only part of a man's head. But if, on the other hand, he'd ducked behind a bush (which worked fine in the livies), a full head-and-shoulders replaced him.

The slow-to-react or stupid, who'd merely flattened on the ground or, still worse, stayed erect when the airhorn went off had man-size silhouettes in their place.

Finally, the howlers-and-chargers had oversize targets – targets that were half again the size of a normal man.

By now the entire company of Companions was standing at the hill's base. Alex motioned them back up into the defensive line and had them take firing positions.

Companion squad leaders now passed out live ammunition.

'Lock an' load ae mag'zine,' Alex bellowed. 'On command, begin . . . firing!'

The hillside rocked to the thunder of weapons. This time Alex waited until all trainees had fired their weapons dry (the projectile weapons used by the Companions and mercs had fifty-round banana magazines, nowhere near the capacity of the unobtainable Imperial willyguns with their 1400-round AM_2 tube mags).

Then he brought the Companions out of their holes, checked to make sure all weapons were unloaded, and went back down the hill. If God gae us tha gift ta see ourselves as others see us, came a misquote from Alex's overly poetic backbrain. He led the hundred men from target to target.

'Noo, y'ken wha' happens whae ae mon dinna find shelter encounterin' ae enemy,' he explained. 'Yama lad, y'dinna find naught to hide behind. Ah' y'see whae would've recked wi' ye?'

The trainee looked at the riddled silhouette, gulped, and nodded.

Alex saved the charging fanatics for last and then gently tapped one of 'them' on his shredded plas.

'Ae dinna be knockit heroes,' he said. 'But a wee hero who's dead afore he closes wi' the enemy be naught but ae fool, Ah think.'

The Companions, who'd now had a chance to see exactly what an enemy unit could do to them – and had done it to themselves – were very thoughtful on the run back to the training camp.

*

A fortieth-century explosive mine looked like nothing much in particular except possibly a chunk of meteorite. It would float innocuously until a ship of the proper size came within range. It then ceased to be innocuous.

The problem with mines, as always, was remembering where they'd been planted and being able to recover them after the war ended. For Sten's mercenaries, however, who had no intention of hanging around the Wolf Cluster for one nanosecond after payday, it didn't matter.

A combined platoon of Vosberh's and Ffillips' men had scattered half a hundred of such chunks of rubble in orbital patterns that Egan's computer boys had suggested, near one of the Jann main patrol satellites. Then they'd withdrawn on the Bhor ship, as silently and unobtrusively as they'd arrived.

The first mine didn't detonate for almost a week. It was fortunate for Sten's purposes that the first one happened to ignite when a full fuel ship was making its approach to the satellite. The small nuke not only took out the fuel ship but its two escorts and the pilot vessel from the satellite.

Mines, properly laid, are extremely cost-effective weapons.

It was nae thae the Companions sang everywhere they went, Alex decided. It was thae they had such bloody awful taste in their music: doleful hymns; chants describing how wonderful it would be to meet death killing Jann.

Ah, well, he realized. Wi' m'own race's history, Ah dinnae hae a lot to complain aboot.

'Seventy seconds,' one of Ffillips' lieutenants said. Egan and his bustling computer people paid no attention.

The twelve of them, with two teams of Ffillips' specialists for security, had taken over one of the Jann observation satellites. The three Jann manning the post had been disposed of, and Egan and his men had gone to work

Wires, relays. laser-transmitters, and fiberoptic cables littered the satellite's electronics room, and now the Lycée people waited while Egan caressed keys on a meter-wide board he'd lugged onto the satellite. He tapped a final key then pulled his board out of circuit. 'Very fine,' he said. 'Let's blow it.'

Ffillips' lieutenant saluted and his men began planting demo charges.

The Lycée gang had used the terminal on the satellite to patch straight into the Jann battle computer. They'd lifted all logs of the mercenary actions from the computer records.

That, Egan thought to himself, will make it a bit hard for the bad guys to get any kind of tac analysis. A good day's work, he realized, as he headed for the Bhor ship hanging just beyond the lock.

He didn't bother to tell anyone that he'd also removed any mention of the Lycée people or Egan himself from the records, and added a FORGET IT command just in case any entry was made. A soldier, after all, has to protect his back – and there was no guarantee that the good guys would necessarily win.

And so the raids continued. A suddenly vanished Jann patrol ship here or a Jann outpost that broadcast pleas for reinforcement before signals shut down. Merchant ships that failed to arrive at their planetfalls. A few 'removals' of Jann administrators.

A man is much larger than a mosquito – and Sten's entire force was less than one-millionth the strength of the Jann. But a mosquito can drive a man to distraction and, given enough time, bleed him dry.

Sten was slowly bleeding the Jann.

'You're sure?' Sten asked dubiously.

'Aye,' Alex said. 'Th' Companions are as trained ae Ah can makit 'em. We're ready to go to battle, lad.'

Excellent, Sten thought to himself. Now all I have to do is figure out where and when.

Chapter Twenty-Seven

Sten eyed Sofia with extreme interest, what she was holding with extreme skepticism, and where they were about to go with extreme terror.

One of the more fascinating things about Sofia – besides how a woman that young could come up with such unusual ways of passing the time when the candles were blown out – was that her body, from the eyebrows down, was completely depilated.

And so she stood, naked and smiling on a black volcanic sand beach, waiting for Sten. Beside her were two three-meter-long pieces of hand-laid clear plas. The boards went from their knife-tip to a curved, half-meter midsection to a suddenly chopped stem. Hanging under each board's tailsection were twin, scimitar rudders.

Sten, whose 'culture' had taught him that the best place for water was in a glass with a healthy dollop of synthalk, had trouble understanding the Nebtans' fascination with see-through watercraft.

'You are hesitating, O my brave Colonel.'

'Clottin' right,' Sten murmured as he turned from the exotic spectacle of Sofia to stare down that beach into the ocean.

Though Nebta normally had mild tides, there were certain places where sharply shelving sea bottoms and undersea reefs made waves build and double on themselves. Such was this beach – one of Parral's seemingly numberless hideaways. Back in the tropic foliage was a small cottage. The beach swept the base of the tiny bay, possibly four kilometers wide at its mouth. And the waves walked in – building to ten- and twelve-meter heights before they crashed into the shore.

One such wave broke, perhaps three hundred meters from the beach, and spume flew high and the air boomed and the ground trembled somewhat and Sten winced.

Sofia had kidnapped him for a three-day break. Sten was quite kidnappable, despite Mahoney's announcement that the timetable was now very, very short – he still hadn't figured out exactly what depredation he and the mercs planned next.

'This is a sport?' Sten questioned. 'It looks more like ritual suicide.'

Sofia didn't answer; instead she dropped one of the long planks on the sand, picked up the other, and dashed into the surf crawling on the shore.

Why, Mahoney, do I have to kill myself practicing these quaint local customs? Sten wondered. He picked up the second board, ran into the water, flat-dove on top of the board, and paddled after Sofia through the surf.

Sten, in spite of Sofia's giggled harassment and example, was not naked. He wore a pair of briefs, having semi-successfully argued that he would not need a third rudder even if he was dumb enough to try this.

But still, he thought as he awkwardly paddled out behind Sofia's board, the view was worth it. And suddenly the backwash caught him and suddenly the board was on top of him and suddenly he was wading back to the beach to pick up his board.

Looking out to sea, he then noticed how Sofia caught her board in both hands and rolled upside down when a wave came over her.

Learning is such fun, he thought as he began the long paddle out again.

And somehow the gods were kind and somehow the waves were quiet and somehow Sten ended up sitting on his board, outside the breaker line next to Sofia.

'Oh, Princess,' Sten began, sputtering out water that tasted very salty, 'this is a wonderful sport which you have shown me. Now I assume we sit out here until UV rays burn us, paddle back in, and do what all sensible animals in their mating season do. Correct?'

As a wave swept in behind them Sofia laughed and started paddling vigorously. The wave caught her board and picked it up. The wave grew to seven meters in height, curling, cresting, and – Sten never having been around the ocean much – sounding an ominous boom as it drove toward shore.

You could get killed doing this, Sten thought in astonishment as he saw Sofia get to her knees, then her feet, riding the wave as her board skimmed down its face. He watched Sofia as she back-and-forthed on the board, always keeping it just ahead of the breaking wave as it self-destructed.

Impossible, Sten's mind told him flatly. You are expected to mount a piece of flotation gear, riding an ocean current as it moves toward shore at perhaps 80kph, stand up, maintain your balance, and also be able to do what . . .

Sofia had her toes curled snugly over the board's front edge, still as her board curved up and down on the still-unbroken wave front.

And then the wave broke and somehow Sofia was out of the wave, and behind it and waving Sten on.

Why in the Emperor's name, Sten whimpered to himself, did I have to fall in love with a macha woman?

And then he dropped back on the board, hearing his words echo in his mind. Love? Sofia? You are here on the Emperor's Mission. Sex is one thing. Love? Sten, do you know what love is?

Indeed I do, his mind answered. I remember you mourning for Bet when you thought she was dead. I remember Vinnitsa. And then Bet's being alive. But also remember the love fading with Bet and you suddenly finding yourself as friends.

Nice thinking, another part of his mind mocked. Good way to keep you from having to do what Sofia did. There is no way that this can be done without a meta-balance computer, Sten's mind continued as he dug for the next wave.

And it built and Sten crawled cautiously to his feet and suddenly he was standing and just as suddenly the wind was roaring like the wave below him and Sten wondered why all the excitement since this wave is not moving me all that fast and suddenly he moved his board to the top of the wave and it crested and . . .

The wave curled and smashed, carrying nondescript bits of debris with it, several logs, Sten, and his board.

The board was on top of Sten, then Sten was on top of the board, then the board was lost and Sten was quietly chewing sand and small beach creatures, then he was picking himself up in the spume and quiet of the beach and Sofia was laughing at him.

He spat a mouthful of seaweed and waded to the shore

'Ready to try it again?' Sofia asked

'In a moment,' Sten managed. 'But first let's have a taste.' And he staggered up the beach toward their picnic outfit, with Sofia behind him. With luck, wine, and a certain amount of technique, Sten felt sure he would never have to get near that killer ocean again.

Chapter Twenty-Eight

Sten and Mathias walked out onto the floor of the massive hangar where Sten's mercs and the Companions were assembled.

'People of the Prophet,' Mathias roared, and Sten wondered where the extra set of vocal chords came from as his boyos thundered their agreement.

'Now we strike against the heart of the Jann,' Mathias shouted. 'Against Ingild. We shall destroy the heresy. We go forth to die for Theodomir and the True Faith of Talamein.'

While Sten listened to the howl of glee from Mathias' legions, he wondered if he was riding another wave of the kind that Sofia had seen him destroyed on. He almost discarded the notion, but over the years, Sten had learned never to scrap that kind of thought. He filed it away to ponder later.

Then Mathias smiled and bowed to Sten. 'Our Colonel. Our leader. The man who has led us in victory. He will now tell us how we shall destroy the falseness – the evil – of contra-Prophet thinking that is the empire of the Jann and Ingild.'

'Aye, Colonel,' Alex semi-whispered from behind him. 'How you plan ae bein' ae braw hero ae tha, Ae dinna ken.'

Hell if Sten knew, as silence fell in the huge hangar. Hoping for inspiration, he eyed the wall-size sit chart that showed in multicolor projections, the garrison worlds of the Jann. And then he had what might be an idea.

And slowly began composing the battle plan . . .

Chapter Twenty-Nine

Otho poured Sten and Alex another liter of stregg, rumbled a laugh, and said, 'No. I don't want to hear it the way you presented the situation to those fanatics. But since you're here, and all . . .' His voice gurgled off as he downed the liter. Alex followed suit.

Sten carefully ignored the mug. 'Situation, Target – Urich. The Jann shipbuilding world. The only world they've got that can produce starships.'

'Och,' Otho agreed.

'This is our target. We'll take out this entire complex.' The plot board hummed into life and the holographic projection vibrated into existence.

'Urich,' Sten continued. 'Ship docks are' – he touched a control – 'in green. Landing facilities, blue. AA lasers, surface-to-air missiles, and multibarrel projectile weapons in red.'

Otho stood and peered down at the projection. Then belched thoughtfully. 'By my mother's beard, but the black ones guard themselves well.

'Having none of your knowledge, Sten,' Otho went on, 'and being but a simple trader, I would have no idea of how you humanoids could capture such a place.'

'We aren't. This is another smash-and-destroy run.'

'You'll use nuclear hellbombs?'

'Negative.'

'If I were a warrior,' Otho said, 'which, praise the beard of my mother, I am not, I would need a host of Bhor and several planetary cycles to destroy this Jann nest.'

'We aren't going to take everything out,' Sten said. 'Just this.'

His finger went through a huge, imposing structure in the center of the complex. One kilometer by two kilometers long by one kilometer.

'This is the engine-hull mating plant. Destroy it, and the whole port's nothing but a yacht repair yard.'

Another control fingered, and the plotting board cleared then refocused, this time with only the mating plant on the board. A brooding, dark-gray mass.

Above the projection hung a list of the plant's vital details. Ti-ferroconcrete construction, tetra-beam reinforcement. The walls were, at their base, fifty meters thick, tapering to a thickness of twenty meters at the roof curve. At either side of the structure were huge clamshell doors, with control booths centered in the midpoint of each panel.

'Environment controls, damage controls, and admin are in a long tube, running lengthwise down the plant's interior, halfway up the walls,' Sten continued.

'You're a world of information about this, Sten,' Otho said admiringly. 'Could I wonder your sources?'

Alex preened slightly. 'In th' propit light, Ah look quite dashin' ae a Jann.'

Otho touched mugs with Kilgour, and they downed the contents and refilled the mugs.

'I can feel the time-winds touch me,' Otho said as he gazed intently at Sten. 'What will you require of the Bhor?'

'Two things. Most important, fifty planetfall lighters, with pilots.'

'Which will be used for?' Otho was growling now.

'You'll land the unit. Then you and your pilots will provide supressing fire.'

'No.' Otho pushed his mug away and hunched, beetling face now locked in merchant/skeptic/negative expression. 'Perhaps you do not understand the Bhor position,' he growled. 'Admitted, we are not fond of the Jann and, when possible, find an excuse to alter their existence cycle. But we are still only minor body parasites to them.

'And while we admire your cause, Colonel, we must be . . . your word I believe is "pragmatic" about the situation.

'Sometimes the cause of righteousness does not win, as I am sure you are aware. And if you lose – and by the fortune of your fathers survive – you and your soldiers will merely lick your wounds and move on to another war.

'But we – the Bhor – must remain to reap the wrath of the Jann.

'We will convoy you and your forces, Colonel, quite willingly. We will even provide resupply. Both functions are those of a merchant. But join your war? No.'

Alex purpled and was about to say something but Sten quickly shook his head. 'I understand, Otho. You do have your people to worry about.'

The hulk looked puzzled, then relieved. As Otho reached out for the mug, Sten added quietly, 'Your people – and your ancestors.'

Otho glowered and took his hand off the mug.

'My apologies, Otho. Now if you will excuse us . . .' Sten stood and Otho rose also, moving slightly reluctantly toward the port.

'We have our own streggans to fight.'

And before Otho could react, Sten eased him out. Came back to the plotting board.

'Ae m' gran' said, y'catchit more haggis wi' honey thae vin'gar,' Alex said, with mild admiration. Sten frowned then shrugged and sat back down at the table.

Then swinging a computer terminal down from the ceiling and eyeing the plotting table's holography, he began writing his operations order.

The port slid open and Otho loomed in the way.

'Your streggans indeed! By my father's icy buttocks!'

He stalked back to his half-finished mug, drained it, refilled it, drained it again, and then growled, 'If the Bhor must take sides, then at least we must have all information,' and hovered over Sten's terminal . . .

OPERATIONS ORDER 14

EYES ONLY. DISTRIBUTION LIMITED TO FOLLOWING OFFICERS AND CONCERNED INDIVIDUALS. ALL RECIPIENTS TO SIGN RECEIPT THIS ORDER. ALL RECIPIENTS TO ACKNOWLEDGE RECEIPT ON ACCEPTANCE. OFFICERS INVOLVED ARE DIRECTED TO READ THIS ORDER IN PRESENCE OF ACCOMPANYING GUARD. NO COPIES PERMITTED. UPON COMPLETION, THIS ORDER TO BE RETURNED TO ACCOMPANYING GUARD FOR RETURN THIS HEADQUARTERS.

Distribution: STEN, OC. BN-2 SECTION, FFILLIPS OIC FIRST COMPANY, VOSBERH, OIC SECOND COMPANY.

Note: Eyes Only: Involved indigenous personnnel (committed Bhor tac/air personnel, Command structure MATHIAS' COMPANIONS) will be verbally briefed by OC.

This order is not to be discussed in their presence.

Situation:
Since the first operational commitment of FIRST STRIKE FORCE, now operating in conjunction with MATHIAS' COMPANIONS, Intelligence estimates of a high order suggest that JANNISAR command elements and hierarchic elements of INGILD's theocracy have accepted a defensive posture. Destruction of THE CITADEL, a primary part of JANN morale, must be considered a factor, as well as this conflict, which has lasted for several generations, and now is entering an active phase.

The above have produced not only tactical inertia on the part of the JANN but a significant increase in officer suicides among JANN ranks. Four systems previously lightly garrisoned by JANN patrol wings have been abandoned as JANN elements regroup in force on main garrison worlds. Intel-estimates suggest a JANN offensive will be mounted in sixty Standard days (estimate plus-minus: four days). Such an offensive will most likely be directed either at NEBTA or SANCTUS. Such an offensive will not be allowed to occur.

The mission:
The operation against THE CITADEL was effective in partially destroying esprit among the JANN. This operation will destroy the JANN ability to physically patrol systems under their control. The target world is URICH, the center of JANN fleet activity. (See FICHE A for Planetary Details of URICH.) FIRST STRIKE FORCE, operating with MATHIAS' COMPANIONS, will force a landing on URICH and destroy as completely as possible URICH's fleet support, ship construction, fuel, and maintenance capabilities.

EXECUTION:
This assault will be a combined operation:
Initial transhipping to 4 planetary diameters off URICH will be provided by Armed Merchant shipping, to be provided by PARRAL. (Details – FICHE B). These ships will deploy assault and tac/air elements, assume an out-atmosphere orbital pattern, and, on completion of strike, will land on URICH to pick up assault and tac/air elements. Combat deployment will be provided by 50 modified Bhor planetfall lighters. Lighters will be assault armed with available medium-range weaponry (Details – FICHE C), provisioned,

maintained, and manned by provided BHOR personnel (Details – FICHE D). Mentioned BHOR lighters will both land second element assault units and provide active suppression of enemy fire. (Details on strike formation and specific tac requirements – FICHE E.)
The Main Strike element will be quartered on a heavily modified PRITCHARD-class freighter, ex-MS ATHERSTON (Modification details – FICHE F). This ship will be crewed by volunteers, as well as selected first-strike assault troops. In addition, Command Headquarters will be located on it. The freighter will be lead element, first wave, and will make a direct crash-assault on Target One, the JANN engine-hull mating plant. The freighter will be provided with extensive demolition capability and triggered to detonate less than one hour after strike forces land. In addition, deployed assault troops will provide demolition on selected other targets, engage ground troops, and attempt to aid Bhor tac/air in supression of enemy surface/air launches.

COORDINATION . . .

And Sten shut down the terrninal. 'Coordination' on this cobbled-together mess, he thought. First I'm going to take a bunch of Parral's cholesterol-heavy traders, get them to take us into the heart of the Jann empire. Then I'll manage to offload my surly thugs onto the Bhor lighters, somehow without having a grand melee between the Bhor, my mercs, and Mathias' fanatics.

If I get away with all that, then I suicide-dive the clottin' freighter – which I still haven't seen – right into the middle of this bloody great hangar, somehow live through the crash, somehow come out shooting, and somehow hang on and be an active menance for the Jann until Parral's ships heave down to pick all of us up.

This will not work, Sten, my friend, his mind told him. Of course it won't. You got any better ideas?

Go see what Sofia's doing, his mind suggested. And, since Sten couldn't find any argument with that, he put the security lock on the computer and headed for a grav-sled and Parral's mansion.

Maybe I'll come up with something better after a few hours lurking in her grotto.

Chapter Thirty

Parral scrolled through Sten's latest reports. Everything was going exactly as the man had promised. The series of lightning raids had the Jann reeling. And now the young colonel was preparing for the master stroke: a daring attack to gut the Jann's resolve to continue the war itself.

Parral chuckled to himself. Yes, he thought, Sten had proven to be a remarkable investment. Of course, Parral didn't believe for a minute that the man would honor his entire contract.

The young fool. Doesn't he realize I know that when the final battle is won, Sten will do exactly what I would: seize the cluster for myself?

It was a final move, Parral had to admit, that any businessman would admire.

He sighed. Too bad. He was really beginning to like the man.

Parral keyed up the analyses his spies had put together and checked them once to see if any details had been omitted, any scenario untried.

No, there would be only one possible solution to Sten's forthcoming challenge. He and his mercenaries would all have to die. And as for Mathias? Another misfortune of the business of war.

Parral also congratulated himself for making sure there could be no possible threat from the Jann – or whatever would remain of them after the final raid. He thought fondly of the powerful armored combat vehicles he had secretly purchased and turned over to his own men. They could crush any attack from any source.

Parral flicked off the computer, pleased with himself. Then he poured a glass of wine and toasted Sten and the men who were about to win him a new empire.

Chapter Thirty-One

Sten thought the freighter gave ugly a bad name.

Pritchard-class freighters were one of those answers to a question no one had asked. Some bright lad, about one hundred years earlier, had decided there was a need for a low-speed, high-efficiency deep-space freighter that also had atmospheric-entry capabilities.

The designer must've ignored the existence of planetary lighters, high-speed atmo-ships for the more luxurious or important cargoes, and the general continual bankruptcy-in-being of any intrasystem freighter company.

The *Pritchard*-class ships were well designed to be exactly what the design specs stated, so well that it was nearly impossible to modify them. Therefore, they trickled down from large-line service to small-line service to system-service to, most often, the boneyard.

This particular example – the *Atherston* – had cost somewhat less than an equivalent mass of scrap steel.

The Bhor had towed the ship to a berth in a secluded part of Nebta's massive equatorial landing ground, and Parral's skilled shipwrights and Bhor craftsmen, directed by Vosberh, had gone to work.

The *Atherston*'s looks hadn't been improved any by the modifications. Originally the ship had a lift-off nose-cone and drop-ramps for Roll On, Roll Off planetary cargo delivery.

The nose had been solidly filled with reinforced ferroconcrete, as had fifty meters of the forward area, so that the dropramps were now barely wide enough for troops to exit in double column. The command capsule had been given a solid-steel bubble with tiny vision slits, and the bubble was reinforced with webbed strutting. And finally, just to destroy whatever aesthetic values the tubby rust-bucket had, two Yukawa drive units were position-welded and then cast directly to either side of the ship's midsection. Steering jets made an anenome-blossom just behind the nosecone.

'Beauty, isn't it, sir,' Vosberh said briskly. Sten repressed a shudder.

'Best design for a suicide-bomber I've ever seen,' Vosberh went on. 'I figure that you'll have a seventy-thirty chance when you crash into that plant.'

'Which way?' Sten asked.

'You pick.' Vosberh smiled. Then he turned serious.

'By the way, Colonel. Two private questions?'

'GA, Major.'

'One. Assuming that you, uh, miss, and by some misfortune pass on to that Great Recruiting Hall in the Sky, who have you picked as a command replacement?'

Sten also smiled. 'Since both you and Ffillips will be grounding with me on the *Atherston*, isn't that a pointless question?'

'Not at all, Colonel Sten. You see – a little secret I've kept from you – I believe I am immortal.'

'Ugh,' Sten said.

'So the question is very important to me. Under no circumstances shall I turn over command of my people to Ffillips. She is arrogant, spit-and-polish, underbrained . . .' and Vosberh ran momentarily short on insults.

'I would assume that Ffillips feels about the same toward you, Major.'

'Probably.'

'I will take your first question under advisement. Second question, Major?'

'This raid on Urich. Is there any chance it will end the war?'

'Negative, Major. We'll still have scattered Jann to mop up – and Ingild to deal with. Why?'

'I warned you once, Colonel. The minute that Parral or that stupid puppet prophet he's running get the idea they're winning . . .' Vosberh drew a thumb across his throat.

'Mercenaries,' he went on, 'in case you haven't learned, are always easier to pay off with steel to the throat instead of credits in the purse.'

'Good thought, Major. Answer – as I said. This war has not even begun.'

Vosberh saluted skeptically and turned away.

'What is that supposed to be, Sergeant?' Mathias asked, staring up at the wood-plas-concrete assemblage in front of him.

'Yon contraption's ae fiendish thingie, Captain,' Alex said. 'A' tha' Ah'm supposit t' tell ye is it's som'at nae longer needs t' exist. Ye're trained noo, Captain. Takit y'r squad an' destroy yon device.'

Mathias scowled but obediently shouldered the demopack filled with plas bricks weighted to simulate demo charges and cord that simulated fusing and primacord.

He motioned his squad forward and, as Alex stepped back, they swarmed up the structure, hesitating at certain key points to lay 'demo charges' and connect the fusing and primacord.

Alex checked his stopwatch and grudgingly admitted to himself that even fanatics can be good. The mockup was actually one of the tube-latches that the raid was intended to destroy on Urich.

Mathias and his men dropped off the structure and doubled up to Alex. Mathias and one other man were trailing simulated det fuse. Not even breathing hard, Mathias snapped to a halt and saluted.

'Well, Sergeant?'

'Ah reckit y'r times fair,' Alex said. 'Noo. Twicet more an' ye'll hae i' doon pat. Then, t'night, w' comit back an' run th' drill again. Wi'oot light.'

The landing field was scattered with more of these practice structures, and, on each of them, a mixed group of mercenaries and Mathias' Companions rehearsed what they would have to be able to do drunk, wounded, gassed, or blind when the strike force hit Urich.

Otho's howls of rage were moderately awesome, Sten realized, listening to the Bhor rage on about what had been done to his trading lighters.

'Armor! Projectile cannon! Shields! Chem protection! By my mother's beard, have you any idea how long it will take us to reconvert our lighters to useful configuration?'

'Don't worry about it, Otho,' Sten said. 'Probably we'll all die on Urich and then there won't be any problems.'

'Och,' Otho agreed, brightening and slugging Sten on the back. 'By my grandsire's womb, I never thought about that. Shall we share some stregg on the thought, Colonel?'

'Mathias?'

'Six hundred trained men, present, ready.'

'Vosberh?'

'We're ready.'

'Ffillips?'

'All teams trained, aware of targets, ready for commitment.'

'Egan?'

'Intelligence, ECM, sensors all on standby.'

'Sergeant Kilgour?'

'No puh-roblems,' Alex purred.

'Order group number one,' Sten said. 'All troops are restricted to base camp area, effective immediately. You may inform your troops that Parral's units are patrolling our perimeter with instructions to shoot on sight any soldiers attempting to take French leave.

'We board ship in two days. I expect all men to be fully converted to all-protein diet, water-packed, and all equipment to be double-checked and shock-packed. We will board ship when Mathias and I return from Sanctus.

'That is all, gentlemen.'

Chapter Thirty-Two

Sten stood at full attention before the tiny altar in the Prophet's study. Next to him was Mathias. Theodomir was chanting a steady stream of prayers and waving the incense wand to all points of the compass.

Finally he approached Sten himself and stopped in front of him. 'Who brings the candidate?' he intoned.

'I do,' Mathias answered.

'Have the proper purification rites been performed?'

'They have.'

'And has this man proven himself worthy of Talamein and all we hold holy?'

'This I swear,' Mathias said.

'Kneel,' the Prophet commanded.

Sten did.

Theodomir touched the wand lightly to each of Sten's shoulders, then stepped back. 'Rise, O Faithful One. Rise as a Soldier of Talamein.'

Sten barely had time to climb to his feet before Theodomir had palmed the switch that slid the little altar out of sight. The Prophet slopped a chalice full of wine and guzzled it down. Sten thought he caught a quickly masked flash of distaste from Mathias.

'Drink, Colonel, drink,' the Prophet said. 'An honor like this does not come every day.'

Sten nodded his thanks and poured himself a cup of wine and sipped at it.

Theodomir beamed and rubbed two hands together. 'Tell me, Colonel. What runs through a soldier's mind on the eve of battle?'

Sten smiled. 'As little as possible.'

The Prophet nodded in what he thought was understanding. 'Yes, I imagine all thoughts would be of an earthly nature. Thoughts of the flesh. Personally, as your spiritual leader, I could not agree more.

'And Colonel, a little advice. Man to man. I know that there are any number of young women, or . . . ahem . . . men . . . on Sanctus who would be willing to share your last hours.'

Again Sten thought he caught a faint look of displeasure from Mathias. 'Thank you for your advice, Excellency.' Then, after a moment: 'Now, if you will excuse me, sir, I have many things to do.'

The Prophet laughed and waved his dismissal. 'Go to it, Colonel. Go to it.'

Sten bowed, saluted, wheeled, and exited. Theodomir's smile vanished as the doors hissed closed, and he looked thoughtful. 'You know,' he mused to his son, 'that could be a very dangerous man.'

'I assure you,' Mathias protested, 'he is fully committed to our cause.'

'Still,' the Prophet said. 'During the heat of battle, if you should have the opportunity . . .'

Mathias was appalled. 'What are you saying, Father?'

The Prophet's eyes bored into him, reminding the young man of his place. Mathias stood nervously, but with a determined expression on his face. Finally the Prophet chortled and refilled his wine cup. 'Just a thought. I'll take your word on Colonel Sten's dedication.'

Then he waved his son away, and Mathias left. The Prophet began chuckling, drank down his wine and poured more.

'You have a great deal to learn, my son. A great deal indeed.'

Chapter Thirty-Three

Urich was as well designed and laid out as any Imperial Guards Division depot. It was the only development on an otherwise deserted world. From two hundred kilometers overhead, it looked like an enormous U. At the open end of the U was shallow ocean, useful for engine testing, a fixed approach pattern, and also, of course, a 'soft' place for crash landings.

At the curve of the U lay the shipyard itself and, at its center, the enormous bulk of the engine-hull mating plant. Alongside that plant were the machine shops, shielded and bunkercd chem-fuel dumps, steel mills, and so forth.

Along one side of the U were docked the major elements of the Jann fleet – a few former Imperial cruisers, some rebuilt light destroyers, and a host of small in-atmosphere and patrol ships. Plus, of coursc, the necessary support craft – tankers, shopships, ECM ships, and so forth.

On the other side of the U were endless kilometers of barracks for the Jann troops when they were off-ship. As the raiding force approached Urich, there were approximately nine thousand Jann on Urich, an equivalent number of yard workers and yard security, and General Suitan Khorea, the commanding general.

Chapter Thirty-Four

Otho watched the screen time-tick seconds until dropaway with half his attention. The other half was listening to the droned story from behind him, coming from the humanoid that Otho sometimes found himself wishing to be a Bhor:

'Ahe,' Alex went on. 'S' th' Brit gin'ral hae order't ae squad up tha' hill f'r Red Rory's head. An' aye, a pickit squad wan' roarin' upit tha' hill.

'An tha's screekit an' scrawkit' an' than, bumpit, bumpit, bumpit, doon tha' hill comit th' heads ae th' squad.

'An' th' Brit gin'ral lookit up tha' hill, an' on th' crest still standit thae giant.

'An' he skreekit, "Ah'm Red Rory ae th' Glen! Send up y'r best comp'ny!"

'An' th' Brit gin'ral turnit a wee shade more purple, an' he say, "Adj'tant!"

'An' th' adj'tant sae, "Sah!"

'An' th' Brit gin'ral sae, "Adj'tant, send up y'r best comp'ny! *Ah wan' that mon's head!*"

'The adj'tant sae "Sah!"

'An' he sendit oop th' hill th' reg'mint's best comp'ny!'

And the timeclick went to zero and Otho touched the button. Alex cut his story off as the Bhor captain got busy.

'By Sarla, Laraz, and . . . and all the other gods,' Otho muttered, then swiveled his shaggy head to eye Sten.

'You know what's going to happen, Colonel. Those chubbutts who brought us here will probably skite for safety the minute we enter Urich's atmosphere.'

'I doubt it.'

'Why not?'

'Because I haven't paid them and because Parral will have them thin-sliced if they do.'

'But what happens if they do do?' Otho heard what he'd just said and grunted. 'You see, Colonel, you try to make me a soldier and then I lose everything. Pretty soon I'll be grunting primordial Bhor.'

'Which is ae differen' frae th' way y' talkit noo,' Alex asked interestedly. Otho just sneered.

Otho, three Bhor crewmen, Alex, Sten, Mathias, Egan with two com specialists, and the ever-present Kurshayne overfilled the control room of the *Atherston*. Packed safely away in shock-mounted compartments were the first wave, two companies of Mathias' troops and Vosberh's men.

Hanging in space around them were the fifty Bhor lighters, filled with Ffillips' commandos and the remainder of Mathias' force.

Otho stared at Sten, as if waiting for him to say something noble. Sten had a mouth too dry for hero speeches; he just waved, and Otho ratcheted the drive to full power and targeted the ship toward Urich's surface.

The Jann picket ships were quickly destroyed by low-speed interdiction missiles that the Bhor lighters had launched two hours before. They had no chance to warn the planet below.

The first clue the main base had was when five one-kiloton nukes flared, just out of the atmosphere. No fallout, no shock, no blastwave, but a near-continuous electromagnetic pulse that, momentarily, put all the Jann sensors on *burble*.

By the time the secondary circuits had cut in, the *Atherston* and the Bhor assault lighters were in-atmosphere, coming in on a straight, no-braking-pattern approach.

As the attack alarm blatted, Jann gunners ran for their posts. One Jann, faster or better trained or more alert, reached his S/A launch station and, on manual, punched five missiles up into the sky.

Above him, a Bhor tac/air ship banked, turned through ninety degrees, and, at full power, blasted toward the field. Its pilot had only time enough to unmask his multicannon before the first Jann missile went off, spinning the lighter sideways.

The gee-force went over 40. Too much even for the massive Bhor. The pilot and copilot blacked out. A millisecond later, the second and third Jann missiles impacted directly on the lighter.

A ball of flame flowered in the morning sky as other ships dove in to the attack.

'Your mother had no beard and your father had no buttocks,' a Bhor tac pilot grunted as he brought his control stick back into his gut, and the lighter flattened out, barely a meter above the landing field. The pilot locked a knee around his stick and both hands flashed across the duck-foot cannon mounted in the lighter's nose.

Fifty mm shells exploded from the duck-foot's six barrels, then the weapon recoiled, dropping the first set of barrels down into load position and bringing the second set up.

The antipersonnel shells from the cannon, warheads lovingly filled with meta-phosphorus and canister, ricocheted off the thick landing ground's concrete and exploded, shrapneling through the Jann running for their combat stations.

The pilot lifted at the end of his run, keeping the stick all the way back, and the inverted lighter came back for another pass, the pilot's laughter roaring louder than the slam of the cannon firing.

'We should be receiving fire by now,' Otho said cheerily and dumped the ship atmosphere. Sten swallowed hard as his ears tried to balloon – they were still some six thousand meters off the deck.

There was a dull crash from somewhere in the stern, and indicator lights turned red. The internal monitor terminal scrolled figures that everyone ignored.

A radar belched and flames began curling out.

Sten keyed the ship's PA mike. 'All troops. We are taking hits. Minus thirty seconds.'

In the troop compartments the soldiers tucked themselves more tightly into their shock capsules, tried to keep their minds blank and their eyes off the man next to them, who probably looked as scared as they were.

Below them, on the field, most Jann AA stations were manned and coming into action, in spite of the intense suppressive fire from the strafing Bhor ships.

Missiles swung on their launchers, sniffing, and then smoked off into the air. Multibarreled projectile weapons nosed for a target.

There was only one good one:

The chunky, rusty mass of the *Atherston*, now only four thousand meters above the field, drive still billowing heatwaves into the air, crashing toward them.

*

'Station three . . . we have a compartment hit. All units inside counted casualties,' a Bhor officer said.

'Whose?' Vosberh asked. Before he heard the reply, a missile penetrated the control bubble and exploded. A meter-long splinter of steel split his spine just above the waist.

Sten pushed the body out of the way and checked Otho. The Bhor's beard was bloody and one eye seemed to be having trouble. But his growl was loud and the grin was wide as he reversed drive on the two Yukawa drive units that had been added for braking force.

'Two hundred meters—'

And Sten dove for his shock capsule.

As it drove downward, the *Atherston* looked as if it were held aloft on a multicolored fountain of fire, and every weapon on the field swung and held on the unmissable target. Quickly the *Atherston*'s compartments and passageways were sieved; Bhor and men died bloody.

Otho's second in command dropped, blood gouting from a throat wound as he slumped over the controls. Kurshayne was out of his capsule, staggering against the gee-force and at the panel. He ripped the dead Bhor away from the controls, then flattened himself on the deck just as one Yukawa braking unit, still under drive, was shot away from the ship and skyrocketed upward.

Most of the Jann guns and missiles diverted onto the drive tube as it arced up into the sky.

And then there was nothing in Sten's eyes but the massiveness of that huge hangar as the ship closed and the doors rose up toward him and became the center of his world and his universe and:

The *Atherston* smashed through the hangar's monstrous doors as if they were wet paper. The ship hung, impaled in the concrete, and then, as if in slow motion, the doors to the engine-hull mating plant broke away and tumbled the ship down into a ground-shuddering impact on the field itself.

'Come on! Come on!' Sten was screaming as he heard the det charges blowing the crumpled nose cone away and then the dry grinding of broken-toothed gears as they tried to lower the landing ramps.

Alex had Otho over one shoulder and was pushing a limping Kurshayne ahead of him as they dropped out of the control room, into the swirling mass of Mathias' and Vosberh's soldiers as the latter ran out onto the landing field.

But no panic, no panic at all. Sten watched proudly as the weapons came off the men's shoulders and the perimeter specialists hit it, set up their crew-served weapons and began spattering return fire into the Jann units.

A vee-bank of Bhor lighters swept across the field at the height of a man's chest, cannon and rockets pumping and fire drizzling out of their sterns.

Smoke began roiling up from the Jann positions.

'Let's go! Let's go! Move! Move!' *And why the clot can't I do anything more inspiring than shout* as Sten and his team doubled around the corner of the hangar, toward their own assigned demo targets.

And why the hell am I shouting when it's so quiet? Clot, man, you're deaf. No, you aren't, as Sten realized that the only fire was coming from his own troops as they moved out, blindly following the assault plan.

Alex was shouting for cease-fire, and Otho grumbled his way toward Sten, bloodily grinning.

'We have one hour, Colonel, and then by my mother's beard this whole world of the black ones will go down and down to hell.'

Less poetically Sten decided that Otho was telling him he'd set the timer on the ship's charges – conventional explosives, but enough to equal a 2KT nuke.

Khorea briskly returned the salute as he entered Urich's main command post. The command staff in the bunker were calm, he noted with approval, and all observation screens were on.

'Situation?'

'We have approximately one thousand invaders on the ground,' an officer reported. 'No sign of major support or asssult ships entering atmosphere. All ships are tac/air support. No sign of potential nuke deployment.'

'The invaders – the mercenaries?'

'It would appear so, General.'

'And that' – he gestured at the screen, where the crumpled hulk of the *Atherston* lay, still buried in the mating plant's shattered doors – 'was their mission?'

'Yes,' another Jann said. 'Evidently their intelligence incorrectly estimated the thickness of those doors. No plant damage is reported. In fact, General, after the raiders are removed, we can have the plant operational in three, perhaps four cycles.'

'Excellent.'

Khorea mused to himself as he sat down at the main control board. The cursed of Theodomir have tried another raid. This time they failed, but they will try to commit as much damage as possible. With no pickup ships reported, they must expect to be able to take and hold Urich. Which means they expect us to surrender.

Impossible, his mind told him. The mercenaries cannot know so little about the Jann. So they are suicide troops? Equally impossible. Well, possibly not for those – he eyed a screen – red-uniformed ones we have heard reports about, who call themselves Mathias' Companions. But the others are mercenaries. Mercenaries simply do not die for their clients.

Therefore – analysis complete. Further input needed, Khorea's mind told him as he issued a string of orders intended to close the Jann circle about the raiders and destroy them utterly.

'Out. You people must get out of here.' Ffillips chided. She stood, weapon ready, over a cluster of workmen kneeling in one shop. Behind her two of her teams reeled det wire across the shop.

'We do not kill civilians,' Ffillips said. 'Now you run. Get very far away from here.'

The workmen came to their feet and shambled toward the exit. Ffillips sighed in satisfaction and turned back to watch her teams at work.

But one Jann workman stooped hastily near a dead commando and had a projectile weapon up, raised, aimed at Ffillips as the white-haired woman leaped sideways, turning and firing. The spatter of rounds cut the man in half.

Ffillips got back to her feet and shook her head sadly.

'But still, you must admire dedication,' she told herself.

'Kill them! Kill the Jann!' Mathias raved as a wave of his Companions poured into a barracks door. The barracks, however, was a dispensary. Lying in the beds were the normally injured and sick of any industrial center.

None of them was armed.

It did not matter to Mathias or to his Companions.

The patients died as they squirmed for shelter under their beds.

From overhead, as the Bhor strafing ships dipped and swooped, firing at anything resembling a black uniform, the port of Urich was in chaos. Here smoke or flame flared: there a building mushroomed outward. Troops scuttled from shelter to shelter.

The raid was progressing very well.

'Pretty,' Kurshayne said.

They were. Sten/Alex/Kurshayne's own target was the Jann design center, specifically the complex design computers in the building's basement.

But the booths for the designers were hung with sketches and models. Some of them, Sten knew, must have been made by people who loved the clean, swept beauty of interstellar ships.

So? Sten pulled the toggle on the twenty-second timer, and electricity pulsed through the portuguese-man-of-war-swirl that the det blocks and wiring made across the building's floor.

Kurshayne was still staring, fascinated, at one ship model.

Sten grabbed the model and shoved it deep into the man's nearly empty backpack. 'Move, man, if you don't want to go into orbit.'

As the three men doubled-timed out of the building, the charges rumbled and then went off and the center fell into its own basement.

No, Ffillips decided. No man, even a Jann, should die like that.

She and three commando teams were crouched behind a ruined building. Across the square from them was a skirmish line of Jann. And, above them, a huge tank of chem fuel.

Between the two forces one of Ffillips' men lay wounded in the center of the square.

'Recovery!' one of Ffillips' men shouted, and she sprinted out into the open. A Jann calmly broke cover, aimed, and put a shell through the would-be rescuer. Then switched his aim and gut-shot the wounded man.

Which effectively made up Ffillips' mind, and she sprayed rounds into the chem tank above the Jann. Liquid fire turned the black-uniformed killers into dancing puppets of death.

'All first-wave units committed, General,' the Jann said.

'Thank you, Sigfehr,' Khorea returned, and eyed his battle screen. Very well, very well. My first wave has held the mercenaries in place. Now my second wave will break their lines and the third wave will wipe them out.

He was curious as to what possible intentions the mercenary captain had – he still could see no rationale for the suicide raid.

*

The charges on the *Atherston* were quadruple-fused, just to make sure nothing could go wrong. Even so, two of them had been smashed out-of-circuit in the landing.

But two more ticked away their small, molecular-decay timers.

Brave men of the Jann reinfiltrated back to their AA positions, and slowly the weapons pits returned to life. Suddenly it was worth a Bhor's life for him to lift his lighter higher than the port's buildings.

The commando team edged forward, out of the shadows toward their target. As they moved into the open, a Jann missile lost its intended target – a Bhor lighter – in ground-clutter and impacted into a building.

All those commandos might have heard was the explosion of the missile and then the crumble as the ten-story structure poured down on them.

Their target would not be destroyed, and, for years afterward, some of their friends would wonder, over narcobeers, just what had happened.

The second wave of Jann, Khorea observed, was moving most efficiently. They did seem to be making inroads against the raiders' perimeter.

The third wave, now that the Bhor tac/air ships had to keep their distance, was drawn up in attack formation on the landing field, close to that ruined freighter.

Very well, Khorea thought. Now the Jann will show their courage.

Sten sighted carefully through his projectile weapon's sights and touched the trigger. Eight hundred meters away a Jann Sigfehr convulsed, threw his weapon high into the air, and collapsed.

Sten slid back into the nest of rubble he, Otho, Kurshayne, and Alex were occupying.

Kurshayne had dug out the model Sten had given him and was evidently staring at it in fascination. Sten started to snap something about children, toys, and their proper places when he noticed the small blue hole just above one of Kurshayne's eyes.

Alex crawled up beside Sten, and they looked at Kurshayne's corpse, then at each other. Wordlessly they clambered back up to the top of the rubble heap.

Contrary to the livies, even good men died at the least dramatic time.

*

A dusty and battered Egan checked his watch, peered out at the wreckage of the *Atherston*, then decided to see how far under the nearest boulder he could crawl.

'Men of the Jann.' Khorea's voice rang through the PA.

'You have the enemy before you. I need not tell you what to do. Sigfehrs! Take charge of your echelons and move them to the attack!'

As that third wave of Jann doubled forward – more than three thousand elite soldiers – past the wreck of the *Atherston*, a decay switch ran out of molecules.

For the first time in Sten's experience. Alex had been doubtful about what would happen when charges went up. 'Ah ken i' th' door's gone, we'll hae ae wee fireball inside yon plant. But wha'll happit whae yon fireball hits yon *back* door ae th' plant, ah lad, Ah dinna ken. Ah dinna ken.'

What did happen was quite spectacular: as intended, the shaped charges on the *Atherston* blew straight out the open-nosed bow of the ship into the engine-hull mating plant, creating a quite impressive fireball – almost half a kilometer high. It rolled forward, at something more than 1,000kps, toward the back door.

But the back door to the hangar did not drop, contrary to everyone's expectations. Instead, the fireball back-blasted, back up through the plant and back out, over the *Atherston* and onto the landing field itself.

From overhead the explosion might have resembled a sideways nuclear mushroom cloud as the now unrestricted blastwave bloomed across the enormous landing ground. Directly over the charging Jann troops.

About the best that could be said is that it was a very, very quick way to die, mostly from the pressure wave, oxygen deprivation, or by being crushed by debris hurled from the hangar. Only the unlucky few on the blast's edges became human torches.

But in less than two seconds, three thousand Jann ceased to exist. As did the engine-hull mating plant. Nothing less than a high-KT nuke blast could have actually obliterated that huge building. But Sten's demo charges lifted the building straight up – and then dropped it back down on itself.

Some of Sten's men, in spite of specific orders, were too close to the blast area. They died. Others would never hear again without extensive surgery.

Sten's raid was more than satisfactory.

A side benefit – one which would ultimately save Sten's life – was that the Jann command bunker's com net was cut and Khorea, together with what little Jann command staff still lived, would be buried for at least three days.

Chapter Thirty-Five

Parral leaned closer to the vidscreen, watching the action from Urich with a great deal of interest. Sten's plan had more than succeeded.

But Sten had done much too well. As far as Parral was concerned, the war was over. Only one final blow was needed, and that Parral would take care of himself.

He switched circuits and keyed the command mike to his transports hanging in space off Urich. 'This is Parral. All ships will break orbit. I say again: All ships will break orbit. Navigators, plot a course for home. That is all.'

None of Parral's skippers, of course, protested. They were all too well trained. And, as the ships turned on Parral's vidscreen, the merchant prince was mildly sorry he didn't have a pickup down on the planet's surface, to watch Sten's final moments.

He was sure they would be terribly heroic.

Chapter Thirty-Six

Sten shoved a chunk of melted plas off his legs and staggered to his feet. Across the crater, Otho stared in befuddlement as Alex grinned at him.

'Dinna tha' go, lad?' Alex said proudly. 'Dinna tha' be't tha most classic-like blast Ah hae e'er set?'

Sten groggily nodded, then turned as Egan stumbled into the crater, his eyes wide in panic. 'Colonel,' the boy shouted. 'They've abandoned us!'

Sten gaped at him.

'We're stuck here! They've abandoned us!'

Then Alex was beside Egan, shaking him and not gently.

'Tha be't nae way to report, so'jer,' he reproved. 'Dinna y'ken hae t'be't ae so'jer?'

Egan brought himself back under control. 'Colonel Sten,' he said formally, but his voice was still shaking. 'My com section reports a loss of contact with Parral's freighters. Plotting also shows all the pickup ships have disappeared from their orbits.'

And then Egan lost it again. 'They're leaving us here to die!'

BOOK FOUR

RIPOSTE

Chapter Thirty-Seven

'What do you think?' Tanz Sullamora asked proudly.

Clot polite, the Emperor thought. 'Slok,' he said, quite clearly.

Sullamora's face began falling in stages.

The painting, like the others, was what the Eternal Emperor could have called Russian-heroic. It showed a tall, muscular young man, with dark hair and blazing blue eyes. Good muscle tone. The young man was armed with what the Emperor believed to be an early-model willygun and was using it to hold off a mixed horde of crazed alien- and humanoid-type fanatics.

The gallery itself was stupendous, almost a full kilometer long, and hung with what Sullamora had assured the Emperor was the largest and most valuable collection of New Art in the Empire.

The paintings were all massive in canvas and theme, all painted in the superrealistic style that was the current rage. The medium was a high-viscosity paint whose colors shifted with the light as the viewer moved. Always the same color, but slightly different in tone. The 'paintbrush' itself was a laser.

Each of the paintings that the Emperor had stared and then scowled at showed another heroic moment in the History of the Empire.

And each one was so realistic, a cynic like the Emperor wondered, why bother with a paintbrush when a computer-photoreconstruction would do just fine?

Sullamora was still in shock, so the Emperor decided to elaborate. 'It's abysmal. A vidcomic, like everything else in this gallery. Whatever happened to the good old days of abstract art?'

Sullamora headed one of the largest entities operating under Imperial Pleasure, a conglomerate that was, basically, a vertical mining discovery-development-exploration sub-empire. He was very successful, very rich, and very pro-Empire.

Privately his tastes ran to the horrible art the Emperor was looking at and prenubile girls taken in tandem. Which was why he had invited the Emperor to the gallery opening, and which was also why he now slightly resembled a Saint Bernard who'd discovered his brandy barrel was empty.

Sullamora managed to cover his first reaction of pure horror and his second, which was to tell the Eternal Emperor he was a fuddy-duddy with no appreciation for modern art.

Instead, looking at the muscular, mid-thirties-appearing man who was the ruler of stars beyond memory, he backed down. Which was his first mistake. He whined, which was his second. The Eternal Emperor liked nothing better than a good argument, and he loathed nothing more than a toady.

'But I thought you would be pleased,' Sullamora tried. 'Don't you recognize it?'

The Emperor looked at the painting again. There was something familiar about the man, but not the incident. 'Clot, no.'

'But it's you,' Sullamora said. 'When you turned the tide at the Battle of the Gates.'

The Eternal Emperor suddenly recognized himself. A little better looking, although he always considered himself moderately handsome and certainly more heroic than he felt. The Battle of the Gates. however, had him stumped.

'*What* battle?'

'In the early days of your reign.'

And then, suddenly, the Eternal Emperor remembered. His laughter boomed across the yawning gallery. 'Do you think I did that?' he chortled, pointing at the drawn blaster and the screaming hordes.

'But it's well documented,' Sullamora protested 'It was you who made the final stand during the Uprising seven hundred years ago.'

'What kind of a fool do you think I am? Hell, man,' the Emperor said, 'do you think – when the drakh hit the ducts – I stood out in front of anybody with a gun?'

'But legend—'

'Legend me arse,' the Emperor said crudely. 'You should know you can always buy a man with a gun. Nope, Sullamora this is not me. During that Uprising I made clottin' sure I was far behind the lines with the bribes.'

'Bribes?'

'Of course. First thing I did was put a price on the heads of the Uprising leaders.

'Like good capitalists, the rebels turned in their own leaders.' He smiled at the memory. 'It was horrible,' he said. 'Blood everywhere.'

'And then what did you do with the rebel soldiers?' Sullamora blurted out, despite himself.

'What do you think?'

Sullamora puzzled this over and then smiled. He had it. 'Execute them all?'

The Eternal Emperor laughed again. Sullamora shuddered; he was beginning to hate the Emperor's mocking laughter. Although he knew it wasn't directed entirely at him, his skin crawled at the feeling that it was aimed at the entire human condition.

In that, he wasn't far wrong.

'No,' the Eternal Emperor said, 'I hired them. Gave them all double raises. And now, next to the Imperial Guard, they're the most trusted regiment in my forces.'

Sullamora filed that odd logic away. Perhaps this kind of personal insight might be of use to him. But, no, it would never work. How could you ever trust men who had tried to kill you? Better to crush them quickly, and get it over with.

He looked at the Eternal Emperor with new disrespect.

'You got anything decent to drink?' the Emperor asked.

Sullamora nodded, boldly grabbed the Emperor by the elbow, and led him to his private chambers.

The Eternal Emperor had been drinking steadily for two hours, telling obscene stories about incidents in his reign. Sullamora forced a laugh at the Emperor's latest joke and, with a great deal of distaste, realized that the Emperor always made himself the butt of all his jokes. The man's a clotting fool, he thought, and doesn't mind anyone knowing it.

Quickly he buried the thought. It was about time to make his move, he realized, noting the fact that the Eternal Emperor had consumed enough spirits to stun a mastodon, without benefit of anti-inebriation pills. With that reminder, Sullamora secretly popped the fourth pill of the evening. He looked at the Eternal Emperor's bleary eyes and decided the time was right.

'I hope this has been a pleasant visit,' he ventured.

'Shhure. Shalla . . . I mean . . . Sha . . . no . . . Tanz. That's it, Tanz.' The Emperor sloshed out another glass and belted it down.

'Great night. Now. Lesh . . . I mean . . . Let's me and you go hit a coupla port bars. Get into a fight. Get into trouble . . . then finda coupla ladies.

'I know some ladies with figures like' – he made curving motions – 'and minds like . . . like . . .' He snapped his fingers – obviously these women were sharp, sharp. 'We'll argue all night, then . . . then . . . you know . . . all night.' The Eternal Emperor gave Sullamora a sudden, sharp, terribly sober look. It came to the man as a shock.

'Unless,' the Eternal Emperor said, 'you have something else on your mind.'

'But . . . but . . .' Sullamora protested. 'this is just a social occasion . . . to show you my new gallery.'

The Eternal Emperor laughed that mocking laugh again. 'Give me a break,' he said and, ignoring Sullamora's bewilderment at the anachronism, pushed on. 'You're the head of the largest mining company in this region.

'You got something on your mind. And you don't have the cojones to ask for an audience. Instead you give me all this royal treatment. Clotting artsy garbage – and lousy art at that. Try to get me drunk.

'Now you're just trying to get up the nerve to dump on me.'

'I haven't the faintest—'

'Context, Tanz. Context. Clot, what do they teach corporate executives these days? Why, in my time— Hell with it. One more time – what's on your mind, Tanz?'

And Tanz, haltingly, told him. About his company's plans to follow up on the rumors in the Eryx Cluster. His spies (although he did not use that word) had assured him that the gossip about the potentially superwealthy fields was a fact . . . And Sullamora wanted to personally hand in his company's application for exploration to the Eternal Emperor.

'Shoulda asked me straight out,' the Eternal Emperor said. 'Can't stand a man who hems and haws.'

'All right,' Sullamora said. 'I am asking you – "straight out," as you say. My company is willing to invest the credits to exploit this new area.'

The Eternal Emperor didn't even think about it. 'No,' he said flatly.

He took pity on the man, filled up Sullamora's glass, and gave the corporate president time to choke down a huge swallow. 'What I had in mind,' he said, 'was a consortium.'

Sullamora spewed his drink across the table. 'A consortium!' he gasped.

'Yeah,' the Emperor said. 'You get together with other big mining companies – I've already put out some feelers,' he lied. 'Put together a consortium and go at Eryx as a unit – then you can exploit the clot out of it.'

'But the profits,' Sullamora protested. 'Too many companies . . .'

The Eternal Emperor raised a hand, interrupting him. 'Listen, I've already made my own studies. Any single mining company that attempts to exploit Eryx on its own is heading for bankruptcy. It's a frontier area, after all. Now, if you people pool your resources, you might make a go of it. That's my suggestion.'

'Your suggestion?'

'Yeah. Take it or leave it. Just a thought. Oh, by the way – your latest request for an increase in your company's AM_2 supply? . . .'

'Yes?' his voice quavered.

'Think about this consortium deal, and I might consider it.'

Since the source of all power (AM_2) was supplied and controlled by the Eternal Emperor, Sullamora had just been kicked in the place where it would hurt the most.

The Eternal Emperor took another drink. Slammed the glass down, making Sullamora jump about two feet.

'Tell you what,' the Eternal Emperor said. 'If you like my consortium suggestion, I might even double your AM_2 quota. What do you think of that?'

Sullamora was not as dumb as he appeared. He liked that offer very much, thank you.

'Double their quota?' Mahoney asked in amazement.

'Clot, no,' his boss said. 'I hate these mining companies. They're almost as bad as the Old Seven Sisters . . .'

He waved a 'forget it' at Mahoney's ignorance.

'Actually, for old times' sake, I might halve it once they put this consortium together.'

Mahoney was aghast.

'You mean you're actually considering letting people into the Eryx Region? Don't you remember how far away we are—'

The Eternal Emperor held up a hand, stopping him. He grinned at Mahoney and mock-tugged at his forelock.

'Where's the congratulations for your brilliant boss? I just bought you more time, Mahoney.'

Mahoney was silent.

The Emperor caught it, leaned forward across his desk. Steepled his fingers. 'Something wrong, Colonel?'

Mahoney hesitated.

'What's going on, dammit!'

'Our operative. Sten. I can't raise him.'

The Emperor sagged back. 'Which means?'

'Hell if I know. sir. All I know is Mercury Corps Appreciation: All bets are off.'

And the Emperor reached for his own bottle. 'Clot! I just may have outsmarted myself.'

Chapter Thirty-Eight

'He . . . he's . . . dead?

'I'm afraid so, dear.'

And Parral bent forward to comfort his weeping sister. Sofia leaned into him for warmth and then jolted away. She wiped away her tears.

'But how?'

Parral gave her his best warm, brotherly smile. 'Oh, he fought bravely, as did the other men. But I'm afraid it was just too much for them. A trap. They died to a man.'

Sofia held her brother's gaze for a moment, wondering if it was true, wondering if her brother had— No, that was too much even for Parral.

With a great heaving sob she collapsed into his arms.

Chapter Thirty-Nine

'Egan's dead.' The Lycée girl said in a monotone.

Sten just nodded. There wasn't time or energy to mourn.

'He's dead,' the woman continued. 'He was just walking out of the shelter for rations and they flamed him.'

Viola shut up, and sat looking at and through Sten with the thousand-meter stare. Before Sten could make appropriate comforting noises, Alex had led her away, taken the computer terminal from her pack, and set the woman to figuring out some kind of strength report.

Not that it was needed. The figures were already thoroughly graven into Sten's mind:

TROOPS COMMITTED: 670 (Sten had landed with 146 of his original mercenaries, plus 524 Companions.)

TROOPS REMAINING: 321.

Clottin' great leader you make, Colonel, his mind mocked. Only 50 per cent casualties? Fine leadership there. And now what are you going to do?

He heard a scraping sound behind him and turned to see Mathias crawling up. He crouched beside Sten, staring at him intently, his face pale, his eyes full of anger and hate. Hate . . . not at Sten . . . but . . .

'My father,' he said. 'Did he give the orders to abandon us?'

Sten hesitated and then said quite truthfully, 'I don't know.'

'His own son,' Mathias hissed. 'My Companions . . .'

Sten put a hand on the young man's shoulder. 'It was probably just Parral,' he said. 'Parral playing his own game.'

Mathias dragged a sleeve across his grimy face. 'I should have suspected . . .' His voice trailed off. Sten steeled himself. He had to start thinking, not talking, not feeling sorry for himself.

'Mathias,' he snapped, and the young man jolted to semi-reality. 'Get back to your men. Await my orders.'

Mathias nodded numbly and slithered back to his position.

Sten cautiously lifted his head above the boulder and eyed the perimeter. After they'd realized Parral's transports had abandoned them, the force had found a defensive perimeter in the four-block-wide chunk of demolished machine-shops. They had dug in and waited for something to happen.

They were completely surrounded by the surviving Jann – a force that Egan, in the last estimate before his death, had surmised to be about five thousand.

Only about twenty to one odds. Easy – if you're a hero in the livies. So you have a little more than three hundred troops left, most of them wounded, Colonel. By the way, you forgot the Bhor.

Indeed. The thirty or so Bhor, since they could no longer fly, had fought on the perimeter as berserkers. Sten was only sorry that, evidently, Otho must've died in the original withdrawal. No one had reported seeing him or his body. Add thirty hulks. So, Colonel? What, then, are your options?

There are only four possibilities in battle:

1.–Win.

2.–Withdraw.

3.–Surrender.

4.–Die in place.

It didn't take a battle computer to run the options. Winning was out, and there was no way to withdraw. Surrender wasn't even an option – five of Sten's mercenaries had tried that tactic. Now they were out in the middle of no-man's land between Sten's perimeter and the Jann lines. Crucified on steel I-beams. It had taken them almost a day to die – and most of them had been helped by grace rounds from the mercenaries.

No. Surrender to the Jann was not possible.

So here it is, young Sten. After all your cleverness and planning. Here you are, facing your only option – to fight a holding action that'll go down in history beside Camerone, Dien Bien Phu, Tarawa, Hue, or Krais VII. Wormfood, in other words.

And then anger flared. Well, and his mind found the phrase from Lanzotta, the man who'd punted him through basic Guards training: 'I've fought for the Empire on a hundred different worlds and I'll fight on a hundred more before some skeek burns me down, but I'll be the most expensive piece of meat he ever butchered.'

He spun back toward the command circle. 'Alex!'

The voice command – and Kilgour found himself at attention.

'Sir!'

'Six hours to nightfall. I want you and five men – volunteers from Ffillips' unit – standing by.'

'Sir!

'We have location on the Jann command post?'

'Aye.'

'Tonight, then. We go out.'

And a smile spread slowly across Alex's face. He knew. Indeed he knew. And it would be far better to die in the attack than huddled in this perimeter waiting for it.

Chapter Forty

It had taken almost two days to dig Khorea and what little remained of his command structure out of the bunker. They'd found him, huddled under a vee-section of the collapsed ceiling, deep in trance state.

The Jann medics had quickly brought him out of it, and Khorea had refused further aid. He'd insisted on taking charge of the final destruction of the mercenaries.

Khorea was probably still in minor shock, delayed battle stress. He had ordered the slow death of the mercenaries who'd deserted and insisted that all Jann be ordered to take no prisoners. He was determined to wipe out the far-worlders who'd shamed the Jann – to the slow death of the last man and woman.

Khorea now sat behind the hastily rerigged computers and screens in the command post. He hated them and longed for the days when a leader led from the front.

Then he half smiled. Realized that all of his electronics, all of his analysis, produced only one answer – the mercenaries would not, could not, surrender.

He shut down his command sensor and stood.

'General!' An aide.

'Tomorrow. We will attack. And I will lead the final assault.'

The aide – eyes wide in hero worship – saluted.

'Tonight, then, assemble my staff. We shall show these worms what Jann are, from the highest to the lowest. But tonight – tonight we shall assemble for prayers. Here. One hour after nightfall.'

Chapter Forty-One

'. . . But before we could stalk the streggan,' the ancient Bhor creaked, 'there was preparation. We fasted and considered the nature of our ancient enemy. And then, once we had determined our mind upon him, we feasted. Then and only then would we set out across the wave-struck ice to find him, hidden deep in his lair . . .'

Ancient, Otho thought, wasn't the word for the old Bhor. One sign of approaching death for a Bhor was for the pelt on his chest to begin turning gray. Shortly thereafter, the Bhor would assemble his family and friends for the final guesting and then disappear out onto the ice to die the death, lonely but for the gods.

This Bhor, however, was almost totally white-haired from curled gnarly feet to beetled brow. He was, as far as anyone knew, the last surviving streggan hunter.

And so they listened in council.

Just as the council had patiently listened to Otho, still being bandaged from the wounds incurred as he'd pirouetted his lighter up and out-atmosphere when he heard of Parral's abandonment.

Just as they had listened to the youngest Bhor discuss why the entire Bhor people must immediately support the marooned warriors.

Just as they had listened to the captain of a merchant fleet discuss calmly – for a Bhor (only two interruptions and one hospitalization) – why the mercenaries should be abandoned and attempts made to reach reapproachment with the Jann. The merchant also happened to be Otho's chief trading rival.

But the council listened, as they would listen to any Bhor. The Bhor were a truly democratic society – any of them could speak at any council. The decision, which could take weeks to reach and involve several minor brawls, would have been discussed, argued, fought over, and then settled.

Once decided, the Bhor moved as of one mind. But the time it took! For the first time – and Otho realized his inspiration was a corruption gotten from those beard-curs't humanoids – Otho wondered whether his was an excessively longwinded and indecisive society.

And the ancient droned on, making no point at all, but telling the old stories. Normally Otho would have been the first to sit at the ancient's right, keeping him full of stregg, fascinated by talk of the old days. But his friends – friends, by my mother's beard, friends who are humanoid – were dying.

Otho ground his fangs. The debate might continue for another four or five cycles. Since Robert's Rules hadn't penetrated to the Bhor, there was only one customary way to force a vote. And generally it meant the death of the Bhor who did it. By my father's chilly bottom, Otho groaned, you owe me, Sten. If I live through this, you owe me.

The ancient creaked on. He was now describing exactly how you tasted a streggan's fewmets to determine whether the creature was seasonable or not.

Otho rose from his bench and stalked into the center of the council ring, his meter-long dagger leaving its belt harness.

Without warning, Otho pulled the long, trailing beard straight out from his chest and, with a dagger-flash in the firelight, cut it away. He tossed the handful of fur down, into the center of the ring, then, as custom dictated, knelt, head bowed.

To the Bhor, the length and thickness of one's beard signified personal power, much as the length of other appendages has signified similarly to other cultures and beings. To chop off one's beard, in-council, meant that the issue was life-defining.

And, since none of the Bhor appreciated threatening situations, normally the beard-cutter lost his measure and, shortly afterward, his head.

Grumbled comment built to a roar covering the ancient's reminiscences.

Otho waited.

And now – the issue on whether or not to support the human soldiers would be voted on. Otho would most likely lose and then a volunteer would separate Otho from his head. Most likely the volunteer will be his Jamchydd-cursed competitor

But, contrary to custom, someone spoke.

It was the old streggan hunter.

'Old men' – and his voice was a rumbled whisper – 'sometimes lose themselves in the glories of their youth. Most of which, I recollect by the beard of my mother, are lies.'

Bones creaked as the old Bhor rose. And then, in a blur his own dagger flashed and the long icefall of the ancient's beard fell onto the flagstone's atop Otho's own beard.

The council was silent as the old Bhor knelt – nearly falling – beside Otho, head bowed.

Chapter Forty-Two

The snap of the man's neck was not all that audible, Sten knew, watching as Alex let go the first Jann's helmet and snap-punched a knuckled paw against the second man's face. Still, it *sounded* loud.

He lay to the side of the Jann observation post, flanked by the five volunteers – Ffillips' men, including their commander – waiting for Alex to finish his minor massacre.

The tubby man from Edinburgh made sure both Jann were dead, then rolled out of the OP.

They crawled on.

The Jann, very sure of themselves, had structured their defense line as a series of strongholds, with possibly fifty meters between posts. Sten wished that he had Mantis troopies instead of mercenaries and somewhere to go – it would have been simple to exfiltrate an entire battalion through those lines.

But he didn't and he didn't, and low-crawled on, below the unsophisticated EW sensors, pressure traps, and command-det mines that linked the strongholds.

Two interlocked Jann lines had been established, but the raiders had no trouble penetrating both of them.

Then, behind the lines, Sten and Alex eyed each other.

Sten wondered what Alex was thinking – and wondered why he hadn't found any words before they left the perimeter. The second would always remain unanswered and it was as well for Sten's battle confidence that the first wasn't either.

Because, Alex was crooning, in his mind's voice, his death song:

> 'Ah sew'd his sheet, making my mane;
> Ah watch'd the corpse, myself alane;

Ah watch'd his body, night and day;
No living creature came that way.

'Ah tuk his body on my back
And whiles Ah gaed, and whiles Ah sat;
Ah digg'd a grave and laid him in,
And happ'd him with the sod sae green . . .'

The raiders came to their feet and moved toward the command bunker. The low murmur of Khorea's vigil filtered through the entrance as they moved toward the structure.

Of the two sentries proudly braced at attention before the entrance, the first died with Sten's knife in his heart. The second caught a sweeping circle-kick as Sten whirled, kicked, recovered, and drove a knuckle-smash into the sentry's temple.

And then Sten was standing above the bunker's steps, watching Alex's ghoul grin as he pulled a delay-grenade from his harness.

And then the Bhor arrived.

Their ships hurtled in low from the east, landing lights full-on. They burst over the ruined spaceport barely ten meters above the ground. Fire sprayed from their every port.

An efficient atmosphere trader also makes a fairly decent gunship, Sten realized, when all the off-loading ports are open and there are a dozen Bhors using laser blasts, multibarrel projectile cannon, and explosives.

Sten had time to wonder where their intelligence came from as the ships banked, curving just above the Jann lines, hosing death as they went, before the world exploded and Jann officers came tumbling up the bunker steps and Alex had the grenade among them and was spraying fire from his weapon and then the shock of the firewaves caught Sten and he was pitched forward, into the softness of corpses and tumbling down the steps and then . . .

He was inside the bunker.

Sten rolled off a sticky body, to his feet, then went down again as he caught sight of the black-bearded Khorea, weapon at waist-level, and a burst chattered across the bunker at him and the lights went out.

Above him, Sten could hear the howls and screams of battle. Forget it. Forget it, as he moved, softly forward in the blackness.

In the hundred-meter-square bunker there was no one but Khorea and himself.

Sten's foot touched something. He knelt and picked up the

computer mouse. Tossed it ahead of him, and then nearly died as fire sparked out of the blackness not at the mouse's thunk where it hit something, but in a level arc behind the sound.

Sorry, General, Sten realized. I thought you were dumber than you are.

Lie here on the concrete and think about things. Ignore the war going on topside. You are here and blind in the dark trying to kill a blind man who has designs on your body.

Breathing from the diaphragm, eyes scanning emptiness. Sten crawled forward, knees and hands coming up, sweeping down, feeling for obstructions. Ah, a microphone with a cord attached . . . Interesting . . . A long cord.

Sten moved to a wall support and looped the cord around the support. A strand of the cord ran through the trigger guard of his hand weapon, and there was enough extension for him to slither five meters away.

The weapon was now lashed to the vertical beam. Sten pulled the cord experimentally. The weapon flashed, and the round ricocheted wildly off the ceiling, floor, and walls.

And Khorea triggered a burst at the flash.

Sten yanked the cord as hard as he could, and the weapon went back to full-automatic, and the darkness became a strobe-flare of flashings as the hand weapon spurted its magazine into the bunker and Khorea came up from behind a terminal, aiming carefully at the flashes and was aiming for the shot that would end the duel in blackness having only time to catch the blur of Sten in the air toward him and the flicker of the knife in Sten's hand and the knife drove into the side of his head and Sten smashed into the dead general and then painfully into a careening table.

And then there was no sound except from outside as the Bhor began their victory chant and grenades and small-arms fire resounded and Sten could hear the howl of his mercenaries and the Companions as they broke out from their death perimeter and came in for the final slaughter of the Jann.

And then Sten hooked up a chair with his leg and sat in the blackness, plotting his revenge against Parral.

Chapter Forty-Three

The meeting was on neutral ground – a planetoid in the Lupus Cluster's no-man's land. It was a Holy of Holies. It was the first place the founder of the religion, Talamein, landed when he fled to the cluster.

It looked a bit like a park, with broad meadows, gentle streams, and woods thick with small game, and one small chapel, the only building on the planetoid.

Two sets of troops faced each other from opposite sides of the chapel, with ready weapons and nervous trigger fingers. The soldiers were the personal guards of the two rival Prophets. After generations of fighting and atrocities on both sides, they were waiting for the signal to leap at each other's throats.

First Theodomir and then Ingild stepped away from their bodyguards and began the slow walk across the grass toward each other. Both men were edgy, not knowing what to expect. They stopped a meter or so apart.

Theodomir was the first to break. A huge grin on his face, he threw out his arms in greeting. 'Brother Ingild, what joy it brings my heart finally to see you in the flesh.'

Ingild also smiled. He stepped forward and gently hugged his rival, and then stepped back again. Tears streamed from his eyes.

'You said "Brother." How appropriate a greeting. I too have always felt as if you were my brother.'

'Despite our difficulties,' Theodomir said.

'Yes, despite them.'

The two men hugged again. Then turned and walked arm and arm toward the chapel, before which was a small table covered with a white cloth. Shading it was a small, colorful umbrella. And on either side of the table were two comfortable chairs. There were documents on the table and two old-fashioned pens.

The two men sat, smiling across the table at each other. Theodomir was the first to speak.

'Peace at last,' he said.

'Yes, brother Theodomir, peace at last.'

Theodomir did the honors of pouring the wine. He took a chaste sip. 'I know that at this moment,' Theodomir intoned, 'Talamein is smiling down on us. Happy that his two children have heeded him and are laying down their arms.'

Ingild started to take a large gulp of wine, then caught himself. He took a very small, priestly sip. 'We have been very foolish,' he said. 'After all, what are our real differences? A matter of authority, not theology. Mere titles.'

You lying sack of drakh, Theodomir thought, smiling broader.

You great bag of wind, Ingild thought, smiling back and reaching a hand across the table for Theodomir to clasp.

'Brother,' Theodomir said softly, his voice thick with emotion.

'Brother,' Ingild said, tears dripping down his nose, equally emotional, wishing for all the world that he had dared to trank up with a few narco leeches.

'Our differences are so easily settled,' Theodomir said. He shot a glance at Ingild's guards, wanting so badly to grab the wizened little drug addict by the throat and choke the life out of him.

'It came to me in a flash,' he continued. 'From the very lips of Talamein.'

'Odd,' Ingild said. 'At that very moment I was thinking the same thing.' And he thought of his awful casualties, and, more important, the terrible cost to the Holy Treasury. For half a credit he would gut the cheap piece of drakh right now.

'So,' Theodomir said, 'I propose a settlement. An ecumenical settlement.'

Ingild leaned forward in anticipation.

'We cease all hostilities,' Theodomir said, 'And each of us assumes the spiritual leadership of our rightful regions of the Lupus Cluster.

'Both of us will be called True Prophets. And each of us will support the claim of the other.'

'Agreed,' Ingild said, almost too quickly. 'Then we can end this stupid bloodshed. And each of us can concentrate on his primary duty. Our only duty.'

Ingild bowed his head. 'Saving the souls of our brethren.'

And in two years, he thought, I'll raid Sanctus with half a million Jann and burn your clotting throne to the ground.

Theodomir patted the documents in front of him. They were treaties, hastily drawn up by his clerks for the meeting.

'Before we sign there, brother,' he said, 'shall we celebrate together?'

He pointed at the small chapel.

'Just the two of us,' he said, 'in front of the altar, singing our prayers to Talamein.'

Oh, you slime, Ingild thought. You heretic. Is there nothing you're not capable of? 'What a marvelous suggestion,' he said.

The two prophets rose and walked slowly into the chapel.

Parral eased back in his chair, watching the two on the monitor as they opened the door, disappeared inside, and closed the chapel door behind them.

Tears of laughter were streaming down his face. He had never seen anything so funny in his life. Two sanctimonius skeeks with their 'brother this' and 'brother that.' Hating each other's guts.

He rang a servant for a jug of spirits to celebrate. What a master stroke. Theodomir had fought him when he had suggested the meeting. He'd screamed, almost frothed at the mouth.

And then he had become suddenly silent, when Parral explained the rest of the plan.

Parral leaned forward as the hidden monitors in the chapel picked up the two men inside. This is going to be very interesting, he thought.

He congratulated himself once again for having the foresight to remain on Nebta. Because, despite his assurances to Theodomir, he wasn't too sure how things were going to work out.

The two prophets were nearing the end of the ceremony, their chanted prayers echoing through the little chapel. It was taking way too much time, Theodomir thought. Normally a High Joining took about an hour to go through. But each man was trying to outdo the other, keeping the prayers slow and solemn. Each word was enunciated as if Talamein himself were listening.

He thanked Talamein that only the moving of the book and the blessing of the sacrifical wine were left. The two men turned to the altar, out of time, of course, and waved their incense wands at the huge book, which sat in the center.

Then they took two steps forward, both lifting the book at the same time. Ingild started to move toward the right. Theodomir the left. Suddenly the two men found themselves in the middle of a tug-of-war.

'This way,' Ingild shouted.

'No, no, you fool, to the left.'

Then, almost at the same moment, they both realized who they were. Nervous glances around the empty chapel. Theodomir cleared his throat.

'Uh, excuse me, brother, but on Sanctus the book goes to the left.'

'Is it in the treaty?' Ingild asked suspiciously.

Theodomir covered his impatience. 'It doesn't matter,' he said with difficulty. 'In the spirit of ecumenism, you may put it where you like.'

Ingild bowed to him. And shuffled off to the right, pleased with the small victory.

They moved quickly to the last part of the ceremony: the blessing and drinking of the wine. The golden chalice of wine sat inside a small tabernacle with a slanted roof. They opened the tiny doors, pulled it out, and then quickly chanted the last few prayers.

Theodomir pushed the goblet toward Ingild. 'You first, brother,' he said, urging him to drink.

Ingild eyed him, suddenly suspicious. Hesitated, then shook his head.

'No,' he said. 'You first.'

Theodomir grabbed the cup impatiently and chugged down about half of its contents in a very unprophetlike manner. Then he shoved the cup at Ingild

'Now you,' he snapped.

Ingild hesitated, then slowly took the goblet. He raised it to his lips and sipped cautiously. It tasted fine. He drained the rest of the cup and then set it carefully on the altar.

'It's finished,' he said. 'Now should we sign those . . .'

He began to cough. A slight one, at first. Then it came in ever increasing frequency. His face purpled, and then he grabbed his sides and began to scream in pain.

'You fool, you fool,' Theodomir cackled. 'The wine was poisoned.'

'But . . . but . . .' Ingild managed through his anguish, 'you drank, too.'

He toppled to the floor, writhing in agony, blood streaming through his lips from his bitten-through tongue.

Theodomir began dancing around him. Kicking him. Screaming at him.

'It was sanctified for me,' he shouted. 'Sanctified for me. But not for an addict. Not for an addict.'

Ingild tried to struggle to his knees. Theodomir booted him down again.

'Who's the True Prophet, now, you clot? Who's the True Prophet now?'

Parral laughed and laughed and laughed as he watched Ingild's dance of death.

Then he flicked the monitor off. It was over. Oh, indeed it was over.

For a moment he wished young Sten were sitting in front of him. He thought the colonel would have appreciated his plan. There are so many ways to win a war.

And then his heart froze, and he unconsciously ducked, as rockets screamed overhead and sonic waves boomed and jolted his palace.

Chapter Forty-Four

'Gad, colonel,' Ffillips said dryly. 'The villians have armor.' The woman appeared absolutely unworried as the mercenaries and Companions took up fighting positions.

The Bhor, now seeing the commercial potential of backing Sten, had gleefully agreed to help in the landing on Nebta. They had scattered enough window and diversionary missiles over Nebta's capital to confuse even an Imperial Security screen. The Bhor transports had then slammed into the outskirts of the capital. Sten thought that the Bhor skippers had deliberately tried to take out as many monuments, mansions, and memorials as they could.

For once, Sten was glad to note, he'd made an invasion with no casualties – other than one of Vosberh's men, who'd managed to get drunk on stregg and fall headfirst off the landing ramp.

The three hundred soldiers had quickly formed up in battle formation and moved toward Parral's mansion. And then tracks had clanked and the ground rumbled and Sten realized that Parral had given himself a second line of defense. Men against armor.

Panic-factor for any inexperienced soldiers. But for the trained? Sten tried to remember where he'd seen the centuries-old illo of two crunchies staring at a track and commenting, 'Naw. Not for me. A movin' foxhole attracks the eye.' And then turned to a grinning Alex.

'W'doomit,' the man reported. 'Parral's troopies hae fifty wee recon tracks an' twenty or so ACVs. Shall w'ae surrender?'

'Try not to hurt 'em too bad' was Sten's only comment.

The Battle of Nebta – the first and probably only one – lasted barely an hour as the vee-formation of tracks clanked into the attack.

Alex picked up a crew-served, multiple-launch, self-guiding rack, carried it forward until the point of the vee-formation was almost on him. Then he triggered the missiles. The small rockets huffed out the tubes, shed their compressed-air launch stages, turned themselves on, and went hunting. Five of the rockets promptly homed on different tracks and turned them into fireballs. The sixth, for reasons known only to its idiot computer-mind, had decided that a statue of one of Parral's ancestors was a more important target and had taken that out.

The ACV vehicles had been short-stopped by a quickly massed wire screen, two meters high. They'd bumped up against the wire, then drifted back and forth while their only semi-trained drivers fought the controls and then those drivers had been calmly sniped down by Sten's soldiers.

The two command tracks had lasted a few minutes longer – as long as it took the ten remaining Lycée kiddies to cut off all commo and for Sten and three men to slip behind them and launch line-of-sight rocketry into their unarmored rear boarding ramps.

It wasn't much of a battle, Sten realized as he saw Ffillips jam a huge crowbar into one assault vehicle's tracks and step back as the crowbar turned into filings and Ffillips commented disappointedly, 'Some of my older manuals swear that an obstruction in the idler wheels will stop any track,' before she flipped a fire grenade onto the greasy engine exhaust and the track became a bonfire.

And then the tracks were halted and their crews were piling out and Sten now knew why conventional soldiers still wear white undertunics as Parral's last line of defense began surrendering en masse.

So now, Sten thought, it is time to deal with our friend Seigneur Parral . . .

Chapter Forty-Five

Parral was running out of alternate plans. His great scenario calling for the Jann and the mercenaries to pull a Kilkenney cats on each other had somehow failed. Even his high-tech defense scheme with the imported armor was a bust. So Parral was supervising the loading of the last few art treasures into the ship.

The ship – a modified short-haul, high-speed freighter – had been set down in the middle of the mansion's grounds and the most portable and easily convertible of Parral's treasures stowed on board.

His new plan was to get off Nebta, hunt up some habitable world, and go to ground until the screaming and skirmishing stopped. If it ever did. Because with Ingild dead, the Jann no longer a factor, and his own power-play circumvented, the Lupus Cluster faced the threat of peace for the first time in generations.

He was pretty sure that Sten would turn over Parral's trading routes to the Bhor. Which would leave Parral somewhat less than necessary.

Oh, well, he consoled himself, under no circumstances can that drunk fuzz-kleek Theodomir hold things together for very long. Sooner or later he'd need expert help, money, and someone who could stay sober for longer than two hours. The mansion and Nebta could be rebuilt.

The last servant loaded the last painting, and Parral hurried up the ramp. He could hear the rifle fire approaching closer and closer. So? Let them loot the mansion. As the port closed, he managed a tiny moment of concern for his sister, Sofia, who'd disappeared some hours before. Then he shrugged. Perhaps she thinks she can do better with her bedmate Sten than with her brother.

Parral headed for the control room. The exec had been holding the ship on thirty-second-takeoff point for almost an hour. As Parral sank into the acceleration couch, the pilot began final countdown.

Outside, a haze built from the Yukawa drive, and the carefully sculpted gardens of Parral withered and died.

Five seconds and counting . . .

'Talamein has blessed us,' Mathias crooned as he focused the helmet sights across the mansion grounds. 'We are chosen by Talamein for his purpose.' His fingers touched ready-buttons on the firing panel.

Mathias and ten of his Companions had hastily set up the S/A missile ramp on the avenue behind Parral's mansion. Mathias closed the helmet face, and his viewpoint became the restricted dual-eyes of the missile, the launch-tube looming to either side, and, visible at the center, the heat-waved trees of the mansion gardens. 'I have it,' he announced.

His hands went around the twin joysticks of the missile control panel. 'Launch on command sequence.'

'Standing by,' a Companion announced.

'Systems on standby. All systems on ready condition.'

Mathias felt the tremble as, a thousand meters away, Parral's ship lifted from the estate. Prematurely he keyed the launch button on top of one of the joysticks, and suddenly his vision became broad and fish-eyed as the missile came out of the tube, hissing fifty meters up into the atmosphere.

Mathias kept his other thumb poised on the number-two joystick's primary drive switch. The launch button now automatically became the manual-det switch.

Mathias orbited the missile, waiting for Parral's ship to come out of ground-clutter, and then, as the sleek torpedo swept back around, he had the missile's sensors on IR visual.

'Normal vision,' he snapped. A companion flipped the switch on the primary switch and the missile howled up through Mach 8, crosshairs centered on the nose of Parral's ship as it clawed for height. The gray steel closed in Mathias' eyes until there was nothing but the heat-shimmer and the metal and then his eyes went blank.

Mathias yanked the helmet from his head in time to see the fireball sweep down the nose of Parral's ship, catch the fuel tanks, and become an elongated cigar of flame, debris slowly pinwheeling back down toward the ground.

His Companions were cheering as Mathias dropped out of the command seat. Mathias allowed himself a laugh, then turned his face serious.

'Not I,' he said as the cheering suddenly stopped. 'But Talamein. I count myself blessed that Talamein has chosen me as the tool for his vengence, for the beginnings that shall make the Faith into the fire-hardened sword the Original Prophet intended. For this – which I vision as merely the beginning – we shall give thanks.'

Which was why, when Sten and Alex burst through the brush, they found the ten men knelt in prayer, seemingly to an empty short-range portable missile launcher.

Chapter Forty-Six

Sofia sat on a small boulder just at the water's edge. She was staring out to where the huge waves she loved were still continuing their thunder, regardless of man's change.

Twenty meters behind her, just on the fringe of the black sand, Sten waited.

He'd found Sofia in hysterics in the mansion as his troops swept through, moving the servants out from the wall of flame that Parral's crashed ship had started. He'd slammed a med-shot trank into her arm and ordered her moved to his own headquarters. Then, and it was very hard, he forced his mind back to business, to the endless details of what happens when you've won a war and what to do next.

The first, of course, had been a chain-coded message sent on Parral's high-power transmitter, to a clean transponder on some worldlet just outside the Lupus Cluster. The message, a short series of code breaks, read:

GOOD GUYS CHOSEN AND VICTORIOUS. GOOD GUYS ARE THEODOMIR. PHASE A & B COMPLETE. APPROPRIATE ACTION IN YOUR DEPARTMENT NOW

Within three Imperial hours, the message had been through the Mercury Corps chain and was in Mahoney's and the Emperor's hands. And a return message went back:

STAND BY. IMPERIAL CONFIRMATION ON WAY. DO NOT EMBARRASS THE EMPEROR. LAYING ON OF HANDS WILL COMMENCE IN ONE WEEK. DO YOU PREFER PROMOTION,

MEDAL, OR LONG LEAVE? YOUR PERFORMANCE DEEMED IN THE SNEAKY TRADITION OF MANTIS.

Which left only minor details until the Emperor and his entourage showed up to confirm Theodomir as the rightful Prophet and leader of the Lupus Cluster. Minor details like burying the dead, nurturing the sick, keeping the mercenaries from outrageous looting, and . . . and Sofia.

And so they had gone to that black beach. Neither Sofia nor Sten had said anything until the grav-sled set down. Then Sofia dropped her clothes and paced to the boulder where she had sat silently for almost two hours now.

Suddenly Sofia rose and walked back to Sten. She curled down onto the sand beside him.

'You did not kill my brother?'

'No. I did not.'

'Would you have if you had the chance?'

'Probably.'

Sofia nodded. 'You and your soldiers will be leaving now.'

'Yes.'

'I will go with you.'

Sten hesitated – he didn't think it would be a good idea for Bet to meet Sofia even though Bet was no longer his lover. And explaining that Sten was neither a colonel or an ex-soldier would prove interesting.

Sofia shrugged. 'You will be taking a vacation with your pay?'

'Probably.'

'I will spend it with you.' Baronial habits die hard. 'And then,' Sofia went on. 'I shall go. I have always wanted to see the Imperial Court.'

Sten covered a slight sigh of relief. Love is wonderful, but it does not last as long as soldiering. Unfortunately.

'For a while, at least, I will not wish to see Nebta,' Sofia finished. Sten had no comment. She took his hand, and they rose and walked into the small hut on the edge of the beach.

Chapter Forty-Seven

Five *Hero* class Imperial battleships hung in stationary orbit above Sanctus. The hovering sharks were attended by a cruiser squadron and three full destroyer squadrons. The formation was backed by a half fleet of auxiliary ships, planetary-assault craft, and two battalions of the First Guards Division.

When the Emperor came to dedicate a building or to legitimatize a conqueror, he preferred to have no surprises – least of all those that began with a bang and directed some sort of projectile in his direction.

The fiche that the courier ship had delivered weighed almost a full kilo and contained everything there was to know or do about its subject: *Protocol Manual for Imperial Visits*.

It included such pieces of information as to what weaponry an honor guard could carry (no crew-served weapons, no individual edge weapons, individual weapons with their firing-section disarmed, no magazines in weapons); length of welcoming speech (no more than five minutes); number of people permitted to speak on landing (three maximum); quartering requirements for Imperial security (one barracks plus apartments adjoining the Imperial suite); dietary requirements for security element (normal Imperial diet for plainclothesmen; dhal, rice, and fowl or soyasteak for Gurkhas); and so on and on, endlessly.

Embarrassingly thorough and detailed, the fiche was one of the reasons why the Emperor had survived – by his personal estimate – more than 160 assassination attempts, only three of which had been successful.

*

It was, of course, one of Sanctus' few sunny days. On an island continent, this also meant it was muggy enough to swim in.

The assembled hierarchy of the Church of Talamein, who'd been standing on the reviewing stand in their full formal robes since an hour before dawn, collectively and silently wished for a good dense fog or perhaps even a snowstorm.

The Emperor – by deliberate policy – was keeping them waiting.

The worthies stood on the kilometers-square landing ground, with ranked Companions in their full-dress uniforms around them. Across the field, behind guarded perimeters, were those lucky citizens of Sanctus permitted to view the first Imperial visit to Sanctus. Or, for that matter, to the Lupus Cluster.

Mathias and his father stood side by side, sweating ignobly. Neither of them found any reason to talk to the other.

And then the crowd murmured as, high overhead, five specks materialized and hurtled toward the field.

The specks grew larger and became cruisers. The crowd began to cheer – the cruisers were the Emperor's advance guard. The ships sonic-crashed to a halt a thousand meters above the field, then sank slowly, one to each corner of the landing ground and the fifth directly opposite the reviewing stand.

Landing ramps slid out, and uniformed troops double-timed down them, drawing up into line formation across the field. They were Guardsmen, and their locked-and-loaded willyguns were at the ready.

From the fifth ship two other formations ran down the ramp toward the reviewing stand. All of them were in the fairly plain brown livery of the Imperial household. And all of them were former Guards, Mercury Corps, or Mantis operatives.

Swiftly, without worrying about anyone's dignity, they checked the Companions' weapons to make sure they were, indeed, unloaded.

Another squad, murmuring apologies, came onto the reviewing stand and ran mass-detectors over the dignitaries. Theodomir was humiliated. One plainclothesman even had the temerity to confiscate the tiny flask of wine that Theodomir had in an inner pocket as an emergency resource.

Then the head of security took a small com unit from his belt and keyed it. Spoke in an unintelligible code. He listened, shut the com unit down, and turned to Theodomir. He bowed deeply.

'You will prepare to receive the presence of the Eternal Emperor, Lord of a Thousand Suns.'

And Theodomir, reluctantly – he was the anointed Prophet of the Faith of Talamein! – found himself bowing back in awe.

'Colonel,' the Emperor asked, a trifle plaintively, 'would a single drink matter to these clots?'

'Nossir,' Mahoney said – but made no move to the decanter in the dressing room.

Neither did the Emperor.

'One of these eons,' the Emperor continued, 'I shall come reeling down that ramp, declare in a high falsetto that this bridge is now open, and proceed to circumcise the first dignitary I see with the ribbon-cutting scissors. Then I will vomit over the rest of whatever noble thieves are greeting me.'

'No question at all,' Mahoney agreed blandly. 'Excellent idea.'

'Oh. One thing. Your operative, this—'

'Sten.'

'Sten. Yes. He and his mercenaries have been instructed?'

'They're out of sight, sir. You won't see any of them.'

'There were no problems?'

'None at all. Theodomir is embarrassed by them, and a good percentage of the mercenaries are deserters from the Guard. Also, since when did a soldier like to stand at attention until he passes out?'

'Colonel,' the Emperor said, checking for the nineteenth time whether the button-line on his midnight-black tunic was even, 'you know about psychology and all that. Why do I still get nervous doing this kind of thing – after a thousand years?'

'It's your constant youthfulness.' Mahoney said. 'Your charming naivete. The awareness that makes all of us love and serve your Eternal Worryship.'

'Bah,' the Emperor growled, and touched a button. 'Captain. Land this bucket. I'm getting tired of waiting.'

The five battleships, each nearly a kilometer in length, hissed down toward the field, and their black shadows merged and blocked Sanctus' sun.

Four of them hung a hundred meters overhead, but the fifth, the *Vercingatorix*, dropped to ground gently on the landing field. And then, following orders, its captain cut the McLean generators and the ship proceeded to sink twenty meters into the field itself. It was the Emperor's own way of autographing a world.

The side of the ship dropped open and became a twenty-meter-wide ramp.

Theodomir waved wildly, and his band began playing. Twenty bars into the song, the band broke off, as no one had yet appeared at the ramp's top. Just as the band squealed and ground to a halt, the Emperor walked down the ramp. Three beats after him, two Gurkha units came down behind him. As the small brown men spread out to either side, the Emperor walked toward the reviewing stand.

The Emperor gives good ceremony, Mahoney thought to himself, watching the solitary man walk toward Theodomir's stand. Two turrets on the *Vercingatorix* swiveled to cover the stand itself.

The Emperor stopped in front of the stand and waited.

And the hierarchy of Talamein dropped to its knees. Even Theodomir, recognizing he was committing some enormous breach, went down.

Only Mathias stayed on his feet, eyeing the muscular man standing below him.

The Emperor keyed his larnyx-mike and, on the *Vercingatorix*, techs found the symp-frequency of the landing field's speakers and patched the Emperor to them.

'I greet you, O Prophet,' the voice echoed and re-echoed across the field. 'As your Emperor, I welcome you and your people back into the fold of Imperial protection. And, as your Emperor, I recognize the heroism and truth of your beliefs and the long martyrdom of your founder, the Original Prophet Talamein.'

Then the Emperor flipped his mike back off and started up the steps to the stand, wondering how long he could make these fools sweat in the sun before he had to let them move on to the next, totally predictable stage of the ceremony.

'And this,' Theodomir said proudly, 'is a replica of the very gun station Talamein himself manned on the Flight for Freedom.'

Mathias, the Emperor, and Theodomir were deep in the heart of Sanctus' inner fastness, touring the treasures of the faith.

The Emperor was preceded by plainclothes security men to each station, plus leap-frogging squads of Gurkhas. Behind them by about forty meters was an awestruck draggle of dignitaries and Companions.

'You know,' the Emperor said conversationally, 'I knew Talamein. Personally.'

Theodomir blinked and Mathias now felt an urge to kneel. The Emperor smiled at their confusion.

'I found him . . . interesting,' the Emperor continued. 'Certainly it was unusual to find so much dedication in a man so youthful.'

Mathias blinked – the only holos he'd seen of Talamein showed him as an elderly, bearded man. He was not sure which was the greater shock – to realize that, indeed, Talamein had walked the face of the Galaxy as a man, or that the soft-spoken man across from him had actually spoken to the First Prophet.

Far behind the group there was a stir as one Companion heard the echoed words of the Emperor, gasped 'heresy,' and scrabbled for his weapon, momentarily forgetting it was deactivated.

Before his hand touched the holster snap, the razor steel of a Gurkha kukri was at his throat, and he heard a soft hiss: 'Remove your hand, unbeliever. Instantly.'

The Companion did just that, and the young havildar-major smiled politely, bowed a bit, and resheathed his long knife.

The Emperor chose to make his announcement after the services, on the broad steps of the inner fortress itself. This time his speech was recorded and patched into a cluster-wide broadcast.

'I have visited Sanctus,' he said. 'And I have seen the fruits of Talamein and found them worthy of belonging to my Empire

'I further have known and listened to this man, your prophet Theodomir, and find him both good and wise.

'For this reason, I declare that the hand of the Emperor is extended over the Lupus Cluster and its people, and shall assist in whatever means requested.

'And I declare that this Prophet, Theodomir, is the legitimate ruler of the Lupus Cluster and that he and his descendants, until I choose to withdraw the hand of support from over their heads, are the legitimate rulers of this region.

'May the powers of the universe and the First Prophet Talamein bless and approve this decision.'

And then there was mass cheering and hysteria and the Emperor wanted more than anything else to get back to the ship, shed his robes and have several – no, many – drinks.

But he couldn't. Now the banqueting would start.

Chapter Forty-Eight

Mahoney counted tombs as he crept down the Avenue of Monuments. He found the specified crypt and waited. No sign of being followed. No one waiting for him. He came to a crouch and moved into the blackness of the crypt entrance.

'Colonel,' Sten's voice came out of the darkness, 'I think we might have a problem.'

'GA,' Mahoney said flatly.

'No hard data.'

'I said report.'

'Feelings, rumors. There's talk of a holy war. It's nothing I can pin down.'

Mahoney was somewhat grateful for the darkness. Sudden shock is not the appropriate reaction to display before one's underlings.

'Theodomir?'

Sten shrugged.

'How?' Mahoney asked. 'He's an alky. Corrupt. No drive.'

'I know,' Sten said. 'It doesn't make sense.'

'How about Mathias?'

'It's possible,' Sten said. 'Look, I told you it was just talk. Still, it bothers me. I just wish you would have given it more time to settle out.'

Mahoney considered a moment, and then nodded. 'You did ask for more time,' he said.

Sten didn't say anything.

'You were right, lad. We should have waited for the situation to settle out further. I cannot tell you why, but there was no time.'

'All right,' he continued wearily. 'You're the man on the spot, Lieutenant. Prog?'

Sten fingered the lump in his arm that was the knife and thought hard. 'Damfino,' he said frankly. 'But I'd better find some way to keep my mercs together for a while. All I can think of is to hang tough in the situation.'

'You realize what might happen in a worst-case scenario – aside from a half-million slaughtered miners, full-out war in the Lupus Cluster, armed prophets spreading through the Universe, and full commitment by the Guard – don't you? I mean to you and me, lad, to mention the important things.'

'I go to a duty battalion and you go to a field command.'

'Wrong. We both will be swinging pulaskis on some swampworld. You as a private and me as a sergeant,' Mahoney said. 'That's providing, of course, the Eternal Emperor doesn't use our guts for our winding sheets.

'At this stage of the game, though, I guess your prog's right. Hopefully, if the worst comes down, you and your troops can figure a way to shortstop the problem. But I doubt it.'

He shook his head sadly and started out of the crypt.

'Colonel?'

'Yes, Lieutenant?'

'A favor. Actually, two of them?'

Mahoney stopped dead. Lieutenants do not ask personal favors of their commanding officers, not even in Mantis Section. But lieutenants also normally lacked the temerity to tell their commanding officer his battle plan was full of drakh.

'What?'

'I had a man serving with me. A Private William Kurshayne. He died during that last raid on the Jann.'

'Go on,' Mahoney said.

'He was ex-Guard. First Assault. I'd like him reinstated posthumously. And a medal wouldn't hurt, either. If he's got any people it might make them feel better.'

Mahoney didn't ask if it was deserved. Still, he shook his head. 'How do I find his records, Lieutenant? Do you know how many Kurshaynes we must've had in the guard?'

Sten grinned.

'You'll find the right one easily, sir. Busted fourteen times and recommended for the Galactic Cross about four times.'

Mahoney reluctantly agreed. He would do it.

'And what's the other favor, since I'm evidently picked as your dogsbody, Lieutenant?'

Sten hesitated. 'It's more personal.'

Mahoney waited.

'It's about Parral's sister,' Sten finally said. 'Sofia.'

'Beautiful woman.'

'Take her out with you. She wants to be presented at court.'

'You think the situation is that close, lad?'

'I don't know, sir.'

Mahoney considered, then shrugged. What the hell. He'd do that, too.

'Tomorrow night, Lieutenant. Start of third watch. Have her report to the *Vercingatorix*. Ramp C. I'll take care of her.'

'Thank you, sir.'

Chapter Forty-Nine

The island continent of Sanctus seemed to shudder as the Imperial fleet lifted from the ground, hovered for a moment parallel with the reviewing stand where Theodomir and Mathias stood flanked by the Companions. Then the ships hazed and vanished straight up into blackness.

Far down the field, behind a hangar, stood Otho, Sten, and Alex.

Sten waved good-bye to Sofia. She had taken the news of her imminent departure with little surprise. At least she had said very little. But then neither of them had in their last wild flurry of love-making before Sten escorted her to the landing ramp of the huge Imperial battleship.

He put that part of his life into his backbrain and turned to Otho.

'You humans have such a love of farewells,' the Bhor began.

'Not now, Otho,' Sten said. 'I want you to get one of your combat lighters fueled and on ten-minute standby. And I want two ships standing by off Nebta.

'For the lighter, I want two of the gunners you used on Urich as crew and yourself as pilot.

Otho's brow beetled upward. 'Impossible, Colonel. With the war over, I have my mercantile interests, which I've already had to—'

'This is important. Because if you don't, there might not be any Bhor mercantile interests ever.'

Otho grunted, then seemed to understand. 'You have no reasons for this?'

'None I can tell.'

'Then I do understand. It is your weird.'

It was Sten's turn to look perplexed.

'It shall be done. I will have the ships off Nebta in five days. I assume they will be used in case your soldiers need immediate shelter.'

Sten sighed in relief. Now, at least, he'd set up a back door for himself and the mercenaries.

Unfortunately his weird, his fate, would be determined in less than twenty hours. Far too soon for Otho's ships.

Chapter Fifty

Sten grounded the gravsled at the end of the dirt track, climbed out, straightened his uniform, and walked on.

Beyond the track led the path to the camp of Mathias' Companions, a path now newly blazoned with their scarlet banner. And, as he walked past the hanging banners, he remembered something that Mahoney had told him, about there being nothing more dangerous than a soldier who's gotten his first hero ribbon.

'Ten-hut!'

Mathias, flanked by two Companions, was waiting at the path's last bend. The three were drawn up at full attention, holding salutes. Sten, in return, gave them the almost-limp, afterthought salute of a ranking officer.

'As you were,' he said, and the Companions relaxed.

Mathias strode forward, hand outstretched, his face one huge smile. 'Colonel,' he said. 'I am truly happy you could come.'

Sten allowed his hand to be pumped and fixed Mathias with a straight stare. 'The war's over now,' he said. 'I have no official rank, no titles with you.' He dropped the hand and took a slight step back. 'I took your invitation as a command.' Then, after a moment: 'Or did you mean it otherwise?'

'I meant it as an invitation to a friend,' Mathias said, taken somewhat aback. Then he took Sten by the arm and guided him to the tiny gym. 'We have a great deal to discuss.'

Sten raised an eyebrow.

Some changes had been made in the tiny gym's office. A huge, semiheroic picture of Mathias had been added, and an equally large photo of the officers of the Companions – Mathias in the center.

And, Sten noticed, a very small portrait of Mathias' father, Theodomir. A large bulletin board had been added, and it was crammed with very military advice, announcements, and orders from Mathias.

You've been a busy boy, Sten thought. I taught you well. He forced a smile as Mathias poured himself a goblet of water and nodded Sten toward a decanter of wine. Sten ignored the wine, reached for the water, and filled a cup. He raised it in toast to Mathias. 'To victory,' he said, and gulped the water down.

Mathias returned the toast.

'To victory,' he said, sipping at his water. He sat, nodding for Sten to relax as well. Sten sat and waited, something he was becoming very good at.

'You have changed the history of this cluster,' Mathias finally said.

'With some help.' Sten nodded to Mathias.

Mathias looked at Sten across the desk, struggling with something. Suddenly he rose and began pacing the room. 'I look around me,' he said, 'and everywhere I see evil. I see hypocrisy. I see empty mouthings of faith.'

Sten knew Mathias was speaking of his father and kept silent. Mathias whirled on Sten. 'I – we can change that.'

'I'm sure you can,' Sten said. 'Someday you'll be Prophet. When your father dies.'

Mathias gave Sten a look that was almost begging. 'It's still all wrong right now,' he said. 'The war isn't over.'

'I don't know what you mean,' Sten said. 'As far as I am concerned – and apparently the Eternal Emperor as well – it's over.'

He pushed through Mathias' halting objection. 'Be patient,' he advised. 'In a few years – twenty or thirty at the most – you'll inherit this whole thing.' Sten waved his hand around the gym, but he meant the entire Lupus Cluster. 'Wait until you have the power to change it.'

'But the unbelievers—' Mathias blurted out, and then caught himself. Swiftly he changed the subject.

'What are you going to do next, Colonel?'

Sten shrugged. 'Find somebody else to hire me.' What will you do now, Lieutenant? Get your tail back to something resembling civilization where you don't have to check your compartment for bugs or assassins before you pass out every night. Get back in uniform. Go on a roaring drunk with my Mantis people. Pat a tiger or two. Listen to Doc's latest hatred for everything, Ida's schemes to buy up a galaxy, and maybe see if Bet's got the wanderlust out of her.

Suddenly Sten realized he was very, very tired and very glad the assignment was just about over. 'Mercenaries drift a lot,' he said, to cover his silence.

Mathias took a breath and then said, 'Join me.' He sat down quickly, turning his eyes away but waiting for Sten's answer.

Sten took a moment, as if considering. 'There's nothing to join.'

'The Companions,' Mathias pled. 'Join the Companions. I know that deep inside, you are as religious a man as we are. I'll give you rank. I'll give you money. I'll—'

Sten raised a hand to stop him. 'I'm a mercenary, Mathias. Understand that. And a mercenary requires wars. And I've learned as a mercenary it is best to get out of your employer's way when the war is over.'

Sten grabbed the wine and poured himself a drink. He sipped and waited again.

'But it isn't over,' Mathias said.

Sten just looked at him. He drank the rest of his wine and rose. 'Yes, it is. Take my advice. Let it be. This cluster is good for a thousand years of peace. When you become Prophet you – and your descendants – can do as you like.'

He patted Mathias on the shoulder, a young man playing father to another youth. 'And if it doesn't work out then,' he promised, 'let me know. And I'll be yours.'

Sten walked from the room.

Very well, Mathias thought. I am sorry. So sorry for what I am going to have to do.

Chapter Fifty-One

Theodomir had just finished the last prayer of the Joining. He rushed down the aisle, not even waiting for his aides or guards. Theodomir needed a soothing drink in the worst way. He glanced at the people still in their pews and laughed to himself. Just sheep, he thought, and boomed through the temple doors.

Theodomir clacked down the steps, feeling a little light-headed. With Parral gone, he was the Man in the Lupus Cluster. Sanctioned, even, by the Eternal Emperor. There was nothing he could not do. His merest suggestion was law over a thousand light-years.

But what he wanted just then, most of all, was a drink. And then he would think about the evening's entertainment. Who would he choose? he thought. Which child would he take to his bed? The boy dancer? Or the girl singer?

Both, he decided

And then his son loomed up in front of him. Theodomir gave him a quick smile and started to push by.

'Father,' Mathias said.

Theodomir paused on the steps, impatiently wondering what his dolt of a son wanted.

He started back as the young man drew a dagger. And, for the first time, Theodomir realized that Mathias was only one of a half-dozen men, all dressed in the blood-red uniforms of the Companions.

'Can't it wait?' he complained, 'I'm busy.' Oddly enough, he knew what the dagger was for. But it was like a dream. Somehow he couldn't interfere.

Then he noticed that the other men also had unsheathed their daggers.

Theodomir screamed as his son plunged the dagger into his chest. And screamed and screamed and screamed as the others took turns stabbing knives into every available area of flesh.

Theodomir's guards thundered up, weapons out, looking wildly at Mathias and his Companions. Mathias looked down at his father. A final moan, a shudder, and the Prophet was dead.

'He is dead,' Mathias informed his father's personal guard.

A moment's hesitation, and then there was a clatter as the men dropped their weapons and began to cheer.

Mathias was the True Prophet.

Chapter Fifty-Two

Another vague Mantis law: When in Doubt, Give Yourself an Escape Hatch.

Alex had set up the escape hatch immediately after Sten had returned from his meeting in the woods with Mathias. He had no prog but knew something was about to come down.

Since they were quartered in the Temple itself, the back door had consisted of two strands of granite-dyed climbing thread, hung out one window.

Inside a nearby urn were the figure-8 descenders and locking caribiniers necessary to get down that thread in a hurry. Both Sten and Alex had taken to wearing swiss-seat harness under their uniforms, hoping that when it hit the turbines they would be long gone offworld.

They were wrong but they were ready.

So, when the howling/mourning for Theodomir started, Sten and Alex were in motion. The first twenty ambitious Companions who'd come hurtling through the door had run into one of Alex's less pleasant surprises.

He'd hand-cast directional vee-mines, hooked them to sensors, and mounted them on either side of the portal. They made a significant mess, enough of a mess to delay the next wave of Companions.

The pause allowed Alex and Sten to hook the descenders onto the thread and back out the window. Neither of them found great exit lines as they pushed off, straight down the vertical wall of the Temple.

No one but a fool springs ten or twenty meters per leap on a long rappel – no one but a fool or an outgunned Mantis soldier.

They hit the ground at the bottom, Sten slamming down the last fifteen meters and thudding to safety with an *oof*. Then they shed their harness and were running.

'C'mon, lad,' Alex urged. 'W'nae hae truck wi' thae fruitbars nae more.'

And then they were out the gates of the Temple and running toward the town below, swinging into the backstreets toward Sanctus' landing field, where, Sten desperately hoped, Otho had the lighter waiting.

'Dinna worry,' Alex flung back cheerily. 'A' w' hae t'do is get away frae th' fanatics, gie oursel's offworld, an' then nae worries save th' wrath ae Mahoney an' th' Eternal Emp'ror.'

And then a platoon of Companions was running down the alley. They spotted the two men and ran forward. Alex went down on one knee, weapon coming out of its pouch, and double-handed autofire into the men.

Then they were back up, running into a side passageway and Sten thinking, If I can only live through the next fifty minutes I can handle anybody's anger.

BOOK FIVE

FLÉCHÉ

Chapter Fifty-Three

Mathias, the only True Prophet of Talamein, stood before his Companions, a red sea stretching out before him in row upon orderly row.

The Prophet had been talking for three hours, retelling recent exploits, reaffirming their faith in him and Talamein, whipping them into a frenzy. Their voices were hoarse from shouting, their faces flushed, and in a few places there were gaps in the line where Companions had fainted.

Mathias had told them of the betrayal by Sten's mercenaries, who, in league with his father's guards, had foully conspired to assassinate his father.

Theodomir was a martyr to Talamein. Mathias assured the Companions that as long as he lived his father's name would never be forgotten.

Then he had led forward the traitorous members of his father's guard. The guards were silent, beaten. A few were weeping. One by one he had them executed, and the Companions cheered wildly as each man died.

Now Mathias was building to the final moments of his speech.

'This is not the death,' he shouted, 'that I plan for the mercenaries of the Traitor Sten. They are awaiting their fates at this moment in my cells, deserted by their two leaders, Sten and Kilgour, who made cowardly escapes.'

'Kill them,' the Companions screamed.

Mathias held up a hand for silence. 'Not yet. Not yet, my brothers. First we will try them, so all the Empire will learn of their foul crimes. And then we shall convict them and execute them.'

He smiled at his young troops. 'I have appointed a committee of Companions,' he said, 'to determine how they shall die.'

A small pause for effect. 'And I promise you they shall be long deaths. Agonizing deaths. We shall squeeze from them every drop of blood possible to repay them for my father's death.'

The Companions roared their approval.

Mathias lowered his voice, ready now to play his final card. 'Lupus Cluster is ours now, my friends. And I dedicate my life as your Prophet, that all men may worship Talamein and bask in his glory.'

'S'be't,' his men shouted.

Mathias tensed, leaned forward, his eyes seeming to bore into every man's soul. 'But there are huge forces now at work against us. Forces that deny Talamein.'

A low moan of dismay swept the Companions.

'At this moment, our enemies are gathering. Creeping to our gates.'

Another long pause from Mathias.

'I say we should fight," he shouted.

'Fight. Fight. For Talamein,' they screamed back.

'I declare a holy war. A war against heresy. Against treason. Against all who blaspheme against the name of Talamein.'

The men were in ecstasy, breaking ranks and rushing forward to lift Mathias up and carry him away in triumph.

Chapter Fifty-Four

Colonel Ian Mahoney, still commander of the Mercury Corps, stood at attention, his heels locked, his face red, his spine a steel bar. He was receiving the chewing out of his life, a dressing down delivered by the all-time master of dressings down.

'Colonel Mahoney, I do not know what to do with you. I do not know what to say.'

Mahoney refrained from noting that the Emperor had been at no loss for words for at least an hour.

'Do you *realize* what has happened, Mahoney? I have just given my blessing to a fanatic. A fanatic who calls me a heretic. *Me*. ME!'

Mahoney was wisely silent

'Clot it, man, I hung myself out there like a babbling fool. State visit. Empire-wide vid coverage. I clotting declared the Lupus Cluster open.'

He leaned across his antique desk. 'And when I declare something open, by all that is holy in this silly sorry Empire that I was dumb enough to found, I expect it to *stay open*. Do you understand, Colonel?'

'Yes, sir!'

'Don't yessir me!'

'No, sir.'

'Don't nossir me, either.' He glared at Mahoney, trembling with anger. Then a long sigh. 'Ah, clot it, Mahoney. Siddown. Pour us a drink. Something nasty. Something poisonous. Something that will get me good and clotting drunk.'

Mahoney sat – but did not make the mistake of relaxing. If it was possible to sit at attention, he did it. He reached for the Eternal Emperor's latest batch of experimental scotch and poured drinks. He sipped at his with as much military bearing as a man could possibly sip.

The Emperor noticed the scotch. Gave Mahoney a thin smile. 'You never did like this drakh much, did you, Mahoney?'

Mahoney made a noncommital noise. And waited for the Commander in Chief of the greatest military force in human history to finish speaking his mind.

The Emperor shot back his scotch, shuddered, and poured himself another.

'I'm a reasonable man, Mahoney. I know how things can go wrong. All right. So I'm up to my butt in alligators. So what? I've been there before.'

He drank.

'I only have one question,' he said in his most reasonable tone of voice.

'Which is, sir?' Mahoney asked.

The Eternal Emperor rose to his feet.

'WHO PUT MY ARSE IN THE SWAMP, MAHONEY? WHO? WHOSE IDEA WAS THIS DEBACLE?'

Mahoney couldn't tell his boss it was, after all, the Emperor's idea.

'I take full responsibility, sir,' he said.

'You're clotting right. you do, Mahoney. I'm gonna . . . I'm gonna . . . Colonel, I want you to think of the worst command in my empire. A hell hole. A place you won't be guaranteed to survive in for more than a week.'

'Yes, sir.'

'I want a full report on it by tomorrow.'

'Yes, sir.'

'Now, who's that other fellow. Lieutenant what-his-name?'

'Sten, sir. Sten.'

'Right. Sten. Is he still alive?'

'Yes, sir.'

'That was his first mistake, Colonel. Now, Sten. For him I have special plans. Do I still own Pluto, Mahoney?'

'I believe so, sir.'

'No. No. Too soft. I'll think of something. You just leave that Sten to me, Mahoney. You'll be too busy finding that hell hole I'm going to send you to.'

'Yes, sir.'

The Eternal Emperor eased back in his chair. Closed his eyes. Almost as if he were asleep. Mahoney waited a very long, very uncomfortable time. Finally the Emperor opened them again. He gave Mahoney a tired look. For a moment Mahoney could almost see just how very ancient the Eternal Emperor was.

'I'm counting on you, Ian,' the Emperor said softly. 'Solve it. Get rid of this Prophet for me. Get rid of Mathias.'

Mahoney came to his feet, knowing that he had finally gotten the Emperor's orders. He snapped his best salute.

'That, sir, will be my extreme pleasure.' He wheeled and began to march out.

'Mahoney?'

The Colonel stopped. 'Yes, sir?'

'Just don't embarrass me again. Please? As a favor to an old drinking buddy?'

'I won't, boss.'

'Being embarrassed is just one of those things I'm lousy at. Funny thing is, the older I get, the worse I am at it.'

He looked up at Mahoney. 'You'd think it would be the other way around, wouldn't you? You'd think by now I wouldn't give a clot.'

'I wouldn't know, boss.'

'Well, I do, Mahoney. I do care.'

And the Eternal Emperor closed his eyes again. Mahoney silently crept out.

Chapter Fifty-Five

At that moment, the prospect of exile on Pluto – or worse – was the least of Sten's worries. He and Alex were hunched over a com in Otho's castle, the coldest, grayest, dankest building Sten had ever been in. The two of them had been freezing their behinds off for weeks and trying to endure the worst food known to beingkind.

They had been notified two hours earlier to stand by on the com. Mahoney was about to issue his orders.

'It'll be tha gibbett, lad, Ah just know it,' Alex said.

'No,' Sten replied. 'Mahoney won't let us off with anything as easy as death.'

'Me mither always said Ah should'na be a soldier.'

They froze as the com line crackled and Mahoney's scowling face swam into view on the screen.

'I've just been to see the Emperor. He is not pleased.'

'I can understand that, sir,' Sten said.

Mahoney softened. 'Ah, well, at least the two of you are alive.'

He peered out at them through the screen. 'I tried to do the best I could for you, gentlemen,' Mahoney said. 'But . . .' He shrugged. It was the kind of shrug that did not bode well for careers.

'What do we do next, sir?' Sten asked.

'*You* don't do anything,' Mahoney answered. 'Just sit tight. Don't get into any more trouble. I'll have a ship pick you up in a few weeks.'

'But Mathias—'

'Don't worry, Lieutenant Sten. We'll take care of Mathias. By the time you're home, I'll have inserted another Mantis team, and it should be over. One way or the other.'

'Sir,' Sten blurted. 'Let me do it. Give me back my team. Team Thirteen. We'll settle Mathias for you.'

Mahoney frowned. Alex gave Sten a warning nudge.

'Revenge, Lieutenant? I thought we had trained you better than that.'

'No. Not revenge. We just have a better chance. I know Mathias. I know Sanctus.'

'Can't take the chance, lad,' Mahoney said kindly. 'Among other problems, all the mining and exploration certificates were personally approved by the Emperor *before* Mathias decided on patricide. There's a whole fleet of miners heading for the Eryx Region. Straight through the Lupus Cluster.'

'Mathias will kill them all,' Sten said. 'It's even more important that you let us handle it.'

'I don't see how,' Mahoney said.

'I have a plan.' And he began talking quickly. Laying it all out, to an increasingly surprised Mahoney.

Chapter Fifty-Six

It wasn't the first time Ffillips had been dragged, restraints chinking, up from a dungeon by thugs and hurled to her knees in front of Mathias.

But, the woman wondered, as she did a body-tuck, side-rolled away from the expected kick, and came back to her feet, it could well be the last.

The late and less-than-lamented Theodomir's throne room had seen considerable change, Ffillips realized as she glanced around. The tapestries and exotic statues were gone, as were the pillows on the stone chair.

The vidmap of Sanctus was now shadowed by an overlay of the Faith of Talamein – twin hands clasped in prayer, centered over a bare sword.

Only the twin torches to either side of the map remained.

On the stone throne sat Mathias, wearing the newly official uniform of undecorated red Companion full-dress. Ffillips bowed her head respectfully and kept her mouth shut – a delaying tactic that had worked quite well years before at her court-martial.

'I speak in the name of Talamein,' Mathias intoned.

'S'be't,' echoed the Companions ringing the bare walls.

'Here, in the most sacred place, seat of the faith of Talamein, I, Mathias, chosen by the Flame as Talamein's True Successor, I charge you, Major Ffillips, in the absence of your leader the arch-antideist Sten, with treason. Treason against our State, our Faith, and My People.'

Come, boy. Can't you find a more original charge than that? Ffillips thought to herself.

Ffillips knew it was most important to stall for time. Death –

which is the usual result of a treason trial – tends to be long term and without much recourse – unless one believed in the hereafter. After service in twenty wars, Ffillips certainly did not.

Ffillips waited a moment, then lifted her gaze to meet Mathias'. Unexpectedly she fell to her knees. A low buzz of surprise ran through the Companions, and even Mathias was startled.

'I do not understand the charge, O Prophet.'

'You will be apprised of the particulars, but they center around the assassination of our late and most honored Prophet Theodomir and your desire to overthrow this Most Holy Our State.'

'Before you were Prophet, I knew you as a worthy soldier and boon companion. I can only suggest, most humbly, that these charges derive from jealous or misunderstanding underlings.'

'You are incorrect, Major Ffillips. These accusations stem directly from my perception, my prayer, and my lips.'

Umm. He wants us dead, Ffillips thought. Then she tried another gambit. 'Since we are strangers to your system, Prophet, may I ask how judgment of the charges is rendered?'

'In the occasion of high treason,' Mathias said, 'the court is composed of church elders and the representative of Talamein.'

Star chamber with a hanging judge. 'Are the circumstances for trial the same for unbelievers as well as members of the Church of Talamein?'

'Major Ffillips, while the sentence could be the same,' Mathias went on, sounding slightly unsure of himself, 'the manner of execution differs. Those under the Cloak of the Faith are permitted an easier end.' And his eyes gleamed slightly. If he understood what Ffillips was leading toward, this could prove him right in his decision and be an even holier coup.

Got you, you fanatical little bugsnipe, Ffillips thought. 'I understand. But, Prophet, I do not wish to sound as if, are we indeed guilty, we would attempt to allay our doom. I was merely inquiring because of the curiosity that my soldiers and I have shown after seeing the bravery and nobility of those who Soldier for the Faith.'

'What is your request, Major?'

'Perhaps . . . since I assume you will provide us with advisors to ensure that trial will be fair under the eyes of Talamein himself, who will come to judge both the quick, the slow, and the dead,' Ffillips went on, 'it could be beneficial if you could find the wisdom to provide us with religious instructors, so we might know more of Talamein and then reach a decision.'

Mathias considered, then reluctantly nodded. That would slow the show trial, of course. But if some of the mercenaries would convert – a blessing. Also, if some of the lower-ranking soldiers find it in their hearts to follow the Way of Talamein, there might be a way for them to be spared and to assist in the training of his Companions for the jihad. But not Ffillips, not her officers, nor Sten – assuming the man could be found.

'I will take your plea under study, Major,' Mathias said. 'I must say it merits consideration. I will inform you of the Prophet's decision after the Prophet prays, fasts, and asks for confirmation from the aetherian heart of Talamein.'

Ffillips bowed as Mathias stood, arms spread.

'We thank you, Talamein, for overhearing this session, and we pray that justice was and shall be performed. S'be't.'

'S'be't,' came the amen as Ffillips was dragged back to her feet and back to the dungeon. Shambling along, faking a limp, Ffillips' eyes swept across the passageways, looking for ideas.

Not too bad, Major, she thought. You've delayed the headsman, got some possibly bribable or corruptible churchmen to come in, and, most of all, some time.

And she wondered just what Sten was doing and whether the man had abandoned his soldiers and simply fled.

Unfortunately the mercenary, battle-trained side of her agreed that the colonel would be a clotting fool if he'd done anything else.

Chapter Fifty-Seven

Otho was fairly certain that the mercenary who called himself Sten was a great deal more. There was, for instance, the highly modified radioset that was beam-cast in a direction that Otho, checking secretly, determined was close to Galactic Center. There was also the absolute idiocy of an unpaid mercenary sticking around to worry about his less-fortunate underlings.

So it did not surprise Otho at all when a sentry peered over his crennelated walk and screamed loudly.

Standing outside the castle, in the driving snow, were one slight human female flanked by two huge four-footed bulging-skulled black-and-white predators; a truly obese humanoid woman with an interesting moustache; and a tiny, fur-covered being with flicking tendrils. Plus four bulky, gravsleds.

Who they were, how they managed to insert themselves unobserved on the Bhor world, and why they knew where Sten was, Otho felt would be perpetually unanswered questions.

So he just opened the gates, set out an appetizing first meal of dried saltfish, the grain-filled, spiced and baked stomach of herding animals, and what remained of the last night's feast animal, then sent an underling to wake Sten and Alex.

Chapter Fifty-Eight

The reunion with his Mantis team was brief and wild. Munin even rose to its hind legs and licked Sten's face. Hugin – the other, and Sten felt brighter animal – purred once, then jumped on the top of the table and inhaled an entire platter of saltfish.

'Y'see, you overstrong lump of suet,' Ida rumbled to Alex, 'you can't get along without me?'

Alex choked on his grain dish, but admitted that he was, indeed, quite glad to see the hulking Rom woman.

Bet pulled Sten aside. Concern on her face. 'What went wrong?'

'We had to move too fast,' Sten said grimly. 'I'll give you the full briefing in a minute.'

Doc was oddly subdued. Sten managed to hug Bet twice, which brought up some interesting thoughts about what they did in the earlier days of their relationship, then he walked over and knelt to get eye-level with the koala-like Altairian.

'Your revenge is a terrible one, Sten,' Doc said glumly.

Sten looked puzzled.

'Do you know what Mahoney had us doing after you were detached? Do you know what his idea of On His Majesty's Imperial Stupidity consists of?' Doc's voice was rising toward a falsetto.

Sten knew Doc would tell him.

'Easy duty,' the team's anthropologist went on. 'Perfect for an understrength team, Mahoney told us. A tropic world whose government some local humanoids were about to overthrow. All we had to do was guard the embassy.'

'Mahoney said the Emperor thoroughly approved the revolution,' Bet went on. 'We were supposed to keep all the Imperial servants –

and their families – from getting fed down the same grinder the government was about to disappear into.'

'We did it,' Ida added. 'For one thing there was no comscan I could figure out that wasn't monitored. Do you know how many credits I lost? Do you know how many of my investments – our investments – have turned to drakh because we were stuck on that armpit?'

'That was not the worst,' Doc continued. 'We were disguised as Guards security – and we even managed to convince those clots who call themselves Foreign Service people that Hugin and Munin are normally part of a Guards team.

'Pfeah,' he sneered, ladling an enormous steak down his maw. And chewing.

'It was hilarious.' Bet took over as Doc glumly chewed. She was trying, without much success, to keep from laughing.

'The indigenes took the palace. Besieged the embassy. Usual stuff. We fired some rounds over their heads and they went home to think about things.'

Through a rapidly disappearing mouthful that looked more suitable for Hugin, Doc said, 'We had, of course, prepared an escape route – out the back gate, through some interconnected huts, into the open, through an unguarded city gate and then walk twelve kilometers to a Guard destroyer.'

'So,' Sten wondered, 'what was the problem?'

'The children,' Doc said. 'Ida, who somehow has time-in-grade on me, ordered me to be in charge of embassy dependents. Nasty, carnivorous, squeaky humanoids.'

'They loved him,' Ida put in. 'Listened to his every word. Made him sing songs. Fed him candy. Patted him.'

'With those *sticky* paws of theirs.' Doc grunted. 'It took me three cycles to comb out my fur. And they called me' – he shuddered – 'their teddy bear.'

Sten stood up, keeping his face turned away from Doc, and thumped Hugin off the table. He composed himself and turned.

'Now that you've had your vacation, would you like to get back to work on something nice and impossible?'

Doc levered himself another steak, and the team squatted, listening as Sten began the back-briefing.

Chapter Fifty-Nine

The escape plans were going extremely well, Ffillips thought. Those mercs with any experience at losing war had secreted some kind of minor edged weapon on their uniforms. These had been put into a common pool, and those most suitable for digging or cutting assigned to the smallest, beefiest, and least claustrophobic of the mercs.

The flagstones that made up the dungeon floor had taken only two nights to cut around and lever up, and the digging had commenced. At each prisoner count and guard shift change, they were dropped back into place and false cement – made from chewed-and-dried bread particles – went around them.

Viola, who'd taken over the Lycée section after Egan's death, had triangulated a tunnel route using trig and what little could be seen from the barred windows at the upper portion of the huge dungeon.

Some of the more devout mercenaries and those who could sound religious had entered study groups with Mathias' instructors.

While listening, asking intelligent questions, and pretending to be increasingly swayed, they also pulled loose strings that held their uniforms bloused over boot-top and scattered earth from the tunnel across the pounded-dirt courtyard.

It was going very well, Ffillips thought, as one shift of naked, grimy soldiers oozed out of the hole and was replaced by another. The first team immediately began swabbing themselves clean in the last remains of the liter-per-day wash-and-drink water ration that their captors allowed.

Very well indeed, Ffillips thought. We have only three-hundred-plus meters of rocky earth to dig through before we stand the possibility of being beyond these walls. Then, once we break out, which should be in the cliff edge, all we need to do is figure out how to rappel down one hundred meters of rock and disappear into the heart of Sanctus' capital. All of which we can easily accomplish given, say, ten years.

Sten, Sten, where are you, Colonel? Ffillips shucked her tunic and, in spite of fairly pronounced claustrophobia, dropped into the tunnel and crawled toward its face, past the sweating, pumping airshaft workers, to begin her own digging shift.

Chapter Sixty

The team sat, considering. Each was working, in his or her own mind, possible alternate solutions to the one Sten had presented. The tigers had thought out the prospects through their somewhat single-track minds, had presented paws with claws out, had the kill-everything plan rejected, curled up, and started cleaning each other's face.

Ida summarized the situation: 'A fanatic. With soldiers. Declared religious war. After our awesomely perceptive Emperor blessed any little atrocity they would want to commit, unto the seventh generation, amen.

'We have mining ships on the way – ships that shall surely be ambushed by these Companions.'

'Ae braw summation,' Alex agreed.

'One solution,' Doc tried. 'We wait until the mercenaries are tried, sentenced to death, and brought out for execution. Your Mathias will undoubtedly attend, and it will unquestionably be a public ceremony. At the height of the roasting, or however he chooses to kill your former subordinates, we take him.'

'Negative,' Sten declared flatly. 'The plan depends on saving as many of them as we can.'

'Does Mahoney know you're figuring it like that?'

'No,' Sten said. The other members of the team dropped the subject. Secretly all except Doc agreed with Sten's romanticism.

'Agreed,' Bet said. 'The only option is to take out Mathias before the holy war can start.'

'Joyful day,' Ida said dubiously. 'By the way, as long as we don't know how we're going to get onto Sanctus, let alone how the clot we'll slither into the capital, has your brilliant mind considered how we'll get into this Temple fortress to take out Mathias, assuming we can do all the rest, O my commander?'

'Not my brilliant mind,' Sten said. 'My cold butt.'

'What?' Ida asked.

'My cold sitter – plus Mahoney sent a geo-ship over Sanctus three days ago, for a seismochart.'

'You realize none of us has the slightest idea what you're talking about, Sten.'

'Of course not, Bet.'

'All right,' Bet shrugged. 'That'll be your department. My department – I just figured out how we get onto Sanctus and inside the capital.

'No creepy-crawly, by the way,' she went on. 'First of all, it's hard on my delicate complexion.'

'Ah dinna ken whae y'be goint,' Alex said. 'You pussycats, Doc, an' th' braw gross fishwife be hard to hide in th' open.'

'Not when we're completely in the open,' Bet said. She tried to keep a straight face and failed. 'Boys and girls, we are going to have a show.'

Puzzlement, and then Sten and Alex got it, and the room dissolved in laughter, except for the tigers, who looked upset, and for Doc, who had no idea what they were talking about.

'You have it,' Sten said when he stopped laughing. 'Also do you know what that gives us?'

'Of course,' Bet said. 'You set things up for what happens after we burn Mathias, his Companions, and the Faith of Talamein into ashes. The solution to the whole Lupus Cluster.'

Sten shrugged. So his thunder was stolen. He'd never believed much in the livie detective who said 'ah-hah' and then everybody else sat listening in awestruck wonder.

'Otho is going to love this,' he said, heading for the door.

'By my mother's beard,' Otho roared, and one chandelier swung and two suits of streggan-hunting armor rocked on their stands, 'you are making a fool of the Bhor and of me.'

'My apologies,' Sten said. 'But it is one solution and, should it work, it will keep you from having buttocks as frozen as those of your father.'

'I will not do it,' Otho said.

Sten poured two stregghorns full and pushed one to Otho. He knew the shaggy Bhor would eventually agree. Sten just hoped he'd be able to handle the hangover that was about to be constructed.

*

Sten huddled in the bed under the heavy furs. His mind was fuddled with too much stregg, but he couldn't sleep. His mind wouldn't shut off as he reviewed the plans for the hundredth time.

He heard the soft-scraping sound outside the door and then came fully awake as it creaked heavily open. His fingers curled for his knife and then relaxed as the small figure stepped in.

It was Bet. She shut the door, walked to the bed, undid her robe, and let it slide to the floor. She was naked under it.

Sten had almost forgotten how beautiful she was. Then she was under the furs and cuddling up to him.

'But I thought . . . we were going to be just friends.'

'I know.' She laughed. 'I was just feeling—'

Sten gulped as she began kissing her way down his bare chest.

'—real friendly.'

With logic like that, who was Sten to argue?

Chapter Sixty-One

The bearded man stood at the mouth of the beach, his net and fishing pike across one shoulder. He stared without much curiosity at the odd assemblage on the edge of the surf. Then he thoughtfully sucked at a tooth and ambled forward to the brightly painted cluster of boxes in front of which stood the Mantis team and a glowering Otho.

With a single island continent, it had been very easy for a Bhor ship to make planetfall on the far side of Sanctus. Sten and his people had then offloaded to a lighter that had blazed only meters above the sea to land them on a beach near the northern tip of the island. Sten knew that was the easy part – any merchants as skilled as the Bhor would also be capable smugglers, easily able to insert anyone almost anywhere without triggering a radar alarm.

'Yahbee ghosts, Y reck,' the fisherman said, unsurprised.

There were far more people on Sanctus' main island than just church officials and Companions, and, Sten hoped, they would provide the key for the success of the operation.

Mostly the residents were illiterate rural or seacoast providers. Peasants. And, as with peasants everywhere, they had the virtues/failings of suspicion, superstition, skepticism, and general pigheadedness However, this fisherman was a little more superstitious and stupid than even Sten thought possible.

Sten figured that if he himself was a fisherman and wandered down at dawn to his favorite fishing spot to find a short bear, a large hairy being, two oversized cats, and four humanoids, the most logical option would be run howling to the nearest church of Talamein for shriving.

Instead the local sucked at his teeth again and spat, almost hitting Hugin, who growled warningly.

'No, gentle sir,' Sten began. 'We are but poor players whose coastal ship was wrecked early this morn. Fortunately we were able to salvage all our gear, though, alas, our faithful ship was lost.'

'Ahe,' the fisherman said.

'Now we need assistance. We need help in assembling these our wagons – and can pay in geld. Also we shall need beasts of burden, to draw the wagons.

'In return, not only shall we pay in red geld, but shall perform our finest show for the folk of your village.'

'Shipwrecked, y'sah?'

'That we were.'

'Stick to beint ghosts,' the fisherman said. 'It hah a more believable ring to it.'

And, as Alex's hand slid smoothly toward the miniwillygun slung under his red/blue/green tunic, the fisherman turned.

'Y go t'mah village. P'raps one hour b'fore Y hae beasties an' workers for you.' He spat again, turned, and trudged, still without panic or hurry, back the way he had come.

Puzzled, the Mantis soldiers and Otho looked at each other, then they started breaking down their gear – five ten-meter-long wagons, hastily built by Bhor craftsmen. They were loaded with the various properties needed for Bet's 'show,' plus det-set lockboxes full of full-bore Imperial weaponry, including tight-beam coms, willyguns, and exotic demo tools.

Theirs was no longer a deniable operation, Sten knew. Either he would succeed, and it wouldn't matter, or he would die. In which case, within six months the Emperor would be forced to commit a full Guard assault into the Lupus Cluster.

And if that was the necessity, something as minor as a blown Mantis team would be the least of the Emperor's worries.

Besides, Sten told himself, if the worst came down, they'd all be dead anyway.

Chapter Sixty-Two

The campaign that Doc projected had a twofold aim. First and most important was to provide a means for some extremely odd-looking beings to be able to insert themselves into Sanctus' well-guarded capital in time to lift the mercs and end Mathias' dreams of a holy war. One of the most effective ways to run a clandestine operation is to run it in plain sight, since the opposition generally figures no one can be *that* stupid and obvious. Covert-ops specialists frequently lose themselves in a maze of double-crosses and triple-thinking.

The second purpose was to emphasize the increasing split between the people of Sanctus and their church. So the jokes, the play, and the after-performance casual asides were designed to make the Companions and the hierarchy look abysmally stupid – so stupid and corrupt that no self-respecting peasant would give a damn if the regime fell. At least no self-respecting peasant who hadn't been able to figure a way to get his paws on some of the graft.

Doc knew that in a largely illiterate, partially repressed culture, a good joke or whispered scandal would spread almost as fast as if it had been broadcast on a livie.

If the campaign succeeded and most peasants were chuckling over the latest anti-Companion joke, and the Mantis section successfully penetrated the capital to start the shooting, hopefully the local populace would stay neutral. If they rose up in support of Mathias, Sten, all his team, and the imprisoned mercs would probably have very brief lifespans. And of course, if they decided to overthrow the palace in support of Sten, the result could well be civil war, and a civil war with religious overtones can last for generations and totally waste a culture.

Doc had spent long hours with his computer before the Bhor

inserted the Mantis team. Working within the 28 Rules of Humor (Doc, like other Altarians, had less than no sense of humor), his innate dislike of humanoids, and his massive contempt for any cause beyond basic selfishness, Doc had come up with half a hundred jokes, some fairly juicy scandals, and one play.

The play was less normal drama than a cross between the Medieval Earth mystery cycles and the early, crudely humorous commedia dell'arte, with a great deal of improvisation.

Casting the play was somewhat of a problem. Since Sten and Alex were well known by the Companions, their onstage and off-stage presences had to be disguised.

For the play, it was easy. Sten and Alex were force-cast as the troupe's clowns and were completely unrecognizable under white-mime makeup, black-outlined facial features, and fantastic fright wigs and costumes. Offstage, though, there was a bit of a problem.

A basic rule of makeup is that it's unnecessary to change much of a person's features for him to be unrecognizable. And Mantis knew those rules very well indeed. So Sten shaved his head and put a rather unsightly blotch on one cheek. Alex grew a walrus moustache and trimmed his hair into a monkish half tonsure.

The plot of the play was idiot-simple. Bet played an orphaned village girl whose virtue was threatened by a corrupt village official (Alex, with a long beard and a battered non-accent), in cahoots with a somewhat evil churchman of the late and not-much-lamented regime of Theodomir. The official was played by Ida in drag.

Bet's only hope was her handsome lover, who had left the village to join the crusade of Mathias and his Companions against the evil Jann. By then official doctrine wasn't admitting that the mercs had done anything but sit on their duffs, pinch chaste women, and swill alk.

The lover would never be seen, which was a relief since the casting potential was running a little slender.

About twenty minutes in, after appropriate menacings by the official and the churchman, the girl sobbed and caterwauled and sank in prayer to Talamein. And the voice of Talamein – Ida again – spoke from offstage and told her to flee into the forest.

There she was menaced by hungry tigers and saved by a shipwrecked mendicant Bhor, played by Otho – who roared when told that he would have to make nice noises about what he considered to be a ridiculous faith, and then roared louder when told that he also had lines suggesting that *all* the Bhor felt the same about Talamein.

Then the Bhor mendicant led the girl to the shelter of two clownish woodsmen, Sten and Alex.

Somehow, through a plot twist Doc could never figure out but one which didn't bother the audience at all, the tigers turned into friendly tigers and did amusing stunts to keep the lonely girl laughing between chanted hymns while the woodsmen were out being woodsy.

She was threatened by an evil fortuneteller (Ida again), and only saved by a mysterious cute-and-cuddly furry creature (Doc, despite his howled protests).

More chanting, more prayers, and then the Voice of Talamein spoke again, saying that the evil official and prayerman were coming into the forest with their private army (Sten and Alex, playing peasants drafted as soldiers).

The army killed the woodsmen (very deft rolling from the wagon's stage into the curtained-off backstage and slapped-on steel helms for Sten and Alex), leaving the girl doomed to submit to the embraces of the official.

But then, once again Talamein spoke, the tigers and Otho roared onstage, ate the villians, the soldiers recanted their ways, then, in a blinding finale, word came of the success of Mathias' Crusade against the Jann. Unfortunately, Bet's lover had been killed, doing something unspeakably heroic. But the Faith of Talamein was triumphant. Amid chanted praise, clown rolls by Sten and Alex, prancing tigers, the play came to a close, and *exeunt omnes* amid applause.

Then, of course, Sten and Alex would move among the crowd doing simple magic gags, clown stunts for the kids, Bet would stroll with her tigers, and Ida would set up the fortune-telling booth while Doc barkered.

And it went over in every village, from the opening performance in the fishing town through the farming villages even to a couple of command performances before rural clergy.

Not that it had to be that great to succeed, when the only 'entertainment' available to the villagers was the drone of the Talamein broadcast in the village square screens, church worship, and getting as drunk as possible on turnip wine.

Slowly the troupe moved closer to Sanctus' capital.

'We're two kilometers from Sanctus' gates,' Ida announced from inside the cart.

Sten nodded politely at a glowering guard team of Companions as they passed in their gravsled, then tapped the reins on the hauling beasts' backs. They grudgingly moved from a stagger into a slow walk.

'An' noo,' Alex said, 'w'be't goint into tha' tiger's maw.'

'Hugin and Munin's maw's back on Prime World,' Bet added from her position, sitting just behind Alex and Sten, who were on the cart driver's bench.

'Sharrup, lass,' Alex replied. 'Ah'm dooncast. Ah fearit this scheme wi' nae workit oot f'r th' benefits of Kilgours.'

'You're probably right,' Sten agreed. 'We're doomed. And doomed without hearing the last of Red Rory.'

'Red Rory, aye?' And Alex brightened. 'W'noo. Wh'n last w'sawit Red Rory, an entire Brit comp'ny wae chargint up thae hill, a'ter his head, aye?'

Sten nodded wearily. The things he did to keep morale up.

'So tha' screekit, an' scrawit, an' hollerint, and ae kinds ae goin' on, an' then heads come doon thx hill, bumpit, bumpit, bumpit.

'Anh't' thae Brit gin'ral's consid'r'ble astonishment, here's his wholit comp'ny, lyin' dead in thae dust.

'But b'fore he hae a chance to consider, yon giant on tha hillcrest screekit again:

'"Ah'm Red Rory ae th' Glen! Send up y' entire rig'mint!"

'An the gin'ral turnit sa red hi' adj'tant fearit he gae apoplexy. An' he holler, "Adj'tant!'

'"Send up tha' wholit blawdy reg'mint! AH WAN' THA' MON'S HEAD!"

'An' tha' whole reg'mint fixit thae bay'nits an' thae chargit up thae hill. An' thae's screamint, an' screekit, an' shoutint. an' carryint on, for aye half ae day.

'An' thae's dust, an' thae's shots, an' thae's aye battle.

'An' th' gin'ral's watchint frx doon below.

'Ah sudden, thro' thae dust, he see't his adj'tant comit runnin doon thx hill.

'An' tae adj'tant screemit. "Run, sah! Run! It's ae ambush! Thae's two ae 'em."'

Very complete silence for many minutes.

Finally Sten turned to Alex, incredulous. 'You mean, *that's* the story I've been waiting for, for the last year?'

'Aye,' Alex said. 'Dinnae it b'wonderful?'

Even more and longer silence . . .

Chapter Sixty-Three

Mathias watched as they led another of Ffillips' mercs into the chamber. The man was naked and sweating heavily under the bright, revolving interrolights. His body was covered with bruises and cuts from many days of beatings. The soldier was exhausted; his eyes were rolling in fear.

Mathias nodded at the chief interrogator, and the man was muscled into a chair and strapped down. Coldly and efficiently, an interrogrator's aide snapped electrical leads to the prisoner's body.

The Prophet stepped forward, looming over the man. Then spoke gently. 'Son, don't let this go on. It grieves me to see a poor sinner submit to such an ordeal. End it for yourself. I beg you in the name of our gentle Father, Talamein.'

He leaned closer to the man.

'A simple confession of your sins and the sins of your leaders is all we require . . . Now, will you confess? Please, son.'

Weakly the soldier shook his head, no.

Mathias nodded for the inquisitor to start. And the first screams ripped from the soldier's body.

An hour later Mathias walked from the chamber, a tight little smile of satisfaction on his lips.

From a crystal decanter, Mathias poured himself a goblet of pure, cold water. Its source was one of the clear mountain springs that he had recently declared holy.

It was night on Sanctus, and Mathias was alone in his spartan chamber. Outside the room he could hear the faint sounds of the pacing guards.

Mathias reviewed his plans once more before going to sleep on the small, hard, military cot he favored.

He realized unhappily that his plans for the resettlement of Sanctus was not proceeding as swiftly as he would like.

The idea had come to him like a vision. He saw a series of small, isolated spiritual communes, devoted to reflection and worship. To create these communes, he would empty the cities and villages. Move the peasants off the farms.

The latest reports said that the idea had met a huge amount of resistance, especially from the farmers and artisans. Who would till the land? they complained. Who would mix the mortar and build the buildings?

This kind of small, ungodly thinking would have to stop Mathias decided. He would not let the unenlightened of his planet stand in the way of a glorious future.

He scrawled an order for Companions to sweep into the villages. What he could not do with reason, he would accomplish by force. He added a suggestion to the report: Burn the homes and destroy the farms. That way the peasants would have no place to return.

Mathias was more pleased with his progress involving the matter of the mercenaries. Of course, he had personally handled that. He had scheduled the public trial to begin the following day. Enough mercenaries had confessed to insure its success.

One by one, each man would be found guilty. And Mathias would order their executions. Those, too, would be public.

It would be a solemn occasion, followed by a great celebration. Mathias had already announced that some of the rules of Talamein behavior would be relaxed during the festival.

A wise Prophet, he told himself, had to understand that his people were only weak human beings.

Mathias began to scrawl a few notes concerning the planet-wide month of purification that he would declare to take place immediately after the festival.

He had some interesting ideas on this subject. Floggings, for instance – all voluntary, of course.

Chapter Sixty-Four

Ffillips stood at stiff attention before her ragged band of men. They were drawn up in the temple's central courtyard. Ffillips could sense the hidden vidmonitors that were broadcasting the event across the planet. Around them were row after row of spidery bleachers filled with red-uniformed Companions. Seated in front of the bleachers were the ten judges handpicked by Mathias from his officer corps.

On one side sat the Prophet himself. He was seated on a small onyx throne. He wore a simple uniform, with only two small golden medals – the torch symbol of Sanctus – to mark his rank.

The evidence had been given – mostly, the humiliating confessions forced from men and women who couldn't bear up under torture. The judges had weighed the verdict. And it was about to be delivered.

Ffillips knew she was dead.

Mathias raised a hand for silence. Instant hush. He leaned slightly forward in his throne. His face was serene, almost kindly. 'Do you wish to say anything in your behalf?' he asked Ffillips. 'In the interest of justice?'

Ffillips looked coldly at Mathias and then at the judges. 'I don't see her here.'

'Who?' Mathias asked.

'Justice,' Ffillips said. 'Now, as one soldier to another, I'll ask you to end this sham. My men and I await your decision.'

But before Mathias could give the signal, Ffillips shouted: 'DETACHMENT, TEN-HUT.'

And her sad, ragged troop suddenly became soldiers again. They snapped to, throwing off the exhaustion and fear. Even those crippled by torture drew themselves up. A few had to be helped. Some grinned at Mathias and the Companions through broken teeth.

Mathias hesitated, then turned.

'What is the verdict?' he asked the judges.

And the same word hissed out along the line of ten.

'Guilty . . . Guilty . . . Guilty . . .' And so on until the last judge pronounced their fate.

Mathias rose, bowed to the judges. 'I have agonized over this,' Mathias announced. 'The evidence was overwhelming, even before the trial. And, as you all know, I counseled compassion.'

He paused for effect.

'No doubt,' Ffillips said, loudly enough for the vidmonitors to pick up.

Mathias ignored her.

'But,' the Prophet continued, 'I must bow to the wisdom of the judges. They know best the desires of Talamein. I can only accede. And give thanks to our Father, for his guidance.'

He turned to Ffillips and her men. 'With great sorrow, I must pronounce judgment—'

Ffillips shouted the order: 'TROOP, RIGHT FACE.'

Her troops wheeled as one. Proud men and women ready to go to their deaths. Their guards broke rank and dignity, rushing over to them, shouting, waving their weapons.

Mathias had to rush out the words:

'You are all sentenced to die,' he shouted. 'Within five days. Before the people of Sanctus, and—'

Ffillips broke through his ranting: 'FORWARD . . . MARCH . . .'

And the soldiers stepped out in perfect time, heading back for their prison and their doom.

'And Talamein . . .' Mathias screamed.

Ffilhps shot him the universal gesture of contempt. And, in her best parade-ground voice: 'CLOT YOU.'

All was confusion. As the mercs disappeared, Mathias was yelling instructions at his guard and fruitless explanations at the vidmonitors.

Ffillips might have been a dead woman, but she knew how to go out in style.

Chapter Sixty-Five

The giant funeral chimneys of Sanctus belched out ash, smoke, and fire, working overtime as the very wealthy and highly nervous ruling class of the Lupus Cluster poured in their donations to the new Prophet.

Sten, Bet, Alex, and the others jockeyed their gaudily painted wagons through the crowds that were pouring into the holy city.

Red-uniformed Companions made cursory attempts to check out the pilgrims. Here and there they pulled people aside to run scanners over their bodies and belongings. But mostly they were just waving the hordes of people through, barely able to keep up with the traffic, much less look for malcontents.

Once they got through the gates, Sten waved his people to one side. He took a fresh look at the Sanctus of Mathias.

To either side of the Avenue of Tombs and its eye-ear-nose-and-throat-polluting monuments spread the city itself. Sandwiched between the mix of small homes, tenements, and the occasional gabled mansion were the narrow streets and alleyways. Sanctus' capital had evidently not had much of a planning commission.

And now the barely passable streets were roiling with visitors. Sten's back prickled as he realized that all of them, whether peasants, artisans, or merchants, were in their colorful best clothes. Also, Sten noted, here and there, other entertainers' wagons.

The chaos was worrisome. It was a perfect cover, to be sure, but the spontaneous partying meant that Sten and his team had less time than they thought. None of them had seen or heard about the sentencing cast, but from the festive tourists, Sten realized he would have to act quickly.

Bet slid across the seat toward him and nuzzled his neck. 'Mathias acted more quickly than we thought,' she hissed. Sten forced laughter and pulled her close for a kiss. A Companion stared at them curiously for a moment, then moved on. A drunken beggar stumbled past, waving a sheaf of tickets.

'THE EXECUTIONS,' he shouted. 'SEE THEM IN PERSON . . . STILL A FEW SPACES LEFT IN THE PUBLIC SQUARE.'

He staggered on.

'SEE THE EXECUTIONS . . . THE TRAITORS OF TALAMEIN . . .'

His voice was finally drowned out by the crowd. Bet broke away from Sten and slid off the wagon seat. Sten gave her a slap on the rump.

'See what you can find out,' he whispered.

Bet nodded and laughed lustily, then jumped down onto the roadway. In a moment she had disappeared into the throng.

Alex stuck his head out from the wagon's interior, then slid up on the seat beside Sten.

'Best be movin', lad,' he said.

Sten took another look at what faced them before he gigged the beasts into motion.

The Temple sat at the end of the Avenue of Tombs, atop a gently rising hill about three hundred meters higher than the city gates. Its spire towered over thick, protective walls. Below the Temple was what had been a monastary. Years past, it had been a place of silent devotion for Talamein priests. More recently Theodomir and now Mathias used it as a prison.

Sten pointed it out to Alex.

'Tha's whae th' be't keepint our Ffillips,' Alex said. He passed Sten a wineskin. Sten upended the bag, letting the wine pour into his mouth. Then it went back to Alex, who raised it, eyes scanning the landscape over the tanned leather.

'Over there.' Sten said, nodding to the skeleton of a building going up beside the old Talamein monastery/prison. 'That's our way in.'

Alex peered at it for an instant, then turned away.

What he had seen was a slim, towering needle of steel, very much out of place next to the ancient monastery. They had heard it was going to be the new barracks Mathias was building for his Companions. Ironically, it was also to be named for Theodomir.

They noticed there were no workers around the building. Obviously they had been given time off for the holiday. They also noticed that although most streets were filled with partying citizens of Sanctus, the area around the prison was carefully being avoided.

Down the hill from it, still on the Avenue of Tombs, they spotted the main armory for the Companions. That area, too, was deserted.

'Got it?' Sten asked Alex.

Alex considered for a moment.

'A wee dicey, lad,' he said finally. 'But it'll hae t' shift.'

Sten gave the signal, then his wagon and the others tumbled forward, deeper into the Holy City.

On a side street farther down the hill from the Companions' armory was what had once been a park. Before Mathias it had been a small green area for pilgrims. A place to rest and, after worship, to picnic after the long fasting. It was three-quarters screened by a ring of tall, slender trees.

But the Companions had put it to a more practical use. Where once had been a sprawling green lawn was now a sea of well-churned mud. The park was filled with small, tracked self-propelled cannon, whose honeycomb armor allowed them high speed and maneuverability. The tracks were built for two men, had small, open turrets, and were armed with quad, full-auto 50mm projectile cannon.

They were powered by old-style low-friction engines that gave maximum performance to a fairly cumbersome little package.

Milling and relaxing in the myriad aisles between the track columns were Companion drivers, mechanics, gunners, and general gofers. Though most of them were pretending to be busy at their duties, they were actually rubbernecking at the crowds of funseekers cavorting a hundred meters or so away in the street.

Ida and Doc broke out of the crowd. A few giggling children followed them for a moment or two, delighted at the spectacle. But as they wandered toward the track park, anxious parents called them back.

Ida was dressed in her rainbow gypsy best. And she was dragging Doc along on a short, silver leash.

'Alley-oop,' she shouted.

And Doc did a ponderous somersault.

They paused near one SP. A few curious Companion privates moved forward a bit to see better.

'Play dead,' she said.

Doc flopped to the ground and stiffened his limbs. 'Don't go too far!' he hissed.

'Your idea,' Ida whispered back, enjoying every minute of it.

A few young men, glancing nervously over their shoulders for superiors, came closer.

'Now, beg.' Ida commanded.

'No,' Doc whispered. 'I don't do begging.'

Ida jerked the leash while she glanced around the park, instantly filing layout, security, and, most important, eyeing the track's individual locks.

'I *said* beg.' Ida smiled sweetly.

Doc did as he was told, trembling on hind legs and waving his paws. He swore to himself that Ida would die many deaths for this disgrace.

'What are you doing here?' shouted a Companion lieutenant.

Instantly young Companion privates jolted in their boots, looked nervously about and started to drift away.

Ida looked at the young lieutenant, then at Doc.

'It's a new act, sir,' she said. 'He's a bit wild yet. Don't know how to behave.'

Before the glowering officer, she half-dragged Doc away on the leash.

'Next time,' Doc hissed when they were out of earshot, 'you go on the chain.'

As they melted back into the crowd, Ida noticed that the lieutenant was still watching them. Just for cover, naturally, she gave Doc a little kick.

Chapter Sixty-Six

The small gravsled hissed up to the Theodomir Barracks-to-be. On it was an untidy assortment of crammed tool boxes and chaotic mounds of electrical spare parts.

Sten and Alex stepped off and, ignoring the guards, began to fill two duffle bags with tools and spidery electrical parts. A bored chief guard wandered over.

'Here now. What're you two doing?'

Sten just grunted at him. Alex handed the guard a grease-stained permit. Both grease and permit had first met less than an hour ago. The guard peered at the permit.

'Says here,' he commented, 'they got problems with the welder on floor fifteen.' He glared at the two men, trying on his cop-suspicious look.

'I ain't heard about that,' he said.

Sten wrestled on his toolbelt.

'Whaddya expect,' Sten said. 'It's a clottin' holiday, ain't it? Nobody don't hear nothin', unless you're like my partner and me.

'Clots We were gonna party tonight. But no. Whadda they care? We spend all those credits on some approved quill. We gotta couple ladies lined up. We're gettin' heated up. Then we get the call. Problems with the clotting welder on the Theodomir building.

'Fix it, they say. I say send somebody else. They say fix it or don't show up tomorrow. So here we are. And we're gonna fix it and get back to the party.'

The guard was a bit stubborn. He, too, had a party planned and hadn't expected the day to be a duty day.

'Still,' he said. 'I wasn't notified. No work done 'less I'm notified.'

Sten shrugged. He and Alex climbed back into the gravsled. Sten keyed a report on the tiny onboard computer, then printed it and handed the hard copy to the guard. 'Sign it.'

The guard stared at it, his eyes widening.

'This says I refused you entrance. You're blaming me 'cause you can't fix the welder.'

'Gotta blame somebody,' Sten said. 'Might as well be you. Look. Be a nice guy. Sign it. We leave. And then it's party time tonight.'

The guard handed the report back, shaking his head. 'Go do your work.'

'Ah, come on,' Sten said. 'Give us a clottin' break. I wanna go home.'

But the guard was firm. He pointed at the building. 'Fix it.'

Reluctantly Sten and Alex climbed back out of their gravsled, loaded up their tools, and, with a few 'clots' thrown over their shoulder, began the weary climb to the fifteenth floor.

Ida and Doc piled over the turret top, into the track. On the ground beside it, the Companion lieutenant was moaning into unconsciousness. After the two had done a quick fiddle with one of the Mantis Section's Hotwire Anything Kits, they'd crept back into the track park. It was unfortunate – for the lieutenant – that he'd come around the wrong corner at the wrong time. Ida'd forearmed him in the gut and Doc had tranked the man, but not before nearly biting through his leg.

Ida fumbled the box out of her purse, looking at the controls.

'Over there,' Doc said, pointing at the SP cannon's security/ignition case. Within seconds Ida had the box epoxied on the case, and the box had analyzed and broken the three-sequence number code that brought the track to life.

As Ida fired the engine up, she settled into the gunner/driver's seat then pushed the track controls forward and hunched a little.

'Hang on, Doc. This is gonna be a clottin' great ride.'

The SP cannon's tracks raised great gouts of spray, and then, as Ida yanked one control stick all the way back, the track spun in its own length and churned out of the park toward the armory.

Alex allowed himself one genteel Edinburghian wheeze as he and Sten dumped their duffle bags on the wooden planking covering the Theodomir building's fifteenth story.

Sten fished through one bag and took out a grapnel gun. He fitted the spool line to the grapnel's shaft while Alex neatly coiled cable from the second duffle bag.

Then Sten took careful aim at the prison's roof below through the gun's vee-sights. He fired and with a whoosh the grapnel drifted toward its target, spooling out light silver line.

Bet signaled the tigers. Hugin and Munin flashed forward out of the alley mouth, bounding in rippling shadows toward the gate of the armory. A few meters from it, they split and darted unnoticed to either side of the gate. They slipped into shadows and became invisible, the only movement an occasional flash of a whipping tail.

Bet patted Otho on his hulking shoulder. She walked out from the alleyway and began ankling toward the steel guardshack.

She was wearing her most prim-but-revealing peasant costume. A summer dress that hugged her body but allowed her long limbs to flash out freely. She acted unsure, vulnerable, little-girl-lost. Without hestitation she walked straight toward the guardshack.

A young, handsome Companion stepped out. 'May I help you, sister?'

She opened her eyes as wide as they could go. 'Oh, yes, sir. I'm hoping you could. I've never been to the Holy City before, and . . . and . . .'

'You're lost?'

Bet gulped and gave a shy nod.

'We were all with the village priest,' she gushed, all over-explanation 'The Talamein youth group – and one of the boys got, well, you know . . . too friendly, and – and . . .' Bet stopped doing the galaxy's best blush.

'You left the group.' The guard was all understanding, and protective.

Bet nodded.

'And now you need to know how to get to the hostel?'

Bet nodded again.

The guard pointed down the street. 'Just down there, sister. A few hundred meters.'

Bet gulped her thanks and began, with an innocent wiggle, to head for the hostel.

'I'll stand right here,' the young Companion shouted after her, 'and make sure you're all right.'

Bet waved her thanks and moved on, tentatively, slowly. Tripping over little potholes – all Princess and the Pea. She heard gates clang open behind her and then the sound of bootsteps. The changing of the guard was right on time.

She nodded at the mouth of the alley. A moment later Otho staggered out, a shambling, stumbling drunken Bhor. He bleared at Bet, gave a huge smile, belched, and trundled forward. 'By my mother's beard,' he shouted. 'Here's a find.'

Bet shrieked, tried to run, and caught a heel in the cobblestones. She fell heavily. An instant later Otho was falling on her. Laughing and gathering her up in his huge and hairy arms. The theory was that no one dumb enough to be a Companion would be bright enough to realize that, to a Bhor, breeding with a human was only slightly less revolting and impossible than with a streggan.

Otho pretended not to hear the shouts from the onrushing Companion and the other guards.

'Just my luck,' he chortled at Bet. 'Now, don't be afraid, little lady. Otho is going to—'

He grunted in pain as the Companion slammed into him. He twisted off Bet, wrapped a mighty arm around the Companion and there was a sharp crack as the man's back broke.

Just behind him, a second Companion gaped in surprise. Bet shot him and he dropped without a sound.

Shouts. Clanking. Sounds of confusion. Bet looked up to see the guards gaping. There were about twenty men pointing and yelling. Weapons were coming up.

Bet put two fingers in her mouth and whistled loudly. The entire street seemed to rumble as the tigers roared and bounded out of their hiding spots, straight into the guards.

Guts trailing, three men went under before the rest knew what was happening. Hugin and Munin bounded among them, ripping, clawing, and tearing. There was immediate panic.

Guns went off, and bullets ripped into Companions instead of tigers.

Then, as a melée, the Companions fled back into the guard tunnel, fighting each other to be first.

It was a long, narrow tunnel with gates at each end. The one on the street side had been opened for the changing of the guards. Security required that the other – the only other exit – be closed.

Companions on the inside of the armory gaped in horror as their friends charged toward them and beat on the bars helplessly as Hugin and Munin tore into them.

Panicked men were climbing the portcullis, trying to squeeze through the slots. And being dragged down.

A guard on the inside violated orders and slapped a button to open the interior gates. As the few Companions still alive spilled through, the guard raised his weapon to fire at the tigers. Before he could shoot, his head exploded.

Bet and Otho ran yelling and firing into the interior courtyard. The way to the armory was open.

Sten and then Alex clipped wheeled guides to the slender cable. The monastery was about twenty meters below them and about one hundred meters away.

Sten tugged experimentally on the wheel's tee-handles. Then held on tight and, without a word, he lifted his feet and began the long, fast slide down toward the monastery roof. He held his breath as his speed grew with every meter of drooping cable. Behind him he heard a low hum as Alex followed.

The roof was coming up fast, and Sten got ready for the shock of landing. Just before he hit, he was textbook-perfect limp and ready. As he slammed into the prison roof, he heard alarms begin to howl. He tumbled back to his feet and was scrabbling a grenade from his pack as he heard the loud thunk of Alex's landing.

Alex did a shoulder roll, Sten pointed, and they sprinted across the roof.

One roof guard got a shot off at them, and Alex cut him in half with a burst from his willygun. They paused about thirty meters from the roof's inside edge. Sten quickly checked for the proper vent, making a mark on his mental map.

'This one,' he yelled, simultaneously spinning the timer wheel on the grenade's primer to seven seconds. Alex had three more grenades out of his pack and ready. They dropped the cluster down the shaft and double-timed away.

Four, five, six, and the grenades exploded. The blast sent Alex and Sten sprawling, their ears thundering. Smoke billowed as they ran back to the hole in the roof.

Alex dug a can of climbing thread from his small backpack, anchored one end on the roof, and, holding the can, 'sprayed' himself down into the prison.

Sten snapped a special figure-8 descender on the thread – it would have cut through any conventional piece of abseiling gear – and followed. He dropped the last few meters clear, landing beside the heavy-worlder. Then Sten was up and running down a long, stone-walled corridor.

Through the thick walls they could hear the drumming of booted feet. A door smashed open, a confusion of men rushed out, firing.

Bullets splattered around them as Sten and Alex opened fire at the same instant. Sten leaped over dead and dying men and sprinted toward the end of the corridor.

A solid metal door stood between them and Ffillips. Sten slapped a demo pack to the door, thumbed the button, and ducked. There was an explosion and the door dropped in one molten sheet.

Sten and Alex fired two deadly bursts at a group of Companions behind them and thundered down the corridor toward the main cells.

The alarms were screaming help . . . help . . . help . . . through the emptying streets.

Ida and Doc waited for help to come up the Avenue of Tombs, either for the armory or the prison beyond it. Ida had quickly figured out the simple twin-stick controls and Doc had worked out the loading mechanism of the track's quad cannon.

They shared a bar of protein and, in the eating of the foul stuff, had agreed to not disagree. Then they heard the rumble of the reinforcements coming. Ida started to fire up the track.

'Wait,' Doc advised.

Ida buried an impatient obscenity and waited.

Then, through the acquisition scope, Ida saw the reinforcements coming. The first to spin into the street were SP tracks identical to the one they rode in. Next came a mass of Companions on foot.

'Now,' Doc said.

Ida shoved the track-brakes/throttles forward, and, tracks-clanking, the SP cannon moved out into the middle of the street. Before the others had time to react, she had begun firing.

The street became a sudden volcano as shell after shell crashed into the oncoming tracks and men.

Doc was a flurry of unending activity as he loaded the guns almost as quickly as Ida could fire. He did wish, however, that he could take a look through her scope at the gore in the streets.

Sten shoved the tiny demofinger into the cell door and shielded his eyes. A low glow, then a ping, and the door swung open.

Ffillips stepped out and gave Sten a long, steady look. 'You took your time coming, Colonel,' she said.

'A little close,' Sten admitted.

'Excellent. Now we're free. Where are our weapons?'

Sten grabbed her by the arm and led the way. Behind her thronged the other mercenaries.

*

The mercenaries poured out the gates of the prison. The guards might have been able to handle a break by convicts. But not by trained, experienced soldiers who armed themselves as they went, from dead guards.

Once free, they pounded down the street toward the armory. Just beyond it they could see the blazing track that Doc and Ida were using to hold off the Companions.

Then they were through the tunnel and inside the armory itself. Bet and Otho had already broken open the arms room and they were passing out weapons, grenades, and belts of ammunition.

It was like candy.

Professional soldiers don't have much use for battlecries but the time spent in Mathias' dungeons had made the mercs a little less than cold-bloodedly professional. Shouting and cheering, they spread out through the gates of Sanctus, always after their ordered goal, but keeping an eye out for humiliations that had to be repaid:

> The tortured men;
> The beaten men;
> The men who had been condemned for their faithfulness.

Ffillips was the first to spot a small company of Companions. She motioned to a squad of her men, and quickly, silently they slipped forward.

And the mercenaries gave the Companions a far easier death than they had planned for the mercenaries.

It was the same across the city, as the mercs fanned out, killing efficiently and coldly. Hunting out the Companions and swinging their guns aside when civilians stumbled into their sights.

Chapter Sixty-Seven

The Companion lunged at Alex with a bayoneted rifle. Alex sidestepped the lunge, stopped the follow-through buttstroke, and took the weapon from the Companion's hands.

Smiling hugely, he took the rifle in both hands and snapped it in two. Then as an afterthought he broke the bayonet off its mounting and politely handed the weapon's pieces back to the bulging-eyed Companion.

And then Alex howled and charged.

The Companion as well as the flanking members of his squad, broke and ran, pelting through the streets of the city. Behind them pounded Alex, some of the mercenaries, and a high-speed-limping Ffillips.

The street dead-ended into a large marketplace, lined with barred shops. Only one, the largest mart, was still open. The Companions dashed toward its entrance but the owner was hastily dropping thick steel shutters over the shop.

'In the name of Talamein,' the lead Companion howled.

'Clot Talamein,' the shopkeeper growled, and slammed the last steel shutter in their faces.

And the Companions turned as Alex thundered into them. A few of them had the brains to collapse and fake death. But most of them died as Alex's meathooks thrashed through the platoon.

There, finally, was only one left. Alex lifted him in one hand, started to practice the javelin throw, and then considered. He lowered the man and turned to Ffillips.

'M'pologies, Major,' he said. 'Ah thinkit's y'r honor.'

'Thank you, Sergeant,' Ffillips said. 'The man is someone I remember. You' – turning to the Companion – 'were the person who thought it humorous to fill our water supply with drakh, were you not?'

Without waiting for a reply, Ffillips fired. The highpower slugs cartwheeled the Companion into a blood-red spray of death, then Alex and Ffillips were headed back down the street, toward the Temple and the fleeing Companions.

Mathias breathed deeply. Find the Peace of Talamein, he told himself. Find the Truth of the Flame, he reminded, watching as his Companions retreated through the gates of the Temple, far below him.

This is but a challenge. Talamein will not fail you, he thought as the gates crashed closed and he saw the ragged, limping mercenaries take positions around the walls of the Temple.

Talamein will prove my truth, he told himself, and turned from the window to soothe his panicked advisors.

Situation:

One temple. A walled, reinforced fortress, built on a ridge. Defended by motivated, fairly skilled soldiers. Provisioned for centuries and equipped with built-in wells.

A civilian populace outside was desperately trying to stay neutral.

A small band of soldiers, besieging that fortress, armed only with personal weapons and light armor.

Prog? A classic siege that could go on for decades.

Without the nukes the Eternal Emperor forbade, it should have been.

Sten was determined to break the siege and end the war – and Mathias – within a week.

Chapter Sixty-Eight

A given for any port city, and most especially for one on an island continent, is that the watertable will be quite close to the surface. This makes building anything over three or four stories an interesting engineering problem, particularly if there's any seismic activity, as there was on Sanctus.

Not only was the water level barely fifty meters below ground level (which meant about 350 meters for the Temple itself), but the ground composition was mostly sand. Which, in the event of an earthquake and in the presence of water, goes into suspension and becomes instant quicksand, a flowing, unstable, gluelike substance.

But tall buildings must still be anchored, which means columns must still be buried deep in the earth. This is, however, not an easy solution since, during an earthquake, these columns will react to the shifting, slurrylike sand and water mix, tilting or collapsing.

The solution, then, is to use hollow columns. During a quake, the sand/water mix will flow up the interior of the columns and give increased stability. This very basic element of structural engineering was known as far back as the nineteenth century.

Hollow columns work very well, except that they duct cold air – air that is chilled to the temperature of the water table or outside ocean – straight up the inside of the column to the building above. The hollow columns under the Temple had chilled Sten's buttocks as he shifted before that first, memorable interview with Parral, Theodomir, and Mathias.

And those hollow columns, coupled with Mahoney's geo-survey, gave Sten the way into the Temple.

A few feet away from where he and Alex stood, sewage gushed from an open pipe, down a gully, and into Sanctus' ocean. The gully widened past the sewage pipe (fortunately, Sten thought) and then narrowed, to disappear into a cleft in the sandy cliff.

From his position in Alex's small backpack, Doc peered down into that cleft. In addition to the Altairian, the pack contained a small light matching the one already on Alex's shock-helmet, some comporations, and a spare set of gloves. Clipped to his belt Alex also had a minitransponder and a spraycan of climbing thread.

Sten was similarly equipped. But he also had a vuprojector reproduction of the cave system below the Temple. The system had been mapped by the Imperial geoship, and Sten was fairly sure that it would lead him to one of the hollow columns – and from there straight up into the Temple itself.

The minitransponder was one of those wonderful chunks of high-tech that most soldiers were never able to find a usable situation for. In theory, it worked fine. Plant two or more senders in given locations at least one kilometer and thirty degrees apart. Those senders would transmit and tell the wearer of the transponder exactly when he was going in the wrong direction. It was sort of a compass with a built-in not-that-way-idiot factor.

The reason that most soldiers were never able to use this wonderful gadget is its designers had never been able to figure a way to plant those senders deep in enemy territory, and therefore the system couldn't work. It was a fortieth-century Who'll Bell the Cat.

Sten flipped on the transponder and touched the SYSTEM CHECK button. They had already planted four transponders around the Temple and should know exactly where they were at any time. However, Sten, having a deep and abiding lack of faith in technology, carried a conventional compass on his belt, as did Alex.

'Ah dinna ken wha w' be't hangin' 'boot, watchin' drakh.' Alex grumbled. 'Ah'm ready t' test m' claustrophobia.'

And he eased forward, down into the cleft. It was a tight fit, and Doc squealed as they went out of sight. Sten lowered himself into the blackness after him.

Doc's comfortable ride in Alex's pack didn't last much beyond the narrow entrance. The first chest-squeeze in the passage brought a gurgle out of him and a breathless insistence that he was quite capable of walking.

And so Doc scuttled out of the pack and took the lead. Alex went second and Sten behind. Doc could ferret out the passageways, and, with Kilgour second, the team wouldn't enter any passageways they couldn't get out of.

The cave went exactly as the geosurvey map said and was easily negotiable by bear-walking – bent over, moving on hands and feet. Only two sections required descent to hands and knees. They quickly penetrated about one-thousand meters into the cave. It was far too easy to last.

It didn't.

Doc *eep*ed in alarm as the crawlway came to a sudden end a few centimeters in front of him. He dropped to all four paws and shone his minilight down into the blackness.

Far, far below, water gleamed.

Sten and Alex crawled up beside him. Sten moved his head, and his helmet-mounted light flashed across the vertical walls below. 'Another passageway. There.' He pointed with the light. The passageway started about four meters above the dark pool that marked the water level.

Alex unclipped the can of climbing thread from his belt, checked the hardener at the can's tip, then sprayed a blot of the adhesive on the rock ledge. Then he slid his hands into the built-in grips on the can and wriggled over the edge, letting himself down with short blasts. He dropped until nothing could be seen of him but the bobble of light from his helmet. Doc took two custom-built jumars from his pack, fitted his hands into them, and went down the same thread. Sten, using more conventional jumars, did the same.

Alex kept going down until he was below the passageway, then clipped and glued the climbing thread to the rock ringing the passage before hoisting himself up into it. The other two were close behind.

The crawlway became rapidly worse, the roof slowly flattening down on them, until they were forced to hands and knees, elbows and knees, and then to a basic slither.

The rock ceiling ripped Sten's uniform as he pushed himself along.

'I am no geologist,' Doc observed, 'but does the fact that the ceiling of this passage is wet signify what I suppose?'

Sten didn't answer him, though the dampness did imply that the passageway they were snaking along had been recently underwater. If it began raining outside (there would be no way for the cavers to realize this in time), the water level would rise. Sten did not want to consider the various ramifications of drowning in a cave.

And then he stuck.

The rocky ceiling bulged and without realizing it Sten had moved under the bulge while inhaling. Stuck! Impossible. That tub Alex made it!

Sten kicked at the sides of the passageway. Nothing. He felt his chest swell and then his muscles started a hyperventilating beat.

Stop it. He began the pain mantra. Panic died. He exhaled and slid easily under the obstruction. And the crawl went on.

Then the cave opened up, its ceiling soaring far beyond the reach of the soldiers' lights. Crystal of a million colors refracted from their lamps as they got to their feet and walked forward, soft, beachlike sand crunching under their boots.

Salt and rock formations climbed crazily around them, here a giant morel, there a spiraled gothic cathedral, still another a multicolor twisting snake.

None of the three found words as they walked through the monstrous room, their light illumining treasures seen by man for this first and only time. And then the treasures fell back into darkness as they went on.

The stunning chamber came to a rapid end with a vertical wall, a roaring waterfall, and a deep pool. No side passages. No alternates. The cave just stopped.

Sten puzzled over his map. According to the projection, the chamber should have a lower passage out. And there probably should be no river and waterfall.

He swore to himself as he realized what had happened. Sometime in the past, an underground river had worn through into the chamber and then dumped straight into the lower passageway. In caver's jargon, it was called a siphon. Naturally the survey by the geoship could not show something as insubstantial as water.

So the cave they had to follow did continue. And if the three Mantis soldiers had gills, they would be in no trouble whatsoever . . . Sten's thoughts were interrupted as Doc shed his tiny pack and dove into the pool, disappearing.

'Ah suggest w'be watchin' our wee timepieces,' Alex said. 'Since Altairians no ken people dinnae hae th' ability to stop breathin' f'r hours a' ae time.'

It was four minutes by Sten's watch when Doc resurfaced and hauled himself, shivering, out of the frigid water. Alex, in spite of protests, shoved the Altarian inside his own shirt to warm him up.

'It goes down three meters, then level for possibly another four. There is one narrow place, but I would think it passable. Then you hulking beings will have to turn your bodies through ninety degrees, into a small chamber with an exit to atmosphere directly overhead.'

Sten and Alex eyed each other. Then Sten motioned for Alex to go.

'Na, lad. Y'mus do't. Ah'll bring up th' rear.'

Sten took a dozen deep breaths, enough to saturate his lungs but without going into hyperventilation. He unslung his pack and belt, clipped them together, and jumped, feet first, into the water.

Blackness. Muddy water. Light just a glow. Down. Down. Cold. Sten could feel the rock close in as he hit the bottom of the passage, rolled, and kicked himself forward. The floor came up, grinding against Sten's gut, then he was through, his heart throbbing, then his fingers touched rock. He felt to the side and found the tight spot. Sten jackknifed and inched his way into the chamber. Skin shredded as he struggled through, hung in the tiny rock womb, then kicked off from the bottom, hand above his head and through the crack and up through dark waters, eardrums pounding and heart throbbing and lights beginning at the back of his eyes. He surfaced, gasping deeply, then swam for a beach illuminated by his helmet light.

As he crawled up onto the beach something splashed beside him, and Doc flopped onto dry land, then sat, looking miserable, his fur wet and bedraggled.

Back in the passage, Alex was well and truly trapped. His body simply would not bend far enough to make the jackknife turn. Alex wondered to himself why he could never remember times like these when some Mantis quack suggested he could stand to shed a few kilos.

As yet, he was unworried. His enormous lungs had more than enough air. P'raps, laddie, Ah'll turn aboot an' go back an' consider whae t' do next. P'raps, e'en, Ah'll hae t' let young Sten carry on w'oot me.

Alex then discovered he couldn't turn back around, either. So he kicked forward and tried the jackknife again, with even less success.

Alex realized he was starting to drown.

Th' hell Ah am, he thought in sudden rage. Ee yon mountain comit nae t' Mahamet, he thought, as he brought his knees up to touch the rock wall in front of the passageway, gripped the rock rim, and thrust.

It was not true, despite stories told later in Mantis bars, that the earth moved. But what did happen is a half-meter-square square of living rock ripped free, coming toward the dim glow of Alex's light.

And then he was rolling into the chamber and frogging his way up for air and light.

He surfaced like a blowing whale, then thrashed his way to shore. Sten, sheepishly treading water just above the hole Alex had come out of, had been getting ready for a nonsensical and impossible rescue dive. He swam toward the small beach, in Alex's considerable wake.

'Ah thought Ah sae aye fish't Ah knew' was Alex's only explanation for the delay, and the team continued.

From there it was easy. The transponder pointed them directly to where one of the enormous poured-and-reinforced columns came through the cave's roof. A small demo charge cracked the side of the column enough for the three to enter.

Then it was just a matter of the three exhausted, bedraggled beings chimneying their way up seven-hundred meters of glass-smooth wet concrete.

Chapter Sixty-Nine

It wasn't much of a diversionary attack. But then it wasn't supposed to be. But battle plans, including phony diversions, never work out exactly as they should. Mantis section and the seventy-odd mercenaries who weren't immediately hospitalized had planned to assemble outside one of the Temple's secondary gates, snipe any Companion stupid enough to stick his head above the walls, fire all the available pyrotechnics and light artillery at the gates, and, finally, whoop and holler a lot while Sten and Alex went for Mathias.

Even though she probably belonged in an intensive care capsule, Ffillips insisted on being present. She was quite happily functioning as Ida's loader while the Rom woman directed bursts of 50mm fire at one of the Temple's gates.

'Of course I'm not saying there's no place for mercenaries,' Ida explained. 'It's merely a dumb way to make a credit.'

'Some of us,' Ffillips managed as she dumped another clip of shells into a loading trough, 'don't have any other choice.'

'Clottin' hell!' Ida snorted. 'There's always a choice.'

'Even for a mercenary?' Ffillips asked dubiously.

'Certainly. A good killer would be a wonderful banker. Or diplomat. Or in commodities, which I can tell you privately is a guaranteed mill-credit career.'

Ffillips was trying to decide whether Ida was joking when a burst caught the Temple gate on one of its hinges and proved that the contractor who had built the Temple had been no more honest than most public-works builders.

The entire gate pinwheeled into the air, leaving a clear entrance to the Temple. Suddenly the diversionary attack turned quite real as the mercs howled – a long, curdling wolfpack sound – and ran forward.

Lean, bloody men and women with death in their eyes and revenge in their guts.

Ida flumped into the self-propelled gun's seat and cranked the engine. With Ffillips still loading, Ida gunned the SP track into the Temple's main courtyard.

Behind her Bet and the two tigers followed silently.

Chapter Seventy

'Which way will it blow?' Sten whispered while examining the tiny ring charge that was anchored to the top of the hollow column.

Sten, Alex, and Doc were five meters below the charge that when set off should let them into the Temple. They were locked in place with treble strands of climbing thread.

'Ah, lad, questions ae thae be't whae makit life in'trestin',' Alex breathed as he triggered the demoset.

The column's cap lifted, as did the floorbeams above it and then the flagstone that was the central Temple's actual flooring.

The flagstone tumbled in the air and chopped down two guards, one Companion, and a statue of the late Theodomir.

Alex, Sten, and Doc shinnied their way up the last few meters, and then they were inside the Temple.

They went looking for Mathias.

Chapter Seventy-One

Ida was leaning half out of her seat and completely unprotected by the track's armor when the Companion finished reloading. She was reaching for a banner that looked like it was made of gold when four rounds slammed into the Rom woman's chest. She sagged across the track's bow and rolled sacklike to the ground as the unmanned track stalled. A look of surprise, anger, and vast disappointment was frozen on her face.

Bet cradled Ida in her arms as Hugin and Munin finished their slow savaging of the Companion who had shot her. Then Bet lowered Ida to the ground and jumped to her feet, mind blank and firing, and the ground rocked and thundered as the Anti-Matter-Two rounds poured out of her willygun, exploding the platoon of Companions running toward her.

Chapter Seventy-Two

Mathias' advisors died in the first burst of fire as Sten and Alex charged through the double doors, into the conference room. The advisors had been too busy watching the debacle in the courtyard one-hundred meters below the balcony to hear the death-rattles of the guards outside the chamber. For which minor error they became very dead.

Mathias stood, looking unsurprised at the carnage, as Doc slid out of Alex's pack and unlimbered the hypo. Alex kept Mathias in the sights of his willygun as the Prophet walked slowly forward.

'I have been expecting you,' Mathias said. 'My best friend and my worst enemy.'

He shrugged out of his red tunic and flexed his muscles. His hands knotted into fists. Sten waited.

'And now we decide the Truth of Talamein,' Mathias said softly as he came in.

Sten thought of the careful reasonings and appeals to friendship that he'd come up with to avoid this confrontation. Useless. He shrugged out of his pack and moved forward.

As Mathias' hand flashed back, behind him to his belt, and came out with a small projectile weapon. The pistol came up and Sten double-stepped into him, right foot coming up in a sweep-kick, and the weapon pinwheeled out of Mathias' hand.

Sten kept the kick moving, then recovered, his back to Mathias. Sensing Mathias was coming in he crouched, arm high, and half-spun back to face the Prophet, arm raised to block the snap-punch Mathias had launched.

Both men recovered and side-paced.

'You don't have to die,' Sten said.

'Of course,' Mathias agreed. 'And I shall not. Not now, not here, not ever. This is the Test of the Flame.' And, gymnast that he was, he came straight in, a mae-tobi-geri flying frontal attack.

Sten one-stepped under Mathias, snap-punched straight up into his thigh, rolled away as the Prophet crashed back down, then recovered as Mathias drove a knife hand toward Sten's head.

Sten flicked his head to the side, and Mathias' killing punch slammed across his temple and ear.

Sten knife-blocked before Mathias could recover and thudded a flat palm into Mathias' temple. Temporarily stunned, the Prophet back-rolled twice and came to his feet, half smiling.

'You *are* a worthy opponent.' He drove in again. Sten blocked his swing-punch, and then Mathias' fist-strike came down on Sten's skull.

The world blurred and went double. Sten snapped his blocking hand into Mathias' gut and, contradicting conventional tactics, dove flat-forward, ball-rolling, rising, and turning as Mathias attacked.

A punching attack, blocked twice, in eye-blurring motion. Sten snapped a knee up into Mathias' diaphragm, and the man sagged back.

Then Sten's single, half-cupped hand swung, slapping Mathias' eardrum. A two-hand stroke would have killed him, but the single blow merely sent his mind spinning, and, for the first time, Mathias lost his balance, stumbling backward.

And Sten paced in, step . . . punch . . . step . . . punch . . . knuckled fist turning and thudding in below the Prophet's ribcage. Mathias doubled.

A final feint as his fisted, coupled hands came up for Sten's face. Sten locked wrists, drove the strike up, and then, howling, leaped straight up into the air, his foot coming up and out and buried into the Prophet's chest.

Mathias back-flipped and struck the floor behind him with a dull *thud*.

Then Doc was at Mathias' side, quickly checking his pulse. 'Adequate, adequate,' he murmured, as he pressed the hypo's trigger and the drug sprayed into Mathias' veins.

'You probably broke some bones, but you didn't kill him.'

Sten was not listening. He was dropped down into semilotus, lungs sucking in air as he recovered.

Chapter Seventy-Three

Bet's flashes in the courtyard: Ida's body; Ffillips calmly sniping down Companions as they came into sight; Otho, evidently trying to find a Companion who could be thrown completely through a stone wall; the tigers, impossibly low, crawling under a firewall of tracers, then darting into a weapons pit. End tracers. Begin screams.

And then she heard the voice – the boom that turned the din of battle into a sudden hush as Companions, mercs, and Mantis people turned, to look up the looming wall of the Temple to the balcony.

On the balcony stood Mathias, with a hailer-mike hung on his chest. 'I SPEAK AS TALAMEIN.'

The battle stopped instantly. The Companions flinched upward, then recovered, waiting for the war to start again. But the mercenaries were as captivated as any, staring up at the red-clad figure high above them.

The Companions made obeisance as the voice continued. Stiff, metallic, but forceful.

'I have chosen to temporarily inhabit this envelope of flesh to speak to you, people of the Faith and the Flame.

'And I have chosen to manifest myself in this sin-riddled flesh to keep my people from falling into the pit of heresy.

'I, Talamein, took the Flame to give those I love freedom. And though I have passed beyond, I still have love for you people of Sanctus, and, beyond you, the peoples of the Lupus Cluster.

'But I see you as a spider on a slender thread, hanging over the terrible chasm of destruction. My faith was of a crusader – a crusader who sought peace and also freedom.

'And then, once having found freedom, each of us would tend his own, whether farm or mercantile, each of us tending the Flame of Talamein deep within each of us.

'Because my Faith is that of the person, not of the race of the world.

'I thought, when I chose to pass into the Flame, that I could rest, knowing I had given my own freedom, wealth, peace, and security. And so I rested for half an eon,' Mathias continued.

The speech wasn't bad, Bet noticed, watching the frozen Companions. Doc would be very proud of his composition.

'But then, from my resting, I felt a rumbling, a disturbance. And I was forced to remove myself from the warmth of the Flame, to examine my people.

'To my shame, I found destruction looming for my people. And I found a young man who was attempting to speak in my name.

'Not an evil man was your Prophet Mathias. He did suppress the heresy of the Jann. But he was a man who went beyond his mission.

'But now I, Talamein, do declare the error of his ways.

'I, Talamein, order my people to lay down their arms and return to seek happiness and their homes. Because only in peace and security can the true beliefs of Talamein come to fruition.

'Only in freedom and security will the Flame of Talamein blossom through the universe.

'I now declare anathema the man or woman who picks up arms in my name.

'I declare anathema the man or woman who attempts to convert an unbeliever by any means other than persuasion and example.

'I now declare anathema the being who uses the words of Talamein to imprison, enslave, or deprive any other being of those rights that all of us realize in our hearts are due us.'

The Companions were, by now, on their knees, heads on the pavement.

'And now I leave you, to return to the Sanctity of the Flame. I adjure you to follow my instructions.

'If you so do, when your earthly envelope decays, I will welcome you to the Fellowship of the Flame.

'I also admonish you not to despise this man Mathias, from whom I speak. Though in error, he sought the truth. In his memory I require you to raise monuments and memorials.

'And now I shall return to the Flame.

'Having used this envelope and therefore sanctified it, I shall also take its occupier with me to the Sanctity of the Flame.

'And we, Talamein and the mortal Mathias, declare this envelope no longer suited to the uses and purposes of the flesh.

'Any such could only be desecration.

'My final blessings, and may peace pass among you.'

The hailer clicked off, and Mathias, gaze fixed on the horizon, took four steps forward, off the balcony. His body silently curved downward through one-hundred meters of space to the courtyard flagstones below.

Chapter Seventy-Four

The courtyard was empty, save for bodies, the stunned mercenaries, and the arms hastily abandoned when the Companions stumbled past the broken gates, toward the city below.

Bet was slumped against Hugin, carefully digging a piece of shrapnel from Munin's paw, when Ffillips squatted before her.

'Mantis Section, eh?'

Bet covered her reaction, then looked up. 'Pardon?'

'I am a logical woman,' the battered soldier said carefully. 'When a mercenary officer returns to rescue me, my men and women, against all odds, bringing with him some of the – forgive me – oddest beings I have ever had the pleasure to encounter and then wins the war by making its tyrant recant publicly, I hear echoes of things.'

'Such as?'

'Such as tales I heard before I, ahem, separated from the Imperial Guards. Are you not Mantis Section, and was this not an Imperial Mission?'

'Clottin'-A, buster,' someone croaked from behind Bet. 'Now, if someone'll stop playing with their triumphs and get me a medic, I'll be quite satisfied. I got four holes in my chest and investments to protect.'

Absolute astonishment, and then Ffillips and Bet were running for the Temple to get Doc as Ida miraculously wobbled up into a sitting position. One of the tigers walked over to her and, purring, began to lick the blood from her neck.

Chapter Seventy-Five

'You must understand the hesitation of this council,' the graybeard croaked as he tottered to his feet. 'I mean no contempt, Colonel . . . I believe you said that was the way to refer to you?

'But you must know the perplexity that the past few years have brought to us, those of us who have recanted the ways of the world to study Talamein in peace.'

'I do,' Sten agreed.

Sten stood in front of twenty of the most carefully selected theologicians of Talamein – men selected for their age, expertise, honesty, and longwindedness. They were in the former throne room of the Temple. It looked much as it had when Mathias was occupying it, except the two-handed sword over the vidmap was gone. The twin eternal flames blazed alone.

Two other beings were in the room.

'These matters,' the elder continued, 'must be studied. Must be considered. Certainly none of us is arguing the truth of the appearance of Talamein himself . . .'

There was a muttered 'S'be't' from the elders.

'What puzzles us is the necessity to consider these actions. The necessity to evaluate them, as to their truth and as to how they pertain to the Truth of the Flame.

'These matters may require some time to consider, and, in that time, what will happen with the ways of the world?

'We assembled here are elders. Men of silence and thought. But we must realize that beyond this Temple and these walls, there are beings and worlds to reckon with. To govern. And, I think I speak for my colleagues, we do not consider ourselves capable of performing this task. I assume, then, that perhaps you . . .' The graybeard let his words trail off delicately.

'No,' Sten said. 'I am but a simple soldier. A man of the earth. I shall continue on my own path, seeking my own destiny.

'But you are correct,' he said, wondering where the drakh he found this smoothness and deciding he'd been too long with churchmen, hypocrites, and noblemen, 'in that you and the people of Talamein shall need protection and assistance.

'This shall be my gift to you.' And he turned to the two other beings in the chamber.

'This first person shall keep your government honest and your people free from the threat of invasion.'

Ffillips smiled.

'And this other being shall handle the necessities of trade, merchandising, and, most important, dealing with those beings from beyond the Lupus Cluster who merely wish sustenance and a chance to pass through.'

Otho grunted.

Sten lifted the medallion that Theodomir had given him months before, when he was made a Soldier of Talamein.

'I am a soldier, as I said. But perhaps, when I was made a Carrier of the Flame, I was given a gift to see into the future a bit.

'I see two things: Strangers shall come into the Lupus Cluster. Travelers. Men who seek strange matter, beyond these worlds. I see that your duty is to give them succor and to show them, by example, the peace that Talamein can bring.

'And I see one other thing: Mathias, it was true, followed the ways of ice and cold and flesh. But somehow I sense that in his final moments, he achieved what few men have gifted to them.

'In his words from the balcony, he truly became what he had intended – Talamein reincarnate.'

And Sten bowed his head, waited five seconds, then strode for the exit. He needed Alex's jokes, Bet for more interesting reasons, and about five liters of pure alk.

This salvation thing was a thirsty and wearisome business.

Chapter Seventy-Six

'No, Mahoney,' the Eternal Emperor purred, 'I do not wish to read the full fiche. I want to consider what you just told me.'

'Yes, sir,' Mahoney said in a carefully neutral voice.

'You will kindly stand at attention while I review this, Colonel.'

'Sir.'

'Your Mantis team, and this young lieutenant . . .'

'Sten, sir.'

'Sten. Yes. He managed, with a handful of mercenaries, to topple a religious dictatorship, to convince its fanatics to go grow whatever they grow out there, and to arrange things so that my miners will be treated well.'

'Yes, sir.'

'I am correct, so far?'

'You are, sir.'

'Admirable,' the Emperor went on. 'Promote him to Captain. Give him a couple of medals. That is an order.'

'Yes, sir.'

'Now, leave us to consider his solution to the whole mess. He turned over the military and political affairs of this whole stinkin' Lupus Cluster to a mercenary. Correct?'

'Yes, sir.'

'A woman, I discovered, who deserted from the Imperial Guard facing court-martial, after stealing an entire division's supply depot and blackmarketing it. One Sergeant Ffillips. Am I still correct?'

'You are, your Highness.'

'Very good. And the diplomatic, intrasystem, galactic, and mercantile end of the operation was handed to an alien?'

'Yes, sir.'

'An alien who looks like a Neanderthal – don't look puzzled, Mahoney, go to the Imperial Museum and you'll see one – and comes from a race of freebooters. One Otho?'

'Yes, sir.'

'I want this Sten on toast,' the Emperor said in a low monotone. 'I want him busted from Captain – I did promote him to Captain, did I not?'

'You did, sir.'

'I also ordered you to pour me drinks, did I not?'

'Sorry, sir,' and Mahoney headed for the cabinet.

'Not that bottle, Colonel. The Erlenmeyer flask. One hundred eighty proof. Open us two beers to go with it. I think I may find myself very drunk while I'm trying to find out if I can legally torture one of my officers.'

Mahoney was starting to enjoy this. But he kept his smile buried as he poured shotglasses and cut the tips off beerjugs.

'Sten. Sten. Why do I know the name?'

'He killed Baron Thoresen, sir. Against your orders. You remember, the Vulcan affair.'

'And I didn't send him to a penal battalion then?'

'No, sir. You promoted him to lieutenant.'

The Eternal Emperor threw down the shot, shuddered, and sipped beer as he fed the mission report fiche into his viewer.

'Interesting ideas this Sten has,' he mused, sipping beer.

'Overthrow the tyrant and then appoint a council of church elders to study the matter. They should have their report *ex cathedra* in, what, Mahoney? A thousand years?'

'More than that, sir.' Mahoney gurgled, still recovering from the pure alcohol. 'He said he chose the longest-winded theologicians he could find. More like two thousand.'

The Emperor shut off the viewer, got up, grabbed the flask, and poured two more shots. He gasped his down, then mused aloud:

'Mantis Section. Why do I keep you people around, since you insist on doing exactly what I want, exactly in the manner I don't want?'

Mahoney stuck with beer drinking and silence.

'Correction to my last order, Colonel,' the Emperor said, smiling in a moderately evil manner. 'Do not court-martial this Sten.

'I want him.

'Detach him from Mantis and Mercury. Give him some kind of acceptable hero background in the Guard.'

'Ummm,' Mahoney insubordinated.

'Captain Sten is now the commander of my personal bodyguard. The Gurkhas.'

And Mahoney's shot went across the room and the beerjug gurgled out, unnoticed, on the carpet.

'God damn it, your Majesty, how the clot can I run an intelligence service when you keep stealing my best men?'

'Good point, Colonel.' The Eternal Emperor took a tiny order fiche from his desk and Mahoney realized just how badly he'd been set up.

'These are your orders: congratulations, General Mahoney, and my further congratulations on your detachment and reassignment from Imperial Headquarters to command the First Guards Assault Division.'

Mahoney threw the fiche to the floor, which was an ineffective gesture, since the tiny bit of plas insisted on drifting downward.

'You can't clottin' do this to me! I just spent seventy-five years building up this clottin' Mercury Corps, and—'

'And I am the god damned Eternal Emperor,' the man growled and came around his desk. 'I can do what I clotting well please, General, and congratulations on your new post and am I going to have to whip your ass to get you to drink with me?'

Mahoney considered for a second, then started chuckling.

'No, sir, your Imperial Majesty, sir. Thank you, sir. Since I have no choice, your Imperial Majesty, sir, I accept.'

Besides, Mahoney was not at all sure he could take the Emperor. Let alone what would come afterward if he did.

The Emperor grunted and poured more drinks. 'You served me well, Ian. I know you'll continue to do the same in your new position. And clot it, don't make things so hard for me when I want to be nice for a change.

'But don't forget this Sten,' the Eternal Emperor said, reaching for the flask. 'I have an idea he is going to go very far indeed.

'In fact, I'll give you one of my predictions.

'Sten will either end up on the gallows or as a Fleet Admiral.'

And the two men drank deeply.

STEN 3:
THE COURT OF A THOUSAND SUNS

To
Elizabeth R. & Leo L. Bunch
and
the brothers four: Charles, Phillip, Drew,
and David

Note

The titles of Books 1, 2, 3, and 4 are Parisian slang for various parts of the guillotine. The 'bascule' is the board on which the condemned man is laid; the 'lunette' is the circular clamp fitted around the man's neck; the 'mouton' is the cutting blade, plus its eighty-pound weight; and the 'declic' is the lever the executioner hits to drop the blade.

The title of Book 5, 'The Red Mass,' comes from a phrase used by a French deputy during the Terror of the A.D. 1790s, one Monsieur Amar, in a letter inviting his fellow deputies to witness an execution 'to see the Red Mass celebrated . . .'

– AC and CRB

BOOK ONE

BASCULE

Chapter One

The banth purred at the quillpig, which, unimpressed, had firmly stuffed itself as far as it could into the hollow stump.

The banth's instinct said that the porcupine was edible, but the six-legged cat's training told it otherwise. Meat was presented by two-legs at dawn and dusk, and came with gentle words. The quillpig may have smelled right, but it was not behaving like meat. The banth sat back on its haunches and used a forepaw to pry two needles from its nasal carapace.

Then the animal flattened. It heard the noise again, a whine from the forest. The banth looked worriedly up the mountain, then back again in the direction of the sound before deciding.

Against instinct, it broke out of the last fringe of the tree line and bounded up the bare, rock-strewn mountain. Two hundred meters vertically up the talus cliff, it went to cover behind a mass of boulders.

The whine grew louder as a gravsled lifted over the scrubby treetops, pirouetted, searching, and then grounded near the hollow stump.

Terence Kreuger, chief of Prime World's police tactical force, checked the homing panel mounted over the gravsled's controls. The needle pointed straight up the mountain, and the proximity director indicated the banth was barely half a kilometer away.

Kreuger unslung a projectile weapon from its clips behind his seat and checked it once again: projectile chambered; safe off; ranging scope preset for one meter, the approximate dimensions of the banth's chest area.

He checked the slope with a pair of binocs and after a few seconds saw a flicker of movement. Kreuger grunted to himself and lifted the gravsled up the mountain. He'd already missed the banth once that day; he was less than pleased with himself.

Kreuger fancied himself a hunter in the grand tradition. Time not required for his police duties was spent hunting or preparing himself for a hunt, an expensive hobby, especially on Prime World. The Imperial capital had no native game, and both hunting preserves there charged far more than even a tactical group chief could afford – until recently.

Kreuger's previous hunts had been restricted to offworld, and mostly for minor edible or nuisance game. That was well and good, but provided Kreuger with little in the way of trophies, especially trophies of the kind that the gamebooks chronicled. But things had suddenly become different. His friends had seen to that. After thirty years as a cop, Kreuger still prized his honesty. He just rationalized that what his new friends wanted wasn't dishonest: look at the benefits! Three weeks away from Empire Day madness. Three weeks on a hunting reservation, expenses paid. Tags for four dangerous animals – an Earth rhino, a banth, a male cervi, and a giant ot.

He had already planned on which wall each head would be mounted. Of course, Kreuger did not intend to mention to his soon-to-be-admiring friends *where* those trophies had been taken.

The gravsled's bumper caromed him away from a boulder, bringing Kreuger back to the present. Concentrate, man, concentrate. Remember every bit of this day. The clearness of the air. The smell of the trees below. The spray of dust around the gravsled.

Kreuger guided the gravsled up the slope, following the homing needle toward the sensor implanted in the banth.

Below, a second one-man sled coasted through the trees. Clyff Tarpy did not need binocs to follow Kreuger's sled. Contour-following, he lifted his sled after Kreuger.

The banth was cornered.

Ahead of him to the right, the ground fell away steeply, too steeply for even his clawed legs to descend. To the left was a sheer cliff. The banth huddled behind a boulder, puzzling.

Kreuger's gravsled landed just outside the nest. Weapon ready, Kreuger moved forward.

Again, the banth was perplexed. The whine had been the cause of a loud explosion and searing pain earlier, the pain that sent the banth fleeing through the forest toward the mountains.

But the smell was two-legs. Two-legs, but not familiar. Had the banth done something wrong? The two-legs would tell him, feed him, and then return him to the warmth of his pen.

The banth stood and walked forward.

Kreuger's projectile weapon came up as the banth walked into view. No errors now. Safety off, he aimed.

The banth mewed. This was not his two-legs.

'Bastard!'

Kreuger spun, the banth momentarily forgotten. He had not heard the second gravsled land behind him.

From five meters, the barrel of the weapon was enormous. Tarpy allowed just enough time to pass for terror to replace the bewilderment on Kreuger's face. And then he fingered the stud. The soft metal round expanded nicely as it penetrated Kreuger's sternum, then pinwheeled through the tac chief's rib cage into his heart. Kreuger, instantly dead, sat down on a small boulder before slowly toppling forward onto his face.

Tarpy smiled as he took a thick chunk of soyasteak from his beltpak and tossed it to the banth. 'Eight lives to go, pussycat.'

Tarpy took a small aerosol can from his pak, and, backing up, erased his footsteps from the dusty rock. He paused by Kreuger's gravsled long enough to shut the power off and disconnect the beacon. The longer it took to find the body, the better. Tarpy mounted his own sled and nudged it back down the hill.

The banth's tail whipped back and forth once. He did not like the smell from the strange two-legs. He picked up the slab of soyasteak, sprang over the rock wall, and went back down the mountain. He would eat on the ground he was familiar with, and then perhaps unravel the puzzle of the other soyasteak, the one with needles that walked.

Chapter Two

The man in the blue boiler suit had his long knife against the throat of Admiral Mik Ledoh. With his other hand he forced the Eternal Emperor's Grand Chamberlain closer to the edge of the battlements.

'Either our demands are met immediately, or this man dies!' His amplified voice echoed across the castle's stonework, down the 700 meters of emptiness and across the parade ground.

One hundred meters below and to the right, Sten checked his foot/handholds. His clawed fingers were barely clinging to mortar notches in the stone. One foot dangled over emptiness, the other was firmly braced on the face of Havildar-Major Lalbahadur Thapa. Sten's willygun was slung from a clip-strap on his dark brown combat suit. Snapped to one arm was a can of climbing thread. At its end was a grapnel.

From above them the terrorist's voice came again: 'You have only seconds left to reach your decision and save this man's life!'

Sten's left hand went up and out, stretching for a new hold. At first he thought he had it, then the mortar crumbled and he almost came off. Sten forced his body away from its instinctive clutch at the wall, then inhaled deeply.

'Kaphar hunnu bhanda marnu ramro,' came the pained mutter from Lalbahadur below him.

'But cowards live longer, dammit!' Sten managed as he one-handed out, lifting both feet clear. Then his climbing boots found a hold, and Sten was momentarily secure. Breath . . . breath . . . and he once again became a climbing machine. Below him, Lalbahadur and the rest of the Gurkha platoon moved steadily up the vertical granite wall toward the two men above them.

Five meters below the parapet. Sten found a stance – a protruding knob of rock. He touched the second can of climbing thread attached to the swiss seat around his waist, and a spidery white line spat out, touched the rock facing, and bonded to it.

Sten motioned outward then toward his waist, signaling that he was secure and could belay the rest of the troops below him. From a third can, on the rear of his harness, a thread descended to the Gurkhas below.

Lalbahadur came up into position, on a single line to Sten's immediate right.

Sten paid no attention. He touched the nozzle of the thread can on his arm, and allowed about fifteen meters of thread, the grapnel at the end, to reel out. He freed one hand from the wall and weaseled it into the thread glove clipped to a carabinier sling, then began rhythmically swinging the grapnel back and forth. Suddenly he cast upward.

The twenty-gram-weight grapnel flickered upward and then caught, spinning twice around the muzzle of an archaic cannon which protruded from the crenellation above him.

Sten clipped his special jumars on the thread and snaked upward while the man in the boiler suit was staring out, into the lights. He never saw Sten lizard up, past the cannon and onto the battlement.

'We have waited for enough time,' the voice boomed, on cue. The knife arm came back for the fatal stroke, and Sten came out of the shadows low, coming straight up, one clawed hand slamming into the man's face and a blocking hand snapping into the knife.

The man in the boiler suit staggered away, and the Chamberlain tottered for a minute on the edge of emptiness, then caught his footing. The man with the knife recovered, long blade ready.

But Sten was already inside his attack, double-fisted hands swinging. The strike caught the terrorist on the side of his head, and he dropped limply.

Behind the battlements, the other terrorists spun toward the threat. But they were far too late. The Gurkhas swarmed up from the darkness and came in, 30-cm kukri blades glittering in the spots. And, once again, the cry 'Ayo Gurkhali' rang around the castle, a battle cry that had made thousands of generations of violent men reconsider their intentions.

To a man, the terrorists were down.

Lalbahadur checked the downed men to ensure they were,

indeed, out. Naik Thaman Gurung unslung the rocket mortar from his back and positioned it. Sten nodded, and the mortar bloomed fire as the round lofted up, out into blackness, and then curvetted down to thud onto the parade ground far below.

Gurung bonded the line that ran back from the mortar, impacted far below in the parade ground to a battlement, then grinned at Sten. 'We barang now, Captain.'

'Platoon up,' Sten shouted. 'By numbers – *move*!'

The first to go was Thaman. He attached jumar clamps to the thread that reached more than 700 meters down to the parade ground, swung his feet up, and was off, whistling down the near-invisible thread to safety.

Sten saluted the Chamberlain. 'Sir.'

Admiral Ledoh grimaced, shoved the ceremonial cocked hat more firmly on his head, took the pair of jumars Sten handed him, and then he, too, disappeared down the thread.

Sten was the next to go, freewheeling off the tiny clamps toward the solid concrete ground. He braked at the last minute, took his hands from the jumar handles, hit, and rolled twice.

Behind him, Lalbahadur and the others descended the thread, hit, recovered, and doubled into platoon formation. Admiral Ledoh, a bit breathless, took two steps forward and saluted. Above him, the Eternal Emperor applauded. Following his cue, the half a million spectators filling the grandstands that lined the five-kilometer-long parade ground broke into cheers – applauding as much for the 'terrorists,' who were taking *their* bows high above, as the Gurkhas, Ledoh, and Sten.

Ledoh broke his salute and puffed toward the steps that led to the Imperial stand. By the time he'd made it into the stand itself, the Emperor had a drink waiting for him. After Ledoh shuddered the alcohol down, the Emperor asked with a grin, 'Who had the idea of that stupid hat?'

'I did, Your Majesty.'

'Uh-huh,' the Emperor snickered. 'Howinhell'd you hold it on down that Slide for Life?'

'A superior, water soluble glue.'

'It had better be. No way am I going to live with that – that – bedpan attached to the head of someone I must see every day.' Without waiting for a response, he added, 'Have another drink Mik, for godsakes! It isn't every day you play Tarzan.'

The second order was followed quickly and thankfully.

*

The Emperor was celebrating an invention of his own. Empire Day.

He'd begun the ceremony more than 500 years earlier to celebrate winning a war that he'd since forgotten.

The premise was simple: Once a year, every year, all Imperial Forces put on a display, on whatever world they happened to be assigned to, with everyone welcome.

There was, of course, more purpose to Empire Day than just a parade. There was a second or tertiary purpose to almost everything the Eternal Emperor did. Not only did the display of armed might reassure the citizens of the Empire that they were Protected and Defended, but also, Empire Day served to discourage potential Bad Guys from developing Evil Schemes, at least toward Imperial Interests.

The most massive display on Empire Day occurred on Prime World. Over the years, Empire Day had become the culmination of a two-week-long celebration of athletics and the arts as well as of military might. It was a cross between Saturnalia, Oktoberfest, the Olympics, and May Day. For that one night, the Imperial palace was thrown open to everyone, which by itself was a major encouragement.

The Emperor's main residence and command center on Prime World, the palace, was set in a fifty-five-kilometer-diameter circle of gardens. The fifty-five-kilometer measure was significant, since that was the line-of-sight horizon limit on Prime. The Emperor was not fond of stumbling across people whose presence he had not planned on.

At the center of the circle of manicured and wildly varying parklands was the main palace itself, possibly the ultimate motte-and-bailey design, occupying an area six by two kilometers.

The 'bailey' consisted of high, fifty-degree-banked walls that vauban-vee-ed back and forth, from the main entrance gate toward the palace itself. The walls were 200 meters high, and buried within was a high percentage of the Emperor's bureaucracy. They were not entirely nukeproof, but it would take direct hits to wipe out the structure, and the Emperor could continue operations even if his palace was completely sealed off; decades worth of food, air, and water were tanked below the walls for his staff.

The palace itself, a large-scale copy of Earth's Arundel Castle, stood at the far end of the five-kilometer-long parade ground that made up the center of the bailey.

Even more so than the bailey walls, the castle had been built on the iceberg principal. Imperial command barracks/living quarters tunneled underground below the castle itself for more than 2,000 meters.

The castle was faced with huge stone blocks behind which were nuclear-blast shielding, and meters of insulation. The Emperor liked the look of Earth-medieval, but preferred the safety and comfort provided by science.

The palace was open to the general public on Empire Day, when huge Imperial Guard gravlighters carried the tourists in. During the remainder of the year, only palace employees boarded a high-speed pneumosubway thirty-four kilometers away in Fowler, and were blasted to their duty stations.

Since attendance at Empire Day on Prime World was roughly akin to being presented at Court, the Emperor had figured out long ago that many more millions of his people would want to go than there was space for. So he'd set up attendance much like what he'd described to an uncomprehending official as a 'three-ring circus.' Nearest to the castle were the most desirable seats. These the Emperor allowed to be assigned to Court Favorites, Current Heroes, Social Elitists, and so forth.

The second 'ring,' and there was no easy way to tell where the dividing line was, went to the social climbers. Those seats could be sold, scalped, threatened for, and otherwise acquired by those people who knew that seeing Empire Day on Prime World was the culmination of their entire life.

The third area, farthest from the Imperial reviewing stand itself, was carefully allotted to Prime World residents. Of course, many of these tickets ended up in the hands of outworlders rather than in those of the Prime Worlders they'd been assigned to, but the Emperor felt that if 'local folks' wanted to make a credit or two, he certainly had no objections.

Seating was on bleachers that were installed weeks before the ceremony, on the banked walls of the bailey that surrounded the parade ground.

Technically, it didn't matter where the attendees sat; huge holographic screens rose at regular intervals atop the walls, giving the spectators access to instant closeups as well as to occasional cut-arounds to those people in the 'first circle' who were somehow Noteworthy.

Some events, such as Sten's 'rescue,' were only held at the far end of the parade ground, next to the castle itself. But most were set up to run continuously, down each area to an eventual exit at the far end of the parade ground.

Empire Day was the most spectacular staged event of the year. The Court still proclaimed itself the Court of a Thousand Suns, even though the Empire numbered far more systems than that, and Empire Day was when those suns shone most brightly.

It was also a night on which anything might happen . . .

Wheezing, Sten leaned against the wall of the concrete tunnel – a tunnel normally sealed by heavy collapsed-steel blast doors. Now the doors were raised to permit the Empire Day participants entry onto the parade ground.

Beside him, panting more sedately, was Havildar-Major Lalbahadur Thapa. The other Gurkhas had been praised and dismissed, to spend, for them, a far more enjoyable evening devoted to gambling and massive consciousness-alteration by whatever substances they chose.

'That was a famous display,' Lalbahadur grunted.

'Yuh,' Sten said.

'I am sure that, should any evil man desire to hold our Chamberlain for ransom, he will never do it on the edge of this castle.'

Sten grinned. In the three months he'd commanded the Emperor's Own Gurkha Bodyguard, he'd learned that the Nepalese sense of humor matched his own, most especially in its total lack of respect toward superior officers. 'You're cynical. This has given us much honor.'

'That is true. But what puzzles me is that one time I made my ablution in one hand, and waited for the other hand to fill up with honor.' Lalbahadur mocked sadness. 'There was no balance.

'At least there is one thing,' Lalbahadur brightened. 'Our heroism will be shown to the parbitayas back home, and we shall have no trouble finding new fools who want to climb walls for the glory of the Emperor.'

Sten's comeback was broken off as a band crashed into noise behind him. The officer and the noncom straightened as the Honor Guard of the Emperor's Own Praetorians thundered forward. Sten and Lalbahadur saluted the colors, then shrank back against the wall as the 600 plus men of the palace guard, all polished leather, gleaming metal, and automata, slammed past.

At the head of the formation the Praetorian's commanding officer, Colonel Den Fohlee, ramrodded a salute back at Sten, then snapped his eyes forward as the honor unit wheeled out onto the parade ground, to be met with cheers.

'My father once told me,' Lalbahadur observed, 'that there are only two kinds of men in the world. Normally, I do not listen to such nonsense, since it is my thought that the only two kinds of men in the world are those who see only two kinds of men in the world and those who do not.' He stopped, slightly confused.

'Two kinds of men, your father said,' Sten prompted.

'Yes. There are those who love to polish metal and leather and there are those who would rather drink. Captain, to which group do you belong?'

'Pass, Havildar,' Sten said with regret. 'I'm still on duty.'

Sten and the noncom saluted, then the small, stocky man doubled off. Sten had a few minutes before guard check, so he walked to the end of the tunnel to watch the Praetorians parade.

They were very, very good, as befits any group of men and women whose sole duties and training consisted in total devotion to their leaders, an ability to stand motionless for hours on guard, and colorful ceremonious pirouetting.

Sten was being unfair, but the few times he'd been told off for parade duties, he'd found it a pain in the moulinette. Parading soldiers may be interesting to some types, but those people could never have spent the endless dull hours of shining and rehearsal that a parade takes.

Although Sten had to admit that the Praetorians were highly skilled. They paraded with archaic projectile weapons; the stubby, efficient willygun wasn't spectacular enough for any manual of arms. And the willygun had no provision for a bayonet. By the fortieth century, the benefits of mounting a can opener on the end of a rifle were long gone, save for ceremonial purposes.

And so the Praetorians jerked to and fro in intricate array with near-four-foot-long rifles.

The soldiers initially had their weapons at the shoulder. On count, the weapons came down to waist-carry, the bayonets gleaming before them like so many spears.

Marching in extended order, on command, each rank would wheel and march back toward the next rank's lowered bayonets. Sten winced to think what would happen if a noncom missed a beat in the continual chant of commands.

The unit pivoted back on itself, then wheel-turned in ranks. By chant, they began a progressive manual of arms; as each line's boots would crash against the tarmac, that rank would move from carry arms to port arms to shoulder arms to reverse shoulder arms.

Simultaneously, squads broke apart and began doing by-the-count rifle tosses – continuing the progressive manual, but after the shoulder arms command each soldier would pitch his weapon straight up and backward, to be caught by the next person in ranks.

Sten, watching with give-me-strength cynicism, had never studied history enough to have met the old line: 'It's pretty, but is it war?'

Chapter Three

Certain beings everyone loves on first sight: they seem to live on a slightly higher plane than all others. And yet those noble ones find an echo of themselves in all other living things. They see life as art, so therefore can be somewhat pretentious. Yet they also mock their own pretensions.

Marr and his lover, Senn, were two such beings, twittering superlatives over the Praetorian Guard.

'My, what lusty fellows,' Marr said. 'All those muscles and musk. Almost makes a creature want to be human.'

'You wouldn't know what to do with even *one* of them if you were,' Senn sniffed. 'I should know. It certainly has been a long time since you tried your wicked way with me.'

'I was merely admiring those wonderful young men. They please the eye. Nothing to do with sex. A subject you always seem to have on the cranium.'

'Oh, gonads. Let's not fight, Marr, dear. It's a party. And you know how I *love* a party.'

Senn softened. Perhaps he *was* behaving like an off-cycle human. He leaned closer to Marr and let their antennae twine. Parties always got to him, too.

In fact, there were very few beings in the Empire who knew more about parties than Senn and Marr. Celebrations of all kinds were their speciality – a little glitter, a little tack, interesting personalities tossed into a conversational salad. Their official function on Prime World was that of *the* Imperial Caterers. They were always deploring the fact that the Eternal Emperor's get-togethers put them in the red. They were, however, much too good businessbeings to deplore too loudly; the Emperor's 'custom' was the reason their catering service was booked years in advance.

In an age not generally known for permanent bondings, the two Milchen stood out. They had been sexually paired for more than a century and were passionately determined that the relationship should go on for a century more. However, such stability was not unusual in their species; for the Milchen of Frederick Two, pairing was literally for life – when one member of a Milchen pair died, the other would always follow within a few days. Long-term pairings among the Milchen were always of the same sex. For want of a better description, call it male. The other gender – put the 'female' label on it, it's easier – was called Ursoolas. Of all things in the many universes, the Ursoolas were among the most beautiful and delicate, beings of gossamer and many-changing perfumed colors. They lived only a few short months, and during that time it was all loving and sexual intensity. If a Milchen male pair was fortunate, it might enjoy two or three such relationships in its lifetime. Out of each bonding came a 'male' pair and half-a-dozen dormant Ursoolas. The mother would whisper a few last loving words to her broodsac and then die, leaving the care of the young to the father pair.

For the Milchen, life was a never-ending breeding-cycle tragedy that bred the kind of loneliness that can kill a loving race. And so they evolved the only system open to them – same-sex bonding. Like most of their people, Marr and Senn were passionately devoted to each other, and to all other things of beauty.

They were slender creatures, a meter or so high, and covered with a downy, golden fur. They had enormous liquid-black eyes that enjoyed twice the spectrum of a human's. Their heads were graced with sensitive smelling antennae that could also caress like a feather. Their small monkeylike hands contained the Empire's most sensitive tastebuds, and were largely the reason for Milchen's being among the Empire's greatest chefs. The Eternal Emperor himself grudgingly admitted they surpassed all other races in the preparation of fine meals. Except, of course, for chili.

The two Milchen cuddled closer and drank in the ultimate spectacle that was Empire Day. Busybodies that the Milchen were, the beings around them were at least as interesting to them as the Imperial display.

Marr's eyes swept the VIP boxes. 'Everyone, but *everyone* is here.'

'I noticed,' Senn sniffed. 'Including a few who ought not to be.'

He pointed to a box across from them as an example – the box that held Kai Hakone and his party. 'After the reviews of his last masque, I don't know how he can even hold up his pate in public.'

Marr giggled. 'I know. Isn't it delicious? And the silly fool is such a bore, he even agreed to be the guest of honor at our *party*.'

Senn snuggled closer in delight. 'I can hardly wait! The blood will flow, flow, flow.'

Marr gave his pairmate a suspicious look. 'What did you do, Senn? Or dare I ask?'

Senn laughed. 'I also invited his critics.'

'And?'

'They were delighted. They'll all be there.'

The two chuckled over their evil little joke, and glanced at Hakone again, wondering if he suspected what was in store for him in few short days.

Marr and Senn would have been disappointed. Kai Hakone, a man some people called the greatest author of his day – and others the greatest hack – wasn't even thinking of the party.

Around him were a dozen or more fans, all very rich and very fawning. A constant stream of exotic dishes and drinks flowed in and out of the box. But it was hardly a party. Even before the celebration had begun, everyone had realized that Hakone was in 'one of those moods.' And so the conversation was subdued, and there were many nervous glances at the brooding master, an enormous man with unfashionably bulging muscles, a thick shock of unruly hair, heavy eyebrows, and deep-set eyes.

Hakone's gut was tightening, his every muscle was tense, and he was perspiring heavily. His mind and mood was ricocheting wildly. Everything is ready, he would think one minute, and his spirits would soar. But what if there's a mistake? Gloom would descend. What has been left undone? I should have done that myself. I shouldn't have let them do it. I should have done it.

And on and on, as he went over and over each detail of the plan. Thunder arose from the crowd as another spectacular event crashed to its conclusion; Kai Hakone barely heard it. He touched his hands together a few times, pretending to join in the applause. But his mind churned on with constantly changing images of death.

The last of the marching bands and dancers cleared the field, and the crowd slowly chattered its way into semi-silence.

Two huge gravsleds whined through the end gates – gravsleds loaded with steel shrouding, lifting blocks, and ropes. They hummed slowly down the field, each only a meter from the ground, halting at frequent intervals. At each pause, sweating fatigue-clad soldiers jumped off the sleds and unloaded some of the shrouding or blocks. Ropes and cables were piled beside each assemblage. By the time the gravsled stopped next to the Imperial reviewing stand, the long field looked as if a child had scattered his building blocks across it. Or, as was the case, an obstacle course had been improvised.

As the sleds lifted up over the castle itself, two large targets – solid steel backing, plus three-meter-thick padding – were lowered from the castle walls to dangle 400 meters above the field. Then six bands marched in through gates and blasted into sound. Some military-trivia types knew the tune was the official Imperial Artillery marching song, but none of them knew the tune itself was an old, bawdy song sometimes titled 'Cannoneers have Hairy Ears.'

Two smaller gravsleds then entered the parade ground through the gates. Each carried twenty beings and a cannon. The cannons weren't the gigantic combat masers or the small but highly lethal laserblasts the Imperial Artillery actually used. The wheeled cannons – mountain guns – were only slightly less ancient than the black-powder, muzzle-loading cannons staring down from the battlements.

After the forty men had unloaded the two mountain guns, they doubled into formation and froze. The leader of each group snapped to a salute and held it as a gunpowder weapon on the castle battlements boomed and a white cloud spread over the parade ground. Then the forty cannoneers began.

The event was variously called 'artillery competition,' 'cannon carry,' or 'impressive silliness.' The object of the competition between the two teams was fairly simple. Each team was to maneuver one mountain gun from where it sat, through the obstacles, to a site near the Imperial stand. There it was to be loaded, aimed at one of the targets, and fired. The first team to complete the exercise and strike the target won.

No antigrav devices were allowed, nor was it permitted to run around the obstacles. Instead, each gun had to be disassembled and then carried/hoisted/levered/thrown over the blocks. The competition required gymnastic skills. Since each team was moving somewhat over a thousand kilograms of metal, the chances of crushed body parts was very high. Nevertheless, qualification for the Cannon Carry Teams was intense among Imperial Artillerymen.

That year the competition was of particular interest; for the first time the finals were not between two of the Guards Divisions. Instead, one team of nonhumans, from the XVIII Planetary Landing Force, would challenge the top-ranked men and women of the Third Guards Division.

Another reason for spectator interest, of course, was that the cannon carry was one Empire Day event that could be bet on. Official odds were unusual: eight to five in favor of the Third Guards. However, actual betting ran somewhat differently. Prime World humans felt that the nonhumans, the N'Ranya, were underdogs, and preferred to invest their credits accordingly; non-humanoids felt somewhat differently, preferring to back the favorites.

Sometimes the gods back the sentimental. The N'Ranya were somewhat anthropoidal and weighed in at about 300 kilos apiece. Plus, their race, having developed as tree-dwelling carnivores on a jungle world, had an instinctual eye for geometry and trigonometry.

Working against the N'Ranya was a long tradition of How a Cannon Carry Should Work. The drill went as follows for the Guardsmen: the gun captain took the sight off, doubled to the first obstacle. Waiting for him there were two men who'd already secured the gun's aiming stakes. They literally pitched the gun captain and sight to the top of the wall. He helped his two men up, then went on toward the second obstacle.

By this time the gun had been disassembled into barrel/trail/carriage/recoil mechanism and was at the foot of that wall. Ropes were thrown to the first two men, and they became human pulleys and the guns went up the wall. Other men free-scaled that wall, grabbed the guns, and eased them down to the other side.

The N'Ranya, however, were more simple. They figured that two N'Ran could lug each component, and worked accordingly. Each part of the gun was bodily carried to the obstacle and 'thrown' to two more N'Ran who waited at the top. Then it was dropped to two more on the far side.

And so it went, clever teamwork against brute force. The N'Ran moved ahead on the net lift, since the carrying N'Ran, without bothering to hand off their parts, simply swarmed up and over the net.

The Guards, on the other hand, went into the lead on the steel spider by uniquely levering the skeleton structure *up* and moving the cannon underneath it.

By the time the two teams staggered over the last obstacle and began putting the gun back together, the Guards team was clearly ahead by seconds.

The N'Ran barely had their cannon assembled when the Guards gun captain slammed the sight onto his gun and powder monkeys slotted the charge into the breech. All that was needed for the Guards team to win was for the aiming stakes to be emplaced and the gun laid and then fired. Obviously this competition fired somewhat out of 'real' sequence.

And then the N'Ran altered the rules. The gun captain ignored the sightstakes, etc., and bore-sighted the gun. He moved his head aside as the round was thrown home, then free-estimated elevation. The N'Ranya dove out of the way as their gun captain toggled off the round. It hit dead center in the target.

Protests were lodged, of course, but eventually the bookies grudgingly paid off on the N'Ranya champions.

At the same time, orders were circulated within the Guards Divisions that recruiters specializing in artillery would be advised to spend time on the N'Ranya worlds.

Tanz Sullamora wasn't happy with things, especially since his Patriotic Duty had just cost him a small bundle.

When he'd heard that for the first time ETs were to be permitted to compete in the cannon carry, he'd been appalled. He did not feel that it was good Imperial policy to allow nonhumanoids to be publicly humiliated on Empire Day.

His second shock was finding that Prime World betting was heavily on the N'Ranya. Patriotism required Sullamora to back the Guards team. It was not the loss of credits, Sullamora rationalized. It was that the contest had been unfair. The N'Ranya were jungle dwellers, predators just one step above cannibals. Of course they had an unfair advantage. Certainly they would be better at carrying heavy weights and so forth. The Emperor had better realize, Sullamora sulked, that while nonhumanoids were a necessary part of the Empire, they certainly should understand how far down the ladder of status they were.

Which inexorably brought to Sullamora's mind where he was sitting. After all he'd done for the Empire, from charitable contributions to funding patriotic art to assisting the Court itself, why had he not been invited to the Imperial box for Empire Day? Or even assigned a box that was close to the Imperial stand, instead of being far down the first circle, almost in the second-class area?

The Emperor, Sullamora thought, was beginning to change, and change in a manner that, the merchant thought righteously, was indicative of the growing corruption of the Empire itself.

Tanz Sullamora was certainly not enjoying Empire Day.

Of course, one major set piece was always planned for Empire Day. And, of course, each year it had to be bigger and better than the previous year's.

Fortunately the current celebration didn't have much to worry about. The previous year, the set piece had been assigned to the Eighth Guards Division, who planned to display the fighting prowess of the individual infantryman.

To that end, McLean units were taken off gravsleds, half powered, and lightened to the point that a unit could be hidden in one soldier's combat tucksack. The end result – a flying man; flying sans suit or lifebelt.

In rehearsal it looked quite impressive.

The plan was for the Eighth Guards to pull one massive swoop, with each soldier functioning as a cross between a tiny tacship and a crunchie.

The Eighth Guards, however, forgot to check on the weather. Prime World was windy. And the normal twenty-gusting-to-thirty winds that blew across the parade field were magnified by the enormous ground's own weather effects. The end result was many, many grunts being blown into the stands in disarray – not bad for them, since many made valuable instant friends – some bruised egos and bodies in the second area of seating, and an enormous gust of laughter from the Emperor.

That gust of laughter blew the Eighth Guards to the Draconian Sector, where they were spending morose tours keeping that group of dissident pioneer worlds in something approaching coherence.

This year, it was Twelfth Guards' turn in the barrel. And, after she spent considerable time in thought, the commanding General found a unique way to do a massive display. Laser blasts lanced into the arena and ricocheted from pre-positioned surfaces to bounce harmlessly into the atmosphere. Explosions roared and boomed. And then elements of the Twelfth Guards fought their way back into the arena.

The Emperor nodded approvingly; very seldom had he seen anybody schedule a fighting *retreat* for display.

Antennas went up, and signalmen began flashing. From over the horizon tacships snarled and realistically strafed the area just behind the parade ground.

Pickup ships snaked in as anti-aircraft fire boomed around them (lighter-than-air balloons, painted non-reflective black and set with timed charges). The ships boiled in, grounded, and, in perfect discipline, the troops loaded aboard. The pickup ships cleared, hovered, and suddenly the air just above the parade ground hummed and boomed and echoes slammed across the field. Screams rose from the stands, and the Emperor himself almost went flat – then reseated himself, while wishing he could figure out how anybody could fake a maser cannon.

Then the stars darkened and two Hero-class battlewagons drifted overhead, their kilometer-long bulks blackening the sky. Lasers raved from the two battleships, and missiles flamed from the ships' ports. Eventually the 'enemy ground fire' stopped, and the pickup ships arced up into the heavens and into the yawning bays of the battleships. Then the ships lifted vertically, Yukawa behind them, and suddenly vanished, sonic-booming up and out of Prime World's atmosphere.

The crowd went nuts.

The Eternal Emperor poured himself a drink and decided that the Twelfth Guards would not go to Draconia.

Godfrey Alain watched the battleships vanish overhead and shivered slightly. In his mind those same battleships were lifting away from the ruins of his own world. His private calculations showed that such an invasion was no more than a year away. Death in the name of peace, he thought.

Alain had faced Imperial Guardsmen before, both personally and strategically – he *knew* the might of the Empire. But, somehow, seeing those battleships and the smooth efficient lift of an entire division of 12,000 struck more immediately home.

And I'm the only one who'll keep that invasion from happening. The Tahn will not do anything. My own people will just die. And my cause will be lost for generations to come.

Alain was not an egotist. All projections showed that he was the only one who could stop such an invasion.

Unfortunately, Godfrey Alain had less than twenty-four hours to live.

Everyone loves clowns and acrobats. Almost a thousand of them filled the parade ground. Doing clown numbers:

A new group of 'drunk soldiers' deciding to salute the Emperor, not knowing how to do it, and building toward a fight that built toward a pyramid display, with the 'drunkest' man atop the pyramid saluting perfectly and then doing a dead-man topple to spin through three tucks and land perfectly on the balls of his feet.

Men in barrels, rolling about and narrowly avoiding destruction; tumblers, spinning for hundreds of meters on their hands; gymnasts using each other, themselves, and sometimes, it seemed, thin air to soar ever upward in more and more spectacular patterns; boxers, who swung majestically, missed, and went into contortions of recovery to get back to the mock-fight; crisscross tumbling, with bodies narrowly missing other bodies as they cartwheeled over and over.

The crowd loved them.

The announcer's text said that the thousand clowns were part of the 'Imperial Gymnastic Corps,' but that corps never existed. Of those present, only the Emperor knew that the display of clowns was as close as his Mantis Section men – the super-elite, super-classified commandos that did the Emperor's most private and dangerous skulking – could get to any kind of public display.

Besides, the children – which included the Emperor – loved that part of the evening.

In normal times, Dr. Har Stynburn would have attended Empire Day from a private booth. At the very least, it would have been in the second circle. More than likely he would have been a guest in the first area, a guest of one of the important people who were his patients.

But those were not normal times.

Stynburn sat far to the rear of the landing field in one of the uncushioned, unupholstered seats that were reserved for the Prime World residents themselves.

Residents. Peasants.

Stynburn was surely a racist. But the gods have a certain sardonic sense of humor. The entire row in front of him was filled with longshoremen: octopod longshoremen. Not only that, but drunk octopod longshoremen, who waved banners, unspeakable food, and even more unspeakable drink in Stynburn's face.

Still worse, the longshoremen expressed enthusiasm by opening their tertiary mouths, located atop their bodies, gulping in air, and then emitting it suddenly and explosively.

Stynburn had, he thought, expressed polite displeasure after one longshoreman had inadvertently shoved a snack that looked like a boiled hat into Stynburn's face. Instead of agreeing, the longshoreman had asked if Stynburn would like to be a part of Empire Day, and wound up two pitching tentacles to provide the means.

He ran fingers through his carefully coiffed gray hair – like his body, still young, still needing neither transplants nor injections.

Stynburn consciously forced his mind to another subject, and stared at the holographic screen across the way. The screen showed close shots of the clowns as they moved toward Stynburn's area, then a momentary shot of the Emperor himself, rocking with laughter in his booth, then other celebrities in their very private booths.

Stynburn was not feeling at his best. As he'd moved into the arena, carefully looking and thinking anonymous, he thought he'd caught a glimpse of the man he had hired.

He was wrong, but the moment had upset him. How did he know that the man was in fact on his assigned post? Hiring professional criminals for a job was valid, he knew, but he also knew through experience that they were extremely unreliable.

Stynburn's train of depression was broken as a security guard came through the stands and told the longshoremen to pipe down or get thrown out. The guard continued up the steps, but paused to give Stynburn a sharp glance.

No, Stynburn's mind said. I know I do not belong here. It is possible that I do not look it.

But continue on, man. Do not stop, for your own life.

Stynburn was not exaggerating. Years before, other surgeons had implanted a tube of explosives where his appendix had been, and a detonator between his shoulder blades. All it took to set off his suicide capsule – and to destroy a twenty-meter-square area – was for Dr. Stynburn to force his shoulders back in a superexaggerated stretch.

But that would not be necessary; the guard continued up the steps and Stynburn forced his eyes back onto the arena, and his mouth to produce very hollow laughter at the antics of the clowns.

Icy fingers tailed up Marr's fragile spine, an instinct that had saved generations of Milchen from death in the long-ago days of Frederick Two. His heart fluttered, and he pulled slightly away from Senn.

'What's wrong, dear?'

'I don't know. Something is . . . I don't know.'

Senn tried to pull him closer to comfort him. Marr shook his head and rose to his full slender height.

'Take me home, Senn,' he said. 'It doesn't feel like a party anymore.'

Chapter Four

The sniffer stirred as Sten approached the closet, micro-gears whirring and throbbing like a small rodent. The security bot hesitated a half second, filament whiskers quivering, and then scuttled inside, its little metal feet clicking on the floor of the closet.

Sten stepped back and examined the Emperor's wardrobe. It was crammed with hundreds of uniforms and ceremonial robes and suits, each item meant for a specific occasion, some as simple as a dazzling white togalike garment, others as complex as a form-fitting suit of many and changing colors.

A vid-book in Sten's room told the history of each piece of clothing. The toga, he remembered, had been for the Emperor's visit to the small system of Raza, where his official title was Chief Philosopher. And the suit of many colors, he was pretty sure, had something to do with something called Mardi Gras. Sten hadn't had time to memorize them all yet, since he'd only been on the job officially for a few months and his mind was still learning the hundreds of duties required of the captain of the Emperor's Own Bodyguard. So far, he had been concentrating on his primary function, which was to keep His Majesty safe from plotters, schemers, groupies, and other fanatics.

The Emperor's security was a many-layered force. First were the military and police forces on Prime World. Within the palace itself was an elaborate mechanical and electronic blanket. The Imperial Household had three Guards units. The most noticeable were the Praetorians. Not only were they used as spit-and-polish, highly visible palace factotums, but they could double as riot police in the event of major disturbances, if there ever were any.

Second were the members of the Imperial Household itself,

recruited to a man (or woman) from the ranks of Mantis Section, Mercury Corps, or the Guards.

Lastly were the Gurkha bodyguards, one company of 150 men from the Earth province of Nepal. Most came from the Thapa, Pun, Ala, and Rana clans, all char-jat aristocracy. They were technically mercenaries, as many of their people had been for more than two thousand years.

Small, stocky men, the Gurkhas combined cheerfulness, humor, devotion to duty, and near-unbelievable personal fortitude in one package. The Gurkha company was led by one Havildar-Major, Lalbahadur Thapa, who was overseen by Captain Sten, the official commander and liaison with the Emperor and the Imperial Household.

His new post was not like being in Mantis Section, the superthug unit that Sten had so far spent most of his military career assigned to. Instead of dressing casually or in civilian clothes, Sten wore the mottled-brown uniform of the Gurkhas. Sten was somewhat grateful that he was assigned a batman, Naik Agansing Rai, although he sometimes – particularly when hung over – felt that the man should be a little less willing to comment on the failings of superiors.

Sten would, in fact, through the rest of his military career, maintain two prideful contacts with the Gurkhas – his wearing of the crossed, black-anodized kukris emblem on his dress uniform and the kukri itself.

Now, waiting for the sniffer to finish, Sten was armed with a lethal kukri on one hip, and a small, Mantis-issue willypistol on the other.

The sniffer completed its tour of the closet and scuttled back out to Sten, squeaking its little 'safe' tone. He palmed the off-plate, tucked the bot away, and stepped back. His Majesty's personal quarters were as safe as he could make them.

Sten began mentally triple-checking the security list for the rest of the wing. Changing of the guard had already passed . . . He had trusted lieutenants posted at . . .

'Captain, I don't like to bother a man at his work but—'

And Sten was whirling around for the voice just behind him, the fingers of his right hand instinctively making the claw that would trigger the knife muscles in his arm, and—

It was the Eternal Emperor, staring at him, a little bit amazed, and then relaxing into humor. Sten felt himself flush in embarrassment. He stiffened to attention, giving himself a mental kick in the behind. He was still a little too Mantis hair-trigger for palace duty.

The Emperor laughed. 'Relax, Captain.'

Sten slid into a perfectly formal 'at ease.'

The Emperor grinned, started to make a joke about Sten's way-too-military understanding of the word 'relax,' buried it to save Sten further embarrassment, and turned away. Instead, he plucked at the party clothing he was wearing and sniffed distastefully. 'If it's okay with you, I'd like to change out of this. I smell like a sow in heat.'

'Everything's fine, sir,' he said. 'Now, if I may be dismis—'

'You disappoint me, Captain.' The Emperor's voice boomed back from the changing room. Sten flinched, running over his potential sins. What had he missed?

'You've been on the job now – how long is it?'

'Ninety-four cycles, sir.'

'Yeah. Something like that. Anyway, ninety-odd days of snooping around my rooms, getting on my clotting nerves with all your security bother, and not once – not once have you offered to show me that famous knife of yours.'

'Knife, sir?' Sten was honestly bewildered for a second. And then he remembered: the knife in his arm. 'Oh, *that* knife.'

The Emperor stepped into view. He was already wearing a gray, nondescript coverall. 'Yeah. *That* knife.'

'Well, it's in my Mantis profile, sir, and – and . . .'

'There are a *lot* of things in your Mantis file, Captain. I reviewed it just the other day. Just double-checking to see if I wanted to keep you on in your present position.'

He noted Sten's look of concern and took pity. 'Besides the knife, I also noticed you drink.'

Sten didn't know how to answer that, so he remained wisely silent.

'How well you drink, however, remains to be seen.' The Eternal Emperor started for the other room. He stopped at the door.

'That's an invitation, Captain, not an order. Assuming you're off duty now.' He disappeared through the door.

Sten had learned many things from Mantis Section. He knew how to kill – had killed – in many ways. He could overthrow governments, plot strategic attacks and retreats, or build a low-yield nuclear bomb. But one thing he had learned more than anything else: when the CO issues an invitation, it's an order. It just so happened that his current CO was the Big Boss Himself.

So he made an instant executive decision. He throat-miked some hurried orders to his second and rostered himself off duty. Then he braced himself and entered the Eternal Emperor's study.

*

The smoky liquid smoothed down Sten's throat and cuddled into his stomach. He lowered the shot glass and looked into the waiting eyes of the Emperor. 'That's Scotch?'

The Emperor nodded and poured them both another drink.

'What do you think?'

'Nice,' Sten said, consciously dropping the sir. He assumed that officer's mess rules applied even with the Eternal Emperor. 'I can't figure why Colonel – I mean General – Mahoney always had a problem with it.'

The Emperor raised an eyebrow. 'Mahoney talked about my Scotch?'

'Oh, he liked it,' Sten covered. 'He just said it took getting used to.'

He shot back another glass, tasting the smoothness. Then he shook his head. 'Doesn't take any getting used to at all.'

It was a nice thing to say, at that point in the conversation. The Emperor had spent years trying to perfect that drink of his youth.

'We'll have another one of these,' the Emperor said, pouring out two more shots, 'and then I'll get out some heavy-duty spirits.' He carefully picked up Sten's knife, which was lying between them, examined it one more time, and then handed it back. It was a slim, double-edged dagger with a needle tip and a skeleton grip. Hand-formed by Sten from an impossibly rare crystal, its blade was ony 2.5 mm thick, tapering to a less-than-hair-edge 15 molecules wide. Blade pressure alone would cause it to slice through a diamond. The Emperor watched closely as Sten curled his fingers and let the knife slip into his arm-muscle sheath.

'Clotting marvelous,' the Emperor finally said. 'Not exactly regulation, but then neither are you.' He let his words sink in a little. 'Mahoney promised me you wouldn't be.'

Sten didn't know what to say to this, so he just sipped at his drink.

'Ex-street thug,' the Emperor mused, 'to Captain of the Imperial Guard. Not bad, young man. Not bad.'

He shrugged back some Scotch. 'What are your plans after this, Captain?' He quickly raised a hand before Sten blurted something stupid like 'at your Majesty's pleasure,' or whatever. 'I mean, do you really like all this military strut and stuff business?'

Sten shrugged. 'It's home,' he said honestly.

The Emperor nodded thoughtfully.

'I used to think like that. About engineering, not the clotting military, for Godsakes. Don't like the military. Never have. Even if I am the commander in clotting chief of more soldiers than you could . . . you could . . .'

He left that dangling while he finished his drink.

'Anyway. Engineering it was. That was gonna be my whole life – my permanent home.'

The Eternal Emperor shook his head in amazement at this thousand-year-old-plus memory.

'Things change, Captain,' he finally said. 'You can't believe how things change.'

Sten tried a silent nod of understanding, hoping he was doing one of his better acting jobs. The Emperor caught this, and just laughed. He reached into the drawer of his antique desk, pulled out a bottle of absolutely colorless liquid, popped open the bottle and poured two glasses full to the brim.

'This is your final test, young Captain Sten,' he said. 'Your final, ninety-cycle-on-the-job test. Pass this one and I okay you for the Imperial health plan.'

The Emperor slugged back the 180-proof alcohol and then slammed down the glass. He watched closely as Sten picked up the glass, sniffed it briefly, shrugged, and then poured white fire down his throat.

Sten set the glass down, then, with no expression on his face, slid the glass toward the bottle for some more. 'Pretty good stuff. A little metallic . . .'

'That's from the radiator,' the Emperor snapped. 'I distill it in a car radiator. For the flavor.'

'Oh,' Sten said, still without expression. 'Interesting . . . You wouldn't mind if I tried some more . . .'

He poured two more equally full glasses. He gave a silent toast, and the Emperor watched in amazement as Sten drank it down like water.

'Come on,' the Emperor said in exasperation. 'That's the most powerful straight alcohol you've ever tasted in your life and you know it. Don't con me.'

Sten shook his head in innocence. 'It's pretty potent, all right,' he said. 'But – no offense – I have tried something stronger.'

'Like what?' The Emperor fumed.

'Stregg,' Sten said.

'What in clot is Stregg?'

'An ET drink,' Sten answered. 'People called the Bhor. Don't know if you remember them but—'

'Oh, yeah,' the Emperor said. 'Those Lupus Cluster fellows. Didn't I turn a system over to them, or something like that?'

'Something like that.'

'So what's this Stregg swill like? Can't be better than my pure dee moonshine – you got any?'

Sten nodded. 'In my quarters. If you're interested, I'll send a runner.'

'I'm interested.'

The Emperor raised the glass to toast position.

'By my mother's,' he said through furry tongue, 'by my mother's . . . What was that Bhor toast again?'

'By my mother's beard,' Sten said, equally furry-tongued.

'Right. By my mother's beard.' He shot it back, gasped, and held on to the desk as his empire swung around him.

'Clot a bunch of moonshine,' the Eternal Emperor said. 'Stregg's the ticket. Now what was that other toash . . . I mean toast. By my father's . . .'

'Frozen buttocks,' Sten said.

'Beg your pardon. No need to get – oh, that's the toasshtt – I mean toast. By my father's frozen buttocks! Sffine stuff.' He lifted his empty glass to drink. He stared at it owlishly when he realized it was empty, and then pulled himself up to his full Imperial Majesty. 'I'm clotting fried.'

'Yep,' Sten said. 'Stregg do that to you. I mean, does that you to – oh, clot. Time is it? I gotta go on duty.'

'Not like that, you don't. Not in this Majesty's service. Can't stand drunks. Can't stand people can't hold their liquor. Don't trust them. Never have.'

Sten peered at him through a Stregg haze. 'Zzatt mean I'm fired?'

'No. No. Never fire a drunk. Have to fire me. Sober us up first. Then I fire you.'

The Emperor rose to his feet. Wavered. And then firmed himself. 'Angelo stew,' he intoned. 'Only thing save your career now.'

'What the clot is Angelo stew?'

'You don't need to know. Wouldn't eat it if you did. Cures cancer . . . oh, we cured that before, didn't we . . . Anyway . . . Angelo stew's the ticket. Only thing I know will unfreeze our buttocks.'

He staggered off and Sten followed in a beautifully military, forty-five-degree march.

Sten's stomach rumbled hungrily as he smelled the smells from the Eternal Emperor's private kitchen. Drunk as he was, he watched in fascination as the equally drunk Emperor performed miracles both major and minor. The minor miracles were with strange spices and herbs; the major one was that the Emperor, smashed on Stregg, could work an antique French knife, slicing away like a machine, measure proportions, and . . . keep up a semi-lucid conversation.

Sten's job was to keep the Stregg glasses full.

'Have another drink. Not to worry. Angelo stew right up.'

Sten took a tentative sip of Stregg and felt the cold heat-lightning down his gullet. This time, however, the impact was different. Just sitting in the Emperor's super-private domain, added to the fact that it was indeed time to get his captain's act together, had the effect of clearing away the boozy haze.

The kitchen was four or five times larger than most on fortieth-century Prime World, where food was handled out of sight by computers and bots. It had *some* modern features – hidden cabinets and environmental food storage boxes operated by finger touch. It also was kept absolutely bacteria free and featured a state-of-the-art waste disposal system that the Emperor rarely used. Mostly he either swept what Sten would have considered waste into containers and returned them to storage, or dumped things into what Sten would later learn were simmering stockpots.

The most imposing feature of the room was a huge chopping block made of rare hardwood called oak. In the center of the block was an old stainless steel sink. Set a little bit lower than the chopping block, it was flushed by a constant spray of water, and as the Emperor chopped away, he swept everything that didn't make Angelo stew into the sink, where it instantly disappeared.

Directly behind the Emperor was an enormous black cast-iron and gleaming steel cooking range. It featured an oven whose walls were many centimeters thick, a single-cast grill, half-a-dozen professional-chef-size burners, and an open, wood-burning grill. From the slight smell it gave off, the stove obviously operated by some kind of natural gas.

Sten watched as the Emperor worked and kept up a running commentary at the same time. From what Sten could gather, the first act of what was to be Angelo stew consisted of thinly sliced chorizo – Mexican hard sausage, the Emperor explained. The sausage and a heaping handful of garlic were sautéed in Thai-pepper-marinated olive oil. Deliciously hot-spiced smells from the pan cut right through the Stregg fumes in Sten's nostrils. He took another sip from his drink and listened while the Emperor talked.

'Never used to think much about food,' the Emperor said, 'except as fuel. You know, the stomach complains, you fill it, and then go about your business.'

'I understand what you mean,' Sten said, remembering his days as a Mig worker.

'Figured you would. Anyway, I was a typical young deep-space engineer. Do my time on the company mission, and spend my Intercourse and Intoxication time with joygirls and booze. Food even seemed to get in the way of that.'

Sten understood that as well. It was pretty much how he had spent his days as a rookie trooper.

'Then as I went up the company ladder, they sent me off on longer and longer jobs. Got clotting boring. Got so the only break you had was food. And that was all pap. So I started playing around. Remembering things my dad and grandma fixed. Trying to duplicate them.'

He tapped his head. 'Odd, how all the things you ever smelled or tasted are right up here. Then all you got to do is practice to get your tongue in gear. Like this Angelo stew here. Greatest hangover and drunk cure invented. Some old Mex pirate taught me – clot, that's another story . . .'

He stopped his work and took a sip of Stregg. Smiled to himself, and tipped a small splash in with the chorizo. Then he went back to the task at hand, quartering four or five onions and seeding quarter slices of tomatoes.

'Jump to a lot of years later. Way after I discovered AM_2 and started putting this whole clottin' Empire together . . .'

Sten's brain whirled for an instant. AM_2. The beginning of the Empire. What this mid-thirties-looking man was talking about so lightly was what one read about in history vids. He had always thought they were more legend than fact. But here he was having a calm discussion with the man who supposedly started it all – hell, nearly twenty centuries in the past. The Emperor went on, as if he was talking about yesterday.

'There I was, resting on my laurels and getting bored out of my mind. A dozen or so star systems down and working smoothly. A few trillion-trillion megacredits in the bank. So? Whaddya do with that kind of money?'

He motioned to Sten to top up the Stregg glasses.

'Then I realized what I could do with it. I could cook anything I wanted. Except I don't like the modern stuff they've been doing the last six or seven hundred years. I like the old stuff. So I started experimenting. Copying dishes in my brain. Buying up old cookbooks and recreating things that sounded good.'

The Emperor turned and pulled a half-kilo slab of bleeding red beef from a storage cooler and began chunking it up.

'What the hell. It's a way to kill time. Especially when you've got lots of it.'

The Emperor shut off the flame under the sausage and garlic, started another pan going with more spiced oil, and tossed in a little sage, a little savory and thyme, and then palm-rolled some rosemary twigs and dropped those in on top. He stirred the mixture, considered for a moment, then heaped in the tomato quarters and glazed them. He shut off the fire and turned back to Sten. He gave the young captain a long, thoughtful look and then began talking again, rolling the small chunks of beef into flour first, and then into a bowl of hot-pepper seeds.

'I guess, from your perspective, Captain, that I'm babbling about things of little interest, that happened a long time ago. Old man talk. Nothing relevant for today.'

Sten was about to protest honestly, but the Emperor held up an Imperial hand. He still had the floor. 'I can assure you,' he said quite soberly, 'that my yesterdays seem as close to me as yours do to you. Now. For the crucial question of the evening.'

He engulfed half a glass of Stregg by way of pre-punctuation. 'How the clot you doing, Cap'n Sten. And how the hell you like Court duty? . . .'

Sten did some fast thinking. Rule One in the unofficial Junior Officer's Survival Manual: When A Senior Officer Asks You What You Think, You Lie A Lot.

'I like it fine,' Sten said.

'You're a clotting liar,' the Eternal Emperor said.

Rule Two of said bar guide to drinking with superiors: When Caught In A Lie, Lie Again.

'No, really,' Sten said. 'This is probably one of the more interesting—'

'Rule Two doesn't work, Captain. Drop the con.'

'It's a boring place filled with boring people and I never really gave a damn about politics anyway,' Sten rushed out.

'Much better,' the Emperor said. 'Now let me give you a little career advice . . .'

He paused to turn the flame up under the sausage and garlic, then added the pepper-rolled beef as soon as the pan was hot enough.

'First off, at your age and current status, you are luckier than hell even to be here.'

Sten started to agree, but the Emperor stopped him with a hard look. He stirred the beef around as he talked, waiting until it got a nice brown crust.

'First tip: Don't be here very long. If you are, you're wasting your time. Second thought: Your current assignment will be both a huge career booster and an inhibitor. Looks great on the fiche – "Head of the Imperial Bodyguard at such and such an age."

'But you're also gonna run into some superiors – much older and very jealous superiors – who will swear that I had a more than casual interest in you. Take that how you want. They certainly shall.'

The Emperor finished the beef. He pulled out a large iron pan and dumped the whole mess into it. He also added the panful of onions and tomatoes. Then he threw in a palmful of superhot red peppers, a glug or three of rough red wine, many glugs of beef stock, a big clump of cilantro, clanked down the lid, and set the flame to high. As soon as it all came to a boil, he would turn it down to simmer for a while.

The Emperor sat down next to Sten and took a long swallow of Stregg.

'I don't know if you realize it or not, but you have a very heavy mentor in General Mahoney.'

'Yeah. I know it,' Sten said.

'Okay. You got him. You're impressing the clot out of me right now. Not bad. Although I got to warn you, I am notorious for going hot and cold on people. Don't stick around me too long.

'When all is lost, I sometimes blame my screw-ups on the nearest person to me. Hell, once in a while, I even believe it myself.'

'I've been there,' Sten said.

'Yeah. Sure you have. Good experience for a young officer. Drakh flows downhill. Good thing to learn. That way you know what to do when you're on top.'

The stew was done now. The Emperor rose and ladled out two brimming bowlsful. Sten's mouth burst with saliva. He could smell a whole forest of cilantro. His eyes watered as the Emperor set the bowl in front of him. He waited as the man cut two enormous slices of fresh-baked sourdough bread and plunked them down along with a tub of newly churned white butter.

'So here's what you do. Pull this duty. Then get thee out of intelligence or anything to do with cloak and dagger. Nobody ever made big grade in intelligence. I got it set up that way. Don't trust them. Nobody should.

'Next, get thee to flight school. No. Shut up. I know that's naval. What I'm saying is, jump services. Get yourself in the navy. Learn piloting.'

The Emperor slowly buttered his slice of bread and Sten followed suit, memorizing every word.

'You'll easily make lieutenant commander. Then up you go to commander, ship captain, and – with a little luck – flag captain. From there on in, you're in spitting distance of admiral.'

Sten took a long pull on his drink to cover his feelings. Admiral? Clot. Nobody but nobody makes admiral. The Emperor topped the glasses again.

'I *listen* to my admirals,' the Emperor said. 'Now do what I say. Then come back in fifty years or so and I may even listen to you.'

The Emperor spooned up a large portion of stew.

'Eat up, son. This stuff is great brain food. First your ears go on fire, then the gray stuff. Last one done's a grand admiral.'

Sten swallowed. The Angelo stew savored his tongue, and then gobbled down his throat to his stomach. A small nuclear flame bloomed, and his eyes teared and his nose wept and his ears turned bright red. The Stregg in his bloodstream fled before a horde of hot-pepper molecules.

'Whaddya think?' the Eternal Emperor said.

'What if you don't have cancer?' Sten gasped.

'Keep eating, boy. If you don't have it now, you will soon.'

Chapter Five

The Emperor had two problems with Prime World. The first was, Why Was His Capital Such A Mess? He had run an interstellar empire for a thousand years. Why should a dinky little planet-bound capital be such a problem?

The second was, What Went Wrong?

Prime World was a classic example of city planning gone bonkers. In the early days, shortly after the Eternal Emperor had taught people that he controlled the only fuel for interstellar engines – Anti-Matter Two – and that he was capable of keeping others from learning or stealing its secret, he'd figured out that headquartering an empire, especially a commercial one, on Earth was dumb.

He chose Prime World for several reasons: it was uninhabited, it was fairly close to an Earth-normal habitat; and it was ringed with satellites that would make ideal deep-space loading platforms. And so the Emperor bought Prime World, a planet that until then was nothing more than an index number on a star chart. Even though he controlled no more than 500 to 600 systems at the time, the Emperor knew that his empire would grow. And with growth would come administration, bureaucracy, court followers, and all the rest.

To control the potential sprawl, owning an entire world seemed a solution. So the finest planners went to work. Boulevards were to be very, very wide. The planet was to have abundant parks, both for beauty and to keep the planet from turning into a self-poisoning ghetto. Land was leased in parcels defined by century-long contracts. All buildings were to be approved by a council that included as many artists as civic planners.

Yet somewhat more than a thousand years after being set up, Prime World looked like a ghetto.

The answers were fairly simple: greed, stupidity, and graft – minor human characteristics that somehow the Eternal Emperor had ignored. Cynically, the Emperor realized he did not need the equivalent of the slave who supposedly lurked on Caesars during their triumphal processions to whisper 'All this too is fleeting.'

All he had to do was travel the 55-plus kilometers to Fowler, the city nearest to his palace grounds, and wander the streets. Fowler, and the other cities on Prime World, were high-rise/low-rise/open kaleidoscopes.

To illustrate:

A building lot, listed in the Prime World plat book as NHEB0FA13FFC2, a half kilometer square, had originally been leased to the luxury-loving ruler of the Sandia system, who built a combination of palace and embassy. But when he was turned out of office by a more spartan regime, Sandia sublet the ground to an intersteller trading conglomerate which tore down the palace and replaced it with a high-rise headquarters building. But Transcom picked the wrong areas and products, so the building was gradually sub-sublet to such 'small' enterprises as mere planetary governments or system-wide corporations. And as the leases were sublet to smaller entities, the rent went up. Annual rental on a moderate-size one-room office could take a province's entire annual product.

The Transcom building turned into an office slum until all the subleases were bought up by the Sultana of Hafiz, who, more than anything, wanted a palace she could use on her frequent and prolonged trips to Prime World. The high-rise was demolished and another palace built in its place.

All that in eighty-one years. Yet the Imperial records still registered the President of Sandia, who by then had spent forty-seven years forcibly ensconced in a monastery, as the lease-holder.

Given the subleasing system, even rent control did not work. 'Single' apartments sometimes looked more like troopship barracks because of the number of people required to meet the monthly rent.

The Emperor had tried to help, since he was quite damned aware that even in an age of computers and bots, a certain number of functionaries were needed. But even Imperial housing projects quickly changed hands and became examples of free enterprise gone berserk.

After nearly 800 years of fighting the sublet blight, in a final effort to control the pressure that drove such destructive practices, a limitation was placed on immigration to Prime World. Prospective emigrants were required to show proof of employment, proof that a new job had been created for them, or proof of vast wealth. The regulations were strictly enforced.

That made every Prime World resident rich. Not rich on Prime World, but potentially rich. Anyone, from an authorized diplomat to the lowest street vendor, could sell his residence permit for a world's ransom.

Prime Worlders being Prime Worlders, they did not. Most preferred to sit in their poverty (although poverty was relative, given guaranteed income, rations, recreation, and housing) than to migrate to be rich. Prime World was the Center, the Court of a Thousand Suns, and who would ever choose to move away from that if he, she, or it had any choice?

Sometimes the Emperor, when he was drunk, dejected, and angry, felt the answer was to nationalize all the buildings and draft everyone on the world. But he knew that his freelance capitalists would figure a way around that one, too.

So it was easier to let things happen as they did, and live with minor annoyances such as population density or city maps that were outdated within thirty days of issue.

In addition to the cities and the parks, Prime World was full of estates. Most of the leased estates were situated as close to the Imperial ring as possible. The proximity of one's living grounds to the palace was another measure of social stature.

There was one final building located on the grounds of the Emperor's main palace. It was about ten kilometers away from Arundel, and housed the Imperial Parliament. It had been necessary to build some kind of court, after all. After the Eternal Emperor authorized its structure, he'd immediately had a kilometer-high landscaped mountain built between his castle and the parliament building. He may have had to deal with politicians, but he didn't have to look at them when he was on his own time . . .

Prime World was, therefore, a somewhat odd place. The best and the worst that could be said is that it worked – sort of.

The pneumosubways linked the cities, and gravsleds provided intrasystem shipping. Out-system cargoes arriving in Prime System were off-loaded to one of the planet's satellites or the artificial ports that Imperial expansion had made necessary. From there, they would either be transferred to an outbound freighter or, if intended for Prime World itself, lightered down to the planet's surface.

Five shipping ports sat on Prime World. And like all ports throughout history, they were grimy and violent.

The biggest port, Soward, was the closest to Fowler. One kilometer from Soward's main field was the Covenanter.

Like the rest of Prime World, Soward had troubles with expansion.

But warehousing and shipping had to be located as close to ground level as possible.

Ancillary buildings, such as rec halls, offices, bars, and so forth, were built over the kilometer-square warehouses. Ramps – some powered, some not – swept up from the ground level to the spider-web steel frameworks that held the secondary buildings.

The Covenanter sat three levels above the ground. To reach the bar required traveling one cargo ramp, one escalator, and then climbing up oil-slick stairs. Despite that, the Covenanter was usually crowded.

But not in the night.

Not in the rain.

Godfrey Alain moved into the shadows at the top of the escalator and waited to see if he was being tailed.

Minutes passed, and he heard nothing but the waterfall sound of the rain rushing down the ramps to the ground far below. He pulled his raincloak tighter around him, still waiting.

Alain had left his hotel room in Fowler. Four other rented 'safe' rooms had given him momentary safety, a chance to see if he was followed, and a change of clothes. He appeared to be clean.

A more experienced operative might have suggested to Alain that he should have tried less expensive costuming; his final garb and his final position, a warehouse district, made him a potential target for muggers.

But Godfrey Alain was not a spy; the skills of espionage were secondary to him. To most of the Empire, he was a terrorist. To himself, his fellow revolutionaries, and the Tahn worlds, Alain was a freedom fighter.

What Alain was, oddly enough, was less a factor of politics than population movement. The Tahn worlds having originally been settled by low-tech refugees guaranteed that the Empire left them alone. The Tahn worlds being what they were – a multisystem sprawl of cluster worlds – guaranteed no Imperial interference. But the Tahn's lebensraum expansion also was a guarantee that sooner or later the Empire and the Tahn would intersect, as had happened some generations before when Tahn settlers moved from their own systems to frontier worlds already occupied by small numbers of Imperial pioneers.

The two very different cultures were soon in conflict, and both sides screamed for help. The Tahn homeworlds could not provide direct armed support, nor were they willing to risk a direct confrontation with the Empire.

The Empire, on the other hand, could afford no more than token garrison forces of second- and third-class units to 'protect' the Imperial settlers from Tahn colonials.

The Caltor system Alain was born into was on one of those in conflict. Since the Tahn settlers ghettoed together socially and economically, they were guaranteed an advantage against the less united Imperial inhabitants. But the Imperial pioneers had Caltor's garrison troopies to fall back on and they felt that Imperial presence lent them some authority.

Such a situation breeds pogroms. And in one such pogrom Alain's parents were slaughtered.

The boy Alain saw the bodies of his parents, saw the local Imperial troops shrug off the 'incident,' and went to school. School was learning how to turn a gravsled into a kamikaze or a time bomb; how to convert a mining lighter into a transsystem spaceship; how to build a projectile weapon from pipes; and, most important, how to turn a mob into a tightly organized cellular resistance movement.

The resistance spread, from pioneer planet to pioneer planet, always disavowed by the distant Tahn worlds yet always backed with 'clean' weaponry and moral support; always fought by the Imperial settlers and their resident 'peace-keeping' troops; always growing.

Alain was a leader of the resistance – in the fifty years since he had seen his parents dead in the ruins of their house, he had become the chief of the Fringe Worlds' liberation movement.

And so he went by invitation to his home worlds as the representative of a huge, militant movement. Going home – to a political and ideological home he had never seen, the Tahn worlds, turned Alain into a lost man, because the Tahr system – those worlds the fringe worlds would unite with if his movement was successful – were not at all what he expected.

The government-encouraged population explosion was part of his disenchantment, as were the rigid social customs. But the biggest thing was the very stratification of the Tahn society. Coming from a pioneer world, Alain felt that any person should be able to rise to whatever level he was capable of. Intellectually he knew this was not part of Tahn culture, but what grew in his craw was the populace's acceptance of the stratification. As far as he could tell, the warrior had no intentions of becoming nobility, the peasant had no interest in the merchant class, and so forth.

It was the classic confrontation between a man from a culture which is still evolving and a society that has fixed on a very successful formula.

That was the first problem. The second, which he had been reminded of at gut level during the Empire Day celebration, was that, if the Eternal Emperor desired it, his revolutionary movement could be obliterated – along with the Tahn settlers Alain's freedom fighters moved and lived among.

Six months before, Alain had made very secretive overtures to an Imperial ambassador-without-portfolio. Initially, he had wanted to discuss a truce with the Empire, and with the fringe worlds that the Empire supported. And, over the months, the concept of truce had evolved.

Alain's final proposal, to be put before a direct representative this night, was broader. He wanted not just a cease-fire, but a slow legitimization of his people and his movement, recognizing the fringe worlds as an independent buffer zone between the Tahn worlds and the Empire itself.

Alain had only discussed the proposition among his oldest friends and most trusted advisors. It would be all too easy for Tahn intelligence to learn of the proposition, proclaim Alain a counter-revolutionary, and arrange for his death.

It would also be convenient for some of his long-term enemies on the Imperial side to have him killed. Alain was not afraid of dying – nearly fifty years as a guerrilla had blanked that part of his psyche out – but he was terrified of dying before his plan was in front of the Emperor.

The meeting had been most secretively arranged. Alain had been provided with false credentials, authorized 'at the highest level,' and arrived as just one more tourist to see the Empire Day display and sample the exotic life of the world that was home to the Court of a Thousand Suns.

Sometime during the Empire Day festivities, he was passed instructions on where the meeting was to occur, but the handoff was so subtle that even Alain was unsure how or when the time-burn message came into his pockets.

He felt relatively secure about the meeting, which had been set at a ship-port dive. It might prove fatal to Alain to have met with an Imperial representative in the long run, but it would certainly be damaging to the Emperor himself if anyone were to know his representative was meeting with a terrorist, especially a terrorist who had been the unsuccessful target of two Mantis Team assassination runs.

There were no followers.

Alain walked lightly up the stairs. His hand on the projectile pistol under the cloak, he checked behind him once again. Then he went down the ten-meter-wide catwalk of pierced steel plating. Alain could see the ground long meters below. On either side of the catwalk hung the structural-steel plating which supported offices and small industrial shops. Gaps yawned between them.

The only overhead on the catwalk was also over the only lit building, a bright red bar faced with pseudo-wood. Its holographic display morosely blinking T E COV ANTER.

He moved quite slowly down the catwalk, slipping from shadow to shadow. He saw no one and nothing outside the bar.

The man was diagonally across the catwalk from the Covenanter, on the open second floor of an unfinished warehouse. He stood well back from the window, just in case anyone was scanning the area with heat-sensitive glasses.

For two hours the bomber had been alternately sweeping the catwalk with light-enhancing binocs and swearing at the rain and his stupidity for taking the job – just as he had every night for three weeks from two hours after nightfall until the Covenanter closed.

This is a busto bum go, the bomber thought not for the first nor the five-hundredth time. Showed what happened when a man needed a job. The clots could sense it, and crawled out from the synth-work every time, somehow knowing when a real professional needed a few credits and didn't have much choice how he got them.

The bomber's name was Dynsman, and, contrary to his self-image, he was quite a ways from being a professional demolitionist. Dynsman was that rarity, a Prime World native. His family did not come from the wrong side of the tracks, because his older brothers would have torn those tracks up and sold them for black-market scrap. Dynsman was small, light on his feet, and occasionally quick-minded.

All else being normal, Dynsman would have followed quite a predictable pattern, growing up in petty thievery, graduating to small-scale nonviolent organized crime until a judge tired of seeing his face every year or so and deported him to a prison planet.

But Dynsman got lucky. His chance at real fame came when he slid through a heavy traffic throng to the rear of a guarded gravsled. When the guards looked the other way, Dynsman grabbed and hauled tail.

The gravsled had been loaded with demolition kits intended for the Imperial Guards. The complete demo kit, which included fuses, timer, primary charges, and the all-important instructions, had zip value to Dynsman's fence. He had sadly found himself sitting atop a roof and staring into a box that he'd gone to Great Risk – at least by Dynsman's scale of danger values – to acquire. And it was worth nothing.

But Dynsman was a native Prime Worlder, one of a select group of people widely thought capable of selling after dinner flatulence as experimental music. By the time he'd removed three fingers, scared his hair straight, and been tossed out of home by his parents, Dynsman could pass – at a distance, after dark, in a fog – as an explosives expert.

Soon Dynsman was a practicing member of an old and valued profession – one of those noble souls who turned bad investments, buildings, spacecraft, slow inventory, whatever, into liquid assets – with more potential customers than he had time for. Unfortunately, the biggest of those turned out to be an undercover Imperial police officer.

And so it went – Dynsman was either in jail or in the business of high-speed disassembly.

He should have known, however, that something was wrong on *this* job. First, the man who had bought him was too sleek, too relaxed to be a crook. And he knew too much about Dynsman, including the fact that Dynsman was six cycles late on his gambling payment and that the gambler had wondered if Dynsman might look more stylish with an extra set of kneecaps.

Not that Dynsman could have turned down the stranger's assignment at the best of times; Dynsman was known as a man who could bust out of a dice game even if he was using his own tap dice.

According to the gray-haired man, the job was simple.

Dynsman was to build a bomb into the Covenanter. Not just a *wham*-and-there-goes-everything bomb, but a very special bomb, placed in a very particular manner. Dynsman was then to wait in the uncompleted building until a certain man entered the building. He was then to wait a certain number of seconds and set the device off.

After that, Dynsman was to get the other half of his fee, plus false ID and a ticket off Prime World.

Dynsman mourned again – the fee offered was too high. Just as suspicious was the expensive equipment he was given – the night binocs, a designer sports timer, a parabolic mike with matching headphones, and the transceiver that would be used to trigger the bomb.

Dynsman was realizing he was a very small fish suddenly dumped into a pool of sharks when he spotted the man coming down the catwalk toward the Covenanter.

Dynsman scanned the approaching figure of Alain. Ah-hah. The first person to come near the bar in an hour. Expensively dressed. Holding the glasses in one hand, Dynsman slid the headphones into position and the microphone on.

Down on the catwalk Alain stopped outside the Covenanter's entrance. Another man stepped out of the blackness – Craigwel, the Emperor's personal diplomatic troubleshooter. He wore the flash coveralls of a spaceship engineer, and held both hands in front of him, clearly showing that he was unarmed.

'Engineer Raschid?' Alain said, following instructions.

'That is the name I am using.'

Across the street, Dynsman almost danced in joy. This was it! This was finally it! He shut off the mike, dropped it, and scooped up the radio-detonator and the sports timer.

As the two men went into the Covenanter, Dynsman thumbed the timer's start button.

Chapter Six

TEN SECONDS:

Janiz Kerleh was co-owner, cook, bartender, and main waiter at the Covenanter. The bar itself was her own personal masterpiece.

Janiz had no poor-farm-girl-led-into-trouble background, though she was from a farming planet. Fifteen years of watching her logger parents chew wood chips from dawn to dusk dedicated her to finding a way out. The way out proved to be a traveling salesman specializing in log-snaking elephants.

The elephant salesman took Janiz to the nearest city. Janiz took twenty minutes to find the center of action and ten more to line up her first client.

Being a joygirl wasn't exactly a thrill a minute – for one thing, she could never understand why so many people who wanted sex never bothered to use a mouthwash first – but it was a great deal better than staring at an elephant's anus for a lifetime. The joygirl became a madame successful enough to finance a move to Prime World.

To her total disappointment, Janiz found that what she had figured would be a gold mine was less than that. Not only were hookers falling out of Prime World's ears, but more than enough amateurs were willing to cooperate for something as absurd as being presented at Court.

Janiz Kerleh, then, was on hard times when she met Chief Engineer Raschid. They'd bedded, found a certain similarity in humor, and started spending time in positions other than horizontal.

Pillow talk – and pillow talk for Janiz was the bar she'd always wanted to open. Twenty years' worth of dreaming, sketching, even putting little pasteboard models together when the vice squad pulled the occasional plug on her operation.

Paralyzed was probably the best way to describe her reaction when Raschid, a year or so after they'd known each other, and sex had become less of an overriding interest than just a friendly thing to do, handed her a bank draft and said, 'You wanna open up your bar? Here. I'm part owner.'

Raschid's only specification was that one booth – Booth C, he'd told her to name it – was to be designed somewhat differently than the others. It was to be absolutely clean. State-of-the-art debugging and alarm devices were delivered and installed by anonymous coveralled men. The booth itself was soundproofed so that any conversation could not be overheard a meter away from the table. A security service swept the booth once a week.

Raschid told Janiz that he wanted to use the booth for meetings. Nobody was permitted to sit there except him – or anyone who came in and used his name.

Janiz, who had a pretty good idea how much money a ship's engineer made, and knew it was nowhere near enough to front an ex-joygirl in her hobby, figured Raschid had other things going. The man was probably a smuggler. Or . . . or she really didn't care.

The Covenanter was quite successful, giving dockers and ship crewmen a quiet place to drink, a place where the riot squad never got called if evenings got interesting, and a place to meet colorful girls without colorful diseases. Raschid himself dropped by twice a Prime year or so, and then would vanish again. Janiz had tried to figure what ship he was on by following the outbound columns in the press, but she could never connect Raschid with any ship or even a shipping line. Nor could she figure who Raschid's 'friends' were, since they ranged from well-dressed richies to obvious thugs.

So when the two men, Alain and Craigwel, asked for Booth C, in an otherwise totally deserted bar, she had no reaction other than to ask what they were drinking.

SEVENTY-TWO SECONDS:

When Dynsman had broken into the Covenanter to plant the bomb a week earlier, he had also paced out the detonation time. His man would enter the bar. Ten seconds. Look around. Fifteen seconds. Walk to the bar. 7.5 seconds. Order a drink. One minute. Pick up the drink and walk across the room to Booth C. The bomber made allowances for possible crowding – which the Covenanter certainly was not that night – then gave his time-sequence another two minutes just to be sure.

Alain eyed the vast array of liquors on display, then picked the safe bet. 'Synthalk. With water. Tall and with ice, at your favor.'

Craigwel, the professional diplomat, ordered the same. His next statement would kill both men. It was intended only to lubricate the discussion that was to follow. 'Have you ever tried Metaxa?'

'No,' Alain said.

'Good stuff on a night like this.'

'Non-narcotic?' Alain asked suspiciously.

'Alcohol only. It's also a good hullpaint remover.'

Janiz poured the two shots, then busied herself making the synth-alk drinks.

Alain lifted his shot glass. 'To peace.'

Craigwel nodded sincerely, and tossed his glass back.

Time ran out. On timer cue, Dynsman touched the radio det button.

The bomb exploded.

High-grade explosive, covered with ball bearings, crashed.

The three humans died very quickly but very messily. Dynsman had erred slightly in his calculations, since the bearings also slammed into the bar stock itself.

Across the street, Dynsman dumped his equipment into a case, ran to the rear of the building, dropped the thread ladder down two levels, and quickly descended. When he hit the second level, he touched the disconnect button, and the ladder dropped down into his hands. That ladder also went into the case, and Dynsman faded into the shadows, headed for his own personal hideaway, deep inside one of Prime World's nonhumanoid conclaves.

Ears still ringing from the explosion, he did not hear the clatter of boots on the catwalk above as they ran toward the shattered ruin that had been the Covenanter.

Moments before the explosion, Sergeant Armus had been trying to soothe the injured feelings of the other member of his tac squad. The sector was so quiet and the duty so boring that it felt like a punishment tour. They were an elite, after all, a special unit that was supposed to be thrown into high-crime-potential areas to put the lid back on, and then turn the area over to normal patrols.

Instead, they had been on nothing duty for nearly a month. Sergeant Armus listened to his corporal run over the complaints for the fiftieth time. Tac Chief Kreuger must really have it in for them. Nothing was going on in the sector that one lone Black Maria couldn't deal with. Armus didn't tell the man that he had been making the same complaint nightly! He had to admit there was a great deal of justification for his squad's complaints. Kreuger must be out of his clotting mind, assigning them to a dead sector, especially with the festival going on. Maybe the crime stat computer hiccupped. Maybe Kreuger had a joygirl in the area who had complained about getting roughed up. Who could fathom what passed for the mind of a clotting captain?

In the interest of maintaining proper decorum, Armus kept all that to himself. Instead he ran the overtime bit past his squad members again – which was another thing that was odd. Because of the pressures of the festival, there were very few tac soldiers to spare, and the entire unit had been on overtime from almost the beginning. Now, how the clot was the chief going to explain that?

And then came the shock wave of the explosion. Almost before the sound stopped, the squad was thundering down the rampway and turning the corner – sprinting for the ruin that had been the Covenanter. Armus took one look at the shattered building and three thoughts flashed across his brain: fire, survivors, and ambulance. And, as he thought, he acted. Although no flames were visible in the ruins of the bar, he smashed an armored fist into an industrial extinguisher button and a ton or more of suds dumped into the building. He shouted orders to his men to grab any tool in sight, and thumbed his mike to call for an ambulance. Then he stopped as an ambulance lifted over the catwalk and hissed toward the bar. What was *that* doing here? He hadn`t even called yet! But he had no time to waste; he unhooked his belt prybar and plunged into the ruins after his men.

BOOK TWO

LUNETTE

Chapter Seven

Dear Sten:

Hiya, mate. Guess you're surprised to hear from the likes of me. Well, yours truly has finally landed some much-deserved soft duty. This is duty, I might add, befitting a clansman of such high rank. Sergeant Major Alex Kilgour! Hah, *Captain*! Bet you never thought you'd live to see the day!

Sten pulled back to give the letter a disbelieving glance. Kilgour! He didn't recognize him without the thick Scots accent. But then, of course even Alex wouldn't write with a burr. He laughed, and dove back into the letter.

Of course, a sergeant major still can't drink at the fancy officer clubs with an exalted captain, but an honest pint of bitter is an honest pint of bitter, and it drinks much smoother when it's never your shout. I've never seen such a brown-nosing clan of lowly noncoms as I've got here. Although I do not dissuade them of this practice. I'm sure that buying a pint for the sergeant major is a ceremony of ancient and holy tradition in these parts.

To be honest with you, this tour is beginning to wear thinner than a slice of haggis at a Campbell christening. The powers that be have posted me as curator of the clotting Mantis Museum. Now, as you well know, it requires a Q clearance to even see the lobby of this godforsaken place, so we don't get a lot of visitors. Just blooming security committee politicians getting their clotting expense tickets punched on the way to some gambling hell. Although there was one lass . . . Ah, never mind. A Kilgour doesn't kiss and tell, especially when the bonny one outranks him.

Anyhow, here I am, performing the safest duty in my wicked career as one of the Emperor's blackguards. I'm going out of my clotting mind, I tell you. And the only thing that keeps me sane is that you can't be doing much better in that fancy-dan job of yours on Prime World. No, I'm afeared it will never be the same since they broke up our team – Old Mantis 13. They better well retire the number, I tell you, or there'll be some explaining to do to a Kilgour.

Have you heard from the others? In case your news is wearier than mine, I'll fill you in on what I know. Bet has been promoted to lieutenant and is running her own team now, although I'm not too sure what nasty business she's about at the moment.

As for Doc, well, that little furry bundle of sharp edges managed himself a sabbatical leave. Do you recall the Stra!bo? You know, The People of the Lake? Those horrendous tall blokes who supped on blood and milk? Sure, I thought you would and wasn't Doc more than a giggle the way he got blotto on all that blood? So, what Doc is doing is getting drunk and staying that way all in the name of Mother Science.

The only one I haven't picked up any particulars on is Ida. When her hitch was over, she refused to reup and did a bloody Rom disappearing act. Although I imagine she must have gnashed her teeth over all that filthy lucre they were waving at her. One thing I have to say for her, though, she did come through on my share of the loot she was investing for us. It was a clotting big heap of money that took almost all of one leave for me to go through. If you haven't got yours yet, I suspect that it's probably winging its way to you. Truly, it's a nice bundle of credits. If by chance she's holding out on you, howsoever, check the futures market columns. Any big jump or dip in the exotics, and you'll find the plump little beggar.

Well, I've about run out of time to get this into the next post. Hope all is well with you, mate.

Yours, Aye.
Alex Kilgour

Sten chuckled to himself as he blanked out the letter. Same old Alex, grousing when the tour is too hot, and grousing when it's too soft. He did, however, have a point about Prime World. It looked soft, and felt soft – dangerously so. Sten had pored over the records his predecessors had left. For the last few centuries, they were almost depressing in their lack of action. However, the few times things did happen, he noticed, the situation tended to get very bloody and very potitical. After his years in Mantis Section, blood didn't bother Sten much. But potitics – politics could make your skin crawl.

Forgetting how small his quarters were, Sten leaned back in his chair, bumping his head against a wall. He groaned as the thump reminded him of the royal hangover he was suffering from. The only effect the Angelo stew had was to mask the alcohol and allow him to stay up even later with the Emperor. Somehow, he had stumbled through his job the next day, leaving him no other cure the following night than to try to drink the residual pain and agony away. Sten had sworn to himself last night that today he would be pristine pure. Not a drop of the evil Stregg would wet his tips. That was the only way out of it. The trouble was, just then, it wasn't Stregg he wanted, but a nice cold beer.

He scraped the thought out of his mind, drank a saintly gulp of water, and looked around his room. The homely-looking woman on the wall stared back at him. Sten gave another mental groan and searched for another place to rest his grating eyes – only to find the same woman giving him the same stare. In fact, wherever he looked, there she was again, the skinny-faced homely woman with the loving eyes.

The walls of the room were covered with her portrait, a legacy, Sten had learned, from the man who had proceeded him. Naik Rai, Sten's batman, had assured him that the previous CO had been an excellent Captain of the Guard. Maybe so, but he sure was a lousy painter – almost as lousy as his taste in women. At least, that's what Sten had thought at first, when he had stared at the murals crowding his walls. After the first week living with the lady, he had ordered her image removed – blasted off, if necessary. But then she began to haunt him, and he had countermanded the order – he wasn't sure why. And then it came to him: the man must have *really* loved the woman, no matter how homely.

The records proved it: the captain had been every bit as hardworking, dedicated, and professional as any being before him. Although older than Sten, he had been assured of a long and promising career. Instead, he had pulled every string possible to win a lateral transfer into a deadend job on some frontier post. And, just before he left, he had married the woman in the picture. The emperor had given the bride away. In his gut, Sten knew what had happened. In the few months he had been there, Sten had realized that his particular post was for a bachelor, or someone who cared very little about spouse and family. There just weren't enough hours in the day to do the job properly. And the good captain had realized that enough to throw it all away for the homely lady in the pictures.

Sten thought he had been a very wise man.

Once you got past the murals, the rest of Sten's room dissolved into a bachelor officer's dilemma: a jungle of items both personal and work-related. It wasn't that Sten didn't know where everything was; his was a carefully ordered mind that heaped things into their proper mounds. The trouble was, mounds kept sliding into one another, a bit like his current interests. His professional studies, for example, blended into a gnawing hunger for history – anyone's history, it didn't matter. And, along with that, the obvious technical tracts a fortieth-century military being might need, as well as Sten's Vulcan-born tech-related curiosity. Also, since leaving Vulcan, he had become an avid reader of almost everything in general.

Two particular things in the room illustrated the personal and professional crush. Filling up one corner was a many-layered map of the castle, the surrounding buildings, and the castle grounds. Each hinged section was at least two meters high, and showed a two-dimensional view of every alley and cranny and drawing room of the entire structure. Sten had traced the sectional map down in a dusty archive after his first month on the job, when he realized that the sheer size of the castle and its grounds made it impossible for him to ever see it all on foot. And without personal, detailed knowledge of every Imperial centimeter of the area, he would not be able to perform his primary function – which was to keep the Emperor safe.

Crammed a few meters away from the map was the other major feature in Sten's current life. Sitting on a fold-up field table was a very expensive mini-holoprocessor. It was the biggest expense in Sten's life, not even counting the thousands of hours of time invested in the tiny box lying next to it.

The little box contained Sten's hobby – model building: not ordinary glue-gun models set into paste-metal dioramas but complete, working and living holographic displays ranging from simple ancient engines to tiny factories manned by their workers. Each was contained on a tiny card, jammed with complex computer equations.

Sten was then building a replica of a logging mill. He had imprinted, byte by byte, everything that theoretically made the mill work, including the workers, their job functions, their tools, and the spare parts. Also programmed were other details, such as the wear-factor on a belt drive, the drunken behavior of the head mechanic, etc. When the card slid into the holoprocessor it projected a full-color holographic display of the mill at work. Occasionally, if Sten didn't have his *voilà* moves down, a worker would stumble, or a log would jam, and the whole edifice would tumble apart into a blaze of colored dots.

Sten glanced at the model box guiltily. He hadn't worked on it more than a few hours since he started the job. And, no, there wasn't time now – he had to get to work.

He palmed the video display and the news menu crawled across the screen. TERRORIST DIES IN SPACEPORT BAR EXPLOSION.

Sten thumbed up the story and quickly scanned the details of the Covenanter tragedy. There wasn't much to it at the moment, except for the fact that Godfrey Alain, a high-ranking Fringe World revolutionary, had died in an accident at some seedy bar near the spaceport. It was believed that a few others had also died, but their names had not yet been released. Mostly the article talked about what was *not* known – like what Alain was doing on Prime World, especially in a bar like the Covenanter.

Sten yawned at the story. He had little or no interest in the fate of terrorists. In fact, he had marked PAID to many terrorist careers in his time. Clot Godfrey Alain, as far as he was concerned. He noticed, however, that there were as yet no official statements on Alain's presence.

The only thing he was sure of was that the press had it wrong about the explosion being an 'accident.' Terrorists do not die accidentally. Sten idly wondered if someone in Mantis Section had sent Alain on to meet his revolutionary maker.

Sten yawned again and began to scroll on just as he got the call. The Eternal Emperor wanted him. Immediately, if not sooner.

Chapter Eight

The Eternal Emperor was an entirely different person from the man Sten had drunk with. He looked many years older, the flesh on his face was sagging, and pouches had appeared beneath his eyes. His complexion was gray underneath the perfect tan. More importantly, the man Sten was observing was stern and grim, with hatred burning just beneath the surface. Sten stirred uneasily in his seat, goose-bumps on the back of his neck. Something was frightening there, and although Sten hadn't the faintest idea what was going on, he hoped to hell it didn't involve a transgression on his part. Sten would not have liked to be the being the Emperor was fixing his attention on at the moment.

'You've read this,' the Emperor said coldly, sliding a printout across his desk.

Sten glanced at the fax. It was an update on the death of Godfrey Alain. Puzzled, Sten scanned it, noting that although there were a few more details, they involved mostly color, with few hard facts. 'Yes, sir,' he said after a moment.

'Are you familiar with this man's background?'

'Not really, sir. Just that he's a terrorist and that he's been a thorn in our side for some time.'

The Emperor snorted. 'You'll need to know a lot more than that. But no matter. I've given you clearance for his files. You can go over them after we've talked.

'I want the people responsible,' the Emperor snapped. 'And I want every single swinging Richard of them standing before me, not tomorrow or the next day, but yesterday. And I want them delivered in a nice neat package. And no loose ends. Do you understand me, Captain? No loose ends.'

Sten started to nod automatically. Then he stopped himself – no, he didn't understand. And his survival instinct told him he'd better not pretend otherwise. 'Excuse me, sir,' he finally said, 'but I do *not* understand. Perhaps I'm missing something, but what does Godfrey Alain have to do with the captain of your guard?'

The Emperor's face clotted with anger, and he started to rise to his feet. Then he stopped, took a deep breath, and sat down again, the anger barely under control. 'You're right, Captain. I'm getting ahead of myself.' He took another deep breath. 'Fine, then. Let me explain.

'This . . . accident has put all of us in a world of hurt. And if you do believe that it was an accident, then tell me now, because I obviously have the wrong man for the job.'

Sten shook his head. 'No, sir. I don't think it was an accident.'

'Good. Now let me fill you in on the background. And I'm sure I don't have to warn you that not one word I say is to be repeated.

'To begin with, Alain was here to see me.'

Sten was surprised. The Eternal Emperor meeting with a terrorist? That was absolutely against Imperial policy. But then Sten remembered who *set* Imperial policy, and kept his mouth shut.

'He had a proposal – and I'm sure it was a serious one, or I wouldn't have hung myself out like this – to defuse our problems with the Tahn System. Simply put, he wanted to set up a buffer zone, his Fringe Worlds – under my aegis – between the Tahn and the Empire.'

'But wouldn't that make him a traitor to his own people?'

The Eternal Emperor gave Sten a grim smile. 'One man's traitor is another man's patriot. The way I see it is that it finally got through the thick heads of Alain and his people that they are the ones doing all the bleeding.

'Every time the Tahn act and we retaliate, they're the ones who get it in the neck. And they are also the ones who take all the blame and get nothing in return.'

'And so he set up a secret meeting with you?' Sten said, filling in the gaps. 'The Tahn found out and short-stopped him.'

'Not quite that simple. Yes, he was going to meet with me. Eventually. But first off, there was to be an initial meeting with one of my best diplomatic operatives. A man named Craigwel.'

'One of the unidentified bodies in the bar?' Sten guessed.

'Exactly. And he's going to stay unidentified. Officially, that is.'

'Any other victims in the bar I should know about?'

There was a long hesitation. And then the emperor shook his head, firmly, no.

'Just worry about Craigwel and Alain. Now, it was supposed to work like this. After exchanging the usual password, Alain and Craigwel were supposed to request Booth C. It had already been reserved for them and secured.

'Alain was then going to lay out his plan, and if he convinced Craigwel of his sincerity, we would have gone to the next step. A personal meeting with me.'

'But then the Tahn stepped in,' Sten said.

'Maybe. But don't be too sure of that. There are about five sides too many in this thing, each one of them with a reason to prevent any negotiations.

'Perhaps it was the Tahn. Perhaps it was someone from our camp. And who knows – perhaps it was one of Alain's own people. Regardless. That's what I want you to find out.'

'But why me, sir? it sounds like a job for a cop. And that I'm not. Clot, I wouldn't even know—'

'No, Captain. This is *not* a job for the police. It's much too delicate a situation. The police *are* investigating. And officially, they will round up a few suspects and those people will be publicly punished.'

He leaned closer to Sten to emphasize his next point. 'And those people will be scapegoats. I don't even care how guilty they are. Just as long as we have somebody to feed the public lions. Because there is a good chance that what you find out will remain classified for the next hundred years.'

He fixed Sten with a cold stare.

'Do I make myself absolutely clear, Captain?'

'Yes, sir.' Sten came to his feet. 'If that will be all, sir.' He snapped a salute.

'Yes, Captain. That's all. For now.'

Sten wheeled and was out the door.

Chapter Nine

'Drink up, cheenas,' Dynsman shouted. 'It's all on me today.' He pounded on the table for the bartender's attention and made motions for six more brimming schooners of narcobeer with synthalk backs. His companions hissed their approval. Dynsman watched in fascination as Usige, his best pal in the group, grabbed a liter jug, unhinged his jaws, and poured down the whole thing without a gasp or even breathing hard. 'That's it Usige, old buddy. Drink 'em down and make room for another.'

Of course, downing a liter of narcobeer at a gulp was not a great accomplishment for Usige or the others. Their scaled abdomens could swell to almost any proportions, and the only visible signs of inebriation the Psaurus ever displayed was to turn a slightly darker shade of purple.

'I tell you, cheenas, today begins a whole new life for yours truly. I hit it lucky for a change. And I'm gonna keep hittin' that way. I can feel it in my bones.'

Usige's grin framed serrated rows of needle-sharp teeth. 'I don't want to pry, Dynsman dearest,' he hissed, 'but you've been flashing a wad of credits around that would even choke one of us.' He waved at his yellow-eyed companions. 'Your obvious good fortune delights us all. But . . .'

'You wanna know if I can put you in on it,' Dynsman broke in.

'That would be lovely, old fellow. Business, as you no doubt know, has been a touch slow.'

'Sorry, pal. This was a one-time number. The kind we all dream of. I pick up the rest of my pay in a couple of hours, and then it's party time for the rest of my life.'

Usige tried to hide his disappointment, not an easy task; the skin of a Psaurus glows when the creature is disturbed. Dynsman noticed the change and leaned over to pat his friend's claw.

'Don't clottin' worry. Dynsman never forgets his cheenas. Fact, I might make a business of it, now that I'm comin' into all these credits.

'What the clot, you boys come up with somethin' tasty, need a little financing, you can always hit me up. Low interest rates, and maybe a small cut of the action if the deal's really sweet.'

Usige's color returned to normal. There was an idea that appealed to him. Rates for the criminal element in Prime World tended to be not only enormous but also more than painful if payment was delayed.

'That is certainly worth considering, friend. We can discuss it later. Now, meanwhile . . .' Usige rose to his full two-and-a-half-meter height and snaked out his foot-long orange tongue as a signal to the others to follow.

'Unlike you, we still have to pay the rent.'

'Anything nice?'

'Not really. Just a little warehouse B&E.'

Dynsman sighed his understanding and watched his friends slither out of the bar, their long tails scraping the floor after them. He checked the time: still a little more than two hours before his meeting. He had been hoping that Usige would keep him company, because he hated waiting alone. He was itching with impatience, and although he didn't realize it yet, a tiny warning bell was still tinkling at the back of his mind.

He ordered up another drink, dumped a credit coin in the newsvid, and began scanning the sports menu. He stifled a yawn as he picked through the sparse offerings. Not much happening so soon after Empire Day – especially if you wanted to get a bet down. Bored, he flipped over to the general news section. Dynsman had less than no interest in anything involving the straight workings of Prime World. But what the clot, maybe something juicy was going on in his profession. He scanned the menu, looking for anything involving crime.

He didn't have to scan far. The Covenanter bombing headline jumped out at him like a holovid. Clot! Clot! Clot! His target had been clotting political! Dynsman automatically gulped down his shot of synthalk and then almost equally as automatically found himself gagging on his own bile. He fought to keep it back.

Steady, man, steady. Gotta clotting think. Gotta clotting— And the first thing he realized was that he was as good as a dead man. No credits would be waiting for him when he met with his contact. Although the payment, he was certain, would be quite final.

He ran over the possibilities. Obviously, he would have to be satisfied with the roll in his pocket. Would it be enough to pay for a hideout? How long would it take before pursuers forgot about him? Dynsman groaned; he knew the answer. It had been set up just as skillfully as Godfrey Alain. There would be no forgetting.

There was only one solution, and the thought frightened him almost as much as the cold-faced man he knew would soon be tracking him. Dynsman had to get off Prime World.

Chapter Ten

Lieutenant Lisa Haines, Homicide Division, wanted to kill someone. At that particular moment, she wasn't particular who it would be, but she wanted the method to be interesting, preferably one that involved parboiling.

And *evisceration*, she added, as the combat car with the Imperial color-slash on it grounded on the crosswalk.

The man who climbed out wasn't the pompous beribboned bureaucrat she'd expected when her superiors advised that an Imperial liaison officer would be assigned to the case. The man who came toward her was young and slender, and wore only the plain brown livery of the Imperial Household. He appeared to be unarmed.

Sten, on the other hand, was nursing his own attitude. He barely noticed that the woman was about his own age and under different circumstances could have been described as attractive. Sten was flat irked. He still had no idea why the Emperor had picked him for the assignment, since he knew less than nothing about police procedures and murder investigations. He'd spent more of his career on the other side.

From his earliest days Sten had hated cops – the sociopatrolmen on his home world of Vulcan through the various types he'd encountered in Mantis to the military policemen who attempted to keep control on the Intoxication and Intercourse worlds.

'Captain, uh, Sten?'

Two could do that. 'Uh, Lieutenant . . . what was your last name again?'

'Haines.'

'Haines.'

'I assume you'd like to see the report,' Lisa said, and, without waiting for an answer, shoved the plate-projector at him.

Sten tried to pretend that he knew what the various forms and scrawled entries meant, then gave up. 'I'd appreciate a briefing.'

'No doubt.'

2043 Tacunit 7-Y reported an explosion, arrived at scene at 2047, Tacunit commander reported ratcheta-ratcheta, response ratcheta ratcheta, ambulance, no suspects, description, blur.

Sten looked at where the Covenanter had been. The entire baseplate the bar had stood on was enclosed in what appeared to be an enormous airbag. On one side, next to the catwalk, was an airlock.

'Step one,' Haines explained, 'in any homicide is to seal the scene. We put that bubble around the area, pump all oxygen out, and replace the atmosphere with a neutral gas, if you're interested in details.'

'I am interested in details, Lieutenant.' Sten began once more with the report. On second reading, it was no more (or less) confusing than any military afteraction report. Sten reread it a third time.

'Would you like a guided tour, Captain? It's messy, by the way.'

'If I start to get sick, I'll let you know.'

The bubble suits looked a little like close-fitting shallow-water diving dress, except that the lower chest area had a large, external evidence bag and the upper chest area bulged, making the wearer look somewhat like a pouter pigeon. Inside the bulge was a small alloy table where an investigator could put notes, records, etcetera. The suit also had a backpack with air supply and battery plate.

Sten thumbed his suit closed and followed Haines through the airlock into the ruins of the Covenanter. Of course it wasn't the first time Sten had examined a bomb site, but it was the first time he wasn't busy running away from it or expecting another one momentarily. He'd learned, years ago, not to consider that gray, pink, or yellow dangling ropes, snail-like particles, and bas-relief facial bones had once been human. Sten oriented himself. There . . . there was the door. That low parapet would have been the bar. Along . . . there . . . would have been the booths.

Two other cops were inside the bubble, laboriously scraping firefoam from the floor and walls.

'You're right,' Sten said conciliatorily. 'A mess.'

'Two of them,' Haines said bitterly.

'Ah?'

'Captain, I'll—' Haines caught herself, shut off her radio, clicked Sten's off, and touched faceplates. 'This is for your information only.

This crime scene is so mucked up that we'll be very lucky if we ever get anything on the case.'

'You know, Lieutenant,' Sten said thoughtfully, 'if you'd said that with an open mike I'd have figured you were setting up an alibi. So GA. I'm not sure I track you.'

Haines thought that maybe the liaison type wouldn't be quite the pain in the sitter she'd expected. 'SOP, Captain, is very explicit. Whatever officer comes on a homicide scene, he is to first take appropriate action – looking for the killer, requesting med, whatever.

'Second, is to notify homicide. At that point, we take charge.

'But that isn't what happened.' She waved her arm helplessly.

'That tac unit responded just before 2100 last night. Homicide was not notified for ten hours!'

'Why not?'

'Hell if I know,' Lisa said. 'But I could guess.'

'GA.'

'Our tactical squads think they're the best. The Imperial Guards. I guess, since they were first on the scene they wanted it to be their case.'

Sten thought back through the report. 'Is tac presence normal in this area?'

'Not especially. Not unless there's some kind of disorder, or maybe for security on some classified shipment. Or if the area's high-crime.'

'And?'

'The tac sergeant said his squad had been pounding these catwalks for three weeks, and nothing had happened.'

Odd. Sten wondered: since the last two weeks had been the pandemonium before Empire Day, it did seem as if the tac unit was misassigned. However, in Sten's experience cops had always found a way to stay away from where they could get hurt. But the tac squad's assignment could be something to ask about.

'Look at this,' Haines continued. 'No fire, but the tac sergeant opened up the extinguishers. He and his people went in. Three bodies. Dead dead. And so he and his people spend the next ten hours galumphing around trying to play detective. For instance . . .'

Lisa pointed down at the flooring. 'That size-fourteen hoof is not a clue – it's some tac corporal's brogan right in the middle of that bloodstain.'

Sten decided that he still didn't like cops that much and cut her off. 'Okay, Lieutenant. We've all got problems. What do you have so far?'

Haines started a court singsong: 'We have evidence of a bomb, prior planted. No clue as to detonation method, or explosive. The bomb specialists have not arrived as yet.'

'You can hold on them,' Sten said dryly. 'Maybe I know a little about that.'

He'd already spotted the blast striations on what remained of the ceiling. Sten lifted an alloy ladder over to the center of the striations. Sten may have been ignorant of police SOP, but he knew a great deal about things that went *boom*.

'Lieutenant,' Sten said, turning his radio back on, 'you want to put a recorder on?'

Haines shrugged – now the Imperial hand-sitter was going to play expert, so let him make an ass of himself. She followed orders.

'The bomb was mounted in the ceiling light fixture. We've got . . . looks like some bits of circuitry here . . . the explosive was high-grade, and shaped. The blast went out to the sides, very little damage done to the overhead.

'Your bomb people should be able to figure out whether the bomb was set off on a timer or command-det. But I'd guess it was set off by command.'

'We have a team checking the area.'

Sten got down off the ladder and reexamined the striations. They occupied almost a full 360 degrees. But not quite. Sten hummed to himself and ran an eyeball azimuth from that area toward the wall.

'Thank you, Lieutenant.' Sten went toward the airlock and exited. Outside, he stripped off his suit and walked well away from the bustling techs around the bubble.

Haines removed her suit and joined him. 'Are you through playing detective, Captain?'

'I'll explain Lieutenant Haines. I got stuck with this drakh job and I don't know what the hell I'm doing. That sends me into orbit, Lieutenant. Now what lit your stupid fuse?'

Haines glowered at him. 'Item: I'm in the same mess you're in. I'm a cop. A very good cop. So I come down here and see what I've got to work with.

'And *then* I get some – some—'

'Clot?' Sten offered, half smiling. He was starting to like the woman.

'Thank you. Clot, who comes down here, says one thing, and then is going to go back to the palace and get his medal. Let me tell you, Captain, I do not need any of this!'

'You through?'

'For the moment.'

'Fine. Let's get some lunch, then, and I'll bring you up to speed.'

The restaurant sat very close to Landing Area 17AFO. Except for clear blast shields between the field and the patio area, it was open-air. The place was about half-full of longshoremen, docking clerks, and ship crew. The combination of one man in Imperial livery and one woman who was obviously the heat guaranteed Sten and Haines privacy.

Dining was cafeteria-style. The two took plates of food, paid, and went to the far edge of the dining area. Both of them saw the other reflexively checking for parabolic mike locations, and, for the first time, smiled.

'Before you get started, Captain,' Haines said through a mouthful of kimchi and pork, 'do you want to talk about that booth?'

Sten chewed, nodded, and pretended innocence.

'Thank you. I'd already spotted that the bomb was directional. Actually, semidirectional. It was intended to garbage the whole joint – except for one booth.'

'Good call, Lieutenant.'

'First question – the one booth that wasn't destroyed was rigged with every antibugging device I've ever heard of. Is there any explanation, from let us say "top-level" sources? What was a security setup like that doing in a sleazo bar?'

Sten told her, omitting only Craigwel's identity and position as the Emperor's personal troubleshooter. He also didn't feel that the lieutenant needed to know that Alain was planning a meeting with the Emperor himself. Any meeting with any Imperial official was enough for her to work on, he felt. Sten finished, and changed the subject, eyeing a forkful of kimchi cautiously. 'By the way – what is this, anyway?'

'Very dead Earth cabbage, garlic, and herbs. It helps if you don't smell it before you eat it.'

'Since you know about bombs,' Sten asked, 'did you figure out why no shrapnel?'

Haines puzzled.

Sten dug into his pocket and set a somewhat flattened ball bearing on the table. 'The bomb's explosive was semidirectional. To make sure the bomb took care of anyone in the bar, the bomber also taped these on top of the explosive. Except the area facing that booth.

'Prog, Lieutenant?'

Haines knew enough military slang to understand the question.

She pushed her plate aside, put her fingers together, and began theorizing.

'The bomber wanted everybody in that bar dead – except whoever was in that booth.'

'If Alain and your man *had* been in that booth when the bomb went off, they would have been . . . concussed, possibly, or suffering blast breakage at the worst, right, Captain?'

'Correct.'

'The bomber knew about that booth . . . and had to have known Alain would be in that booth on that particular night.'

Haines whistled tunelessly and drained her beer. 'So for sure we have a political murder, don't we, Captain? Clot!'

Sten nodded glumly, went to the counter, and brought back two more beers.

'Not just a political murder, but one done by someone who knew exactly what Alain's movements were supposed to be, correct?'

'You're right – but you aren't exactly making my day.

'Drakh!' Lisa swore. 'Clottin' stinkin' politics! Why couldn't I get stuck with a nice series of mass sex murders.'

Sten wasn't listening. He'd just taken the reasoning one step further. Impolitely, he grabbed the plate-projector from under Haines' arm and began flipping through it.

'Assassination,' Lisa continued, getting more depressed by the minute. 'That'll mean a pro killer, and whoever hired it done will be untouchable. And I'll be running a precinct at one of the poles.'

'Maybe not,' Sten said. 'Look. Remember the bomb? It was just supposed to knock Alain cross-eyed, yes? Then what was supposed to happen?'

'Who can tell? It never did.'

'Question, Lieutenant. Why did an ambulance *not* called by this tac sergeant show up within minutes of the blast? Don't you think that maybe—'

Haines had already completed the thought. Beer unfinished, she was heading for Sten's combat car.

Chapter Eleven

Port Soward Hospital bore a strange resemblance to its oddly shaped cnidarian receiving clerk. It just grew from an emergency hospital intended to handle incoming ship disasters, industrial accidents, and whatever other catastrophe would come up within a ten-kilometer circle around Soward itself. But disasters and accidents have a way of growing wildly, so Soward Hospital sprawled a lot, adding ship-capable landing platforms here, radiation wards there, and nonhuman sections in still a third place.

All of that made Admissions even more a nightmare than in most hospitals. In spite of high-speed computers, personal ID cards, and other improvements, the hospital's central area went far toward defining chaos.

Sten and Haines waited beside a large central 'desk,' the outer ring of which was for files and such. The second ring contained a computer whose memory circuits rivaled an Imperial military computer. In the center swam the clerk(s), a colony of intelligent polyps-cnidarians, beings which began life as individuals and then, for protection, grew together – literally, like coral. But most cnidarians did not get along. The one in front of Sten – he mentally labeled it A – burbled in fury, snatched a moisture-resistant file from Polyp B, tossed it across the ring to Polyp R, Sten estimated, brushed Polyp C's tentacles off A's own terminal, and finally turned to the two people waiting. Its 'voice' was just shrill enough to add to the surrounding madness as white-clad hospital types steered lift gurneys past, patients leaned, lay, or stood against the walls, and relatives wailed or wept.

'You see what it's like? You see?' The polyp's feeder tentacles were bicycling wildly against the bottom of the tank.

'Police,' Lisa said dryly, holding out a card with one hand. She touched the card with an index finger, and the 'badge' glowed briefly.

'Another cop. This has been one of those days. Some wiper comes in, bleeding like – like a stuck human. Drunk, of course. He doesn't tell me that he's union, and so I send him to the Tombs. How was I know to he was union? Job-related and all that, and now I've got all this data. He'll probably die before I get the paper work through. Now what do *you* want?'

'Last night, around 2100 hours, an ambulance responded to a call.'

'We have thousands of ambulances. For what?'

'An explosion.'

'There are many kinds of explosions. Ship, atomsuit, housing, radiation. I *can't* help you if you don't help me!'

Haines gave the polyp the file. The being submerged briefly, only the plate-projector, held in one tentacle, above the surface. Then another tentacle wove behind the being to a terminal and began tapping keys.

'Yes. Ambulance GE145 it was. No input on who summoned it. You see what my trouble is? No one seems to *care* about proper files.'

Sten broke in. 'Where would this ambulance have been routed to?'

'Thank you, man. At least someone knows the proper question. Since it was sent to a . . . drinking establishment . . . unless other data was input, it would have gone to the Tombs.'

'The Tombs?'

'Human emergency treatment, nonindustrial.' The polyp pulled a square of plas from the counter and touched the edges of it. An outline of the sprawling hospital sprang into life on it. Further tentacling and a single red line wound its way through the corridors.

'You are . . . here. You want to go *there*. They'll be able to help you. Maybe.'

Sten had one final question. 'Why is it called the Tombs?'

'Because this is where our – I believe the phrase is down and under – go. And if they weren't before, they are when they get to the Tombs.'

'GE145. Weird.' The desk intern was puzzled. 'No entry on who dispatched it – came from out-hospital. Three DOA's. They're . . . um, being held for autopsy results, Lieutenant.'

'Question, Doctor. Assuming this ambulance had arrived with live victims, what would have happened then?'

'Depends on the injury.'

'Blast. Shock. Possible fractures,' Sten said.

'Um . . . that would have gone to – let me check last night's roster . . . Dr. Knox would have treated them.'

'Where is he?'

'Let me see . . . not on shift today. Pity.'

'Would he be in the hospital?'

'No, not at all. Dr. Knox was hardly one of us. He was a volunteer.'

'Do you have a contact number on him?' Lisa asked.

'It should be right— No. No, we don't have anything on his sheet. That's unusual.'

'Two unusuals, Doctor. I'd like to see your files on this Knox.'

'I'm sorry, Lieutenant. But without a proper court order, not even the police—'

Sten's own card was out. 'On Imperial Service, Doctor.'

The intern's eyes widened. 'Certainly . . . perhaps, back in my office. We'll use the terminal there. Genevieve? Would you take the floor for me?'

Ten minutes later Sten knew they had something.

Or rather, by having nothing, they had something.

KNOX, DR. JOHN, began the hospital's scanty info card. No such doctor was licensed on Prime World, as Sten quickly learned. Yet somehow a 'Dr. Knox' had convinced someone at Soward Hospital – either a person or a computer – that he was legitimate. His listed home address was a recently demolished apartment building. His supposed private clinic was a restaurant, one which had been in existence at that address for almost ten years.

'So this Knox,' Sten mused, still staring at the fiche, 'shows up from nowhere as a volunteer two weeks ago.'

'He was an excellent emergency surgeon,' the intern said. 'I prepped some patients for him.'

'What did he look like?'

'Tall,' the intern said hesitantly. 'One eighty-five, one ninety centimeters. Slender build, almost endomorphic. Seventy kilograms estimated weight. Eyes . . . I don't remember. He was very proud of his hair. Gray it was. Natural, he swore. Wore it mane-style.'

'Not bad,' Haines said. 'You ever think of being a cop?'

'In this job I sometimes think I am one.'

'You said he was "hardly one of you." Did you mean just because he was a volunteer?' Sten asked.

'No. Uh – you see, we don't exactly get Imperial-class medicos here. The pay. The conditions. The patients. So when we get a volunteer as good as Dr. Knox, well . . .' And the intern interrupted himself: 'His room!'

'Knox had a room?'

'Of course. All of us do – our shifts are two-day marathons.'

'Where would it be?'

'I'll get a floor chart.'

'Very private sort, this Knox,' Lisa said. 'His room card specifies no mechanical or personal cleaning wanted. Maybe *we'll* get something.'

Sten suspected they would get nothing, and if they got as thorough a nothing as he feared . . .

'Four thirteen.'

Lisa took the passcard from the back of the room file.

'Hang on. And stay back from the door.'

Millimeter by millimeter, Sten checked the jamb around the slide-door's edges. He found it just above the floor – a barely visible gray hair stretched across the doorjamb.

'We need an evidence team,' Sten said. 'Your best. But there won't be a bomb inside. I want this room sealed until the evidence team goes through it.'

Lisa started to get angry, then snapped a salute.

'Yes, sir. Captain, sir. Anything else?'

'Aw drakh,' Sten swore. 'Sorry. Didn't mean to sound like, like—'

'A cop?'

'A cop.' Sten grinned.

The room was ballooned, then gently opened. Finally the tech team went in.

The three spindars – one adult and two adolescents – were not what Sten had thought expert forensic specialists would look like. As soon as the room was unsealed and the adult lumbered into the bedroom, the two adolescents rolled out of its pouch and began scurrying about with doll-size instruments and meters taken from the pack strapped to the adult's pouch.

The adult spindar was about two meters in any direction and scaled like a pangolin. It surveyed the scuttlings of its two offspring with what might have been mild approval, rebuttoned the instrument pack with a prehensile subarm, scratched its belly thoughtfully, and sat down on its rear legs in the center of the room. The being chuffed three times experimentally, then introduced itself as Technician Bernard Spilsbury. Spindars having names unpronounceable to any being without both primary and secondary voice boxes, they found human names a useful conceit – names selected from within whatever field the spindar worked in.

'Highly unusual,' it chuffed. 'Very highly unusual. Recollect only one case like that. My esteemed colleague Halperin handled that one. Most interesting. Would you be interested in hearing about it while my young protegés continue?'

Sten looked at Haines. She shrugged, and Sten got the idea that once a spindar started, nothing short of high explosives could shut him up.

'Out on one of the pioneer worlds it was. Disremember at the moment which one. Pair of miners it was. Got into some unseemly squabble about claims or stakegrubs or whatever miners bicker about.

'First miner waited until his mate got into a suit, then shot him in the face. Stuffed the corpus into the drive, suit and all.'

One young spindar held up a minidisplay to his parent. Columns of figures, unintelligible to Sten, reeled past.

The young one chittered, and the older one rumbled.

'Even more so,' the spindar said. 'If you'll excuse me?' His forearm dug larger instruments from the pack, then he waddled to the bed, half stood, and began running a pickup across it. 'Curiouser and curiouser.'

'Speaking of curious,' Haines said quietly to Sten. 'You wondered about that tac squad? I think I'll check on just *why* they were assigned to that area.

'I owe you a beer, Captain.'

They smiled at each other.

Before Sten could say anything, the spindar was back beside him. 'That took care of one sort of evidence, of course.'

'You found something?'

'No, no. I meant the miner. To continue, he then dumped the ship's atmosphere and disposed of all of his mate's belongings and went peaceably on his way.

'Questioned some months later, said miner maintained that he had shipped solo. Contrary to the ship's lading, no one had been with him. Claimed the other party had never showed at lift-off, and he himself had been too lazy to change the manifest. There was, indeed, no sign that anyone had ever been on the ship besides this individual.

'But Halperin produced evidence that it was physically impossible for one human to have consumed the amount of rations missing from the ship. The miner contradicted him. Swore that he was a hearty eater. Pity.'

Evidently that was the end of the spindar's story. By then, Sten knew better, but asked what happened anyway.

'The planetary patrols in the frontier worlds are some what pragmatic. Not to say ruthless. They purchased an equivalent amount of rations and sat the suspect down in front of them. Gave him thirty days to prove his innocence. Trial by glut, I suppose you would refer to it. A definite pity.'

Again the spindar dug out instruments and, attaching extensions to them, swept the ceiling area. 'The man died of overeating on the third day. Odd system of justice you humans have.

'This case,' the spindar continued, reseating himself, 'is even stranger. You do, just as you warned me, Lieutenant, appear to have a great quantity of nothing.'

For Sten, that was the first positive lead toward finding the disappeared Dr. Knox.

Chapter Twelve

'And what, Captain, does nothing give you?' the Eternal Emperor asked.

The Emperor might appear less angry, but Sten was determined to keep the briefing as short as possible. As long as he stuck to business, he probably couldn't get in much trouble.

'This Knox did not want the room cleaned. My theory is that he was afraid some personal evidence might still be in the room's automatic cleaning filters.

'We found no fingerprints. No traces of dead skin, no urine traces in the bed, no sweat or oil stains in the pillow. Also, there was no IR residue in the bed coverings.'

'Thank you, Captain. I will now assume you and the techs produced every sort of zero-trace science can look for. Explain.'

Sten did. Knox not only cleaned the room minutely, but also used sophisticated electronics to remove *all* traces of his occupancy.

'So. Your, uh, Knox character's more than just a professional doctor.'

'That's the assumption,' Sten said carefully. 'Haines – she's the police OIC on the case – is tracing doctors who might have learned another set of skills.'

'If your Knox is as good as you say, Captain, I'd assume he was an offworlder.'

'Haines is checking all Prime World arrivals within the last E-year, sir.'

'Good luck. Prediction, Captain: You're going to draw a big fat blank.'

'Probably. Which is why we're working angle B – the bomber.'

The Emperor shrugged. 'If you've got one pro, why couldn't the bomber be just as faceless?'

'Because the bomber' – Sten caught himself before he could say 'blew it,' – 'made a mistake.'

The Emperor considered. 'All right. Work that angle. Is there anything else?'

Sten shook his head – there was no point in mentioning the tac-squad's mysterious presence until Haines had more information.

'One more thing, Captain. For your information only. The Tahn Embassy's Principal Secretary has requested an interview with me. I think we may both assume what it will be regarding.

'And I really would like to be able to tell him more than "I got plenty of nothing."

'That's all, Captain. You may go.'

Chapter Thirteen

Sten fingered the pore-pattern key on his mailbox and absent-mindedly fished out its contents. It was the usual junk – *The Imperial Guard Times, Forces Journal*, the palace's daily house organ, the latest promotion list, an ad from a military jeweler – all of which went into the disposal. Sten tucked one fiche – reminder of his somewhat past-due bill from a uniform tailor – into his belt pouch and started to close the little door. Then he saw something else and fished it out curiously.

It was a real paper envelope, addressed by hand to 'Captain Sten, Imperial Household.' Sten fumbled the envelope open. Three other pieces of paper dropped into his hand. The first was a blank envelope. The second was a thick engraved paper card:

MARR & SENN
Request the Honor of
Your Attendance
At a Dinner Reception
for
KAI HAKONE

RSVP Guest

Perplexed, Sten stared at the invitation. Of course he knew Marr and Senn as the Imperial caterers and unofficial social arbiters at Court. The brief meetings he'd had with them had been purely official, even though he was personally intrigued by their bitchy humor and warmth. He wondered why they'd invite a lowly captain, regardless of position, to what must be a Major Social Event.

The third piece of paper, also hand-written, explained it. The card said simply, 'It's time for old friends to meet again,' and was signed Sofia.

Umm. Sten knew that the woman he'd had a brief but very passionate affair with during a previous assignment was on Prime World – he'd been responsible for getting Sofia off Nebta before the shooting started – but had semideliberately not looked her up, having no idea any longer what he felt toward her.

Sten decided he needed some advice. In the Imperial Household, unofficial advice for officers was the province of the Grand Chamberlain. His offices were only a few hundred meters from the Emperor's own business suite.

The Grand Chamberlain, Fleet Admiral Mik Ledoh (Ret.), looked like everyone's favorite grandsire. Sten, however, had looked up the admiral's record as part of his routine security check while settling into the job.

A hundred years before, Ledoh had been a fireball. Literally. During the Palafox rising, his tacship flight was ordered to provide cover for a small planetary landing. Unfortunately, intelligence had erred, and the planet was strongly defended by hardened orbital satellites.

Ledoh had supervised the conversion of the tacships into pilot-aimed nuclear missiles, and then led the strike himself. He and three other pilots managed to jettison their capsules successfully.

Then, over the next decades, he'd become the Imperial fleet's prime specialist in planetary assaults. Promotion came rapidly for a man who, basically, specialized in logistics. By the time of the Mueller Wars, Ledoh was a fleet admiral.

The Mueller Wars were one of the more confusing conflicts of the Empire, since the battles were fought near-simultaneously on dozens of different worlds. During the wars, Ledoh commanded the landings in the Crais System, and in a war noted for its bloodiness and ineptness, took the system with minimal losses – minimal, at least, compared to the fifty to seventy per cent casualties the war's other battles produced.

After peace was signed, Ledoh retired for some years, then emigrated to Prime World. When the previous Grand Chamberlain died in office following an unfortunate surfeit of smoked eels, Ledoh, with his combat record and, more important, logistical ability, was a natural for the job.

Sten could never figure out how Ledoh managed to juggle the various official and unofficial requirements of a household the size of a medium city and still maintain benevolence. Sten was very grateful that he had nothing more to worry about than keeping the Emperor alive, and the welfare of 150 Gurkhas.

Sten stepped inside Ledoh's office and paused.

Ledoh, Colonel Fohlee, CO of the Praetorians, and Arbogast, the Imperial Household's paymaster, were staring at a wallscreen readout.

'Colonel,' Arbogast said, 'I am not attempting to involve myself in militaria. All I am doing is trying to clear this inquiry from Himself regarding the, and I quote, inordinately high desertion rate in your unit.'

'What does the Emperor expect to happen when you dump a lot of young soldiers into the middle of Prime? Any virgin can be seduced.'

'Another area which isn't my expertise,' Arbogast said. He and Fohlee quite clearly hated each other. Ledoh attempted mediation.

'There were four desertions this month alone, Colonel. Perhaps you should examine the selection method for your Praetorians.'

Fohlee turned on Ledoh. 'Does not compute, Admiral. Candidates for the Praetorians are personally vetted by myself or my adjutant.'

Arbogast came in before Ledoh could respond. 'No one is trying to assign blame, Colonel. But your records indicate that almost forty men from your unit have disappeared in the last E-year alone. And none of these deserters has turned himself in or been arrested. The Emperor feels that something is wrong.'

'I'm aware of that,' Fohlee said. 'My staff is devoting full attention to the problem.'

'Perhaps,' Ledoh said, 'we're putting too much demand on the young soldiers.'

'Perhaps,' Fohlee said reluctantly. 'I'll look into it myself.'

'Thank you, Colonel. I'll report to the emperor that you have taken over full personal responsibility.' Arbogast gathered his file, nodded to Ledoh and Sten, and disappeared back toward the rabbit-warren filing system.

'Clotting clerks,' Fohlee snarled, then turned and saw Sten. 'Captain.'

'Colonel Fohlee.'

'I've been trying to contact you for most of today.'

'Sorry, Colonel,' Sten said. 'I was under special orders.'

Fohlee snorted. 'No doubt. I've been observing your troops, Captain. And, while I never believe in telling another commander his business, it appears to me that some of your soldiers are less than adequately concerned about their appearance.'

'Gurkhas are pretty lousy at spit and polish,' Sten agreed.

'It's been my experience, having commanded soldiers from every race, that none of them cannot be taught proper military appearance.'

Even though Fohlee was nowhere near Sten's chain of command, there was little benefit in getting into a slanging match with a superior officer.

'Thank you for bringing the matter to my attention,' Sten said formally. 'I'll check into it.'

Fohlee nodded a very military nod. Once up, once down. He collected his file, came to attention, saluted Ledoh, and brushed past Sten.

Ledoh waited until the colonel's metal-tapped boot-heels resounded down the corridor, then smiled. 'Offload, young Sten. What's the prog?'

Sten was still staring out the door.

'Don't fret the colonel, boy. He's just grinding his molars.'

'I see. But what the hell do I have to do with why his toy soldiers are disappearing?'

'Jealousy.'

'Huh?'

'Colonel Fohlee is deeply disturbed that – by Fohlee's thinking at least – the Eternal Emperor puts so little faith in his Praetorians, and chooses the Gurkhas for immediate security.'

Sten blinked. 'That – no offense, sir – is damned silly.'

'The smallness of the military mind in peacetime, young Sten, should never be overrated. At any rate. Your problem, now.'

'It's, well, unofficial. And personal.'

'Oh-hoh.' Ledoh touched a key on his desk and the door behind Sten slid shut and the CONFERENCE light on the exterior went on. 'Timecheck?'

Sten looked at his watch finger. 'Seventeen forty-five.'

Ledoh sighed contentedly and fished a flask out of his desk. Two pewter cups went beside it, and Ledoh gestured with the bottle. 'Join me in a libation of this substance our Eternal Distiller refers to as Scotch.'

'Uh, I'm not sure if I'm off duty.'

'As my prerogative as Household Chamberlain, you are officially off duty.'

Sten grinned as Ledoh filled the cups.

'I have no idea,' Ledoh said plaintively, 'why His Highness insists on gifting me with this vile swill.'

The two men drank.

'GA, young man.'

Sten passed Ledoh the invitation.

Ledoh's eyebrows slithered slightly in amazement. 'Great Empire, but you rate, young man. I wasn't invited to this bash.'

Sten handed the personal note across.

'Ah. Now I see. Who is this Sofia?'

'A, uh, young woman I am – was – friendly with.'

'Suddenly it all becomes very clear. Pour yourself another, son.'

Sten followed orders.

'Firstly, this event is, as the vid-chatter says, the primo social event of the season.'

Sten didn't want to seem ignorant, but – 'Who is this Hakone?'

'*Tsk*. Young officers should read more. He is an author. Very controversial and all that. Writes about, generally, the military, from, shall we say, a somewhat unique point of view.

'Were the Eternal Emperor not who he is, in fact, Hakone's writing might be termed borderline treason.'

'That settles that, then.'

'Negative, young man. The Emperor encourages dissent – short of anyone's actually putting it into practice. And as you may have discovered after Empire Day, he likes his officers to think freely.'

'So I should go?'

'You should go. Excellent visibility for career and all that. However, there remains one problem. This young lady . . . Sofia.'

'Yeah,' Sten agreed.

'Without prying, young Sten, what are your current feelings toward the lady?'

'I'm not sure.'

'Then there *is* a problem – besides the fact that both our glasses are empty. Thank you.

'Marr and Senn believe in keeping, shall we say, a lively household. By this I mean that they have in residence some of the most marriageable beings in the Empire.'

'Oops,' Sten said, almost spilling his Scotch.

'Exactly. If this Sofia is able to invite you to the fete, she must be one of Marr and Senn's Eligibles.'

Sten couldn't believe it. 'Me?'

'Of course, Captain. You could be considered very desirable. I assume this Sofia comes from some off-planet nobility or other, and probably has wealth. For her, marrying someone who has the appropriate hero awards, someone who is part of the Imperial Household, and, most important, someone who has been selected at a very young age for a fairly important command, might, shall we say, signify?'

'I'm not going!'

'Do not be so absolutist, Sten. Consider the invitation. It says "Guest," does it not? The answer to your problem is simple. Contact an incredibly lovely young lady of your acquaintance and take her. That should defuse the Sofia situation handily.'

Sten poured his drink down and shook his head sadly.

'Admiral, all I've done since I've been on Prime is my job. I don't know any young ladies – let alone any incredibly lovely ones.'

'Ah well. Perhaps the Emperor will be willing to give the bride away, then.'

Sten blanched.

Chapter Fourteen

The tower was a shudder of light at the end of a long, narrow valley. A gravcar flared over the mountains, spearing the valley with its landing lights – hesitating as the autopilot oriented itself, and then *whoosh*ed toward the tower along the broad avenue that was the valley. Moments later, other gravcars followed its route, hovering momentarily then bursting for the tower in a rush.

Marr and Senn had invested half their credits and most of their ultra-artistic souls in the tower. It needled up from a broad base to a slender penthouse perch. The tower was constructed of every imaginable mineral, metal, or crystal that responded pleasingly to light. For *their* living quarters, Senn and Marr had had no interest in conventional building materials. Nor were the materials uniform in shape or size – a vaguely oval lump might be placed next to a perfect square. Light in all its forms was all that counted. Red light fired by emotional changes; blue from the musk of wild valley animals; and all the other primary colors from the constantly changing humidity and temperature of the valley itself. Some lights flickered from hue to hue in constantly shifting moods; others stayed one color for hours on end – the bass notes in the color orchestra.

Marr and Senn thought of the tower as a simple place, a place they called home. And that night it glowed more frantically than most others as the guests arrived. Because that night they were having a special party.

Sten's throat was suddenly filled with abrasive phlegm. Cough as he would, he couldn't clear it, it just seemed to clog his throat more. What's more, his ears burned and his toes and fingers felt frostbitten and his tongue plas-coated. He was trying to figure out what to do with the gorgeous woman pressed up against him. His arms waggled on either side of her body, trying to make up their minds whether to paddle in or paddle out. It didn't help that the woman's musk was designed – well designed – to incite lust in any male dead less than ninety-six hours. Finally, he put his hands on the woman's slender hips, hugged them slightly for politeness' sake, and then pushed her away. 'Uh . . . nice to see you, too, Sofia.'

Sofia stepped back and took him in with melting eyes. She was looking at him with, well, approval, Sten thought, wishing a guy could wear something resembling underwear beneath the skin-tight formal uniform of a Gurkha officer.

She crammed herself against him again in another full-body melt and whispered in his ear. 'It's been so long, Sten, love . . . I could . . . I could— You know . . .'

Yeah, Sten *did* know. He could remember quite well, thank you, and all of his memories were pleasant. The trouble was, he almost hadn't recognized Sofia when she appeared before him. Not that she was unpleasant to look at; far from it. But he had fixed in his mind a portrait of the straightforward woman of nineteen or twenty, with a dark short-cropped halo of hair and eyes that questioned and judged things as they were. Instead, he was staring at a surgically perfect curve of a woman, with a glittering tumble of hair that reached just below her buttocks. It was also her only covering. Sofia was fashionably naked, her skin pricked here and there with highlights of color. Still, it was Sofia, after a fashion, a Sofia with hungry, knowing eyes.

Sten was sorrier than hell that he had ever had her introduced at Court. 'You . . . look great, Sofia,' he said, trying again to edge her gently away. It wasn't that he didn't like having a naked woman in his arms, he just liked it better without everyone watching him.

'We have so much to catch up on,' Sofia draped an arm in his. 'Let's go someplace private and talk.'

Sten felt himself being led away like an obedient little dog.

'Here's our drinks, Sten,' came the welcome voice from behind him. 'You can't believe the cute little roboserver they . . . oh . . . uh . . . Sten?'

And Sten turned with great relief. Police Lieutenant Lisa Haines was standing with two drinks in her hands and a puzzled-going-to-hurt look on her face.

With the numb but still nimble fingers of a born survivor, Sten jumped for the rope she was dangling out. 'Lisa,' he said, his voice a little high, 'you're just in time to meet an old friend of mine, Sofia Parral.'

Sofia stared coldly at the woman. 'Oh,' she said, her voice steel-edged.

'Sofia, I'd like you to meet Lieutenant Haines. She's uh . . . I mean, we're . . . uh . . .'

Lisa extended a hand to Sofia. 'I'm his guest – a *new* friend of Sten's,' Lisa purred. 'So nice to meet an old one. Knowing the captain, I'm sure we have a great deal in common.'

Sofia coldly took her hand and shook it. 'Yes,' she said. 'I'm sure we do.'

She turned her attention back to Sten. Frost coated her eyes. 'Forgive me, Sten, but I simply must not ignore the other guests. Perhaps we can talk later.' She turned a smooth, lovely back to him and ankled away. Sten was not quite sure what he had escaped, but was clotting glad he had. He absently reached for one of the drinks Lisa was holding and was brought up short by the smile on her face.

'I didn't realize you knew anyone here, Sten.'

He swallowed his drink and then found the other one being thrust into his hand.

'Oh, maybe one or two.' Then he laughed, suddenly at ease. 'Put it at one. Just one. And thanks a hell of a lot.'

He looked Lisa over approvingly. Her body was curved richly and deep, and displayed in a very un-cop-like white gown that hugged and hollowed in all the proper places. She took the glasses from him.

'Now, let's go find a refill,' she said. 'And enjoy the party. Assuming there are no more surprises. Mmmm?'

'No. No more surprises. I hope.'

Sten couldn't have been more wrong. In seconds he had a refill, Lisa was close against him, an orchestra was playing, and there was just enough room on the dance floor. Sten figured he could fake it, especially since the orchestra was playing what even Sten could recognize as a three-quarter-time slow dance.

He bowed to Lisa and led her onto the polished metal floor. That, he realized later, should have been the key.

But there he was, settling gently into Lisa's arms, moving his feet along the floor, and then he started to understand why Marr and Senn's events were superparties.

When the band began the song's reprise, someone turned the generators on and surprised dancers found themselves floating straight up, then drifting sideways into counteractive generators.

The ballroom instantly became less a dance floor than a flurry of slow-motion acrobatics.

Sten blessed his null-grav training when Lisa, looking bewildered as her gown billowed around her waist, floated past him. He tucked and swam toward her, grabbing an ankle first, then working his way up until he had her by both hands.

Lisa recovered, smiled, and resorted to the traditional ''Nother fine fix.'

Sten had no idea what she was talking about, but decided to seize the instant.

Weightless kisses taste about the same, even if there does seem to be a sudden excess of saliva.

Seizing the instant also meant that Sten, watching out of the corner of his eye, dolphin-bent his legs, waiting. Until a flustered matron floated nearby.

Sten used his feet as a kickoff point, and the drive sent Lisa and him spinning down toward the floor. They bounced near the edge of the field, close enugh for Sten to pirouette Haines sideways onto a normal-grav floor. She in turn dragged him out of the McLean field.

'Nice party,' Sten managed.

'Mmm,' Lisa said. 'So zero-gee winds you up, Captain?'

'Isn't heterosexual love odd in its incarnations?' Marr whispered after closely watching Lisa and Sten's slow orbit.

'Perambulations is the word you're looking for,' Senn corrected. 'Shall we arrange those for later?'

'Regardless. We should take them under wing, and – Sr. Hakone! You honor us!'

Hakone had approached them unnoticed. He sipped from his half-empty glass of quill.

'As the guest of honor, may I comment on the evening thus far?'

Senn opened his liquid-black eyes in mock astonishment. 'Is anything wrong?'

'For a party that purported to be in my honor,' Hakone said, 'I find too many people here who would like to use my bones for toothpicks.'

'We made our invitations before your masque was previewed, Sr. Hakone,' Marr said. 'We had no knowledge—'

'Of course you hadn't,' Hakone said dryly. 'You two aren't the sort who believe a party is best gauged by the number of duels it creates.'

'You offend!' Senn hissed.

'Perhaps.' Hakone was indifferent. He drained his glass and fielded another from a passing tray. 'My idea of a gathering, after all, is a group of comrades, with something in common to share. Evidently we differ in that regard.'

'If we had known,' Marr pacified, 'that you wished a group of fellow ex-soldiers to sit around and become comatose while sharing lies of your long-gone youth, we would have done so.'

Hakone allowed a smile to crawl across his face. The writer was dressed entirely in black, close-fitting trousers and a flowing tunic. 'As I said before, we differ. By the way – one man I would like to meet.'

'There is someone we didn't introduce to you? Our failing.'

'Him.'

Hakone waved a hand toward Sten, who was recovering his sense of gravity with a full glass.

Marr flicked a glance at Senn. Puzzlement. Then took Hakone by the hand and led him over to Sten.

'Captain Sten?'

Sten, who was about to kiss Lisa again, turned, recognized his hosts and, thanks to his cram course in the palace files, the guest of honor.

'Sr. Hakone.'

'This is a young man,' Marr said, 'who we believe will progress greatly. Captain Sten. And?'

'Lisa Haines.' Like most good cops, Lisa didn't believe in unnecessarily letting anyone know what she was.

Hakone smiled at her, then effectively shut Lisa, Marr, and Senn out of the conversation. 'You command the Emperor's bodyguard, isn't that correct?"

Sten nodded.

'It must be interesting work.'

'It's . . . different.' Sten said neutrally.

'Different? What were you doing previously?"

Sten's background, as a member of the Emperor's Mantis Section, was of course never to be admitted. For that period his record showed service on some far worlds, enough to justify a double row of medal ribbons that had been won for far stealthier and dirtier deeds.

'Guards. Mostly out in the pioneer sectors.'

'Unusual,' Hakone said, 'for someone – and I mean no offense – as young as yourself to be picked for your current post.'

'I guess they needed somebody who could climb up and down all those stairs in the palace without having heart failure.'

'You have a mentor,' Hakone pursued.

'I beg your pardon?'

'Never mind. Captain, may I ask you something frankly?'

'Yes, sir.'

'I note from your ribbons that you've seen combat. And now you're here. At the heart of the Empire. Do you like what you see?'

'I don't understand.'

'You joined the service, I assume, like all of us. Expecting something. Expecting that you were serving a cause.'

'I guess so.' Sten knew damned well why he'd joined – to get the hell off the factory world known as Vulcan and to save his own life.

'When you look around' – and Hakone's expansive hand took in the bejeweled Court denizens that had flocked to the party – 'does this match what you expected?'

Sten kept his face blank.

'Don't you find this all a little, perhaps, decadent?'

Not a chance, Sten's answer should have been. Not when you come from a world where boys and girls go into slavery at three or four. But that wasn't the right thing to say. 'Sorry to be so thick, Sr. Hakone,' Sten said, 'but on the world I come from, *animals* are normal sex partners.'

Hakone's face flashed disgust, then he realized. 'You joke, Captain.'

'Not very well.'

'Do you read?'

'When I have the leisure.'

'Perhaps at another time we can discuss this further. In the meantime, I would like to send you some of my works. Will you receive them at the palace?'

Sten nodded. Hakone bowed formally and turned away. Sten looked after him. Question: Why would the guest of honor decide to look him up? And then stand there and play games? The evening was increasingly surprising.

The party was ending on a muted note. It had gone from a mass of egos forced together to a swirl of excuses for other appointments. Sten and Lisa, not being very experienced in Prime World high society, were among the last to add themselves to the swarm of beings making a polite exit.

Marr grabbed them just before they hit the pneumotube to their sled. 'Too soon, my loves,' he cried. 'Much too soon.'

And he latched on to their hands and began pulling them back through the crowd. Sten tensed – soldiers, like cats, don't look back. He felt equal tension through Lisa's fingers. Somehow that made him feel more at ease and very close to her. It was a sharing of distrust.

'Really, Marr,' Sten said. 'We gotta go. We both have duty tomorrow, and there really isn't time for—'

Marr broke in with a sniff. 'As you might say, clot duty. And as for time – that's just something the science types use to keep everything from happening at once.'

He pulled them forward, out of the crowd and into a long, pulsing yellow hallway. Sten hesitated once again, and then felt Lisa's fingers tense before tugging him on. They turned a corner and were instantly confronted with a tricolored split, tunnels leading in different directions. Marr urged them toward left – blue – and Sten realized from the tension in his calves that they were moving upward.

'Senn and I have had our eye on you,' Marr said. 'Through the whole party. Both of you are a bit out of place, aren't you?'

'I'm sorry,' Sten apologized. 'I'm not very used to—'

Marr waved him down. 'Don't be foolish. Our gatherings are not about social niceties. In fact, people's general appreciation is that we provide just the opposite.'

'Oh, my god,' Lisa said. 'I knew I'd foul this up.' She glanced down and checked the gossamer that was her dress. 'You can see through it, right? I knew I should have—'

Sten pulled her close to him, shutting her off.

'I think he's trying to tell us something else,' he said.

Marr pulled them onward, seemingly ignoring their hesitations. They rushed past rooms gleaming in haunting colors or dimmed to impossible shades of blackness. They were near the top level – the gallery section – and although the two guests didn't realize it, each room represented a fortune in art works. Scents and sounds slipped out, taunting, urging, but Marr pressed on, babbling all the time.

'This is special,' Sten realized Marr was saying, 'Something only the two of you would understand. You'll see – see for yourselves – why Senn and I built our home here.'

The hallway suddenly blossomed into the open and Sten fell a soft, perfumed breeze.

'See,' Marr said. 'See.' He waved a small, furry arm around, taking in . . . everything.

They were standing on what could most easily be described as a roof-top garden. Strange and exotic plants shadowed in close to them, nestling their bodies, caressing . . . what? Lisa, a bit fearfully, tucked in closer to Sten.

'Through here,' Marr said.

And they followed him along a winding, darkened path. It was like walking through a series of bubbles. Scent and perfurmed light tugging . . . tugging . . . and then bursting through into another pleasure. Sound, perhaps, or a combination of sound and light and tingling feeling. Sten felt Lisa's body loosen in his arms.

Then the violin curve tensed and stopped. For a moment all Sten could feel and know was the swell of her hip. Marr was talking again, and as he talked, Sten found himself looking upward.

'It only happens three times a year,' Marr was saying. 'A work of art that can only be seen, not purchased.' He pointed to the shimmer of glaze that separated the roof garden from the real world.

Sten saw the huddle of mountains, picked out by moonlight, that pressed in toward the dome sky. He shifted his weight and felt his leg brush a flower. There was a slight hiss of perfume, and he felt Lisa's body ignite his skin every place it touched.

'Watch,' Marr said.

And Sten and Lisa watched. The crag of cliffside just beneath the moon suddenly darkened. It became a deeper and deeper blackness until it formed into a knotted, pulsing ball.

'Wait,' Marr droned. 'Wait . . . wait.'

And then the black ball exploded. A soundless fury of storm clouds formed themselves into crayon swirls of black against the Prime World moon. Then they began to twist into a funnel shape that powered across the valley, hurling itself against the mountains on the other side of the valley.

This, Sten and Lisa didn't see. Because all they could observe was the broad, open end of the funnel, sweeping across the lights of the night sky.

It was over very quietly and softly. Somehow, Sten found himself holding Lisa in his arms. Above them, the dome was dark. Beneath them, the garden was shadow soft. Sten looked at Lisa, a dim halo of light, just below his height. 'I . . .'

Lisa held a finger to her lips. 'Shhh,' she whispered.

He pulled her closer, and he felt the garden around him hush and soften even more . . .

Marr and Senn watched the two lovers embracing under the dome. They cuddled closer in bed when they heard Lisa's soft 'Shhh.'

Senn turned to Marr and pulled him nearer. 'There's only one thing nicer than a new love,' he said.

Marr palmed the switch and the vidscreen went respectfully blank. He leaned over Senn. 'An old love,' he finished. 'A very old love.'

*

As Sten tightened his embrace, he could almost feel Lisa blush a very unlieutenantlike blush. A hand on his chest gentled him away a step. And Sten watched as the white gown shimmered off. Then there was only Lisa.

Chapter Fifteen

'You clottin' incompetent,' Lisa hissed at the corpse. Sten had an idea that if he and the spindar techs weren't present she might have kicked it a couple of times.

Former Tac Chief Kreuger grinned up at them, blackened scavenger-gnawed flesh drawn back from his teeth. One arm had been torn off and, half-eaten, was lying almost five meters from the body, near the edge of the cliff.

'You humans have the most unusual idea of sport,' Spilsbury rumbled, his subarms tapping busily on a small computer keyboard. 'What pleasure can conceivably be derived from the stalking and slaughter of fellow beings? Beyond me. Quite beyond me.'

'Sometimes they taste pretty good,' Sten offered.

'Cause of death?' Haines asked. She was not in the mood for philosophical discussion. The phone call had, fortunately, come not quite at the crucial moment, but rather early the next morning, just as Sten and Lisa were awake enough to be getting reinterested in each other again.

'Hunting accident. We have an entry wound characteristic of that from a projectile weapon.

'Plus – and this will please you, Lieutenant – there are no signs of an exit wound. I would assume the projectile remains in the body.

'Shortly one of my offspring should have it retrieved for you. Cause of death, therefore, I would theorize as emanating from a hunting accident.'

'Very clottin' convenient,' Haines said. Spilsbury's computer rattled, and the spindar handed the readout to the policewoman.

'Time of death . . . time of death. Here.' Haines mentally ran time back. 'One cycle prior to the bombing.'

'Plus or minus three hours,' Spilsbury said. 'The precise time will be available momentarily.'

Haines started to say something else, and Sten nodded her away from the tech. They walked to the cliff edge.

'Like you said, Lieutenant. Real convenient.'

Since it was the first time it had happened, Haines had been wondering just what one called a person you worked with who you'd just made love to. She decided Sten's reversion to formality was probably the most sensible. 'Cops don't believe in coincidence,' she said.

'I don't either.' Sten was trying to keep his theorizing under control. Coincidence *did* exist – every now and then.

Spilsbury waddled up behind them, holding a vis-envelope out. 'This is the projectile.'

Sten took the envelope. The projectile – a bullet – was evidently made of some fairly soft metal; its tip had mushroomed until the bullet was fully twice as wide at its tip as at its base.

'I cannot identify the exact caliber,' Spilsbury went on, 'but it is indeed a hunting-type bullet.

'From the entry wound it appears that the corpse turned to face down the mountain just before the bullet struck him.

'It is a pity you humans were constructed with such soft epidermi, unlike more cleverly designed beings.'

'Yeah. Helluva pity.' Sten said. 'Lieutenant, do you have any idea what kind of critters they hunt on this preserve?'

'Dangerous game.'

'Like what, exactly?'

'I'll call the preserve center.' She busied herself with a belt talker.

Sten chewed on his lower lip. Haines, the talker to her ear, turned and began reciting the list of target game the preserve featured. Two or three times Sten had to ask particulars about an animal. Lisa finished the list and waited. Sten nodded at her, and she broke com.

'Dangerous game,' he said. 'All designed to be real efficient.'

Lisa looked puzzled.

'Efficient like the tech just said. Hairy, scaled, armored or whatever. The kind of critter that'd take some serious killing.'

Haines still didn't get it.

'When you are trying to stop something big and nasty, especially something that's got skin armor, you use a big bullet,' Sten explained. In his Mantis career, there had been times he'd encountered said big and nasties in the performance of his duties and had to drop them. 'A big bullet,' Sten went on, 'made out of some heavy dense alloy. You don't want the bullet to mushroom when it hits skin armor.'

Lisa took the envelope from Sten. 'So you wouldn't want a nice soft slug like this one. Not unless you were hunting a nice, soft-skinned animal.'

'Like a man,' Sten finished.

'I don't like this, Captain. Not worth a drakh.'

Sten had to agree.

'You know what my bosses are going to say,' Haines continued, 'when I report that Tactical Chief Kreuger was involved in this conspiracy? That he put a tac squad in position knowing what was going to happen – and then got his chest blown in as a payoff?'

Sten looked at her, and knew that wasn't what the homicide detective was worried about. If one high-level police officer was involved, was he the only one?

'Something tells me there's going to be more than one boss with his tail out of joint,' Sten said.

'Drakh, drakh, drakh, Captain. Come on, let's get back and see what else can ruin our day.'

Chapter Sixteen

'Dynsman is our mad bomber, ' Lisa said glumly.

Sten wondered why no joy, but that was less important than making sure the police identification was correct. He knew it would be far better to give the Emperor a 'no report' than a wrong one. 'Are we operating on a most-likely suspect or do we have the clot nailed?'

'Nobody's ever nailed until they confess. But I don't see anybody else but Dynsman being the nominated party. Item: he's the only professional Prime World bomber who's unaccounted for.'

'How do you account for mad bombers?' Sten asked curiously.

'People who blow things up for a living tend to get watched pretty closely by us,' Haines said. 'And since they tend to be self-eliminating, there aren't that many of them.'

'We're assuming that the bomber was a Prime World native?'

'We've got to start somewhere – plus no outworlder who pays the rent that way has come to Prime World within the past year.'

'GA.'

'This Dynsman specializes in insurance jobs. Using military explosives.'

'Whoever blew the Covenanter used military demo.'

'Second, this clown's never been offworld in his life. A few cycles before Alain got hamburgered,' Haines went on, 'Dynsman was in hock to his eyebrows to every loan shark around.

'Then he paid his debts and was flush. He hung out with the Psauri – don't bother asking: they're small-time lizards and even smaller-time crooks.

'Suddenly he was picking up the tab and promising even bigger parties to come.

'All at once he hit up every ten-percenter in Soward. Since he'd paid them off, his credit was good.

'Then he disappeared.'

Sten ran through what Lisa'd given him. Contemplating, he walked to the railing of her 'houseboat' and stared down at the forest below.

Since housing on Prime World was at a shortage, and strictly controlled, some fairly creative homes had been developed. Lisa lived in one such. Her landlord had leased a forest that was legally unsettleable. No one, however, said anything about overhead. So large McLean-powered houseboats were available, moored above the forest. They were built in varying styles, and rented for a premium. The occupants had supreme privacy and, except in a high wind, luxury.

The interior of Haines' houseboat was a large, single room, with the kitchen and 'fresher located toward the stern in separate compartments. Lisa divided the room with movable screens, giving her the option of redesigning the chamber with minimum work any time she had a spare afternoon.

Furnishings consisted of static wall hangings of the single-stroke color school, plus low tables and pillows that served as chairs, couches, and beds.

Sten, on the whole, wouldn't have minded living there without changing a thing. He went back to business. 'You've got more.'

'Uh-huh. This Dynsman went to the port and ironed a securicop who was guarding some richie's yacht. Exit yacht, two minutes later.'

'Where'd Dynsman learn how to run a spaceship?'

'You've been in the military too long, Captain. Yachts are built for people with more money than brains. All you have to do is shove a course card in the computer; the boat does everything else. So the boat did everything else, and Dynsman was offworld.'

'Clottin' wonderful.'

'Yeah. Well, I got more. Including where Dynsman went.'

'So why the glum?' Sten asked.

'The glum is for the real bad news. Background, Sten. When I made Homicide, I figured out that sometime I'd want to file something that nobody could access. So I set up a code in my computer. And just to be sneaky, in case somebody broke the code, I set up a trap. If somebody got into my files, at least I'd know it had happened.'

'Drakh,' Sten swore, seeing what came next. He stalked across the room.'

'Pour me one, too. Right. Somebody got inside my computer. Somebody knows everything I've got.'

Haines shot her drink back.

'Still worse, babe. I ran a trail on the intrusion. Captain, whoever broke my file's inside the Imperial palace!'

Chapter Seventeen

'I do not think I needed this,' the Eternal Emperor said, quite calmly.

'Nossir,' Sten agreed.

'Congratulations, Captain. You're doing an excellent job. I'm sorry as all hell I gave you the assignment.'

'Yessir.'

'Go ahead,' the Emperor continued. 'From the gleam, I know you've got something worse than just having a spy here in the palace.'

'Yessir. This Dynsman took the yacht as far as the fuel would go, then abandoned the ship.'

'Do you have a track?'

'Lieutenant Haines's report said that Dynsman signed on a tramp freighter in that port – Hollister, it was – and transshipped.'

'How in the blazes could he get a berth? You didn't say this jerk has any deep-space experience.'

'He doesn't. But the tramp, according to Lloyds, shouldn't be too particular. It carries high-yield fuels.'

'Mmm. Continue.'

'Uh . . . the tramp's single-load destination was Heath, sir.'

'You are truly a bundle of joy, Captain Sten.'

Heath was the capital of the Tahn worlds.

'Captain, have you been drinking?'

'Nossir. Not yet.'

'We'd better start.' The Emperor poured shots from the 180-pure flask and drained his.

'Captain, I will now let you in, on an example of Eternal-Emperor-type reasoning. Either (a) the Tahn *were* responsible for greasing Alain' – the Emperor's tone changed – 'plus some . . . others, and are running this whole operation; or (b) this whole thing is turning into the most cluster-clotted nightmare going.'

'Yessir. I dunno, sir.'

'Lot of help you are. Fine, Captain, very fine. Pour another one, don't come to attention, and stand by for orders.

'I'll start with the assumption that I can trust you. You're too damned young, junior, and fresh on the job to be involved with whatever's going on.

'I trust the Gurkhas. By the way, how good a man is your subudar-major? Limbu, isn't it?'

'None better, sir.'

'I want you to turn the guard over to him. You're detached. I will be quite specific since I remember from your Mantis days that you sometimes . . . freely interpret orders. You are to go find this Dynsman; you are to bring him back unharmed; he is to be capable of answering any and every question that I can come up with.

'I do not want revenge, I want goddamned answers, Captain. Is that clear?'

'Yessir.' Sten touched the glass to his lips. 'I'll need support, Your Highness.'

'Captain Sten, you figure out your ops order. You can have any clottin' thing you want, up to and including a Guards Division if you think it'll help.

'I want that Dynsman!'

Chapter Eighteen

The portal slid shut behind Tarpy's back. Reflexively, he moved to put a wall at his back while his eyes adjusted to the semiblackness. His pupils dilated, and now he could see overhead the spots of light that were stars and spaceships.

The scene in the hemispherical chamber shifted, and it was daylight, as one sun swam into close-up, and the Imperial landing force hung 'below' it, above the slightly larger dot that was the planet.

Across this moved the black strut-beam that supported the chamber's control chair, and Tarpy could make out the figure of Hakone outlined in the seat.

Again the scene shifted, and now the battleships and assault transports floated above the planet's surface, which swept to either side of the chamber. Tacships flared out and down, and remote satellites engaged them.

Five battleships split from the main force, their Yukawa-drives pushing them up toward the planet's pole, as the transports drifted down toward the landing.

Tarpy ran battles through his head, then snickered as he got it. Of course. Saragossa.

He could never understand why soldiers couldn't let go of the past. To him, the battles he'd fought in were meaningless. All they gave him was promotion, perhaps a medal, and that never-to-be-admitted satisfaction of close-range killing.

Saragossa. As far as Tarpy was concerned, the battle was not only long-lost but one that never could have been won. Hakone's laboring for some kind of culprit had never signified. But he caught himself. Not to reason why as long as somebody's paying the bills. He dug out a tabac and, making no move to shield the flame, set fire to its tip.

Hakone caught the reflection from a dial in front of him and spun the booth on its arm. 'Is that you?'

Tarpy did not bother answering. He couldn't be bothered with nonsense – none of Hakone's servants had entry permit to the battle chamber. Therefore, whoever was inside would be whoever was expected.

The long beam swung down, out of the chamber and level with the chamber's lobby. Hakone climbed out, walked to Tarpy, and brought his hand through a 360-degree loop. The 'battle' above died as the lights came up in the chamber. 'The Emperor has saved us all some research,' Hakone said. 'We now have a line on this bomber our associate used.'

He took a handful of fiches from his coverall's breast pocket and passed them to Tarpy. 'The man fled into the Tahn worlds,' Hakone said.

Tarpy half smiled. 'It should be hard for him to go to ground there.'

'You have whatever resources you need. If you wish, take a few of our Praetorian deserters with you for backup.'

'Will it matter how I do it?'

'Not at all. He's a small-time criminal, adrift in a verv violent society. No one will inquire.'

Tarpy palmed the exit switch, and the chamber's portal swung open.

'By the way – the Emperor also has a man in pursuit.'

'Do I worry?'

'No. He's inconsequential – some captain named Sten. I met him. Quite sloppy for an Imperial soldier.'

'But if he gets close?'

Hakone shrugged. 'The issue at stake is a great deal larger than the life of one Imperial grunt, Tarpy.'

Tarpy stepped through the portal, palmed it shut, and was gone.

BOOK THREE

MOUTON

Chapter Nineteen

Sergeant Major Alex Kilgour, detached Mantis Section Headquarters, parent unit First Imperial Guards Division, glowered down at his tasteful purple and green loose tunic and pantaloons and then across the cobbled street at the schoolyard. In the yard, a uniformed and elderly Tahn officer was drilling eight-year-olds in some sort of arms drill. When y' gie th' bairns pikes before th' war starts, Alex thought sourly, p'raps y' should be thinkit ae nae fighting.

The march-and-countermarch he was watching, however, was very low on Kilgour's piss-off list. There were many, many others. Waiting for Sten, he ran through them.

There was nothing wrong with being detached for special duty. In the back of Alex's mind, he had been considering a certain sense of morality. He'd spent enough years in Mantis to realize that sooner or later the ticking clock would stop. Just lately Alex had been hearing his personal clock slowing.

But that, he protested to himself furiously, was nae the prime reason. Ah join't th' Guard ae ah soldier, he went on. An' somehow now Ah'm on some strange world, dressed ae a panderer. One of these aeons, Alex promised himself, prob'ly on my retirement, Ah'll gie th' Emperor what Ah serve the full story. The poor wee lad cannae know.

The strange world was Heath, capital of the Tahn worlds. Alex and Sten had gone in covertly. Kilgour, however, quibbled at their cover – Sten had figured that high-credit pimps would never be questioned as to their real motives.

Whatever Alex had been expecting, in a long career that specialized in inserting him in the middle of bizarre cultures, Heath proved a great deal more.

The Tahn culture consisted of rigid, stratified subcultures. At the top were the warlords, landed hereditary politico/commanders. Under them fell the lieutenants, the tactical leaders and warriors. Then the merchant class, and, finally, the peasants. The peasants did all the drakh work, from spear-carrying in the growing Tahn military to agriculture to menial jobs.

That, Alex thought to himself furiously, dinna makit me fash. But th' stinkit peasants no seem to *mind* bein' serfs. A thousand years earlier, Alex Kilgour would probably have made a very acceptable revolutionary.

An' not only that, he went on, th' food's nae whae a civilized body should eat. Ocean weed, food frae' bottom-scuttlin' beasties, drakh-planted carbos dinna make a diet frae a human, he thought, and burped.

Alex, not being the sort who could keep himself at the bottom of a brooding barrel for long, was consoling himself with the thought that at least the Tahn beer and alk were strong and readily available, when Sten slouched up beside him.

'Y'r mither dresses you funny,' he said. Sten's garb was even more extreme – which in Heath's underworld culture meant even less noticeable – than Alex's. His knee-length smock was striped in orange and black, and the leotards under them were solid black. It was, Sten had been assured, the height of fashion among those who sharked through the sexworld of prostitution.

Sten merely grunted at Alex's sally. He, too, stared at the schoolyard. The Tahn warrior had discovered an error in some child's performance and was systematically shaming him in front of his fellow. Sten motioned his head, and the two men moved away, headed toward the red-light district they were quartered in.

'Hae'y found our mad bomber?' Kilgour asked.

'Yeah.'

'Ah, Sten. P'raps y' dinna be telling me. It's aye worse'n Ah thought.'

'Even worse,' Sten began angrily. 'The clottin' idiot went and did it again.'

Lee Dynsman was an idiot. After he'd jumped ship on Heath, found a hidey-hole, a drink, a woman, and a meal, which consumed what was left of his credits, he'd put the word out in the under-culture bars that he was an expert bomber and Very Available. A small gang with large ambitions had quickly recruited him to blow the vault on a Tahn credit repository. For once in Dynsman's career, the job had gone flawlessly, dropping the thick cement/steel back wall into rubble. The gang scooped up the loot, took Dynsman to their hangout, and drank him into celebratory oblivion. No dummies, they realized that since the Tahn 'police' (actually paramilitary, seconded for special duties from the army) needed a culprit, they narked Dynsman.

'So our wee lad's in the clank,' Alex said.

'Still worse.'

'Ah, lad, lad. Dinna be makit aye worse. Y'know, Sten, when Ah was runnin' th' museum, Ah was considerin' m'leave. M'mum's castle's in Koss Galen Province, aye the loveliest part ah th' planet a' Edinburgh. An the castle sits on a wee loch, Loch Owen. Ah could'a gone there instead't bein' here wi' these barbarians.'

'Shut the hell up.' Sten was in no mood for Alex's meanderings. 'Dynsman isn't in jail,' he went on. 'The clot's been transported.'

'Oooh.' Alex understood.

'I thought you would, you refugee from a clan of criminals. Transported. To a clottin' prison planet.'

'Ah need a drink.'

'Many, many drinks,' Sten agreed. 'While we figure out how the hell we tell the Emperor there is no way in the world to lift Dynsman off the Tahn worlds' worst penitentiary.'

Alex then saved the day by spotting a bar that was just opening. The two men pivoted and swerved inside.

Chapter Twenty

Tarpy, too, had tracked down Dynsman. His cover for travel to Heath hadn't been nearly as clever as Sten's. He and the five Praetorian deserters with him masqueraded as a touring public fight team. Arriving unannounced, they had very few bookings, which left the assassin and his men more than enough time to look for the disappeared bomber.

Tarpy twirled the cup of tea in his hands and wished for something stronger in celebration. But he had rules – absolute rules that had kept him alive for nearly seventy-five years, rules that were never broken. Among the strongest was no mind alterants on the job.

He shot the tea back and motioned for his legman, a former corporal, Milr, to continue.

Milr did, and the warm glow that spread inside Tarpy came from more than the tea.

Very seldom had he taken a job that did not require violence, toil, and blood. But the current one showed every sign of being simple, painless, and well-paid.

Tarpy scanned the fiche on the prison planet. Pre-hominid. All prisoners sentenced for life. Average prisoner life expectancy – five years, local. Number of escapes – zero.

Unlike most people who kill for a living, Tarpy believed an old adage – Kill Without Joy. He had taken the adage one step further – don't kill if there's no need.

Dynsman's chances of returning to the Imperial worlds were near zero. All these people, Tarpy thought. Running around scheming after something, and none of them realize that the gods always take care of those who play with fire.

Tarpy stood, pulled the fiche from its reader, and crossed to the hotel-room sink. He rinsed out his cup, opened a cupboard, and took out a bottle of pure quill. He poured a cup for himself, then, as an afterthought, a glassful for Milr. Milr swilled the alk, without bothering to wonder about the unannounced suspension of The Rule.

He drained his glass. 'Reassemble the team, Corporal. We'll tranship back to Prime World on the next available.'

Dynsman was no longer a factor, nor was that Imperial officer. Tarpy next considered exactly how much of the commission he would have to pay the ex-Praetorians to keep them from feeling cheated.

Chapter Twenty-One

A wry joke on Heath was that the huge river running through the middle of the capital city was the only river that had ever caught on fire.

It burned for days, seriously scorching the surrounding waterfront. But even after the fire on the polluted channel had died, the Tahn lords had done nothing to clean it up, in spite of their loud and frequent avowals of love for simplicity and nature. After all, the warlords had immaculate gardens to wander through and in which to compose the Tahn's superstylized poetry. The peasants could – and sometimes did – eat drakh.

On the other hand, since all waterfronts throughout history have been the same, perhaps the fire could have been considered instant urban renewal. Not that it took long for the same abattoirs to spring back to life.

The Khag was a prime example. Its popularity was twofold: not only was it close to both the onworld water shipping and the spaceport, but at the port anything or anyone illicit was available.

The two men at the bar fit right in – except for their soiled gray uniforms and pants bloused in knee-high swamp boots. They were armed, but so was almost everyone else in the Khag. Their weapons – stunguns, truncheons, fighting knives, and gas sprays – were hung on leatherette Sam Browne belts. Their voices were as raw as they were loud and semidrunk. One of them – Keet – owled at the ticket packet on the bar in front of them.

'Last day, partner. Last day.'

His cohort Ohlsn nodded. 'You know, I have been figuring our problem, Mr. Keet.'

'We sure have a lot of them.'

'Not really,' Ohlsn continued. He was in that stage of drunkenness where brilliant ideas occur, still sober enough so that some of them make some degree of sense. 'The problem with us is we're betwixt and between.'

'I don't track.'

'Keep drinking. You will. We sit out there for three planet-years at a stretch, and what do we want more'n anything?'

'To get our butts back to homeworld.'

'Shows why we aren't warrior-ciass. 'Cause that's dumb.'

'You've been sluicing too heavy.'

'Not a chance. Look at it. Out there, we got power, right? How many times you tapped somebody 'cause you didn't like his looks? How many times you had some konfekta show up at your quarters wanting anything but to go out there with Genpop?'

'That's part of the job, Ohlsn.'

'Sure it is. So look at the two of us. We're peasant-class, right? But when we're walkin' our post, for three years we do better 'n any warrior or warlord I know.'

'This is a new assignment. Maybe it's gonna be a drakhheap.'

'Come on, man. Think about it. The job's the same as we been doin' for years – how in hell could the two of us do any better?'

Keet considered. Part of his consideration was emptying the liter-size carafe of quill in front of them into their glasses.

That was what Sten and Alex had been waiting for. They were at a small table, about three meters behind the two men. Sten waved, and the previously overtipped waitress was beside them.

'Those two,' Sten said. 'Buy them another round.' He slipped her more than enough credits, then looked at Kilgour.

'Och aye,' Alex agreed to the unspoken question. 'Those are our boys.'

By that time, another carafe had been set in front of Keet and Ohlsn, and they'd quizzed the barmaid on who was buying. Keet turned and puzzled at them. Sten hoisted his own mug and smiled. Keet and Ohlsn exchanged glances, considered their diminished drinking fund, and came to the table. They both were highly unimpressed with Sten and Alex, who were glowing gently in their pimpsuits.

'Don't like to drink alk from somebody I don't know,' Keet growled.

'We're the Campbell brothers,' Alex smoothed.

'Yuh. And I know what you are.'

'In our trade, it pays to advertise,' Sten said. 'You don't get the girls if you don't look like you can afford them.'

'Got no use for pimps,' Ohlsn said. 'You ought to see what happens to 'em out there.'

'An experience I plan to avoid,' Sten said, refilling their mugs.

'Knock off the drakh,' Keet said. 'You know what we are. You ain't buying us 'cause you like our looks.'

'Nope,' Sten agreed. 'We've got a problem.'

'Bet you have.'

'We thought maybe to take care of it before it happens.'

'Lemme guess,' Keet said. 'One of your whores got staked, right? And she's headed out.'

'This man's a mind reader,' Sten mock-marveled to Alex.

'You know the rules, chien. Once they're gone, they don't come back. Unless they're stiff. So don't bother trying to buy us so that you can rescue your hole. Don't happen. Never has happened.'

'We're no stupid,' Alex said.

'So why the free?'

'Our friend, see,' Sten began haltingly. 'She's cuter'n leggings on a k'larf. But she ain't too swift. She went and got hooked up with somebody up there.' Sten jerked his thumb upward, in the Heath-universal sign for any class above your own or the people you were dealing with.

'His third wife didn't like it. My friend ended up being took as a receiver.'

'Hard hash,' Keet said.

'She was a real moneymaker,' Sten sighed. 'And so I'd like to see she gets taken care of. She's the delicate type.'

Keet and Ohlsn eyed each other.

'What are you looking for?'

'Somebody to take care of her. Don't want to see her end up on the wrong side.'

'You want one of us to tuck her under a wing?'

'You have it.'

'Don't make sense. Why do you care? She ain't never coming back.'

'It's an investment. See, Din's got sisters growing up. And they're even cuter'n she is. So if I protect the family . . .'

Ohlsn grunted happily. From his point of view, he was in the bargaining chair.

'Fine, chien. We take care of her. But what's in it for us? Now? Here?'

Alex lifted a roll of Tahn credits from his pocket.

'Drakh,' Keet said. 'Should'a hit us at the beginning of the leave.

That won't do us any good for the next three plan-years out there, now will it?'

'Drop an offer.'

Keet lifted the ticket packet. 'This says we ship eight hours from now. Means if you're trying to buy us, you got to come up with something we can do 'tween now and then. And something that won't mess us. Which means don't even bother offerin' something in your own . . . organization?'

'Man drinks quill, he starts thinking about other things,' Ohlsn steered them.

Sten widened his eyes. 'Sorry, men. I guess I'm a bit slow. That's clottin' easy.'

'Bro,' Kilgour added. 'We could set 'em um wi' any piece a' fluff. But these gens sound like they're willin' to treat us on the square. What about Din's sisters?'

Keet licked his lips. 'You've already got them?'

'Clot yes,' Sten said. 'Folks don't care. They breed 'em like k'larf. Wait till they hit ten, then sell 'em. We've had two for about a month. Breakin' 'em in right.'

'Then there's the deal,' Keet said. 'Plus you provide the rations and the drink – and make sure we hit the transport on time.'

The four beamed at each other, and Sten signaled for another pitcher to seal the arrangement.

Outside, the salt air hit and instantly sobered Sten. He'd had just enough drink to seriously consider telling the two men in gray what was going to happen to them, and why. Instead, he fell back from Keet one half a pace and dropped his hand. His curled fingers freed the muscle holding the knife securely in his arm, and the blade dropped free into his hand. He gave the nod to Alex.

Alex spun and swung, knotted three-gee muscles driving his fist straight into Ohlsn's rib cage. Ribs splintered, and the punch-shock impacted the man's heart.

Ohlsn was dead, blood gouting from his mouth, before he could even realize.

Keet's death was somewhat neater, but no less sudden, as Sten's knife slid into the base of the man's skull, severing the spinal cord.

Old Mantis reflexes took over. They caught the corpses as they toppled and eased them to the boardwalk.

The bodies were quickly stripped of weapons, uniforms, and ID packets. From a nearby piling, Alex grabbed weighted bodybags they'd stashed earlier; and they struggled the corpses into them.

Minutes after they'd died, the two bodies splashed into the harbor to sink tracelessly and dissolve quickly. Ten hours, and nothing but a revolting slush would remain for forensics specialists.

Alex bundled the uniforms together and tucked them under one arm. 'Of a' the sins Ah hae on m'conscience,' Alex mused. 'Ah never consider't pollutin' th' ocean'd be one a them.'

'Alex, help,' Sten said plaintively.

'A min, lad. A min. Ah'm lockit up noo.' Alex was indeed quite busy in the tiny slum flat they'd rented. Kilgour was feeding the ID cards, personal photos, and such from Keet and Ohlsn into one of the few Mantis tools they'd brought with them. The machine was copying the ID cards and personal data from the two originals then altering them so that Sten and Alex's pictures and physical characteristics were implanted on the documents.

'Sergeant Major Kilgour, I still outrank you, damn it!'

The final photo clicked out a shot of Keet arm in arm with some female-by-courtesy who must have been the love of his life. The new photo, however, showed Sten as the erring lover. Kilgour beamed and fingered a button. The machine began hissing – in less than a half a minute the original documents in the machine, and the guts of the machine itself, would be a nonanalyzable chunk of plas. He turned to see what Sten's problem was.

'I am not,' he said firmly, 'a clottin' seamstress. I am a captain in the Imperial Guard. I do not know how to sew. I do not know how to alter uniforms to fit, even with sewing glue and this clottin' knife. All I know how to do is glue my fingers together.'

Kilgour *tsk*ed, poured himself a now off-duty drink, and sadly surveyed Sten.

'How in hell did y'manage to glue *both* hands together? M'mum w'd nae have trouble wi' a simple task like that.'

Before Sten could find a way to hit him, Alex solved the problem by dumping his mug of alk over Sten's hands, dissolving the sewing glue, which Sten had rather ineptly been using to retailor Keet and Ohlsn's uniforms. The mug was swiftly refilled and handed to Sten, who knocked it back in one shot.

'Ah,' Alex pointed out wisely after Sten had finished choking and wiping the tears from his eyes. 'Y've provit th' adage.'

Sten just stared lethally at his partner.

'Ah y'sew, tha's how y'weep.'

Kilgour, Sten decided, was definitely rising above his station.

Chapter Twenty-Two

His muscles complaining as he automatically tensed his legs against the greasy tug of the water, Dynsman waded out through the receding tide. He was still way too new at the game yet, and hadn't learned to let the steady pull of the sea help him walk. It was the same at Conch time, when the day was officially ended by the shoreline horn. Then it was a matter of walking with the incoming tide and trying to keep one's balance. Dynsman still fought it. And the penalty was sleepless nights of agony as his legs knotted and cramped.

Adding to his problems was the knife-sharp sea bottom, littered with gnarled rocks and razor-edge mollsk shells. He had only thin plas boots to protect his feet.

'Clot!' A misstep, and a tiny slice of flesh was nipped off by a shell. He stopped, dragging himself back against the tide. His heart pounded wildly for an instant as he looked about him. He could almost feel the blood oozing from the tiny abrasion. Dynsman thought about all the things that sniffed for blood in the mollsk bed and shuddered.

He fought back the panic and tried to regain his bearings. On each side of him, forty other prisoners of Dru eased out through the surf like slow-beating wings. They moved cautiously through the water, watching for the telltale bubbles of frightened mollsks.

Dynsman had never worked so hard or been so frightened in his life. He would much rather disarm a sloppy bomb then pursue the wily mollsk. Dynsman really wasn't good with his hands even when working on the delicate mechanisms that make things go bang; his seven remaining fingers were mostly numb, blunt objects. He had lived at his trade as long as he had by being canny and what-the-hell-let's-go-for-it lucky.

'Dynsman!' came the bellow from the shoreline. 'Get your ass behind it or I'll put my boot in.'

The bellow hit him like an electric shock, and Dynsman stumbled clumsily forward, his mollsk-plunger held somewhat at the ready.

Like most tasks on Dru, what Dynsman was about involved a product that was exceedingly exotic, expensive, and lethal. The tender mollsk was prized in many systems for its incredible taste and mythological aphrodisiac qualities. It was a mutant Old Earth bivalve creature, containing on average a kilo of delectable flesh, guarded by a razor-sharp shell about a half meter in diameter.

It had been bred to its present delicious state over many centuries. The problem being, for the hunter, that the same genes that made it so large and tasty went along with a highly efficient system of mobility. The creature lived in the mud and preferred chill; krill-swarming seas. When it fed, it opened its huge top shell like a fan, guiding the microorganisms into its stomach-filter system. The mollsk could not see or feel, but judged the environment for mating or danger by a highly evolved system of smell. Which, in addition to convenience, is why mollsk hunters worked as the tide rushed out. In theory, the smells of the decaying shore life would mask the odor of an approaching mollsk hunter. But only until the last moment, when the hunter was a meter or so away. Then the mollsk would smell the hunter, take fright, and burrow deeper into the mud, leaving a trail of roiling bubbles. That's when the hunter captured it. Or if you were Dynsman, tried for it.

Like the other hunters, Dynsman was provided with a mollsk-plunger. It consisted of two handles, a little more than a meter and a half long, that connected to a pair of very sharp shovel jaws that were spring-loaded and sieved. The plunger was held at the ready as the intrepid hunter waded out through the surf watching very carefully for the bubbles that marked panicked mollsks. Aiming at the point where the bubbles just disappeared, and making allowances for light refraction, the tool was plunged into the mud at just the right moment, triggering the spring. Then the mollsk-plunger was hauled to the surface spewing mud and water, and the creature was popped into the bubble raft towed behind the hunter.

Dynsman was about as bad at the job as anyone could be. He could never time the bubbles correctly, and, about every other shift, he dumped his raft over as he was wading to shore. That meant he lived on very, very short rations because on Dru, a prisoner's food intake and the availability of luxuries depended upon performance. After only a month on Dru, Dynsman's ribs stood out from his hollow stomach at about a thirty-degree angle. To add injury to starvation, every time he fouled up, Chetwynd, the behemoth who was the boss villain, put his wrist to the nape of Dynsman's neck and made him do what Chetwynd called 'the chicken.'

Dynsman moved slowly forward again, his feet feeling for the uncluttered spaces along the bottom. A streak of bubbles suddenly shot for the surface and Dynsman almost panicked. Blindly, he slammed the mollsk-plunger downward and triggered the release. A myriad of bubbles exploded upward and then Dynsman was laughing almost hysterically as he tugged up on the plunger, a large mollsk snared in its jaws. He pressed the release lever and hurled the creature into the raft. There, he thought to himself. You're finally getting it. With a great deal more confidence, he strode forward. But then the old doubts and fears came crowding back. All the stories he had listened to in the village about the things that wait for a guy and are most likely to attack during rookie false confidence.

Dynsman had yet to witness one of the attacks, but he had seen the bodies dragged up on shore by Chetwynd and his cronies. There were many, many beings to fear in those waters, it was said, but two creatures in particular were the source of constant conversation and mid-sleep perspiration. The second most deadly being that *also* preyed on the mollsk was the morae. It was shaped a bit like a serpent and powered its three-meter length through the seas by constantly moving ribs – the tail streaming out behind for a rudder, or more awfully, as a brace in attacking.

The morae had an enormous head with jaws that could unhinge, allowing it to rip into morsels much larger than the circumference of its tubular body. And, like most animals of the deep, its flesh was very dense, giving it enormous strength, even for its size. Eyewitness accounts had one morae going for a leg dangling out of a boat and dragging leg, boat, and all under water. Fortunately, Dynsman reassured himself, the morae rarely fed during an outgoing tide. It was during the return home, with the seas pounding back at the shore, that the hunters worried.

Most dreaded of all, however, was the gurion. This was a *thing* that was always hungry and hunted at all times. Dynsman noticed that he was about waist-deep, a depth most favored by the gurion when it was on the stalk. He had never seen a gurion, and sure as hell wanted to keep it that way. Apparently they looked a bit like an Earth starfish but enormously larger – perhaps two meters across. On their many legs they could rise up out of the water over a three-meter tide. A gurion could run through the water as fast as a human being could on land. It was impossible to escape them. They were an almost obscene white, covered with a thick bumpy skin. The huge sucking discs on their legs could rip a mollsk apart then evert its stomach, which was lined with rows of needle-teeth, over its prey, grasp the soft flesh, and pull it back into its body, ripping and digesting the living organism at the same time.

Dynsman never wanted to meet a living gurion.

All in all, after being condemned to Dru, Dynsman wasn't sure if he wouldn't have been better off facing Prime World justice. He felt that he had always been an unappreciated man, but on Dru his talents were going completely without use. He thought of himself as the kind of a fellow who could get along in any society. He had not a prejudice in him. He just wanted to be allowed to do what he did best – blow things up – and then enjoy the companionship of his fellow professionals in a bar after the bloody task was done.

Chetwynd had changed all that. Dynsman did not blame the Tahn system for his present state. He had made a misstep and then been caught. Dynsman blamed it on evil companions. What happened later was only to be expected.

Chetwynd was only one of many prisoner bosses who ruled the isolated villages sprinkled across Dru. The Tahn, fascists that they were, created the prison colony of Dru for only one purpose: to imprison criminals, both political and societal. Rob a bank or hoist a picket sign, it was all the same to the Tahn. But, fascists or not, they were also eminently practical. If they had to have a prison world, it should pay for itself. Better yet, it should make a profit.

In Dynsman's area, the Tahn had seeded a vast mollsk bed. Twenty grams of mollsk flesh went for a small fortune in Tahn high society. Deeper inland, musk-bearing plants rolled like tumbleweeds across an enormous desert landscape. Since they also sprayed a highly caustic acid all about them when they were halted, it cost many prisoner lives to harvest them. And across the face of Dru, ranches, farms, and mines produced items worth a warlord's dowry at the cost of many 'worthless' lives.

Dynsman had figured out the system even before he was transported to Chetwynd's village, and was determined to keep himself alive. With Chetwynd, it was a plan that almost could have worked.

Chetwynd had been a labor organizer on the docks at the Tahn's main spaceport. In his somewhat colorful past there had been more than a modicum of murder and robbery and mayhem. But when he led his fellow workers out on strike over some now obscure benefit-parity issue involving in-flight feelies for deep-space workers, it was just the final straw for the Tahn. He was put in manacles and told there were many many *many* mollsks in his future.

By the time Dynsman came on the scene, the enormous being that was Chetwynd had staked out the village for himself. He dressed in the best of clothes, confiscated all the luxuries for himself and his cronies, and had gathered a little harem of prisoner lovelies. The ladies were there, it would be noted, more for his charm and prowess than his relative riches as boss thug.

Dynsman himself had fallen under the giant's spell when he was dumped from the flitter and assigned to Chetwynd's work party. The big man had already pored over a stolen copy of his rap sheet. 'Bomber, huh?' he had mused. 'You gotta be the clot I was always lookin' for back on Heath.'

Chetwynd had immediately put Dynsman to work building bombs. The materials were far from right, but Dynsman did his damnedest to produce, bragging all the while about the sophisticated things he could do if given the right tools and materials.

He never asked Chetwynd what the bombs were for because the obvious targets – the guards – would bring thousandfold retaliations if any of them were even scratched. Eventually Dynsman managed to produce a double-throw-down explosive device, triggered by the narcobeer breath that always seemed to exude from Dru guards. The test was unfortunate. The problem was, Dynsman had made a minor error involving the pheromone trigger, and when Chetwynd threw a party for the first blast, the musk favored by Chetwynd's latest passion set the bomb off well before schedule.

Dynsman expected to be killed on the spot. Instead, Chetwynd merely smashed him about for a while and then, after a long conference with his bullyboys, assigned him to the main mollsk work party. As he waded through the surf, waiting for the first *crunch* of the morae, or the gurion, Dynsman had mixed feelings about his reprieve.

There was a shout from his left. Dynsman whirled to see that entire side of the work force flailing at the water, desperately struggling to reach shore. Another shout rose to his right, and Dysnman knew that somehow it was too late. The others were already heading back, and he had been daydreaming about his problems, ignoring everything about him.

He tried to get his feet to move, but instead stared in awful fascination at the black shapes that were whipping through the sea toward them. Morae! By clotting hell, morae! Somehow he turned and started plunging his knees up and down, but made almost no headway against the outgoing tide. His heart was hammering, his muscles straining, and still it wasn't enough; he could almost feel the gaping jaws moving in on his legs. The legs felt so thin and brittle. Then he was on the shore, and people were pulling him onto the beach and he was gasping and laughing and messing himself in fear. They dumped him and ran back. Dynsman heard a scream and rolled over to look.

Chetwynd was standing in the surf, his huge body braced against some terrible pulling weight as he tugged at one of the mollsk hunters. Chetwynd had the man beneath both arms, and the hunter's body was wracked back and forth in fast, terribly agonizing motions. The man screamed and screamed and screamed. But Chetwynd kept his hold. He kept pulling, and finally whatever had the man let go. Chetwynd staggered back with him and collapsed on the sand to a ragged cheer from the others. Dynsman himself almost yelled out in relief until he saw the thing that was in Chetwynd's arms. The morae had won. Nothing existed below the waist. The worker grinned at Chetwynd, and then his eyes rolled up in his head and blood burst out of his mouth.

Dynsman turned aside to vomit.

Chapter Twenty-Three

'One to you, Mr. Ohlsn!
'Acknowledged, Mr. Keet!'

Prodded by Sten's club, the prisoner double-timed from the white line chalked on the ground across the compound toward Alex. Kilgour saluted, in the flat-hand outstretched salute of the Tahn, then motioned the prisoner out the gate, onto the world of Dru itself. He slammed and triple-print-locked the gate, then doubled, knees high, toward his partner. Again they exchanged salutes, then started toward their quarters.

'Ah ha' been a lot of things f'r the Emperor, young Sten,' Kilgour said heavily, 'but y've forced me into roles Ah dinna ken a' all. I wasna bad bein't a cashiered soldier when we were dealin't wi' those mad Taliemaners. But this time y'hae me ae first a pimp, an' noo a screw.

'M'mum w'd nae likit you.'

Kilgour had been sniveling since the two had boarded the guard transport for Dru. Their identities hadn't even been questioned. Evidently even the security-conscious Tahn could not figure why anyone, for any reason, would want to go to the prison world of Dru.

Not that a guard's life was without its comforts. A good percentage of Dru's luxury goods were filtered into the guards' compound. And of course there were human amenities, since any prisoner condemned to Dru quickly learned that his or her life expectancy would be significantly enlarged by volunteering to share a guard's bed.

Sten and Alex had evaded the situation by claiming that on leave they'd both bedded the same woman, and been given the same social disease, which was slowly responding to treatment.

Ohlsn had been right – for the peasant-class men and women the Tahn routinely recruited as prison guards, life was very sweet indeed.

'Young Sten,' Alex whispered, just outside the security door to the guards' barracks, 'are you *sure* that all we hae t'do is lift this mad bomber? Wha' would happen if we set a wee bomb ae our own in the center ae this compound before we hauled?'

'Good idea, Sergeant Major. No.'

Kilgour sighed and they entered their quarters.

Alex waited until the machine finished cycling, lifted the plas door, and took the two mugs of narcobeer to the table he and Sten were sitting at.

All of the recreation rooms in the barracks were the same – overly plush chambers that attempted to copy what the vids showed of warlord quarters. With additions. Like the narcobeer machines. Alex winced, and sipped. Coming from a free world and the Imperial military, he'd never experienced the dubious joys of narcobeer. Sten had slugged down more than his share on the factory world of Vulcan.

'Nae only d' these Tahn no eat right,' Alex grumbled, 'but th' dinna ken beer.'

'That's not quite beer.'

'Aye. A camel pisseth better ale than th' Tahn make.'

'It's fermented grain of one sort or another. Plus about five per cent opiate.'

Alex chugged the mouthful he'd been swilling straight back into his glass. 'Y'r jokin't.'

Sten shook his head and drank. It tasted even worse than he remembered.

'Wha's the effect?'

'You get glogged, of course. Plus there's a slight physical addiction. Takes . . . oh, may be a cycle or two of the cold sweats to shake.'

'Bleedin' great. First Ah'm a pimp, then Ah'm a screw, an' noo Ah'm becom'it a clottin' addict. The Emp'll ne'er know wha' troubles Ah seen.'

Sten noticed, however, that the information didn't keep Alex from finishing his glass. Further complaints were broken by loud, raucous cheers from the other guards as they welcomed two others into the rec room – guards Sten and Alex hadn't seen during their three weeks on Dru.

'The Furlough twins!'

'How'd the luck of the draw play?'

The slightly older and beefier of the two women motioned for silence. Eventually, the other guards shut up.

'Y'wan a report? Awright. The late prisoner, our lamented whatever his clottin' name was – or was it her? – successfully passed to his reward and was recycled.'

'Clot the villain. Who cares?'

'Me'n Kay found a new way to spend time back on Heath.'

Great interest was obvious among the other guards.

'You people been using the body detail to hit the resorts. Lemme tell you, there's somethin' better. With the fleet bein' built up, there's a whole bunch of recruits.

'Young they are. Stuck on post. Me an' Kay figured that they got credits, and nobody to spend 'em on.'

'Tell you, they spent 'em on us, since we used our guaranteed right an' spent time on base, in the R&R center.'

'Good times,' someone snickered.

'Tell you,' the woman went on. 'Back there, it's better. They sack with you 'cause they want to, not 'cause there's pressure. Tell you women a little secret,' she leered. 'It's a lot . . . stronger that way. Plus *they* pick up the tab.'

A watch sergeant stood and ceremoniously waved his mug at them. 'We're glad to see you people back. Sounds like your stories are gonna be great. But the next time the lottery rolls around, if you guys take it again, somebody's gonna get dead. This is the third time in two years you two went back to Heath.'

Sten and Alex were looking at each other. There wasn't any need to discuss matters. They tabbed new narcobeers from the machine and joined the fray.

The problem they'd never solved was, once they found Dynsman, how to get him – and themselves – offworld. Being experienced covert operators, they'd always assumed there was a way. But in three weeks they had not yet been able to find one. Dru was ringed by manned and unmanned guard ships. The only way on or off was in prisoner transshipments or on robot freighters lifting out the luxury exports. The prisoner ships were manned by heavy guard contingents, and not even Sten and Alex felt competent enough to take over a ship guarded by a hundred people. The export ships were uniformly refrigerated and nitrogen-atmosphered. This 'lottery' sounded interesting.

It was. The Tahn were very proud of Dru. Not only was the prison planet operating in the black, but the prisoners themselves were used, even beyond their death.

Under stress, the human animal's pituitary gland produces a painkilling drug. The greater the stress, the greater the production. Since most prisoners who died on Dru died under extreme stress, their bodies were filled with the drug. The problem was acquiring the body, and freezing it before corruption set in. Prisoners died on Dru very frequently – but all too many of them died under conditions that made body recycling impossible. That was one reason why any of the prisoners sent to Isolation never reemerged, except in bodybags.

A 'good' body, Sten and Alex found out, went offworld, to Heath. The cycling was not done on Dru; for two reasons: the difficulty of getting skilled techs to accept assignment to an armpit like Dru, and the fact that the pituitary gland extract was, like all painkillers, a joyful opiate. Whichever one of the Tahn warlords came up with the idea of using prisoners for opiates, he or she was bright enough not to want an already troubled world like Dru to have access to a supernarcotic. When enough prisoners had died and been frozen and bagged in time, the bodies were escorted offworld by two guards. That was the only way off Dru other than the normal Recreation leave following the three-year tour of duty. And the escorts were chosen by lottery.

By the end of the evening Sten and Alex were eyeball-crossing on narcobeer. But they had their way out. For Dynsman and themselves.

Chapter Twenty-Four

Step one was Alex's story. 'Ah,' he mock-yawned. 'Nae a month on Dru, an a'ready Ah heard y'r best stories.'

'You got a better one, Ohlsn,' a guard jeered. The tubby Scotsman had already established himself as a character and a favorite among the guards. Especially since he was more than willing to buy his round and another.

'Since Ah'm buyin't, shouldna ye be shuttin' y'r mouth?'

Silence fell.

'Ah'm tellin't a story aboot Old Earth. Before e'en the Emperor. Back when we Scots ran free an bare-leggit on a wee green island.

'But e'en then, afore the Emperor, there was an Empire. Romans, they were call't. An because they were sore afrait a' the wee Scots, they built this braw great wall across the island. Wi' us on one side, an' them on the other.

'Hadrian's Wall, it was namit.

'But e'en then, bus'ness was bus'ness. So a' course, tha' were gates in th' wall, for folks to go backit an' forth.

'A' course there were guard on th' gate.

'On th' evenin' in question, there wa' two guards on th' wall, Marcus and Flavius . . .'

Step Two was Sten.

The first thing they needed was to find Dynsman. The third thing Sten and Alex needed was a way to mickey the lottery.

Either task depended on having a terminal and accessing Dru's central computer.

Guards were not encouraged to have personal terminals, and the terminals that existed were carefully controlled and voice-sealed to the appropriate authorities.

However, Sten had discovered that the game machines in the recreation room were very sophisticated. If a guard won on them, he could be paid immediately in narcobeers (delivery through the slot) or by credits added to his or her banked salary. Losses, of course, meant immediate deductions. Sten had grinned in glee – the machines were exactly like those he'd grown up with on Vulcan – and exactly like those the Mantis team had boogered in their destruction of that factory world.

So while Alex was occupying the guards, Sten seemed to be pinballing his heart out on one of the machines. Actually he was taking over the machine and using its lines to access the central computer itself. His tools were a microbluebox that they'd smuggled onto Dru in the guise of a music machine, a secondary high-power source that also had been smuggled, and Sten's occasional bashing left foot against the game machine itself.

Sten reacted as the game screen flashed; he tapped keys and cut himself out of the circuit. Anti-access device, but toad simple. He considered for a minute, then tried an alternate code. Another step forward.

'. . . Now here's Marcus, who's been on this wee isle for years an' years. But puir Flavius, he's only been there for a month or so. An' the puir lad's scarit solid. He dinna like th' food, he dinna like th' weather, an' most a' all, he's messin' his tunic aboot th' Scots.

'"Dinna Fash," Marcus tells him. "Aboot nine a' th' evenin't, y'll be hearin't a braw whoopin't an' hollerin't an' carryin't on.

'"Tha'll just be the Scots comin't oot a' th' grogshops. But y'll noo have to worry."

'But Flavius is worrin't . . .'

Sten was also worrying. He looked around – every eye in the rec room seemed intent on Alex's story. Sten slithered a microdrill from his pocket and touched it to the rear of the game machine. The drill whined in. Sten plugged the connection on the drill handle into an outlet on the microbluebox and keyed the ANALYSIS button. The bluebox hummed concernedly.

'. . . So noo it's nigh nine, and sure enow, there's whoopin't an hollerin't an' carryin't on. And aye, doon the street toward our wee Romans comit this braw great cluster a' Scots. An' they're hairy an' dirty an' wearin't bearskins and carryin't great axes a' claymores.

'And Flavius knows he's gone to die, here on this barren isle light-years from his own't beautiful Rome. So he's shakin't an' shiverin't.

'But Marcus, he's got this braw smile on his face a' this horrible horde comit staggerin't up.

'"Evenin'", he says.

'"Clottin' Romans," comit th' growl, an' somebody unlimbers a sword.

'"You're lookin't good a' this night," Marcus goes on.

'"Clottin' Romans" is th' solo thing he gets back, an' th' Scots are e'en closer, an' Flavius can smell their stinki't breath, an' he's a dead mon.

'"Nice night tonight," Marcus keeps goin't.

'"Clottin' Romans," comes again.

'Flavius hae his wee eyes shut, not wantin' t' see the blade tha' rips his guts out an' all. But nae happen't. All th' braw hairy killer monskers pass through the gate.

'An Flavius is still alive.

'He relaxes then. Takit twa deep breaths, grins a' Marcus, an' says, "Y're right. Tha Scots na be so bad."

'"Aye, lad. You're learnin," Marcus comes back. "But in another hour, when their *men* get done drinkin't, p'raps there'll be a wee spot a' trouble."'

As usual when Alex finished one of his stories, there was uncomprehending silence. Broken by two things:

The game machine flashed the correct code. Sten now was inside the main computer; and:

His microdrill had evidently gone too far, since the PAYOFF sign started flashing, and narcobeers began dropping down the slot. As Sten quickly palmed the bluebox and microdrill, the guards whirled at the *whirclunkthud* of beermugs dropping into the serving pickup. A throng gathered instantly around the machine.

'Clottin' luck,' one guard said. 'I've been ringing this game for a year, and the most I got was two beers. Look at that.' The PAYOFF sign read 387 narcobeers.

'And what the hell am I gonna do with all that?' Sten wondered.

'Mr. Keet,' one guard said, 'you been takin' dumb lessons? We're gonna drink 'em, that's what we're gonna do.'

Sten and Alex exchanged glances, then braced themselves for what would prove a very, very long evening . . .

Chapter Twenty-Five

The big man lolled on the beach, lazily watching the mollsk hunters plod across the bed. He was surrounded by half-a-dozen lovelies who were sunning themselves, but keeping one eye out in case Chetwynd should want something. Chetwynd barely stirred when he heard the flitter dust up behind him. And he pretended not to notice the whine of the engines cutting off, then bootheels grounding through the sand.

'Chetwynd?'

'Yar.'

'Get up when I talk to you!'

Chetwynd slowly turned his huge head, then pretended surprise when he saw the two guards. Just as slowly, he creaked to his feet and struck a mock pose of respect.

'Sorry, mister – I didn't know . . .' He let his voice trail off in pretended nervousness. 'We wasn't expecting a visit.'

'Yeah, well too bleeding bad. Hate to inconvenience an important villain like you.' Sten measured the bulk that was Chetwynd with his mind. Only the insolence in his eyes gave Chetwynd away. Everything else was as humble and respectful as any guard could wish from a villain of Dru. A very dangerous man, Sten thought.

'We're lookin' for a villain,' Sten snapped.

'Came to the right place, mister,' Chetwynd drawled.

Sten ignored the subtle rudeness. 'Name's Dynsman.'

'Dynsman . . . Dynsman . . .' Chetwynd puzzled, then he let his eyes brighten. 'Yar. He's still alive. We got a Dynsman.'

'Where?'

Chetwynd pointed, and Sten turned to see their target at the shoreline cleaning out a flat-bottomed skiff.

'Useless bugger. if you don't mind me saying so, mister. Can't do a clotting day's decent work. I'd put him washin' pots if I didn't figure he'd poison us all with his carelessness.'

Sten and Alex ignored Chetwynd and began stalking across the beach, their bootheels grating heavily.

Dynsman barely had a chance to see them coming. Just as he raised his head, Alex grabbed him by the base of the neck and lifted him off the ground.

'Villain Dynsman?'

'Yeeeesss, mister.'

'Wanna talk wi' y', lad.'

Alex tossed the little man into the boat, gave Sten a glance, caught the nod, and climbed in after him. He picked up the oars as Sten tossed off the tie, and clambered in after him. Alex began rowing out into the sea.

'Honest, mister,' Dynsman wailed. 'I didn't do nothin' . . .' Then in a flash of inspiration, he pointed an accusing finger at the receding mountain that was Chetwynd. 'He *made* me build that bomb!'

'Is that right?' Sten said. 'You're a bomb builder, are you?'

Dynsman was in instant terror. Maybe they didn't know . . . oh, clot, what was he into?

'Tell us aboot it, lad,' Alex soothed.

'Well, see, he asked me . . . and . . . and I said I had some experience at explosives . . . and . . .'

'Shaddup,' Sten hissed. 'We don't give a clot about Chetwynd.'

Dynsman just stared at Sten as it occurred to him that something terrible was about to happen.

'Tell us about the Covenanter,' Sten snapped.

'Oh, my god,' Dynsman breathed.

Alex gave him a cuff. 'Ah canna abide blasphemy.'

'Forget it,' Sten said. 'Let's just kill him now. Get it over with.'

Sten curled his fingers and let the slim needle that was his knife spring into his palm. Dynsman saw it and began to sweat in real horror. 'I didn't know it was political. I never do political work. Ask anybody. Ask 'em, and they'll tell you. I'm just a . . . just a . . .' He looked Sten full in the face, then burst into tears. 'I don't do political,' he sobbed.

Sten felt like a bugsnipe.

'For clot's sake's, Alex! We got the right guy. Do him, would you?'

Alex nodded and reached into the pocket of his uniform.

Dynsman screamed, coming halfway to his feet. It was the most chilling sound Sten had ever heard – despite enormous experience in listening to soon-to-be dead men scream Then he realized that Dynsman wasn't screaming because of them.

Sten turned his head.

A *thing* was running toward the skiff through the water at about fifteen knots, closing so quickly on its spindly legs that it almost appeared to be walking on the surface of the water.

Dynsman screamed again. 'It's a gurion!'

Alex desperately tried to spin the clumsy skiff around, but it had no centerboard and just spun freely on its axis. Sten grabbed for a punting pole, and just as the creature rose to its full height, vomiting out the awful stomach mouth with its bleeding veins, he heard the sound of rushing water behind him.

Whatever *that* was, he had to leave it for Alex, and he rammed the pole straight into the gurion's maw. The tip of the pole splintered and gave as it speared past the scores of rows of teeth into soft flesh. The gurion howled but continued its rush forward, lifting the skiff upward and slamming it over.

Alex had even less time than Sten to react. A second after Dynsman's scream, he saw another gurion charging his side. He flailed out at it with an oar, and then felt a huge wave pressing under him, the sky rushing down at him, and then he was gobbling water. A thick arm clasped his body and squeezed hard as a tentacle tore at his uniform. He tried to get his feet under him – the water wasn't very deep at this point – and desperately fought for a grip on the animal.

Sten was afraid he was being dragged toward the gurion's maw, and he lashed out at the thing in front of him with his knife and slit straight across the delicate membranes of the gurion's stomach. Suddenly he was hurled away. He twisted his body in midair, and then was plunging into the water. He landed with a jolt and found himself standing thigh-deep in water. A geyser of blood was fountaining from the first gurion. Sten immediately put the creature out of his mind and whirled in the water, looking for Alex.

The heavyworlder's lungs were bursting, but he had managed to get a hand on a frontal ray, and another on a ridge graining upward from the gurion's back. Other rays were closing around him, suckers grasping his thick body. Under the water, Alex saw the blood-red maw, centimeters from his face. He strained mightily, a huge bubble of what little remained of the air in his lungs bursting out. Slowly, very slowly, he began forcing the ray toward the gurion's own stomach-mouth. Reflexively, the needle teeth began swarming as they sensed flesh approaching. Finally with a last mighty shove, the tip of the ray entered the maw.

A high whine almost pierced Sten's eardrums. Then the gurion that had Alex rose to its full height out of the water, and Alex kicked off from the creature's body. The gurion had one of its own rays crammed into its mouth and was gobbling it down, shrieking in pain as its own digestive juices and teeth ripped into its own flesh. The animal was devouring itself; and its weird physiology – especially the peristaltic motion of its rows of inward-pointing teeth – would not let it stop.

Sten felt something thump at his side, and he grabbed into the water for Dynsman. The man was struggling hysterically; Sten felt for his carotid, pinched, and after a few moments Dynsman went limp. Sten began hauling the man to shore.

'There's more!' Alex shouted.

About a quarter of a klick away, three more shapes had risen out of the water and were charging toward them. Alex was at his side now, and the two of them grabbed Dynsman by the collar and began wading for their lives.

On the shore, Chetwynd and the others had been watching the battle with great interest. Chetwynd saw the two Dru guards rescue the little creep they called Dynsman. He glanced lazily over at one of the skiffs. If he gave the word, he and his cronies could rescue the three.

From many meters away, Sten could read Chetwynd's mind: the other skiffs, just lying there, plenty of hunters, and many makeshift weapons to boot. Even before it happened, Sten knew what Chetwynd was about to do.

The laugh came from his toes and burst up along his tremendous bulk. Chetwynd had never seen anything so funny. He collapsed to the ground, howling with mirth. Around him, the other prisoners caught the humor of the whole thing. If they didn't help, the guards would die. And there was no way Chetwynd and his mates could be blamed. The entire shore rippled with laughter.

Sten and Alex dug in for one last effort as the water prowed behind them and a gurion closed in. With a final yank, they dragged out of the last few meters of muck and collapsed on the beach.

Sten lay there for a very long time. He could hear the laughter all around him. He waited there, gathering his breath, his eyes closed. Finally there was silence. He turned over on his back and looked upward. Chetwynd was grinning down at him.

'Anything I can do to help, mister?' Chetwynd said.

Sten stared up into the mocking eyes. He felt the thin haft of his knife in his hand, and thought about how it would feel to . . .

'What the clot!' Sten gasped.

And the feeling was gone, and Sten found himself convulsed with laughter. All one had to do was to look at events from Chetwynd's point of view.

The aircar slid across the barren landscape, Alex at the controls. Dynsman was stuffed safely between them and a course was set for headquarters. There was a groan, and Alex glanced down at the stirring Dynsman. 'A hard lad to kill,' he commented.

'Yeah, well I guess we can settle that. Gimme.'

He motioned to Alex, and Kilgour fished through a pocket and came up with a tiny hypo. He handed it to Sten, who began peeling up Dynsman's sleeve. The little bomber opened his eyes, spotted Sten, and tried to struggle up. Sten pushed him down with a hard hand and pressed the hypo to his flesh.

'Sweet dreams, you little clot,' he said, and plunged it in.

Chapter Twenty-Six

Sten thought it was too easy. The max-variation chip in Dru's central computer that determined the draw of the escort lottery turned out to be near-Stone Age, its random-variable generator only controlled by a pickup that measured the magnetic flux from Dru's sun and the other two worlds in the system.

His fellow guards didn't.

'Clottin' hell. I said this man was lucky,' a guard marveled. 'Not two months on-post, and you get the bag detail.'

'Ah, tha's m'partner Mr. Keet,' Alex covered.

'He cannae play cards worth a whistle, an' his choice on the racin' beasties is horrific.

'But gie the wee lad a pure-chance game, an' he always walks.'

Their shift sergeant was more then irked.

'Mr. Keet. Mr. Ohlsn. I find it upsetting that you two new assignees to Dru are this lucky.'

'Yessir,' Sten said. He and Alex, in formal grays, were locked at attention.

'Consider this, gentlemen. While you're escorting this prisoner's body back to Heath, I plan on a full investigation.'

'Investigation? A' wha?' Alex said.

'Of . . . we'll just call it luck. But I expect, when you two return here, there shall be great surprises.'

'Aye, Sergeant,' Alex put in fervently 'When next y' see us, surprises will be all around.'

Before Alex could continue, Sten side-kicked him into silence, saluted, and the two about-faced and exited.

The robot ship, just out-atmosphere, automatically shut off the Yukawa drive and kicked in the AM_2 drive for the stars.

Alex and Sten had already broken the lock to the control chamber and were standing over the pilot.

'Th' Tahn dinna be a' bright a' they think,' Alex said. 'This autopilot's a' easy to reprogram a' bacon through a goose.' And Alex busied himself at the tapeplotter, changing the ship's course. 'Dinna y' want to be unfreezin't wee Dynsman?'

'Why bother,' Sten said. 'A dead villain's not a worry.'

'Aye. Time enow to lazarus the lad when we rendezvous.'

Rendezvous was with a superspeed Imperial destroyer lurking just outside the Tahn sector, with instructions to monitor a given wave frequency for pickup. Once Alex and Sten were picked up, the robot ship would be returned to its old course for Heath. But a spacejunk fragment lay in its future. The robot ship would never arrive at its destination.

'W' hae our mad bomber, w' hae our health, wha' more could a man want?'

'A good healthy drink,' Sten offered, and headed for the guards' living section to see if anybody had been humane enough to pack a liter or so of alk.

Chapter Twenty-Seven

The blue panel on Ledoh's desk began blinking. Ledoh quickly shut down the inconsequential conversation he'd been having with the Imperial Commissariat, hit the buttons that locked the entrance to his office, and set off the CONFERENCE lights. He crossed to the doorway into the Imperial chambers and tapped with a fingertip, then entered.

The Emperor had his chair swung around and was staring out at the parade grounds as Ledoh entered. Two full flasks sat on the Emperor's desk, one of what the Emperor called Scotch, the other – Ledoh shuddered when he recognized it – pure medical alk.

Without turning, the Emperor growled, 'You feel like a drink, Admiral?'

'Uh . . . not particularly.'

'Neither do I. What's the worst thing that's happened to you this shift?'

Ledoh sifted through unpleasantries. 'The Tahn Embassy's Principal Secretary expressed dissatisfaction with the meetings.'

'He thinks *he's* dissatisfied?'

'To continue, sir. His dissatisfaction has been communicated, through the usual channels, to the Tahn lords. I, uh, have here their response.'

'Go ahead. Ruin my day.'

'The communiqué is on my desk, if you'd like the exact wording,' Ledoh said. 'No? Roughly, in view of the situation on the Fringe Worlds, the Tahn lords would like to meet with you.'

'Is that all?'

'Not quite. Because of the death of Alain, they are reluctant to meet here on Prime. They request a meeting on neutral ground in deep space, further conditions, to include the proper security by both sides, to be negotiated. Said meeting to occur within one Prime year.'

'Clot, clot, clot. They are shoving it in my face.'

'Yessir.'

'What about the riots on the Fringe Worlds?'

'Four capitals overrun. No word from provincial capitals. Guard support units are moving into position. Casualties? We have an estimate of somewhere approaching twelve thousand. On both sides.'

'You know,' the Emperor said evenly, 'at one time I figured that any problem I faced could be met with sweet reason, the Guards, or enough alk to blind me out. Turns out I was wrong, Admiral. This appears to be one of those situations. I'll summarize. See if you agree: Fact A: The Tahn worlds are using the death of Alain to pressure me. They want the Empire to back out of the Fringe Worlds. Correct?'

'Very possibly,' Ledoh said.

'I pull out – and that'll leave those settlers who moved in dumb, fat, and happy on the assumption that the Empire will protect them forever and ever amen swinging in the wind. Im-clottin'-possible, even if I could convince those yokels to uproot and haul.

'Fact B: Alain's dissidents, who never got the word that unification with the Tahn worlds would probably mean their instant demise or at least the destruction of everything they're fighting for, are equally beyond reason. Check me, Admiral.'

'You are making no mistakes that I can see.'

'So the only solution that I've got is to figure out who murdered Godfrey Alain – and it *better* be nobody Imperial – and then go off and meet with these Tahn. On their turf. And eat a measure of drakh. Is that the only way out?'

'No comment, sir.'

'You are a lot of clottin' help. Mahoney would have had an idea.' The Emperor glared at Admiral Ledoh, and then his expression softened. 'Sorry. That was a cheap shot.

'What I'm thinking is that, way back when I was a ship engineer, I had another solution to things.'

'I'm very interested in hearing it.'

'That was to drink all the alk in sight and then punch up everyone involved.'

'Very humorous,' Ledoh said.

'You are a clottin' heap of help,' the Emperor snarled as he got up and headed for the door into his private chambers.

Ledoh, before he left, carefully replaced both flasks in their cabinet.

Chapter Twenty-Eight

The gurion rushed straight for him, its blood-red stomach brushing across his face, leaving a trail of digestive saliva that burned through the first layer of skin. Dynsman screamed in horror and hurled himself backward. From the corner of his eye he saw the Dru guard plunge a pole into the creature's maw, and then the boat flipped over against the combined weight of the gurion and Dynsman's panicked attempt to escape.

He clawed his way to the bottom. He was in total hysteria, breath bursting out of his lungs, yet too frightened to surface. Blindly, he grabbed hold of a razor-sharp outcrop and felt the edges bite deeply into his hands. Despite the pain, he held on as long as he could. He could feel the awful roil of the water and taste the rusty sweetness of blood. Something hard touched him and Dynsman screamed again, losing the little hold he had over his sanity. Water rushed into his lungs and he battled his way to the surface. A huge *whoosh* of air knifed in, and Dynsman saw the guardsman closing on him, gore dripping from a slim flash of silver in his hand. Dynsman struck out at the man in a panic. In slow motion the knife hand reached toward him. Dynsman was helpless, and watched in awful fascination as the knife slid into a mouth beneath the arm, and then the hand shadowed past his head. There was a sudden heavy pressure between his shoulder blades and neck, and Dynsman felt himself . . . dying . . . dying . . . dying . . .

His body flopped against its restraints on the table. A huge flipper appeared and just barely touched the slidepot, and soothing sedative trickled into his veins. Dynsman's body went very still again.

Rykor's face was a portrait of odobenus-contemplation. She woofed at her dripping whiskers and then daintily brushed them aside with a front nip. Rykor sighed and leaned back into her gravchair. The bot mechanism shrilled in complaint as it tried to adjust itself to her enormous bulk.

'It's difficult, young Sten,' she said. 'The man keeps replaying the same memory patterns.'

Rykor was one of the Empire's chief psychologists, specializing in the Imperial military. Her subspecialty, never publicly mentioned, was screening people for the Guard's Mercury Corps – intelligence – and for the secret Mantis teams. She also handled the occasional special project, such as Dynsman's in-progress brainscan. But Dynsman's brain was locked in trauma and insisted on rerunning the moments of his near-death.

Sten glanced at the helpless bomber, almost obscene in his nakedness, dripping with a myriad of probes and intersyn connects. He had seen Dynsman relive the moments a dozen times, and so far nothing went past the gurion attack. Even the moment when he came awake on the flit was a ghostly instant that flashed back again and again to the terrible moment of the gurion.

Sten rose and walked to Rykor's side. She reached out an affectionate flipper and gently caressed him. 'You were always one of my . . . special people,' she said softly.

Sten ran his hand across the bulk that was her shoulder.

Rykor brought her mind back from the Dynsman place. 'Do you still have the knife in your arm?' she asked suddenly.

Sten just grinned and kept patting, bringing her down from the link.

Rykor hoisted herself up suddenly, the gravchair groaning. 'We must go deeper. Smash past the trauma block.'

'It's important,' Sten said. 'Others have died.'

Rykor nodded and eased back into a full rest. She concentrated fully on the brainscan and gave the slidepot a heavy tap. Dynsman moaned.

Above him, the screen came to life again. First it was in black and white, and then a swirl of color bars. The bars fuzzed together and formed a picture. Softness at first, and then the gurion threatened for an instant, and then gradually collapsed against a persistent crease of yellow. Stan watched as Dynsman relived his life, in full color.

The tall slender man with the thick shock of gray hair leaned a narcobeer across the table. Dynsman's screen hand reached in and pulled it forward.

'Next shout's on me,' Dynsman's voice echoed.

The man smiled into the screen at 'Dynsman,' and from the monitor's empathy-banks Sten could tell that it was a smile Dynsman didn't quite trust. In fact, he was more than a little frightened.

'. . . If you don't mind, Dr. Knox,' Dynsman continued, his voice trembling a little.

The gurion extended a long ray toward Dynsman, and he shrieked as he felt the cold band whip around his neck—

'Stop!' A shout from Sten.

Rykor took one look at the frozen horror on the screen and leaned her flipper onto the slidepot. Dynsman's body relaxed on the table. Rykor waited for Sten's instructions.

'Knox,' Sten said. 'Enhance.'

The mind-vid screen blanked then blurred as it reversed itself to Knox. It held there as Sten studied the figure. 'That's our boy,' he said. 'Fits the hospital description. Now, what else can we find out about him? Smell? Any special scent he uses?'

Rykor keyed in the sniffers. 'Nothing at all,' she said. 'Quite out of the ordinary for a man who obviously cares so much about his appearance.' She ran her cursor up to his carefully coiffed hair for an example.

'As a matter of fact,' she said, after studying her monitors, 'there is nothing about this man at all – except for his visual appearance – that should attract any being . . . smell, no register . . . voice, firm, but no register . . . aura press, no register . . .'

She turned her head lazily toward Sten. 'Nothing marks this human at all. Highly suspicious. Body motion empathy . . . verbal . . . forget it. It's all zed, zed, zed.'

Sten studied the frozen picture that was Dr. Knox. At the moment, Knox was the complete cut-out man. No one, except a superpro, is completely two-dimensional. Then Sten noticed something: a dull of yellow on Knox's left hand.

'Enhance, left hand,' he told Rykor.

The hand filled the brainscan screen. The dull yellow was a ring, with a very clear emblem stamped on its flat surface. Sten peered at it, knowing what it was, but not quite believing it. The stamped emblem was a foot, elongated with its emphasis on the heel. And on the heel . . .

'Magnify,' Sten said.

Blossoming from the heel were two wings.

Sten groaned and relaxed back into his chair. Matters had gotten even worse than he had expected.

Even Rykor was a bit overcome. She sneezed loudly. 'Mercury Corps,' she said, puffing through wet whiskers.

'Yeah,' Sten said. 'And I hope to god he's just a renegade.'

The gurion's ray encircled Dynsman's neck . . . nestling, and then with a sudden burst, pulling him close. Dynsman felt his lungs collapse and saw the last precious stream of air explode outward. And then a knife hand – Sten's? – swept into view . . . and . . .

'The rest of the way!' Sten ordered.

Rykor's flipper paused at the slidepot. She glanced over at Dynsman's flopping body, where he was reliving the horror again and again. Her empathy glands were weeping at the edges of her eyes.

'I don't know if I can,' she said.

'Do it!' Sten said.

And Rykor startled, sliding the pot full on. The brainscan flurried far ahead . . .

The holograph to one side of the screen that was Dynsman's brain was the body of a curling worm. On its main body, winking colors of blue and red and yellow, mapped the parts that Sten and Rykor had already explored. The gurion marked the only red. The blue points were connected by thin capillary pink. Those blue spots already touched were blinking at them.

'Where?' Sten urged. 'Where?'

Rykor studied the holograph. An infinite number of blue spots to go . . . empathy . . . empathy . . .

'There,' she breathed. And Rykor wept as she zeroed in.

The image of the bar that was the Covenanter filled the screen. The laser brights of the sign were swallowed by the fog that drifted in from the nearby spaceport. Dynsman didn't know the scientific reason for it, but at night many kilometers surrounding the main port were surrounded by fog. And, this was a special night. He was waiting for . . .

'This is a busto bum go,' Dynsman's thoughts whispered across the screen to Sten and Rykor.

Dynsman was as unsure of himself as he had ever been. A huge picture of one hand suddenly filled the screen. Two missing fingers stubbed out.

'Come, on,' Sten said impatiently. Rykor twisted the scroll.

The screen furred and then Dynsman was watching two men greet each other in front of the bar.

'Push the sound,' Sten snapped.

Alain looked at the man in engineer coveralls, made his assessment, and then said, 'Engineer Raschid?'

Sten and Rykor watched the two men go inside, and then flashing shadow hands as Dynsman armed his bomb and waited for the final moments. There was no sound from the bomb's timer, but Dynsman could hear the ticking in his mind. The words 'Engineer Raschid' were the key. He had paced out the seconds it would take for them to be greeted by Janiz and then seated in Booth C.

Dynsman beat out the last moment of several people's lives in his mind. Not now . . . almost now . . . now . . . and the brainscan room was filled with muted white light and ear-shattering explosions.

Then the screen became a gurion, pulsing its stomach-mouth toward Dynsman's face. The man that was Dynsman strained against his straps and screamed once again.

Rykor watched him, her eyes filling with tears. 'What should I do with him?' she asked.

Sten shrugged. Rykor wiped her eyes. Then she reached out her flipper and pushed the slidepot down the rest of the way. On the table, Dynsman was suddenly very still. He was peaceful then, for the first time in his life.

'Do you believe in ghosts?' Rykor asked.

Sten thought for a minute. 'Maybe . . . but not his.'

Rykor considered that, and then pressed the buttons that ordered the chair to deliver her back into her soothing deep-water bath. And just before she disappeared into a explosion of water, Sten heard her say, 'You're an optimist, young Sten.'

And Sten imagined a hoot of laughter exploding out of the tank. Sten exited the chamber, wondering exactly what she meant.

Chapter Twenty-Nine

Sten shifted the bulky file from one arm to another and stood patiently in the doorway to the work area. He watched with no little amazement as the Eternal Emperor bent low over the strange boxlike object held gently in his hands. The curled right fingers of his hand plucked at first cautiously at the strings, and then with more confidence.

He sang in a soft, husky voice:

> 'Now with this loaded
> blunderbuss
> The truth I will unfold.
> He made the mayor to tremble
> And he robbed him of his gold . . .'

One string buzzled against a fret and the Emperor broke off in frustration. 'Clot!'

He slammed the instrument down with a loud bang and an echoing of stringed chords. He stared at the thing for a long moment and then kicked it over to a heap of similar objects. Then he spotted Sten. He frowned deeply, and then his face cleared. 'Don't *ever* try to build a guitar,' he growled.

'I wouldn't dream of it, sir,' Sten said as he walked into the work area.

He looked at the pile of discarded instruments and glanced around the room. Hung here and there were other attempts. Some were partially completed. Some consisted of just the cut-out backs. And scattered about were necks in a variety of sizes, drilled for rods. Sten sniffed at the evil-smelling smoke boiling from a pot of goo that was bubbling over an open fire.

'Excuse me, sir, but what's a guitar?'

'A musical instrument,' the Emperor said. 'Or at least that's what some devil called it when he invented the fretted thing.'

Sten nodded thoughtfully. 'Oh, that's what you were doing.' He picked up one of the discarded guitars. And studied it. He peered past the strings and inside the hole.

'I don't see any circuitry. How do you make it work?'

'With great bleeding difficulty,' the Emperor said. He rose and pulled one of the blank backs from its wall hook. Then he sat again and laid it across his knees. 'Hand me the sandpaper.'

Sten looked around, wondering what his boss meant. Then he connected: Sand. Rough. Some kind of abrasive. He reached down to the litter on the floor and picked up something that he believed would fit the requirements.

'It's all in the inside shape,' the Emperor said. 'Something to do with how the sound bounces against the box. Trouble is, nobody was very scientific about it back in those days.' He took the sandpaper from Sten and began polishing inside the box.

'They did it to taste,' the Emperor went on. 'So much here . . .' He rubbed along one curving line. 'So much there . . .' He began sanding at the brace of the strut itself, smoothing and removing spots of what appeared to be glue.

In sudden disgust, the Emperor set the thing down on the floor. Sten saw, however, that this time he was careful to place it on a thick rug. The Emperor noticed where he was looking.

'Lebanese,' he said by way of explanation. 'Two square yards from said folk. You don't even want to know what it cost.'

He looked up at Sten. 'Okay,' he finally said. 'You want a safe place to talk. This is it.' He swept his hand around the workshop, crammed with antique tools and materials. 'This is the most secure place I know of. I have it swept daily.'

Sten smiled thinly. He picked up the thick file folder and slid out a small, slender device. 'And I just swept it again, sir,' he said, showing him the debugging device.

The Emperor looked at him. 'And?'

Sten picked up the guitar that the Emperor had recently dismissed as poor quality. He shook his head.

'Maybe that's what made the, uh, guitar buzz,' he said. 'Sorry about that, Your Highness.'

The Eternal Emperor thought for a moment, considering whether he ought to get mad. After a while, he grinned at Sten. Then he grabbed a pair of tongs, lifted up the pot of evil-smelling goo, and dabbed it on the guitar with a brush.

He looked up at Sten. 'Well?'

Sten checked his snooper, and then shook his head. 'Clean.' Then he opened the remainder of the file and palmed its contents across the desk in a gambler's swirl. 'Are you ready, sir?' Sten asked.

The Emperor studied him. 'You mean am I through clotting around?'

'Yes, sir,' Sten said.

The Emperor picked up the unfinished guitar body again and started stroking its sides. 'Go.'

Sten pulled out a photograph – a still taken from the brainscan room. 'That's our boy,' he said.

The Emperor studied the picture of Knox. 'Mr. Big,' he said dryly.

'If by that you mean the main fellow behind this thing no, sir, I don't think so. He was merely Dynsman's control. Fortunately for us, he wasn't satisfied with just that role.' Sten handed over another photo.

The Emperor peered down to see a tight shot of Knox's ring hand. He caught the emblem instantly. 'Mercury Corps!'

'Yes, sir. Not only that, we know for a fact that this man – call him Knox for the moment – was a doctor. That means he was probably a Mercury Corps trained medico.'

'Former or current?'

'Hopefully, former. We don't know. I've got Lieutenant Haines checking on it.'

Sten ran down for a second, watching the Emperor sitting very quietly, rubbing the abrasive against the wood. The Emperor reached into a slit pocket and pulled out a small object. Sten peered forward. The object appeared to be made of metal, and forked. His boss shifted the object around in his hand and then gently tapped it against the side of the instrument. A low, muted tone *thum*ed . . . for many heartbeats. The Emperor pressed it against his cheek, quieting it.

'The harmony,' he said, 'still isn't right. Go on, Captain.'

Sten took a deep breath. What he had to say next was putting him on very dangerous ground. 'May I speak freely, sir?' Sten asked, knowing it for a fool question. No one should ever speak freely to a superior. But it was a chance he had to take.

'GA.'

'A large piece of this puzzle is missing. Right from the middle.'

'What do you need to find it?'

'An honest answer.'

'Someone is holding back?'

'Yes, sir.'

The Emperor had caught the point long ago. Still, he liked to play things out.

'Would that someone be me?'

'I'm afraid so, sir.'

'Ask away,' the Emperor said, his face strangely softening.

Sten sighed.

'Thank you, sir. But let me lay the rest of this thing out first. Then I'll ask.'

'Okay, we'll do it your way. But hand me the glue.'

Sten puzzled at him, and then realized the Emperor was pointing at the evil-smelling pot. Sten picked it up and handed it to the boss.

The Emperor reached over to a dusty shelf and slid out a small wood-handled brush. He let it float on top of the goo pot and reached down between his legs for the top of the guitar. He thumped it with his knuckles. Then he scraped the tuning fork across it, listening intently for the humming sound. He nodded with satisfaction. 'This one might be right.'

Then he dipped the brush deeply into the hot mixture at his feet and began brushing the goo along the ridges of the guitar's shoe.

'To start with,' Sten said, 'there was some kind of code phrase that seemed to trigger the bombing. Dynsman's vital functions jumped about twelve beats every time we mind-scrolled it back.'

'Which was?'

The Emperor listened closely as he continued working. He fit the top of the guitar to its box and then clamped it into place.

Sten glanced at his notes. 'Raschid,' he said. 'The action was supposed to begin when someone used the name Raschid. To be exact, the phrase was Engineer Raschid.'

Sten didn't notice the Emperor's face cloud over in anger. 'Go on,' he prodded, almost in a whisper.

'Then there was Booth C,' Sten said. 'Dynsman was supposed to trigger the time bomb when he next heard someone ask for Booth C.'

'Stop,' the Emperor said. He said it quietly, it was as clear a command as Sten had ever heard. 'So I killed her,' the Emperor said to himself. 'It was me.'

'Sir?'

By way of an answer, the Emperor pulled a bottle from underneath his stool. He took a long shuddering drink and then handed it to Sten.

Sten just waited, staring at him. If there was any way of getting through to this man, Eternal Emperor or not Sten was hoping it was then. 'Engineer Raschid?' the Emperor said. 'Yeah. That's me. One of my many disguises, Captain. When I like to get down among them.'

It all came together for Sten after that admission. 'Then sir, it follows that you were the target. It had nothing to do with Godfrey Alain. Or the emissary who went to meet him in your place.'

The Emperor smiled a sad smile. 'Yeah. He was supposed to identify himself as Engineer Raschid. Instead of the bar, they were supposed to ask Janiz for Booth C.'

'Janiz?' Sten asked. 'Who was Janiz?'

The Emperor just waved him on. So Sten continued linking the chain of evidence together.

'Fine. So here was how it was supposed to go. Dynsman had the bomb set up at Booth C. It was shaped to destroy the bar, but only stun its key occupant. Meaning you. The rest is easy. The ambulance was supposed to take you to Dr. Knox.'

'And then they figured I'd be in their control,' the Emperor said. 'Dumb clots. It's been tried.'

He started to take a sip from the bottle, then shook his head, corked it, and shoved it under his stool. 'Sometimes,' he said, 'I don't like myself. You ever feel that way?'

Sten figured it was better to ignore this and just press on. 'Sir,' he said as carefully as possible, 'it seems to me that the Tahn have got clot all to do with this. Somebody – probably one of your own people – wants to replace you as Emperor. The Tahn just got dragged into it because of Alain.'

He waited for a response, but the Emperor remained silent, thinking his own thoughts. Sten decided that it was time to ask the key question. 'Who was she, sir?'

The Emperor raised his old/young eyes. 'Janiz,' he said. 'Just Janiz. We used to be lovers. Quite a few years ago. When I was feeling . . . who the clot cares how I felt.

'I told her a few stories. About what a badass I was. How rich I was gonna be. And she . . . she . . . Hell, son, she listened to me.'

'But you were the Emperor,' Sten said softly.

The Emperor shook his head, no. 'I was Engineer Raschid,' he said. 'A bully dreamer. A liar. Hell, she believed me. I used to roll into town pretty regular – every year or two. Then I kept promoting myself. And then it was Captain Raschid, ma'am. Captain Raschid.'

'But that was a long time ago,' Sten guessed.

The Eternal Emperor nodded. 'We stopped being lovers. But we stayed friends. I put up the credits for the bar. I was to be a very silent partner. Except for Booth C. I had her keep that just for me, or people I sent there. I had the best anti-snooping equipment in my Empire installed.

'Godfrey Alain wasn't the first covert meet I set up there. Strange what you make of old lovers.'

He thought for a long moment and then pulled the bottle out from under his feet. He took a small drink to clear his head. 'What is your advice, Captain?'

Sten rose to his feet. 'We know there's a leak, sir.' He began pacing. 'We have to shut down everything. Someone, sir, is very definitely trying to kill you.'

The Emperor smiled an odd smile. He started to speak but kept it to himself. Sten wished to God he had said what was on his mind. What was he still hiding?

'Okay. You are the target. We don't know how many conspirators there are. So we trust no one. I follow the Knox trail. And, you, sir . . .'

'Yes, Captain? What exactly do you propose I do?'

Sten caught himself, and wondered if he had gone too far.

The Emperor raised several fingers in a mock salute. 'Don't worry about me, Captain,' he said. 'I'll be perfectly safe. Although sometimes I wish . . .' The Eternal Emperor picked up his last discarded guitar. He bent low over it and began fingering out a complicated string of chords.

Even to Sten's untrained ear, it sounded pretty good. It also sounded like a final dismissal.

Chapter Thirty

Kai Hakone ground his palms together and the tabac leaves shredded down onto the leaf below. Carefully he sprinkled water onto the leaf, then rolled the leaf around the shreds, folding the ends in on the roll. He finished, inspected the cheroot with satisfaction, then dipped it in the nearly full snifter of Earth cognac before him. Satisfied, he clipped the end and, using a wooden firestick, lit the cheroot and leaned back, looking across the chamber. It was a private room in one of Prime World's most exclusive clubs, where it was very easy for Hakone's fellows to meet, and for Hakone to keep free of monitoring devices.

The other men in the room – perhaps fifty – were Hakone's age or older. Industrialists, retired high-rankers, entrepreneurs with laurels to rest on. To an outsider, they reeked of wealth. To Hakone, they smelled like death.

But to Kai Hakone, that nostril-scorching scent like lamb, like burnt pork, was the smell of his life, and his writing.

Some people are formed by a single experience.

Such was Kai Hakone.

Almost from birth he had wanted to fly. To fly in space. The world he was born on was comfortably settled, as were his parents. His mother had one great idea – that it would be possible to establish a store where persons could walk in, fit themselves into a booth for measurement, then pick a pattern and, within minutes, have a custom-tailored garment. That idea made the Hakones very wealthy and very satisfied.

They had no understanding – but also no disagreement – with their son's desire to go out; and so Kai Hakone ended up commissioned as a lieutenant in command of a probe vessel at the start of the Mueller Wars.

Hakone had taken all the lessons of the Academy to heart and was earnestly trying to lead, inspire, and be an authoritarian friend to the thirty-eight men on the tiny ship. But his probe ship was picked for close-in support of the landing on Saragossa. Five Imperial battlewagons died that day, as did most of the Seventh Guards Division committed on the troopships. Among the million dead spewed into lung-spilling space or endlessly falling onto a rock-hard planet, were the men and women of Hakone's ship.

His probe ship had died slowly, cut to ribbons by missiles, close-range lasers, and finally projectile-blast guns. Lieutenant Kai Hakone was the only survivor. He'd been dug out of the ruins of the ship and slowly psyched back together.

After the Mueller Wars ground down, the Emperor found it very convenient to allow anyone in the Imperial Service who wanted out, out. Kai Hakone found himself a young civilian, with a more-than-adequate separation allowance, no desire to return to his home world, and the reek of death in his nostrils.

That reek had led him to his current career as a writer.

His first vid-book – a novel on the rites-of-passage-via-slaughter – bombed. His second, a sober analysis of the Mueller Wars, became a best-seller, being published ten years after the war ended, just at the correct time for a revisionist appraisal. Since then, Hakone's works, all grim, all tinged with the skull, were received and reviewed as coming from a major creative artist.

His sixth volume, a return to nonfiction, soberly analyzed what went wrong at the battle of Saragossa, taking the scandalous viewpoint that the young admiral-in-place was a scapegoat for the Emperor's own failings. The work was, of course, cleverly worded to avoid any semblance of political libel.

But that, Hakone realized, was another turning point. That was the reason he was sitting in a rich man's club, smelling rich men's lives and feeling like a spectre at the banquet. But Hakone shut that thought off, much as he closed off the perpetual wonderment of what would have happened to Kai Hakone had the battle of Saragossa been an Imperial triumph.

He clicked fingernails against the table for attention, and the room fell silent.

Again he looked around at the fifty-odd men in the room. If Hakone were brighter, or more analytical, he might have wondered why none of the former military people had rank above one-star, why the industrialists were all people who had inherited their businesses from their forebears, and why the entrepreneurs were those who hustled borderline deals. But the nature of conspiracy is not to question.

'Gentlemen,' he began, his quiet voice a contradiction to his bear-like presence. 'Before we begin, let me advise you that this room has been proofed against any known electronic eavesdropping, as well as any physical pickups. We are able to speak freely.'

A man stood. Hakone identified him as Saw Toyer, who'd increased his riches supplying uniforms for the Guard.

'Time has passed, Sr. Hakone,' he accused. 'We – and I think I speak for us all – have given more than generously. We expected . . . something to happen following Empire Day. As you promised. Instead, and I am not asking to be privy to the secrets, nothing has occurred. At least nothing which we can see.

'Were I not committed, I might ask if my credits are being poured into a black hole.'

'That is the purpose of the meeting,' Hakone answered. 'To inform you of what has happened.'

Hakone could have gone into detail: that the attempt to shock and then kidnap the Emperor had gone awry. That the assassin had successfully fled Prime World. That his control and their operative doctor, Har Stynburn – 'Dr. Knox' – had disappeared. But that as far as Hakone knew, the dangling tails of that conspiracy had either been cleaned up – such as the murder of Tac Chief Kreuger – or had cleaned themselves up. But he knew that the secret to success is never to worry the money-men with minor problems.

'Phase One, as you've said, went awry. But, you'll notice, without any suspicion on the part of the Emperor, other than his assigning one of his personal soldiers to investigate. As guaranteed, we left no traces.

'There is one problem, however. And that is that our normal source of intelligence has gone dry. We no longer have input to the Emperor's next moves.'

Hakone swizzled his cheroot in the cognac and relit the cigar, waiting for the buzz of dismay to die. Gutless. Gutless, he thought. These men have never learned that there is always one more kilometer that you must go. So, his optimistic side answered, you learned long ago that you run with what you brought.

Hakone tapped for silence again. The buzz was louder as fear grew in the room. Hakone wetted a finger in the cognac and began moving it around the rim of the glass. The high whine silenced the throng.

'Thank you,' Hakone said. 'What is past is past. Now for the good news. Our coordinator is most pleased with what is going on.'

'Why?' The snarl was unidentifiable.

'Because in spite of our actions, and in spite of Imperial motion, there have been no breaks.'

'So what do we do next – find holes and pull 'em in after ourselves?' That came from Ban Lucery, one of the few industrialists Hakone respected.

'That is a firm negative. Our coordinator – and I heartily agree with his decision – has said that we move to Phase Two of what we've dubbed Operation Zaarah Wahrid. Relax, gentlemen. The days of this intolerable Imperial control are numbered. There is no way Phase Two can fail.'

Chapter Thirty-One

The little men purveyed the logs from the pond, hooked them into the chain hoist, and the drunk sat against a pile of peeled logs and cheered. Naik Rai and Subadar-Major Chittahang Limbu watched approvingly.

Sten shut his model box down and the figures disappeared instantly, although he was sure that his 'drunk' had time to take another swig from the bottle before he vanished.

'This is not good,' Haik Rai said. 'How will you remember which socks to wear?'

'You are sure this is correct?' Limbu echoed in Gurkhali.

'Goddamn it,' Sten swore. 'I am not sure of anything, Subadar-Major. All I know is that I am detached on Imperial Service. All I know is that you are to take charge of the Gurkhas.

'And all I know is that if you shame me, on Dashera it shall not be bullocks but ballocks that are cut off. By me, Subadar-Major.'

Limbu started to laugh, then saluted. 'Captain, I have no idea what is happening. But I do have this feeling that none of us shall meet short of Moksa.'

Sten lifted a lip. 'Thank you for your confidence, Chittahang. But I wave my private parts at that feeling. That is all. You are dismissed.'

The two Gurkhas saluted and were gone. Sten continued packing. Again the door signal buzzed, and Sten palmed it open.

It was Lisa. Sten noticed that she carried a debugging pouch that was on. The door closed, and he decided the first order of business was to kiss her thoroughly.

Eventually they broke. Lisa smiled up at him. 'Everything is ga-ga.'

'No drakh,' Sten said. 'You sound like the Eternal Emperor.'

'You're leaving.'

'I say again my last. I know I am leaving. For the safe house.'

'Nope,' Haines said, coming back to the point. 'I mean you're *leaving* leaving. You and that tubby thug of yours.'

'Uh-oh.'

'We've found our famous Dr. Knox.' And Haines threw a fiche onto Sten's table.

'Tell me about it.'

'Dr. John Knox is actually named Hars Stynburn. Broken out of the Mercury Corps. Court-martial sealed: I quote "for the good of the Service" end quote.'

Sten felt a first wave of relief: at least the conspiracy didn't involve the current Imperial military.

'It seems that Dr. Stynburn, who always was fairly militant about his views, was assigned as Med Off to a pacification team. Some world – it's in the fiche – that the Empire had trouble bringing under control.

'The natives on this particular world didn't want much of anything,' Lisa said. 'Except steel weapons. Dr. Stynburn somehow arranged that the spearheads and so forth were highly radioactive. Is that what you people really do?'

'Knock it off, Lisa.'

'Sorry. It's been a long day. Anyway, so the natives kicked – the female ones, since the planet was a matriarchy. Native life span was real short, so by the time Stynburn's team was taken off, the planet was clean for settlement.

'Unfortunately somebody sang like a vulture, and Dr. Stynburn got a court-martial.'

By this time, Sten had fed the fiche into his desk viewer, listening to Haines with only a quarter of his attention.

'Busted out. No prison . . . clot it . . . should'a spaced him . . . drifted . . . no record of employment . . .' He shut off the viewer and looked at Lisa.

'No record,' she said. 'But we found him. He's off Prime.'

'Where?'

'A little hidey-hole of a planet named Kulak.' Haines handed Sten another fiche.

'How'd you find him so fast?'

'Since you pointed out that our Dr. Knox appeared more 'n a bit egocentric, I wondered if he wasn't also dumb enough to keep his career going instead of disappearing as a potwalloper.

'Sure enough. Dr. – his new name's William Block – is the contract medico on Kulak.'

Sten fed more fiche into his viewer, scanned the overall description, and was scared several different shades of white. 'I should've stayed in Mantis,' he said to himself. 'All I'd be doing is making a drop into some swamp with no more than ten thousand to one odds. But not dummy me.'

'You've heard of Kulak?'

Sten didn't bother with the full explanation, since it was fairly involved. Kulak was a small planetoid with a poisonous atmosphere and a killer environment. Its location was approximately between Galaxy's End and Nowhere. Its only interesting feature was that crystalline metals on the planet had a life of their own, growing like plants. One of those metals was incredibly light, yet far stronger than any conventional metal known to the Empire. Its chemical properties and description were included on the fiche.

But Sten was quite familiar with that substance – he'd 'built' the knife hidden in his arm from it, back on Vulcan, in 'Hellworld' – the punishment sector for Vulcan's slave laborers. The work area – Area 35 – had duplicated Kulak's environment exactly, down to the point of killing over 100 per cent of the workers sentenced to it.

And now Sten was required to go back to Area 35. He was as terrified as he'd ever been in his life.

Sten told his swirling stomach to shut up and scanned on. After discovery, Kulak had been abandoned by the discovering company, but it was reopened years later by independent miners, tough men and women who were willing to crapshoot their settlement on Kulak. Since Kulak was not considered a plush assignment, their co-op had jumped at the chance to get a for-real doctor, especially one willing to pact on a two-E-year-contract. Since many of the miners were themselves on the run from Imperial justice, no one was much interested in exactly what Dr. 'Block' – Hars Stynburn – had done. On Kulak, Imperial treason rated up there with nonpayment of child support.

Sten corrected his features and yanked the fiche. 'Yeah I've heard of Kulak.'

'I have a tacship standing by,' Haines said. 'Destination sealed, even for the pilot. And I ordered the necessary environmental suits.'

None of the replies that occurred immediately to Sten was suitable – and then Kilgour thundered through the entranceway, tapping a fiche angrily.

'Wee Sten,' he said. 'Y'dinna ken where this daft lass is tryin't to send us noo.'

'Yes, I do.'

'Sorry, Lieutenant. Ah dinna see you f'r a mo.'

'Never mind, Sergeant. Your fearless leader doesn't look as if he's any happier than you are.'

'Sten, d'we hae t'do this? Canne we noo con a wee battalion ae Guards to winkle this dog oot?'

'And put him on the run again?'

'Aye, lad. Aye. Ah guess y'hae a point. Nae a good point, but ae point. So where does this leave us?'

'It would appear,' Sten said dryly, 'that we're doon th' mine.'

'Dinna be makit fun ae th' way Ah speakit,' Alex said. 'Ah'll hae m'mither on y'.'

And Sten went back to packing.

Chapter Thirty-Two

Jill Sherman was the only law on Kulak. Sherman had been chosen by the Kulak cooperative to provide some species of order in the single-dome village that was home base for the miners. She was at least as mean as any miner on the planetoid, she was generally brighter than the miners, and she had a laissez-faire attitude toward law enforcement. She had only three rules: no weapons that could injure the dome; no crooked gambling; every miner got an honest count on his crystals.

Sherman had found it expedient to take the contract as the only law on Kulak after her previous assignment had become somewhat spectacular. She'd been a police subchief on a world plagued with continual riots – understandable, since that world was *entirely* composed of minorities, each of which put its foot down the throat of the less fortunate after achieving power. Eventually Sherman decided she had seen one too many riots and dropped a mininuke. The explosion had not only blown the current party out of power, but Sherman into flight just ahead of a wave of charges – murder, malfeasance in office, and attempted genocide.

She eyed Sten's credentials, then looked at the two men, who were still recovering from landing sickness.

'Dr. Block's done a fine job here. Why in clot should I help you two Imperials take him out?'

'I won't read the warrant again,' Sten said tiredly. 'But there's little things like treason, multiple murder, conspiracy, flight to avoid prosecution – you know. The usual stuff.'

'This is Kulak, my friend. We don't *care* about what someone did back in civilization.'

'Lass,' Alex began. 'P'raps we could buy you a dram and discuss—'

'That's enough, Sergeant,' Sten snapped, perhaps unwisely, but his stomach was still doing ground-loops with the tacship that had fought its way to a landing on Kulak. 'You people operate under an Imperial charter. The charter could be lifted with one com message by me, and Imperial support would be on its way. Are you prepared to escalate, Officer Sherman?' If Sten's guts hadn't been sitting in his throat, he probably would have found a different way to go. He had certainly made a mistake as Alex's near subvocal moan underlined.

'Sorry, uh, Captain was it? Dr. Block can be found in C-Sector, Offices 60.'

Sten then made his second mistake. He nodded brusquely, took Alex by the arm, and was on the way out.

Sherman, of course, waited until the double lock on her office cycled closed, and then was on the com.

Even the streets of the domed city were primitive. They were temp-controlled and oxygenated, but that did not keep the condensation within the dome from continually fogging, raining, and creating much mess underfoot.

'Y'blew it, lad,' Kilgour murmured as he and Sten slogged through the mire. 'Yon lass wa' admirable. In one wee hour, Ah could'a had her eatin' out'a mah hand.'

Sten probably snarled at Alex because he was scared – scared of the world, scared of what it brought up in his past, and scared of the many ways to die slowly that Area 35 had shown him.

He may also have been afraid of the suits they wore. Everyone on Kulak wore suits, even in the dome, unless immediate physical necessities suggested otherwise. The suits were interesting – large, armored, so bulky that even a lithe man like Sten had to waddle in them. One reason they were so bulky is that each limb contained a shut-off element. If a suit limb was holed, the wearer could cut off that segment, instantly amputating and cauterizing the affected limb.

Regardless of the reason, Sten was as afraid as he had been for years.

Dr. Hars Stynburn/Dr. John Knox/Dr. William Block had gotten the tip from Sherman. He hastily finished strapping himself into his suit then armed himself with the usual long, evilly curved near-sword and 'harvesting tool.'

When a miner harvested a 'ripe' chunk of the metal that grew outside the dome, he used a spade-gun, a double-handed, spring-powered rifle that fired a spear about one meter long and faced with a 25-centimeter, razor-edged shovel tip. The spear's velocity approached 500 meters per second, which made it quite a lethal tool.

Stynburn had been expecting an attack – not from Imperial law, but rather from one or another of Hakone's pet thugs. He wasn't angry either way, since he felt it was perfectly legitimate for a covert operation to police up all traces. That was why he'd fled Prime World in the first place.

That was also why his office/quarters had its back wall close against the dome itself, and why Stynburn had set his inner office door as an airseal.

Stynburn closed his faceplate and checked the readout. No leaks. He dumped his office atmosphere back into the dome and kept his hand ready on the button. His eyes were on the vidscreen over the entrance, the vidscreen that showed his outer office.

He did not wait when the door opened and he saw two men enter.

His hand went down on the red switch, and instantly his back wall and the dome's outer seal exploded outward, pinwheeling Stynburn out onto the surface of Kulak.

Even through the chamber, Sten could feel the *chumph* as the inner office decompressed. Reflexively, both he and Alex slammed their faceplates shut. And waited.

The gauges, present in every room and every office in the dome, dipped then recovered.

'Th' lad's gone out,' Alex said through the suit com.

Sten didn't bother to answer – he was headed back through the entrance, for the nearest dome lock.

But the mucky street outside was filled with miners. Sherman was at their head. Sten stopped and flipped his faceplate open.

'We've decided,' Sherman began, sans preamble, 'that you have your law, and we have ours. We need a doctor. And we've got one. And we're going to keep him.'

Sten couldn't think of a lot of threats that made sense.

'We'll take whatever comes down afterward when it comes down. If it comes down.'

'Which means, lass,' Alex put in sadly, 'y'hae nae intention ah lettin' us gie away?'

Sherman nodded.

Sten's suit roughly duplicated the same type the miners and Sherman wore. But being of Imperial design, there were small changes. Sten hoped desperately that one of them wasn't known.

He took a square container from his belt and twisted the cap open as his faceplate closed. A thin, visible spray hissed out, and Sten tossed the container into the midst of the miners. He flipped his com level button to full and roared 'Gas! This is a corrosive gas!' as he began running. For a few seconds the miners were too busy seeking shelter from the squat container as it hissed, buzzed, and danced around the street to worry about where Alex and Sten were headed.

By the time Sherman's outsuit analyzer had figured out that the container was nothing more than an emergency air supply – carried as a liquid for compactness – Sten and Alex were at the dome's outer lock.

'Och,' Alex moaned, booting Sten into the inner chamber. 'Ah'll be th' wee lad wha' hold 'em a' the bridge.'

Before Sten could answer, Alex cycled the lock closed, leaving no option for Sten but to go out after Stynburn.

Alex turned, as the near-mob elephanted up to him. 'Aye noo, an' who'll be the first?'

The first was a miner who dwarfed Alex and his fellows. Alex blocked his blow and then swung. The block smashed the man's suit arm, and the punch cartwheeled the monster back through the air into the middle of the crowd. Kulak was a light-gee world – and Kilgour was a heavy-worlder. The mob closed in, and the situation became desperate.

Moderately desperate, since the knives that most of the miners carried were inside their suits, and they didn't have enough room to aim and fire their spade-guns – at least not without taking the chance of sending their bolts through the nearby dome wall.

So Alex-at-the-lock deteriorated into a vulgar brawl. In any other society, it would have been called a massacre, but on Kulak it was merely a fight that would be told about for a few years until the people involved struck it rich and moved off or died.

And there was nothing that Kilgour enjoyed more than a vulgar brawl. In motion, he looked like a heavily armored ball that ricocheted away from the lock entrance to connect with a target and then spun back to position, an armored ball confusedly quoting half-remembered and terrible poetry.

'Tha' oot spake braw Horatius.
Th' cap' ae th' gate:
T' every man upon the airt,
A fat lip cometh soon or late.'

The fat lip was a miner's smashed faceplate and a near-fatal concussion. Alex was too busy to see the man fall as he grabbed a swinging, grab-iron-wielding arm and shoved the grab iron into a third miner's gut, exploding the pressurized suit.

> 'Ae Astur's throat Horatius
> Right firmly pressed his heel . . .'

That miner gurgled into oblivion.

> 'An' thrice an four times tugged amain . . .

Sorry lad for the poetic licence.

> 'Ere he wrenched out the steel.'

The miners pulled back to regroup. Alex turned his suit oxy supply to full and waited.

The mob – only half of it was still interested in fighting – grew hesitant.

> 'Wae none who would be foremost
> To lead such dire attack;
> But those behind criet "forrard."
> An' thae before cried for their wee mums.'

That was too much, and the miners phalanxed forward. A phalanx works very well, so long as nobody takes out the front rank. Alex went flat in the dome's muck and rolled toward the onrushing miners. The front rank stumbled and went down, effectively blocking the airlock. And Alex was running amok in their rear. The ram of his helmet was as effective as his feet and fists, and then the mob was hesitating, turning, and running down the narrow passageways, away from Alex.

He collected himself, chopped his suit's air supply, and opened his faceplate, breathing deeply to let the euphoria and adrenaline ebb somewhat.

> 'It stands some'eres or other
> Plain for all to see.
> Wee Alex in his kilt an' socks
> Dronk upon one knee
> An' underneath is written
> In letters ae of mold

How valiantly he kept th' bridge
Ee the braw days ae old.'

Alex looked around, hoping for an appreciative audience. There was none – the battle casualties were either terminal, moaning for a medico, or crawling away at speed. But Alex wasn't bothered.

'Tha,' he went on, 'wa a poem Ah learn't a' m' mither's knee an' other low joints.' He looked worriedly at the lock behind him. 'Now, wee Sten, if y'll be snaggi't th' doc so we can be away afore thae dolts realize Ah'm guardin't a lock 'stead of a bridge . . .'

The dust was metal filings, quickly being blown into the yellow fog that clouded the outside of the dome. Sten briefly looked at the exploded walls that had been Stynburn's chambers, then went after the footsteps in the dust.

They sprang, one every ten meters, up into what might have been called – had they not been swelling constantly, pulsating, then collapsing into ruin – hills.

The trail led around a boulder. Intent on the ground, Sten almost died, jerking aside only as the growth on the boulder matured, blossomed, and explosively 'spored.'

The trail led along the edge of those hills, then down into a widening valley past a river of liquid metal.

Too easy, Sten's mind warned him. Sten fought to see through the yellow haze, trying to track the quickly vanishing prints as they led up from the valley, then disappeared on a germinating pool of rock. Sten used his hand to sweep in a circle around the last truck, his arm-stretch a rough indicator of a man's tracks.

He looked up. Below the rock bed was a small grotto. The winds hadn't yet brushed the metal dust on the floor, and Sten could see footprints leading out of the cleft, headed down toward the river.

He was in the grotto, pacing carefully. Three steps in, and all systems went to red with an old joke: How can you tell a Mercury Corps man? By his tracks. He always walks backward. Sten rolled awkwardly in the suit as Stynburn dove at him from ambush at the edge of the grotto.

Stynburn's clubbed spade-gun went for Sten's faceplate, but Sten's smashing feet sent Stynburn sailing over his head to roll in the dust.

Sten righted himself just as Stynburn came up firing the spade-gun. Having seen the spade-gun, Sten was turning, to offer as small a target as possible; by chance his suited arm intersected the spear's trajectory, deflecting the projectile harmlessly.

Two men, wearing suits that turned them into blobbed caricatures of humans, faced each other in an arena of metal dust that whirled and dissolved in the yellow wind.

Stynburn turned on his com. 'Who are you? Who am I facing?'

Stan was not a man for dramatics. 'Captain Sten. On His Imperial Majesty's Service. I have a warrant, Dr. Stynburn.'

'You have a warrant,' Stynburn said. 'I have a death.'

'We all do, sooner or later,' Sten said, looking for a strike point.

'I will tell you one thing, Captain – Sten, was it?'

'Doctor, you sound like a man who wants to die. I want to keep you alive.'

'Alive,' Stynburn mused. 'Why? Evidently it's all failed. Or perhaps it has not.'

Sten's eyes widened. This wasn't the first time he had faced someone who appeared mad, and Stynburn's words were proclaiming just that.

'Failed? What's failed?'

'You want me to talk, don't you?'

'Of course.'

'Captain, you must know what I was.'

'Mercury Corps. So was I,' Sten offered, maneuvering toward the man's left.

'In another world, another time, we could have been friends.'

Sten deliberately stood straight, as if considering. 'Yeah,' he said slowly, musingly. 'Maybe we could have. Clot, I always wanted to be a doctor.'

'But that would have been another time,' Stynburn said. Sten realized the man was playing games.

'I have two deaths is what I should have said. Yours and mine.'

'Then it's your move, Doctor.' Sten braced in suit close-combat position.

'Not that way, Captain. You shall die. Here and now. But I shall give you this. No man should die in ignorance. I shall give you an explanation. That is Zaarah Wahrid.'

Sten keyed his mike then realized that the two words were explanation enough for Stynburn. He saw the man contort in his suit.

Years of Mantis training had taught Sten the various ways an agent could kill himself, and he knew full well that the contortions were Stynburn's attempts to cramp his shoulders back. Sten was in motion, diving and rolling behind a growing/shrinking rock, hoping that the living mineral would stand as—

The first crash was not that loud. The bomb that had been

implanted between Stynburn's shoulder blades wasn't very effective. The most powerful explosion was the oxyatmosphere in Stynburn's suit fireballing across the grotto.

And then there was nothing except the gale's howl in Sten's outer pickups as he lifted himself over the rock and stared at the few tatters of suit that were scattered across the dusty floor.

Zaarah Wahrid, Sten thought as he picked himself up. One lead. Sten had a fairly good idea that one clue would not be enough.

He headed back down the trail, checking his helmet compass for bearings back to the dome.

The first job was to rescue Alex. If he was still alive, that'd be easy.

Because the next job was to face the Emperor with almost nothing.

BOOK FOUR

DECLIC

Chapter Thirty-Three

The Blue Bhor was a two-story, rambling building that sprawled along the banks of the River Wye. Built nearly a century before, it was an inn that catered to the local fisherfolk and small farmers on the Valley Wye. The valley was gentle, with rolling, rocky hills that climbed up into low, gray-blue mountains – a place where someone could make a passable living fishing or a grumbling living digging out rocks from ground that sprouted stones faster than potatoes. Still, it could be a pleasant life in a place that was good to raise a family.

Then the sportspeople of Prime World discovered it. And fishing season after fishing season, people streamed into the valley to catch the elusive golden fish that darted along the river. New roads were built. Many, many businesses sprouted up, and even a town – the Township of Ashley-on-Wye – was created where only farms had existed before.

As the valley boomed, so did the Blue Bhor. It began as a single, not very comfortable bar with a rent-a-room above. Owner after owner expanded the inn to handle the growing business and then sold out. Eventually the Blue Bhor boasted two bars, a ramshackle kitchen the size of a house, and more than a dozen rooms, each with a wood-burning fireplace of a different design. Since every new owner of the Blue Bhor had added a room, a patio, or a fireplace, there was nothing unusual about the Blue Bhor this particular day as the construction sleds hovered up and unloaded materials and workers.

They were greeted and guided by the newest owner, one Chris Frye, Prop. He was a tall, rangy man with little use for any BS except his own. Frye had purchased the place with his pension monies, and things had not really been progressing very well. His biggest problems were that he was exceedingly generous and had a tendency to pick up the tab for people he liked; he mostly preferred to close up the joint and just go fishing; and the only people he really got on with were fisherfolk – serious fisherfolk like himself who rarely had money and were always putting their bills on the tab.

Frye had just about been ready to toss the whole business over, sell out, and then spend the rest of his life fishing, when Sten showed up. Sten and Frye only knew of each other by reputation. They formed an instant liking for each other on first meeting, as only two old hands from Mantis Section can.

Frye had spent the last years of his military career in Mantis Section overseeing the transition of Lupus Cluster from a fanatic religious culture to a trading system loosely ruled by the shaggy Bhor. He'd spent many cycles drinking Stregg with the shaggy Bhor, toasting mother's beards and father's frozen buttocks. He had also heard a thousand different stories about how the Bhor had come to rule the Lupus Cluster. Mostly, the stories were not to be believed. They all came down to a single root: a young man named Sten. Sten, they all agreed, was the greatest fighter, lover, and drinker in Bhor history. Besides, they liked the little clot, even if he was human.

'In the whole time I was there,' Sten confessed to Frye, 'I only got laid twice, and I lost almost every battle except the last.'

'The one that counts,' Frye said.

'Maybe so,' Sten said, 'but my ass was seriously in a sling the whole time I was there. Clot! You can't drink with the Bhor! Unless you sneak some sober pills, and even then I was flat on my back after almost every party.'

Frye decided that Sten was a pretty nice fellow. Of course he was a clotting liar from Mantis, taking on the persona of the *real* Sten. He had long ago decided that the Sten of legend would have been a royal pain. Who the clot would ever want to drink with the perfect being the Bhor were always going on about? So Frye just smiled when Sten introduced himself, and accepted without a giggle the cover name he was using. Frye figured the name Sten was about fifty different people. Mantis did things like that.

Over one long night of hospitality Blue Bhor-style – which meant groaning platters of fresh fish, game, and side dishes, all from the Valley Wye – they struck a bargain. The Blue Bhor was to be Sten and Haines's safe house. Since it was off-season in the Valley Wye, the cover was near perfect. Frye would close for remodeling, just like every other new owner of the inn. To cut the cost of the extensive repairs, he would house and feed the construction crew.

It was a great bargain on both sides. To make the cover work, they *really* would have to remodel the old place. Not only that, but the bill for the rooms and the food would have to be paid, in case there was a smart bookkeeper snooping around. This allowed Haines to bring in a fairly large crew of experts to work on the case. It also allowed her to haul in as much sophisticated equipment as she needed, hidden between the stacks of construction materials.

The deal would make Frye's best year ever – especially coming during the off-season. He was even thinking about maybe staying on a few years longer; on the kind of credits Sten was stuffing into his account, Frye would be able to entertain fisherfolk for eons to come.

Haines stumped into the main bar and slid onto a stool. Behind her the last group of workpeople were unloading the last gravsled of equipment. She sniffed at her foreman's coveralls and wrinkled her nose. 'I smell like I been dead for two weeks.'

Frye gave one more swipe with his rag at the gleaming wood bartop, grabbed a tall glass, and frothed out a beer. He slid it in front of her, then leaned over and gave an ostentatious sniff. 'Smells better to me,' he grinned. 'Less constable and more good, honest sweat.'

Haines gave him a hard look and slugged down a healthy portion of beer. This put her in a better mood, especially since Frye topped it up again. 'You don't like cops, huh?'

Frye shook his head. 'Does any sensible person?'

Haines considered this for a moment. Then she gave a short laugh. 'No,' she said. 'Even cops don't like cops. That's why I got into homicide. When you're really doing your job, other people don't like to associate with you.'

Frye's retort was interrupted by the sound of footsteps, and they turned to see a grizzled man, in battered clothing and old-fashioned waders. He was lugging what appeared to be archaic fishing equipment.

'Bar's closed,' Frye sang out.

The man just stood, peering into the place, as if letting his eyes adjust from the bright, clear Valley Wye sun outside.

'I said the bar's closed,' Frye repeated.

'Remodeling,' Haines threw in.

The man shook his head, and then shuffled slowly over to the bar and sat down on a stool. 'Worst fishing I seen in years. I need a beer.'

He clinked some credits on the bartop. 'A tall cool one. No. Give me a whole damned pitcher.'

Frye shoved the credits back. 'You haven't been listening, mister. I told you, the bar is closed. For remodeling.'

The man wrinkled his brow in a frown. 'Well, I'm not walking to Ashley for a beer.' He glanced over at Haines' frosty mug. 'She got one, so you must be serving. So gimme one. I'll pay double! Tap's working. What the hell do you care?'

Haines felt her neck prickle. Something wasn't quite right here. She slid a hand into a coverall pocket and touched the small weapon nestled there. Then she slid off her stool and stepped a few paces to the side, covering both the man and the door. 'Listen when you're being spoken to, mister,' she said. She nodded at his gear by the side of the stool. 'Now, the place is closed. Pick up your things and go.'

She noticed that Frye was reaching under the bar for something.

'So,' the grizzled man said. 'What if I don't?'

Then he casually reached across the bartop, grabbed Haines' beer, and calmly chugged it down. He slapped the glass down and looked up at them. Haines had her gun out.

'Lieutenant!' a voice barked behind her.

Hearing Sten's voice, she partially turned, keeping the grizzled man in view. He grinned broadly, and then Sten was plucking the weapon from her hand.

Haines was ready to roundhouse Sten. She gaped as Sten stepped past her and came to attention in front of the beat-up old fisherman.

'I'm sorry, Your Highness,' Sten said. 'We weren't expecting you until tomorrow.'

Haines chin started to fall toward the swell where her breasts began.

'No problem,' the man said. 'Thought I'd stop by a little early. Get in a little fishing. Check things out.'

Sten stepped behind the bar and drew the man a beer. He slid it over and the fisherman took it in one long shallow. He turned to Haines and gave her a little wink.

'Lieutenant Haines,' Sten began, 'allow me to introduce you to—'

'It's the Emperor,' Haines croaked. 'The clotting Eternal Emperor.'

The Emperor bowed low over the stool. 'At your service, ma'am.'

Sten had to grab for Haines's elbow as the hard-bitten lieutenant of homicide felt her knees buckle.

'Zaarah Wahrid.' The Emperor rolled the phrase over on his tongue, puzzling at it, searching his memory. He shook his head. 'Doesn't mean a thing to me. That's all he said?'

Sten sighed. 'I'm afraid so, sir. I'm sorry, but the whole thing has been nothing but a mess from the moment you put me on it.'

He drew his beer toward him, and then pushed it away. 'Sir, I really think I ought to—'

'*Quit*?' the Emperor thundered. 'No clotting way! I'm up to my neck in drakh and you want me to relieve you?'

'With all due respect, sir,' Sten pushed on, 'I *have* failed to carry out every portion of this assignment to any kind of satisfaction.'

The Emperor started to jump in, but Sten raised his hand, calling on his rights as a free individual to quit a job if he wanted. 'I've done nothing but spend a shipload of credits for zed information. All we've still really got are much supposition and too many rumors.

'Beautiful. I hit Stynburn. Raise a whole lot of hell. Probably take you two years to settle those miners down. And all I come back with is a phrase nobody's ever heard. If this were a Mantis operation you or Mahoney would have had my head and sent me to deep freeze as well.'

The Eternal Emperor thought for a moment. Whether it was for effect, or whether he was indeed considering an evil future for Sten, the young captain would never know. Finally, he gave a loud snort. Then he held out his glass for Sten to fill with some of Chris Frye's finest.

'I am *where* I am,' he said, 'because I make quick decisions and then follow them through, no matter how lousy the robe of many colors turns out to be in reality. I've blown it once in a while. But mostly I win. Check the history archives and see if I'm not borne out by this little flight of ego I'm allowing myself.'

Sten decided it would be far from politic to comment on the 'little ego' remark. Instead, he drained his beer, took a deep breath, and then leaned forward across the table. 'Very well. Orders, sir, if you please.'

The Emperor hesitated for a nanosecond, considering how much he should really tell the young man in front of him. And then he caught Sten watching and knowing the hesitation for what it was, and just plunged on.

'It works like this,' he said. 'The Tahn are all over my royal behind for some kind of a meet. My advisors argue that no one of any real diplomatic stature has even recognized their odious system, much less sat down and talked to them.'

'But,' Sten said, 'I get the idea you agree there ought to be some kind of meet.'

The Emperor sighed. 'Has to be. I've been trying to stall. If they want to talk to my exalted self, maybe I'll do it, or maybe I won't. That would be the ultimate recognition of those warlords. Cause me no end of problems with the rest of the Empire. For clot's sake, the Eternal Emperor can't just be at the beck and call of every Tom Dick, and ET.

'Fouls up the whole system. There is my Imperial mystique to be considered. And that, Captain, is not ego, it's the glue that keeps this whole mess together.'

'So you're stalling them,' Sten said.

The Emperor smiled. 'Isn't that what diplomacy is all about? It's either stall or war.' He shrugged. 'A couple of my high-priced lawyers might disagree, but I've always found "going to court" cheaper than a war.'

He finished his beer and rose. 'And I don't think a war with the Tahn will be a little one.'

The Eternal Emperor turned to go. Then he stopped and gave Sten one of his most charming grins. 'I sure could use a good barely-living guilty party to throw off the sleigh right now.'

'How long can you keep stalling?' Sten asked.

'Less and less,' the Emperor said. 'I want you to grind it until the last minute.'

Sten nodded. 'I'll find your boy, sir.'

'Yeah. You will.'

And then the Eternal Emperor picked up his fishing gear and shambled out the door. Sten watched him go. For just a second, the Emperor wondered what would happen to young Captain Sten if he failed.

Even if it had been a Mantis operation, the safe-house System Sten, Alex, and Lieutenant Haines had worked out at the Blue Bhor would have been a wondrous thing. Just to begin with, it involved several different departments, a task usually impossible under almost any circumstances. Even cynical Alex was impressed about how well everyone blended in.

To begin with, security was an absolute must. Sten and Alex needed some definite thugs to keep trigger watch on anyone who might show an interest in the old inn.

So they carefully felt out old Mantis Section buddies who were either on I&I or using up sick leave. There were never any snarls from these people. They either smiled and kissed you or smiled and cut your throat.

Next, there were the police/Imperial people. Haines had carefully selected known trustworthy police people.

The way the safe house worked was that the security people patrolled the outside and Haines's group ruled inside, with occasional bursts of temper when Alex or Sten put in their two credits. The talents inside unfortunately guaranteed that everyone was potentially at the other person's neck. They were all mostly cops. But they were all super-specialists. The talents ranged from hackers to real computer techs to archivists to com-line snoopers. All were very bright, trustworthy, and friends of Haines.

One thing Sten had to give them – they were damned good. They were the beings who had tracked down Dynsman and finally located Stynburn.

And the way they had gone about it had been something to behold. In a similar operation, if Mantis had been assigned, the most sophisticated, high-powered computer would have trashed through millions of files in the search. The big problem with Prime World was that anything of even medium industrial power sent out red signals in all directions. Prime World was also the capital of all spydom, including the fortunes that were spent on industrial snooping.

So Liz Collins, the head cop computer tech, had proposed that they supply themselves with fifty or so tiny computers, each with the IQ of a five-year-old. Then she and her aides had strung them all together, resulting in a system as sophisticated as anything on the planet. More important, because of the way they were linked, they could dive in and out of information systems without being detected and usually without leaving a trace. As a side benefit. Liz had set the system up so that it could steal power. A constant monitor/feeder slipped in and out of power sources like a burglar, stealing just enough to keep the entire system operational, but not enough to show up significantly on individual power bills.

Alex also decided that Liz Collins was a woman he might want to get close to. She was slightly taller than he, and was built with all the proper and more than ample curves that Alex liked, plus many rippling muscles. Alex had been in ecstasy when he met her while setting up shop at the Blue Bhor. A gravsled had got itself mired near the riverbank. Before he could respond, Liz had leaned down and, with some cracking of bones, had lifted the sled from the muck then patted it on its now frictionless way. Alex could imagine those shapely, powerful arms around his heavyworlder body. It had been a long time, he realized, since he had felt himself *really* hugged.

The main readout Collins had set up in the computer linkage system was in the largest room of the Blue Bhor – King Gilly's Suite. Alex walked into the room and tried desperately not to be a beast and to keep his eyes off her muscular apple-shaped behind. Her structure narrowed then, he thought, licking dry lips, to proper lady's proportions before blooming to the most wonderful set of shoulders, and frontal mammary structure. It was the kind of sight that made a Scotsman *know* what he had under his kilt. She was the most beautiful woman Alex had ever seen.

She turned away from the screen and gave Alex a look that melted his heart, as well as a few other areas. 'Could we hold on that drink a bit? I should be getting something from the linkup soon.'

Alex would have given her anything in the world. 'Nae too thirsty mysel', lass,' he cracked. 'Now, wha' be we s' far?'

Liz turned back to the computer, all business again. We're running two main search patterns right now. The first is the most difficult.'

'Zaarah Wahrid?'

'Stynburn's last words. And so far they don't mean a thing anyplace we're checking. And I mean anyplace. We've gone through a couple of thousand languages. Every encyclopedia. Religious tracts. All of it.'

'Could it be—'

'Don't even bother. We're covering all possibilities. Trouble is, "all possibilities" means a hell of a lot of time, even with this setup.' She smiled fondly at the main terminal of her elaborate computer linkup system.

Alex warmed, wishing he were the computer. 'Lass,' he said, 'dinna y' think it's aboot time y' rested y'r wee mind wi' a bit ae th' hops?'

He leaned casually on the table supporting the computer readout screen, carefully keeping himself from encircling her rounded waist. Liz smiled over her shoulder at him, and Alex thought it lit up the room. His heart always thumped on her rare smile, and he beamed a cherub grin from his own round, red face.

'I think we're coming in on something now,' she said.

Alex peered at the words and figures bubbling up on the screen. He had to free his mind for the high-speed scrolling, and then he had it.

'Appears you have the late Doc Stynburn in th' crosshairs.'

Liz nodded enthusiastically. Alex loved her even more when she was on the hunt.

'Do we! Look at this. He set up about a half dozen cutout corporations. Based in frontier banking planets. Each time he took a new job or consultancy, he ran it through one of the corporations.'

'A wee tax scam,' Alex said.

'You got it. Foolproof one, as well. Leave it to a doctor.'

He cleared his throat loudly, bringing himself back to some sort of reality. 'An' th' second search,' he said 'Stynburn, Ah s'pose?'

Liz nodded. 'That's killing time for opposite reasons. Instead of too much, we've got too little. The guy knew every Mercury Corps trick in the book.'

'Then you thought of the corporate cutout business,' Alex said admiringly.

Liz blushed. 'I thought it was a small stroke of genius.'

Alex could barely keep himself from patting her. What if she took it wrong? Or right? Or . . . He tried to pull his mind away from the swirl of figures on the screen. He cleared his throat again. 'Anything else, lass?'

Liz handed him a thin sheaf of printout. 'I'm not sure, but since I picked these up my cop brain's been sneezing.'

Alex scanned them – very dry police-jargonese reports of four deaths. All had two things in common: they were accidental, bizarrely so; and they had all occurred within the vicinity of the palace. Alex rechecked the first death: Female victim. High blood alcohol. Strangled on own vomit. Slight bruise on throat. He buzzed past the name to the woman's history. Deserter from the Praetorian Guard. Alex felt a small mental tingle. He quickly thumbed through the other reports and the answer glared up a him. 'You were right, lass, police officer tha' y' be.'

Then he showed her the common thread.

'Every swinging Richard is a former government,' Collins realized. 'Ex-clerk. Ex-tech. Ex-museum security. And all with—'

'—palace connections,' Alex finished for her.

Liz slumped into her chair and gave a long exasperating sigh. 'Murder. Murder, murder, murder. Aw clot.'

Then, just as deep depression was about to fog the entire room, the vid-screen began blinking red. Liz leaped to her feet and studied the screen. After thousands of computer hours, the first major break in the case was staring her in the face. They had finally broken through Stynburn's elaborate corporate cutouts.

'Sweet Laird,' Alex whispered. 'Th' clot worked for Kai Hakone.'

Chapter Thirty-Four

'I have never seen one of these before,' Kai Hakone said. 'May I examine it more closely?'

Sten handed him the Imperial Service card. The Imperial emblem on the card, keyed to Sten's own pore and pulse pattern, blinked as Hakone took it, held it for a moment, then passed it back to Sten.

'Actually, Captain, while I've no idea what you need, your appearance is fortunate.'

'Ah?'

Hakone was about to explain, but his words were cut by the loud whine of a ship lifting on Yukawa drive barely half a kilometer overhead.

Hakone's mansion was located on the largest hill overlooking Soward, Prime World's biggest port. It had been built as an off-voyage hobby by the captain of a tramp freighter, who intended it to be his retirement home.

That trader's retirement never came about, since he made the tactical error of offering play-pretty beads to a primitive culture more interested in sharp-pointed and deadly objects. But since most people, let alone those who could afford the price of a Prime World mansion, weren't fascinated with the sound and bustle of a space port, Hakone had been able to lease the sprawling house cheaply. Since then, he'd finished the interior and added his own concepts, which included the hemispherical battle chamber in its rear.

The Yukawa-drive cut off, and in the utter silence of AM_2 drive, the ship disappeared. 'I like to hear what I write about,' Hakone half explained as he led Sten into the house. 'Is it too early for a tod, Captain?'

'The sun's up, isn't it?'

Hakone smiled and led Sten through the large reception area, the even larger living room, and into his own den.

Hakone's 'den' – office and writing area – was styled after an Old Earth library, with innovations. Vid-tapes, reports, even bound antique books lined the twenty-meter-high walls. The center of the room was a long, flat table. But from there, the resemblance to eighteenth-century Earth was gone, since the table was lined with computer terminals, and the laddered access to the shelves was automated.

At one end of the room was Hakone's bar, and it extended across the width. Sten scanned the bottles as Hakone motioned for him to make his choice.

'You happen to have any, uh, Scotch?'

Hakone was up to it. 'You have adopted the Emperor's tastes!' he said, reaching down a bottle and pouring two half-full glasses of the liquor.

Sten touched the glass to his lips, then lowered it. Hakone, too, had barely drunk. 'You said fortunate, Sr. Hakone?'

'Yes. I was planning to contact you, Captain.' Hakone waved Sten toward a wide couch nearby. 'Did you happen to see my masque? The one which was performed prior to Empire Day?'

'Sorry, I was on duty.'

'From what the critics say, perhaps you were lucky. At any rate, I now find myself between projects. And then I discovered something most fascinating. Are you aware that no one has ever done a history of the Imperial palace?'

Sten pretended ignorance, shook his head, and sipped.

'Not only the building, but the people who are assigned to it,' Hakone went on, with what seemed to be a writer's enthusiasm.

'An interesting idca.'

'I thought so. As did my publisher. Especially if the tape deals with the people who are assigned to it. I want to tell a history of people, not of stone and technocracy.'

Sten waited.

'As you know,' Hakone continued, 'I am primarily a military historian. I have, frankly, my own sources. So when I conceptualized this project, the first thing I began investigating was the people assigned to that palace.

'That is, by the way, why I made such a point of wanting to meet you at Marr and Senn's party. You are a peculiar man, Captain Sten.'

Sten looked solemnly interested.

'Are you aware that you are the youngest man ever assigned to head the Imperial bodyguard?'

'Admiral Ledoh told me that.'

'That interests me. Which is why I availed myself of your military record. Wondering, quite frankly, why you had been chosen.'

Sten didn't bother smiling – he knew that his phony file was intrusion-proof. Only Mantis headquarters, the Emperor himself, and General Ian Mahoney knew what Sten's real military history was.

'You have a perfect record. *No* demerits at OCS. Commissioned on such-and-so a date, all qualifications reports rated excellent, all commanding officers recommending you most highly, the appropriate number of hero-moves for the appropriate awards.'

'Some people are lucky.'

'If I may be honest, Captain, perhaps too lucky.'

Sten finished his drink.

'Captain Sten, what would you say if I told you I suspected your whole military background was a tissue?'

'If I were not on Imperial business, Sr. Hakone, and depending on the circumstances, I would either buy you a drink or a nose transplant.'

'I did not mean to be insulting, Captain. I am merely suggesting that you have been assigned to your present post because of previous performance in either Mercury Corps or Mantis Section.'

Sten pretended stupidity. 'Mercury Corps? Sorry, Hakone. I was never in Intelligence, and I've never heard of Mantis.'

'The response I expected. And I appear to have offended. Change the subject. What brings you here?'

Hakone replenished the drinks.

'You once employed a Dr. Hars Stynburn,' Sten said, trying the sudden-shock approach. Hakone reacted indeed, but quite obviously, sending the top of the liquor decanter spinning to the floor.

'Clot! What's the imbecile done now?'

'Now? Sr. Hakone, I must advise you that this conversation is being recorded. You have a right to counsel, legal advice, and medico-watch to ensure you are not under any influence, physical or pharmacological.'

'Thank you for the warning, Captain. But I don't need that. Dr. Hars Stynburn did indeed work for me. For a period of four months – Prime months. At the end of that time I discharged him, without, I might add, benefit of recommendation.'

'Continue, Sr. Hakone.'

'My household normally consists of between fifty and three hundred individuals. I find it convenient to employ an in-house medico. That was one reason I initially employed Dr. Stynburn.'

'One reason?'

'The second reason was that he was, like myself, a veteran. He served in the Mueller Wars, the battle of Saragossa.'

'As did you.'

'Ah, you've scanned my tapes.'

'On précis. Why did you dismiss him?'

'Because . . . not because he was inefficient or incompetent. He was an extremely good doctor. But because he was a man locked into the past.'

'Would you explain?'

'All he wished to talk about was his time in the service. And about how he felt he had been betrayed.'

'Betrayed?'

'You're aware he was cashiered from the service? Well, he felt that he was fulfilling the exact requirements of the Empire, and that he was used as a Judas goat after those requirements were fulfilled.'

'The Empire generally doesn't practice genocide, Sr. Hakone.'

'Stynburn believed it did. At any rate, his obsession became nerve-wracking to me. And so I found it easier to release him at the expiration of his initial contract.'

Sten was about to ask another question, then broke off. Hakone's eyes were hooded.

'Locked into the past, I said, didn't I?' Hakone drained his drink. 'That must sound odd to you, Captain, since you've reviewed my tapes. Don't I sound the same way?'

'I'm not a historian, Seigneur.'

'What do you think of war, Captain?'

Sten's first answer – blatant stupidity – was something he somehow felt Hakone didn't want to hear. He held his silence.

'Someone once wrote,' Hakone went on, 'that war is the axle life revolves around. I think that is the truth. And for some of us, one war is that axle. For Dr. Stynburn – and to be honest, Captain, for myself – that was Saragossa.'

'As I said, I'm not a historian.'

Hakone picked up the two glasses, fielded the decanter from the bar, and started toward a nearby door.

'I could tell you, Captain. But I'd rather show you.' And he led Sten through the door, into his battle chamber.

The Mueller Wars, fought almost a century before Sten's birth, were a classic proof of Sten's definition of war. The Mueller Cluster had been settled too quickly and was too far from the Empire. The result was a lack of Imperial support, improperly defined and supplied trade routes, and arrant ignorance on the part of the Imperial bureaucracy administering those worlds.

And then war, war by the various worlds, fighting under a banner that might have been headed 'Anything but the damned Empire.' By the time the Emperor realized that the Mueller Cluster was a snowball rolling downhill, it was too late for any response except the Guard.

But Imperial overexpansion had reached into the military as well. The battles that were fought were, for the most part, on the wrong ground, with the wrong opponent, and at the wrong time.

The Emperor still, when he began feeling self-confident, had only to scroll his own private log of the Mueller Wars to deflate himself to the proper level of humanity. Of all the disasters, before the Mueller Cluster was battered into semi-quiescence, the worst was Saragossa.

Saragossa should never have been invaded. Its isolationist culture should have been ignored until the Saragossans asked to rejoin the Empire. Instead a full Grand Fleet and the Seventh Guards Division were committed. The invasion should have been easy, since it involved landing on a single world, which had only a few low-tech satellite worlds for support.

Instead the operation became a nightmare.

The grand admirals who ordered the assault might have wondered why initial intelligence reported some seven moonlets around Saragossa, and the landing surveys reported only one. But no one wondered, and so nearly a million men died.

The landing plan was total insertion, so the Guards' transports were committed, and the heavy support – five Imperial battleships – were moving toward the ionosphere when the question of the missing moonlets was solved.

They'd been exploded, quite carefully, so the fragments maintained planetary orbit. And then any fragment larger than a baseball had been manned with Saragossans who were less interested in living than keeping the Empire away. Imagine trying to push a landing force through an asteroid belt that is shooting back.

The first battleship was holed and helpless more than three planetary units offworld. The admiral in charge of the landing – Fleet Admiral Rob Gades – transhipped with what remained of his staff to a command ship in time to see his other four battleships explode into shards.

At that point it was too late to recall the troopships. Even before the ships split into capsules, most of them were destroyed. The landing caps that entered atmosphere without support lasted bare seconds under the ravening fire from the surface.

That, Hakone explained to Sten as he swung ships through the battle chamber, was when his own probeship was destroyed. He never saw the end of the battle. What ended it was Admiral Gade's order – *sauve qui peut*, save what you can. One third of the assault fleet was able to pull off Saragossa.

'One third, Captain,' Hakone said, as he shut down the battle chamber. 'Over one million men lost. Isn't that enough of an axle?'

Sten flashed briefly to the livie he'd undergone before basic training – experiencing the heroic death of one Guardsman Jaime Shavala – and his subsequent decision that he had less than no desire to see what a major battle felt like, ignored his gut agreement, and used the safe answer of stupidity. 'I don't know, Sr. Hakone.'

'Perhaps you wouldn't. But now do you understand why I hired Stynburn? He went through the same hell I did.'

Sten noticed with interest that Hakone, while he'd been sitting behind the control chair of the chamber, had gone through half the decanter of Scotch.

'By the way, Captain, do you know what happened to Admiral Gades?'

'Negative.'

'For his – and I quote from the court's charge – retreat in the face of the enemy, he was relieved of command and forcibly retired. Do you think that was fair?'

'Fair? I don't know what is fair, Sr. Hakone.' Sten brought himself to attention. 'Thank you for your information, Seigneur. Should we have any other questions, may I assume your further cooperation?'

'You may,' Hakone said flatly.

Sten was about to try a wild card and ask if the phrase Zaarah Wahrid meant anything to Hakone. Instead, he shut off his recorder, nodded, and headed for the exit.

If he had left a few seconds earlier, he might have caught one of Hakone's men clipping a tiny plas box to the underside of Sten's gravsled.

Hakone walked out of the battle chamber, back into his library. Colonel Fohlee was waiting, and looking distinctly displeased.

'You think I erred,' Hakone said.

'Why were you giving him all that, dammit! He's the Emperor's investigator.'

'I was fishing, Colonel.'

'For what?'

'If he'd shown one iota of understanding – one flicker of what is important – we might have been able to make him one of us.'

'Instead you ran your mouth and got nothing.'

'Colonel! You are overstepping.'

'Sorry, sir.'

'As a result, I found that this Captain Sten is unreachable. I have a tracer attached to his gravsled. Put a team of the deserters after him. Track the sled until we have the location of the safe house he's using for his investigation. Then kill this Captain Sten. That is all!'

Fohlee found himself saluting, pivoting, and exiting and never wondered why he had that response to the command voice of a man who had not worn a uniform for almost a hundred years.

Chapter Thirty-Five

The vid-screen glowed in the darkened room. In one corner, the computer held its target: the phrase ZAARAH WAHRID. The rest of the screen was filled with line after constantly changing line of information. At the moment, the computer was postulating that the phrase meant some kind of commercial product. It was searching the Imperial patent office for everything registered since the department was founded.

Liz Collins, the hunter, tried to keep her eyes glued to the screen, looking for some kind of connection or vague reference. As each line rolled up the screen, her eyes followed, and then automatically clicked down a stop for the next. At the moment, she was scanning a catalogue of household bots, almost all of them a century or more out of date.

She had to fight to keep her brain on her job. Steady on, woman, she thought to herself. If you think this is boring, guess what comes next. Then she groaned as the finis asterisks rolled up and the next and a worse category came up: Defense.

The air stirred behind her and then she heard the door open and soft footsteps pad in. She turned to see Alex standing behind her, two mugs of frothy beer in his hands.

''Bout that drink, lass?' he said softly. 'Ah whidny be disturbin' y' noo, would Ah?'

'Oh, my god, yes,' she said, meaning the drink. Then she caught Alex's crestfallen face and corrected herself. 'I mean, no. No, I mean . . . right, I could use a drink.'

She palmed the computer to automatic, setting up the search alarms, and then rose to take a glass out of Alex's hand. She took a small sip and gave a bit of a start. 'This isn't just beer!' She grinned. And then she noticed the shot glass sitting in the bottom of the mug.

'A wee boilermaker,' Alex explained. 'Beer and a good single-malt Scotch that'll oil th' bubbles.'

Liz took a long, slow swallow. 'Mmmm, I don't mind this at all.'

She crossed over to the fur-covered couch and sat down, crossed her legs, then started to tug her uniform skirt down over her knees. She stopped when she saw the wistful look in Alex's eyes as the slight flash of thigh started to disappear. 'What the clot.' She patted the place next to her. As if almost suddenly coming awake, Alex shook his head then took the few steps required to reach the couch and sank hesitatingly down beside her. He carefully studied the wall opposite them, afraid to meet her eyes.

'So,' he finally said, 'do y' think we'll be finding this Zaarah whatever it is?'

Liz remained absolutely silent. She just took another sip of her drink.

'Ah mean, y' been workin't your pretty, beg your pardon, y' been workin't hard, lo these many—'

'Alex,' Liz whispered, breaking in.

He turned and looked directly at her for the first time since he entered the room. 'Yes, lass.'

'Do we have to talk?'

'No, lass.'

'Well, then . . .'

Alex finally got the point. He reached out his arms to enfold her, and he felt the muscular but somehow so soft arms go around him. Slowly they sank down into the couch.

Once again, Liz didn't bother about the flash of thigh as the uniform skirt rose higher and higher and . . .

Unnoticed by them, the computer screen began winkng red. It sat patiently, pulsing that it had found it . . . found it . . . found it . . .

The screen read:

ENT: JANES, Historic Records. BATTLESHIP: ZAARAH WAHRID (Flower class – 14 constructed).

The entry went on, covering the ship's dimensions, crew, armament, launching date, and history, ending with the information that *Zaarah Wahrid* had finished her illustrious career as flagship on the Saragossa invasion during the Mueller Wars. The ship was totally destroyed, with a loss of 90 per cent of its crew . . .

Fortunately for the lovers, it would be many hours before they read the entry. Because once again the case had come full circle. *Zaarah Wahrid* was a ship that no longer existed.

Chapter Thirty-Six

Sten lifted the gravsled away from Hakone's mansion and set his course directly from Soward across the city of Fowler toward the Imperial palace.

Once past the city limits he dropped the sled's height to 50 meters. Thus far, he was doing exactly what Hakone had predicted, and would next set his course for the safe house in Ashley-on-Wye.

But several hundred people, were they not deceased, might have advised Kai Hakone never to predict Sten's actions.

The gravsled may have appeared standard Imperial issue, but it was not. The man who planted the tracer on the sled should have noticed its fairly elaborate com gear. But he didn't.

So while Sten put the sled's controls on auto, and hung the aircar in a slow orbit over the trees, he checked himself and his vehicle for bugs. At 22.3 Hz, his detector sounded off like a banth in heat. Sten unhooked the directional transponder from the board and went over the sled. It took only a few seconds to find the tracer unit.

Sten went back to the controls and considered the various possibilities. He decided, turned the sled onto manual, and lifted it to 1000 meters. Then he set a new course directly for the Great South Sea. This was, on compass, 80-plus degrees, magnetic, away from his proper destination, the Blue Bhor. Sten had no idea what the tracer was intended for, but he had decided to play the hand, at least for a few thousand kilometers.

It didn't take that long.

Sten's prox-radar blipped at him and advised that an object was rapidly approaching from his rear. He turned and scanned through the sled's binocs.

Ignoring the modifications, Sten's gravsled was a standard combat car: McLean-generator-powered, ten meters by five meters in dimension, seating four people in the open. The object coming toward him was also a standard Imperial combat vehicle, about twice the size of Sten's gravsled, and intended for a combat platoon of twelve or so beings.

Sten counted six men in the sled, which was closing on him at a rate of about 60 kph. He decided to make their job a little easier, and slowed his own sled. The sled behind also slowed.

Tacmind thinking, Sten automated: They are trying to track me. Given mission: Find the safe house and . . . six men in that sled . . . take me out.

Sten *tsk*ed to himself and snapped the double safety harness around him.

He shoved the control stick forward for full-speed and snapped the built-in dopplering radar off. On normal combat cars, this was permanently on, insuring that no matter how much an idiot the pilot was, he could not run into something in fog, smoke, rain, or drunkenness. But Sten's car *was* a modified one.

Another modification went on, a second, also doppler-stupid radar. It fixed on the platoon gravsled coming up on Sten, giving a closing speed of nearly 80 kph. Very slow reactions, Sten decided.

Before the pilot of the sled realized what was intended, Sten chopped the control stick, then lifted the stick into control attitude and yanked it back again, almost into his lap. Standard combat cars – gravsleds – had no such capability. Which may have been the reason that the pursuing pilot gaped as Sten's sled curved straight up and around in a perfect Immelman, then dropped directly toward the pursuers.

Sten saw fear, panic, and motion as he dove straight for the other sled. The platoon sled's pilot cut power and sank, barely in time to avoid Sten's seemingly kamikazze dive.

It banked and recovered. Doors on the smooth side of the vehicle opened, and missile banks whirred into sight. Fire, smoke, and four air-to-air (atmo) missiles blasted out.

Sten already had his combat car on its back. As forces yanked at his face, his hands clawed for the distress flare button.

The flares bloomed out, multicolored phosphorus fires. And obediently, the pursuers' heat-seeking missiles homed on the flares. Four missiles impacting at the same time made a helluva bang, enough to send the platoon sled skidding out of control momentarily, the five passengers grabbing for handholds. And then out of the smoke dove Sten's combat car. The platoon sled's pilot panicked and pirouetted his sled on its own axis. Again late, since Sten's car was now just above him.

And then the last thing the six thugs in the sled might have expected happened. Sten flipped his combat car to orbit, unsnapped his safety harness, and jumped straight over the side, into the other gravsled.

He twisted in midair, his clawed hand bringing out his knife, while his mind looked for a soft landing.

The landing was on the first man, Sten's heels crushing his rib cage and Sten going down to his knees – under the clubbed willygun swing of the second man – and then straight up, spread fingers going into eyeballs and brain.

Sten whirled as the second corpse fell. His knife swung across the wrist of the third man, whose hand fell away, blood hosing across the sled. He gaped at the spouting blood, stumbled, and fell away into nothingness.

Sten never saw that he was on automatic pilot, realizing a man was swinging a long, issue Guards combat knife at him. Sten blocked with his own crystal blade – and sheared through the alloy steel. The fourth man didn't even have time to react before Sten's steel bootheel slammed up, crushing his skull.

Air ionized, and Sten went flat, skidding across the checkered metal of the aircar's deck, the willygun projectile sizzling overhead, and Sten was diving forward, and his foot went out from under him as he skidded on a patch of blood.

Sten took the fall, but his knife hand lashed out, braced at the wrist. The speared knife caught the fifth man just below the belt, then slashed through his spinal cord. The living corpse spasmed backward over the sled's pilot, who was trying to unbuckle himself.

Sten slammed into the copilot's seat, then tucked his feet under him and snapped up.

The sled's pilot had fought his way free of the body and was standing. Sten came in on the man. His intentions were to take one prisoner and ask very serious questions.

But the pilot took one look at the gory Sten and that small sliver of metal that was death itself, screamed, and hurled himself over the side of the combat car.

Sten grabbed for the man, but too late. He watched the screaming form pinwheel down toward the parkland far below.

Collect . . . collect . . . and no-mind died, combat madness went away, and Sten swore to himself. Breathe . . . breathe . . . and he sat down, not noticing the blood that swirled and trickled across the gravsled's deck.

Rationality returned, and Sten looked at the five dead men in the sled. Haines can find something out about them, one part of his mind decided. Less important, another told him. You don't believe in coincidence. You went to Hakone. You were given a song-and-dance. On your leaving, someone attempted to kill you.

Considering the Imperial warrant he had been given, Sten had enough to arrest Hakone and use any means necessary, including brainscan, to find out how Hakone tied into the conspiracy to assassinate the Emperor.

But that was too easy a solution.

Somehow Sten had the idea that no one as highly visible and vocal as Kai Hakone would be the mastermind behind the attempt.

Chapter Thirty-Seven

Fog swirled over the long, brilliant-black ship that sat on a landing field barely longer than itself. Lights haloed around the loading ports as men and women loaded equipment and themselves on board.

The landing field was carried on Prime World's books as an Imperial Fleet tacship/emergency field, but it was actually used only by the Emperor for arrivals and departures he did not want to see blazoned on the vid-screen

The ship itself was equally obscure. According to the record books, it had been constructed as the Imperial Merchant Ship (Passenger) *Normandie*. A luxury, super-speed liner that had been mothballed after its third voyage.

The *Normandie* did appear, from the outside, to be a conventional liner, but it had been built for one purpose only – to be the Emperor's vehicle, whether for secret missions or for vacations. It had the armament of a fleet destroyer and the power drive of a fleet cruiser.

It took less than a hundred men to run the *Normandie*, which was state-of-the-art automated. That did not mean the ship was cramped, since the largest percentage of the *Normandie* was taken up with Imperial accommodations. Movable bulkheads and decking insured that the Emperor could hold anything from a private party for himself and a lady to an Imperial summit meeting.

Since the ship officially did not exist, it did not have to worry about proper clearances. When necessary, it was easy for the *Normandie* to assume one or another of the identities of its supposed sister ships.

It may have been the biggest cloak-plus-dagger ever built.

*

'Marr, you are being a daffodil. There is no possible pollution here.'

'You talk and talk,' Marr sniffed, 'but I tell you, I can *smell* the fumes from the drive.'

Marr and Senn were possibly the only caterers in history given an EYES-ONLY security clearance.

They stood near the waist of the *Normandie*, watching as their supplies rolled up the conveyor into the guts of the ship.

'All right, so there is pollution. I touch your delicate nostrils. But what will that matter to the fish? They are in tanks, not standing out here in the murk catching their death.

'I am merely concerned that these Tahn beings will find our food offensive,' Marr said. 'How would you like to be responsible for this conference's falling apart because of indigestion?'

Their predawn bickering was broken off as Subadar-Major Limbu strolled up. The Gurkha officer was in full combat gear, including willygun and kukri hung in its sheath in the middle of his back. He saluted. 'These fish,' he indicated. 'They are not for my men?'

'They are not, Chittahang. I have enough dahl, rice, and soyasteak to turn every one of your naiks into balloons such as the one you are starting to resemble.'

Chattahang glanced at his stomach reflexively, then recovered. 'Ah. Very good. But I shall tell you a secret. That bulge is not from my stomach. I find it necessary to coil some of my other organs above my belt.' He grinned, winked, and went back to supervising the loading of his men.

'Marr, do you ever think we shall get the better of these small brown ones?'

'Probably not.' Marr turned and reacted. 'Our fearless leader has arrived.'

Five large flitters settled beside the *Normandie*, and people unloaded.

'See, it's that glut Sullamora with the Emperor,' Senn hissed. 'Why was he invited?'

'I am not the Emperor, darling, but I assume that, since he is an Imperial trader there must be something involving trading rights with these Tahn – Senn, are you *sure* we are prepared?'

Marr and Senn had been alerted to provide rations shortly after the Emperor-Tahn meeting had been set. They had immediately researched the tastes of the Tahn, particularly of their lords. Fortunately, vid-tapes on exotic cooking were still popular in the fortieth century. They had provided everything from live brine shrimp to starch to still-growing vegetables. Plus some surprises of their own, since every chef feels he can improve on anyone's diet.

Bootheels thudded on the tarmac, and the contingent of Praetorians doubled in from the security perimeter. They were ordered and counted by Colonel Den Fohlee, and paraded on board.

'Do we have enough?' Marr worried.

'We have enough! One hundred fifty Praetorians, and we have enough starch and raw protein to keep them happy for a millennium. Thirty Gurkhas. The crew, with its own rations. The Emperor – who knows what he'll want – Sullamora . . . I procured his favorite recipes from his cook. Extras enough for these Tahn, even if they feed their starving hordes. We are *ready*, my love.'

'Yes, but what are *we* – you and I – going to eat?'

Just as Senn's membranes wrinkled in alarm, the boarding alarm gonged.

The last of the rations went on board, and the ship's ports swung shut. The flitters cleared the field, and then the *Normandie*'s Yukawa-drive hissed more loudly, and she lifted away.

Offworld, *Normandie* would rendezvous with a destroyer squadron and a cruiser element. Those Imperial sailors had been told only that they were to escort a ship to a location, prevent anything from happening to that ship, and then return it to its base. They had no idea that the Eternal Emperor was on board, nor that the meeting with the Tahn lords was the only chance of avoiding an eventual intergalactic war.

Chapter Thirty-Eight

The group sat silently around the huge table that was Frye's main groaning board. Solid depression had set in. At the far end of the table Haines was idly doodling on her miniscreen. At the other end sat a strangely quiet Alex. He gloomed across the table at Liz, who was punching in a few last commands at her ever-present control unit.

Sten entered, a sheaf of print-outs under his arm, and saw the expectant looks come suddenly up at him. 'No,' he said, 'I don't have a thing . . . but maybe I've got some kind of weird map we can all jump off from.'

People came alive again. Sten began handling out the eafs of paper. 'One thing I learned as a crunchie – when you're stuck in it, make a list of what you know. And what you don't know.'

He gave them all a sickly grin and shrugged. 'Keeps you looking busy and important, anyway.'

They began going over Sten's list. The facts had been boiled down:

1 The original plot was to assassinate the Emperor. All information indicates a wide-ranging conspiracy.
2 The plot is continuing. Otherwise, why the mysterious deaths near Soward – all former Praetorians or palace employees? Also, why the attack on Sten? By former Praetorians – mostly deserters Subfact: At least forty Praetorians disappeared in the last E-year.
3 The plot seems to involve someone in the palace itself. Consider the multitude of computer taps and scans on the outside that lead, and then disappear, in there.
4 To repeat, the plot is continuing, and the Emperor logically is still the ultimate target.

'As a cop,' Haines broke in, 'it sure would make me feel better if I knew the target was out of the way.'

'At least that has been solved,' Sten said. 'The Emperor has left Prime World. I can't tell you for where but he is absolutely safe and surrounded by trusted advisors and security.'

Alex breathed a sigh of relief. 'Thank th' lord,' he said. 'No clottin' Romans.'

'Has the Emperor been informed how deep in the drank we are?' Liz asked.

'Negative,' Sten answered. 'We've agreed on absolute com silence. I can only reach him in an emergency. There is a line established at the palace.'

They waited for him to say more, and then when ht didn't, continued reading.

5 Kai Hakone is obviously one of the main conspirators. Key indicators here are Stynburn and the many other connections to the Battle of Saragossa. Also, Sten was attacked immediately after interviewing the suspect.
6 *Zaarah Wahrid* is another connection to the Battle of Saragossa. Question: What does a destroyed ship have to do with the conspiracy?
7 Complicating factor: Hakone had no connection with the palace. He is a known adversary of the Emperor and is not welcome.

'When do we arrest this clot, lad? Ah'll twist his guts into a winding sheet an' find out what we mus' ken.'

'Not a chance, Alex,' Sten said. 'To defuse this thing we've got to pick up everybody at the same time. Especially the inside man at the palace.'

'Take Hakone now and we blow it,' Haines agreed.

They bent their heads to read the rest.

8 Should we be checking the archives for more on Saragossa? Could other connections be hidden?

'Have you got a year?' Liz said dryly. 'I don't know a computer in the Empire that could run that scan sooner.'

'Forget it, then,' Sten said.

'Is that all?' Haines asked.

'Yeah,' Sten answered. 'Except Hakone.'

'I'm running him now,' Liz said, pointing at her monitor screen.

'A stupid suggestion to the expert,' Sten said to Liz.

Liz gave a low chuckle. 'When all else fails,' she said 'stupid works with a computer.'

'He's got to have a headquarters somewhere,' Sten said. 'Hakone can't be running plotters in and out of his home, or meeting them on street corners or some such rot.'

'A vacation home?' Haines postulated.

'Someplace remote?' Liz said.

Collins was already keying in an ownership search. She used the same program she had jury-rigged to break through Stynburn's corporate maze.

'Th' mon's a military fanatic,' Alex said. 'There's where we'll upend him. Certain a' he wrote his bloody great work on the Mueller Wars—'

Before he could finish, the answer swarmed up and curled into place on the screen. Alex's guess had hit close.

'*Zaarah Wahrid*,' the screen entry began. 'Register No. KH173. Berth 82. DO YOU REQUIRE DESCRIPTION?'

'Clotting yes,' Sten shouted as Liz typed in the orders.

Kai Hakone was the owner of the tiny and well-worn space yacht *Zaarah Wahrid*, which was berthed in a private port only a hundred or so kilometers away.

'Get the ship's computer on the line,' Haines snapped.

'Not so fast, Lieutenant,' Liz said. 'What if the onboard's been rigged?'

'She's right,' Sten said. 'We've gone too far to get in a hurry now.'

'I'll ask the computer if the ship needs servicing,' Liz said. 'Real routine.' The answer came back negative.

'Okay, now something official but innocuous.'

'When's the last time the ship left port?' Sten suggested.

Liz tapped her keys. 'Not for more than a year. But that's fine. I can do a log search. Nothing pushy. Just the surface info. That'll keep *Zaarah Wahrid* on the line.' The little boat began running through its log as Liz gently inserted a few of her probes – always keeping just out of the way, hovering and buzzing like an electronic fly.

'Will you look at this?'

Liz had run an IQ scan on the onboard.

'This little putt-putt has a computer big enough to run a liner!'

'Why would a little yacht need something that size?' Haines asked.

'Ah – ah, ah, no you don't, *Zaarah* clotting *Wahrid*.' Liz shut down fast. 'She's also got more booby traps then you can drink beer,' she said to Alex. 'I hang on anymore, and the least she'll do is wipe.'

Sten slumped down, exasperated. 'Is that all you could get, Liz?'

'No, I tricked it into giving me its key.' She scribbled it down.

Sten climbed to his feet. 'Come on, Alex. I think we better do a little lightweight breaking and entering.'

They headed for the door.

'Oh, Captain?' Liz said.

'Yeah.'

'You probably ought to know something else.'

'Go.'

'Apparently *Zaarah Wahrid*'s got a bomb on board. Seems like a pretty big one.'

'Thanks.'

'Don't mention it.'

Sten and Alex slouched out.

Chapter Thirty-Nine

It was a tiny main cabin aboard an equally tiny speedster. Although the speedster was only of moderate value, at one time someone had put a great deal of care and work into it, maintaining the plaswood floor and walls and deep ebony fittings and cabinetry. But it had become a mess. Clothing was littered about, and it was cluttered with dirty food containers that the current occupant hadn't even bothered to dump into the waste system.

Tarpy was sprawled across a bunk, his eyes closed and a small smile on his face. He was swarming with cats. In another age they might have been called alley cats. Certainly their pedigree would have been questioned. Tarpy called them spaceport cats, and they were every size and color imaginable. He was stroking the furry bodies that threatened to bury him, and idly monitoring the goings on of the *Zaarah Wahrid*, a rust bucket berthed about half a klick away.

Somebody *urr*ed beneath his left shoulder, and Tarpy lifted it enough for a kitten to escape. The kitten joined several others nursing at Momma's teats. Momma was permanently enthroned on Tarpy's stomach.

The cats were the only thing keeping Tarpy sane. Nothing, absolutely nothing had happened around the *Zaarah Wahrid* since he had taken up post. He had backup muscle stashed just on the other side of the *Zaarah Wahrid*, but Tarpy had kept contact with them to the absolute minimum. He considered them all dim-witted clots, whose only value was a willingness to die in place.

For company, on the long watch, Tarpy preferred his pussycats.

He felt a slight tingle at his left ear and heard a faint *beep-beep-beep*. Tarpy's heart raced and he ordered his pulse to slow. Finally something was happening!

He gently disentangled himself from the cats and sat up in the bunk. He punched in the visual monitor and began sweeping the area around the ship's berth.

The space-yacht port was fairly easy to survey. It looked like a two-kilometer-high metal tree with many branches. The trunk of the tree was devoted to shops, restaurants, maintenance and fueling. The branches were divided into private registry berths housing everything from yachts of near-liner size to little put-abouts.

Just to the side of the *Zaarah Wahrid* Tarpy saw something move. He scoped in on the movement as Sten and Alex walked out of the shadow of an overhanging ship and sauntered vaguely toward the craft. Tarpy grinned in recognition and hit the alarm buzzer to alert his muscle.

He rose from the bunk and slipped on his weapon harness. He strolled toward the door then paused for a moment. Tarpy looked at the open containers of food on the floor. It was more than enough to keep his friends happy until the job was done.

The door hissed open and Tarpy disappeared.

Alex gave the berth area one more quick visual check. No one. Not even a tech around. 'Gie it a go, lad, we're clean as the queen's scantlings.'

Sten walked straight to the lock panel near the ship's entrance, flipped it open, and began punching in the lock code Liz had given him. He entered the first three numbers and then waited for the computer to check them and give him the go-ahead for the next group. 'Get ready to jump, Alex. Can't tell what's on the other side of the door.'

Alex nodded and made his visual sweep again. Almost before he spotted the muscle, the heavyworlder felt his muscles bunch and a cold chill beneath his spine. 'A wee lot a' comp'ny,' he hissed to Sten, and stepped quickly away from the ship's lock.

Sten whirled in time to see a figure dash from one conex to another. Alex and Sten gave it one heartbeat then two, then three, swiftly looking for and finding cover and quietly slipping willyguns from tunic holsters and palming them.

'There!' Alex said.

Sten slowly turned his head as Tarpy stepped out alone.

'Help you, bud?' Tarpy drawled, moving toward them. Sten noticed that the casualness masked a professional and subtle half-circle. He wasn't coming directly at them but moving to one side.

'The fuel tank,' Sten whispered to Alex.

Alex nodded, catching the fact that Tarpy was putting a huge supply container within range of an easy belly dive. They heard the rustle of footsteps to either side as Tarpy's thugs moved into position.

'A few wee rats,' Alex said.

'How many?'

'Four. Maybe five.'

Sten forced a grin at the approaching enemy. 'You have a name, friend?'

'Tarpy, if anyone cares.'

Sten just nodded, keeping the stupid grin going. 'You got something to do with this rustbucket?'

'Might,' Tarpy said. 'That is, if you have business with it, I do.'

'I could,' Sten said. 'Me and my partner have been looking for something cheap. Something we could fix up.'

Tarpy smiled a lazy smile back. 'She's a fixer-upper, all right,' he agreed. 'But whatcha gotta do is talk to the owner. Get permission and all that.'

'Now!' Alex shouted.

Sten brought his willygun up and snap-fired at Tarpy as he dropped to the ground in a shoulder roll and came up behind a tumble of ship iron. A round spattered against the hull behind him and almost simultaneously he heard a shriek of pain.

'Ah was right, lad,' Alex called from the other side. ''Twere definitely five wee rats. Four noo.'

Tarpy had easily made it to cover. Sten chalked up another mark under the professional column and began checking the area for the others.

There was a clatter of footsteps on plating beneath him, and Sten glanced down through the gap between the *Zaarah Wahrid* and gravslip. Right beneath was a large and very expensive yacht. One of Tarpy's yahoos was stalking him below. It was like playing three-dimensional chess. The enemy could come from every side as well as down and up. Sten signaled to Alex. He had the left flank and Sten the right. They would take care of the bullyboys first and *then* worry about Tarpy.

He heard a heavy thud as Alex dropped ten meters down to the next berthing slip. Above Sten was a ladder leading to the next deck, half shielded from prevailing winds by a curving metal reef. Sten took two steps to one side to draw fire and then leaped for the ladder and began clambering upward. He was hoping to hell no one was in position, and his back crawled under imaginary sights as he monkey-sprinted up the rungs.

Sten spotted the first man's buttocks almost immediately as they slowly disappeared across the hull of a moored gravflit. The man *was* trying to find the high ground. Sten shot him through the bowels.

Then he stalked on, looking for one more, and knowing that he was still probably following Tarpy's plan. It was obvious from their clumsy creeping that Tarpy's backup troops were unskilled grunts. If Sten were Tarpy, he'd use them as a screen: gun-fodder for him and Alex. That would leave Tarpy in complete control. *He* would then set up the killing ground.

Sten heard a whisper just above him. He glanced up at the overhead catwalk, running out to a slip. Tarpy? Sten didn't think so. He waited until the footsteps stopped. Whoever it was, he was next to a fuel conex. A tube led from the conex to the berthed craft, and Sten could just make out the square edges of a robofueler manipulating the tube. The footsteps moved a pace or two more as the man above took up position.

Port regulations forbade on-board presence during refueling. Sten took careful aim at the conex and hoped that whoever owned the boat was a law-abiding citizen. He squeezed the trigger.

Flames exploded in all directions. Sten took one step to the side and dropped back down to the *Zaarah Wahrid*. Instinctively, he rolled as he hit, expecting return fire. As he came to his feet, something black and charred and vaguely human dropped past him with no sound, just a black thing with a gaping red hole where a mouth should be.

A little shaken from the drop, Sten paced forward along the slip, back toward the front of the *Zaarah Wahrid*. He peered cautiously out and saw Alex moving between a jumble of tie-up cables. Alex spotted him and gave a thumbs-up sign. The other two wee rats had been taken care of. Sten felt an itching in his right hand and looked down to see a slight coil of blood oozing out. Sometime during the fight someone had pinked him. Remarkable how you don't feel things on an adrenaline rush, Sten half thought. He switched the willygun from one hand to the other and raised his hand to suck on the sore spot.

All the while he was thinking of Tarpy. Somehow, he was sure, they were still playing the pro's game. Sten was positive Tarpy was just out of sight, waiting for the perfect shot. Was he stalking Alex?

Then Sten saw his friend's expression change, and at almost the same moment sensed someone just behind him. He spun, trying to bring up the willygun, but knowing the gun was in the wrong hand. He curled his fingers as he pivoted and tried desperately to drop . . .

Tarpy had him. He saw the man called Sten just in front of him. The huge man, Alex, was in a direct line. It was a perfect chess move, Tarpy thought as he pulled the trigger. The first shot would take out Sten, and then all he had to do was keep squeezing and the big man would fall less than a heartbeat later.

Then Tarpy felt himself suddenly go cold. It was a desperately weakening kind of cold that seemed to start at the shoulder and move quickly down the body. His knees buckled under him and he fought to keep his mind from blacking out.

Tarpy looked down and saw his own gun lying beside Sten. A hand was clutching the gun, and its fingers reflexed on the trigger and the gun fired.

Tarpy wondered *whose* hand was holding the gun. He heard the sound of flies and felt buzzing around his face. Tarpy reached up to brush the flies away. And then he saw his own arm, spouting bright red arterial blood.

Oh, Tarpy thought as he fell. It's my hand holding the gun.

Sten stared at the sudden corpse that had been Tarpy. He double-reflexed his fingers and the knife shot back into its sinew sheath. He felt Alex's heavy presence move up behind him, and let his friend help him to his feet.

Sten looked at Alex. 'He had us both. You know that, don't you?'

Alex gave him a slight squeeze and then pushed him forward to the *Zaarah Wahrid*'s lock panel. 'So he did, laddie. But then, some-one hae t' sometime, dinnae they?'

With a loud creak of old, unused metal, the yacht's door groaned slowly open. Sten barely waited for room to spare and dived inside. Alex turned back to stand guard.

The interior was a gutted hulk, a jumble of valueless machinery and dangling wires that led nowhere. Sten cautiously edged his way through what had been the main cabin toward the pilot's cubbyhole. Though he encountered no booby traps, Sten realized that no one had ever intended to use the craft.

He checked the doorway to the pilot's center. Nothing of danger that he could spot. He peered around the corner and his eyes widened in amazement.

Someone had laser-torched away the entire control board. Sitting in its place was an enormous computer. Unlike everything else aboard the ship, it was gleaming spotlessness. Even as he watched, a tiny duster bot hummed out and made its mindless little trek across the main board. It shot out a thin polarized mist in front of it and then efficiently sucked up the motes of dust.

Sten stepped up to the board. He still had no idea what would trigger the bomb. All he was really concerned about was when. Sten was betting that the thing was set up on some sort of a timer. That was logical, if for no other reason than to prevent an accident that would also wipe out the computer's files.

His fingers ran across the keys: ATTENTION! ZAARAH WAHRID! The vid screen lit up. IDENTITY? Sten hesitated, and then made a fast guess: HAKONE. More digestion followed then: HAKONE, G.A.

Sten sighed in relief. So far, so . . . and he continued tapping on the keys without hesitation. There was always a chance that a lack of instant response from the operator was the trigger. REVIEW FILES. The computer went at its task, calling up endless data. At first Sten couldn't figure out what he was seeing, and then he realized it was a list of main subheadings, hundreds of them, and they were repeating themselves, scrolling up the screen and then off. Sten tried to focus on the headings. Finally one scroll up: WAHRID COMMITTEE, DETAILS OF.

Sten cranked the cursor up and froze the heading. REQUEST DETAILS, he punched in.

The screen blinked twice, and then names and figures began sliding up the screen. Something else also appeared. Five overly large letters, forming a word or a name, began flashing urgently in the right-hand corner of the vid-screen. GADES! GADES! GADES! Over and over again, it repeated itself: GADES! GADES! GADES!

Sten's insides went frigid. The bomb had been triggered. Obviously, he was required to punch in a code response to shut it off. He had no idea where to begin. Therefore, he did the most logical thing. Logical, if you are not particularly worried about living.

He stared at the screen, concentrating as hard as he could on the blur of names and numbers and other details.

A warning horn began to hoot. The bomb was moments away from going off. But still Sten remained there, frozen – taking in all his mind could hold. The hooting dimmed. It became only a minor annoyance in the back of his brain. He read on, and on.

He heard an odd growling sound behind him. And then an enormous hand encircled his body and Sten felt himself being lifted up from the floor. All he could see was the swirl of data, and he realized that someone was carrying him through the ship at a dead run.

An explosion of light burst into his face as they cleared the door.

Alex stopped for a microbeat just short of a large loading container. Then he hurled Sten fifteen feet through the air. Sten felt himself soaring over the top and then saw the ground rushing up at him on the other side.

An enormous explosion shook the area, deafening him.

He came woozily back to reality, shaken by the blast. Somehow Alex was lying beside him.

His friend stood up slowly and dusted himself off. Sounds of sirens wailed in the distance. Alex helped Sten to his feet. 'Ah mu' talk to y', lad,' the Scotsman said, 'aboot th' nasty habit y' hae a' nearly killin' us.'

Chapter Forty

The grounds around Hakone's mansion looked like a military base as uniformed men loaded weaponry into gravsleds, boarded, and the sleds sidled around, like so many dogs ready for a nap, into combat formation.

The uniformed men were not ex-soldiers, since they were still carried on the roles of the Imperial military. They were deserters from the Praetorians who had been seduced or subverted into disappearing and used for long months for the conspiracy's dirty jobs.

They were gleefully back in uniform, and in motion. After all those years Hakone should have been delighted; it was finally happening!

But, like most things in life, it was happening at the wrong time. Even though Haines and Collins had thought every link to *Zaarah Wahrid* had been cut, one alarm link had remained. When the ship exploded, Hakone knew immediately.

Kai Hakone, not unsane, prided himself on his ability to instantly scope a situation. *Zaarah Wahrid*, both the computer files and the ship itself, were gone. He was under orders from the conspiracy's coordinator to wait until a certain signal was received from the *Normandie* before he moved. But things had changed, and he had no way to consult the coordinator, then aboard the *Normandie*.

Hakone took command responsibility and put his people into motion. After all, the Emperor's death was a certainty, and the worst thing that might happen was that his people might have to hold in place for a limited amount of time.

Hakone forced himself into cheeriness – he'd long recognized a tendency to brood – and bounded down the steps as his own personal combat car slid up to them and grounded.

'You know the route, Sergeant.'

'Damn well better after all these years,' the grizzled ex-Praetorian said. The car lifted off. The assembled gravsleds followed, tucking themselves into an assault diamond as the sleds hissed over the port of Soward.

Chapter Forty-One

The pilot checked his proximity screen and radar, then grunted to himself in satisfaction. He touched controls, and the crane-mounted pilot's chair swung back and around from the banked array and deposited him at ground level. He unbuckled, and then decided his honor deserved a display. As he stood, his fingers brushed a control that turned the huge main screen to visual.

Light-years away from the pulsar was a glare, visually and on all instruments. The Tahn pilot heard a murmur of discomfort from the lords standing before him, then he blanked the screen and bowed. 'Our coordinates are those ordered. We have the Imperial ships onscreen, and rendezvous is expected within ten ship-hours.'

Lord Kirghiz returned the pilot's bow before he and the other leaders of the Tahn system solemnly filed out of the control room.

The pulsar – NG 467H in the star catalogs – was the third option given to the Emperor by the Tahn for the meeting. It had been the only one approved. The Emperor realized that the pulsar insured total radio silence from all parties. So unless an ambush was already set – and the Empire had more than enough confidence in the superiority of Imperial sensors to eliminate that possiblity – no surprises would await, beyond whatever the Tahn dignitaries might want.

Also the Emperor had a hole card. Imperial science being a notch ahead of the Tahn, the Emperor had a complex com-line out, all the way to the palace. The Emperor was desperately hoping that the line would be used during the summit. Not by him, but by Sten. If Sten managed to produce the main conspirator who had inadvertently caused Alain's death, negotiations would proceed far more smoothly.

The *Normandie* and its flanking ships had picked up the incoming Tahn fleet hours before. An Imperial supersecret was responsible for that. Not only was the fuel AM_2 solely controlled by the Emperor, but before it was sold the fuel was 'coded.' Only Imperial ships ran pure fuel. All others ran modified AM_2. Imperial scoutships could pick up and identify at many light-years' distance the existence and rough identity of any non-Imperial ship.

On the screens, the Tahn ships pushed a violet haze behind them as they moved toward the rendezvous.

The Emperor shut down the monitor screen in his quarters, looked at Ledoh, and took several deep breaths. 'And so now it begins.'

Chapter Forty-Two

'Are y' finished, wee Sten,' Alex inquired gently. Sten coughed and straightened from the commode. Too quickly his guts spasmed and he heaved again.

'Advice, lad,' Kilgour went on. 'When y' feel a wee furry ring comin't up on y', swallow fast, since it's y'r bung.'

Sten recovered. Everything seemed stable. He rinsed his mouth at the sink then glared at Kilgour. 'Your sympathies are gonna be remembered, Sergeant Major. On your next fitness report.'

He wobbled into the large central room of the Blue Bhor, then dropped into the nearest chair as the world swam about him again.

Across the room Haines looked at him in concern, as did Rykor, her thick, whiskered face staring over the top of her tank.

'Bein't brainscanned is aye no a pleasure. Ah know y'll nae be wishin' naught.' Alex poured drinks for Collins, Haines, and himself and extended the jug toward Rykor, who shook her head.

'What did we get?' Sten managed. Less than two hours after the *Zaarah Wahrid* had blown, Sten had reluctantly put himself under Rykor's brainscan – as, earlier, he had done for Dynsman.

'We have a complete list,' Rykor began, 'of all conspirators.'

Sten groaned in relief.

'I amend that. We have a list of all sub-conspirators.'

Haines swore. 'The little guys. Who's at the top?'

'We already know that,' Sten said. He was very, very tired. 'Kai Hakone.'

Rykor whuffled through her whiskers. Somehow she'd gotten the idea that the salt-spray might be taken as an expression of condolence. 'You are incorrect.'

Alex broke the silence. 'Clottin' Romans!'

Sten suddenly felt much better – or much worse. He fielded the decanter and poured about three shots straight down. His stomach immediately came back up on him, and Sten let his brain concentrate on not being sick for a moment.

Haines muttered and stared at her carefully drawn conspiracy chart.

'There was a link from the ship directly to the palace, just as there was a feeler into your files, Lieutenant,' Rykor went on. 'Unfortunately the palace end was not an information link, as you thought. It was a command input terrninal.'

Sten started to blurt something, then caught himself. 'Rykor, logic control.'

'As you wish.'

Sten forced his mind to reason clearly. 'If Rykor's right, then our "inside man" is actually the one we've got to take before we can nail all these little guys.'

'Correct.'

'And we have zed clues at present. Therefore, we need to snatch Hakone and drain him.'

'Error,' Rykor said. 'There is one possible clue. Also, since Hakone is near the top, should we not assume that any attempt on Hakone would immediately send all our conspirators to flight, leaving the dry rot still in place within the palace?'

'Correction,' Sten said, and then reacted. 'Rykor what's the clue, dammit?'

'The computer bomb.'

'Gades,' Sten remembered, pronouncing it as it appeared flashing on the *Zaarah Wahrid*'s screen.

'Try the same word with the accent on the first syllable,' Rykor went on. Haines, Collins, and Alex were puzzling – and Sten was the only one who knew that Hakone, when he was describing the battle of Saragossa to him, had used the name.

Rykor allowed herself the pleasure of submerging while Sten reacted, but she surfaced and continued before Sten could explain. 'Second point. The conspirators are entirely too – cute, I believe was the word you used. They insisted on giving meaningful names to their scurryings.

'Third. Somehow, the battle of Saragossa links all these beings together.'

'Collins,' Sten barked. 'The name is Gades. He was some kind of admiral at Saragossa. I want his file. Everything. Hell, is the clot alive? Is this the clown we're looking for?'

Collins was headed for the nearest terminal.

'Watch the references, Sergeant,' Haines said, going after her. 'The file might be booby-trapped.'

Since his stomach wasn't actively coming up on him anymore, Sten felt he deserved another drink.

Alex went to Rykor's tank and looked properly respectful. 'Lass, since y' no drinkit, Ah dinnae ken wha' y' should have as ae reward. Perhaps a wee fish?'

Rykor heaved, flippers coming out of the tank and smashing down, salt water cascading over the room. For a moment Sten thought she was in convulsions.

'Sergeant Kilgour!' Rykor finally managed as the waves subsided, 'and for all these years I felt you humans lacked humor. You are a good man.'

'Alex,' Sten crooned as he walked over and draped an arm around his sergeant. 'At last we've found someone who understands your jokes.

'Your next assignment will be as a walrus.'

Unfortunately Sten's hopeful easy solution was not to be.

Admiral Rob Gades was very, very dead, by his own hand, three years after being relieved by an Imperial court after the debacle at Saragossa.

Despite testimony that Gades's order for retreat had salvaged a full third of the invading force, the Imperial Navy was in no more mood than was the Empire itself to listen to a loser's explanations. Though the testimony was enough to keep the man from being stripped of his rank and awards and sentenced to a penal battalion, it was insufficient to keep him on active service.

He'd used his retirement money to purchase a small planetoid in a frontier system and outfit it rather luxuriously. Then he'd disappeared. The mail ship that toured the planetoids three times a year had discovered the body, six months after Gades had put his parade sword against his chest and leaned forward.

The Saragossa episode was his only black mark. He had been one of the youngest officers to reach flag rank, even allowing for the service-expansion the Mueller Wars had brought.

Son of an Imperial Navy officer . . . superior records in crèche . . . admitted to a service academy at the minimum allowable age . . . fourth in his graduating class . . . commissioned and served on tacships, fleet destroyers, aide to a prominent admiral, exec officer on a cruiser, commander of a destroyer flotilla, Command and General

Staff school, military liaison on three important diplomatic missions, commander of a newly commissioned battleship, and then flag rank.

'Th' lad hae luck, until th' last min,' Alex considered.

Sten nodded.

Rykor *tsk*ed. Given the otarine structure of her head it came out more like a Bronx cheer, but the proper intention was obvious.

'You two disappoint me. Mahoney told me that you' – Rykor was about to say Mantis soldiers, but reconsidered, unsure whether Haines and Collins knew. – 'people don't believe in luck.'

Sten looked at Alex.

'We're missing something.'

'Aye. The wee crab-eater hae somethin'. Gie her th' moment a' triumph.'

Rykor savored it a minute before continuing. 'Who recommended Gades to that exclusive military school? Who suggested to a certain admiral that Lieutenant Gades would make an excellent aide? Who boarded him for the flotilla command? Who got him those – I think you would use the phrase "fat" – diplomatic assignments? . . .

'One person – and one person only.'

Sten scrolled Gades' record and read the signatures at the bottom of those glowing recommendations and requests.

'Oh Lord,' he whispered softly.

The rank and even the signature changed over the years. But the name was the same. Mik Ledoh. Imperial Chamberlain and the man closest to the Emperor!

'And now we know who is at the peak of the conspiracy, do we not?'

'But why Ledoh? What in blazes did he have to do with Gades?'

Rykor flipped her own computer terminal open. ORDER: COMPARE LEDOH AND GADES, ALL CATEGORIES. REPORT ALL SIMILARITIES.

And eventually the computer found it.

In the gene pattern . . .

Regicide sometimes springs from very small beginnings – small, at least, to those not immediately involved. Philip of Macedon died because he chose public instead of nonobjectionable private sodomy; Charles I could possibly have saved his head if he'd been more polite to a few small business people; Trotsky could have been less vitriolic in his writings; Mao III of the Pan-Asian Empire might have survived longer had he not preferred the daughters of his high-ranking officials for bedmates. And so forth.

Admiral Mik Ledoh's attempt to kill the Eternal Emperor was

rooted in equally minuscule events. Ledoh's first assignment in logistics was as supply officer on a remote Imperial Navy Base.

The base sat outside even what were then the Empire's frontier worlds. Though a long way from nowhere, the base was positioned on an idyllic planet, a world of tropical islands, sun, and very easy living. Since the base's function was merely to support patrol units, dependents were encouraged to join wives or husbands on that assignment.

Understaffed, the patrols and patrol-support missions were long. A probe ship would be out for four months or more before returning to duty. Compensation was provided by an equivalent time on leave.

There was not much for those soldiers and sailors assigned to this tropic world, beyond fueling and maintaining the probe fleet. Bored men and women can find wondrous ways of getting into trouble. Ledoh, a handsome lieutenant, found one of the classics – falling in love with the wife of a superior officer.

The woman was an odd mixture of thrill-seeker, romantic, and realist. Two months into their affair, one week before her husband returned from long patrol and subsequent transfer, she told Ledoh that she had chosen to become pregnant. While the young officer gaped, she listed her other decisions – she would have the child; she loved Ledoh and would always remember him; under no circumstances would she leave her upward-bound husband for a young supply officer.

First real love affairs are always gut-churners. But that woman managed to make the memories even worse for Ledoh. He never saw her again, but he managed to keep track of her – and his son.

The woman's husband burnt out young, and became just another alky probe-ship cowboy. Ledoh had hopes that . . . but she never left the man. The best that Ledoh could do was to shepherd his son's career. He was delighted to find that, from an early age, the boy wanted to follow in his 'father's' footsteps. Ledoh made the necessary recommendations.

When Rob Gades graduated from his military academy, a very proud Mik Ledoh watched from the audience. But he was never able to approach Gades, even later in the man's career.

Someday, he promised himself. Someday there'll be a way I can explain.

Someday, he felt, was shortly after Gades was promoted to admiral.

But the Mueller Wars happened, and Ledoh found himself organizing and leading the Crais System landings. He succeeded brilliantly – unlike his son, who was relieved of command after Saragossa.

Ledoh protested the board's decision, but uselessly. At that point he wanted to go to his son and tell him what would happen – that sooner or later sanity would return.

But he couldn't find the words.

Before he did, his son died, a suicide.

Two weeks after hearing of the death, Ledoh applied for retirement, to the shock of the Imperial Navy. Since the Crais landings were one of the few bright spots of the Mueller Wars, there was an excellent possibility that Mik Ledoh was in the running for Grand Admiral.

The conspiracy might even then have been avoided if anyone had known of Ledoh's ties to Gades. But Mik Ledoh hewed close to the old and stupid military adage: 'Never explain, never complain.'

Men who have spent most of their lives in company do not handle the solitude of retirement well, and Ledoh was no different. Retirement only gave him the chance to brood at leisure, and brooding led him to the conclusion that the reason for his son's death, the reason for the deterioration he had come to see in the Empire since the Mueller Wars, and the reason for his own unhappiness was the Eternal Emperor himself.

Kai Hakone's sixth vid-tape, built around the premise that Admiral Rob Gades had been a true hero and a scapegoat, provided the spark.

The rest, from his use of the old-boy's network to return from retirement for a position in the Imperial household to his subversion of bright Colonel Fohlee to his friendship with Hakone to the building of the conspiracy's octopus-links made perfect sense.

Or would have, if any historian had been permitted to dig into what happened that year on Prime World.

Instead, two policemen, two soldiers, and one walrus-like psychologist sat in a room over a rural pub, staring at two displays on a computer screen: father and son.

In an age when limb transplants were as commonplace as transfusions, and a medico needed to know the proper factors to prevent rejection, gene patterns were automatically recorded for any member of the Imperial military, just as blood type had been recorded a thousand years before.

Sten finally got to his feet, blanked the screen, considered a drink, and regretfully decided against it.

'Orders group,' he said. 'Haines, I want a full strike force available. Kai Hakone is to be secured immediately. Imperial warrant.

When you have him in custody, all other conspirators on Rykor's list are to be taken and held incommunicado.

'Sergeant Kilgour.'

'Sir!'

'We're to the palace.'

And Sten and Alex were in motion, headed for the only com-link to the Emperor.

Chapter Forty-Three

Sten's alarm should have gone off when he and Alex doubled into Arundel's gates. But the fact that the two Praetorians on duty were in parade battle dress instead of their normal monkey suits just did not register. Nothing else would have given away the revolt. Clerks scurried about, dignitaries mumbled in corners, and the palace was normal.

Normal, until Sten and Alex came out of the lift on the Emperor's private level. And then it was Alex who realized something was wrong.

'Captain,' he said. 'Wha' be y'r Gurkhas?'

And Sten came back to immediacy. Those Gurkhas the Emperor hadn't taken with him on the *Normandie* should have been patrolling the corridors. Instead there were Praetorians, all in full Guards combat dress.

The realization was very late, as four of the Praetorians snapped out of an alcove, willyguns leveled.

'Lads,' Alex started. 'Ye're makin't a wee mistake.'

And then Kai Hakone, in uniform, stepped out of the chamberlain's office. He nodded politely to the two. 'Captain Sten, you are under arrest.'

Chapter Forty-Four

NG 467H was a maelstrom of blinding light and howling interference that blanked the two fleets hanging in the white shadow of the spinning neutron star.

The *Normandie* and the Tahn battleships were motionless in their orbits, support and escort ships patterning around them. Since the pulsar eliminated conventional navigational methods, the ships maneuvered using computer-probability screens, computers that were normally used only for navigational instruction and simulated battles. Communication between ships was either by probe ship or by unmanned message-carrying torpedoes.

Pilots, whether Tahn or Imperial, were of course well-skilled in instruments-only conditions, but so near NG 467H, most instruments were equally useless. So, using known (by computer projection) locations, cruisers eased around the bloated hulks of the *Normandie* and the Tahn ship, hoping none of the Big Ugly Clots had altered their orbits, and the destroyers and probe ships ran infinitely variable patrols using a central plotting point cross-triangulated from the three nearest stars, and crossed fingers.

The vicinity of NG 467H was the ultimate whiteout, and the two leviathans and their pilot fish and remoras were as blind as if at the bottom of a deep.

BOOK FIVE

THE RED MASS

Chapter Forty-Five

Sten lay on his bunk, running progs.

After their arrest, Alex had been frog-marched away to join the Gurkhas in their dungeon. However, to his initial surprise, Sten was merely ordered to his quarters. But after analysis, the move seemed to make sense – at least sense from Hakone's point of view.

Hakone was obviously thinking beyond the obvious next moves.

Nevertheless, having been involved in more than a few coups d'etat, Sten thought Hakone had his head up. If *he* were Kai Hakone, he would have ordered Sten, Kilgour, and the Gurkhas shot instantly, and worried about explanations later.

Sten may have been sent to his quarters, like any officer ordered under Imperial hack, but Sten's room had been fine-combed for weaponry and three armed former Praetorians had been stationed outside. Sten's only real weapon was the knife in his arm, which had gone undiscovered.

Sten was somewhat uncomfortably coming to the conclusion that he was gong to die rather quickly. He'd already checked his layered maps of the castle, but the nearest chamber that accessed the wall passages and tunnels was some fifty meters away.

Sten didn't even consider the window, assuming that Hakone would have a couple of hidden sharpshooters on the ground below ready for Sten to try that exit.

Keep thinking, Sten. Assume, for the sake of stupidity, that you can go out the door, immobilize three guards, and then get into the palace's guts.

Ho-kay.

Then you head for the radio room, the room with the sole link to the *Normandie*. Further assume that you have time to broadcast a warning to the Emperor; that your broadcast gets through to the ship; and that the call isn't fielded by Ledoh.

Clottin' unlikely again.

But assume it, lad. Assume it. Then what happens?

What happens then is Hakone kills you. Then the Emperor comes back (hopefully), retakes his own palace, and, if that happens, gives you some sort of medal.

A very big medal.

Sten had never wanted the Galactic Cross. Especially posthumously.

He dragged his mind back. Hell with it, man. You can't even get out of your room yet.

A fist thundered against his door, and Sten rolled to his feet.

'Back against the far wall, directly in line with the doorway.'

Sten obeyed.

'Are you against the wall?'

'I am.'

'This door is opening. If you are not immediately visible, I have an unpinned grenade ready.'

The door opened, and there stood a man he was already considering his chief warden, grenade ready. The other two guards stood slightly behind him, willyguns up.

And behind them was Kai Hakone.

Sten stayed motionless as the guards came in and flanked him, carefully staying meters to either side, as Hakone paced into the room.

'Captain Sten, a word?'

Sten grinned – a lot he had to say in the matter.

'Outside. As an officer in the Guard, will you give me your parole?'

Sten considered lying, then discarded it. He still had a job, and being inside the palace made its accomplishment slightly more possible. 'No.'

'I thought not.' Hakone beckoned, and four other guards came into the room. 'But I still would like to discuss matters with you.'

Sten had a fairly good idea that, if the Emperor survived and returned, he would have a major case of the hips. His gardens were being busily dug up and entrenched or sited for ground-to-air missile launchers by Praetorians. Hakone seemed to notice none of the activity as he walked beside Sten.

The seven Praetorians held diamond-formation around Sten, their weapons leveled and aimed.

These also Hakone ignored. He was, like any thinker-turned-activist, in the middle of a near-compulsive explanation. 'It would have been simpler if Phase One had been successful.'

Sten, equally compulsive an intelligence officer, wanted more information.

'Phase One, Sr. Hakone? I don't have all the pieces. You were intending the bomb to stun the Emperor, correct? He was then to be hustled to Soward Hospital, where Knox would take over the case.

'What would that have given you?'

'The Emperor traditionally withdraws from the public after Empire Day for a rest. One, perhaps two weeks. During that time he would have been reconditioned.'

'To follow whose orders?'

'Ledoh and others of us who recognize that the Empire must be redirected to its proper course.'

'But now you're going to kill him.'

'Necessity is a harsh master.'

Sten mentally winced – Hakone couldn't *really* think in those clichés.

'So he dies. Why did you take over the palace?'

'Once the Emperor is dead, and with us holding the center of all Imperial communications, no false information will be broadcast.'

'Like who really did it?'

Hakone smiled and didn't bother answering.

'By the way, Hakone, if you don't mind my saying, who is going to be your judas goat?'

'The Tahn, of course.'

'Don't you think that those delegates might have their own story? And be listened to?'

'Not if they're equally deceased.'

Sten's poker face melted. 'You're talking war.'

'Exactly, Captain. With a war starting, who will be interested in a postmortem? And a war is what this Empire needs to melt the fat away. That would also settle the Tahn question.'

'When is this going to happen?'

'We have no exact timetable. The Praetorians and I were supposed to take the palace three days from now. Your discovery of the *Zaarah Wahrid* forced us into premature motion. The actual termination of the Emperor will be decided by Admiral Ledoh.'

'You really think this committee, or whatever you're calling it, *could* run the Empire?'

'Why not? Twenty minds are obviously superior to one, aren't they?' Sten could have answered by stating the obvious – no, because any junta becomes an exercise in backstabbing as each leader tries to take out the others. Instead he went in another way.

'Twenty minds don't know the secret of AM_2.'

'Captain, you really believe that drivel?'

Drivel, hell – Sten had spent enough time around the Emperor to realize the man *had* that ace up his sleeve.

'There is no way I can believe that one man – one mortal man – controls AM_2. That the answer is nowhere in his files.'

They continued to walk, Sten maintaining silence, waiting for the offer.

It came.

'The reason I wanted to talk to you privately,' Hakone finally continued, 'is that after the . . . event, there will probably be a certain amount of resettlement. You could be of service.'

'To you personally, or to your committee?'

'Well, of course, for us all. But I would want you to report to me.'

Sten didn't let himself smile. Already Hakone was figuring on having his own people to guard his back. The man didn't even believe his own theories. 'What would be my new job description?'

'You would be allowed to maintain your present position. But I – I mean we – would have you detached for special assignments in the intelligence area.'

'You're forgetting I swore an oath. To the Emperor.'

'If the Emperor no longer existed, would that oath be valid?'

'Suppose I say no?'

Hakone started to beam, then studied Sten closely. 'Are you lying to me, Captain?'

'Of course.'

Hakone's smile was subtly different as he beckoned to the guards.

'You are a careful man, Captain. Let us leave things as they are. You are restricted to your room until notified otherwise. After the Emperor's death, perhaps we should rehold this conversation.'

Sten bowed politely, then followed the guards back toward his quarters. He was not interested in Hakone at the moment; he'd figured a way out of his confinement – and a way that gave him almost a 10 per cent chance of surviving the ensuing debacle.

That was better odds than was normal for Mantis.

Chapter Forty-Six

Lord Kirghiz ignored the grumblings of his fellow Tahn lords, fitted himself into the lighter's bare-frame jumpseat, and buckled in. After getting Kirghiz's curt nod, the co-pilot hissed orders to the pilot, and the lighter broke lock with the Tahn battleship and arched toward the *Normandie*.

Kirghiz was showing less the stoicism required of a man worthy of ruling the warrior Tahn than that of a man with worries far more serious than the indignity of being chauffeured in a troop transport. To begin with, less than one third of the Tahn council had agreed to the summit meeting, and those who had deserted him were the most adamantly anti-Empire, pro-war faction of the Tahn lords.

Kirghiz's control of the Tahn council was very tenuous, based on an uneasy agreement among a majority of the various Tahn factions. In his absence, he knew that the ruling council might very well change its entire structure.

Still worse were the demands he was required to make on this, the first day of the summit. Several were deal-killers, conditions which Kirghiz knew, from his decades as a diplomat and power broker, the Emperor could not agree to.

In fact, if he were the Emperor, Kirghiz would consider breaking off the meeting moments after hearing those demands.

He prayed, to whatever gods he disbelieved in, that the Emperor was the consummate politician he should be, and would recognize the demands as nothing more than cheap grandstanding for the Tahn peasants and the peasant-mentality of those lords who proposed them. Because if the talks broke down, Kirghiz saw no other alternative than war between the Tahn worlds and the Empire.

No computer he'd used could predict the outcome of such a war, but all of them showed one thing: Defeated or victorious, the Tahn worlds would be in economic ruin at the war's end.

Kirghiz being a Tahn, a Tahn warrior, and a Tahn lord, he did not even think about the other result to the talks breaking down – the certainty of his own trial for treason and execution if he returned without a treaty.

Chapter Forty-Seven

If he survived the breakout attempt, which was very unlikely, Sten made a note to put the cost of replacing his mini-holoprocessor on somebody's expense account. Because sure as death and dishonesty, Sten's hobby machine was ruined.

The holoprocessor was intended to create the illusion of very small – no more than 100-centimeters-high – figures, machines, or dioramas.

Cursing his ineptness at electronics, Sten had replaced all of the holoprocessors's fuses with heavy-duty wiring stripped from a shaving light and cut the safety circuits out. He had searched through the holoprocessor's memory looking for some sort of horrible beastie to use, then laughed and input the description and behavior of the wonderful gurions he and Alex had met shortly before.

That complete, the mini-processor was pushed to a few meters from the door. Its actuating switch was boogered to a remote, under Sten's foot.

Sten took the required position, directly across from the door opening, and then considered cheap lies. Sick? Nobody's that dumb, not even a Praetorian. Hungry? Still worse. Then Sten was struck by inspiration. He tossed a vid-tape at the door and got an appropriate clunk.

'What is it?' came the guard's suspicious voice.

'I'm ready now.'

'For clottin' what?'

Sten allowed puzzlement to enter his voice. 'For Sr. Hakone.'

'We have no orders on that.'

'Hakone – you must have heard – told me to contact him immediately after our meeting.'

'He didn't tell us that.'

Sten let silence work for him.

'Besides, he's given orders that no one is to see him until further notice.'

'Kai Hakone,' Sten said, 'is in the Imperial com bunker. I think he would like to speak to me.'

Any sergeant can fox a grunt, just as any captain can fox a sergeant. Or at least that's the way it had worked when Sten was on duty in the field. He hoped things hadn't changed much.

'I'll have to check with the sergeant of the guard,' came the self-doubting voice.

'As you wish. Sr. Hakone told me that he wanted nobody to know.'

There was an inaudible mutter, which Sten's hopeful mind translated as a conference, consisting of *yeah, Hakone works things like that, nobody told us nothin', that figures, what'th'clot we got to worry about if we just take him to a com center*. And then the louder voice: 'Are you back against the wall?'

Sten held out his hands. Indeed, he was standing, obviously unarmed, against the far wall. The guard eyed him through the freshly drilled peephole, then unbolted and opened the door. He was three steps inside, his backups flanking him, when the two-meters-high image of the gurion rose from the holoprocessor and walked toward the guards.

The reaction was instant – the guards' guns came up, blasting reflexively and tearing hell out of the ceiling.

Sten's reaction was equally fast: he flat-rolled, hit, half rose over the self-destructing holoprocessor, his knife lanced before him, and then buried it in the chest of the lead guard.

Sten used the inertia of the guard to stop himself, and the knife came out, splashing blood across the room, through the rapidly fading gurion. And Sten was pivoting, his left, knuckled hand smashing sideways, well inside the second guard's rifle reach, into the man's temple, while his right arm launched the knife into – and through – guard number three. Cartilage and bone cracked and broke in guard number two, and Sten recovered into attack position before any of the three corpses slumped to the floor.

Wasting no time in self-congratulation, Sten catted down the corridor, heading for the palace's catacombs.

Kilgour, too, was trying moves.

'Clottin' Romans,' he bellowed down the corridor. 'Y'r mither did it wi' sheep. Wi' goats! Wi' dogs! Clottin' hell, wi' Campbells!' No response came from the guards outside the cell.

He stepped back from the window and looked apologetically at the 120 Gurkhas sharing the huge holding cell with him.

'Tha' dinnae ken.'

Kilgour's plan, for want of a weaker word, was to somehow anger the guards so much they'd come into the cell to bust kneecaps. Alex hoped that, regardless of weapons, he and the 120 stocky brown men in the cell could somehow break out.

Havildar-Major Lalbahadur Thapa leaned against the wall beside him. 'In Gurhali,' he offered helpfully, 'you might try one pubic hair.'

Alex laughed. 'Now that's the stupidest insult Ah've heard in years.'

'Stupider, Sergeant Major, than calling someone a Campbell – whatever that is?'

Without warning a section of seemingly solid stone in one wall slid open, and Sten was suddenly leaning nonchalantly against the far wall. 'Sergeant-Major, I could hear your big mouth all the way down the corridor. Now if you'd knock off the slanging and follow me.

'The arms room,' Sten continued, as the Gurkhas recovered from their astonishment and bustled into the low tunnel Sten had emerged from, 'is three levels up and one corridor across.'

'Ah'm thinkit Ah owe y' a pint,' Alex managed, as he forced his bulk after the Gurkhas. Sten looked very knowing as he palmed the rock wall shut.

Chapter Forty-Eight

Years later, Sten and Alex would have a favorite pondering point. They could understand why the Emperor built Arundel. They could also understand why a man who believed in romance required a castle to have secret passages.

The problem was the *why* for some of those passages. Both men thought it very logical that a backstairs went from the Imperior chambers to feed into the various bedchambers. Sten could even understand why the Emperor wanted a tunnel that provided secret egress from cells in the dungeon far below.

They were never able to explain to everyone's satisfaction why a few of the tunnels opened into a main passageway.

Some of the former Praetorians involved in the revolt might have wondered, too, if they had survived. Most did not.

A Praetorian paced down a seemingly doorless corridor, then a panel swung noiselessly open and a small grinning man swung a large knife that looked to be a cross between a machete and a small cutlass.

There were only a little over a thousand Praetorians facing 120 wall-slinking Gurkhas. The battle was completely one-sided.

The reoccupation of the palace went quickly, silently, and very, very bloodily, as Sten deployed his troops in a slow circle, closing on the Imperial chambers, the communication center, and that one room with the com-link to the Emperor.

The armored door to the com center was sealed, which offered no potential problem to the Gurkha squad deployed around it. The lance-naik already had his bunker-buster loaded and the rocket aimed at the door's hinges when Sten kicked him aside. 'Yak-pubes,' he snarled in Gurhali, 'do you know what would happen if you discharged that rocket in this passageway?'

The lance-naik didn't seem worried. Kilgour was already slapping together a shaped charge from the demopack he'd secured from the armory.

'Best w' be all hangin't on th' sides ae the corridor,' he muttered, and yanked the detonator. Sten had barely time to follow the suggestion before the charge blew the door in. The Gurkhas, kukris ready, leaped in the wreckage but could find nothing to savage. The Praetorians inside had been reduced to a thin paste plastered across the room's far wall. Kukri in hand, Sten ran past them, leapt, and his foot snapped into the thin door leading to the com room itself. He recovered and rolled in, low, to find himself looking at a shambles of crushed circuitry, looped power cables, and spaghetti-strung wires.

And Kai Hakone, standing in an alcove away from the doorway, mini-willygun leveled at Sten.

'You're somewhat late, Captain.' Hakone motioned with his free hand, eyes and gun never moving away from Sten.

'You have the palace, but we have the Emperor. The com-link is destroyed. Before it can be rebuilt . . .' and Hakone gestured theatrically. His eyes flickered away as he scanned for Sten's accomplices – enough time for Sten to grab the end of a severed power cable and throw it into Hakone's face.

Hakone fried, and in his convulsions the willygun went off, its projectile whining away harmlessly as his flesh blackened then sizzled before the circuit-breakers popped and the body collapsed, leaving Sten in the ruins of the com room.

''Twould appear th' only hope our Emp hae is us bairns doin't o'er th' hills t' far away.'

Sten nodded agreement, and then he and Alex were moving, headed for the palace's command center.

Chapter Forty-Nine

'. . . And lastly, the Aggrieved Party solemnly petitions His Imperial Majesty to publicly display his historic sense of justice, and deep feelings for individual tragedy, by recognizing the heroic and tragic death of Godfrey Alain. Alain was a man respected by . . .'

Admiral Ledoh droned on and on, reviewing once again the demands of the Tahn. His audience consisted of two very bored men: the Eternal Emperor and Tanz Sullamora. Sullamora was fighting to stay awake, and doing his best to remain attentive. He kept watching the Emperor for a signal of his feelings. It was an impossible task. The Eternal Emperor's face was a complete stone.

'. . . and, by an agreed time, the Emperor will read, or have read, an agreed-upon message to his subjects, whose basic points should consist of—'

'Enough,' the Emperor said. 'Clotting *enough*. I got their point. Now, the question is, what is our response?'

Admiral Ledoh raised an eyebrow. 'I was about to suggest that if we agree that we are completely familiar with their demands, we should have them analyzed by the diplomatic computer.'

The Emperor laughed. 'Relax, Ledoh. You're starting to sound like the damned Tahn.' He picked up a pot of tea and refilled three cups. 'As for the diplomatic computer, forget it. I can run it down faster and more accurately. I've been doing this kind of thing for more centuries than I've got stars.'

Sullamora nodded. 'I was waiting for you to say just that, sir. And I hope that you don't think me immodest to point out that I have had many years of experience with these people.'

'That's why I brought you along. They trust you about as much as they can trust any non-Tahn.'

Sullamora smiled. 'It isn't trust, sir. On their part it is pure greed. After all, I am the only person you have sanctioned to trade with them.'

'That's why you're my ace in the hole,' the Emperor said. 'Because you are gonna be my well-baited hook.'

Sullamora hadn't the faintest idea what the Emperor meant, but he recognized praise when he heard it, and smiled back graciously.

'Now,' the Emperor said, 'let's translate some of this into plain talk. They have five basic demands, and I believe all of them are negotiable.

'Starting with number one: they want my Imperial contract to administer the Fringe Worlds. Translation: they want a gift of all those systems.'

'You'll say no, of course, sir,' Sullamora puffed.

'Sort of, but not quite.'

Sullamora started to protest, but the Emperor held up a hand. The Emperor barely noticed that Ledoh had been strangely noncommittal.

'Let me boil the rest down, and then I'll tell you how we probably ought to play it.

'Second demand: open immigration. My objection: they can pack the system with their own people. That's a double giveaway.

'Third: unconditional amnesty for Godfrey Alain's people. No problem. Granted. I can always round up the real hard-core types later, on the quiet.

'Fourth – and here's another sticking point – they want to set up a free port in the Fringe Worlds.'

'That has a lot of commercial possibilities,' Sullamora said.

'Sure. But it also means I'm supposed to increase their AM_2 quota. Which means they can stockpile even more and give me much bloody grief down the line.

'Last of all, they want me to publicly apologize for Godfrey Alain's death.'

Ledoh raised his head and gave the Emperor a thin smile. 'You never apologize, do you, sir?' he said bitterly. No one noticed his tone.

'Clotting right. Once I start apologizing I might as well start looking around for someone to take my place.

'Last time I admitted I was wrong, it cost me half my treasury.'

'A firm no, sir,' Sullamora advised. 'Frankly, I don't see a single point we can give on. My vote is to send them packing.'

'On the surface, I would agree with you, Tanz. But let me run back what I propose. Then see what you think.'

Sullamora was suddenly very interested. He could sniff a profit.

'To start with, I flip their last point to my first.'

'You mean the apology?' Sullamora was aghast.

'Sure. Except I do it this way. I propose that we build a memorial to Godfrey Alain. To commemorate his death and the many deaths on both sides of this whole mess.

'Instead of an apology, I put it to them that all peace-loving peoples are responsible for this ongoing tragedy.

'For frosting on the cake, I fund the whole clotting shebang. I build a memorial city on the Tahn capital world. A sort of Imperial trade center.'

Sullamora grinned wolfishly.

'In other words, you get to put a garrison on their home planet.'

The Eternal Emperor laughed loudly. 'Good man! Not only that, but I guaran-clotting-tee you that every man and woman will be from my elite troops.'

'Excellent! And if I know my Tahn, they'll swallow the whole thing,' Sullamora said.

'Next: Instead of letting them administer the Fringe Worlds, I propose a peacekeeping force. Manned fifty-fifty.'

Sullamora shook his head.

'Not so fast, Tanz. I let them appoint the commander.'

Sullamora considered. 'But that would be the same as handing it over to them.'

'It would appear that way. Except, since I provide the ships, and those ships would be commanded by my people, their top guy would be helpless when it came to any action.

'And to copper my bet, I double the basic pay of my troops.'

Sullamora especially liked this. 'Meaning, compared to the Tahn, they'd be relatively rich. Also meaning, you'd be undermining the morale of the common Tahn soldiers.'

He made a mental note to try this tactic in some of the more difficult trading posts under his corporate command.

The Eternal Emperor continued. 'Open immigration, fine.

'Now, for the free port concept, I'll agree. With the proviso that I get to appoint the man in charge.'

'They'd have to go for that,' Sullamora said. 'After you let them pick the chief of the peacekeeping force. But who would you propose?'

'You,' the Emperor said.

That rocked Sullamora back. The profits he had been sniffing were soaring to the sky.

'Why me?'

'You understand them, but your loyalties are to me. Therefore, I keep complete control of the AM_2 supply. Through you, of course.'

'Of course.' Sullamora knew better than to cook his books as far as energy supplies were concerned.

'Finally,' the Emperor said, 'I have a magnanimous proposal. It'll really sound that way when the diplomatic fools get through flowering it up.

'The Tahn's main problem, besides being plain fascist clots, is they're under heavy population pressure. That's why we're knocking heads in the Fringe Worlds.'

Sullamora nodded.

'Therefore, to take the pressure off, I agree to fund an exploration force. I will bankroll the entire thing and provide the ships and crews.'

Even the silent chamberlain came forward for that one. 'But what advantage—'

'The ships will be ordered to explore away from the Fringe Worlds. If we find anything . . .'

If there was to be any further expansion, the Tahn would be moving the other way. With luck, that pioneer rush to other systems would bleed some of the tension out of their military culture.

'Well?' The Eternal Emperor leaned back in his seat, looking for comments from his two key men.

'It seems fine to me,' the chamberlain said quickly.

Sullamora, however, thought for a very long time. Then he slowly nodded. 'It should work.'

'I sure as clot hope so,' the Eternal Emperor said 'Because if it doesn't—'

The light next to the hatchway blinked on-off-on.

Ledoh frowned annoyance and touched the annunciator key.

'Communication officer, sir.'

'This conference was not to be—'

'Admiral,' the Emperor interrupted. 'This may be what I'm expecting.'

Ledoh palmed the door to open.

The watch com officer didn't know whether to salute or bow to the Emperor, so he compromised ridiculously.

The Emperor didn't notice – he was hoping that the signal was from Sten, announcing that he had the conspirators nailed, on toast, and ready for delivery to the Tahn.

'Uh . . . sir,' the officer said, finding it easier to deliver his message to Admiral Ledoh. 'This signal isn't from the source we expected. It's a distress signal. Standard sweepband broadcast. Our satellite just happened to pick it up.'

'Clot,' Ledoh swore, and took the printout. 'We didn't need this. No response.'

'Hang on. Let me look at it.' Ledoh passed the sheet to the Emperor. According to the burst-broadcast signal, the merchant ship *Montebello* was in a desperate situation, a number of light-years, estimated, off the radio pulsar NG 467H. Fuel explosion on-board ship, all officers injured, most crewmembers severely burned, request immediate assistance from any receiving ship.

'Jerks!' the Emperor said. 'Cheapjack shippers, trying some kind of econo slingshot orbit, and they're not capable of finding their way out of a closet with a torch.'

'Your Highness,' Sullamora said. 'Admiral Ledoh is correct. There are far more important things happening than a few dozen burnt spacebums.'

The Emperor would probably have made the same decision. But, characteristically, Sullamora put it wrong, and the Emperor flashed back more than a thousand years to when he himself hadn't been much more than a spacebum.

'Lieutenant,' he said to the com officer. 'Transfer this message to the ComDesRon. Order him to dispatch one destroyer immediately.'

The officer only saluted this time, then scurried out of the Imperial presence.

The Emperor turned back to business. 'Now, Admiral, would you please put all of our common-sense into the appropriate diplomatic drakh, so Lord Kirghiz won't think that we've gone insane?'

Chapter Fifty

'Thank you, Mr. Jenkins. I have the con.'

The hell I do, Commander Lavonne considered as his deck officer saluted and stepped back. That lousy game machine we're using to keep us off the BUCs is telling me what to do.

He rechecked the computer-prob screen that was giving him his course. 'Nav-point zeroed?'

'Zeroed, sir,' his executive officer said.

'From zero . . . course left thirty-five degrees, down fourteen degrees.'

'Course left thirty-five, down fourteen.'

'Secondary drive . . . quarter-speed.'

'Secondary drive at quarter-speed.'

Lavonne mentally crossed his fingers and hoped the next few seconds didn't produce anything unusual, such as an intersection orbit with another destroyer. 'Engage drive.'

'Drive engaged.' The Imperial Destroyer *San Jacinto* hummed slightly as the ship's gyro clutched in, turning the ship into the correct direction, and the Yukawa drive shoved the *San Jacinto* away from the thronged fleet.

Lavonne let thirty seconds elapse. 'Increase secondary drive to half-speed.'

'Secondary drive at half-speed,' came the toneless echo from his quartermaster.

'Mr. Collins . . . from the count . . . now! Five minutes to main drive.'

'Five minutes until main drive, Captain, and counting.'

Five minutes gave the skipper of the *San Jacinto* brooding time. He considered slumping into his command chair, then brought himself up. We are all getting a little sloppy out here, he reminded himself. He then concentrated on his brooding.

Under normal circumstances Commander Lavonne would have been biting handrails in half when he'd gotten his assignment. He had spent entirely too many years pulling tramp steamers' tubes out of cracks to enjoy another rescue. As far as he was concerned all merchant fleets should be under military control. Lavonne was not at all a fascist – he'd just seen too many freighters permitted to off-planet with out-of-date or nonexistent safety sections, red-lined emergency gear, and officers who weren't competent to command a gravsled.

But the new assignment would give the commander and the men and women of the *San Jacinto* something to do.

Basically Commander Lavonne was ticked. Originally he and his ship had been pulled from their DesRon and ordered to rendezvous and escort a liner to its destination.

Initially Lavonne felt very proud. Somebody Up There – Up There with Stars – felt that the *San Jacinto* was as good a ship as the commander and his crew knew it to be. Lavonne, in his few selfish moments, also recognized that the whole enterprise, whatever it was, would probably look very good in his record jacket when it came time for promotion.

Ship's scuttlebutt soared when they reached the destination – off NG 467H – and then peaked when the incoming Tahn ships were identified. Lavonne figured out that he and his men were participating in something Terribly Significant and Probably Historic. The question was, what? Lavonne had a mental image of himself as a frizzly old admiral taping his memoirs and saying: 'And then I was permitted to participate in the Empire-shaking (whatsit) located off a distant radio star, in which (nobody ever told me) happened.'

What made it worse was the radiation from NG 467H. Since all vid-ports and com-screens were sealed, the sailors felt even more than usual like sardines in a tin.

Orders from the squadron commander arrived in the messenger torps but were less than helpful: patrol from such a point to such a point, then return exactly on orbit.

It's a sailor's right to piss and moan, but not within earshot of his division commander. Sailors went on report. Several paired sailors requested permission to join the general mess decks, breaking up long-standing relationships. Lavonne's most trusted bosun's mate, who only got busted when the *San Jacinto* berthed in a liberty port, was reduced to the ranks after he modified one of the ship's water purifiers to produce something that, when drunk, hit with the potency of AM_2 fuel.

The *San Jacinto* was not a happy ship, so Lavonne was actually grateful when he got the orders to break from the fleet, operate under independent command, and relieve the disaster-stricken MS *Montebello*.

'Four minutes, thirty seconds.'

Lavonne brought himself back to the ship's bridge. 'At fifteen, give me a tick count.'

'At fifteen, aye, sir. Coming to fifteen . . . fifteen, mark! Twelve . . . eleven . . . ten . . . nine . . . eight . . . seven . . . six . . .'

'On order, engage main drive.'

'Standing by.'

'Two . . . one . . .'

'Mark!'

And the *San Jacinto* shimmered as the AM_2 drive smashed the ship into the orbit that would arc it very close 'over' the pulsar toward the nearest intersection point with the *Montebello*.

'Ah, lad,' Alex mused. 'Th' remind me ae m' ancestor.'

Though it appeared to be a tramp steamer that had far more owners than semiannuals, the ship was really a Mantis Q-ship, an intelligence ship mounting as much power as an Imperial destroyer and far better electronics. In addition to the normal four-men crew, Sten, Alex, and forty Gurkhas were crammed into it.

Before he punched the panic button that had alerted the fleet, Sten had prepositioned several remote satellites outside NG 467H, satellites that hopefully would report the drive-flare of any ship headed in his general direction. Then he'd sent the distress signal, knowing that the satellite originally intended to field the tight beam from the palace would respond and communicate with the fleet itself, even though the ships were inside NG 467H's interference blanket.

'I did not know, Sergeant Major Yeti, you were aware of just who your ancestors were,' Naik Gunju Lama said in seeming innocence.

Kilgour sneered at him. 'Frae off'cers Ah hae t'take drakh like tha', but no frae a wee private who hae to gie back to Katmandu to have his pubes pulled.

'As ae was sayin't, Captain. One ae m'ancestors went on th' dole, an'—'

'What the hell's a dole?' Sten asked. There'd been no signals from his remotes, and so they had time to kill. Listening to another of

Kilgour's absurd stories seemed as good a way to pass the time as anything.

'A wee fruit, shaped like a pineapple. Now dinna be interruptin' me, lad. So it's necessary tha' m' ancestor sees a quack, to certify he's nae able to ply his trade.

'The doc looks a' m' ancestor, one Alex Selkirk Kilgour, an' blanches. "Lad," he says. "Y' be missin't parts!"

'M' ancestor says, "Aye."

'"Why'd y' nae hae transplants?"

'"It was nae possible," Selkirk explains. "Y' see, till recent, Ah was a pirate."

'The doc thinkit tha' makit sense, an proceeds wi' th' exam. Whae he's done, he says, "Sir, y'be't healthy aye a MacDonald."

'"Exceptin' tha' missin't parts."

'So Selkirk, he explainit: "Y'see't tha' missin't leg? Wi' the peg? Ah was boardin't a richun's yacht, an' th' lock door caught me."

'Th' medico listen't, mos' fascinated.

'"Th' hook?" Selkirk gie on, "Tha' be from't ae laser blast. Took m' paw off clean't ae whistle."

'"An' the eye?" the doc asks.

'Selkirk, e' fingers th' patch. "Th' eye? Tha's frae seagull crap."

'Th' wee surgeon's a' puzzled an' all.

'"Seagull crap?"

'"Aye. Ah was dockyard, starin't up ae a crane, an a gull go't o'er an' deposits."

'"But how can seagull crap . . ."

'"Ah, doctor, y'see, Ah'd only had the hook twa days."'

Sten sought for the proper response and then found it. 'Clottin' Romans!' And then he focused his attention back on the warning screens.

The *San Jacinto,* keeping itself sunward of the tumbling tramp freighter, matched orbits with the pinwheeling ship and nudged closer. Then a volunteer officer, his suit visor at maximum opacity, jetted a line across to one of the *Montebello*'s tie-down pads. Then the destroyer's winches, at their lowest gearing, drew the two ships together.

Lavonne had assumed that the *Montebello*'s lock system would not match his, in spite of Imperial design regulations, so he had the accordion tube ready. It inflated and spread out, fitting and sealing over the *Montebello*'s lock.

Lavonne, an officer who believed in leading from the front, was suited and waiting inside the *San Jacinto*'s lock. Behind him twenty sailors were suited up. The lock, one passageway, and a room were set up for the anticipated burnt crewmembers of the *Montebello*.

'Ten kilos, sir.'

'All hands, seal suits.' He, his twenty sailors, and the rest of the crew of the ship snapped their faceplates closed.

'Open the outer lock.'

'Outer lock door opening, sir.'

Air whooshed from the lock chamber into the accordion tube as the atmospheric pressures equalized. Lavonne grabbed the line running down the center of the tube and hand-over-handed to the *Montebello*'s lock.

He keyed it open then he and his chief medical officer stepped inside. Lavonne punched the emergency code that allowed both lock doors to open simultaneously, and waited as atmosphere reequalized. He was braced for almost anything – null-atmosphere with exploded bodies; fire-blackened men and women; mutiny; chaos. *Almost* anything.

What he saw was three men. All wore Imperial uniforms. The slender man in front had the rank tabs of a captain in the Imperial Guard. All three men had willyguns aimed at his chest.

Lavonne gaped, but before he could recover, the captain said, 'Imperial Service, Commander. I am commandeering your ship!'

Chapter Fifty-One

The meeting room was a hush of diplomats. It was packed with the Tahn contingent and the Emperor's aides. In the far corner of the room the Emperor himself huddled in conference with Lord Kirghiz and Tanz Sullamora. Underlings on both sides were waiting for the final word. Was there to be an agreement or were they about to go to war?

If they had been inside the Emperor's head when the Tahn delegation arrived for the final meeting, there would have been no question. He had noted that everyone, from the lowest-ranking Tahn lord to Lord Kirghiz himself, was dressed in formal uniform. They were decked out in emerald green cloaks, red tunics, and green trousers. The tunics were covered with a rainbow of ribbons and dangling medals.

The Eternal Emperor covered a smile when he saw them; people put on their best for a party, not a declaration of war. He himself was dressed in his most simple uniform: It was a rich, light gray. And he wore only one decoration: his rank as head of state – a small gold button with the letters AM_2 over a background of the null-element's atomic structure. The Eternal Emperor had pointed out to Mahoney once that the way to stand out in a crowd of gold braid was to upstage with simplicity. 'When you're the ultimate boss,' he once observed, 'you don't have to announce it.'

The Emperor rose to his feet and extended a hand to Kirghiz. 'Then we're agreed?'

Lord Kirghiz fought to maintain a dignified face. But he couldn't help his smile of victory. 'Agreed.'

'Then let's leave the details to our staffs,' the Emperor said. 'We can dot our i's and cross our t's on a mutually beneficial date.

'Now, I have taken the liberty of anticipating our peaceful solution to the late difficulties. Gentlemen. Ladies. If I may invite you to a small dinner of appreciation.'

He waved his hand and huge doors hissed open behind him. The Tahn craned their necks to see a richness of food and drink yawning out behind the Emperor. There were loud cheers, much laughter, and the Eternal Emperor led his guests into the banquet room.

The banquet was the highlight of Marr and Senn's long career. They had spared nothing to lay out one of the most exotic official dinners in Imperial history.

To begin with, they had been faced with the task of making the enormous ship's banquet hall feel cozy. So they'd ordered the bulkheads moved in, and then draped them in soft colors to warm the atmosphere. The tables were artfully placed so that no one felt cut off from the main attraction, the Emperor and Kirghiz, who were seated across from one another at the head table. They had also gutted the lighting system and installed indirect illumination that picked out the gleam of silver and polish of plate and highlighted the appetizing dishes being served.

The greatest miracle was the food itself. Naturally, since the Emperor was the host, the menu consisted of Tahn dishes, offering condiments and spices that the caterers knew would compliment and entice the Tahn palate.

As for service, they went one step further. The ultimate in luxury was to be served by a person, rather than a machine or even a high-priced waiter bot. Therefore, Marr and Senn had pressed the Praetorian Guards into service. Behind each diner was a Guardsman in full dress who, at the slightest gesture, would pour wine, change a dish or sweep something out of the way.

The man most pleased with the arrangement was Admiral Ledoh. He couldn't have planned it better himself. He picked up his wine goblet and took a small sip. He had to admit that Marr and Senn were a very talented pair. It was unfortunate that their greatest banquet was to be their last.

Ledoh glanced over to Colonel Fohlee, who was seated at the far end of the table. Ledoh raised his glass to Fohlee in a silent toast. Fohlee returned the salute.

Chapter Fifty-Two

In a time when subspace communication was nearly perfect, the ship-to-ship wire-line was as archaic as a speaking tube. But not off NG 467H. And so the bot jetted out toward the *Normandie* on peroxide rockets, trailing wire behind.

Its circuitry may have been thirty years old and out of use, but it still told the bot to home . . . home *there* . . . on that ring of sensitive metal . . . closing . . . reverse . . . jets . . . and the com-line clicked home and the line was open to the *Normandie*.

'This is Dr. Shapiro,' came the voice from the *Normandie*. 'How many casualties do you have?'

'This is Commander Lavonne. Thirty-five. My med officer says twelve are critical, third-degree flash burns, unstable. All others second- or third-degree burns, semistable.'

'Stand by.'

Half-moon clamps slid out from the *Normandie*, locked onto the *San Jacinto* and pulled the two ships' cargo doors into proximity mating, and the doors opened.

Sten's forty Gurkhas spilled out into the *Normandie*'s hold firing. Each carried not only his kukris and willygun, but a stungun hung on a retracting combat sling around his neck.

Sten's orders had been simple: (1) anyone you see is to be taken out; (2) if they are unarmed, stun them – if they are armed or violent, kill them; (3) find the Emperor and secure him; (4) no one, emphasis *no one*, is to approach the Emperor under any circumstances – anyone, no matter what explanation or rank, who tries is to be killed.

Gurkhas being Gurkhas, and appreciating simple orders, every person in the hold was down and unconscious in five seconds. Even the 'talker,' linked to the *Normandie*'s command center, had no time to report that the ship was being attacked.

On command, as if it were a drill, Corporal Luc Kesare stepped forward with a napkin-covered platter. Kirghiz turned and smiled, awaiting the new dish, as Kesare's left hand retained the platter and his dagger-holding right shot out, the blade going through Kirghiz's smiling mouth, through his palate, and into his brain.

And so the slaughter started . . .

Chapter Fifty-Three

The column of Gurkhas, Sten at its head, was doubling silently through the crew quarters central corridor when the ship's PA system blared: 'All hands . . . the banquet room . . . somebody . . . they're trying to kill the Emperor—' The voice stopped and confused sounds chaosed for a moment before the system went dead.

Crewmen stumbled out into the corridor and went down as the Gurkhas stunned them.

At a lift tube Sten raised a hand and the forty men were motionless. He issued orders sending half his men, under Havildar-Major Harkaman Limby, up through officers' territory with orders to secure the *Normandie*'s com center and control room. The other twenty followed Sten toward the banquet room.

The huge main doors to the banquet room were yawning open when Sten and Alex sprinted up. Sounds of fighting raged somewhere deep inside the room. At Sten's signal, Alex and the Gurkhas cautiously edged their way inside.

The work of art that Marr and Senn had created was gone. Tables were overturned and smoking. The room was ankle-deep in smashed plates and smeared food. Horribly mutilated corpses grinned up at the Gurkhas.

Sten and the others crept through a long, twisting aisle of gore. It was hard for them to keep their footing in the nightmare mess. Sten noted the many dead Praetorians and Tahn. Sprinkled here and there were the bodies of Gurkhas who had died fighting for their Emperor.

Alex viewed the massacre, his eyes hard and cold. 'Aye,' he said. 'Tha be ae betrayal worthy a' th' Campbells.'

Sten noted with relief that the Emperor's body was not among the carnage.

Just past the end of the head table was a circle of perhaps fifteen Praetorian traitors, all dead, and all with gaping wounds. In the center of the circle was a Gurkha who had been shot through the throat. Sten recognized him as Jemedar Kulbir. He had died on his oath to protect the Eternal Emperor.

'Yon lies a hero, lad,' Alex whispered reverently.

Before Sten could answer, a sudden blaze of fire erupted from a corridor off the banquet area.

'Go!' Sten shouted, and they hurdled the remaining bodies and charged across the room.

As they turned the corner, they found a squad of Praetorians mopping up the last of a three-man team of Gurkhas. Sten had just enough time to see Subadar-Major Limbu draw his kukri and suicide-charge the knot of men. Two Praetorians died before they even had time to open fire, and then Limbu fell.

Sten's Gurkhas sprayed the Praetorians from behind. In a blink, fifteen more were dead, and Sten's people were sprinting past on the trail of the Emperor.

Chapter Fifty-Four

The Emperor booted Tanz Sullamora's chubby body down the companionway, then turned, willygun in hand and went down the ladder after him. As his feet went off the risers onto the handrails, braking his sliding descent, part of his mind was mildly amused that his body still remembered how to move in an emergency.

The Emperor hit the gun-deck plates and threw himself to one side as an AM_2 round exploded where he should have been standing. Four rounds went back up the companionway before the Praetorian's chest exploded. The Emperor kept his finger twitching on the trigger, and hosed the gunblast across the top of the companionway. The antimatter rounds ripped the top of the ladder away, and the Emperor shoulder-blocked it down.

'That'll give 'em a minute, figuring how to get down,' he said.

The Emperor took half of that minute considering his position. When the Praetorian had killed Kirghiz, the Emperor had frozen momentarily. A tiny segment of his mind snarled at him: Maybe it's time to get in a couple of bar brawls and get the moves back.

The Gurkhas had saved his life during that blur of death, as short brown men swarmed the central table. Naik Thaman Gurung had wrapped the Emperor in his arms and brought him to the floor, taking a willygun blast in his own body. Subadar-Major Chittahang Limbu had a willygun on full auto, spraying rounds into the banquet room.

The Emperor had rolled out from under Thaman's corpse, grabbed the Gurkha's weapon, and put his troops into motion. Find a barricade, he kept thinking, as his group fought their way toward the exit. The Emperor might have chosen to retreat toward his own quarters, but the ex-engineer part of his mind propelled him toward the ship's stern, toward the *Normandie*'s engine spaces.

He realized the handful of Gurkhas under Subadar-Major Limbu, who set up the rear guard, could only hold for a few moments. But those few moments would give him a start toward the engine room. Once there, the Emperor knew, he could run any number of assassins round and round into oblivion.

The Emperor surveyed the gun deck. Except for the missile launchers, gun racks, and gun positions studding the passage that curled from near the ship's nose back to end before the fuel/engine areas, the *Normandie*'s gun deck would have looked like any conventional liner's promenade deck. Not here, he decided. This isn't a place for even a moment's stand.

Ledoh was already waiting at the next hatchway that led down toward the kitchen areas.

The Emperor motioned, and his men moved. He was mildly startled to realize that he had only Sullamora, Ledoh, and two Gurkhas left.

And even more surprised when he caught himself enjoying what was going on.

Sten, Alex, and the Gurkhas dropped down to the gun deck through an overhead shell hoist. Fifty meters away a knot of Praetorians was crowding a down-passage.

Twenty of them – and Sten's eyes registered that one of the Praetorians had seen him and was shouting an alarm.

As Sten went down, his hand slapped a red switch on the wall. The switch read LOAD.

A Goblin missile sitting on the overhead of the gun deck slid smoothly down track toward a launcher on the far side of the Praetorians.

The system could launch one missile per launcher every six seconds, so the missile moved very, very rapidly down the loading track, approaching a speed of nearly 60 kilometers per hour when it intersected the Praetorians. One thousand kilos of steel contacting a few hundred kilos of flesh at that speed produces casualties.

By Kilgour's count five Praetorians were down before the remaining fifteen found shelter behind launchers, gun tubes, and such, and opened up.

'Ah hae quite enow a' this drakh,' he muttered and took action.

The *Normandie*'s armament was intended not only for deep space but also for planetary action. Of course atmospheric weapons such as chain guns were normally mag-locked in place behind the sealed ports they fired through. An assortment of weapons was racked on the bulkhead, but all were intended for firing from a mount, and – of course – out-ship. One of those devices was a flare projector which, under normal circumstances, took four men to wrestle to the firing port.

Sergeant Major Alex Kilgour, heavy-worlder, was not normal under any circumstances. He had the projector off the wall, loaded, aimed, and the firing switch keyed before anyone could react.

The flare burst down the long corridor, hit the far bulkhead, ricocheted, and . . . flared.

A signal flare that is intended to be seen for about half a light-second makes quite an explosion when it goes off in a ten-meter-by-ten-meter passageway. The Gurkhas and Sten had barely enough time to flatten ahead of the oncoming fireball before the *Normandie*'s automatic extinguishing system *yeek*ed and dumped several tons of retardant on what it perceived as a fire.

Too late for the fifteen little mounds of charcoal that had been Praetorians.

Sten and his troopies hot-footed down that melted companionway to find their Emperor.

Chapter Fifty-Five

Marr and Senn had taken refuge inside an enormous sonic oven. They were in the vast stainless-steel kitchen of the liner when the massacre began. When they heard the hysterical shouts on the PA system, they had wisely decided to stay put.

Senn hugged Marr close. 'When they're done,' Senn said with a shiver, 'they'll hunt us down and kill us, too.' He stroked the fur of his lifelong companion. 'Oh, well. It's been a good love, hasn't it?'

Marr suddenly rose to his full height. 'Bugger them,' he said.

'Do we have to?' Senn asked.

'One thing we know, dear,' Marr said, 'is kitchens. And if those brutes invade my kitchen they are going to be a sorry set of humans.'

He began bustling about, getting himself ready for the final confrontation. Senn saw what he was doing and leaped up, all thoughts of a tender death swept from his mind.

They started with the sonar oven. It was about three meters high and as many wide. Inside were many cooking racks and a retractable spit that could hold an entire bullock. The cooking source was a wide-beam sound projector, which looked somewhat like a large camera, mounted on hydraulic lifts. When the oven was operated, thick protective safety doors automatically locked, and the projector swept across the food, spitting bursts of ultrasound to cook whatever was inside.

The first thing Marr did was smash the safety lock. Then the two of them muscled at the sonar cooker.

Many boots thundered just outside the kitchen, and the two turned to see the Eternal Emperor back into the huge room. He was dragging Tanz Sullamora with him, and firing back through the doorway. A split second later they saw first the chamberlain and then the two remaining Gurkhas follow. Naiks Ram Sing Rana and Agansing Rai shouted defiance at their pursuers and sprayed them with their willyguns.

They ducked as the Praetorians returned fire. Behind them, the stainless steel walls of the kitchen hissed and bubbled and turned to molten metal.

'This way,' the Emperor shouted, and he led his tiny group toward the kitchen's emergency exit. Just beyond that was a tunnel leading to the main storehouse area and then the engine rooms.

A thunder of Praetorians followed them. Ram gave a soft cry and dropped as a willygun round sizzled into his abdomen. The rest of the Praetorians crowded toward the Emperor's group, who were just disappearing through the emergency-exit door.

Without hesitating, Senn turned his body into a furry ball and rolled out of the oven they'd retreated to. He palmed the KITCHEN STEAM-CLEAN button and then dove back into the oven.

Steam hissed from nozzles in the walls. Sanitation sniffers instantly analyzed the area for foreign – meaning biological – objects and then directed the huge volumes of steam on the invading organisms.

Eleven Praetorians opened their mouths as one to scream. Their lungs filled with intensely hot steam and were parboiled before sound could reach their lips. Their flesh swelled and blistered, then the blisters broke and ran.

The cleaning process took only thirty seconds – just as the instruction manual predicted! – before shutting off. By then, all eleven Praetorians were dead. Or dying. The human body is tough.

More bootheels, more firing, and another group exploded through the doorway, Fohlee at the head. He saw Senn's small face peering from the oven. 'Kill them!' Fohlee shouted. A squad leapt forward as Marr and Senn rolled out of the oven. Fohlee and four of his Praetorians ran for the emergency exit the Emperor had taken. But the door was momentarily blocked.

Meanwhile the flying squad of Praetorians was pounding toward Marr and Senn.

'Help me!' squeaked Marr, and Senn slid his tiny shoulders under the sonar cooker and strained upward.

Slowly . . . slowly . . . it came up.

'*Now*!' Marr shouted, and the two of them jumped through a rain of willygun fire. Marr just had time to hit the cooker button before they were safe behind a steel food bin.

The lens of the sonar cooker blinked and then glowed full on. The invisible but deadly beam coned outward as the squad of Praetorians charged directly into it.

Marr and Senn huddled behind the bin, listening to the terrible sounds of the Praetorians dying. Within seconds every member of the squad had been cooked. The high-frequency waves heated from the inside out, and so, even before the flesh began to curl and smoke and brown, their internal organs exploded outward, spattering fifty meters of kitchen wall with gobs of flesh.

Marr peered out at the gore and shuddered. Senn tried to peek out after him, but Marr pushed his lover back, saving him from what he knew would be a lifetime trauma. Marr felt a small place of beauty shrivel inside him.

Many shouts and thundering. Marr looked up at the main entrance to the kitchen and repositioned himself at the cooker control button again. Whoever came through the door would die like the squad of men before. His finger was almost hitting the button when he saw the slim figure crash into the room.

In one heartbeat he recognized Sten and his finger brushed past the button. Marr didn't even wait to see what happened next. He dropped back behind the bin, beside Senn.

Marr looked at the large luminous eyes of his friend. 'I almost killed our young captain!'

He buried his face in Senn's soft fur and wept.

Sten and Alex back-shot the four Praetorians who were straining at the emergency-exit door. Fohlee had just enough time to spot them, and crammed his body behind the butchering machine, a free-standing bot of red-enameled steel. Its three-by-five-meter bulk stood motionless, razor-sharp knives and meat-gripping claws still and lifeless.

Sten dropped to his knees and edged his slender body into the gap between the machine and the walls. He pushed slowly down the dark tunnel. Would Fohlee keep moving, or was he waiting just around the turn? There was almost no room to maneuver, and Sten had to shift his gun to his left hand to move forward.

There! He saw the black snout of Fohlee's weapon, and Sten struck out at it, losing his balance and falling to the floor. But his knuckles hit cold metal, and he felt the weapon rip from Fohlee's grip, then heard the gun clatter to the kitchen floor. Sten kick-rolled out of the narrow tunnel and started to his feet. A heavy blow sent him down again, and he twisted his body clumsily as he fell, just avoiding Fohlee's dagger. He saw the shadow of a boot flashing down at him, but he managed to get three fingers on a heel and twist. Fohlee staggered backward, slamming against the bot.

Machinery came to life with a shriek, and the bot's upper body whirled, meat-grabbing claws searching for flesh. Before Sten could recover, Fohlee dodged the claws and picked up his gun. The two brought their weapons up at the same time. But a meat hook on a chain swung out of the bot and caught Fohlee in the throat. He screamed in agony as the hook dragged him into the butcher bot's claws.

Sten found himself watching in awful fascination as the machine skillfully dealt with Fohlee. Within seconds, many knives had skinned him while still alive. Tiny hoses snaked out to suck up the blood. Saws whirred in to cut the joints, and boning knives flicked in and out to separate the flesh.

Fohlee's final scream was still echoing through the kitchen when the last of him had been carved, packaged, and shipped into cold storage.

Absently, Sten reached out and shut off the machine. Then he walked heavily around the butcher bot to find Alex.

Chapter Fifty-Six

Power sources and engines may have changed immensely, but any twenty-first-century deep-space black-ganger would have been at home in the *Normandie*'s engine room. The chambers were the same huge echoing metal rooms, throbbing with unseen power. The gleaming AM_2 drive units could have been diesel-electric or nuclear, and the same walkways spidered up, around, and over bewildering machinery and arcane gauges.

Since the *Normandie* wasn't under drive, only one watch officer and a wiper had been on shift, and they lay in pools of blood.

The Emperor spotted the two Praetorians one level up, crouched behind an AM_2 feedway. He considered, then aimed carefully and fired four times. The four rounds hit on either side of the spiderwalk and cut it free, and the Praetorians dropped. Just like skeet, the Emperor thought as he snap-shot both men before they crashed to the deck.

'Come on, Admiral. CYA,' he shouted, and Ledoh and the last remaining Gurkha helped him weasel a portable welding rig to the emergency door. The Emperor was slightly proud of himself as his body-memory adjusted the oxy-gas mix, fired the torch, and spot-welded the emergency hatchway they'd come through shut.

'That'll give us some more time, Mik.'

Ledoh was glaring at him, and another part of the Emperor's brain wondered what the hell was going on with the man. When the shooting had started, Ledoh'd been one of the first to pull out a service pistol, but it had been knocked from his hand by what the Emperor considered an overly protective Gurkha. The man couldn't be scared, the Emperor thought. But maybe he is, he went on, as he led the three men up catwalks. Maybe it's been too long since he'd had somebody shooting directly at his tail.

Maybe he's as scared as Tanz Sullamora, who was wheezing up behind the Emperor, his face near-coronary flushed.

Ledoh waited until all four men were on the next platform. Now, he decided. Now. That damned Gurkha had spoiled his first chance. Now was the time, and his ceremonial sword was in his hand and he was lunging, the blade aimed for the middle of the Emperor's back.

But just as the conspirators had underestimated the lethality of the Gurkhas, so did Ledoh underestimate the reaction time of Naik Agansing Rai.

Rai – Sten's ex-batman – somehow leaped between the Emperor and the blade – and was spitted neatly through the lungs. He sagged down, almost dragging the blade from Ledoh's hands.

Ledoh stepped in, pulled the blade from the man's chest, and came back for a swing – and then Tanz Sullamora became a hero.

The fat man somehow managed to wildly swing his willygun – the willygun he had no idea how to fire – into Ledoh's ribs, staggering him into the platform's side railing. Sullamora was still reacting to his own bravery as Ledoh pivoted back and slammed the sword's pommel into his neck. Gasping for air, Sullamora went down, and Ledoh was in lunging position . . .

To find the Emperor standing four meters away, at the end of the platform. He was empty-handed, his willygun still slung across his back.

'That figures,' the Emperor said. 'Do I get to know why?'

Ledoh could barely speak – all those years, all the plans, all the hatred. But he managed, 'Rob Gades was my son.'

And then he was attacking.

Again the bystanding part of the Emperor's mind was wondering who in hell Gades was as he pulled a breaker bar from the emergency fire kit on the bulkhead behind him, held it two-handed in front of him, and parried Ledoh's blade clear.

Ledoh's eyes glittered as he stop-stanced closer and slashed at the Emperor's waist, a cut that was again deflected, and then the Emperor was in motion, left foot kicking out into Ledoh's chest.

A sword against a crowbar appears an unequal fight – which it is, as several people who'd pulled blades on the Emperor during his ship engineer days had found to their considerable surprise.

As Ledoh tried to recover, the Emperor slid one hand down the bar and swung, two-handed. The steel crashed against Ledoh's sword, snapping the blade just above the hilt, before the Emperor changed his swing and the bar smashed back against Ledoh's forearm.

The bone snapped loudly and Ledoh screamed in pain. Clutching his arm, white bone protruding through his tunic sleeve, he went to his knees.

The Emperor studied him. 'You poor bastard,' he said, not unsympathetically. 'You poor, sorry bastard.' He stepped back, to the emergency com next to the fire kit, and considered the next step.

Kilgour was wrenching mightily at the welded-shut hatch into the engine spaces when Sten elbowed him aside.

The knife popped from its sheath into his hand, and he held his wrist in a brace then forced the knife through the hatchway itself. The crystal blade sliced through the steel as if it were plas. Sten made two cuts around the blackened areas that marked the weld, then shoulder-blocked the hatch open and was into the engine room, kukri in one hand, his own knife in the other.

Four bodies . . . no Emperor. He scanned above him, then was up the ladders, moving like a stalking cat.

Levels overhead he could see two more sprawled bodies and two men.

Emperor. Still alive. Praise a few dozen gods. Around the walkway. Other man . . . on his knees. Ledoh.

Neither the Emperor nor Ledoh heard Sten.

Sten was on the catwalk just below the two when he saw Ledoh force himself out of his pain. His unbroken hand went back into his waistband and emerged with a tiny Mantis willygun, and Sten was only halfway up the ladder as Ledoh aimed the pistol.

A kukri cannot be thrown. It's single-edged, and its bulbous-ended off-balance blade guarantees that, once thrown, the knife will spin wildly.

It is, however, almost a full kilo of steel.

Sten overhanded the long knife at Ledoh, in a desperate last chance to save the Emperor's life.

At best the blade should have clubbed Ledoh down. But the whirling blade sank point first into the back of Grand Chamberlain Mik Ledoh, severing his spine.

Ledoh, dead before his finger could touch the willygun's trigger, spasmed through the guardrails to thump finally, soggily, on the deck plates many meters below.

Sten came up the last few steps and stood looking at the Emperor. One or the other of them should probably have said something terribly dramatic. But dramatic gestures happen, most often, during the retelling. The two bloodstained men just stared at each other in silence and relief.

Chapter Fifty-Seven

Naked under a bright summer sun, Haines considered perfection. The drink comfortably close at hand was icy; the sun was hot; a cool breeze from the forest below kept her houseboat comfortable.

Almost perfect, she corrected herself.

One thing missing, and one problem.

The last months, after the Emperor had returned to Prime World, had been very long indeed, and the attempts to clean up the mess had begun.

Haines was fairly grateful that she'd only been witness to part of them; Sten had told her about the rest.

Evidently, after the last Praetorian had been hunted down on the *Normandie*, the Imperial fleet had immediately scudded since even the Eternal Emperor couldn't cobble together any believable explanation that the Tahn would accept for the deaths of their chief lord and his retinue.

Kirghiz or one of his underlings must have been under orders to report regularly, because barely two days out, the fleet found itself pursued. One Tahn battleship and cruiser and destroyer escorts should have been an overmatch for the *Normandie* and its escorts. But the Emperor had already called in reinforcements and two full battleship squadrons rendezvoused with the *Normandie*.

The Tahn fought bravely and in ignorance. Despite all attempts to communicate, they fought to the last man under complete radio silence. Sten never knew if they thought they were rescuing Kirghiz or revenging him.

On return to Prime, the Emperor immediately attempted to explain to the Tahn, but diplomatic relations were severed and all Tahn personnel were withdrawn.

Haines had barely noticed, since she'd been too busy rounding up the surviving conspirators. She'd never arrested so many wealthy, high-ranking people in her life.

Then there was a show trial because the Emperor was hoping that somehow the Tahn would listen to the truth. Of course they wouldn't – any good totalitarian knows he can always find somebody to pin a crime on. Even attempts to convince the Tahn of the truth by neutral diplomats from cultures constitutionally incapable of dishonesty were ignored.

The series of trials was mind-numbing. At least Haines had the opportunity to testify in open court. Sten, under Imperial orders, gave his testimony from a sealed chamber, his voice electronically altered to prevent any possibility of identification.

In spite of the defense counsels' howls about star chambers, ninety-five per cent of the conspirators were found guilty – and treason and attempted regicide were still capital crimes.

Even the acquitted five per cent weren't free of the Emperor's vengeance. Just the day before a small item on the vid reported that a recently freed industrialist's yacht had exploded with him aboard . . . Haines closed down that line of thought. She was contemplating perfection, and to her even Imperially ordered assassination was still murder.

The sun was slowly moving her toward sleep, and she was musing on casually lustful thoughts when a flit hummed nearby. She forced herself awake and up, reaching for a wrap. Then she recognized Sten in the flit and lay back, her thoughts becoming somewhat less casual.

Sten tied up to the houseboat, wandered through the kitchen, fielded a beer, and joined her on the deck.

'How'd it go?' she asked.

'Hell if I know,' Sten said. 'Better and worse.'

'Shed and tell, Captain.'

'Uh . . . well, that's part of the good news. I just got promoted.'

'Well pour the bubbly and get naked, Commander.'

Sten followed orders, stripped, and lay down beside her. He grunted in animal satisfaction. Haines waited as long as she could.

'Come on, Sten. Talk to me!'

The day had, indeed, been better and worse than Sten expected.

After the *Normandie* returned to Prime, while Sten had been retained as commander of the Gurkhas, he'd actually been detached for special duties, which included the endless appearances in court.

The Gurkhas had been built back up to the strength and were

headed by Subadar-Major Chittahang Limbu, even though he was still technically recuperating from his wounds.

Sten had only been in the palace to eat and sleep, and the few hallway encounters he'd had with the Emperor had been worrisomely formal and brief.

Until the day's Imperial summons.

When Sten entered, saluted, and reported, the Emperor had been sitting, completely still, behind his desk.

Long moments passed before he spoke.

Sten had been expecting several things to be said. None of them were right.

'Captain, are you ready to go to war?'

Sten blinked, found that all his potential responses sounded dumb, and stayed silent.

'I will make a prediction, Captain. Ex Cathedra Eyes Only. Within five E-years we will be fighting the Tahn.'

The Emperor took slight pity. 'At ease, Captain Sten. Sit down.'

Sten was somewhat relieved. He didn't figure that the Emperor ever busted somebody out of the service if he allowed the clot to be seated first.

'Well, Captain? Your thoughts?'

Sten was perplexed. Like any professional military man, he truly believed the somewhat contradictory line that a soldier's job is to avoid war.

The Emperor seemed to be slightly prescient. 'It's gonna be a bitch when it comes.

'By the way. No way am I wrong. Intelligence says that every Tahn shipyard has converted to warship construction. The Tahn are buying up every particle of AM_2 they can get, no matter what the price.

'Also – and I'm keeping this off the vid – there've been a whole clottin' group of skirmishes with my normal patrol ships around the Tahn worlds. Aw hell. Why am I lying to you? Every spy ship I send in they send back full of holes.'

The Emperor then took out a flask from his desk. Sten felt slightly more relieved – first sit down and then maybe a drink. Maybe he would keep his captain's bars. 'The reason I have been avoiding you, Captain, is that this whole sorry-ass mess is something I've been trying not to think about.

'So anybody who had anything to do with it was on my drakh list, frankly. Being an Emperor means never having to say you're wrong if you want things that way.'

He poured into two small metal cups, and Sten recognized the smell of Stregg.

'This stuff gets to you after a while,' the Emperor said, but he made no move to offer a cup to Sten. 'Remember when we got loaded on Empire Day?'

Sten did.

'Remember what I told you?'

Sten remembered.

'Well, I took the next step *for* you.' The Emperor took from his desk drawer a set of orders and tossed them on his desk.

'Don't bother reading them now. You're reassigned. Flight school. Oh yeah. By the way. That chubby thug of yours?'

'Sergeant Major Kilgour?'

'Him. You wonder where he is?'

Sten had. Alex had disappeared most mysteriously a month or two earlier.

'Yeah. I lifted him because he was actually applying through channels to get married. To some cop or other. Clottin' idiot. Neckbreakers like him shouldn't ever get married. Anyway, he's now learning how to make like a big bird, too.

'Also he ain't a sergeant major anymore. I kicked him up to warrant officer. If he's gonna be in the clottin' navy, at least he won't have to put up with their silly class system.'

The Emperor picked up and fingered his cup. 'Captain, you might want to return to some kind of position of attention.'

Sten was standing, locked and rigid in an instant.

'The other thing' – and the Emperor reached into his desk yet again and took out a small blue box – 'is you're now a commander. Here's your insignia.' He shoved the box across to Sten. 'Now, pick up that cup.'

Sten obeyed.

'I'm gonna call the toast – it's to you, Commander. Because no way I'll ever see you again.'

The Emperor stood. 'To your health, Commander Sten!'

To Sten, the Stregg tasted very odd indeed.

Haines was running all this input – less the Emperor's certainty of imminent war, which Sten had not mentioned – as Sten finished his beer, went back into the boat, and got another.

'Another thing I picked up,' he went on after he sat. 'You're going to get some kind of promotion, too.'

But Haines was considering something else. 'So you're going to go off and become a junior birdman. When?'

'That's the rest of the good news,' Sten said. 'It seems, uh, I've come into some money.' Ida's illicitly acquired and invested funds had finally caught up with him, and Sten was sitting on more credits than he believed existed.

'Also me and you're on long leave before we report to our new duty stations.'

Haines smiled, took a sip of her drink, and then winked. 'Hey sailor. You want to fool around?'

Sten started laughing and knelt beside her. She pulled him down, and he felt her breasts and her lips, and then there was nothing but the blinding warmth of the sun itself.

Chris Bunch is the author of the Sten series, the Dragonmaster series, the Seer King series and many other acclaimed SF and fantasy novels. A notable journalist and bestselling writer for many years, he died in 2001.

Allan Cole is a bestselling author, screenwriter and former prize-winning newsman. The son of a CIA operative, Cole was raised in the Middle East, Europe and the Far East. He currently lives in Boca Raton, FL, with his wife, Kathryn. For details see Allan's website at www.acole.com

Find out more about Chris Bunch and Allan Cole and other Orbit authors by registering for the free monthly newsletter at www.orbitbooks.net